THE PANDAHEM CYCLE I

The Dray Prescot Series

THE PANDAHEM CYCLE I

Kenneth Bulmer

writing as

Alan Burt Akers

Published by
Bladud Books

First published in 2011 by Bladud Books

Originally published separately by Daw Books, Inc., as:
Mazes of Scorpio (1982)
Delia of Vallia (1982)
Fires of Scorpio (1983)
The short story "Lallia the Slave Girl", first published 1982
in *Fantasy Tales*

This first omnibus paperback edition published in 2011 by
Bladud Books, an imprint of Mushroom Publishing,
Bath, BA1 4EB, United Kingdom

www.bladudbooks.com

ISBN 978-1-84319-869-7

Contents

MAZES OF SCORPIO

A Note on the Pandahem Cycle

Dray Prescot often calls himself a plain sailorman, yet the picture he paints of himself in these narratives is highly enigmatic. In *Mazes of Scorpio,* the first volume of the Pandahem Cycle, a completely new era in his life begins to develop. True, he was a powder monkey in Nelson's Navy, and clawed his way through the hawsehole to the quarterdeck to become first lieutenant of a seventy-four. But he was disappointed with his posting. When the Savanti, those mortal yet superhuman people of the Swinging City of Aphrasöe on far Kregen, called him to serve as a Savapim in their schemes, he crossed the gulf of four hundred light-years more than willingly.

Rejected by the Savanti, he in turn spurned them for the sake of Delia. Only through the machinations of the Star Lords was Prescot brought back to Kregen. He has fought his way on that marvelous and brilliant world of savagery and beauty, and has made a name for himself. But now all that changes.

Called to be the Emperor of Vallia, he, with his comrades, has vanquished poor old mad Thyllis, Empress of Hamal, and now seeks to create a fresh and lasting unity among all the nations of Paz. They all face a common foe in the Shanks, the Fishheads who raid their coasts. And, there are worms within the bud, secret enemies who desire only to drag all down for their own selfish ends.

Dray Prescot has been described as an immensely broad-shouldered man of enormous vitality, a little above middle height, with brown hair and eyes, a man conveying an impression of passion held in check, moving with the savage grace of a wild beast of the jungle. From sources outside his own testimony we know him to be a man of complete integrity, holding within himself a cool center of calm; a passionate, dominant, commanding and yet truly humble man.

Prescot is chivalrous—in what many people would see as a comically old-fashioned way—to any woman deserving of chivalry. He acknowledges, and tolerates and attempts to be sympathetically understanding toward, any woman who is not.

A plain sailorman? Hardly. Life on Kregen under the mingled streaming lights of Zim and Genodras, the Suns of Scorpio, has changed and matured Prescot in ways unknowable to denizens of this Earth. We can guess that his headlong career has barely begun, that the many friends and foes surrounding him, the horrendous experiences he has endured, the future perils he must face, will continue to mold his character, hardening what is already harsh, softening what is already gentle. All we can say is—Hai Jikai!

Alan Burt Akers

One

At The Ruby Winespout

At the beginning of rhododendron time two of my spies were fished out of the river with their throats cut from ear to ear.

The banked masses of leaves, black-green and shining, burst—it seemed in the course of a single morning—into explosions of color. The blossoms scattered flecks and rushes, swathes and coruscations of all the colors of the rainbow across the dark green leaves. Color rioted and scents perfumed the air. And two good men were dead.

Anger and self-contempt were useless. Anger at the waste of human life, contempt that I had asked Nogan the Artful and Lifren the Soft to spy for me; and now they were dead. I told my friends what I intended to do. Their reactions were predictable.

"No!"

"It is impossible."

"You cannot go running headlong into danger!"

But Seg Segutorio, regarding me with his mocking gaze much modified by thought, said, "You probably need to let some of the bad humor out, Dray. Your blood is getting thick. We'll just toddle along to this infamous Ruby Winespout and exercise our muscles a trifle."

Good old Seg!

"And our brains."

"Oh, aye," said Seg. "Brains." His fey blue eyes regarded me with amusement, clearing both mockery and thought. "Between us, we've not used our quota all that well, have we?"

I was surprised.

In all the concerns pressing in on us as we sought to assist a shattered empire to regain its strength with one hand and with the other repel fishlike marauders from over the curve of the world, I had thought Seg secure. He had overcome his grief for his wife Thelda and was now, I was convinced, the most balanced of us all. Except and despite that he could become a wild and raving maniac if he got into a spot of hand-to-hand. As the best Bowman of Loh in all Kregen, in my view, Seg Segutorio could handle himself in any situation. He was a comrade, the greatest comrade any man could have, and I relied on him absolutely.

"I don't know what you're on about for yourself, Seg. But if you're referring to the bother I'm having with Drak over this emperor of Vallia nonsense—"

He interrupted with the ease of valued friendship.

"No troubles you can put a shaft into. I've managed to steer clear of half a dozen designing families with marriageable offspring. Since Thelda—well, Dray, I'll tell you. I feel like those flowers out there."

So that was it.

We were standing in the long room with the serried windows overlooking a panorama of gardens dropping away to the River Havilthytus. The imperial palace, the Hammabi el Lamma, rearing imposingly on its artificial island in the river, had now become a place I could tolerate. The profusion of flowers helped, for the place always struck cold and hard. Delia had with her usual skill contrived comfort from the rooms of the apartments in the Alshyss Tower given over to our use.

Here in Ruathytu, the capital city of the Empire of Hamal, we people of Vallia were never allowed to forget we were strangers. We had concluded a magnificent treaty with the Hamalese and their new emperor, Nedfar, and everything looked promising for the future. We had to patch the empire together again for the Hamalese, and resist with the last drop of blood in our bodies the devilish Shanks who raided us all.

Seg shifted his belt on his hips, settled it. He coughed. "The problem now is those rogues in The Ruby Winespout. They are a notorious gang—"

"So we'll stroll along, as you suggest, and take a look."

The protests from our people, the vehemence with which this hero and that vowed he or she would accompany us—well, I cut all through the babble.

"This is a task for one or two only. Kov Seg and I will go. That is all there is to say."

Deft-fingered Minch, crusty, bearded, my camp commandant, said dourly, "Majister—if the Empress Delia were here she would stop you, for a certainty."

"Well, Minch," I said, somewhat testily, "as she is gallivanting off somewhere and is not here, she can hardly stop me, can she?"

So that decided *that*.

We were going deliberately to put our fool heads into a tavern notorious for murder, foul play and evanishments, where two of our best men

5

had been cruelly done away with, and Seg and I tended to regard it all rather lightly.

We kitted ourselves up to look like mercenaries. This was not a disguise, for we'd both been mercenaries in our time. Our clothes were hard, sober, workmanlike, with much leather and a little metal, for we did not wish to appear grand.

Seg picked up the silken cords from which dangled the representation of a mortil's head sculpted in silver. The ferocious snarling hunting-beast's head looked devilish life-like, a miniature head of destruction. This mortil-head, the pakmort, signified that its wearer was a paktun, a mercenary who had gained fame and notoriety, who perhaps controlled his own free-lance band, although that was more likely to be found among the wearers of the pakzhan, the hyr-paktuns.

"If you like, Seg," I said. "A paktun wearing the pakmort will receive better service than a simple paktun."

"All the same... I don't fancy a knife in my back."

"I agree. You are wise not to wear your pakzhan. The glitter of gold at your throat might tempt a blade."

So, in the end, we hung the silken cords of the pakmorts around our necks and secured the cords to our shoulder points. No mercenary likes an enemy to grip a cord around his neck and choke him to death. Then, flinging short blue-grey capes over our left shoulders and pulling our floppy hats low over our eyebrows, we set off.

We elected to fly saddle birds from the palace.

"We'll have to stable them in a commercial scratching bar establishment," said Seg, "before we get anywhere near The Ruby Winespout."

"True. One wonders if they'd steal 'em to sell as saddle flyers, or steal 'em to roast and feast on."

The two saddle birds flew strongly through the late afternoon air. We flew high over the river and slanted down toward the southeast, leaving the Sacred Quarter to our rear. We flew over the Blind Walls and the little creek beyond. Ahead a maze of streets and alleyways surrounded the Eastern Arena. Here lay the homes and hovels of the working folk, the guls, who yet prided themselves they were far better off than the great mass of the clums, who although free and not slave were poor beyond poverty.

Work on the new aqueduct bringing water from the southeast had halted during the recent wars. There were signs around the piles of stones that the building would soon begin again. Like any civilized city of Kregen, Ruathytu consumed vast quantities of water.

We flew down well short of our destination and stabled the two fluttrells; inconspicuous saddle birds, fluttrells, in Ruathytu. The scratching-bar establishment appeared clean and honest. We set off walking in the last of the light from the twin suns.

The street—Seg said he was sure it was the Street of a Thousand Strangers—wore a faded look, with many of the shops and houses shuttered. The skyline was broken here by the looming overhang of the aqueduct, broken sharply at the point where construction had ceased. The clouds hovered overhead, tinged with crimson and jade. Shadows faded and disappeared and then grew again, hard-edged, twinned shadows from the roofs and walls.

"Well, my old dom," said Seg. "And there it is."

The Street of a Thousand Strangers—if that was its name—opened into a small kyro and the square contained the last of a small outdoor conjuring act packing up. They had evidently not attracted much of a crowd. The fire-eater was disconsolately quenching his little brazier. A lady with spangles and not much else to cover her embonpoint stood with a little dark-haired fellow counting the takings.

Seg laughed. "They'd better be off with their gold before night falls."

"Aye!"

Some jugglers slammed the wicker lids on baskets no doubt containing balls and hoops they could spin with dazzling skill. A little breeze whisked leaves and dust. Seg's nod indicated the tavern across the square. A single tree grew outside, a wilting, drooping, yellowish tree. The tavern was built of grey brick, well-weathered and mortared, and the windows were small and mean. It did not look an inviting place.

Seg's nod, besides singling out this dolorous building, stiffened my resolve. The dump looked the kind of place to pass in a hurry and not look back. A shuttered house stood to its right side, and on its left, an open space still showed the rotted teeth of a demolished building.

No reason, apart from the unfavorable aspect of this place, should have made me feel a breeze of alarm.

Seg started across.

I followed.

The smell? The feel of that little breeze? This place was wrong.

For all that feeling, I was determined and knew Seg shared my determination that we would not be overawed. We were out for a spot of enjoyment. If spying came into it, all well and good. But we'd been rusting for too long after the tremendous battles in which we'd managed to defeat and, for the moment at least, drive off the hateful marauding Shanks. Those Fishheads from the other side of Kregen were the menace for the future. Right now Seg and I were a couple of harum-scarum mercenaries, out for a night on the town.

Seg Segutorio, who hails from Erthyrdrin, is a wild fey brand of fellow, with black hair and bonny blue eyes, feckless and reckless and, with that otherworldliness of his people, shrewd and canny when he has to be. He and I had adventured a very great deal since Seg had first hurled a forkful of dungy straw into my face. I would not be without Seg for—well, for practically anything at all in two worlds.

As so often occurred, Seg must have picked up the empathy of my feelings, for as we approached the door he said, "Now if Inch and Turko were here, and—"

"Aye," I said.

There was no need to lament between us the absence of our comrades. They had their work to do on Kregen, as we had ours.

A smell of roasting ordel reached us as we strode up the steps to the door. The smell of cooking was good. I cocked an eyebrow at Seg and he nodded, firmly.

"I am sharp set."

So, as we entered the low-ceiled taproom, looking around at tables and chairs positioned about the sawdusted floor, we wrinkled our noses, sniffing the aromas. To the smell of roasting meat was now added the divine scent of fresh momolams.

A man with only three arms wiped his three hands on his blue and yellow striped apron. His jowly face and lemon-shaped head bobbed.

"Welcome, horters, welcome. You are hungry? We have the best meal this side of the River Mak. Come in, come, and sit down. Hey, Fluffi! Wine for the horters."

At his call a little serving wench came up with feline grace, carrying a pitcher. If that was the wine, they were rough and ready here.

"A middling Stuvan, tart," advised the little Och, wiping his three hands again. "But suitable. Oh, yes, suitable."

As Seg and I sat down with our backs to the wall, Seg grumbled, "Anyone would think he was expecting us."

"Trade is bad. We are two paktuns with gold. But what you suggest is worth considering."

"So? How do we consider it?"

"For a start—do we trust the wine?"

"A middling Stuvan? Hard to judge."

I laughed. Oh, yes, I can laugh.

"If we don't we'll be thirsty, and suspect—"

"And if we do we could be stuffed down in the cellars, with our throats slit, ready to go out into the river."

"Pre-unfortunately-cisely."

Seg slumped back against the wall and eyed with a most baleful stare the wine the little Fristle fifi had poured for him. I picked up my goblet.

"I'll drink, Seg. You may claim indisposition, religion, temperance—"

"Why you? Why me!"

"You may rearrange the plan, should you wish."

He stared at me.

In a low, a very low voice against eavesdroppers, he said, "You, Dray Prescot, as I have said, are a low-down, devious, cunning, rascal of a devil!"

And I laughed again.

"Landlord!" I called it out between laughs.

He appeared, the apron twisting around two of his hands, the third fidgeting with the table arrangements. "Horters?"

"Would you fetch a fresh bottle of Farfaril, for we have just enough silver between us to pay for a decent wine and our meal." I spoke casually but with emphasis. "After that we will have a pair of copper obs between us."

"At once, horters." He did not sound disappointed.

Although he was a cripple, having only three arms, he was deft enough in removing the two goblets of the Stuvan. Farfaril is a full-bodied red wine, not too sweet. I am not overfond of the wines of Hamal, although a few of their top vintages are superb by any standards.

The little Fristle fifi brought the bottle of Farfaril. It was brought quickly enough, the dust still upon it, and the seals intact. I judged there would not have been time to tamper with it. If it had been drugged ahead of time, and laid by, in store to wreak a mischief, Seg and I would have lost our gamble...

The tavern began to fill up as the twin suns sank beyond the Walls of Repentance. The jugglers came in to spend what little they had earned. A man with a chained Munfoon, all hair and eyes and lolling tongue, came in to make the poor creature dance to the sound of a pipe. The girl who played the pipe was clad in mere rags, her naked feet raw and red, her face a pinched white blot. The Munfoon danced a little jig and a rattle of copper obs fell about the girl. She snatched them up, and together with the man and the chained pathetic creature shuffled to a dark corner. All evening other entertainers would perform their shows. Some were better not spoken of.

There was no doubt about it. The roast ordel and the yellow momolams were superb. We ate hugely. Our silver insured us good helpings and a second bottle. We sat, watching, waiting for the arrival of the man or woman who had caused the deaths of our two spies.

We had chosen our own dark corner, against the walls. There was a certain amount of horseplay—leeming, Kregans call it—and one or two fights. Only one dagger was used, and that only inflicted a minor wound. The blood was mostly from a slashed scalp, and scalps bleed like broken hearts.

"I suppose your information was reliable, Dray?"

"We thought so. That great rogue Hamdi the Yenakker told us. He swore the man to see was regularly here in The Ruby Winespout. A man with three black pigtails, a nose bent to larboard, and missing his left ear."

"If true, bizarre enough to spot."

"We thought so."

"Well, Hamdi did help us before. He would turn his colors the moment a new lord appeared. How long do we give this fellow with the pigtails and the bent nose and the missing lughole?"

"As long as it takes."

"By the Veiled Froyvil, my old dom! And to maintain our cover we've ordered two bottles, and two bottles only. It will be thirsty work."

And this time we both laughed.

"As for the woman, Hamdi was less precise. Not a serving wench, not a shishi, yet a girl who would come here. With a sword strapped to her waist. And coiled hair. Not an easy mark."

"If she does come here, we'll know her."

The first bottle emptied.

We both felt fine.

We started in on the second bottle.

On Earth, where I was born, and which was some four hundred light-years away, a tavern like this would have been wreathed in tobacco smoke. Thankfully, there were no smokers on Kregen.

At least, not tobacco smokers...

A nasty little fight broke out two tables along, and a fellow was carried out feet first and hurled on his head onto the cobbles outside.

The victor, breathing hard, sat back at his bench.

"Stupid tapo! As though one could not see his dice were obviously loaded."

Another man joined them, flicking his little rods of many colors. If he cheated, he was not discovered as the game of Flick-Flock proceeded with much swearing and bangings of the tables.

Seg looked at the clepsydra perched on a shelf above the door. The water dropped steadily. It was a dark lustrous green.

"If he does not come soon, my old dom, my tongue will begin to crawl about seeking sustenance among the tankards."

"Maybe we could discover, with cries of joy, another few silver pieces?"

"Why not?"

In the manner of old campaigners we had automatically appraised the metal of the roisterers and swaggerers in the wide main room of The Ruby Winespout. Rough artisans, mostly, with tradespeople sitting together along the angled wall to our corner. Three tables along, past the gamblers at Flick-Flock, the five men sitting with their heads together had not escaped our notice. We kept a quick glance on them from time to time. They were not artisans or tradesfolk; they carried weapons and three of the five wore brigandines, the other two wore jacks.

"Hey, Landlord!" exclaimed Seg, half-rising and extending his hand.

"Lookit that! A real beautiful silver sinver graced with the head of the Empress Thyllis, no less." He puffed his cheeks, and added: "The late Empress Thyllis."

The little Och trotted over, looking pleased.

"Late or not, horter, it is all good silver."

"Aye! Another bottle!"

From the corner of my eye, my attention centered amusedly on Seg's antics, I caught movement approaching from the tradespeople's tables. Seg was bellowing: "Caught in the lining! Foul stitching by a half-blind wight, I don't doubt, but I'd kiss his bald pate for him now!"

The movement from my side abruptly manifested itself.

An exceedingly large and extraordinarily hairy man fairly hurtled at me. He knocked over an intervening table. He was purple of face, bulging of eye, foaming of mouth, and screeching something like: "I'll have your tripes out and strangle your scrawny neck in 'em, so help me Uldor the Mighty!"

There was time to observe he wore a shaggy old pelt-like garment, by its bulk probably concealing armor beneath, before he hit our table. Seg toppled away, with his catlike grace recovering instantly. I leaned away from the blow of a ham-sized fist. I dodged. I shouted.

"What the—?"

The hairy mass shoved the table away. The remains of our bottle splashed. The fist swung again, and the maniac roared out: "I know you, Planath the Sly! Now you have reached the reckoning." He lashed out again.

I dodged.

"I'm not—"

"Stand still, Planath, rast, yetch! I am going to scrunch your scrawny neck between my hands! I, Dahram the Bold! Accept your just punishment like a man, cramph!"

He got himself entangled in the wreckage of the table. He kicked out, stumbling, windmilling his arms. He had just the two arms, and was an apim like me, a member of Homo sapiens. But he was large, and hairy, and wrought up. There were precious few options left open to me, by Zair!

His purple face and bulging eyes bore down again. He did not have three black pigtails, his nose was not bent to larboard and his ears were both present and correct.

"Now as Uldor the Mighty is my witness, I have sworn to take payment out on your hide, Planath the Sly! Now is your hour of doom—"

He stopped bellowing rather suddenly.

This was mainly because I placed a hand around his throat and pressed a little. My other hand caught his left arm and bent it back—not cruelly, not viciously, just enough to make him stoop very smartly and rub that squashed and fiery nose against the edge of the overturned table.

I spoke into his ear.

"I am not Planath the Sly, Dahram!"

He grunted. I eased the pressure.

He spluttered. "I know you are not Planath the Sly! He could never do what you have just done! My apologies, dom, sincere apologies—but that physiognomy of yours—"

Seg laughed.

"That'll teach you to monkey with nature!"

Seg knew that I could make subtle adjustments to my face, after a fashion, taught me by a famed Wizard of Loh. I'd altered my own fierce features into what I thought would be a face that would not upset Seg too much. I must have put in too much of the sly look.

I let Dahram the Bold up.

He rubbed his throat and eyed me. He was a fine tall bulky man. There was indeed armor under the pelt. His sword was scabbarded into a plain leather sheath, bronze-bound.

The little fracas had loosened the shaggy pelt at his throat. I caught the glitter of gold.

I said, "Cover your pakzhan, Dahram. We do not wear ours here—"

"Aye," said Dahram. "But I sold my pakmort when I became a hyr-paktun, sold it to the brotherhood."

We righted the table and, as though he'd been waiting for the outcome of the little fracas, the Och landlord appeared with the bottle paid for with Seg's sinver he claimed he'd found lodged in his lining.

Dahram the Bold cocked a bushy eyebrow at me.

"Join us, dom, and tell us your story. I own I would not relish being in the shoes of this Planath the Sly."

We were fated not to drink that third bottle of Farfaril.

The five men at the table we'd been casually observing chose that moment to make their move.

As I have said, only one dagger had flashed in the fights so far.

These five men descended on us with naked steel.

The patrons of The Ruby Winespout drew themselves away. Some looked. Most went on with what they were doing, only sparing a glance to see how the fight would go, making their wagers on the outcome. Murder and mayhem occurred too commonly in The Ruby Winespout to raise an alarm.

And, all this in defiance of the strict Laws of Hamal...

I did not think Dahram the Bold was the betrayer, delivering the metaphorical kiss of betrayal by his antics. The five opened out as they rushed along the cleared space before the tables. One of them pushed his enveloping hood away from his face in order to see better. And, lo! He had three black pigtails, and a nose bent to larboard, and only one ear. And, lo! again.

One of the five men was a woman, with coiled hair under a steel cap, and a sword which was now a bar of glitter in her gloved fist.

"So that's the way of it!" quoth Seg.

Dahram the Bold didn't waste time. He ripped his sword free of that plain scabbard. The sword was the straight cut and thrust weapon of Havilfar, the thraxter. The swords swinging against us were thraxters, also. There were no rapiers and no main gauches in evidence in this tavern brawl.

Seg and I drew. Now we happened to have strapped on drexers, the superior sword type developed in our home of Valka, a blend of the best aspects of the thraxter, the native Vallian clanxer, and the superb and mysterious Savanti sword. Without another word, we set to.

Two

Of Beggars and Emperors

In a tavern fight of this brawling nature you don't have to be too choosy. You don't stand on ceremony. The romantic flicker of glittering blades is all very well, but...

The broken bottle rolled at the side of my boot.

I picked the bottle up, noticed that the end was broken into a satisfyingly jagged array of teeth, and gestured with it in my left hand as though I were about to throw it.

The leading wight rushing upon us dodged. He moved his head and shoulders back to avoid the throw. I waited until he'd moved, was fixed at the end of his balance—and then I threw.

The jagged end chewed up his face.

Dahram the Bold hurled himself forward, all bulk and hair, yelling. His sword flickered.

When you are a brand new young prince, or a brand new young emperor, you will find many people only too willing to patronize you, suck up to you, toady, flatter, all in the best interests of your good self, of course. I had a quick feeling of regret that, for all this hairy magnificence, there had not been a few more men like Dahram the Bold about some of the emperors and kings I'd known. He had assaulted and insulted me; now he did not waste words but just got stuck in to help to redress the balance.

He fought with a panache that overbore the next two assailants. He foined with the thraxter, using the blade as though it were a pea stick. The man with the three black pigtails lost two of them, and half his face with them, as Dahram slashed. The woman turned and ran. The last of the five stood looking with stupid, bewildered eyes at the hilt of the sword. The blade was through his neck. Seg can throw a blade, too, as well as loose a shaft...

As a fight, it was all over almost before it had begun.

"Friends of yours, doms?"

"No, Dahram. Never seen 'em before."

Seg said, "It would seem our journey has been in vain. And the bottle is broken—"

"Yes," I said. "All right, we'll go."

Seg hitched up his belt.

I said to Dahram, "You will take a stoup with us at a more salubrious tavern? We are in your debt."

"For that little bit of knockabout?"

"For disconcerting those damned assassins."

Seg hauled his sword free. He had to put his foot on the dead man's face. "You've seen them before?"

"No," said Dahram. "No. I don't know 'em. I'm tazll at the moment, looking for a job. I heard a merchant will hire guards here."

"There are many taverns where guards are hired."

"True. Very well. And the first drink is on me."

"Are there any sweeter words in any tongue?" quoth Seg.

On that cheerful note we left The Ruby Winespout. No doubt the little crippled Och would have regular arrangements for disposing of dead bodies.

My thoughts became grim. My two spies had been disposed of, their bodies found in the river...

We told Dahram we were called Nath the Hammer and Naghan the Fletcher; but he did not believe us. That did not bother me. Dahram, as I thought, was a chance acquaintance, fine company for an evening on the town away from the Sacred Quarter where the nobles and the gilded youth of the city played. He would sign on as a guard with a merchant and be off in a couple of days...

We swaggered across the square where the jugglers had performed their tricks during the day. We kept a very sharp lookout for the woman who had run off. The way I saw the situation was spelled out by Seg.

"The pigtail fellow Dahram chopped and the woman hired the three thugs to deal with us. Pigtail is dead. Will we ever run across the woman again?"

Dahram boomed. "Aye, doms! She had a nasty mean look about her, did that one."

"All I really saw was that coiled hair and a sharp pointy nose like a witch." As I spoke my gaze probed about among the shadows under the walls where the lights of torches did not reach. "And a ring on her finger the size of a loloo's egg—"

"You exaggerate, dom! As big as a walnut, yes!"

"That'll be a poison ring," said Seg sagely. "She can flip the lid open and pour enough poison into your goblet to shrivel the toes of a regiment of heroes."

"As I remarked," said Dahram the Bold, "a nice class of friends you have." He roared at his own words—a trick some people have that doesn't really offend if you think about them as humans—and then sputtered out: "There's the Calsany and Flea. They hire guards there."

"They sell drinks there," we said together.

Thirsty work, swording.

Although the maniacal wars of the late Empress Thyllis had now ceased, and the civil war was over, there still remained urgent need of fighting men.

The old iron legions of Hamal were being rebuilt. There was still need of mercenaries. Every person, every man woman and child old enough to understand, was aware that the danger from the Fishheads, the Shanks from over the curve of the world, had arrived in full force.

We could only expect this "full force" to become fuller and more powerful in the future.

Dahram the Bold would find a merchant eager enough to hire him.

We settled to our goblets in a quiet corner of the Calsany and Flea.

"Oh, yes, doms," said Dahram, putting his goblet down and wiping the back of his hand across the hair over, below and surrounding his mouth. "I'm from Theakdrin, of which you will never have heard, seeing it is a small kovnate tucked in a bend of the River Os. We were independent for as far back as anyone could remember; then the Hamalese took us over. That was when I was a little shaver. So, I fought for Hamal. Well, it seemed the right thing to do at the time."

"And then?" said Seg.

"Oh, I went for a mercenary. Hyr-paktun. Although you might not believe it—"

"We do."

"In these recent troubles I started off hired out to a kov of Hamal and ended up fighting against him. That's the way it goes in the paktun's trade."

Also, as we saw, though Dahram the Bold might be a hyrpaktun wearing the pakzhan, he had achieved that rare distinction through his own prowess. He was not a leader. He would not control his own band, and hire and fire, seek contracts, conclude deals. He would be in the forefront of the battle, always, earning his hire, fighting with swirling sword, and the pakzhan glittering gold at his throat.

He wanted to know all there was to learn of the black sorcerer and the unholy thaumaturgy that had destroyed the old empress and her followers. We were able to tell him a little of the Wizards of Loh—some of whom are my friends and in no sense black sorcerers—and how the arch-devil had been blown away in a flame of gramarye. He shivered.

"I am a fighting man. Sorcery—no, doms, not for me."

Mere mortals are not allowed the privilege of looking into the future. If it be a privilege, that is. So Dahram the Bold spoke thus, quaffing his ale, with no conception of what fate held in store for him in the way of sorcery...

We were pestered by a Rapa with one arm, whose feathers were mostly bristled off his birdlike face. His beak was dented. He wore rags, and stank.

"Masters—I was once like you—I fought at the Battle of the Incendiary Vosks—masters—an ob, a copper ob, for the sake of Havil the Green—"

Seg threw a few copper obs. The miserable creature scuffled for them. His feathers rustled. He stank.

"I was at that fight," said Dahram, offhandedly.

"Oh?" we said, firing up as your fighting man does at promised reminiscences and soldiers' yarns. "So were we."*

After we decided to leave, Dahram said we were welcome to share his lodgings. A widow woman was most hospitable. We thanked him; but we had our own pads for the night.

So, with the shouted "Remberees!" we parted.

I said, "I must talk to Nedfar about the ex-soldiers. It is cruel that they should be reduced to begging. That Rapa may have stenched worse than a slave-whipmaster's armpit, but he had fought."

Seg has this astonishingly practical turn of mind to set against the fey qualities of his nature. He surprised me yet again.

"Mayhap, Dray. And mayhap he had his own arm chopped off and singed his feathers. The rest is mere play-acting."

"Self-mutilation!"

"Successful begging is an art form. It goes in families. You get your trade, you learn it early, you accept your mutilation, and you are set up as a working beggar for life."

"I don't care for that, by Vox!"

But care for it or not, it was true and it went on. We had obliterated all traces of the self-mutilation bit in Vallia; but, for all our careful planning, we still had our beggars. They diminished, season by season; but they were a blot on our so-called civilization.

For some reason I had no desire to retire to bed this early. Sitting at

---

* Here Prescot gives a résumé of the Battle of the Flaming Vosks, fought against the Shanks, and much old-soldier talk is quoted which I am almost sure is parody. A.B.A.

the desk in a small study, part of the luxurious suite of apartments in the Alshyss Tower, I wrote to various people, counseling, inquiring, giving news, occasionally issuing direct orders. I wrote to Djanduin, and Valka, to Zamra and to Veliadrin, to Zenicce and to my wild clansmen of the plains of Segesthes. The burs passed as the water dropped in the clepsydra, and I did not notice. From this small study I could feel in direct contact with all those places in the world of Kregen that are especially dear to me.

I could not, of course, write to Delia.

Where she was, only the Sisters of the Rose knew.

So, and with strokes of the pen rather harder than softer, I directed a letter to Katrin Rashumin in the pious hope she would see that the SoR forwarded it to Delia.

Then I took a fresh sheet of paper, and hesitated.

Drak.

He still was not the Emperor of Vallia.

Finally, I wrote a letter couched in general terms, inquiring particularly after the trouble in the southwest of the island. I also wished to know the progress of our movements in the north and northwest, where Inch and Turko were involved.

Having written to Drak, I could write to my youngest son, Jaidur, who was the King of Hyrklana, and bring him up to date with the news and inquire what went forward in his realms.

And then I went to bed.

The first person I saw the following morning was cheerful old Ortyg ham Hundral, the Pallan of Buildings. He wore a loose round cape and a close-fitting cap they call a havchun. He beamed at me, sipping the hot milk my people had prepared for him.

"Majister! We have discovered the plans of the Temple of Havil in Splendor!"

"This is splendid news, Ortyg," I said, enthused at once.

"We can rebuild houses to fresh patterns; the priests have been insistent that their temples be restored in toto."

We talked on for a space, for the Pallan of the Buildings was a learned man, brought out of retirement. He had had nothing to do with mad Empress Thyllis, living quietly on his estates. He bustled off, cheerfully, and in came Nedfar.

"Please tell me what you propose in respect of the regular regiments of Djangs still in Hamal, Dray. I value them. But some of the people—well, they—"

"They don't like to see foreign troops in their capital city. Well, that is more than understandable."

"It is not quite that. Of course, you are right; but it has more to do with the very ferocity and build of your Djangs."

I laughed.

"My four-armed Djangs will take most foemen apart, yes, I agree. As for your damned stinking Kataki slaver, with his whiptail and bladed steel, Djangs rejoice to blatter Katakis."

"No one likes Katakis."

"They almost took over your country, Nedfar."

"Only through that mad wizard, Phu-si-Yantong. Well, all that is gone, dust blown with the wind. We admire your Djangs. But we would feel happier if there were apims of Vallia to represent your presence."

"Very good, Nedfar. I'll see to it."

"You had no fortune last night?"

"No." I told Emperor Nedfar what had happened in The Ruby Winespout. "I'm seeing my man today. He has to know more about Spikatur than he has told us so far."

"I could wish the business well away and gone."

"Like your Tyfar and my Jaezila. Is it true that no one knows where they had flown?"

"Perfectly true, for my people. I have asked."

"So have I. When your son and my daughter take it into their heads to plan a little intrigue, all the pressures of Imrien would not pry the secret loose."

"No, by Krun!"

"And," I said, making my voice more courteous, tactful, "the princess Thefi—?"

Nedfar's fierce eyebrows drew down. He had developed as a man wonderfully since he had become emperor, and I was now convinced that the megalomania from which he might easily suffer would be resisted. I'd damned well see to it, if it was not. And, as you will readily perceive, there is the example of my own megalomania...

"My daughter Thefi has been sent to a distant cousin, in the country, to take the fresh air, to recuperate, and to take stock. As for Lobur the Dagger, he is posted at once to a Hamalian Air Service patrol, and is out there over the Mountains of the West fighting the wild men."

"Poor Lobur!"

"And if he can win through, then he may win Thefi. Now, Dray, to business. We must restock the vital arms, we need cavalry mounts, both land and air, we need full-scale production of arrows and varter bolts, we need the mergem process to be speeded up—"

"In short, Nedfar, we need the complete arsenal of a major power in full deployment to beat these confounded Shanks. I agree. So, let us to it!"

Two meal breaks later we surfaced. I said, "I have contracted to go and see Pallan Ortyg ham Hundral. He has found the plans of the Temple of Havil in Splendor—"

Nedfar rubbed a finger along his chin.

"I seem to remember a flying ship of the Djangs dropped buckets of combustibles on that Temple, Dray."

"So I am told. Katakis were shooting varters from it."

In the little ensuing silence we both, in our own ways, regretted the follies and extravagances of battle.

The enormous continent of Havilfar, stretching below the equator, contained many countries and nations, the largest of which was the Empire of Hamal up in the northeast corner. The Kingdom of Djanduin, out in the west, was almost as large. Up above the equator to the north lay the island of Pandahem, divided up into various countries, and divided, also, east to west by a chain of mountains which altered completely the climate of Northern and Southern Pandahem. North of there lay Vallia... And, to the east of Vallia, Valka...

Well, I own it, I sensed the feelings of the people of Hamal. We of Vallia and Valka and Djanduin, with friends from Hyrklana and the Dawn Lands, had rid the world of the mad Empress Thyllis and the arch-fiend, Phu-si-Yantong. But, well and all, perhaps we'd be better off at home? We might be overstaying our welcome here. I sensed this, in the delicate way Nedfar talked, his graceful gestures, and the way those eyebrows manipulated the shadows over his face.

"We must rebuild Hamal, Nedfar. We must be strong to face those devilish Shanks who raid us. But I think you know my feelings on having a country fight its own battles."

"Yes," he said wryly. "I remember."

"And I am restless. I am asked this and that, I do this and that, and yet—"

"The Empress Delia?"

"By Zair, how I miss her!"

"Well, my friend, you must go adventuring, as you love so well to do."

"But—"

He smiled, and in his firmness of feature reminded me of his son, Tyfar, who was a blade comrade and who would, if all our friends could knock some sense into him and her, marry my daughter Jaezila.

"Oh, yes, Dray," said the Emperor of Hamal, "there are always buts."

Then Seg came in after knocking and I was able to dissimulate. By Krun! But Nedfar was right!

"Seg!" I said, and I spoke so that my comrade swung instantly to face me, and I saw that quickly suppressed flick of his hand, ready to draw sword or bow. "Seg, my old dom. You and I are due for some roving again—we have nothing now to detain us here."

"That is true. I have the Kroveres of Iztar, but we are busily recruiting and things go passably well—"

"We will visit Vallia and Valka—"

"Visit?"

Nedfar saw what Seg meant.

"Can you visit your home?"

For me, an Earthman transited across four hundred light-years of emptiness to a marvelous and wonderful new world—to such a one—where did home lie? With Delia, yes. But she was off adventuring, driven by compulsions a mere mortal man was not allowed to share. Home? Yes, Valka was my home, up there in the high fortress castle of Esser Rarioch overlooking Valkanium and the bay. And, too, the gorgeous enclave city of Zenicce was home to me, and so were the tents of my ferocious Clansmen of Segesthes. And, too, so was the windy city of Djanguraj in my Kingdom of Djanduin. I have many homes, many I have not spoken of. But I think in the end a fellow's true home is what he carries in his head. Where his thoughts lie, that is home.

Another knock sounded and the two guards opened the doors with a quick check of the fellow they admitted.

Protocol, at least for the Emperor of Vallia, was deliberately relaxed.

One of the guards, old whiskery Rubin who could sink a stoup of ale without pause and who had been in one or another of my regiments for a long long time, opened his mouth and bellowed: "Majister! Andoth Hardle, the Spy, craves audience!"

I did not burst out laughing. But, by Vox, I own my craggy old beakhead split into a most ferocious smile of pleasure. Good old Rubin. Spies, like anyone else, had to be announced to the emperor unless they were personal friends.

"He," observed Seg, "won't be a spy for long if Rubin shouts any louder."

"Send him in, Rubin," I said.

"Quidang!"

And so my latest spy, Andoth Hardle, trotted in.

Trotted. Well, he was small and lithe and wore a chin beard, and was deft and inconspicuous, quick with a dagger, and wearing link mesh under his tunic. He bowed.

"Majister."

"Sit down, Andoth, and take a glass. Your news?"

"The woman with the coiled hair has been taken up."

"What!" exclaimed Seg. "So easily?"

Andoth Hardle sat in the chair that did not stand next to my desk, and he delicately filled the glass on the side table with parclear. He put the jug down and rearranged the linen cover. He lifted the glass and the parclear sparkled.

One does not ordinarily toast in parclear.

"Taken up, Kov Seg. She was discovered lying in the gutter, drunk and stupid."

At once Seg and I believed we understood.

"Poor soul," said Seg, and he spoke softly.

Nedfar, too, caught the drift.

"Yet, she was an enemy, and would have destroyed us."

"True."

"You will see her, majister?" Hardle drank and wiped his lips daintily with lace-trimmed linen from his sleeve.

"I will see her, Andoth."

Seg looked in my direction, and I nodded. Of course.

Then I said, "Andoth. This is good news. But, before I see her, make sure she is sober and cleaned up, given fresh clothes if necessary, fed and cared for."

"I understand, majister. It shall be as you command."

"Does she give a name?"

Hardle twisted his head sideways. "She is not, majister, the Lady Helvia. At least, she says her name is Pancresta."

"I see. Send for Hamdi the Yenakker. Have him study this woman, and do not let her see him. I feel there is a great deal we can learn from her."

So that was how it was arranged. But privately I wondered just how much we would ever learn about Spikatur Hunting Sword.

Three

Questions for Spikatur

The corridors, sculpted from rock, trimmed with rock, arched and groined with rock, loomed grim and forbidding. The walls ran with moisture. Torches hurled sharp sparks from glittering particles embedded in the walls. The floor slimed slippery underfoot. These were dungeons.

Yet the woman Pancresta had been placed in a room furnished with some comfort, with carpets and wall hangings, with tables and chairs, and a brazier against the underground damp and chill. Her room would not have shamed a middle-class hotel.

She stood up as we entered.

Her coiled hair was neatly arranged. She wore a long blue robe, and the hems were trimmed with fur. A cheap fur, perhaps, but soft and warm. Her face was pale.

While that was natural, the paleness was more a habitual absence of high color than a result of her capture, her present predicament. This, I felt strongly.

Her face was of the long, plain, strong type, with prominent cheekbones, and a tight mouth. She had worn armor, and a sword belted around those lean hips. She would be mean in a fight, and mean elsewhere, and now she was filled with a vindictive desire to revenge herself for the death of her lover.

I said, "Mistress Pancresta?"

She inclined that hard face, and the coiled hair caught the light.

"You will not believe me, Mistress Pancresta, if I express sorrow for the deaths of your companions. But it is so. Needless death offends me."

"Death is not needless when it is such as you who should die."

Seg opened his mouth, and I said, and I think I surprised her, "Why?"
"Why?"

She opened her eyes fully. They were dark with pain.

"Yes. Why is it needful that I die?"

"Because you are one of the lordly ones."

I laughed.

"I? A lordly one? You mock me, Mistress Pancresta."

Her hard face did not flush; but her lips tightened still more.

She fairly spat out: "You are the Emperor of Vallia. That, alone, marks you for destruction."

"As to that," I said casually, "I'm inclined to agree with you. But that has nothing to do with death."

She was puzzled.

"You speak in riddles."

"No. I speak in words that will be understood by those who have the intelligence to understand."

"Now you mock me."

Truth to tell, true though all this was, it was of small comfort to me, knowing that I intended to shift the job of being Emperor of Vallia off onto my fine son Drak. Still, he was born to be an emperor. I had merely gained that job by my sword and by election. There were differences. And, mind you, my way may very well be the better of the two...

"I would like you to tell me what you know of Spikatur Hunting Sword."

She smiled then, a hard and cruel smile. But I fancied there was uncertainty in it, too.

"Spikatur will sweep you and all your kind away."

"You mean you will go around murdering all the people you don't like?"

"No—it is not like that—"

"Then what is it like?"

"It is a Great Jikai!"*

I frowned. The misuse of the word Jikai does not amuse me.

"I allow there are many princes and kings in this world who would be

---

* Jikai: this word here quite clearly carries the meaning of Crusade. A.B.A.

better off out of it. But not all. And not all the ordinary folk you people murder. You are drenched in blood, and most of it is blood of innocent people."

Now, Nedfar was a man of high principles, a man of impeccable integrity, as I knew. He had been talked to long and long before agreeing to become the Emperor of Hamal. But, for all that, he was a natural-born prince, a Prince of Kregen. Now he coughed a dry little cough and spoke firmly. "I am against the use of torture. It dismays and sickens me. But in certain cases—"

Seg said, "Careful, Emperor. Dray is sensitive on that point."

Nedfar's reply was brusque.

"So am I, Kov Seg. But my good friend Trylon Agrival was foully murdered the other week by these monsters. He was a man steeped in the ancient lore of the Sunset People. Why should they murder him?"

"Because," burst out the woman, "he pried into secrets we were never meant to discover."

Extraordinarily difficult, by Krun, to argue against beliefs of this kind!

But argue one must. At least, argue and talk and cajole. Torture—no. I'd have no part of that, and neither would Seg. And, while my regiments remained in Hamal, neither would Nedfar, comrade or no. And there spoke the voice of paranoia, loud and clear...

I said, "I have struggled against unjust authority all my life. I have been slave. I have been whipped and tortured and chained in far fouler dungeons than any you may imagine, Mistress Pancresta. I do understand so much of what Spikatur Hunting Sword originally stood for." I used the Spikatur oath. "By Sasco! I have fought alongside the adherents of Spikatur!"

She looked surprised not so much at what I said, for that could all be a hollow shell of lies, designed to trick her, but at my use of the oath calling on Sasco.

"What do you know, fool, of Spikatur?"

So I told her what little we knew. The Spikatur Hunting Sword conspiracy had begun as a force to defeat Hamal. We believed it originated in Pandahem. It was made up of groups of people and owned no single leader.

At this she leered at me, and her voice thickened.

"This is all over now."

Seg whistled.

I saw what she had let slip.

She, too, saw. Her lids lowered over her eyes. Her mouth clamped to a bar.

"We shall leave now, Mistress Pancresta. But we shall return. I need answers to those questions. If you know, I think it would be wise to answer."

"We of Spikatur Hunting Sword are not afraid to die for what we believe."

"I know," I said, and we went out and left her alone. And then Nedfar, regal, dazzling in his robes, a prince, the Emperor of Hamal, turned at the door as the guards prepared to clang the bars shut.

"Remember, Mistress Pancresta. Dying is easy. It is of the manner of dying that you should think."

Seg started to say as we walked up that dolorous corridor: "You wouldn't really—" Nedfar shook his head.

"Of course not. But dark thoughts loosen tongues." The whole scene here distressed me, because a woman was incarcerated, because we were trying to force her to reveal what she had sworn to keep hidden, because the naked face of force was being used. But remembering old Trylon Agrival did make the point. He had been a Vallian, visiting Hamal and seeking to uncover the riddles of the past. He was gentle, absorbed in his work, a man out of the run of politics. Nedfar and Agrival had struck up a firm friendship. Agrival had tended to wander off into ruins, poking and prying, trying to read the old inscriptions. Such a man was very far from the lordly ones of Kregen, rubbing the noses of the poor in the dirt.

Yet the assassins of Spikatur Hunting Sword had murdered him.

I felt that a new wave of terror would be unleashed, that this new leader the Spikatur adherents had acquired, this dark unknown, would bring down all that we had been struggling to achieve.

Once, I had seen Spikatur as a potent if suspect weapon in the struggle against Hamal. Now that weapon was being turned against the very people who had emerged successfully from the fight against Hamal—the Hamal represented by mad Empress Thyllis—and against innocent people who stood aloof from the conflict. This did make sense. But in the context of Kregen and the future we all faced in dealing with the marauding Shanks, the sense was completely overshadowed by the greater sense of mutual preservation and freedom.

"Cheer up, my old dom," quoth Seg as we emerged into the glorious twinned rays of the Suns of Scorpio. "Now this fresh air after those dungeons gives me an appetite."

"Capital," I said, and off we went to find our second breakfast.

Not in the mood for one of those huge festive meals of Kregen, Seg and I bade a temporary farewell to Nedfar and took ourselves off to our private rooms. There we ate well, quaffed good Kregen tea, and discussed just what we planned to do.

As usual, Seg took up the latest stave on which he was practicing his magic. In due time that stave would become a superb bowstave. There is, as I have said before and will no doubt say again, no finer archer in all Kregen than Seg Segutorio. His face was intent as he worked.

"And you plan to take off, leave all this high life, tramp off into the wilderness?"

"If fate takes me that way. Otherwise, I plan a little jaunt to a few places I know where one may come by some action, a few drinks, good food and a lot of laughs—"

"You will go alone?"

"Only if you elect not to come."

He looked up quickly, and the fey blueness of his eyes struck like daggered lightning through a black overcast. He smiled. He gave the stave a tremendous buffet so that it spun around and around.

"The elections have just taken place," he said.

So that was all right.

Then whiskery Rubin stuck his head around the door and bellowed.

Rubin, incidentally, like so many of my old swods, was a Zan Deldar and would, at his own request, remain so. Not for him the escalation of the dizzy heights. He could become a Hikdar, the next rank up, at once, should he so wish. It would not be long before he was a Jiktar. It would take a little longer, a matter of a decade, if no one got massacred too recklessly, before he made Chuktar. But for whiskery Rubin, being a Deldar, and a Zan Deldar, the top of the tree at that, was ambition, reward and pleasure enough.

"Majister! Hamdi the Yenakker craves audience."

"Show him in, Rubin, please." I glanced across sharply. "You have been on duty a long time."

"Aye, majister. Standing in for young Long Wil, who has a twisted shoulder."

"Oh?"

Rubin looked evasive. The magnificence of his uniform was entirely superficial. All the gold and braids and feathers would not interfere with his sword arm. But he did look splendid. His medals—the bobs—on his chest glittered.

"Fell, majister, twisted his shoulder."

Far be it from me to inquire further. But, just to be devilish and to let my swods know I wasn't senile yet, I walked across, digging out a gold zan-deldy piece. This I placed in the horny palm of Rubin.

"Puggled, winner or loser. You will know, Zan Deldar Rubin, who deserves this acknowledgment from me."

"Aye, majister, may the glory of Opaz shine on us all."

He stiffened up into attention. On Kregen it could not be ramrod attention; but he stiffened up as straight as one of Seg's best shafts. His face, brown and lined and like a chunk of that hard stone they can never seem to break under a year's hard labor in distant Shalasfreel, betrayed nothing. If Long Wil had been in a fight, his comrades would see to it that the deserving of the combatants received the gold. And ten gold pieces, in one zan-deldy coin, was a matter of consideration. I did not think Long Wil had fallen down drunk. That behavior tended to exclude folk from the ranks of my various guard units.

As Hamdi the Yenakker sidled in, I reflected that this little aside with Rubin was not unimportant. Of little incidents like this was the trust between commander and men forged, for there was nothing here of the insulting patronage of handing out money as largesse without reason beyond the buying of men's loyalty. My men and I swore our mutual loyalties by the edge of the sword.

"Well, Hamdi?"

"Majister. She is the woman I warned you of."

"So I gathered. This Pancresta. Sit down and take a glass. What else have you learned?"

"She is from Pandahem. From south. I do not trust her. But she asks for an audience with you, majister."

"Does she? Well, Hamdi, you rogue, as you well know I do not trust you. Oh, we have done business in the past. But mayhap this time... Who knows?"

Hamdi looked hurt. He was still the same tall and upright fellow, carrying himself with a swagger, now sworn to all things Vallian after our victory over mad Empress Thyllis. But he understood we knew he was a rogue. I feel that upset him only in that he felt less free to practice his wiles. Well, nothing much need be said about Hamdi the Yenakker. He sold us information. He provided contacts. He had his uses.

And, so far, he had not betrayed us.

"Have I not served you well, majister? Was it not I who took you and Kov Seg here to The Crushed Toad to meet Nath the Dwa? Have I not provided you with trustworthy information? Did I not save the life of young Strom Nomius?"

"Aye, Hamdi, you did warn us in time to prevent his assassination. But to the matter of the woman—"

"Yes, majister. I think she wishes to trick you by giving you false information." He stood up for himself. "Unlike me."

Seg said, "I could wish Deb-Lu or Khe-Hi were here."

"Aye."

Had our two comrades who were Wizards of Loh been available on hand, they might well have riddled out if Pancresta spoke the truth. As it was, the Wizards were about their own business.

Then Hamdi said, "Has... pressure... been exerted on the woman, majister?"

"No," I said. His look was sly, understanding, a tilt to his head and a side-long glance conveying what he was hinting at. "Nothing like that, and nothing like that will be permitted while Kov Seg or myself remain in command."

"Well, majister, something made her wish to talk."

I would not open out on a speculation on the results of Nedfar's threat. I said, "It is probably as you say. She wishes to trick us. I will see her."

Hamdi screwed up his eyes.

"There is one thing—"

"Yes?"

"—She insists that she meet you privately, in the open, away from spying eyes."

Carefully, Seg said, "Can she insist?"

"She was, kov, most insistent."

"She must be afraid of others of Spikatur. If she sells them, they will surely seek to kill her."

"That is right," I said. "But it suggests there are loopholes in the security here."

"It is all Hamalese, now, apart from this wing of the palace."

"All right." One woman, alone, deserved her fair chance of life. "I'll see her as she wishes."

"1 shall arrange it, majister."

Hamdi rose, finishing his glass of parclear, and bowed. I let him. He put store by these things. When he had gone, Seg said, "All right, Dray. So you meet her and some hidden stikitche puts a shaft through your back."

"So I shall wear a breast and back."

"If it was me, I'd put one through whatever of you was unarmored. That'd be your vosk-skull of a head."

"Most assassins are not as good shots as you."

"Any stikitche worth contracting could hit your head."

The point of this wrangle was perfectly clear. Seg wanted to come along, too. I did not say him nay.

There was time to see Ortyg ham Hundral, Pallan of Buildings, and to join with him in gleeful contemplation of the plans of the Temple of Havil in Splendor. I had only one fleeting thought at the oddness of this. Not so long ago I'd have been straining every nerve to destroy every damned temple erected to Havil the Green.

Times change, by Zair!

When Hamdi the Yenakker reported back the location chosen for the meeting with Pancresta, I own to an odd feeling of the rightness of the choice.

The bloodiness of the Arena in Ruathytu was notorious throughout the length and breadth of the continent of Havilfar. I had not fought there at that time, although the ways of the Star Lords are passing strange and beyond the full comprehension of mortal men; but I had fought in the Arena of Huringa in Hyrklana. Along with many others, I had set my face against the idea of the Jikhordun, the Arena, the killing machinery of deadly games on the silver sand.

In the Great Arena, here in Ruathytu, the arch devil Phu-si-Yantong, that infamous Wizard of Loh, had made his last stand, his final resistance, until blown away in the Quern of Gramarye fashioned by our comrade Wizards of Loh.

Since that awful occurrence, the place had not been popular, we had done all we could to discourage attendance, and the other smaller Jikhorkduns had reopened to patronage we deplored. So the Great Arena lay deserted under the Suns, and the silver sand sparkled unmarked by the tramp of booted feet, the rush of talons, the sprinkle of shed blood.

Here, out on the silver sand, Pancresta chose to meet us and tell us the secrets of Spikatur Hunting Sword.

Four

What Chanced in the Arena

The Emperor of Hamal said in his sternest voice, "Remember, Dray Prescot, you are the Emperor of Vallia. And King of Djanduin. And many other notable titles and ranks. It is not fitting that you should not go attired as an emperor."

"As to that," I said, adjusting the plain lesten-hide belt with the silver buckle, "I never feel comfortable in all that popinjay finery."

Seg let loose a cross between a grunt and a chuckle.

So, quickly, very quickly, I said, "I speak only for myself, Nedfar. You, I am sure, understand that."

Nedfar took it in good part.

He was dressed magnificently, a shimmering statuesque emperor, a lordly one of Kregen, dominating and superb.

Seg and I wore the brave old scarlet, with a cunning coat of mesh-linked mail, and over that we wore a breast and back apiece, since that pleased Seg on my behalf. Our harness was plain, workmanlike, without any of your frills. The smell of rich leather-oil pervaded the chamber not unpleasantly. I say rich—any fighting man will use the best equipment he can lay his hands on, and taking care of weapons and harness is a number-one priority. That oil was expensive.

Seg found himself in something of a quandary.

His strong face looked puzzled. I laughed and said, "Luckily enough I am not in that predicament."

He hefted two bows, one in each hand, and he looked at and weighed one and then he looked at and weighed the other.

Finally, he said, "Were it not thought excessive, what our old comrade Fran the Zappim would call Vulgar Ostentation, I would take them both."

"Even a Djang finds difficulty in shooting two bows at once. They do not recommend the practice, and—"

"And they have four arms! I know..."

"We are only going to speak to a poor woman, alone, out on the silver sand."

"I don't trust her."

"No more do I. Take them both, then. They will snug up over your shoulder well enough, seeing they are so alike."

He made that little grunting chuckle of his, and shook his head, and shoved both bowstaves up over his shoulder.

"I may look a ninny, but that does not bother me."

Nedfar shared the general amusement over Seg and his precious bows.

We strapped up our usual arsenal of weaponry—a rapier and main gauche, a drexer, a shoulder pack of throwing knives, those little deadly weapons the girls of the great clans of Segesthes call the Deldar, a hunting knife, odds and ends of lethal nastiness. Weight had to figure into all this, of course, but a fellow can carry a tremendous load when his life depends on it, and we took nothing we felt we did not need or might not require.

For helmets, which we took because Nedfar insisted, we chose plain, smoothly round, headpieces, rather like basinets, and the gallant red feathers flaunted from minuscule silver rosettes. Over all we each flung a scarlet cape. This was, perhaps, carrying effect to extremes; but I had taken some heed of Nedfar's words.

So dressed up in a curious mixture of men going off to war and men intending merely to impress, we set off.

If I do not mention that snugly scabbarded down my back lay a Krozair longsword, it is merely because whenever the opportunity offers I take a specimen of that great brand as a matter of course. There was, I firmly believed, on Kregen only one pattern of sword superior to the Krozair longsword, and that was the marvelous Savanti sword.

So, dressed and accoutred and with a good meal under our belts, we went down to the courtyard and mounted our zorcas.

As we rode along through the crowded streets after the short haul across the river, our zorcas patient of this delay before we remounted, I reflected on how well I knew this once-hostile city, how great and magnificent a place it was, and yet how different in atmosphere from the other great cities I knew on Kregen.

Everywhere people were busy about the task of rehabitation. The place hummed with activity. Our small bodyguard rode at our backs, a party of Nedfar's personal guards, and a half-dozen files of my duty squadron, which happened to be this day from 1ESW. The First Regiment of the

Emperor's Sword Watch. I knew every man, and every man knew me. But, as we rode, we attracted little attention.

For this I was glad, but it showed all too clearly that the people of Ruathytu might have misinterpreted the attitude of their new emperor.

Nedfar rode between us, and presently he half-leaned sideways and said to me, "The Empress Thyllis would never have ridden through her capital city like this, Dray. There would have been processions, and regiments of guards, and chanting and singing everywhere she went."

I acknowledged the truth of this observation.

"The people do not fawn on me, and that is good. It seems your brand of emperorship works here in Hamal as well as in your Vallia."

"That pleases me. I can't stand the sight of rows of upturned bottoms."

Seg laughed.

The sounds and scents of a busy city surrounded us. But as we neared the Jikhorkdun the clamor fell away. The aqueducts bulked black against the sky. The cobbles rang louder under the hooves of the zorcas. These splendid riding animals, proud, curveting, each with his single spiral horn jutting arrogantly from his forehead, were full of fire and mettle.

And the Arena brooded like a dark blot upon the city.

Hamdi the Yenakker waited for us inside the first of the shadows.

He bowed most respectfully to Nedfar.

"Lahal, Emperor!"

Nedfar acknowledged with a Lahal and a gesture, and then we dismounted and, with the guards closed up around us, went through the first of the warren of courtyards and practice rings and bazaars. Everywhere they lay deserted and empty.

Once, this place would have been frantic with the everyday carryings-on of the Jikhorkdun. The booths were shuttered, the stalls empty. The practice rings gaped blindly.

Through the colossal arches supporting the seating of the amphitheater we went, and our booted feet rang hollow echoes.

And so we stepped out from one of the ring of gateways, out onto the sands of the Arena, out onto the Silver Sand.

One could fancy all those rows and rows of seats, towering up into the sky, filled with the insensate beast-roar of a blood-mad crowd. Thousands of people, screaming with the blood lust upon them, and, down here where we stood, a small forlorn group, the kaidurs would have fought and died.

I gave a little shivery shake of my shoulders.

An airboat drifted in over the stands, lowering down to the sand.

Seg said, "At least she travels in comfort."

"It was thought best, kov, by the Jiktar of the guard." Hamdi spread his hands, saying it was no affair of his. The airboat settled out in the center of the arena.

Nedfar took a step forward.

He halted, and turned to us.

I do not see why—at that stage—we felt tense, jumpy. We were just humoring a proud and willful woman, attempting to gain secrets from her without the use of force. But, all the same, I own to putting my fist down onto the hilt of my drexer, and of looking sharply into the blue-black shadows around the arena.

"Dray?" said Nedfar.

"You are emperor here now, Nedfar."

"Only because of you... Very well. Let us all go out together."

Seg, Nedfar and I walked across the silver sand.

Sometimes, in the old days, the Jikhorkdun of Ruathytu had used golden sand.

Red blood still looked dark and unwholesome, spilt on gold as on silver sand.

The heat beat down. The suns were halfway down, sending mingled shadows across the floor of the arena. All the rows of flagstaffs were bare of treshes, naked and like withered sticks after a gale.

Pancresta alighted from the airboat.

We walked on.

She advanced to meet us. We would meet just over halfway.

She wore her long blue gown, open now at the throat. Even at this distance she gave the impression of hard dominance, of authority, of determination. She walked well.

"We have done well," said Nedfar, "to have caged this one."

"Aye," said Seg.

The way Nedfar observed that we had done well, and my own observation that Pancresta walked well, chimed. One supported the other. The Arena in Ruathytu is large. We took our time walking to this meeting. All the time we strode on, in a strange and affecting way, yet in no sense a weird or eerie way, I could hear the crazed roar of a blood-lusting crowd in my head. I could hear them, and if I half-closed my eyes I could see them—see the rows of inflamed faces and upraised fists, see the spectators as I fought out on the Silver Sand, see them all, by Beng Thrax's Glass Eye and Brass Sword!

In the airboat parked beyond the advancing form of Pancresta, the guards waited. There were not many of them in the small flier; after all, they merely guarded a lone woman. They were Hamalese, decked out in blue and green and with a deal of silver lace and colored feathers.

An airboat flitted in over the western edge of the amphitheatre. Seg glanced up, following my gaze.

Nedfar said, "I gave orders that the patrols should be active."

By the way we walked, the way we talked and, I suppose, by the way we thought, we gave an enormous importance to this woman Pancresta. Incongruous? I was beginning to think so when the airboat abruptly swooped.

She passed directly over the flier that had brought the woman to this meeting.

A small dark object tumbled out, and then another and another.

They dropped down, plummeting into the flier.

They were not pots of combustibles.

"What?" said Nedfar, and he halted.

A man leaped from the parked flier.

He flailed his arms around his head. He danced like a crazy man. Another followed him, and then a third. They swirled and beat their arms. Around their heads a hazy shadow drifted, joining and parting, a grayish shroud lapping them together in a cloud of torment.

"Wasps," said Seg. "Or bees."

"Aye."

We started to run. Seg and I raced over the silver sands, and as we ran so we drew our swords.

No thought of the incongruousness of all this armory could stand now against the stark reality of the trick by which we had been fooled.

Pancresta stopped. She looked up. She held up her arms.

There was tremendous triumph in the gesture.

The voller sweeping through the air dived low, flew above her and a net spun out, a mesh of glinting silver.

The net grasped Pancresta as she grasped the strands.

In a twinkling she was drawn up.

She vanished over the coaming of the voller and the air-boat pivoted, rose and stormed away. She disappeared over the lip of the amphitheatre.

The whole thing was over in the time a rapier takes to pierce a man's lung.

Seg stuffed his sword back into the scabbard and I did the same. There was no need for us to exchange words.

Both of us knew what had happened.

We belted in a straight run for the abandoned flier.

Corruption had been at work, bribery, force. The Hamalese guards had been got at. Pancresta's friends had been in communication with her in her dungeon cell. A guard had acted as a go-between. The chances were strong that he was himself a secret member of Spikatur Hunting Sword. Whatever the truth of that, the result was plain. The patrol had been outwitted, a flier had snatched up the woman, and the guards were reeling about, screaming, stung and bitten and tormented.

Seg and I bundled into the voller.

She went up with Seg at the controls like a stone from a catapult.

Low Seg hurled her, low over the topmost tier of seating. We scraped across and shot away.

"There," said Seg.

Ahead of us, speeding into the sunset fires of red and jade, the dark shape of the voller flitted like a moth against a lantern.

As we watched she turned northward, swinging in a wide arc.

Instantly, Seg swung the levers of the craft over and we hared off to cut the corner.

"We won't lose them now," I said.

"They have a fast airboat. It will be a long chase."

"Aye."

Below us, glimpsed and lost as we sped on, the smoking wreckage of a guard voller appeared and disappeared. She had obviously been burned by Pancresta's friends.

"Just put your foot down to your left, will you, my old dom?"

I glanced down and then did as Seg requested.

The crunch did not please me.

"I'll check if there are any more—"

A few more half-drunken wasps were disposed of.

The strange thing—and I make a particular note of the strangeness of it—was my complete lack of emotion when I saw the brown and red scorpion. He waddled out from under a fold of a flying fur. I just squashed him.

I was so wrought up with mortification at the simple way Pancresta had tricked us, I just did not have time to dwell on the propensities of the Star Lords for sending scorpions to whisk me off to other parts of Kregen, or to send me packing home to Earth, four hundred light-years away.

And, anyway—home?

My home was on Kregen.

Seg said, "Cleansing finished?"

"As far as I can see. Do we keep up with them?"

"Just. The vollers are well matched."

I glanced back over the stern.

"There is no one following us."

"Ha," said Seg. "We did get away smartish."

"Yes."

We were two old campaigners and we worked together as a team. We did not waste words, unless we jested. I know Seg was as affronted as I that we had been so easily sucked in.

Even in the rush of wind the voller held the tang of spilled wine. The Hamalese guards had started their drinking early. I found a simple earthenware jug that might contain ale or water or oil, and prised the stopper out and sniffed.

"A middling Stuvan, Seg. You will join me?"

"The Spikatur rascals used pots of stinging insects and scorpions. They did not, I fancy, poison the wine. Yes, my old dom, I will join you."

As I poured I reflected that the Spikatur people had been clever. They had burned a guard voller outside the Jikhorkdun. They had dropped their little stinging allies on the airboat inside the arena. No doubt the guards were rushing to the burning flier, and Nedfar was having some difficulty in finding guards and fliers to obey his orders inside the amphitheatre. Had they burned the voller that had brought Pancresta, the flier in which we now pursued them, they'd have been swamped by patrols.

As it was, Seg and I were just two people to chase them out of all the patrolling guards.

Ironic.

Yet for me, and I thought for Seg, also, this was just what the doctor ordered, as they used to say.

There exist on Kregen as well as Earth bone-dry pundits who scorn tales of adventure. If these people lack the breadth of imagination to encompass an understanding of the pressures on, condition of, illumination of and triumphs and failures of the human spirit then that is their loss, not ours. The unwillingness to accept defeat tamely does not brand a person as a monster—it may, of course. But then, that is what adventure tends to do, sort the sheep from the goats, the ponshos from the leems, make people face themselves, shorn of pretensions, and—perhaps, if they are lucky— grasp at a little of what the human spirit exists at all for...

Seg and I were off, and we were off on adventure-bent, and Spikatur was only half the answer and hardly any of the reason.

Five

The Hissing of the Star Lords' Chair

How terrible to live in a world without color!

Or, rather, given the universal prodigality of Nature's palette, a world in which you could not see and appreciate color. To live in a monochrome world...

The sheeting lights, rippling and undulating across the sky, the streaming mingled radiance of the Suns of Scorpio, jade and ruby, illuminating everything in fires of crimson and emerald—nothing. You'd see nothing of this in a world without color...

You'd see a pale ghost rising in the sky as the first of Kregen's seven Moons, The Maiden with the Many Smiles, lifted over the horizon. Her pinkish radiance flooded down, adding to the lighting of the world. Soon she was joined by her sister, She of the Veils, whose more mellow golden and rose light mingled and softened the pinkness. The surface of Kregen wallowed in color and light.

And, high through the air, the two vollers bore on.

"We just keep pace," observed Seg.

"The suns will soon be gone—"

"Aye. But we have moons for the whole of tonight."

Not for a single mur this night would real darkness fall. On some nights when not a moon shines in Kregen's sky folk say that it is a Night of Notor Zan. And when all seven moons form their intricate dances into a single configuration of brightness, a line of radiance, folk say that it is the Scarf of Our Lady Monafeyom.

No moon would be at the full tonight, and so Our Lady Monafeyom's Scarf would not be seen.

But there would be ample light for us to track and follow the fleeing airboat.

Like a flitting black bat she darted ahead, fleeting, wispy, a phantom under the Moons of Kregen.

Seg and I took watch and watch, turn and turn about.

We flew North.

The land of Hamal passed away below.

In the small hours the wine ran out.

Seg said, "Soup?"

"I'm with you, Seg."

The Hamalese guards had provided themselves with rations, not being entirely stupid, and in the Kregan way taking care that they were victualed against a long spell of duty. Seg brought out the crockery pot of soup, and undid its linen cover. He shook the pot and sniffed.

"Vosk and Taylyne—"

"Excellent."

Now we were used to drinking this soup hot, whereas many Hamalese drank it cold. We were flying up north toward the equator, and although fairly high in the air, and at night, we were not too cold. All the same, Vosk and Taylyne soup is, in our opinion, best drunk hot.

Taylynes are pea-sized vegetables, scarlet and orange, and they blend with Vosk, which is one of the most succulent meats of all Kregen, to form a truly splendid soup.

Seg found the slate slab and the box of combustibles and then fished around in his pouch and brought out his tinder box.

Fire may be produced by many different methods, on Kregen as on

Earth, and the tinder box Seg happened to have was one of those little devices the Kregans call januls. He struck flint and steel with unthinking skill, and the tinder caught and flared. In no time the combustible box perched on its slate slab was chucking out the heat.

The soup pot went onto the holder, and Seg sat back, rubbing his hands.

"Any bread?"

He rummaged around in the linen bag and came up with a squat, round, flat, brown loaf.

He sniffed.

"It is leavened, but only just."

"Munsha bread, from one of those shops along Baker's Alley, I'll be bound. Well, it may not be done in the bols style, but it will go down a treat."

"Aye."

The soup began to warm up.

We had covered the forward angles with a flap of cloth, both to protect the combustible box from the slipstream and to conceal the glow. A narrow chink of light escaped aft where the box was beginning to corrode and break down.

The shaft of light, smoky orange, fell on the deck.

It glinted from the chape of a sword scabbard, and threw the grain of the wooden deck into relief. I sniffed the aroma of the soup as Seg broke the bread and looked for butter.

Into that narrow bar of smoky light waddled a scorpion.

"I thought," I said in some disgust, "I'd cleared all the dratted things away."

Seg took no notice.

He sat, half-bent, and the yellow butter on his knife remained unmoving just above the munsha bread.

I stared.

"Seg!"

The scorpion waddled forward.

He was russet and black, banded in glisten, and his sting curved up over his back, arrogantly.

I threw a frantic glance at the controls.

The levers were hooked up with their ropes onto a straight northerly course so that we could prepare our meal and eat in comfort. The voller would fly on. I stared back at the scorpion. He halted on the edge of that narrow band of orange light, glaring at me.

I felt sick.

I knew that my foot could not crush this scorpion.

He waved his sting over his back.

"Dray Prescot," the scorpion said to me, "you are summoned to an audience of the Everoinye."

I swallowed.

At least, this was new.

The Everoinye—the Star Lords—actually telling me they wanted to see me! Damned odd. Frightening, too, for usually the Star Lords just sent their damned scorpion, or their equally damned but hugely large blue Scorpion, and whisked me off.

I said, "Scorpion?"

"You are ready?"

I took a breath.

"You mock me, you must do so."

"Perhaps. It is not for you to inquire into my—"

"Save it, you miniature monster, save it. I know all about my own ineptness and stupidity and how I must not pry into things far beyond my intelligence."

The stinger curled and uncurled.

If that showed the scorpion's anger I did not know or care.

"Get on with it, scorpion. Summon your big blue brother. Let's get this thing over and done with."

And, all the time, Seg remained frozen. He poised, static, and the yellow butter slicked on the knife.

That splendid yellow color took on an unhealthy green tinge. The world turned blue. Blue radiance fell about me.

Waiting for the cold, and the rushing wind, and the endless fall into emptiness, my main emotion was one of irritation. This surprised me. Oh, yes, there was fear in there. I was scared practically witless.

These unknowable people, the Star Lords, possessed awful powers. I was well aware of that. They could hurl me about Kregen, naked and weaponless, to fight for them. They could more dreadfully contemptuously fling me back to Earth, where I was born, four hundred light-years away. They could ruin my life—again.

I waited as the blue radiance dropped about me and the leering form of a giant Scorpion reared above me.

Irritated.

That was it. Through all my panic, irritation with the interruption to my own plans was my main feeling.

Deuced odd.

Usually I was mad clean through, filled with anger, roaring and raging against the Everoinye and their Scorpion, or their messenger and spy, the gorgeous bird, the Gdoinye, in his scarlet and golden feathers. As it was, I just felt like hurling my hat to the deck and jumping on it.

The blueness brightened and cleared. The cold ceased. The fall ended.

I stood on a crimson tiled floor. Crimson walls curved up all about me, arching overhead into a crimson vault in which the brilliant white glitter of stars formed constellations unknown to me.

This chamber, I thought, I had visited before.

I tried to swallow and my mouth was as dry as a pauper's tankard.

The voice whispered in from nowhere and everywhere.

"Sit in the chair, Dray Prescot. Sit."

I licked my lips.

"What damned chair—?" I started to bluster.

The chair sizzled out of the enveloping crimson. It rushed toward me like a runaway totrix, flapping draperies, rippling fringes, lurched to a halt touching my knees. I twisted and fell into the seat. The arms reared up and lapped across my chest like the tentacles of an octopus and the chair hared off, hissing, racing away into the crimson shadows.

This was not madness.

No draught animals pulled the chair. It just went howling along across the floor, hissing, and when it careered around an invisible corner neither it nor I leaned over.

Expecting the light to turn from crimson to green and then to yellow, and to finish up in an ebon chamber with three oval pictures on the walls, I did not close my eyes.

No shimmering veils of gossamer brushed my cheeks.

Pungent scents stung my nostrils.

My eyes watered.

My nose ran.

I tried to clean myself up and the straps held my arms fast locked.

So, then, irritated beyond measure, I yelled.

"Everoinye! Star Lords! What footling nonsense is this?"

They heard me all right. I did not doubt that.

But they did not deign to reply.

After a space I gave up raging at them and calling them all the foul names I could put tongue to, and sat in a dull stupor waiting for what nonsense they would bring on next.

Abruptly, the chair stopped.

There was no sudden jolt. My insides did not give a forward lurch as we halted. One moment we were spinning along, the next we stopped. The transition, abrupt, made no difference to my posture or feelings.

The chair hummed to itself.

I looked around.

If I was not deceiving myself in the pervasive glow, the crimson walls curved away to each side as well as fore and aft. The chair and I waited in the center of a great cross, an intersection of crimson vaults.

A green oblong appeared to my right side.

The size of two men, it shone a refulgent greenness into the lambent crimson glow.

I bellowed.

"Is that you, Ahrinye?"

Ahrinye, a younger Star Lord, had made his opposition to the older Everoinye known. And younger and older...? What meanings did those words have to beings whose life spans must run into the millions of years?

With a whining hiss another chair shot out of the green oblong.

It rushed past me.

It hurtled away along the crimson floor, heading the way I had come.

One glance was all I had, one look at the occupant of the other chair.

He, in his turn, had had one good look at me.

His numim roar lashed out as he whistled past.

"Zaydo! You no good rascal! Skulking again, are you—"

And then he was gone, Strom Irvil of Pine Mountain, gone whirling away. His glorious lion-man's face was in full flower, all his wounds healed. His fur, his hide, glowed more brightly than I had seen it before, when he'd been trapped in the bowels of the earth and sorely wounded. His bristling lion mane was a tawny umber. He roared with the righteous wrath of a great lord chastising a lazy body slave.

The body slave had been me, Zaydo, and Strom Irvil had been taken up before my eyes, taken up by the Everoinye.

Well, he'd come belting out of that green door.

I did not think he'd gone in there by choice.

Was it my turn next?

The chair moved.

Hissing, it curved past the green oblong. The greenness dimmed, dwindled, was gone.

I sucked in a breath.

Nothing like this had happened to me before.

The Star Lords had told me they were growing old. How old that might be was beyond my guessing. Were they becoming senile? Were they fumbling? They had made mistakes before. They had made a mistake with a time loop, and dropped me down into the wrong time, and, correcting that mistake, had given me all of Djanduin. Perhaps their powers were failing?

Anyway, they hadn't given me the Kingdom of Djanduin. That wonderful country had come my way first through boredom and then through duty. I was the King of Djanduin.

The chair passed on along the crimson floor, and the vaulting rolled past above, and the whitely glittering star constellations changed and glowed and shone with supernal fires.

Another chair passed, going by in a flicker of movement.

The occupant was a man, an apim like me, a member of Homo sapiens. I add the sapiens in deference to our old friends the Neanderthals, who in these later times have become far more exciting than of yore. He sat hunched, looking ill. He was, as he would have to be to be a Kregoinye and perform the will of the Star Lords, a big strong fellow with a powerful face. His hair was long and blond and confined in braids beneath a steel helmet. His face bore the scars of battle. He wore a badge upon his chest, a thing of gold and silver threads in the form of a rampant graint. The ferocious crocodile-headed bear leered at me as the man whisked past.

He was gone, and I twisted my head around to stare after him.

He stared back at me, turning to look aft. He smiled.

I returned his smile.

This man, this blond warrior with the graint badge, was the third Kregoinye I had seen. The second was Strom Irvil. The first was Pompino, that foxy-faced Khibil of unusual talents, with whom I had shared many adventures. Would I encounter Pompino here? I looked forward to that meeting with genuine joy.

As for this third Kregoinye—his hard warrior face bore marks of illness, deeply indented lines, and a pallor that floated his tan like scabbed paint. What, I wondered, had happened to him? Then I banished all other thoughts, to concentrate on what was happening, as the chair bore me, with horrible suddenness, into total blackness.

Somewhere a loon laughed like a demented creature.

Or, more likely, someone screamed in torment.

Or, that horrendous noise could more likely be merely the hissing rush of the chair, screeching as it bore me on into the unknown.

Sparkling motes of light danced before me, thin and scattered at first, but thickening, dancing in clumps and gyrating nodules of fiery brilliance. We rushed on and through them, motes of diamond dust, brushing them aside in whirls of sparkling specklings. I drew a breath. The dots of light swung away from us. Rather, we swung away from them, surging out to hiss along an ebon floor, with all the sparkles massing and banking away to the left.

The chair stopped.

I turned my head away from the sparkles and looked to find what I expected to see.

Framed in their thick silver rims, three pictures adorned the far wall. Oval pictures, three of them in a line along the blackness, each showed a different face of the planet Kregen.

Silence dropped down. I could hear my harness creaking as I breathed, and that displeased me, a professional fighting man.

Each silver-framed picture showed an aerial view of Kregen. That on the extreme left showed the familiar outlines of Paz, the side of the world I knew.

There were the outlines of the continents of Havilfar, and Loh, of Segesthes and Turismond. The islands, too, showed clearly, Pandahem and Vallia—I stopped for a moment to dwell on Vallia. That small island at the eastern seaboard was Valka, with Veliadrin to the west. Valka! Well, my home was a long way off now, farther off even than from the flier taking Seg and me north across Hamal.

Funny. Here was I, looking down on a picture of Havilfar, and Seg and I were flying across that land.

He would be gripped in a stasis, unmoving, the butter knife in his hand, all unknowing of where I had gone.

But would he?

Perhaps he merely moved and had his being in normal time. Perhaps it was I who was speeded up in some weird way, sent spinning into the gulfs of superhumanity?

I shifted my gaze away from Paz and looked at the center picture.

This showed sea, with the hint of land at each horizon.

The extreme right hand picture showed a pattern of islands and continents I did not know—although a few of the ancient maps in the Akhram had hinted at such configurations.

I knew I was looking at a map of the other side of Kregen. I committed what I could to memory, as I had tried to do before, and a voice spoke in words and also in my head.

"Yes, Dray Prescot. Look well on the world of Kregen. It may be that you will have little time left to look on the world you call home."

Six

The Everoinye Speak of the Savanti

By this time I was past caring about how scared I was.

I said, "I suppose, Star Lords, you will as usual not bother to explain what you mean."

No answering laugh, a bubbling chuckle, hung on the scented air. I had thought that perhaps the Star Lords retained still some elements of a human sense of humor. But the feeling of coldness drove out laughter.

"We do not need to explain, Dray Prescot. It is not a case of bothering."

Well now...!

"Why do I have little time? Do you intend to send me..." My voice trailed. I did not want even to put into words the thought that I might be dispatched back to Earth.

The voice, in my ears and in my head, said, "We do not have a task for you to perform at the moment. We summoned you here to acquaint you with our desires for the future. Also, Dray Prescot, we wish you to know that we are well pleased that you have driven back the Shanks."

There was so much astonishing information in those few words. I sat back in the chair. The straps confining my arms had fallen away, and I had not noticed.

"You—" I said. Then: "You are thanking me?"

By Zair!

The Everoinye, omnipotent superhuman overlords, descending—condescending—to give a mere mortal human being a word of thanks!

Astonishing!

The Shanks, who by a variety of names were bad news, came raiding up over the curve of the world from their unknown homelands. They festered along the coasts of Paz. And they had tried to invade and settle, and we had beaten them and driven them back in the Battle of the Incendiary Vosks.

The voice whispered, "Yes, Dray Prescot. You beat the Shanks. But the Fishheads are not finished."

"That I know only too well."

"We thank you—and your astonishment offends us. Much has happened since you were first brought to Kregen by the Savanti. We are pleased that we discovered you and took you into our service. You have performed well. But if you think that your days of toil are numbered—"

"No, Everoinye," I said. And I let rip a gusty sigh. "I know I am a fool, an onker of onkers, but I'm not onker enough to believe that."

"We do not dispute your self-judgment that you are an onker."

I just let that ride by. At least, it did show that the Everoinye might still have a shaky grasp on a shoddy sense of humor.

"We said we were pleased you beat the Shanks. We did not thank you."

So that was one in the eye for me. I had presumed, and had presumed wrong.

"But we do thank you, as you pointed out by your astonishment. We are offended at ourselves, that we have fallen away from a humanity of which once we were proud."

"Once?"

The voice sharpened.

"We will not say—'still.' We are no longer human."

"You can say that again."

"We are not, Dray Prescot, less than human. We are superhuman."

Some note, some timbre, something, made me say, "You poor devils."

For a time, then, there remained silence between us.

At last the voice whispered: "Look at the—"

The word used meant nothing.

"Look," said the voice, and there was strained patience in its tones. "Look at the pictures on the wall. The right-hand picture."

I looked.

Whatever word the Everoinye had used to mean the pictures, I did not know it and couldn't reproduce it. Afterward, when I discovered alternative meanings for the word "screen," that still was not the word. That came much later. So I looked and the continents and islands of the antipodes swam before my gaze.

"That configuration of lands is very like Paz. We call it Schan. It is a use name. The Fishheads who raid you in Paz sail from the coastal areas. There are many other peoples of the islands and continents. Unpleasant people. Now look at the center picture."

The sea sparkled blue, almost as though it moved and struck the suns light from wave tops.

I peered more closely and then, miraculously, the sea seemed to swarm away around each side of the picture. It was as though I were falling down into the oval frame.

I jerked back in the chair.

The sea came very near. It was clear and sparkling.

A fleet sailed that sea.

A fleet of squat, square, unlovely ships, with high poops and chunky bows, bristling with armaments. I knew the waterline would be sweetly curved, the underwater parts marvels of naval construction. The masts, tall, after the fashion of poleacres, bore the tall, narrow, slantingly curved sails of the Shanks. They did not so much catch the wind and belly out, as on ordinary vessels, as take the wind and plane it over their curves as the wind planes over a gull's wing.

"I see them," I said. "Fishheads, Leem-Lovers—"

"Yes. They sail to Paz. They follow the advance guard which you defeated on the sands of Eurys."

I shook my shoulders.

"I did not beat the Shanks alone. There were many with me, men and women, all brave and valiant, and all who shared in the victory—"

"Yes, yes. Paz turned out its finest."

"I would not forget that."

"The Shanks have been driven out of some of their homelands. They intend to take yours."

I put my fingers to my forehead, and rubbed.

By Krun! I was tired!

"I, for one, cannot condemn them for that."

"If you understood more, you would—"

"Mayhap. All the same, if they try to steal what belongs to Paz, they must be stopped. Or," I added, hoping for a miracle I knew would not be vouchsafed, "perhaps, they could be assimilated, somehow—we have lands they could settle."

"They intend to slay you all. They do not believe in half measures."

So the ugly business persisted, the desires of men that drove out all feeling, that blinded to all save personal gain.

"And," I said, and the weariness slurred my words, "in the half of the world you call Schan there are many more nasties behind the Shanks."

"Very many."

"Is there an end? Will it ever stop?"

"Yes."

"How?"

"When Kregen becomes as the Everoinye and the Savanti wish it to be. Those desires clearly conflict at the moment; when they are as one, the business will end."

"I thought the Savanti merely wished to make the world over—"

"The Savanti wish to make the world of Kregen a world for apims alone. We believed you understood that."

It had been there, a black thought in my mind, to be driven out and banished. Much had pointed to that reading of the way the Savanti operated. They sent their Savapims out into the world to preserve an apim way of life. They had recruited me from Earth, to be a Savapim, and I had failed them and been driven out—rather, I'd told them to keep their paradise and had escaped with Delia. Now I saw the truth. And I sorrowed, for I had loved the Savanti and their Swinging City of Aphrasöe.

I took a breath.

"This is bad news. Tell me, Everoinye, why do you open up these secrets to me now—?"

"We grow old, Dray Prescot."

The fear in me took a strange turn.

If the Star Lords could grow old, perhaps die, how would that affect the fate of Kregen?

"I have a thousand years of life because I bathed in the Pool of Baptism in Aphrasöe. You, Star Lords, must have many and many a thousand years of life—"

"If we have, you would do well to think that perhaps those thousands of years are not to be devoted to Kregen alone."

I felt shattered.

Then a thought came to me that might be connected.

I said, "You told me that the Savanti objected to what the Curshin did on Kregen—"

"Stop, Dray Prescot!"

The voice almost knocked me over with its power.

"You are a rogue, a miscreant, a man with a charisma that can rouse whole nations to do your will and bidding with joy and gladness. But you may not speak of things that you cannot understand. We told you there are Others of whom we do not speak. The Curshin are not of these. But you do not speak of them."

Somehow, I managed to keep my mouth shut.

The Star Lords went on speaking.

"There are forces driving on the Shanks, as we have told you, obvious forces. But there are Powers that drive on the forces that impel those that drive the Shanks. In these things, Dray Prescot, you may not meddle."

I burst out: "By Vox! I don't want to meddle in any of it! I just want to get the business finished!"

"And that is your task to perform. If you do it well, you may remain on Kregen."

"I'll do it," I raged. "By the disgusting diseased left nostril of Makki Grodno! I'll do it or get chopped in the doing—as you damned well know!"

"We know, Dray Prescot. We know. And—we know far more than you think we know of yourself; because you do not understand yourself at all."

By Zair! That was true—confound it...

The arms of the chair began to writhe up. I guessed there was to be an end to this audience. I got a deep lungful of air and said in my old harsh way, "How long do we have before that enormous fleet of Shanks reaches us? And, where will they touch land?"

"As to the latter—that you must wait and see. As to the former—" Here the arms clamped me tightly. "You have a few seasons yet."

"Enough to—?"

"Enough to do what you want to do, what you know you must do. When the time is nearer, we will call on you again—if we do not call on you before that."

Was there that incongruous note of laughter that I have likened to the last bubble in a forgotten glass of champagne? The Star Lords, were they laughing at me?

The chair gripped me. The blackness swirled. All the stars of the galaxy went around in my head and Seg said, "Here, my old dom, catch hold of this bread, will you. The soup is almost done."

Seven

Into Pandahem

The pursuit continued all through the night.

The Moons of Kregen sailed majestically overhead, the stars massed into a pervasive glitter that reminded me uncomfortably of the spanning star-glitter in that crimson curved chamber, and Seg and I in comradely fashion took watch turn and turn about.

As we both half expected, the fleeing voller swung sharp left-handed after passing the northern coast of Hamal. She fleeted westward. Here we were practically on the Equator.

"Pandahem," said Seg. "Has to be."

"I agree. So there's no wager there."

Seg screwed up his face.

Our voller was making a speed equivalent to just under eighty miles an hour, a pretty fast clip for an airboat, but slow in comparison with some of the swift vollers in existence. We continued to head due west. Seg sniffed the breeze, and looked around from south to north.

Then he said, "No wager on Pandahem, that is true. But a wager on which part?" He laughed, his fey blue eyes very merry. "And any loon would suggest we are making for the southern half, I'll wager you we're headed for the northern."

That thought had been in my mind.

"Very well. I had a hankering for the north. They'll turn north, probably, and aim to bypass the Koroles. A due northwest course would suit them. So, I'll wager on the south."

"A gold double-talen?"

I nodded.

"Done."

Past Skull Bay and due west over the sea fleeted the voller. The day passed. We saw no signs of any other aerial traffic, although twice we passed above argenters, their fat sails bellying and their fat hulls punching into the sea.

We sat and talked and fiddled with our equipment and eyed the fleeing airboat.

"He makes no signs of changing course."

"He is well aware we are following."

"Of course. And," said Seg, "I'll wager he doesn't care!"

"You think he wants us to follow into a trap?"

"More than likely." Seg ran an oiled rag down a sword blade that had been polished to a blinding reflection. "He knows you're aboard."

"Maybe," I said, deliberately ignoring Seg's suggestion that if I were around then everyone would be setting traps for me. Mind you, by Vox, it was uncomfortably near the truth... "I'd suggest he's a cautious navigator. He hugs the coast."

"Well, no one is stupid enough to fly northwest from Ruathytu, over the Western Hills and across whatever lies beyond. The wild men out there are plain murder."

"Yes. But it looks as though he's going to fly along the coast and then turn due north for Pandahem. Cautious to a degree."

"It could be," said Seg, looking up, "that he has one of the old Hamalian vollers that always broke down."

I nodded, realizing the justice of the suggestion.

Now that we had formed bonds of friendship with Hamal, we did not have to buy inferior airboats that continually broke down. But there were still a lot about, despite the losses of the Times of Trouble and the wars.

"If his flier does break down, we're nicely situated to go down and haul him out of the drink. And Pancresta."

But the voller we pursued did not falter in her onward rush through the air of Kregen.

Even at ten db* the journey took a goodly time and I said to Seg, fretfully, "You'd think the Hamalese would provide the fastest vollers for their guards. Nedfar evidently overlooked that."

"Had they done so, that flier up front would be going as fast as we are."

Good old Seg! Trust him to sort out the idiotic remark and upend it for all to see. In this case the all was me.

Then Seg stuck his face up, staring ahead.

"Hullo. He's changing course."

I joined Seg and we watched as the flier up ahead swung gently around, not losing distance over a too-acute turn, and headed into the northwest.

"That course will—" Seg paused, and then went on "—take him between Wan Witherm and the Koroles. It looks like South Pandahem, after all."

We turned to follow.

"It's all jungles and stuff there, I believe."

"Well, he may fly on over the Central Mountains."

Settling down again to this stern chase, we brewed up, and ate some more of the rations. We estimated we could eat them all by the time we arrived at the south coast of the island of Pandahem. If the Spikatur people up front escaped from us over a simple matter like the lack of provender, we'd be looking silly.

"Tighten our belts, my old dom. They won't starve us into giving up the chase."

---

* db: Dwaburs per bur. A dwabur is five miles approx and a bur is forty minutes approx. A.B.A.

I laughed.

"They will more likely escape through a lack of potables in this voller—yes?"

And Seg laughed, too.

We found a brass-bound spyglass in one of the lockers and took turns staring after the voller ahead. I summed up her lines, seeing they were identical for all practical purposes to our own voller's. The differences were merely those of ornamentation. The reason why our speeds were so evenly matched was, therefore, simple. We all flew in the same breed of airboat.

"When I worked in the voller yards of Sumbakir," I said, "we built mostly personal fliers. But I recognize like and like. We'll not catch that fellow unless he does something extremely foolish."

"That may be. But he has to come down somewhere, some time. Then we'll drop down on top of him."

"Aye."

The air tanged with heat, now, the sea below a sweltering shimmer. The rush of the breeze blew as a solid wall of heat, hot and choking in our faces.

"Southeast Pandahem," I said. "I don't know that part of the world, Seg."

"I know nothing definite, either. There was a fellow I knew—a paktun with one ear missing and a ferocious squint, old Frandor the Schturmin—told me he'd once served a king or prince down in the southeast. Stinking jungles, he said. Potty as notors, the lot of 'em, so Frandor said."

"I can believe it."

Then Seg let rip his chuckling grunt of good humor.

"I agreed with him, too. That was before you made me a damned notor, a jen, and dumped me in it. All lords are stark staring bonkers. It is a law of nature."

"That," I said, and I spoke mildly, "I do not believe."

"No? Well, maybe. All I will say is that if the jungle is our destination, we'll sweat a trifle."

The dwaburs passed away, and as we had anticipated, the food ran out.

I eyed Seg.

He saw me looking at him.

I licked my lips.

"You look fat and healthy, Seg," I said. "I wonder how much seasoning you will need."

"You could put all the salt on my tail you liked, my old dom. I'd still be too damned stringy."

"As to that, that I do believe."

We almost lost our quarry in a build-up of clouds over the coast.

The voller ahead darted into a white canyon of billowing cloud. We followed, and we had the speed lever notched over past its rightful halting place. We held on; but it was a near thing.

Thunderstorms raged among the clouds.

Twice we were hurled end over end, and twice we righted ourselves, clinging on with gripping fingers, to hurl our voller on in pursuit.

The storms held us both up, pursuer and pursued alike, and presently the flier carrying Pancresta began a series of maneuvers which, apart from wasting time, gained them not a palm in distance upon us.

At last we broke free of the storms and the darkness and sailed on over jungle, steaming in the new radiance.

A wide river rolled along below, brown and smooth, carving its path through the forest.

"If you can believe what old Frandor the Schturmin told me, and if I'm right, that'll be the River of Bloody Jaws."

I nodded. There was no need to enlarge on who owned the jaws in the Kazzchun River.

"She flows down from the Central Mountains all the way to the Sea of Chem." Seg gestured over the coaming. "There is a fair amount of traffic."

On the broad brown surface boats moved, mostly propelled by long sweeps all working in unison. There were a few more rakish craft tacking along. We saw a few small habitations in clearings along the banks. Whoever lived down there made what they could out of their surroundings.

We flew on, deeper into the island. Pandahem, like Vallia, in size is on the order of the size of Australia; there was a lot of it. Hereabouts, quite clearly, the river formed the main and best, possibly the only, means of communication.

Scraps of cloud drifted by. We saw flocks of waterfowl, wide-winged and long-necked, rising in multitudes from the waters. Brown mudflats gleamed. On those banks the ominous forms of risslaca showed. No one was going swimming in the River of Bloody Jaws without regretting the notion.

"I don't expect to see any fliers here in Pandahem," said Seg. "But they must be known. The folk down there do not pay us much attention."

"Hamal and Hyrklana never would sell vollers to Loh or Pandahem, among others. Now we have these damned Shanks to fight I think the Pandaheem will get their vollers."

"They're surely needed in this part of the world."

We flew so grandly over the tops of the trees. What it would be like down there, trudging along, was something I did not wish to find out. Even the river for travel would be a headache.

Up ahead the forest lifted to a shallow range of hills. They were not mountains. But there were a lot of them, serried ranks of rounded slopes, one after another, and every one crammed with the ferocious vegetation of the jungle. The rain forest swarmed up over the rounded hills.

"The river trends away to the east," said Seg.

"I see. Is that a town near the beginning of the bend?"

Seg used the spyglass.

"Yes. Now, I wonder...?"

But the voller flew on, over the town in its riverside clearing, on and rising to soar over the unending roundnesses of the jungle-clad slopes.

We no longer flew a trifle west of north following the course of the river as it rolled down southeast. Now we flew on over solid jungle.

Seg had the spyglass trained neatly on the voller.

I thought I glimpsed a flicker of movement among the trees ahead of the path of the voller.

There was just a sudden movement there, a hint of a cloud of black dots, and then the sky over the trees was clear.

"Seg! Train your glass down, ahead of the voller—there—there where that rounded hill slopes over that valley—"

He did as I said, instantly.

After a moment, he said, "I see only trees."

"I thought I glimpsed—something—there."

"Only trees, now."

He handed me the glass.

I looked. The tops of the closely packed trees jumped into focus. I was looking down onto the crowns of the denizens of a rain forest, and no prying with human eyes would descry what lay on the forest floor.

I handed the spyglass back.

"Nothing, save the trees. But—"

"Yes? What was it?"

I took a breath.

Seg believed I'd seen something.

"Like a flock of birds—"

"All right. Nothing unusual in that."

"Agreed. But at this distance—they must have been large—"

"Saddle birds?"

Seg's tone was sharp.

"Aye."

He looked seriously at me, his fey blue eyes regarding me calmly. "Pandahem does not have flyers."

"I know. So that means..."

"I'll cast loose the guidance ropes. We'll be ready to go down at once."

"Good."

I stared eagerly at the airboat ahead.

But—but the wretched thing just went sailing on, flying high and fast, going pelting along. She just flew over whatever mysteries lay beneath. Perforce, we followed.

Taking up the spyglass I leaned over the coaming and studied the ground underneath. Rather—the tops of the trees...

Anything could be concealed under that luxuriant foliage. We hurtled out over the rounded top of a hill, and on the far side a fair-sized lake opened out. The water was as brown as the waters of the River of Bloody Jaws. A few islands studded the surface. There were no boats. A few birds quarreled on a brown mud spit. The suns light glinted up off the water. Sounds rose, the birds, the roars of hunting beasts, the distant splash of water I took to be a waterfall.

Swiveling, as our voller flashed on, I looked aft.

The edge of the hill fell sheer into the lake. It was buttressed by tall columns of rock, grey and weather-beaten and festooned with lianas. Birds cavorted here, too. A spume of white mist was just visible over a rising shaft of rock.

Even in the rush of the breeze, the strong and pungent smell of flowers stung my nostrils.

"Spiny Ribcrushers," said Seg. "Like syatras."

"They smell—juicy."

"That's right. They'll melt you down to your boot soles."

The lake whisked away below, the tall buttresses of rock vanished aft. Ahead the voller bore on steadily. The rain forest started on the very edge of the lake, and continued, unbroken. Probably there was a small tributary down there.

Seg put the control levers back on the guidance ropes and presently he called: "The hills are flattening out ahead. And we have the river back."

It was clear that the River of Bloody Jaws, coursing down to the southeast, made a vast loop to go around this outcropping of hills.

I stared ahead, far into the distance.

There was no sign of the Central Mountains.

Still the voller sailed on.

At the apex of the curve of the river where it turned to skirt the jumbled upheaval of forest-clad hills stood a town. As we flashed past above we could see the town was stockaded, small but neat, with jetties extending into the river. There was no sign of a single vessel. Smoke rose and the smells of cooking lifted. Seg made a face and rubbed his stomach.

"Old Frandor told me they were a devilishly mixed bunch here, with screaming cannibals in one valley and a high level of civilization in the next. Something to do with the difficulties of communication after the old empire went."

"We saw something of that in the Hostile Territories—Seg? You remember?"

And then I wished I hadn't mentioned the Hostile Territories of Turismond and thus brought up memories of our adventures there. Delia and me—and Seg and Thelda. I said at once, "Look! The fellow's turning!"

Whatever made the voller carrying Pancresta choose that moment to turn, I blessed. Whatever it was saved me from a nasty moment.

Seg said, "He's turning gently—now what is he up to?"

We began to edge out to starboard to cross the angle of the other flier's turn and so meet him. But he was a clever flier and kept away, using all his speed, turned so that soon we were heading directly back the way we had come.

And, still, we followed.

But we had narrowed the gap considerably. If only we'd had a couple of db's more speed—but that was foolish. If we'd had those, we'd have caught Pancresta hours ago.

The reciprocal course was taking us away to one side of the town over which we had passed. Speeds in the air are phenomenal if compared with speeds on land.

Seg abruptly stiffened. The spyglass twitched and was held, rigid. He stared ahead.

Then he said, "You were right about the saddle flyers."

Of course! Pancresta's flier had shot on ahead, over that lake and the rearing columns of rock where I'd imagined I'd seen flyers. The voller had drawn us on, and then gently turned, taking all the time needed, and reversed course. The saddle flyers had risen in a cloud to follow.

And now we were heading smack back into them.

Very carefully, I said, "I think Pancresta will escape. I count thirty birds. By the time we've finished with them, she'll be gone."

"I think you are right." Seg picked up his two longbows, letting the spyglass fall. He looked at each one. "We'll feather them, all of them, I have no doubt. But that scheming woman will be vanished."

"We know where to, though. We'll find her."

"Aye, my old dom. We'll catch up with her, in due time. But, now—" And here Seg selected a bow and drew it gently, and so took an arrow and set nock to string, "—now we have a fight on our hands."

Eight

Seg Quenches a Fire

Shooting through the windrush of a voller's flight is a truly difficult business. Seg had little difficulty aiming with the uncanny marksmanship of a Master Bowman of Loh. Seg had finished off my training as a bowman, after my ferocious Clansmen of Segesthes had taken me in hand, and I tried to match Seg, shaft for shaft.

"One gold piece, Dray, or—perchance—three?"

The wind caught at his dark hair, tumbled the locks over his forehead. His fey blue eyes challenged me right heartily. The wind blew, the hostile saddle birds dropped upon us—and, as ever, Seg was out for a wager or two, a side bet on the outcome in addition to our own lives.

"Three, I think," I said with a judiciousness that brought a delighted curl to Seg's lips.

Up aloft the birds winged in.

They sparkled with light. Radiance reflected from burnished accoutrements. The leading saddle flyer bore brilliant golden ornamentation over his breast feathers. That gold would be wafer-thin, beaten out into hollow shapes, strapped on with narrow leather bands. His wings held stiff in the attacking dive.

Seg sniffed, looking up. "Brunnelleys," he said. He held the new bow down, relaxed, the shaft crossing the stave and beginning that smooth draw of the master bowman.

The wind buffeted into our faces. The birds up there, gaudy of color in mauves and blues and browns, with yellow beaks and scarlet clawed feet—all four legs bore claws—swooped with that eager pounce of the brunnelley. Powerful saddle birds, brunnelleys, and like just about any other kind of saddle flyer, unknown in the island of Pandahem.

"Aye. And the riders are not flutsmen, either."

"No. I fancy Spikatur has a hand in this." And then Seg lifted the bow, drew and loosed.

The shaft missed. I looked not so much amused as dumbfounded.

In his turn, Seg looked at the bow. His brows drew down. He pursed up his lips. I shot and put a shaft through the wing of a brunnelley which wasn't going to do the bird a great deal of harm.

Seg threw the bow down into the bottom of the voller.

He picked up the other bowstave, and shook it.

"Thus do the prideful take a tumble, and the mighty are cast down. The stave does not cast true."

I knew he had no stupid boastfulness in equating himself with pride and mightiness; just that the aphorism fit and appealed to our sense of humor. With his second cast he sent the shaft clean through the breast of the rider.

The fellow screeched and fell off, to dangle all upside down in the straps of his clerketer under his bird's tail feathers.

"H'm," quoth Seg. "That is marginally better," and so shot again, thwack thump and sent a shaft clean through the eye of the next.

I tried to match my companion; but when Seg got himself into a paddy and shot with real intent, there was no man alive on two worlds, I devoutly believe, who came within a million dwaburs of him.

We began to take the diving formation apart, and such was the ferocity of our shooting the plunging birds parted and screamed down with whistling feathers on either side of our voller.

That was merely round one.

In the brief respite before the next attack we glimpsed Pancresta's flier diving steeply ahead, going down with tremendous speed to soar out over the river.

"They're gone," said Seg, arranging his next series of shafts in the quick-release sockets along the gunwale.

"Aye. For now."

"Here they come again."

Once more we shot sufficiently well to drive off the attack. Four shafts plunked into the woodwork of the voller, and a handful more cut through the canvas.

We were aware of height and wind and of rushing progress through the air. The Suns cast light and shadow, and the birds wheeled about us now, their riders shooting down. One or two cast javelins, but I made no attempt to snatch a javelin from the air and hurl it back. At this moment the bow was the superior weapon.

Our voller ploughed on, slowing down, surrounded by the furious cloud of birds.

"They thin out." Seg shot and took up shaft and drew and shot again.

"True."

I put my head over the coaming and looked down.

"The rasts."

Half a dozen riders closed in on their birds, the wings beating perilously close together, aiming to strike up at our exposed underside.

Three quick shafts took three of them out; but the balance bored on. Golden ornaments glittered. The men riding the birds hunched in tightly buckled cloaks, not streaming flamboyantly, and their small round helmets gleamed with purpose. This group carried crossbows. A bolt punched up through the canvas past my nose, and I jumped back.

"I count that as three gold pieces to me," said Seg, and he laughed.

"Indubitably." I looked over again, in time to put a shaft into the nearest fellow. He looked up with the utmost surprise on his face, one-eyed, for the shaft through the other one impeded his vision somewhat.

He fell off his bird, and the brunnelley curved away, carrying the dangling rider like a pendulum clock.

Seg sniffed.

At once disabused of the notion that he was passing a comment on my shooting, I sniffed also.

We looked quickly about.

Shafts hissed in, to feather into the voller and start to turn her into a flying pincushion.

Smoke blew flatly back.

"They've set us afire, my old dom. But where is the flame?"

Smoke suddenly choked back in a great evil-smelling cloud.

"Wherever it is, the wind drives it flat, and the smoke obscures the source."

Then I cursed myself for a ninny, a nincompoop, for the kind of man no captain of a seventy-four would ever employ as his first lieutenant. When I served in the Royal Navy of Nelson's time we habitually doused fires before going into action, and sanded the decks, and took the utmost precautions against being set alight.

And, now, I'd just forgotten to douse the fire in the combustible box, and it had been struck by a shaft, and overturned, and set our voller aflame.

Even as this stupid, time-wasting self-recrimination echoed in my silly old vosk-skull of a head, the fire burst up and enveloped the voller. Flames blew flatly aft. Seg yelled.

He leaped for the controls and threw off the guidance ropes. He shoved the levers down and the flier's nose dropped and we fell out of the sky like a brick.

A flashing glimpse of a bird, upside down and with a broken wing where we'd struck him—a man slashing with his long flexible aerial spear—another fellow loosing and his bolt splintering into the coaming under my nose—and then we were hurtling down and down toward the ground.

We had no flying safety belts. We'd have to ride the voller down.

"Hold on!" bellowed Seg.

A gusting mass of smoke and flame billowed up, a choking confused mass, orange and scarlet and black, coiling and hot—damned hot!

The spectacle we must have made from higher up as the men astride their brunnelleys looked down surely convinced them we were doomed.

I wasn't too sure myself...

"Seg!" I bellowed.

My comrade towered amid the filthy smoke, enveloped in flame, a titanic figure of myth, of the time when men walked among volcanoes and leaped the fire-filled chasms in the earth.

He yelled back, and the words blustered past, lost amid wind and smoke and flame roar.

The trees reared up.

What Seg did with the controls was what any competent aerial pilot would do. He set them for a slanting impact, slowing the speed as much as he could, and then fastened the guidance ropes back on. But, being Seg Segutorio and a wild and fey fellow, he set the voller to a steeper angle than any more circumspect flier would risk.

We went skipping through the tops of the trees.

Tree branches thwacked at us, ripping canvas and gonging against wood.

Leaves fluttered up into our faces, birds squawked and flew for safety, a horde of little red spiders wafted off on balloons of silk. A leafy bough slashed at my head and I ducked and my helmet reverberated as though the Bells of Beng Kishi were all cracked and dissonant.

We toppled out of the last hoary heads of the trees and pitched for the brown river below.

The voller was now a roaring combustible mass and Seg and I crouched in the stern, shielding our faces, waiting for the moment of impact.

Seg gasped out: "I thought—the river—douse the flames—"

Before I could cough out an answer we hit.

We felt as though we'd leaped off a roof onto a brick factory. The thump rattled through the flier, through our backbones and shook the teeth in our jaws.

Water fountained up around us, like a flower's petals, brown and silver, and we were hurled headlong into the water. Even then the hem of Seg's tunic caught alight and hissed madly as he went under.

We splashed to the surface, blowing suds, winded, blinded, singed, our heads ringing and ringing. I felt as though a torturer from the Empress Thyllis's dungeons under the Hammabi el Lamma had been at work on me for a sennight.

Seg whisked the water from his eyes and glared about.

"Back to the bank, sharpish!" I yelled.

We started splashing back.

The flier, burning, drifted away, and the flames flared for a long time before they were doused, as we could see by the reflections.

Over arm we crawled for the bank. Only two fang-jawed creatures had a go at us, and we managed to get a sword down in time to poke them off. They were not harmed. Their scales glistened in the light of the Suns and the licking fire reflections from the burning voller. The smell of the river began to get up our nostrils to replace the stink of smoke. That smell was all dark brown.

Rotting vegetation, slimed mud, bursting gas bubbles all joined in an infernal soup of aromas.

Seg reached the bank first. He grasped at a root sticking into the water and the damned thing came alive and tried to bite him.

He yelped and drew back and swiped at the thing.

It screeched and scuttled off on a hundred or so bandy legs. It turned its flat head as it went, and its eyes promised that it would be back.

We crawled out and flopped face down on mud.

We breathed in and out, and we were alive, and that was miracle enough.

Up aloft against the bright haze there was no sign of the flyers astride their golden-adorned brunnelleys.

The first thing Seg said was, "I regret losing that stave that cast crooked. I would dearly have loved to find out why."

I said, "All I know is that shot gives me three gold pieces."

"We will work the reckoning as soon as we can. I do not recommend swimming in harness—although you, Dray Prescot, are half fish in the water."

"And you—half waterlogged tree trunk?"

He laughed and tossed his head and the water spun from his helmet. We believed in wearing armor, and we believed in wearing as much and as little as would protect us and let us move. I stood up and my foot went into the mud knee deep. A stink gushed.

Hauling my leg out made a loud sucking noise.

"Inland a bit, and then head for the town?"

"Aye."

We lay sprawled for a few moments longer, getting our breath. Our equipment carried on our persons was still with us. That in the voller was gone past redemption.

Eventually we crawled off the mud and onto the first of the less squelchy ground. Trees struggled for existence and the light dimmed to a watery greenness. Rain forests can be gloomy places. The noises of hunting animals—those who hunted by day—echoed among the trunks and from the masses of leaves overhead. There was no real undergrowth. Walking was a matter of selecting a good line, of keeping the eyes wide open and of constantly rotating the head. Seg fussed with his bow, spanning a new string from the watertight pouch. I carried a drexer in my hand. We marched.

We spoke little. Sounds carried even among the maze of trunks. And we walked softly.

If I say without either pride or humility that we two pacing through the forest were probably more dangerous than any animal we were likely to meet, I believe you will understand, and realize that that is the way of it on Kregen—if you wish to survive.

Nine

Jungle Cabaret

Attacks from nasties of the forest came at infrequent intervals. Hereabouts the going was only really difficult where a tree had fallen, taking others with it, and so opened a gap in the canopy of leaves above. Here sunshine could pour down—and with twin suns the extent was measurably greater—and produce a twisted tangle of undergrowth.

Negotiating these places was really cutting a way through jungle.

Here it was—slashing with swords to carve a path, ducking vines and treacherously looping strands of animate vegetable killers—that the risslacas, the dinosaurs, attacked. Their smaller brethren also came panting after our blood.

We did not make a fuss about it.

As Seg, drawing out a fresh arrow and fitting nock to string, said, "They're only doing what Nature intended and trying to fill their bellies."

"Aye. It is their misfortune they choose us for dinner."

"I feel sorry for them. But..."

And he loosed and blotted out the yellow glaring eye of a risslaca whose fanged jaws would, had they closed over either of us or both of us together, have chopped us in half for a neat midday snack.

I loosed to take out another, smaller, dinosaur.

They humped along between the tree trunks, adapted to this environment either by nature or by genetic engineering, and we jumped down into a ravine, choked with vines. The emerald and ruby light lay across the clearing, and the dazzle above precluded looking at the sky.

In this slot of jungle-choked forest we encountered a couple of hairy crachens, and managed to drive them off, their mandibles waving, without killing them. Their faceted eyes regarded us. I took from them the same impression I'd taken from the multi-legged pseudo tree-branch on the bank.

Those eyes said—We'll be back.

Tiny pinhead stingers wrung blood from us, and we had to beat them off, nickering, clinging, clouding wings gauzy in the dim light. Their life span might only be a day or so; they lived it up while they could, and drank their blood off with the best.

Although had it happened it would not on Kregen have been at all unusual, I have to report that we did not find a single princess to rescue from a dinosaur. Or find a single princess, come to that. We plunged on, through the rough areas and going as fast as we could with caution between the aisled trunks of the trees. Old, those trees, old and anciently hoary, festooned with parasitic growths, lush with tree-borne life, and of a normal human scale in height. But they were growing on the island of Pandahem, alongside the River of Bloody Jaws—on Kregen—and, although like jungly trees of Earth, they were different, very different.

When we reached a recognizable trail we halted.

From the cover of a tree trunk we looked out.

His voice pitched so that it would reach me and not listening hostile ears, Seg gave his opinion.

"Well—I'm not walking along *that*!"

"No."

He cocked his head at me.

"Ten gold pieces I spot a trap first."

"Done."

In his home in Erthyrdrin, at the northern tip of the continent of Loh, Seg had lived a pretty wild life before going as a mercenary to earn a living. Out there feuds rankled and a fellow had to keep his wits about him. Seg would probably spot a trap first—unless my own training with my clansmen, and with my Djangs and sundry other rascals and ferocious warriors of Kregen could aid me.

We paced the trail, well away among the trees, following its line. It was headed for the town.

Where it went the other way we did not know, for we'd come across it almost at right angles. It struck inland away from the river.

In any event we both said, "There!" and pointed together.

Instantly, we were both flat on our faces, alongside each other and head to tail, glaring out.

But nothing stirred.

After a time—a goodly time, for to rush in these matters is to court disaster—we stood up and inspected the trap.

"A tie, I think."

"Aye."

"Although I fancy your finger pointed after mine—"

"Never in a month of She of the Veils!"

Wrangling happily, we checked out the trap.

It was a simpleminded enough affair, a pit covered with leafy branches and positioned where enough sunlight dropped through an ancient and almost covered gap to give life to a little lower vegetation around. Simple it might be. It would be effective if anyone—be it animal or idiot human with no right to be wandering around in the jungle—should try to walk across it.

We went on.

A species of medium-sized vosk—larger than a bosk—lived here in the forest, rooting around, and no doubt the trap was laid for them.

They were wild, not domesticated, and they flourished a set of tusks that would part stomach from backbone in a trice.

We debated.

"Not worth it," I said.

"We-ell," said Seg. "I'm sharp set."

"The town cannot be far. They'll have vosk all ready cooked, crisp and golden and with momolams, too..."

"I'll grant we wouldn't have to cook the meal. If the town doesn't show up in a bur or so, I shan't wait."

"Momolams?"

These are the splendid small round golden vegetables, rather like brand-new potatoes with mint and steaming with flavor, that can melt the saliva from granite.

"I tell you, Dray Prescot, if we reach this town and order up a meal of vosk and there are no momolams, I shall seriously consider marmelizing you."

"I am surprised to hear you voice so uncouth a word."

"Yes, it is fit only for savages. But, in these circumstances—"

And then we both held, stark still, poised, as voices floated in from the trees. Laughing voices, shrilling, and with the voices the sounds of bottles and glasses—surely, bottles and glasses?

Cautiously, we crept forward.

The funny thing is, and I was well aware that we might at any moment be fighting for our lives, I was thinking that the golden-yellow tubers, these famous momolams, are more often eaten with roast ponsho than with vosk. We reached a crusty-barked tree and hunkered down, and slowly, cautiously, looked around, one each side.

The trail lay nearer to Seg than to me. I saw a small clearing, uncluttered with undergrowth except for a strange plant rather like a large gourd, from the top of which extended a thick stalk crowned with an orange flower.

From the gourd section came the sound of voices and the rattle of bottle lip against glass.

Perhaps Seg made more noise than I did. Perhaps because he was just the nearer of the two of us... As lean and tough as I was, he would have been no juicier...

I stared out on the strange plant.

Certainly the gourd was of a size to hold two or three people. But I did not think two or three people were inside having a party. The stem bearing its orange flower lifted some fifteen feet from the top of the gourd, swaying gently five meters or so up, and as I took all this in, and realized what this was all about, so I was yelling my head off and jumping forward, sword raised.

"Seg!"

The stem lashed.

The orange flower opened, revealing massed spines.

It struck. It struck full at Seg's head.

I roared in, just bashing in a full-shouldered charge at the stem, and with the sword slashing and hacking, cutting through the fibrous vegetable growth. Thick green liquid gushed. The flower writhed. It twisted in on itself, blindly seeking its tormentor. I took a tremendous swing and the steel bit and then the flower hit me a thwack across the shoulder and head over heels I went into the muck.

It seemed to me only a moment or two later that a woman's voice said, "Well, pantor Seg, your friend is alive, it seems."

And Seg's voice, as though from a distance: "For which I give thanks to Erthyr the Bow, and to all the Lords of Creation." And, then, because he was Seg Segutorio, and the truest blade comrade a man could ever hope for, he added, "And, anyway, he has the skull of a vosk and the hide of a boloth, the speed of a leem and the strength of a zhantil."

The woman laughed.

"I see you two get on together."

"I owe him ten gold pieces for this one—"

I tried to open my eyes, and the woman's voice sharpened.

"You would pay him ten gold croxes for saving your life? Is that what you value yourself at?"

"No, mistress Tlima, it is a bet I lost."

"I see—"

But, it was clear, she did not see at all.

The glue holding my lids down parted with some pain and light flooded in. I blinked, and Seg said, "About time."

Just to keep him going, I said, "Ten gold crox pieces, and not clipped, either."

He laughed.

His laugh rang out, joyous, full.

I sat up.

When my shoulder returned and attached itself to my body, I went to give it a rub, and the woman put a hand out and stopped me.

"Leave it, pantor. It is bandaged."

She was apim, full of face and figure, wearing a dark blue gown with white lace, and her features were those of a woman who has fought through life, and sees some comfort before they ship her off to the Ice Floes of Sicce.

We were in a tavern, with a thatched roof and wooden beams, with wooden walls and wooden floor, and the furniture was plain and simple and clean. I ached all over.

"The poison. A single spine struck past the edge of your armor." Seg shook his head. "Well, you cannot armor every inch of your body and still prance about."

"No."

The orange flower in striking back at me, so Seg related, hit my shoulder where the armor stopped the poisoned spines dead. But a petal flapped up and that solitary damned spine ripped in past the rim of my corselet, past the mesh, and so nicked me in the neck.

"You'd have had your head fall off if I hadn't kissed your neck as though you were a luscious sylvie."

"I trust you enjoyed the experience."

"I am not a fellow for sylvies, as you know."

"You suggested it."

"I was merely trying to be vivid in describing what could have been more awkward if that damned flower thing had upended you."

"Oh? I see."

The woman, this mistress Tlima, looked on in a bewildered fashion.

She addressed us as "pantor" which is the Pandahem way of saying lord. It equates with the notor of Hamal and the jen of Vallia. She called Seg Seg. She did not name me.

By this time Seg knew that I had a whole arsenal of names on which I could call. And for the Emperor of Vallia to be swanning about in a jungle on Pandahem could be awkward for said emperor if avaricious minds got to work.

The gourd emitting its party noises and the orange poison-spined flower formed a symbiosis of plants dedicated to catching and eating people. They grew in handy spots. The Kregish name can most easily be given as the Cabaret Plant.

Cabaret, I think, has the air to suit what they were up to.

Mistress Tlima bent and solicitously pulled and punched at my pillow in the way women have. A tinge of color glowed across her cheekbones.

"The Cabaret Plants are evil to us, for they delude poor drunken folk. Otherwise they live on small animals and their roots."

"Evil?" said Seg, raising one ferocious eyebrow.

"Yes!"

"As to that," I said, and rolled aside to avoid a sharpish straight left to the pillow and then rolled back to dodge the following right hook. "As to that, if a poor deluded folkim is drunk, perhaps he shouldn't be?"

"I shall fetch a meal," said mistress Tlima. The small room in which I lay was furnished as I have said, and was clearly one of her superior guest rooms. Seg had paid her in good gold deldys, which are Havilfarese coins. The local gold coin, the crox, was named after the local king. He, I was to learn, was busy causing the dickens of a stir and an uproar that was to embroil Seg and me willy-nilly. So, I lay back on the severely mauled pillow and smiled up at my blade comrade.

"So you brought me in on your back, hey?"

He looked shifty for a moment, did Seg, and then he hauled out his purse and dished out the ten gold pieces.

"I'll hand it to you, Dray. You spotted that trap first."

I took the gold and let a big smirk contort my features. That rubbed the salt in. Seg suddenly burst out laughing. He gazed down on me as the door opened and mistress Tlima came in with the tray that, quite clearly, had been already prepared. Still laughing, Seg burst out: "You can smirk all you like, Dray! I'm only thankful to have lost the ten deldys! By the Veiled Froyvil! I thought I was consigned to the Ice Floes of Sicce then."

Mistress Tlima placed the linen-covered tray on the side table. She stared reproachfully at Seg.

"Pantor Seg! How could you?"

"Well," said Seg, and that shifty look returned, "you can't afford to give this comrade of mine a knuckle."

"Pantor Dray? He saved you, and you tell him you brought him in all the way through the forest on your back!"

"Oh?" I said. I was enjoying this. "Oh ho?"

"You can oh ho, and oh ho ho, my old dom—I'll tell you—Mistress Tlima's husband came across us and we brought you in flopped out over the back of his cart."

So, I laughed.

By Zair! But it was good to be alive!

The food was good. It was roast rashers of vosk, juicy and crisp, all at the same time. And—momolams. Also there was a pottery dish of palines, and this sovereign berry, cure for melancholy as for dyspepsia, grew just as luxuriously in the rain forests of Pandahem as in the sweet lands of my own Valka.

When she had gone, and the door was closed, mistress Tlima remained Seg's chief concern.

"I had not realized—"

"It is of no consequence."

"But—"

"Perhaps, Seg, I have had my fill of running around under a score of different names. I am Jak—true. But also I am called Dray. And so I shall be."

He sniffed, resigned.

"By Vox! I am glad I don't have to keep track of all your names."

But we both knew the old truth that if you wanted to stay alive on Kregen you had to remember names. If you didn't, you were like to get killed pretty sharpish.

By the next day I was recovered enough to venture on a gentle stroll around this jungle town of Selsmot. I commented that calling the place a smot—meaning town—was rather grand. The stockade kept out the forest, and there was really, all things considered, a fine area maintained free and growing vegetables. The houses of wood and thatch and leaf were open and airy and a surprising number of them crowded within the stockade. But, all the same, the place was rundown and apathetic.

Seg said, "That's because old King Crox has gone missing and no one has the heart—"

"Gone missing?"

We walked along the dusty street—when it rained the dust became a quagmire—and Seg told me what he had discovered.

A band of most unhealthy bandits—drikingers—hung out in the bend of the river among those rolling tree-clad hills over which we had flown in pursuit of Pancresta. King Crox had taken in a strong expedition to deal with them once and for all. Nothing had been heard from him since, and that was two seasons ago. So—he had gone missing.

"Chopped," I said. "Poor fellow."

Then, sharply, I swung about to face Seg, saying, "And a band of drikingers in the jungle—that adds up to—"

"Perhaps. Pancresta and Spikatur—"

"It has to!"

"Except that although the king has gone missing, the drikingers have stopped plundering the trails and the river. He must have been successful."

"Very well." I could see from Seg's manner there was more. "Go on, you great infuriating—bowman—"

"The queen was determined to find the king. There was no love in it, so I am told, rather pride. She was married off for political reasons and the king rode off that night and—"

I smiled. "Not all women are beautiful nor all men handsome."

"This Queen Mab went after the king with her own expedition and—"

I cocked my head up. "She's gone missing too?"

"Aye."

"And some fat regent will be running the country to the benefit of his pocket."

"Kov Llipton—"

"And that gives me even greater assurance that it has to be Spikatur Hunting Sword in the jungle. This Kov Llipton is probably in league with them and the drikingers."

"You, Dray Prescot, have a tortuous and mistrusting mind."

"Useful, at times."

"Oh, aye, useful."

Still there was a hint of mischief about Seg, a bubbling enjoyment of tantalizing me. I did not scowl—Seg was fully entitled to his bit of harmless fun. And, anyway, I did not feel the same urgency. I was feeling slothful. That, mistress Tlima had warned Seg, was the inevitable result of being poisoned by the Cabaret Plant, the final outcome of which was death. Seg had sucked out the poison, there had not been a full flower-freight of spines to strike me, and I was alive. But I was tired.

"Go on then, you will tell me as and when—"

He nodded toward a tumbledown building standing a little back from the line of the other buildings. The place leaned comfortably against an enormous tree, a single intruder from the jungle. Small agile forms sported among the branches. A warm friendly smell wafted from the building, and a hanging pottery jug outside proclaimed the nature of its business.

A few drops of warm rain fell.

In mere moments the deluge would thunder down, and the dusty street would squelch not just underfoot but halfway up our legs. People walked briskly for shelter.

"The Dragon's Roost," said Seg.

"Very good. I need a wet inside me more than outside."

Starting off for the tavern with its low leafy roof and leaning walls of solid trunks, I made Seg step out smartly to follow. There was more to this. He caught me up and we ducked our heads to pass under the curved beam over the open front door. The sound of people talking and the gusty smell of a variety of drinks met us, mingled with the odors of rich cooking and the tang of woodsmoke.

"There is a party of adventurers here, in The Dragon's Roost. They may be braggarts, they may be fools, they may be heroes, but they are determined to chance their fortune among the hills."

The low door gave onto a long enclosed stoop, bowered in greenery, a place sheltered from the heat of the Suns and the rain which, hot and thick, hissed down outside.

We looked at each other.

Seg beamed and I nodded, pleased.

"Right, Seg. They are out to make their fortunes in the hills. They know something, then, that we do not. And we will go along with them. It seems to me that they and us—we all have the same objective, I'll wager."

"That, my old dom, is one wager I'll not take on!"

Ten

At The Dragon's Roost

If we imagined we had only to march up the shallow steps to the stoop and enter The Dragon's Roost and join up with the expedition, we were quickly disappointed.

The obstacle stood, four square at the top of the steps, and glowered upon us.

He appeared to be apim, at least, through the hair that sprouted from every possible point, although his apimishness was not certain. His eyes, most merry and bright, belied the scowl twisting his hair-girt mouth. He showed uneven teeth, yellowed and missing biting chompers here and there, giving him a mouth like the side of one of Nelson's frigates.

"Clear off! Schtump! We've had enough rascals like you to stuff a vosk pie for the feast of Beng Hravimond!"

Our clothes had been in a state of wreckage after our burning and river adventures, and the trek through the jungle, so we had borrowed ordinary clothes from mistress Tlima. These were simple brownish tunics, reaching to above the knee, and open at the throat. Seg carried his bow and a quiver, and I my drexer. We looked, I suppose, ruffians.

"We are not masichieri," declared Seg, somewhat heatedly.

The mass of hair within the leather and metal harness did not give him time to continue.

"Masichieri, thieving rascals, rogues—schtump!"

Seg sighed

"I do not want to teach this hairy flea-bitten mass a lesson. But, by the Veiled Froyvil! He leaves me precious little alternative."

"Tsleetha-tsleethi," quoth I, which is to say, softly-softly. "If he serves his belly, he merely does his duty."

The bright eyes regarded us more closely.

"Comedians, are you?"

"Your name, dom?" I said.

"I should be angry—but you amuse me. I am Hop the—"

"Hairy?" cut in Seg.

"Fambly! One more crude remark and I shall be forced to come to hand-strokes with you—I am Hop the Intemperate."

"Ah!" I said wisely.

"What does that mean?"

"It means," said Seg, "that you are well named."

A girl's laugh intruded. We all turned to look along the stoop, and Hop the Intemperate immediately went into the full incline, his nose rubbing the floorboards, his massive bottom upended.

This kind of bowing and scraping has never pleased Seg or me, so we merely gave the girl a slight polite nod, more, I fancy, in acknowledgment of her beauty than anything else at that time.

She was pretty, rather than beautiful, with a pert nose and red lips. Her hair, of a light corn color, fell in a loose mass to one side, gathered in by a silver band. She wore a green tunic, simple in cut, girt by a silver belt. She carried only a dagger as a personal weapon; but I had no doubt that her other weapons had done the business for many a fine upstanding young fellow. She looked—winsome, I suppose is a good way to describe her. She was not, I judged, the queen of these parts.

"Stand up, Hop, for the sweet sake of Pandrite and his holy mother!"

Hop gathered himself, rather like a sheepdog shaking after a dip in the millpond. He glowed.

"Lady Ilsa!"

She looked at us.

The little dip between her eyebrows darkened.

That—and I sighed to myself—that was a familiar sign.

Her voice, cool, distant, commanding, reached us with the touch of a stroking feather over an open wound.

"And you are?"

Seg spoke up.

"Llahal, young lady—"

"Have you noticed," I remarked in a casual conversational way, "how they don't bother with a polite Llahal as a greeting in this benighted place?"

The girl gasped. She drew herself up, not flinching as much as expressing distaste and hauteur. Hauteur, a comical concept to an honest sailorman, ill-suited her.

Hop the Intemperate blew out, hard, making his whiskers shiver in the breeze.

"Now, then, you rogue—"

"All right, Hop. You have a job to do. This girl—"

She shouted, cutting off my undoubtedly hot-headed and foolish comments. She screamed. She shrieked for the guards and for Hop to take off our heads— Well, it was a silly vapid scene. Poor old Hop the Intemperate went to sleep, very gently, on the warped boards of the stoop. The first guard, a Gon whose shaven head glistened with butter-shine, jumped onto the stoop waving a spear and Seg's bow lined up—exactly.

The second guard crashed into the first, who was trying to run backwards, and the pair fell over.

Lady Ilsa stood, her fists jammed into her mouth, her eyes goggling.

I did feel sorry for her. Sincerely.

Seg said, "We are here to join the expedition. If these guards are going along, maybe we'd better think again."

"Lady Ilsa," I said, and I own I spoke rather sharpish. She jumped as though goosed. "We are friends; at least, we want to join the expedition. You'd better tell your guards to stand down, and quickly, before they are hurt."

She took her fists away from her mouth. She was shaking.

"You—!"

"We are honest fellows needing a job—"

A young gallant, dressed all in a glittering blue, with much gold embroidery, stepped out. His fists were thrust down on his hips. I noticed he was wearing a rapier and left-hand dagger, still unusual at that time on Pandahem. His face was of that pale, aristocratic, hollow, blot-faced self-possession which conceals homicidal characteristics from those who do not wish to look closely upon wealth and position.

"Ilsa? You are safe?"

He kicked the two guards who were groveling away around each other, trying to stand up, their harness in some unfathomable way inextricably intertwined. They made mewling noises. The young dandy kicked them again. He enjoyed that.

Seg started to say, "Llahal, notor. We wish to join—"

The young lord said, "Do not speak to me until I speak to you, offal."

He turned back to the girl, cutting Seg and me out of the world's existence. It was handsomely done, if overdone.

Seg glanced at me, and I smiled, and then we both laughed.

A new voice, a mellow, full voice, not quite a fruity voice, said, "At last. Some excitement to liven things up."

We looked along the stoop.

The owner of the opulent voice half-concealed his face with a large—a very large—yellow kerchief. He was dressed in a simple tunic of dark blue, so dark as to be called black save for the artfully inserted panels of royal blue. He carried no weapons. He sneezed. At once the woman at his side jumped forward with a sprig of the lapinal plant, already smoldering, and waved it under his nose. Coughing and spluttering, he inhaled the aromatic fumes. He sounded like a wine-press at full blast after harvest.

"Oh, oh, by Beng Sbodine, the Mender of Men! I am dying! My lungs burn—"

"A sip of wine, master—"

The woman in some magical way while brandishing the sprig of lapinal produced a spouted wine jug. This the man seized and upended and glug-glugged. We could see his nose was of a splendid size and proportion, a ripe glowing plum color. His whole face partook of pleasure, ripe cheeks, full lips, merry eyes, now squeezed shut as he drank. He enjoyed the good things of life, did this one.

As for the woman, fussing over him, she was not slave, for she wore a decent blue gown, with a bronze-link belt, and the comb in her long dark hair glittered. Her face held a look that might take many years to fathom, and then, when you had descried what she thought, you would be back with your first impressions of half-humorous but dedicated service to the man. And to say she fussed is to do her a disservice. She handled the man well, insuring that what he called for in the way of medicaments and wine and comfort was instantly available.

After he regained his composure, he said, "Why do I risk my health by venturing out here when the rains fall?"

He shivered. Then he said, and his voice no longer whined, "Strom Ornol, it seems you have no use for these two men, therefore I shall take them on."

The noise of the rain on the roof had not ceased all during this farcical scene. Now, in the silence after the words spoken by the man whose glowing nose was once more concealed by the yellow kerchief, the rain beat down. To a fainthearted soul that thunderous rolling barrage might well have sounded like the knell of doom.

"They are of no concern of mine, save that they must be punished for striking my servants."

Seg started to boil up at this, and I put a hand on his forearm. He lowered the bow. The yellow kerchief twitched, so the man had witnessed that little byplay.

"As they are now in my employ, I would not take kindly to their punishment by another hand."

The young lord, pale-faced rigidity personified, reacted in a way that half-surprised me. I fancied I had some, at least, of this particular relationship worked out.

"Very well, Exandu. The matter does not touch my honor. Just see they are punished."

"But, Ornol—" said the Lady Ilsa.

Strom Ornol took her arm. It was a familiar gesture.

"It is a nothing. And you should not have embroiled yourself with the lower orders. Come inside."

I bent down and helped heave Hop the Intemperate to his feet. He rubbed his chin through the hair, and winced.

"You have a fist, dom," he said.

"You have my apologies, Hop. The blow was unexpected. Otherwise you would never have—ah—fallen down."

He rubbed again and shook his head.

"As to that, I am not sure."

So, you see, somewhere along the way the world had turned and I could use the words "I apologize" to someone other than Delia. A thought worth ruminating on, that...

Exandu sneezed again, and the woman went through the pantomime, and the spluttering volcano subsided. He blew his nose, hard, and sniffed, and wiped his eyes.

"Here am I like to catch my death, and all because of two rascally paktuns. Well, Hop, see to them, there's a good fellow. I must find a warm corner and a potion. Shanli! I shall need a double potion of your Special Blood Warming Lightning. As Beng Sbodine, Mender of Men, has turned his face away from me!"

"Now, now, master," soothed Shanli, taking his arm with one hand and waving the aromatic smoldering sprig of lapinal under his nose with the other. "I shall take care of you. I have a warm shirt in the oven, and Old Mother Babli's hot honey punch, with three measures of Harnafon's Fortified—"

"Three measures! Shanli, you do look after me. You are a treasure."

They walked off, and Hop wheezed and sniffed, and rubbed the hair over his chin, and jerked a thumb.

"Come on. If master Exandu wants to take you on, you're in luck."

We disentangled the two Gons, and helped them on their way inside. Their uniforms were of the grand style, with many dangling ribbons and straps, and, somehow, Hop wound up with a goodly length of gilt wire in his fist.

Seg laughed.

"A boon comrade, I swear it!"

"Maybe. You'd do best to keep a watchful eye on that lord. Strom Ornol." Hop looked about. "A right nasty package, that one, due for the unraveling one fine day."

"All the same," said Seg to me as we started off along the stoop after Hop. "All the same, we strolled along here to join the expedition, not to be hired on as paktun guards."

"So we're in luck. We go along—and we get paid—"

Seg's look would have melted down the finest gold coin in all of Kregen. "You're a mercenary hulu, you really are—"

"We've both been slave, we've both been paktuns, we've both been hungry and thirsty—and we've both been fine lords. You take what comes."

"That's right, by Vox!"

"And if you can nudge fate along a little bit—"

"All the same," said Seg, cutting in, having thought this thing through. "Fine lords, you say. We've been fine lords, and we still are! And, you're—"

"Yes. But it will surely suit our purpose better to be simple paktuns hiring out to guard this expedition? Surely?"

Seg sniffed. "Going along as minions? Very well. As you say, we take what comes."

So, into the back entrance of The Dragon's Roost we went to join up with the brave expedition venturing into the jungle-choked slopes of the Snarly Hills.

Eleven

Of Another Fist

The smells of cooking wafted deliciously from the back quarters of The Dragon's Roost. The scurry of slaves intruded an unpleasant note into an idyllic scene; but all in Opaz's good time we would remove the blot of slavery from Paz. We followed Hop the Intemperate through a room stuffed with sacks and boxes of food and hanging garlands of vegetables, and along a corridor. The kitchens lay ahead, and my mouth watered.

Hop opened the door and motioned for us to go through.

Seg went first.

I followed.

As I turned to look back for Hop an object of considerable hardness, some size, of rugged knobbyness and traveling at a goodly speed slap-bang-crashed into my chin.

I went over backwards, upsetting a pile of copper pots.

Girls started screaming. Steam filled the air. I sat up on the floor in a lake of half-cooked cabbages and stared at Hop.

He stood just inside the door, rubbing the knuckles of his right fist. He looked—through the hair—mighty pleased.

"That, I think, makes us even."

I moved my jaw. My eyes watered. I did not shake my head. My chin had click-clicked twice under each ear as I moved it.

"You, Hop the Intemperate," I said. "Have a fist, also."

"Aye."

Seg said, "It is just as well this is all friendly, for you should know, Hop the Rash, your insides would have been strewn across the floor for the cooks to inspect, had I so wished."

That, for Seg, was a long speech.

Hop chuckled.

"You are no paktuns, wandering for hire. I heard from mistress Tlima but did not realize at first. You are rip-roaring lords out for adventure, and I own to some simple pleasure in feeling the tingle in my knuckles."

So that settled all our devious schemes to hire on.

We were accepted into the expedition as members. The unpleasant Strom Ornol had to acquiesce in the wishes of the majority, otherwise he would have been out of the expedition. Exandu expressed sorrow that he had not hired on two fine upstanding rogues to protect him, for, as he said between sneezes and sniffs at the aromatic fumes, and swigs of herbal and honey concoctions: "I am not long for this world. My bones are too frail to support my body, and my poor old heart strains to keep me alive. Why do I venture into so rash an undertaking?"

Privately, Hop said to Seg in a whisper, "The old fraud is after the gold and jewels, that's why."

We were introduced to the other members of the party. The spoils were to be divided into six. Seg and I now came into one share. Strom Ornol and his retinue, including the lady Ilsa, would take another. Exandu would gasp and wheeze, no doubt, while pocketing his share.

When we sat around the circular table in the window alcove corner of

The Dragon's Roost, bottles and jugs nestling on the polished sturm wood, Kalu Na-Fre wrapped his tail hand around his flagon. Before lifting it to his lips, he picked up a single paline from the dish in each of his two left hands. These he popped, and chewed with relish and then the tail hand brought the flagon to his lips. With his right hand he pointed to the map, opened among the litter of bottles.

He took the flagon away and said, "The distance is not great as the flut-trell flies."

Strom Ornol, pale-faced as ever, showed his disgust.

"You are in Pandahem now, Kalu Na-Fre."

The Pachak popped two more palines with his two left hands. The right hand described circles on the map.

"My point precisely."

"It," said Exandu plaintively, "will prove a sore trial for my poor old bones."

The Pachak, Kalu Na-Fre, brushed back his long yellow hair. He used one of his left hands and his right. Before their movements were finished his right-handed tail hand lifted the flagon. These wonderful folk of Kregen with more than an apim's miserable allotment of two arms and two legs must, it is clear, be endowed with lobes in their brains that enable them to coordinate their intricate movements. As for the cunning interlocking shoulder jointing, these are marvels of bio-engineering, in all the different systems found in Kildoi, Pachak, Djang and all the others.

"You do not have a suggestion, then, Kalu?"

"Only that we will have to walk once the animals can go no farther."

Exandu sniffed and consoled himself with a swig of Mother Babli's Home Brew, strongly laced, I fancied, with an expensive wine.

Kalu Na-Fre and his people would come in for their sixth share.

Any puzzlement we might have had that the booty was to be split six ways between the principals, despite the numbers of people they brought as minions, was resolved, at least in my mind, by what I surmised of the relationships here. Strom Ornol, a feckless younger son of a noble house, had been kicked out by his father to make his own way in the world. He was up past his ears in debt to Exandu.

Seg and I had put in our contribution in good Hamalian golden deldys. That currency was well-known down in the south of Pandahem, very well known. We made it crystal clear that we were not Hamalese, and backed that by our appearance as adventurers out in the world and no longer owning allegiance to any one nation.

Over in a corner the patrons of The Dragon's Roost were playing dice. The game was Soshiv and the click of the ivory cubes rattled as a background to our decisions. Soshiv—the word is one of the common ways of expressing the number eighteen—so times shiv, three times six—entails using six dice each per player. Three are thrown, the highest total being eighteen, and then the opposing players take their turns to throw against point. There are complicated betting arrangements and conventions ordering the reading of the dice. The click click and the calls as the numbers fell accompanied our deliberations as we prepared for the expedition.

Skort, the fifth member of the party, said very little. As a Clawsang he was well aware that his appearance could so unsettle and upset some people that at best they would be sick and at worst—well, Skort the Clawsang wore armor and carried weapons.

As for myself, and Seg also, as I knew, Clawsangs were merely another form of human life in the world. If you imagined that their skull-like faces, covered with a tightly stretched pebbly skin of grey and green granulated texture, blunt of jaw, the roots of the teeth exposed, the nostrils mere sunken slits, the eyes, overhung by bony projections, of a smoky crimson, if, then, you imagined this face emerging from a freshly opened grave, you could be pardoned for the thought, unworthy though it was. It was not the Clawsangs' fault they looked as though they were decomposing.

Mind you, even the stoutest hearts might flinch if they bumped into a Clawsang on a pitch-black night of Notor Zan with only the erratic illumination of a torch to pick out the rotting teeth and the decomposed nose and the glaring crimson eyes...

Yet Skort was not ashamed of his appearance. Why should he be? This was the way the gods had fashioned him. Perhaps he found the jolliness of a full-fleshed ruddy countenance as offensive to him; a bloated bladder of blood.

The Clawsang's voice sounded like the rustle of bat wings from a Herrelldrin Hell as he spoke. He did so infrequently. He kept his weapons handy about him. His people maintained a sharp lookout.

Skort said, "We must march. Why do we hesitate?"

The lady Ilsa could not bear to look on Skort. Strom Ornol, over his shoulder, said, "We wait for the sorcerer."

"And if he is not here soon," said Exandu, "I shall retire to bed. I feel faint, and I am sure I have an infection in my right ear. I can hardly hear that side."

The business of the tavern went on, and ale was quaffed and the dice players threw and presently a girl came in to dance. She was a Sybli, and lusciously beautiful in a vapid way, and when she had finished a handful of copper was thrown, and one or two silver pieces. She picked them up gracefully and departed, and the ale went around again.

The local brew, made from plants tended with loving care, was a fine straw-yellow, very clear, not over strong, an ale made for quenching the thirst and not for fighting on.

Had this part of the forested area of Pandahem lent itself to hops production as I knew it, the brew would have been improved considerably. As it was, Seg and I drank a little, and talked, and sized up the people of the party with whom we would soon be risking our lives.

As Seg, speaking quietly behind his ale jug, said, "I judge the Clawsang to be a fighter, and the Pachak, clearly. This Strom Ornol could be useful if he is not wounded. Exandu?"

"He really believes he can catch all the illnesses sent by all the devils there are. But he looks healthy enough."

"Aye. And we are to have a sorcerer with us."

"If all the tales the locals tell are true, that might be not only useful but essential."

"If you believe the stories..."

The inhabitants of Selsmot were riddled with the dread of the Snarly Hills. Travel toward the south went invariably all the way around in boats on the River of Bloody Jaws. The trails went east and west, for a way; not south.

The conversation, such as it was, became general as Ornol, fretfully, exclaimed, "But the bandits have stopped attacking the caravans and the river traffic. Why, then, is there still this superstitious dread of the Snarly Hills?"

The Pachak, Kalu Na-Fre, said, "Perhaps a greater evil has settled there."

The lady Ilsa looked flustered. Skort the Clawsang rubbed a skeletal hand across the rotting roots of his teeth. Ornol's color rose. And Exandu fluttered his yellow kerchief in a wild and vain attempt to halt a tremendous sneeze.

"There is a draught! I am sure of it! Shanli, my pet, find the draught—"

"Yes, yes, master. It is there, over by that window—"

She started to rise, and, in truth, a breath of air did fan in from an ill-fitting window shade. Seg stood up.

"Mistress Shanli. Please allow me."

She flushed.

Exandu, fluttering his kerchief, did not notice and Seg went across and adjusted the shade. We thought nothing of the incident.

No one spoke further on the subject of greater evils.

The risks ahead of us we could guess would be great. There is on Kregen a saying—"Don't dice with a four-armed fellow"—which attempts to caution against taking foreseeable and unnecessary risks. What we would be facing would be perils of the unknown kind.

The locals, while relishing relating to us all manner of ghastly stories of the Snarly Hills and accepting drinks, did not wish actively to be too closely associated with us. They would not sit at our table. Their grimaces and winks, their grave nods, even the way they quaffed the ale we bought for them, all contributed to a creeping horror about to overwhelm us.

One of the locals, a Rapa, having imbibed a skinful, decided it was time to go home. His strongly vulturine face, the sharp beak surrounded by a bristle of brown and grey feathers, turned toward the door before the fellow's body followed the commands of his brain. His plain tunic was ale-stained. He was happy, though.

Tangle-footed, he swayed toward the door and then—and the transition was abrupt—he lurched sideways in terror and crashed into a table. Ale spilled. Tankards flew. The people at the table leaped back; but their protests died in their throats.

Through the open doorway came the sixth member of our party.

"At last," said Strom Ornol. "Fregeff. Now perhaps we can decide." The young lord took no notice of the turmoil the sorcerer's entrance caused.

This Fregeff, one could see at a glance, was an Adept of the Doxology of San Destinakon. Swathed in an enveloping gown of brown and black lozenges that bewildered with their subtle shifts of alignment as he moved, he presented an imposing figure simply because one knew what he was. Set against wizards of other cults, an Adept of the Doxology of San Destinakon appears dark, somber and eclipsed. This is an illusion.

Because he was a Fristle, his powerful catlike features arrogant within the hood, he did not bear a woflovol upon his left shoulder. The bronze cham about his waist connected to a bronze necklet, and that hoop rested securely around the neck of a vicious winged reptile, a volschrin, one of the rissniks. The narrow head lay low beside the Fristle's ear. A red tongue darted. The membranous wings were folded back, and the barbed tail was hidden within the sorcerer's hood. When those wings unfurled and were spread and the volschrin flew wickedly to tear out the eyes of his victim, they spanned a full arm's breadth. But his body was no larger than that of a cat, and, like his catman master, he hissed.

The hissing voice said, "Greetings and Lahal."

We all replied politely. The sorcerer moved toward our table and the empty seat. He placed his wooden-hafted bronze flail upon the sturm-wood table, and sat down. The brown and black lozenges adorning his robe shifted eye-wateringly.

No one ventured to suggest he was late for the meeting.

Fregeff turned his head and whispered to the reptile on his shoulder, and then called, "A dish of blood, and swiftly!"

Without delay a pottery dish awash in fresh chicken blood was hurried in. The serving girl, a plain-faced gentle soul, trembled as she placed the gory dish upon the table.

The volschrin hopped down, bronze links clanking, and lapped.

"Well," said Strom Ornol, his voice quivering from affronted dignity, "perhaps now we can get started."

Twelve

Through the Snarly Hills

"Hold on a moment, Seg," I said, and halted on the forest slope to catch a breath. "My lungs are on fire, and my side burns."

Seg stopped to look back. Some of the others took the opportunity to halt in a straggly line between the trees under the dim green light. Seg didn't believe me.

"It's all uphill and down my old dom, I know. But—?"

Strom Ornol bustled up. His pale face looked greenish in the light and—was that a flush of color along the cheekbones? Possible, although unlikely...

"What are you lollygagging about for? Come on, come on!"

Skort the Clawsang passed me, his bulging knapsack just about finding room between me and the tree I leaned against. I had to pull back to let him pass. His skull face turned toward me, but he said nothing. Only his crimson eyes gleamed as he passed.

"Sink me!" I burst out. "I'll rupture my inward parts if we gallop along like this."

Seg's face was a picture.

The Fristle sorcerer, for whom we had waited for our meeting in The Dragon's Roost, also passed without a word. His winged pet balanced agilely on his shoulder, every now and again flirting a wing out to maintain balance. A right pair, they were...

Exandu waddled up.

His face resembled Zim at the going down of the day, seen through a misty haze, embracing all around him with a roseate glow. Sweat dropped. He puffed.

"I have—" he gasped, and swallowed, and tried again. "I have a thorn through my foot. I am sure of it. And my face—I am bitten through to the bone by these pinheads!"

Shanli helped him. Her face was intent.

"I have ointments, master—when we rest—"

"When! That Ornol strides on like a madman!"

"We rest now, Exandu," I said. I turned as the blue shadow that was the lady Ilsa halted, gasping, her hand to her side. "We rest now."

"Oh" said Seg. He beamed. Then: "Why didn't you just tell the infernal idiot?"

"He believes he leads us. That is fine—" I looked away as Ilsa more fell than sat down. She still did not accept us as equals, and Seg and I couldn't care less. I said to no one in particular, "If I can't have a rest now, I will not answer for the consequences."

When Strom Ornol strode back along the line of struggling people with their burdens he found us sitting comfortably, our backs against the tree, sipping ale.

He frowned.

He picked on the lady Ilsa.

"Up, Ilsa. We must get on. You keep me waiting."

"My feet, Ornol—"

Her moccasins were strong and sensible, supple and resistant to thorns. But no one was in any doubt that marching over this forested range of hills was a laborious and painful business for anyone, let alone a girl. I had ventured, just the once, to suggest that the ladies be left in Selsmot. I had been told by Ornol to shut my mouth and keep out of his business, and by Exandu that, much as he regretted the necessity, Shanli had to go. "It's my insides, you see. Shanli understands them. She keeps me alive."

We crawled to our feet after a bit, following Ilsa, who obeyed the strom. But that was not the first or the last time I called for a halt because I was too fatigued to go farther.

Seg told Ornol, "You see, strom, he was stung by a Cabaret Plant. It has drained his strength."

"If he's this bad, he shouldn't have started."

Walking along, Hop the Intemperate said, sotto voce, "If he's this bad he'd be dead."

Seg walked with Hop for a space after that, and explained the situation. Hop's hairy face moved in an expressive way. He grasped it. Later he was seen talking to Shanli, and later still, when we stopped again, Exandu took the opportunity to say in a quiet voice, "You are a man of parts, Dray the Bogandur. A man of resource."

"I felt for your inward parts, Exandu."

"And my poor feet! And my skin, which is like Shanli's pin cushion—oh, oh, that Beng Sbodine, Mender of Men, should abandon me now!"

"Well, Exandu," said Seg in his hateful voice, "you've got the Bogandur to look after you on that score."

When we'd had a quick word to decide what names we could give these people, for they already knew we were Seg and Dray from mistress Tlima, Seg had suggested the Sublime for me. I'd riposted with the Ineffable for him.

Then I said, "How about Seg the Fearless?"

"Oh, no! Oh, no, a fellow would get into too many fights with a name like that."

"Well, if you're Naming me the Bogandur, I can but suggest the Horkandur for you, my lad."

So that was that.

We pitched camp that night and Ilsa and Exandu were not the only ones to lament their aches and pains.

A long straggly line of people stumbling through a jungle, with those in front hacking a way through when necessary, presents a prime target, but we had only a few desultory attacks from predators to ward off, and we lost only two porters. Having eaten enough food to lighten loads, we could accommodate the dead men's burdens. We carried waterproof packs on our backs, and these, we promised ourselves, would be filled with gold and gems when we returned this way.

Ha!

The reason for Seg's and my presence here was not forgotten by either of us. We even debated if, perchance, one or other of the people here in the party were agents of Spikatur Hunting Sword.

"Somebody could be," pointed out Seg. "Luring us to our doom."

"Wager?"

"We-ell..."

"Who do you fancy?"

"They're all runners."

"That's true, by Krun!"

Seg half glanced about as I used that Hamalese oath; no one paid us any attention. Everyone was too tired.

Everyone except Strom Ornol. From his tent the sound of singing broke discordantly on the night. A lamp gleamed through the canvas. I thought— I was not sure—a woman's shape showed, dancing.

"He likes his comforts, the strom," observed Seg.

"Aye."

"I'd mark him down. A bad egg, kicked out by his father the trylon, taken up with bad company. Anxious to hit back at the aristocratic lot who disowned him. A likely candidate for Spikatur."

"I remember a fellow, a kov, a great hunter, called Kov Loriman the Hunting Kov. He was an adherent of Spikatur. Mind you, that was in the days Spikatur struggled against Hamal and not against all and sundry."

"Well, my old dom, if we get to the place we're going, we'll find out why they changed."

"I feel that, too. But we could be mistaken."

Seg yawned. "Maybe. Just that it feels right. No, I won't back the dandy strom. Mayhap Exandu?" He yawned again.

I said, "I have the middle watch, and so I need my sleep even if you do intend to stay up all night."

In the midst of his reply Seg yawned again, and then, confound it, so did I. We turned in, to be roused out to stand our watch when the time came. At last the next day dawned in a muted green radiance dropping down through the leaves, and we could eat our breakfast and shoulder our burdens, take up our weapons and set off.

The routine of marching and resting, of fighting off predators, of arguing and surmising, and of eating and sleeping continued for a sennight as we slogged through the Snarly Hills.

We were, in truth, an oddly assorted party.

No one in his or her right mind was going to pick a quarrel with the sorcerer.

Pachaks detest quarrels as being indicative of low mental abilities and deplorable moral outlooks.

The Clawsang kept to himself and the people of his small group, and refused to be drawn into a quarrel.

Exandu turned any argument into a complaint about the state of his health, parlous, parlous in the extreme...

Wanting to quarrel with any and everybody, Strom Ornol turned on Seg and me, and we, like Skort the Clawsang, refused to be drawn. We could act like onkers when we wanted to. We enraged the young strom by our obtuseness. All the same, Seg had a word with Shanli, and she had a word with Ilsa, and—by chance or not—the young dandy strom moderated his tone. Again, the hold of unpaid debts restrained him.

"The trouble is," I said, "he's holding himself in. One fine day he'll blow up."

"Let him scatter himself all over," said Seg. He spoke with a bright satisfaction. "All over."

On Kregen the image herein conjured was not that of this Earth, where an explosion means that; on Kregen the image was of a volcano blowing up. And the image pleased Seg mightily. I didn't blame my blade comrade. The truth was, Strom Ornol was well nigh insufferable. He always wanted to be in the right. He always wanted to know it all. He was, in short, a pain in the neck.

One day toward the end of the third sennight in the forest we broke through into a wide upland clearing. Water glimmered near the center, and the jungle ringed the clearing with solid dark green. We all stopped, taking our breath.

"Straight across, and skirt the lake," said Ornol.

"Well, now—" started Exandu.

The strom cut him off. "If you wish to toil through the jungle, you may, fat man. As for me, I take the manly path."

Seg rolled up his eyes. I did not laugh. Ilsa came up to cling to Ornol's arm. Shanli hovered at Exandu's side. Skort stood, impassively waiting. Kalu Na-Fre looked carefully around the clearing and over to the far jungle. Fregeff the sorcerer shook his bronze flail.

"The water is evil," he intoned.

To be honest, that did not surprise us.

The sense of danger scraped at our nerves.

Exandu puffed and heaved out a sigh. "My back! I ache all over! Get out the map and let us see exactly where we are."

Ornol shook out the map and we crowded around.

This famous map, we learned, started it all. From the moment it came into Exandu's possession—he was vague on the exact details, merely mumbling about red gold and slit throats—it set the fire of avarice alight. Exandu's dealings with Strom Ornol brought that young dandy in. Fregeff was known to Exandu, as was the Clawsang, Skort. The Pachak, Kalu Na-Fre, had joined them in a tavern one night when the place burned down and he had been useful in extricating a terrified Exandu. So we had joined the party, and we were all devoted to finding the treasures, and the map pointed the way.

The bandits must have amassed great treasures. They had been put down by King Crox. Alive or dead, he could be dealt with. Queen Mab, too, was missing. No news was good news. I know that Ornol envisaged walking into the bandit lair and kicking rotting bodies aside to fling open their treasure chests and help himself.

Fregeff shook his flail at the lake, and repeated, "The water is evil. You may approach. I shall go the longer way."

Exandu looked longingly at the short open way, and the dimness of the circuit. He shook his head mournfully.

"You put a poor sufferer in a great quandary. My aching feet will never carry me all the way around; yet if we venture across the center—"

"I am going," snapped Ornol. "I shall wait for you at the far side of the clearing."

The map indicated four of these clearings with a central lake. The accuracy of the map was open to question. The paper was rough, thick and coarse-grained, much tattered on the edges, burned here and there, and with rusty brown stains adding a decorative touch. The outlines of the river, lake and hills were sharp enough, and the cross near the center seemed to sit up and beg for attention. That was the lure.

The map folded up along worn creases. I wondered why Exandu allowed Ornol to carry the precious parchment.

The strom started off, long-legged, spry, striding out over the cleared area. He called back, harshly and imperiously: "Ilsa!"

Instantly, the girl ran out to follow.

With some hesitations, the guards and porters followed.

The Clawsang took a fresh hitch to his belt, drew one of his swords, gestured to his people, and followed.

The Pachak looked at Exandu.

"Go on, go on, good Kalu," wheezed Exandu. "I shall struggle across after you. Somehow." He put out his hand and at once Shanli was there, tall and dignified, and with his hand on her shoulder, bitterly complaining about his poor aching bones, Exandu waddled off.

Fregeff lowered his bronzen flail. "And you?"

"I think, master sorcerer, and with no disrespect to you, that our duty lies with the ladies and the main party."

"Then may Destinakon have you in his keeping."

Fregeff gestured to his people, and set off to edge around the clearing.

Seg looked me in the face, half-frowning, and I nodded my head, peaceably, and so we set off after the others.

The ground was covered with myriad gouges, like the imprints of a shovel, laid into the soft spongy soil. The dents overlapped and ran in no ordered pattern. Water glimmered in some of them. We followed along the drier parts.

At the border of the lake Ornol did not pause, but pressed on. The water held a dank oily scum on its surface, and rainbow hues broke blisteringly from the coils. Nothing moved in the lake; only our own onward progress changed the spectrum from each ridge of oily scum. The twin Suns burned down. The air hung flat and humid. We labored on.

When we reached the far edge of the clearing and the hard line of dark green, we stopped, and waited, and presently, panting with the effort, Fregeff joined us.

No one—not even the usually insensitive Ornol—said anything to the sorcerer.

He said, "Why does nothing grow in the clearing?"

Before anyone got up the effort needed to think of an answer, the Fristle went on: "I will tell you. The water is evil. It poisons the ground."

That seemed all too probable.

On that somber thought we all plunged once more into the jungle.

Two more clearings were passed in like fashion, the party having skirted the lake at the center waiting for Fregeff at the far end. When we reached the fourth clearing with the heat of the Suns declining and the green dimness in the forest darker by contrast to the streaming mingled light out in the open area, Seg said, "Three out of four. Good odds. But—four out of four?"

"Fifty-fifty, I suppose, still."

"Fregeff?"

The sorcerer did not shake his flail. His cat face looked exhausted, the whiskers drooping. He was no worse off than the others—all bar Strom Ornol.

"The evil I sensed in the waters of the other lakes is absent here."

"So there is no problem, no hindrance," shouted Ornol.

He started off at once, over the indentations in the mud. His figure looked hard and arrogant, lively, forceful. He led on, and his people with the lady Ilsa followed. He half-turned to shout back: "Come on, come on. We will camp at the far side."

As the porters and guards moved forward, leaving the shelter of the trees and plodding on over the cleared ground, Seg started to follow. I said, "Wait, Seg."

Fregeff turned to me.

"Why do you fear where there is no evil?"

"Why? Perhaps because you have not given your opinion?"

The Fristle sorcerer stepped out onto the mud. He was careful to step on the ridges between the indentations.

"I can tell that there is no evil in the lake. That is all."

The members of the party had by this time advanced some distance across the clearing in the waning light. We followed. The indentations, like the blows of spades, flat into the earth, appeared sharper, less eroded than in the three previous clearings. Here and there a few small green shoots showed, fragile plants growing up along the ridges between impression and impression. There had been nothing growing in the first three clearings.

Here and there, too, lay casual scatterings of bleached bones.

Seg cocked an eye at me. We loosened the swords in our scabbards, unsure, uneasy, quivering against the onset of a dread that should not exist.

As we neared the water we could see the surface was crystal clear and sparkling where it was not covered by broad lily pads, blue-green and velvet with lushness in the low-lying light.

Strom Ornol strode on. At his side the lady Ilsa struggled bravely to keep up. The porters bent under their loads. The guards looked about, white of eye, and their heads turned this way and that as though under imminent attack from the air. The Pachak openly drew his swords. The Clawsang copied him. A sweet and intrusive scent gusted from the lake. The lily pads floated silently.

When I spoke to the sorcerer, my voice was hushed.

"No evil, Fregeff?"

"No evil of a supernatural kind that I can tell."

"There is *something* wrong with this place." Seg pulled his bow off his shoulder, the stave lay clenched in his left hand. He lifted his right to draw an arrow—and the surface of the lake boiled.

Lily pads swirled wildly away. From the sparkling water enormously long stems flailed. Dozens of them, bunched and thrashing, they heaved from the water, scattering glinting drops, slashing frenziedly at the members of the party.

At the tip of each flailing stem a bloated flowerlike object smashed down, hard, splitting into the earth, splashing mud in gouts, leaving spade-like indentations.

A Gon guard was smashed into jelly.

The people screamed. They were running, some fell and were squashed.

Blood oozed into the mud. The hammer-hard flower heads flailed at us, lashed down, smashed into the earth with soggy deadly smacks, driving deep gouges into the mud.

I drew my sword and, raving, leaped forward.

Thirteen

Concerning a Distortion of Reality

Seg leaped alongside, bow thrust back over his shoulder, sword in fist. We burst past Fregeff, who was looping up his bronze chain around the little shoulder-perching reptile. His bronze flail clashed.

Shoulder to shoulder, Seg and I drove forward into the flailing forest of lashing stems. The plate-like mangling flower heads swung with tremendous force. The stink of disturbed mud filled our nostrils, till we gagged.

With ferocious slashes, we cut and hacked at the stems as they swooped near. They were sinewy, not easy to hack through, and from the gashes opened by our swords a thick and slimy brown ooze dribbled.

The screams of the terrified people racketed on never-endingly. Through the whirlwind of stems and the looping darting rock-hard flower-heads we glimpsed Strom Ornol, hacking and slashing. The other members of the party fought back. The porters reacted differently, each according to his race. Some dropped to their knees to pray and were so squashed into the mud. Others put their heads down and ran. Others hefted their bundle or bale and tried to beat off the terrible plants. Most of these, too, were squashed.

Seg pelted on before me, incensed, head up, his sword blurring. He lopped a plant stem clean through, catching it near the head where it was thinner and more tender. He scooped up Shanli in his left arm. He made loud squelching noises as he ran.

Following on as fast as I could I saw Ornol flailing away, and the lady Ilsa hanging to his left arm, hampering him and yet gaining protection from her nearness. She, I judged, would be safer with Ornol than if I attempted to snatch her. Ornol would as lief take a swipe at me, a suddenly appearing attacker in the corner of his eye, as at a plant.

Sword flailing above my head in ghastly parody of the plant stems flailing at us, I ranged up alongside Seg and Shanli. Exandu was just about done for. His face bloated scarlet. His eyes stood out. Yet he was bashing away with a heavy curved single-edged sword. He used it with a cunning skill, and all the time he bashed at the plant stems, he was maintaining a high-pitched catalog of all the complaints besieging his poor abused body.

"Aid me, Dray the Bogandur! Help a poor old fellow who—"

"You appear to be doing well enough," I shouted, sliding and almost going over. "I'll stay with you. Run!"

Then a damned hard-edged flower whistled down at my head. It was useless to stand up to them and cut through the stem. If you did that the head would simply fly straight on and bash you. You had to duck and weave and slash cunningly, avoiding the blows.

"They can't see us!" bellowed Seg. "Yet they strike with uncanny accuracy."

"Magic," said Shanli, under Seg's arm. "It is sorcerers' work."

Puffing and bloated, Exandu slashed along with a will with companions to protect his side.

"No magic—Shanli, my treasure. They strike at noise."

I had to say it, for I was annoyed with myself.

"There is no noise of bottles and glasses, or of people having a good time. It seems these things have no need of enticing us."

"We were—fool enough—to come near them."

The terror and confusion persisted. We had a long way to go. The impressions of the murderous flower heads reached everywhere in the clearing. There was no safety until we reached the hostile jungle.

We lost good men. Mere squashed red puddles, they had to be left as we fought to escape. Even the bundles they carried had to be left. Swishing our swords, taking more care to strike exactly, leaving a trail of decapitated flower heads, we labored on toward the far side of the clearing, for that was the nearest now. I thought to glance back.

The Fristle sorcerer stood stock still. The volschrin clung like a scaled polished statue. His hood was thrown back. His strong cat face was upturned. He did not move; he made no sound—and the devilish killer plants ignored him.

I gasped for a breath.

"Exandu! Stand still. Do not move, do not make a sound."

When he understood, he stopped running. His body shook. Sweat ran thickly down his cheeks. Seg stopped, too, grasping Shanli. We all stood, swords poised, staring about, using our sight, the weapon we had that could trump the killer plants.

The stems wreathed and writhed above our heads, the blind flowers seeking prey. Those stems flailing and lashing at our party continued to do so. We breathed short, watching as more men were felled into red puddles. The stems left us alone. We breathed easier, getting our breath—

And Exandu sneezed.

Instantly two plant heads uncoiled and swished down at the source of the sound.

Seg chopped one, and I chopped the other.

He raised his eyebrows at me. I knew what he meant.

"By the Veiled Froyvil, my old dom!" he was saying silently. "How long are we to stand here like a couple of loons?"

I didn't know. Once Exandu got his breath back—we'd run. Our squelching progress through the muck would alert the killer plants, and down they would swoop.

Fregeff lifted his flail. He lifted the bronze links silently. He looked proud, defiant, the recipient of powers that would blast a lesser man. The whiskers of his catlike face bristled.

He shook the flail.

Above the diminishing screams of the running people and the ghastly swishing sounds made by the killer plants, we in our pool of petrified silence heard the bronzen links of the flail clash together.

Rearing from the crystal waters of the lake, pushing the velvet lily pads aside, swooping out at any sound to smash their victims flat, the pallid stems swayed toward Fregeff. The wizard shook the flail again.

The blind flower heads above him, their edges hard and square, drew back. They wilted. They writhed, and now they writhed as though caught in an open flame. Swiftly, they withdrew, coiled, disappeared beneath the waters of the lake. It was as if, through the agency of his flail the wizard had told them to turn tail, yield, flee...

Again the sorcerer shook the flail of the Scourging of San Destinakon.

The chiming sounded sweetly in our ears, yet, in all truth, it was a sound of utmost horror.

The wizard emitted no brilliant gust of flame and fire, no bolt of lightning, such as the incandescent bolts with which the sorcerer's Quern of Gramarye was formed. And we knew the power came not only from Fregeff and not only from the flail; the thaumaturgy boiled from the conjunction of the two. Invisibly, the power smote a circle of clarity among the swooping pallid killer plants.

Exandu shook himself. He whispered, and he thought he whispered only to himself; but we heard, Seg and I, we heard.

"To Opaz the Nine times Exalted, who has the mastery over all men, be the praise!"

Under my blade comrade's arm Shanli erupted into a violent squirming bundle of womanliness. "And, Pantor Seg the Horkandur! If you would put me down, I shall be about my work!" Her voice was loud, strong, not shrill but overpowering. I understood she spoke and acted thus to cover up the words spoken by Exandu.

Seg stood her up. She did, in that moment, look magnificent. Instantly, she was ministering to Exandu, fiddling with his straps and clothes to put him to rights, soothing his brow, producing a bottle of a honey-gold liquid, which gave him something to stop his querulous complaints.

Seg smiled.

Fregeff joined us, still remote, wrapped in the aura of power. We did not shrink away as we had every right to do; but we were conscious of the dark authority of the man. In the normal course of events I give wizards a wide berth. I count some sorcerers as good friends. Fregeff, a Fristle, a cat-man, might yet number among those. That lay with the gods.

"We give you thanks, San Fregeff."

He inclined that cat head, and with the links of the flail brushed his whiskers. Before replying he whispered to the volschrin perched on his shoulder. The reptile flicked his wings. Fregeff addressed the volschrin as Rik Razortooth. Spreading his membranous wings, the reptile flapped away and sailed toward the nearest severed flower head, trailing his thin bronze chain. He settled and began to rip at the hard carapace of the flower head.

Fregeff said, "I was right when I said there was no evil in the water. The evil in the other lakes had killed the plants. Whoever placed that evil there knew what he or she was doing."

Skort the Clawsang marched back over the mud toward us.

Fregeff went on: "But I own I was slow. We have lost porters and guards. I shall abase myself to San Destinakon this night, and chastise myself in expiation."

"Nonsense, San," said Skort. His ghastly face leered upon us, the ruby eyes slits of smoldering anger. "The fault was ours. You have saved us all."

I said, "You have met these plants before?"

"Aye. Slaptras. They grow in Chem, along with syatras and tenchlas."

"Everything happened very quickly after the plants attacked," pointed out Seg in his superior and endearing way, knowing exactly what he was doing. "I think Skort is right and San Destinakon has no need of a scourged back this night."

"As to that, Horkandur, I can only say my business is my business. I have no need of sermons from others."

I felt the chill.

Exandu, blustering, blowing, sneezing, moaning pitifully and bellowing angrily, broke in. He did not relish, as I saw it, the loss of the limelight. I was wrong in that...

"Let us leave this infernal place and schtump! The spell may not last long enough for my poor aching feet to carry me into that terrible jungle away from the slaptras."

Fregeff gave the bronze chain a single jerk, and the volschrin flew back to his shoulder. Ruby eyes regarded us. "It was hardly a spell," said the sorcerer. "More a distortion of reality—well, my business is my business."

We all made our way across the mud to the trees. The bodies and the bundles would be taken care of. We made camp and more than one of us wondered if the future held more horrors. Most of us were faithfully convinced that the future *did* hold more horrors...

Our faith was justified.

Fourteen

I Receive a Personal Invitation

On Earth, I am informed, the tropical rain forests occupy less than ten percent of the land surface of the planet, yet they contain half of the species of the world. Whether this be so or not, in view of the claims of the sea, is beside the point; the truth remains, tropical rain forests are wonderful, mysterious secret worlds of their own, romantic, pulsating with drama, hot and sticky and uncomfortable and downright dangerous.

Seg and I had no retainers, and we hadn't bothered with a tent or beds or tables and chairs, as the others had. We camped as we had camped on many a night and many a place of Kregen. We were old campaigners.

From the canopy above where the leaves spread out into jigsaw patterns between branch and branch and tree to tree, down to the soft ground where the detritus piled up, and was consumed and carried away, each level contained its own slice of life. We did not venture into climbing. We toiled along the floor, wending a way between massive vine-covered trunks. When we camped at night we formed the tents into a circle and set fires and watches. More often than not we were disturbed; but we had some handy fighters with us, and we were more than a match for the denizens of the jungle.

At least, for some of them...

On the last night before the map told us we would reach the upper lake and the waterfall and the rocky cliff, Seg and I passed a few words about our companions. What those words boiled down to, essentially, was: We didn't know.

"Kalu the Pachak will, like Pachaks, be an honorable man. I am surprised he is mixed up with a rogue like Ornol, or that shuddery fellow, Skort—"

"I," I said, "have Exandu picked for a villain."

"We-ell, you could be right. He is reticent about his trade. And he did pray to Opaz the Nine Times Exalted."

"Which marks him as not being a Pandaheem."

"Unless he's been converted." And Seg laughed.

Usually new lands are visited by the Four M's. The Military, the Merchants, the Mercenaries, and the Missionaries.

"We had some sprightly dealings with the missionaries of the Black Feathers of the Great Chyyan," I said, "and it is sure Skort the Clawsang worships dark gods. But Exandu?"

"Tomorrow we fetch up with the drikingers' lair. We'll find out more then." Seg rolled over in his bag. "G'night."

And, all in good time, on the morrow we marched up to the edge of the forest and looked out across the lake toward the sheer face of rock.

Everyone, instinctively, checked the water first for signs of slaptras. We saw no velvety blue-green lily pads.

Strom Ornol said, "I march around to the right."

Exandu puffed and said. "The way to the left seems shorter."

Skort the Clawsang half drew and then thrust back his sword into the scabbard. This sword was a lynxter, which is a Lohvian sword, something like the Havilfarese thraxter. Skort knew about the jungles of Chem, which is in Loh. But he had not vouchsafed any information of his origins. Like the rest of them, he was reticent on the point, and we were happy to take them all, like us, as plain adventurers.

"I think I will go with Strom Ornol," said Skort.

The lake shimmered in the mingled radiance of the Suns of Scorpio. The jungle pressed in around the perimeter. Directly opposite us the wall of rock towered, smothered in vines, brilliant with flowers. Many birds swooped and called one to the other, cavorting in midair. There seemed, at first glance, little to choose which way we went. The heat shimmered off the lake, and the rock face wavered in heat distortions.

Among the birds flying and disporting I saw—suddenly and quick—a magnificent golden and scarlet bird. He flew up out of the entangling vines, and circled around the edge of the lake. I watched him narrowly, my companions forgotten.

He swerved. In headlong flight he soared straight above my head, wide winged, glorious, the light of the suns incandescent upon his feathers. He was the Gdoinye, the spy and messenger of the Everoinye, the Star Lords.

Among the people clustered at the edge of the forest, I knew only I, of them all, could see the Gdoinye.

He cawed, arrogantly, and banked, wide-winged, magnificent of plumage, and soared away around the right-hand side of the water.

I said, "Master Exandu, I think the right-hand way will be easier on your fragile bones."

His flushed face jerked up, and sweat dropped off the end of his roseate nose.

"You think so?"

"Aye."

"Well, perhaps—you, San Fregeff. What do you think?"

"I will go with Strom Ornol."

The Pachak, Kalu, answered the unspoken question by starting off. He turned to his side where he had one arm only.

Everybody followed.

The distant roar of the waterfall indicated its presence; we could not see it yet. The powerful scent of flowers stung my nostrils. I cocked a wary eye at Seg.

"Yes. Spiny Ribcrushers."

"I fancy Skort will know of them."

We picked our way with great caution around the edge of the lake. Roots of trees snaked into the water. We watched everything with the care of men who have marched through a jungle.

On the brown mudspit the birds quarreled. The brown water shimmered with heat. We kept our weapons in our fists, and we plodded on until we circumnavigated the right half of the lake and so stood before the first of the rocky buttresses.

The lianas twined away above, looping and jumbled, coiling into massy knots and protuberances. The rock dripped with moisture, grey and leprous. The weather-beaten appearance was occasioned by an intricate and enormously extended series of carvings. Faces, birds, fish, animals, risslacas, insects, grotesque and beautiful, the carvings swarmed upon the rock and in the heat shimmer appeared to move and breathe with a pseudo life, at once fascinating and disturbing.

Exandu stopped and wiped his face. Skort moved on, around the end of the buttress. Strom Ornol, at the Clawsang's side, half-turned back and motioned us on.

"There is an opening, a portal."

The sight of the gorgeous bird sent by the Star Lords had, as so often in the past it had not, reassured me. Oh, yes, the Everoinye liked to keep an eye on me from time to time; perhaps in this instance that was all they were doing. Very probably that was the true answer. But, was it not a human weakness to try to see the Gdoinye's actions, flying around the right hand side of the lake, as some kind of assistance?

We all shuffled around the buttress and saw the opening in the rock, square, hard, forbidding.

Seg whispered, "If there are bandits around, are we to go strolling in like players at feast time?"

"I gather Exandu and Ornol believe they will encounter only dead men, and can help themselves to the treasures."

"That's as may be."

The square opening was twice man height, and three times man wide, and the architrave was surrounded by grotesque gargoylish carvings, obscene monstrosities sculpted by a depraved master hand. Inscriptions, etched into the rock, proclaimed the standard curses. Because many of the artisans employed on masonry work were unable to read or write, either the literate master mason would chalk out the words, and the hammer and chisel men would faithfully follow his outlines, or a stencil would be placed on the stone and fuming acid poured on to etch out the words. We all stared at the ritual curses.

Not one of these hardy adventurers would be affected by the blastings and ib-destructions and diseases promised for anyone who entered here. They were accustomed, in the adventurer's trade, to weightier obstacles than mere carven words.

Then Exandu let out a quick, chopped-off cry of alarm. Kalu said, "That is indeed strange." Skort said nothing and Ornol shouted for his people to prepare torches.

Fregeff the wizard pulled his hood up over his head, and he covered his volschrin, Rik Razortooth, with the hood.

I turned back from examining a marvelously carved head of a Medusa to hear Seg say, "By the Veiled Froyvil! I don't believe it!"

So I turned around and saw Seg standing, mouth open, finger pointing, staring in horror at the blasphemous inscriptions.

Three lines of writing in the flowing Kregish script, all beauty and curve and free-flowing line, had been blasted into the rock. They looked black, as though some instrument dispensing enormous heat had simply burned the stone away.

Three lines of writing, and the center line was a mere nothing, a repetition of the rote curses:

ENTER TO YOUR DOOM

Well, one ignored that. But I looked, standing beside Seg, and I saw... I saw! The first line of writing said:

DRAY PRESCOT, EMPEROR OF VALLIA

And the last line of writing said:

PHU-SI-YANTONG

The heavens did not open and darkness did not descend on my senses. But it was a near thing, by Vox!

All manner of impossible thoughts clashed and collided in my brain. Phu-si-Yantong, that arch-devil, the Wizard of Loh who had brought great misery to the people of many lands, and particularly to those of Vallia and Pandahem, was dead. He was dead. He had been blown away in a supernal gout of fire in the Quern of Gramarye, in the Jikhorkdun in Ruathytu. He was dead. How could he have known, so long ago, that I would visit here? Could he have sent his ib in lupu into the future?

Seg took my arm.

"He's dead."

"Yes."

"Horkandur?" said Shanli's gentle voice. "Pantor Seg—you are feeling ill?"

Seg swallowed.

"I am all right, thank you, mistress Shanli. Perhaps the smell of the Spiny Ribcrushers affects me."

We smiled at Shanli. We made ourselves smile for her. She did not flinch back.

"They do have an—an overpowering smell, true. The strom insists on going first. Would you—may I ask—pantors..."

I said, "We will stay with you and Exandu, Shanli."

"My thanks, my lord."

The macabre message, weird, eerie, of another time, had to be pushed away. Yantong was dead and burned to pieces. We were here, chasing the remnants of the followers of Spikatur Hunting Sword. Our task was not finished. Useless to fret over the hows of the message blasted into the rock. Its black-burned letters remained; no one commented on them. Once you've read one ceremonial curse you've read them all. Perhaps the others couldn't see the message, as though it had been blasted out for Seg's and my eyes alone. I hesitated no longer. Shouldering my bundle, my sword in my right hand, I followed on as Exandu's people, carrying torches, plunged into the darkness beyond the portal.

They did not make a great deal of noise; but the sound of moccasins shuffled hushed on the ancient stones, the clink of armored men rang with a subdued tone, the harsh breathing stifled. We walked on, into a chamber cut from the rock. Our lights revealed two doors at the far end, both closed, and I surmised we were in for more argument over choosing the way.

Strom Ornol said, "Right."

Still mazed by the message from a dead foeman—or foe-sorcerer—I couldn't have cared less which was selected. We had to find Pancresta and her friends, and see what we could do to remove the new evil of Spikatur Hunting Sword. Seg and I followed through the right-hand door.

Slaves went past carrying long poles cut from the forest. Seg glanced at the poles and frowned. He spoke to a Rapa slave as the fellow passed.

"How long is that pole?"

The Rapa's beaked face ducked. 'Ten feet, master.'

"H'm," said Seg, as we all walked quietly down a stone corridor. "We shall need a few bundles of those, I shouldn't wonder."

"Aye," I said. "Remarkably useful items."

Kalu, an adventurer well-versed in enterprises of this nature, said, "Where I come from, we often talk of going ten-foot poling." He did not say where he came from. "And of green-sliming. I think we should march together."

"You've done this before, then, Kalu." Seg made it a statement.

"Yes. It is a living."

I said, "So your tavern meeting with the good Exandu was not by chance." Then I laughed, letting Kalu see the laugh was all good-natured. "Mayhap the fire...?"

He shook his head and his wild Pachak hair flared yellow. "No. I would not stoop to that. And, were our position other than it is, Bogandur, I might needs challenge you."

We walked through the right-hand doorway and followed the party, the leaders of whom prodded the floor assiduously.

"You could, Kalu. But I would not fight you over so important a matter. I respect the honor of Pachaks too highly."

Someone up front let out a yell and we crowded on to enter a chamber, robed in black, lit by fire crystal in the roof above, and with a vast and circular stairway leading down positioned at the center. Here was a problem.

"There is no other way forward," said Ornol. "So we go down."

The stairs were broad, hewn from rock, slippery. There was no handrail. The depths below resounded with blackness.

"My heart and lungs," said Exandu. He gasped. "This will do my rheumatics no good at all."

"When we rest, master," said Shanli, "I will poultice your joints with Mother Rashi's Herbal Attachments."

"Oh, yes, Shanli. They always ease the stiffness."

Seg and Kalu exchanged a smile, and we all descended the winding stairs into the depths.

Three-quarters of the way down, with the darkness at the foot of the stairs lightening to the glow of the torches, Skort the Clawsang waited on the steps. He stood bravely enough on the outside as the people walked down against the wall. When we came up with him, with Seg and Kalu still talking together, Skort's hideous decomposing corpse face leered on us.

"The strom bids silence from this point down."

Kalu started to bristle up, but Seg, amicably, said, "That makes sense, good Skort."

From the way my blade companion spoke, I knew he was not plucking feathers, as they say on Kregen. Of course, silence made sense down here. We went on, quietly, and the oppressive stillness of the place began its insidious work on our nerves.

The spiral stairway gave onto a flat expanse of rock, with an opening ahead of us and another to our right. The left-hand side of the expanse was walled off solidly. There were no doors in the two openings. A warrior moved forward with a pole and prodding the floor, prodded past the central opening.

He was a Chulik, with tusks unadorned, and a blue-dyed pigtail. He turned and motioned us. All was well.

Chuliks, trained from birth to be mercenary warriors, may have nothing much of warm humanity in their makeup; they are superb fighters and they are brave, you have to say that of them. This Chulik served Strom Ornol.

We all followed on through the opening and found we had to turn sharply to the left along a fifteen-foot-wide corridor. The walls were solid rock. The ceiling and floor were rock. Our torches flung shards of light along, and the procession of heads cast grotesque shadows ahead of us.

No rooms opened off the corridor. At the far end the pasages turned ninety degrees to the right. Halfway along another opening showed merely blackness to the questing torches. Strom Ornol marched straight past this opening and went with his people around the far corner.

When Kalu reached the corner he used his sword to mark a sign upon the rocky wall.

In one sense he needn't have bothered. Every corner was lavishly inscribed with marks. Numbers, letters, names, exhortations, they crowded the rock as the light from the torches fell across them. Seg nodded at this display of ancient instant cartography.

The Pachak leaned close, whispering, "I have a system."

All I did was to make note of the sign which, by reason of its semi-obliteration of others beneath it, indicated it to be among the most recent additions. This mark was in the form of a heart, lobed, and as we passed various corners I noted that the slashed line through the heart pointed the way we had come.

On we went. Because Ornol insisted on leading us, and Skort stuck with him, and Fregeff shuffled along after, Exandu and Kalu and Seg and me tended to be always bringing up the rear. This seemed a sensible idea. Danger, when it came, could strike from our back as easily—possibly more easily—than from our front.

The onward progression of our party, which, despite the losses we had suffered battling through the jungle and at the Pool of the Slaptras, was still of some size, created enough noise for the prohibition upon conversation to be relaxed. Although I accepted this, I did so with reservations. Kalu, who knew about these things, was cheerful enough as he told us,

"Oh, yes. The guardians of the tombs usually know if folk come adventuring down. We will know when we have found them well enough. Yes, by Papachak the All-Powerful!"

"But we're not delving down tombs!" protested Seg.

Kalu waved his upper left arm, shield slung over his back. "What's the difference? Down here?"

We went on following the leaders until we reached an echoing chamber, vaulted of rocky ceiling, lit by ghostly fires that sent streamers of light disturbingly across the floor. The whole system of rooms and corridors was free of dust. This made me suspicious. In this chamber there were twelve doors, set around the circumference. I noticed the mark of the heart upon the door we entered. Halfway around the chamber lay the corpses of two werstings and two strigicaws, savage hunting beasts, long of fang and claw. The bodies appeared to be mummified. All four throats had been slit.

On the other side, propped against a wall, sat the corpse of a man. He, too, was mummified. He was a Chulik. He had been powerful, and wore scraps of armor. His weapons had been taken from him. Farther along lay a scattering of bones, and the skulls of two Rapas and a Fristle.

"They make you welcome," observed Kalu. He sounded quite cheerful, perfectly at home. But he gazed about alertly, and his group of Pachaks closed up, watchfully.

Just as we were about to follow Strom Ornol through one of the doorways without knowing why he had chosen this particular one, we all stopped, poised. The sound of screaming reached us. The black-paneled door to our left crashed open. A man staggered through. He was a Pachak. His lower left arm was a mere stump, bandage-swathed. He was clad in tatters. He carried a sword, rusty with blood. His Pachak face showed such terror as made the heart leap in shocked sympathy.

He sprang out onto the rocky floor, and swung about, flinging the sword up before his face.

Out from the door after him leaped the forms of fanged nightmares, feral eyes ablaze, razored talons reaching to rip past his feeble defense and tear his head from his shoulders.

Amid the instant pandemonium that shattered about us I saw the bristle hairs of the hellhounds spiking in ungovernable anger. They yowled in frenzy, foam-spitting, their red tongues lolling between those razor teeth.

In the next second the hellhounds leaped, lethal engines of destruction, charged demoniacally full upon us.

Fifteen

In the Maze

Seg loosed and in the same motion he dragged his sword clear of the scabbard. Kalu's shield slapped across in his two left hands, and his right brought the sword up, his tail hand whistling over his head, curved blade glittering. My own sword joined in and we fronted that first crazed charge.

Exandu moaned and drew his single-edged sword and stood with us. Slaves screamed and ran. The warriors of the party stood, back to back, in clumps, or with their backs against the wall. The noise echoed in a racket of snarls and shrieks, of muffled chomping of sharp fangs and the juicy thwunk of blows. Keen steel drew bright red blood.

We fought the hellhounds.

We strewed their bristly lean bodies over the rocky floor, trailing blood. We slashed and hacked at them, and they yowled and snarled, and kept coming, a tide of hairy wolf-like bodies pouring through the black-paneled doorway.

They took their toll of our people.

Striking like a maniac, I tried to keep Exandu and Shanli covered, and Seg ranged up on the other side. We had no shields; but we skipped and pumped and ducked. Our brands stained gory, and the blood splashed up to our shoulders.

At last, at last it was done, and no more hairy hellhounds, teeth ravenous, eyes crazed, leaped for our throats. The black-paneled doorway gaped—empty.

"Now may Beng Sbodine, the Mender of Men, have us in his mercy." Exandu spoke deliberately. He shook blood drops from his sword. Seg glanced at me. We marked Exandu's mode of speech. Nothing here, then, of Opaz the Nine Times Exalted.

Strom Ornol, blood-splashed, kicked the hairy and bloodied corpse of a hellhound. He bent, picked the thing up, and threw it viciously from him.

"Creatures from hell!" His pallor was intense.

"They are mortal, not supernatural," said Fregeff.

At his feet lay four hellhounds, unmarked, but dead, stone dead.

Shanli started to minister to Exandu. Skort bent to one of his retainers. The decomposed appearance of the man was a gruesome reminder that soon he would no longer belie his looks.

"Poor Sangl," said Skort. "How am I to tell his mother of this?"

Others of our party were down; a shaven-headed Gon, an uncouth Brokelsh, a Fristle who served Fregeff. No Pachaks had been lost. Kalu knew his own men well.

"We must push on." Ornol waved his sword commandingly, and blood drops splattered. "Ilsa—you must march."

The girl stood up, trembling, from where she had crouched in the angle of floor and wall. She bore dark smudges beneath her eyes, and the tears coursed down her cheeks.

"Yes, Ornol, yes. Those poor men—those terrible beasts—"

"They can be slain with steel." Ornol waved his sword and strode off, commandingly. We all followed.

Seg shouted. "We can't just leave our own people like this!"

Ornol half-turned.

"Can you bury them in this rock? Do you wish to carry them with you?"

Seg looked furious. I walked over to the Gon and, bending down, gently removed the shield that he had failed to employ properly and so save his life. "At least," I said, "we can say the proper words over them and commend them to their gods, and then take from them what in brotherly comradeship they no longer need and we do."

This, with due solemnity, we did.

These small rites meant that Seg and I were last to leave the chamber, with Kalu and Exandu just ahead.

When in the town of Selsmot mistress Tlima had sent a slave over to The Dragon's Roost with our belongings, we had resumed possession of our equipment and weapons. Our own clothes, being mere rags, we did not bother with, and continued to wear the brown tunics. I own I felt the usual irrational but understandable longing to be wearing the brave old scarlet.

"Good men are dead," I said. "I fancy there will be more before we find Pancresta."

"Aye," said Seg. "And before we get out of this devilish place."

"Well, by Zair!" I said with some force. "Just make sure, Horkandur, that you are not one of them!"

"And you—Bogandur!"

With a suspicious look back, we went on. "And that poor devil of a Pachak. Who was he? Where did he come from?"

We assumed that, as he was a Pachak, he would not be a bandit.

Fresh shouts up ahead hastened our steps, and we arrived in the next chamber to find Strom Ornol and Exandu locked in mulish argument. This room, lit by the pervasive glow of fire-crystal walls, gave off a pungent reek of rotting flesh. A small pool of water at the center, rock-coped, held a miniature slaptra. The thing was slashing about with hard-edged flower heads at the end of stalks some two meters long.

Exandu and Ornol might argue over which door to take next; a goodly number of the folk were standing laughing at the slaptra. They taunted it as though it could understand. A Gon stepped forward, and slashed with his sword. The flower head flew off. They all laughed again.

As though that was the signal, the warriors leaped on the slaptra and hewed it to pieces.

No doubt they felt better after that.

"Very well, master Exandu! Very well. You may come with me, as you wish. I go through the door marked in green."

"But, strom—"

"I shall go with you, Strom Ornol," cut in Skort.

"And I," said the wizard.

When the whole mob advanced on the green door, busily poking the ground ahead of them with their poles, and casting searching glances over their heads, Seg and I, with Kalu, saw no reason why we should not follow along.

Green doors, blue doors, black doors, they were all one.

Three long corridors later, and two rooms containing, one: skeletons piled up in yellow-brown heaps, and, two: rotting wooden chests spilling dust and moths, we came to a blue-paneled door. This the leaders pushed open. At once shouts of dismay echoed down to us in the rearguard.

We pushed along and entered the next chamber, weapons ready for what might leap upon us.

We saw a large circular room, halfway around which lay the corpses of two strigicaws and two werstings. Opposite them sat the corpse of a Chulik. Bones lay scattered near. And by the black-paneled door a heap of still blood-reeking hellhound corpses, and those of men, lay in a shambles.

The variety of oaths that rose was marvelous in its diversity.

"Twelve doors!" shouted Ornol above the din, pressing them down by the pallid force of his face and authority. "We have nine left. Let us take the yellow door."

Yellow seemed a sound enough choice to me. I glanced at the red door. It would not be as easy as that...

By the time we had traced a weary way through rooms and corridors, and reentered the circular room through the orange door, we had rested once, and were still tired and more than dispirited. Exandu was one long moan. Ilsa plumped down, and put her hands to her face, and wept openly.

"The turquoise door!" cried Ornol. "Follow me."

His warriors dragged themselves up from whence they had flopped down, and kicked the slave porters into motion, and obediently started after Ornol. Skort the Clawsang and his people followed. Ornol swung back, his pale face wrathful.

"Ilsa! Where are you?"

I went up to Ornol. My face was perfectly blank.

"Strom. It is needful that we rest."

He sneered at me. "Strom, is it? Is that the way to address me? You call me pantor—"

"Pantor, we rest now. You may go on; but you will go on alone."

He glared about. Exandu tried to rescue the situation, for it was obvious and petty enough, Zair knows.

"A rest, good Ornol, for longer than the ten murs you allowed us in the room of the hanging virgins. I beg you."

I said, "We camp here. Set the guards and let us brew some tea and cook ourselves a meal. Our rations will stand that—"

"Our rations and water are almost gone," said Kalu.

"Aye. We must keep up our strength if we are to escape," said Exandu.

"Escape? We have not yet started!" burst out Skort.

We all stared at him in astonishment. As though alarmed at the vehemence of his outburst, he went off, his corpse face seeming to deliquesce and melt away to teeth and bone, and started bellowing at his people to make camp.

We made camp and set watches and tried to sleep. This place of tunnels and rooms was beginning to become a trial. It reminded me uncomfortably of the Moder I'd been down in Moderdrin, the Humped Land, although— as yet—in nowise as horrifying. And this puzzled me, for I, along with the others, had been set for a trial of strength with the bandits, if they were not all dead. This maze came as a shock.

"Seems to me, my old dom, as though we shall all starve to death."

"I could eat hellhound, if I had to. So could you."

"Aye, and so could the others, if it came to it. They'd drink hellhound blood, too..."

"If Zair wills it."

When we started up again after a camp of some eight burs or so, we rose with much groaning and clicking of joints, and the slaves had to be kicked into motion by equally sore warrior guards. We all straggled off, poking the floor and watching the ceiling, and followed Ornol through the doorway paneled in turquoise.

We had not eaten to break our fast, determining to press on for a few burs before consuming any more of our fast vanishing rations. We entered the next chamber, one of three, at the branch of the corridor. Everyone exclaimed in surprise.

Down two sides of the room, which was clothed in bright tapestries depicting scenes of the hunt, stood two long tables. White damask shone. The service was of silver and the viands smelled so aromatic that the saliva started up in our mouths. Amphorae of wine stood in their tripods racked against the far wall. The place was set for a feast.

Kalu swung to us. "Let no one eat or drink!"

The rush for the tables halted, suddenly. We stared longingly on the viands. Our mouths were parched and our tongues hung out. Ornol clamped his lips. He pointed at a slave, a Brukaj with a stubborn bulldog face. "You! Sit at the table and eat, drink!"

"Master!" quavered the Brukaj, shaking.

Ornol lifted his sword. He placed the point against the slave's neck, under his ear. He twitched. A thread of blood shone. "Eat, drink! Or die!"

Ilsa hurried forward; but Shanli was there, to hold her. Exandu sat down on one of the chairs. Everyone else watched. I watched, for I felt, suddenly, that this place was not as the Moder had been.

The slave ate and drank, quivering with fear. But the food was marvelous, delicious, and the wines superb. Soon he was sweating with enjoyment, and drinking—and singing. He sang merrily, throwing-his arms about, his lowering bulldog face transformed.

"If he dies, he'll die happy," said Exandu, with a sigh.

"If the poison does not torture him too much," said Seg, a savage note in his voice. Fierce and fiery is my comrade Seg, with a heart as soft as a girl's lips—at times.

"We will sit and wait," said Ornol.

I fancied he had not liked the hint of mutiny. This hiatus gave him the chance to allow us a proper rest. If the slave died—but the Brukaj did not die. We fell on the food and drink, and, by Krun it was good, all of it, superb!

At last, stuffing our packs with food and carrying bottles of wine, we set off again.

After a long march in the lambent glow of the fire-crystal walls, a march wherein we met and bested fearsome Bearded Phantoms, whining Mind Leeches and a covey of stinking Dragworms, we returned to the chamber, one of three, where we had feasted.

Our exclamations of surprise and anger, of dejection and fear, were partially mollified when we saw that the tables were again laid as we had first found them. Incontinently, we sat down and feasted once more.

"This will not do," said Kalu, stripping a chicken bone expertly and flinging the naked bone over his shoulder. "We are like to eat ourselves to death."

"There has to be a way," said Seg, drinking heartily. "Aye. But which? To go left is to return to the circular room of the twelve doors. To go right is, mayhap, to return here."

"We had best try to the right. If we do return here we can go to the circular room of the twelve doors and choose again."

So we picked up our gear and set off along the way through the chamber we had not explored previously. The way led on, smoothly, until we came to a low-ceiled room, at the farther end of which was set a large door, and a smaller at its side. One, the larger, was green, and the smaller was red.

Everybody set down their burdens and waited. I felt that same prickling on me as I feel when unseen eyes smolder upon my naked back, as a great beast readies itself to spring. I said, "The red door."

Ornol swung to face me. His pallor shone. "Red? Red—that is no color for a true Pandaheem! I choose the green!"

"Well," I said, forgetting all about niceties of address, "green is not the color of Pandahem. That is blue."

"If you seek a quarrel—"

I drew a breath. I was in for it now. Like a calsany, stubborn and onkerish, I dug my heels in.

"I go through the red door. Those who wish may go with you through the green."

Immediately, Skort chirped out: "I go with the strom."

"And I," said the sorcerer.

Kalu, quietly, said, "I will go with the Bogandur."

We all looked at Exandu. Shanli mopped his brow.

He looked at Ornol and then at me, at the large green door and the small red door. He sweated. He shook. He turned his eyes up piteously.

"Does no one then think of my poor old bones? Of my feet which are blistered to the bone? How I ache!"

Shanli whispered in his ear. He sighed.

"Very well. I mean you no offense, Strom Ornol. You, I think, understand that." And here Exandu jingled the pouch of gold he carried strapped to his waist belt. We did not miss the significance of the gesture. "But I go with Dray the Bogandur, through the red door."

Ornol's head jerked back. His nostrils pinched in.

"Very well." He swung his sword, commandingly. "Come!"

He ordered his slaves to kick the green door open. They did so. A sweet scent wafted and light shone. They all went through, two by two, warriors with swords, porters with burdens, and we heard their excited exclamations of pleasure and wonder gradually fading on the scented air.

"Perhaps..." stammered Exandu.

Seg turned to me, preoccupied. "Why make an issue of it now?"

"The red door just—seems right."

"Perhaps we ought—" Exandu started over. "They sound very jolly."

The green door slammed in our faces.

I kicked the red door open.

A dim blueish light shone at the head of a flight of stairs. Those stairs stretched wide to either side. On each tread a tall golden candelabrum upheld in clenched fists five golden candles. The flames rose, tall, sharp, flowerlike in their involuted calmness. The blue light dropped down, pervading everything that golden light did not reach. The air tanged, harsh, warningly. I stepped through and Hop the Intemperate, so close he pushed me aside a little, thrust his ten-foot pole ahead.

The pole clanged against marble. The floor of the space above the flight of stairs remained firm, unyielding.

We moved through the doorway, and paused, gazing down the stairs into a vast inchoate blueness far beneath.

The red door groaned and closed at our backs.

We were a small party; Kalu and his men, Exandu, Shanli and Hop and their people. Seg and myself. We stood looking down that breathtaking vista.

The red door groaned and closed—and the treads and risers of the stairway rotated and combined into a single long shining sheet, stretching away and away beneath—stretching into stygian blackness as all the candles were extinguished as one, and the blueness vanished.

In a sliding helpless mass we shot screaming down into the blackness.

Sixteen

Red Water

Whoever crafted those steps was a master mason. There was not a fissure between tread and riser you could slide a hair through. Down that slippery slope in the utter darkness we slid, straight down, whoosh, helter-skelter, helplessly.

People slid into me, and whirled away, and the cries bounced from the roof, weirdly, echoing like bats trapped in a vault.

How long we skidded down I do not know. It could not have been much above four or five minutes; it felt like a lifetime. Without warning, smashingly, I went feet first into water. The shock knocked the breath from my lungs.

In a moment or two, with lungs aflame, I surfaced.

Flinging the hair back from my eyes and staring around I saw the darkness relieved by a somber red glow. Even as I watched and the heads began to bob up in the water alongside, the glow grew and deepened and became a blood-red drenching of fire all about.

It was borne in on me that, perhaps, just perhaps, red was not going to be the Prescot color in this pickle.

Hop the Intemperate, flailing away like a pregnant whale, surfaced, spouting.

"Help!"

I put a hand under his armpit. The armor we wore would drag us down if we did not shed it or find a landing place very quickly.

Across from me a ledge of rock showed.

"The rock!" I heaved up and bellowed. "Make for the rock."

We all started splashing. A Pachak at my side, using an economical three-handed paddle, dived away, yelling.

At his side, glimpsed in rosy silver flakings in the red light and the water, a long fish shape darted.

Fangs opened wide, tiny eyes glared black and malevolent. Fins shivered silver. The great fish opened its jaws and bore in, hungrily.

Time, time! There was no time! I drew my old sailor knife and dived under. The sleek belly sped past above, and the legs of the Pachak kicked just beyond. Quickly, quickly! The sailor knife, honed to a wicked edge, sliced all along the guts of the fish. Redness poured out. I drew the knife along, and then turned, flailing my arms, shot for the surface. There was time only to see Hop scrambling up onto the ledge, and Seg hoisting Shanli up, before I'd drawn in a mighty lungful of air and so dived again.

There were more of the giant fish, wicked jaws agape, silver and red in the water, arrowing in.

Three of them, three I took.

Then I surfaced and Seg hauled me out.

Exandu was wailing and moaning—he had a slash along his left calf and he swore that his leg had been taken off for dinner.

Shanli calmed him. I was trembling. The fish had been—had been deadly in their intent.

We huddled on the ledge and dripped water. In that ruddy light the water dropped like blood.

Pieces of fish rose to the surface and reddened the red water, and monstrous shapes fought over them, and devoured them. Hop shuddered. He stared at me as though drugged.

"You saved us all!"

"No," I said. "I took but three."

"But," he said, and pointed, "see!"

And there were many more than three fish corpses being consumed in the bloody water.

I stood up. I clutched the wall for support.

"I am going this way." I started to move. I didn't care which way we went. "Follow me."

Obediently, they stood up, shaking, and followed.

The ledge, slippery with fungoid things, broadened. We passed under an overhang and entered a series of chambers cut from the rock. Here, in the pervasive ruby light, giant and obscene carvings leered at us from every wall, from the roof, pranced at our side, seeming to move and beckon as we passed. I thought to shield Shanli from these awful sights, but she strode on, head up, supporting Exandu, not looking to right or left, but guiding his path.

Then, I thought—the people who construct these places love to put these carvings here, and so was myself again, able to be mocking and cynical and no longer wrought up by the darkness and the ruby light and giant fish and the horror of fangs closing on naked and quivering flesh.

As we passed on I counted the people with us; we had not lost a single soul.

Forcing our way through hanging slimy growths, like seaweed, dangling at the exit to the caverns, on we went. We were attacked by reptilian things that skittered and chirped and slashed their stingers at our legs as we passed. We squashed them and moved on.

We were assailed by stenches released from corpse pits abandoned for centuries, we stopped up our nostrils and pressed on. Skeletons dangled in our path, and came to life and sought to drag us down with bony fingers. These we cut to pieces, bone by bone, limb by limb. We sundered their blasphemous forms, and went on.

In a cavern drenched in a pallid greenish light a giant dragon, a risslaca of horns and scales and tri-tails, essayed the task of slaying and eating us. Him we shot with arrows, from bows freshly strung with dry strings, and cut him with spears, and so drove him sobbing back into a rocky corner. We left him there, cowering from our spite, and did not kill him, and pressed on.

We pressed on. That was the sum of our achievement.

Our clothes were ripped and shredded and torn to pieces. Our limbs were raked by talons, and torn and bloodied. Our armor was dented. Our helmets hung lopsidedly. Many of our weapons were broken. But we pushed on, on...

And, at last, a ragged scarecrow bunch, we stumbled on a stair that led upward.

"I cannot climb," declared Exandu. He sank down. "I am done for."

"Would you have Shanli carry you on her back? Would you bear that shame?"

"Shame? What shame?"

Seg stepped forward. He lifted Exandu. The man was large and well-filled, with a nose of size; Seg lifted him as he would a little child. "I will carry you up."

"Horkandur," whispered Exandu. "Horkandur."

So, up the stairs we went, and we went carefully, for we had had our bellyful of tricks and traps.

At the top a small red door stood before us. I did not kick it in with casual violence. We looked all about, and we prodded with our poles. We pushed the door with a pole from a safe distance. And we were quiet and we listened.

The door eased open.

Red light shafted out.

Kalu, at my side, took a breath. "We have been through much, Bogandur. But there is worse to come."

"In that case," I said, and I own to that old Prescot madness upon me, "we will front it now!"

And I bashed the door open and leaped through.

I did not die. I am here to prove that.

I would have done so if Seg, ready with arrow notched and drawn, had not loosed with deadly aim.

Yet the fellow who would have had me was only a normal human being, a malko, a ferocious gorilla-faced chap with massive muscles, of a stocky, dour, indrawn disposition. He dropped on me from above the door, and his curved sword slashed for my throat.

Seg's shaft took him clear through his back, punched on through lungs and chest and shattered out in a splattering gush of blood. I slashed sideways as I rolled clear.

The room was wide, bright with lanterns, and a dozen more of the gorilla-faced malkos ran up, weapons glittering.

These were only men, ferocious, and armed; they were nothing compared with the terrors through which we had passed. Seg stepped up, shooting like a fountain of shafts, and Hop surged alongside me, with Kalu on the other side, and his Pachaks with him. The fight was brief and exceedingly ferocious. At its conclusion the malkos lay dead, and still we had not lost a warrior.

Sweat and blood bedabbled us. We glared at the high-domed chamber under the lights.

Along one side a row of cages stood, black-barred and empty. A few tables and benches, strewn with discarded scraps of food and warrior trappings, huddled in one corner. Seven doors opened at the far end. Nearer at hand, a door stood in an angle. The air held a cloying, stale smell.

"I must have a drink," cried Exandu. He lay where Seg had dropped him. Shanli cooed over him. Kalu stepped out into the hall, his warriors with him, and they carried out a swift but thorough search. I crossed to the door in the angle.

"Take care, Bogandur," called Seg.

He stood at my back, arrow to string, half drawn, ready.

I did not say, as it crossed my mind to do, "With you at my back, Seg, I have no need for care." Cautiously, I pushed open the door with my sword.

A corridor lay exposed. The light was not as bright. A fresh rotting smell gusted out. Four doors broke the left-hand wall, and one to the right lay recessed, with a red lamp above the arch. I stepped forward.

Stepping with exquisite care, testing every footfall, I inched along to look into the barred opening of the first door. The cell lay empty, straw-strewn and stinking.

The second cell contained a skeleton, cruelly chained to the wall.

The third cell held a woman.

She stared up as I looked in. She held herself with such commanding power, clad in rags, her hair stringy and tangled, that my heart leaped. She stared with a bright and hostile arrogance upon me as I peered in through the bars.

The cell door was barred from the outside. I lifted the bar, in a gesture at once matching her arrogance, and pitiful in my instinctive reaction. I lifted the bar and threw it aside.

A sliding screech sounded in my ears.

Instantly I hurled myself headlong, fingers scrabbling for the edge of the pit the trapdoor beneath my feet opened.

Only a catlike swiftness saved me. I caught the edge and hung. Dangling, I hung there as the harsh croaking voices of malkos sounded, gobbling in glee. They broke from the recessed door with the red light above it. They swarmed across the corridor, their weapons lifted, their gorilla faces alive with sadistic glee at my plight and their solution to my problem.

Suspended over a gulf—which at its floor held a bed of spikes, I did not doubt, if nothing worse—I saw the onrush of the guards. There were six of them. They wielded spears and axes. They rushed.

My muscles cracked as I sought to lever myself up.

Seg's bow loosed. With blurring speed he loosed again. Two of the malkos pitched forward, skewered. Then Seg, with a bellow of pure rage, hurled himself forward. His sword flamed. I got an elbow up, then the other, chinned myself over the lip and rolled. Seg's blade clashed violently with the axe of the first malko, twirled and thrust. A spear slashed down Seg's side and he reeled away, and came back, raging. I was up on a knee. The next malko sought to smash Seg's brains out, and was punctured for his pains. The others closed in, and for a moment Seg was slashing and hacking, leaping and ducking, a magnificent fighting warrior, battling for his life and the life of his comrade.

Then I got myself—tardily, tardily!—into action and dinted the last of them. He fell full length with a clash of armor.

Seg shooshed a great breath, and wiped a bloody hand across his face. His sword dripped.

"Hai, Jikai!" cried the woman, walking from her cell. "I give you the High Jikai!"

"My lady!" said Seg.

"Aye," I said, speaking with a rush. "And I give you the High Jikai, too, Seg."

We stood for a moment, there in that blood-soaked corridor in a place of horrors, and took our breath. Then Seg said, "Llahal, my lady. I am Seg. And this is Dray."

She managed a smile. She did not look at the mangled corpses. "You are welcome. You have come with a strong party of warriors to rescue the king and queen?"

"Well, no, my lady," said Seg.

"But you must have! Why else would you venture into the Coup Blag, this vile place in the Snarly Hills?"

I said, "There is gold, my lady, and treasure."

She looked stunned. Then, "You have not seen the king, the queen? Or any of—their people?"

"Only a poor devil of a Pachak, who died."

We must have looked like very devils, ourselves, Seg and me. We were battle-stained, blood-splashed, grimed and sweaty. Our swords reeked. We were big, muscle-bulging fellows with hardy looks and uncommon quick ways. She sucked in her breath.

Seg said, "My lady. Our swords are at your command."

"Yes, yes, Jikais. But—those poor people—I came here with the queen to look for the king. We did not find him. We found horror and death. And the bandits were too frightened—"

"Yes," I said. "Do not fret over them now."

Seg began to wipe his sword on the tunic of a slain malko. I did the same. We were careful to wipe our hands and the hilts of our sword, scrupulous in cleansing them.

The woman said, "Lahal, you must forgive me." She swayed. "My name is Milsi and I serve Queen Mab. And you are drikingers, also."

"Lahal, Milsi," said Seg. "No. No, we are not bandits."

"But—"

And then Exandu tottered along, staring at the corpses and mopping his brow.

"Careful of that great hole in the floor," said Seg.

"What—" He saw Milsi. "A woman, Seg the Horkandur?"

"Aye," said Seg. "The lady Milsi."

She had said she served Queen Mab and it was quite clear from her demeanor and carriage that she was no serving wench. She looked with some curiosity upon Exandu, and, in truth, he looked like us, a right bundle of rags and blood.

She addressed Seg, and he instantly attended to her, bending only a little, his face intent.

"The next cell. Would you look, please?"

"The bar—" I warned.

"Aye."

Seg looked in and I peered over his shoulder. A corpse of a woman, half-naked, with long dark hair astrew, lay collapsed against the wall. Seg turned at once.

The woman sighed at his face.

"So she is dead, then—a friend—oh, this hideous place!"

And Seg put his arms about the lady Milsi, and comforted her.

Kalu and his people came in then to report that nothing stirred in the chamber. We had seven doors from which to make a choice. Which would it be?

"My lady," said Seg, and I marveled at the gentleness of his voice in these horrific surroundings. "You have knowledge of this place? This maze of the Coup Blag?"

She pulled back a little from him and looked up, and the tears stood in her eyes. "No. No, I do not know—I know only that we must find the king—and the queen—and leave with our lives—if we can."

"We must do more than that," put in Kalu, with his usual cheerfulness. He appeared undaunted by the terrors through which we had gone. "I, for one, do not intend to leave without my fair share of treasure."

"But—your life—?"

"I have risked it many times, my lady. It is a habit."

About to turn away and make a start on the next door, I swung back as Seg spoke. He spoke to the lady Milsi.

"Lady. Your life will be mine—while I live no harm shall come to you if I can prevent it. That I swear."

Abruptly, like lightning striking through thunderclouds, she smiled. She was splendid in that moment. "You will be my Jikai, Seg the Horkandur?"

"If you wish it, lady."

They stood, looking one at the other, and I knew they did not see and were not aware of anyone else. Softly, she said, "I wish it."

Seventeen

Milsi

We stood before the seven doors and Exandu said, "You choose red again, Bogandur? After the travails we suffered because of that red door at the head of the staircase?" He cocked his head at me, his nose red as the door before which we stood. "Blue or green are the colors of Pandahem."

"As they are of Hamal, master Exandu."

"That I grant you. But red—I do not think my aching bones, my head, my feet, my heart or liver will stand any further torments."

"There will be more, Exandu," said Kalu. "Never fear."

The lady Milsi stood close by Seg. She said. "He is mightily cheerful." She turned to Kalu. "Why is that, Pachak?"

"My lady?" Kalu Na-Fre looked perplexed. "Why should one be concerned over death? Papachak has all mortals in his hands. There is treasure here, and my bonny fellows will bring it out."

"Or die in the attempt?"

"If that is willed." Kalu gestured at the doors. "I have followed pantor Dray and with him Exandu and pantor Seg. I do not think I shall change now. They have brought me luck."

"Luck!" burst out Exandu. Shanli soothed him, and Hop the Intemperate let out a gusty kind of laughing groan.

"Certainly. I have not lost a single one of my fine fellows since we left that Strom Ornol."

The lady Milsi put a hand to her face. Seg instantly put his arm about her waist to support her. She was a splendid woman, her body, although grimed with dirt, glowing through the rents in her clothes, full and firm and voluptuous. She was of an age with Seg, I judged, probably a few seasons younger, given that Seg had bathed in the River of Baptism in far Aphrasöe, and therefore one must judge his age not by chronology but by his appearance when he bathed in that magical stream.

"Very well, then," spoke out Exandu, and he drew himself up. "Red it is." Then he said, "It will bring back the memories."

Using the skills we had acquired to stay living people in this place, this abode of horrors called the Coup Blag, we pushed the door open. Only a stone-walled corridor showed before us, ten feet high and broad, stretching some fifty feet to the corner, unbroken by doors. We entered and, prodding and watching, went on.

We found a few traps, things of swinging flagstones in the floor, and spyholes with crossbow bolts fixed to loose at anyone passing, and a metal mirror fixed at forty-five degrees so that what we thought was the end of the tunnel was a pit filled with acid. These traps we negotiated, and pressed on. The sound of voices, and singing, and the clink of bottles and glasses reached us from around the next bend.

"Anyone for the Cabaret?" said Seg, and he laughed.

The lady Milsi walked now with her arm about his waist, and he assisted her along with great solicitude.

I stuck my head around the corner.

The chamber was large, filled with light. There were tables laid for a feast. They were there, sprawled out, eating and drinking and singing. Chests stood ranked and broken open and a profusion of treasures had been pulled out and lay scattered on the marble flooring. The smells of food and wine struck us shrewdly.

Strom Ornol looked up. His pallid face showed a flush along the cheek-bones and he waved a golden goblet high.

"So there you are! We thought you were all dead."

We walked forward.

Fregeff and Rik Razortooth were drinking, one a good rosé and the other a silver dish of blood. I could not see Skort the Clawsang.

"Skort?" said Ornol. "Oh, he disappeared some time ago. We had a wonderful time in a valley choked with fruit trees and filled with flowers. Then we came in here and have been feasting ever since. We move on soon. You are only just in time." He saw the lady Milsi.

"Oh?"

The pappattu was made. Milsi was seated next to the lady Ilsa, and we men heard words concerning fresh clothes.

"It is rest we need!" declared Seg hotly.

"Well, that is your fault for not following me. We have had a splendid time, and we think we know the way out."

"Bogandur!" cried Exandu, collapsing into a chair. "What have you done to me!"

"We will be happy to go with you, Strom Ornol," I said. "After we have eaten and taken our rest."

Fregeff ostentatiously reached for a fresh dish of blood.

Kalu said, "Where is the way out?" He stared at the treasures scattered about. "There is some treasure here. But we have not had a hard time yet, and the end of this is not yet in sight."

"Not had a hard time!" exclaimed Shanli. "Look at my poor master! Shame on you, master Kalu!"

And the Pachak laughed, and swirled his tail hand, and went off with his people to eat and drink.

"The way out lies the way we entered," said Ornol.

"Perhaps," said Kalu, and took up a golden goblet and drank deeply.

Ornol transferred his attention to Milsi, and her story was soon told. Ornol sneered. "Serving a king or queen is a poor man's game. There is no real reward in that."

Seg stiffened. "At least, when they kick out ne'er-do-wells, they usually have their reasons."

There would have been a fight, there and then, if we others had not intervened. Ornol didn't know how lucky he was.

Sucking at a honeyed wine, Exandu moaned as Shanli wiped his brow. "If only we'd gone with Ornol through the green door, think of the misery and terror we would have been spared!"

"Yes," I said. "Perhaps I did not choose wisely—save in one thing."

"Aye," said Seg, with a snap in his voice. "Had we gone through the green door, we would never have—"

Milsi laid her hand on his arm. He turned, at once, looking at her. She smiled. "I will go with the lady Ilsa and make myself presentable. I have much to thank you and Dray the Bogandur for, Seg the Horkandur, Jikai."

Seg rolled his shoulders most uncomfortably under that.

"My lady..." was all he could find to say.

"Anyway," Kalu was saying between mouthfuls to Hop, "where I come from the hellhounds breathe fire. They'll crisp you up like a vosk rasher."

"That is sorcery, Kalu, I daresay."

"Ask Fregeff."

I walked along and took up a piece of meat and ate, what it was I've no idea, and regarded Ornol from the corner of my eye. If the idiot insisted on rushing off at once, I did not think the party with me was in fit state to follow. And, the lady Ilsa provided a pretty problem, too...

Kalu laughed, and so drew my attention. "Very well, Hop the Intemperate. When we all get out of here, I'll make an assignation with you at The Sign of the Jolly Puddler in Mahendrasmot. Is it a bargain?"

"If we get out—"

"You stick with me and my fine fellows. No fear of that."

Some of the warriors were singing "My Love is like a Moon Bloom." A rival party at the other table struck up with "The Two-Tailed Kataki," which made Seg glance quickly down the chamber to where the ladies were fussing over chests of gorgeous raiment.

"She's a grown-up girl," I said to Seg.

He did not flush; but he looked decidedly off key.

"You—like her, Dray?"

"Yes."

"Since I lost Thelda, I've not really bothered to look at another woman. But I'm over Thelda now. She is a part of the past. I shan't forget her; but—"

"Milsi is a splendid woman, Seg. By Vox! She's been through a few horrors down here. Yet she's—well, she's—"

"Aye!"

"All the same. She has a past, too."

"I know. I think she is in much the same case as I am."

I put a hand on Seg's shoulder. This was an unusual and gratuitous gesture between us; but I was deeply moved. He smiled that smile of his, and his fey blue eyes challenged me. "All right, my old dom. I do not forget you owe me a faceful of dungy straw."

"Two!" I said. "Two, by Zair!"

And we both recalled that fraught day in The Eye of the World when the Sorzarts raided the farm and we first met.

110

The merriment thundered on. These people were reacting to moments of horror, snatching a few balancing moments of boisterous pleasure before plunging once more into the terrors of the Coup Blag. We set about filling our bellies and of finding fresh clothing and weaponry.

Needless to say, Seg and I found some scarlet cloth, and so fashioned ourselves breechclouts in the color that—well, that might this time just have proved itself once again.

Among the merrymakers the absence of decomposing corpse-faces was marked. We asked questions, and learned that Skort and his people, with some of the porters, had been bringing up the rear guard when a stone block had fallen across the corridor. The delayed-action trap had squashed only two poor fellows, a Rapa and a Moltingur; but it had isolated Skort from the rest.

"This is a maze," declared Fregeff. "Doubtless we will come upon them again."

"I sincerely hope so," I said, munching on a hunk of roast vosk leg. "The Clawsangs are bonny fighters."

The pressure Exandu could bring to bear on Ornol must now be lessened, at least in the young dandy's eyes, by reason of the treasure here. He could be free of what he owed. All the same, Exandu managed to persuade the strom to wait until we were in better shape to march with him.

At last, fully kitted out and feeling rested, we took up our bundles of loot and started out.

Up ahead along a corridor, and nastily soon after we started, we heard Ornol's strident voice.

"By the Furnace Fires of Inshurfraz!" he screamed. "Is there no way out of this maze?"

We were back in the room of the feast from which we had started.

"We try another door, pantor," said Kalu, equably.

So we did. This time we followed on into corridors we had not penetrated before. The little mark of the heart had long since petered out. Whoever had made it had not ventured these halls and passages of dread.

When we came across levers and buttons and tripwires we left them severely alone. We halted, as our way was impeded by a simple tilting flagstone trap. A prod from a pole dipped the near edge down without effort. It swung lazily back into place. The stone was too wide to clear with a jump. To balance two men would be exceptionally tricky.

Standing in a niche cut from the rock stood the armored skeleton of a Chulik. He looked ferocious, pared to the bone. If he was touched, warned Fregeff, who could guess the magic there, he would probably come to life and we'd have an unwanted fight on our hands with a fearsome representative of the Kaotim, the Undead, who are well known on Kregen.

Kalu stepped forward. "I am not so sure," said the Pachak. "Pantor Dray, would you stand ready to cut his legs away from under him? And, Pantor Seg—?"

We, with others, poised our weapons ready to slash the skeleton to pieces the instant it moved.

Kalu reached out with his sword and, delicately, pushed the skeleton's skull. The jawbone clicked up into place.

Nothing else happened.

"There!" cried Kalu, and his tail hand pointed at the swinging stone trap. "Try it now!"

We did. The flagstone held firmly for us all to cross.

We crossed that trap in safety, but others caught us and men died. I misliked this greatly, but after another blazing row with Ornol over directions, we all went along a smoothly paved and open passageway and I trailed on after.

Seg said, "Should we cut off on our own?"

"Safety in numbers. Anyway—apart from Milsi—he was right about the large green and small red doors."

Around about then the passageway opened into a chamber robed in yellow silk, with an ebon throne surrounded by skulls and with tall candles burning. Kalu looked around and yawned.

When a horned and hoofed demon, of the horrific Kregan variety, appeared from nowhere on that ebon throne, Kalu took a little more interest in the proceedings.

Being of Kregen, the demon was hooved of rear feet, clawed of third feet, tentacled of second feet and bore human hands on his forearms. His horns emitted sparks of light. His tongue licked out like a rattlesnake. Everyone screamed and crowded for the door by which we had entered—everyone save Fregeff, the Fristle sorcerer.

He lifted his bronzen flail and shook it and the demon struck with a twinned bolt of fire from his eyes and poor Fregeff went thump head over heels into the corner.

The pandemonium at the door sorted itself out as the crazed mob fled. More than one wretch fell and was trampled.

Fregeff crawled painfully to his feet. His eyes streamed blood. But he lifted the flail, and shook it.

The twin blue bolts of fire hurled him flat again.

Seg loosed a shaft. It caromed off the demon, who took no notice.

I said, "You'd best take the lady Milsi out, Seg."

"And leave you?"

"Oh, I'll run with the best of you. But—Fregeff—"

"He has met his match."

"I am not so sure—look!"

For the Fristle gathered himself together. His arm lifted. He released the bronzen chain attached to the collar about the reptile's neck. The volschrin on his shoulder spread his wings. Rik Razortooth swooped up in a sudden gusting of membranous wings.

As Fregeff shook his flail for the third time, the demon uttered a screech of pure rage. The twin blue bolts of devil fire slashed from his eyes, burned across the chamber. The sorcerer flopped over, his lozenged robes flapping. He twitched an arm. Again the bolts of fire flew from the demon's lambent eyes. But this time they struck for the volschrin. Rik swerved in midair, dived and weaved and the hissing blue bolts of lethal fire missed. Fregeff shook his flail weakly.

Rik dodged the last outpouring of malevolent energy and then—and then! The reptile simply flew straight at the demon's face. Sharp fangs slashed. First one eye and then the other shredded. They did not bleed. They exploded into blue flame and Rik somersaulted away, wing over wing, to gain his balance in the air and so volplane easily to Fregeff's shoulder.

The Fristle reached up his left hand and caressed the little winged reptile.

The demon stood up. Now blood, blue, smoking blood, poured down his cheeks from his ruined eyes. He shrieked. He tried to fly away with jagged wings and crashed into the throne and darts of glittering steel sliced from the sides of the throne and impaled him. The defense of the throne slew its occupant.

The demon collapsed like a slashed wine sack.

The seven hoops of steel, razor-sharp, met through his gross body.

Fregeff stood up.

Seg, Milsi, and I ran to him.

"San! San—you are unharmed?"

"As well as can be expected." And the Fristle laughed.

The laugh bordered on hysteria; but Rik flapped his wings and Fregeff was instantly himself. His face with its fierce whiskers looked drawn. His hands shook.

"The little volschrin," said Seg, "he is a marvel."

Because wizards, even good wizards, are not all sweetness and light, it was perfectly natural for Fregeff to say, "Yes. Beware lest he take your eyes."

We heard the hiss of indrawn breath at our backs, and, instantly, Seg and I whirled, swords snouting. Kalu stood there, his own weapons raised. His Pachak face, hard, dedicated, revealed more emotion than any we had so far seen him express.

"Demons!" he said. Had the thought not been incongruous, I would have thought he spoke with joy. "Now that is more like an adventure!"

His own people had remained with him; now they began to retire through the doorway. Fregeff shook himself, refastened the bronze linked chain to Rik's collar, and, with the reptile flappingly settling back onto his shoulder, nodded to us and went out. Seg took Milsi's arm.

"Time to go—"

"Yes. A moment, Seg. Those guards, those malkos, down in the cells. They were—different—from the rest of this infernal maze." I faced the lady Milsi. "Were they the bandits, do you know, my lady?"

"I—I do not know. My party was set on and my people were killed, or ran. I was taken up, prisoner, and conducted to that awful place."

"So you cannot know anything of the maze. No, I see that. Still, I wonder why they imprisoned you—"

"I serve the queen—"

"No good will come of this now, Dray! Come on, my old dom. Let's get out of this place and see about looking for the way out. There has to be one, somewhere."

"You are right. Lead on."

I turned toward the doorway and followed Seg and Milsi as they left. A movement caught at the corner of my left eye, and I looked that way, ready for a sudden treacherous onslaught.

One of the tall yellow silk drapes hanging against the wall rippled its sinuous length. I waited for a moment, watchfully. A small brown and red scorpion waddled out from under the drape. He stopped, looked about, waving his tail over his head. Then, as my indrawn breath hissed, he turned around and strutted delicately back, the stinger like a mocking finger upraised. He vanished under the yellow silk.

I felt the blood go thump around my body. A sliding, grating screech of stone on stone sounded in the chamber. I faced the door again. A slab of stone slid down between the door jambs. It hit the floor with a solid thud.

My sword rang uselessly against the stone.

I was alone in the chamber, trapped behind solid rock.

A sound whispered at my back. I whirled. The seven hoops of razor-sharp steel slid back into the ebon throne. They sucked themselves from the demon's body with a bright glitter, unstained by blood, blue or red. The streaks of blood upon the demon's cheeks, smoking, ran upward. They drew themselves up and entered the ruined sockets of his eyes. And when all the blood had been returned, the eyes grew back again, blazing devilish eyes of fearful hate.

The demon hissed. He came to life and roared, and those evil eyes flamed with sorcerous power from another world.

Alone, trapped, I stared with fearful fascination upon the ghastly form of the demon as he prepared to blast me where I stood.

Eighteen

Pitched into the Depths

I, Dray Prescot, Lord of Strombor and Krozair of Zy, felt all the blood in my body congeal. My heart thudded with pain. I trembled. The eyes of the demon mesmerized me. Sparks flew from those orbs, gigantic orbs, swelling and bloating with power. In the next heartbeat—if my heart could ever beat again—supernal bolts of fire would lash from those eyes and burn me to a crisp.

There was just one chance, just the one, and the little brown and red scorpion was my only hope.

Headlong, I dived for the yellow silk curtain from which the scorpion had so delicately waddled.

No time to lift the drape. No time to do anything but hurl myself full at the wall.

My shoulder hit the yellow silk. It bulged inward. For a frightful moment I thought I had thrown myself against solid rock—for I went smashing into a hard surface. Then—and even as I burst in a shower of plaster through the false wall—a scorching fire flamed past my back.

The demon had hurled his bolts of lambent fire and the yellow silk burst into flame. Amid a shower of broken plaster and splintered laths, I tumbled head over heels out of the demon's lair and into a chute down which I slid end over end, spinning around like a Catherine Wheel, arms and legs splaying like a drunken crab.

Lurid flames played above me as the silk wisped and more bolts of fire lashed at the opening I had made.

I hit something soft and furry and warm. Yellow torchlight blazed in my eyes. I felt the warm furry object move and lurch. In the next instant I was gripping on for dear life as a monstrous beast went screeching and trumpeting away along a corridor. Horns lifting before me, tail lashing to my rear, a gross body waddling from side to side beneath me, trapped on the back of an immense and savage beast, I went shooting away along the passage under the streaming light of the torches.

By Zair! This was a nightmare come true! I gripped on and shook my head and swallowed and so looked about to see what I could do—if anything.

What manner of beast it was that I bestrode in so strange a fashion I could not tell. I clung on and got my breath, and saw the roof of the tunnel lowering and narrowing ahead.

In only moments at the speed we were going the beast would be into the lower portion of the tunnel and I'd be scraped off as a dog scrapes off a flea against a rough tree trunk.

I swiveled around. The stone floor whistled past. I took a breath, lay flat and then rolled off aft. A tail lashed at me and winded me, and I hit the floor and bounced like a rubber ball. I tumbled hard, head over heels, and lay for a moment, flat, staring at the disappearing beast. I could see flailing tail and galloping clawed feet, and a mass of shaggy hair, and that was all. The monstrous beast dived into the narrow tunnel and vanished around a corner.

I sat up. The tunnel stopped going around, and settled for up being up and down being down. I felt myself and decided that if I had any broken bones they wouldn't stop me from marching on and out of this Coup Blag nightmare.

And then I realized just where I was.

How often I have said that I like to be off adventuring alone! How often I have boasted emptily that to be off by myself is the height of joy! Well, right now I wished I was still with my companions. This maze of monsters and demons, of savage beasts and cunning traps, was no place to be alone.

No, by Zair!

Still, I had to go on. Quite apart from the mystery of Spikatur Hunting Sword, and the onrushing menace of the Shanks and their tremendous invasion fleet, there was the question of my life. That, I felt, was something I ought to ponder on.

As I picked myself up and settled my gear straight, I found myself wondering if, perhaps, that scorpion was another sign from the Star Lords. Could that incident have been a simple coincidence? It did not seem likely.

In the flaring yellow light of the torches becketed along the walls I looked about carefully. The tunnel contained jagged openings on my right, as though the rock had been broken open. Light splashed inside. Of course, I said to myself with little satisfaction, of course—stupid to imagine the Star Lords would actually help me, even recognize me, despite what had happened to my recent astonishment. Anyway—if that damned scorpion hadn't waddled out so insolently from the silk drape, I would not have hesitated and would have left the demon's lair.

The scorpion had not just saved me, he'd damned well got me trapped in the first place.

Exploring the jagged openings and the maze of tunnels beyond was a chancy business. The torches burned with their yellow light, and I ran constantly across nasties, ferocious animals and beast-men, fanged and clawed, dripping horrors of nightmare. Now, meaningfully, I wielded the superb Krozair longsword and I did not hesitate. The moment any malign creatures confronted me, it was a headlong blattering attack that swept them away in lethal bites of the magnificent Krozair brand.

"By the Black Chunkrah," I said, sweeping my hair back, staring in foul temper at the latest dismembered corpse of a hairy horror, "I can't spend all my life shilly-shallying about down here!"

But that seemed all too likely a prospect as I went stumbling on. In a section of tunnel from which the roof had fallen, to admit a green leprous light like a radiant leaching stripping away flesh from bone, I ran across some poor devil who had not jumped fast enough.

Off to the side and inclined down from a higher level ran a quadruple chute. The slide was of a greenish metal, well-oiled, sharp-angled. On the floor at my feet rested a massive object like a bobbin with four sections, one to fit each part of the chute. The bobbin was man-high in diameter. Under it blood had congealed. A pair of legs stuck out, the sandals worn and with a leather strap broken and tied up over the big toe of the left foot. Also a hand stuck out here, grasping a ten-foot pole.

The fellow's fingers had to be broken to release the pole. He wore no rings.

I pondered.

The ten-foot pole had failed him. It seemed to me that I was on a low level of the Coup Blag, perhaps at the basement level. Up higher—and, by Krun! I was going up higher!—the traps would be clustered thickly to precipitate unfortunates back down here. I took the ten-foot pole and scabbarded the longsword.

In only a few hundred yards I came across stone steps leading up.

I stopped.

Now stairs are the very devil for traps.

You can put your foot down and instead of treading on solid stone, you break through painted parchment and get caught in a bear trap. You can trigger a pressure plate, and the step at your back will gape open and something exceedingly hard and sharp will come flying out and knock you sideways to breakfast time. You can be caught as we had already been caught, in a stairway that snaps shut into a slippery slope. Stairs can be counter-balanced and geared to a pack of half-starved krahniks who tread-mill away like crazy, so that you run and run and the stairway whistles back so that you do not move forward an inch.

And, inevitably, there are the stairways that deluge foul-smelling gunk on you from on high when you reach a certain tread or acid that eats you or nauseating gas that chokes you. As I say, beware of lightly tripping up and down stairs...

Prodding carefully, up I went.

This little beauty was fixed to trigger crossbow bolts through holes in the risers. The bolts were arranged to make diced meat of anyone foolish enough to trigger the bows. The ten-foot pole worked and the bolts hissed over my head. I own I stopped, then, and swallowed. Still, up I had to go...

The corridor at the top was almost like coming home after the jagged uncertainties of the caverns beneath.

The first room contained a single table, spread with fine linen, set out with a sumptuous meal—for one.

Not having a handy slave to taste the meal, and being starving hungry, I set to. If precedent was to be followed, I should be all right. Who or what-ever was monitoring proceedings here was well aware of my predicament. No doubt methods of observations were fixed everywhere. This argued that the powers of a great wizard were at work. The signomants by which Wizards of Loh are able to see events at vast distances must be here, some-where, but I could not discover them.

The little signomant like a bronze brooch with nine differently colored gems given me by my comrade Wizard of Loh, Khe-Hi-Bjanching, had been long since lost. Probably my friends were able to investigate the bot-tom of a river, or the depths of a swamp. I tramped on, wiping my mouth, and twirled the ten-foot pole in readiness for the next set of alarums and excursions.

Worries over Seg had to be pushed aside. He was with the main party and they had Kalu and the sorcerer Fregeff, and they should manage to keep themselves sane and alive. Moving along and prodding and keeping a watchful eye on everything, I considered the consequences of the eruption into our lives of the lady Milsi. Of course, Seg was the finest gentleman you could ever hope to meet, in the best sense, and his natural concern for Milsi was understandable. All the same, she had warmed to him. I'd seen that. She had been incarcerated, in rags, ill-used, expecting a hideous fate, and a hero had appeared and vanquished her enemies and brought her out of her imprisonment. Yes, there had been a spark in Milsi's eyes when she looked on Seg Segutorio.

Praise be to Zair!

If Seg was really interested in Milsi, then I prayed that her reciprocal interest was not merely engendered by the circumstances and a full heart of relief at her rescue, but would continue. That, only the fates and the future could tell.

Just about then, the ten-foot pole came in handy in an unexpected way.

I'd negotiated a silly forty-five-degree metal mirror across the corridor and so had not gone thumping on. Ahead of me the corridor narrowed to something between five and ten feet wide. At its far end, well-lighted, the end wall was covered in two-foot-long spikes. They were clumped together like the spines of a bristle ball. I prodded the floor.

The stone appeared solid. But why stud a vertical end of a corridor with spikes, if they were not to pierce human flesh? And, if that was their func-tion, how was I to be propelled onto them, or they to be hurled at me?

The answer came as the whole corridor tilted down.

Had the trap worked—well, had it worked you would not be listening to my narrative—I'd have gone head over heels down the vertical corridor as it swiveled into a pit, and so spread myself against the spikes, with piercing results.

The ten-foot-pole switched up like a quarterstaff and the ends cracked against the lip of the pit.

I dangled from the pole, balanced, as it held across the mouth of stone. If one end slipped... If I shifted my grips clumsily... I swung about like a pendulum over the spike-shafted pit and started to work hand over hand to the side. With a heave and a grunt I hauled myself out and reclaimed my faithful old ten-foot-pole. By Krun! The trap had been a dilly, a whole corridor suddenly plummeting down to form a deep shaft—and the spikes at the end were sharp enough and close enough to make diced Dray Prescot a reality.

Still, it had not been clever enough. The designer should have disguised the spikes. They had alerted a warning. And, I promised myself, when I met the designer of this maze, if I did, I'd let him investigate a few spikes of my own.

Then the ill-begotten child of a muck farm and a cesspool almost had me.

The trap was the same—a simple-seeming corridor that abruptly pitched down into a deadly shaft. Except that it was different, The shaft gaped before me in the center of a room, with dangling stink-vines and rotting corpses to insure I walked along where I was expected to walk.

And the shaft was ten feet wide.

As I pitched forward, the dangling screen of creepers ahead of me whisked aside to reveal the serried mass of spikes onto which I was supposed to fall.

The good old ten-foot pole caught at both ends on the sides of the shaft and stuck. It jammed across. And I dangled from the middle.

The pole was not exactly diametrically positioned across the pit. The famous ten-foot pole was by a hand's breadth longer than ten feet!

After that it was a hand-over-hand swing to reach the sheer wall. Then a muscle-jerk and a chin-up and then a balancing act on the pole. I stood up on it, pressed against the wall, and hooked my fingers over the lip above me. Hauling myself out and twisting on my stomach at the top, I looked down. I did not wish to leave the jammed pole where it was.

One end was that life-saving fraction higher than the other. I reached down, and then, with a curse at my own stupidity, took off my belt and dangled that down to catch the end of the pole and that was not long enough, either. So I joined up enough of my belts and straps and swung the end down and caught it as it looped, and slid a buckle on, and pulled it all tight.

The faithful pole came up like a gaffed salmon.

An itchy scrabbling sound at my back made me roll over without even looking for the source of the noise. I rolled and came up on a knee and the longsword pointed—and a little schrafter, an animal that sharpens his teeth on the bones of skeletons in dungeons, scuttled away, scared out of his wits.

My breath gusted out in a whoosh.

Fitting my gear together did not take long, and all the time I kept looking under and between the hanging stench vines and the grotesque half-decomposed corpse-shapes. Out there the darkness closed in. And, pair by pair, in fours and eights and scores, lambent yellow eyes gathered. When I fastened the last buckle and was ready, hundreds of pairs of eyes gleamed on me from the darkness.

Flinging a torch snatched from a corpse's withered fingers, I backed off. Careful, careful! The room offered no way forward, so I retraced my steps, turning every now and then to hurl a torch back into the host of eyes which followed in the darkness. The trouble was, flinging torches made the darkness at my back more intense. How long this went on I do not know; I know I felt more tired than a galley slave after a stern chase in a calm.

The traps I encountered when I branched off from the path I had already traversed were of the diabolical and cunning kind. Somehow I survived them, losing bits of skin, and the drexer—which annoyed me— and sundry portions of my gear. By the time I staggered into a room lit by a crystal fire roof, I had shaken off that pack of following eyes, and had also been reduced to a scarlet breechclout, a rapier—the main gauche had been carried off in the throat of a batlike creature that in swooping from the darkness had impaled itself—and the Krozair longsword. I was barefoot. Well, that is normal for a fellow who has been a powder monkey in Nelson's Navy. I staggered into this room to see three walls lined by bronze statues of armored men, apim, diff, all kinds, and the small table laid with a meal. I just flopped down on the chair and stared at the food, summoning my energies to eat and drink.

When I began to eat, if all the statues in the chamber had come to life and rushed upon me, I'd have finished gnawing on the vosk bone and fought the pack of 'em one-handed.

I drank hugely—a light Tardalvoh—and looked around the walls. And then I noticed that dust lay thickly upon the floor.

This was something new in the Coup Blag.

The wall containing the doorway through which I had entered held six other doors, all closed. They were all blue. I sighed. "By Makki-Grodno's disgusting diseased liver and lights! Is there no end to this infernal maze?"

A voice from the air said, "Blue instead of red, will serve me, will serve you, will serve destiny."

No use in looking around. The voice could be coming from anywhere. I shouted, "I'm not interested in serving destiny! I've been doing that ever since I came to Kregen! I just want to get out and go home!"

And then I checked myself. No. No, that was not true. Well, of course it was true—of course I wanted to go home to Delia. But I had to do something drastic about this confounded conspiracy of Spikatur Hunting Sword, if I killed myself doing it. I stood up, hand on sword hilt.

"Blue, you say, you misshapen Opaz-forsaken lump of—"

"If you trust me."

There was no denying the mockery. I drew a breath, stared at the doors—and, lo! All save one turned red.

I stumped across the floor, reaching for the ten-foot pole and remembering it had splintered to pieces down some damned alley. I hefted the Krozair longsword. I have used that superb brand to do all kinds of tasks on Kregen; now it would tap tap tap at the floor and walls as I went along as though I were a blind man. Which, in this place of horrors, I was.

The blue door opened before I reached it.

Blue light spilled.

Sword ready, I stormed through—and was instantly set on by a dozen of the malko guards, raging, weapons bright, gorilla fangs clashing for my throat, swords raking for my guts.

Nineteen

The Game Is Named

The very violence of their onslaught worked in my favor.

The leaders jostled one another to get at me, the blood lust bright and ugly on their lowering gorilla-like faces.

Hard, packed with muscle, malkos, fierce and not to be trifled with. Big, husky fellows, with their tiny black eyes overhung with massive brow ridges, and black fissured lips, dented in by the jut of yellow fangs, glowing with a sullen passion to kill.

They wore studded leather armor, very spiky as to shoulder and elbow, bulging over ribcages, adorned with scaled belts and gilt buckles. Their weapons were spears and shields, swords and daggers, and they gobbled in their passion to slay.

I daresay they had never met a man armed with a Krozair longsword before. I venture to suggest they had never tangled with a Krozair Brother before. Well, few folk outside the inner sea of Kregen, the Eye of the World, have had that dubious pleasure. I did not waste time. The Krozair brand flamed.

When it was done, two, at least, ran screaming. They did not run with all their bodily parts intact or functioning; but they were able to run away. Their companions lay scattered about the chamber. And forgive me, I mean scattered.

By Zair! The things a man does when he is frustrated!

The malko guards, grim with their gorilla faces and their metal-studded leather armor, had been posted to watch over a series of cages. These iron-barred receptacles held an assortment of slaves. They were well enough dressed for slaves, the girls in tissue-thin vestments and strings of cheap jewels, the men oiled and shaved, other men, of a variety of races, although unarmed, unmistakable mercenary guards. They all looked miserable, as slaves look downcast; but they appeared well fed.

A voice called, "Splendid, Jikai. Now let us out of here, in the name of Hiscielo the Chuns."

"Whoever he might be," I said to myself, and went across to the cage from which the woman called.

I knocked the lock off with a single blow. That is always a fine spirited—and empty—gesture. As soon as I'd committed that extravagant act of folly I checked the Krozair longsword, just in case... The edge was unmarked from the iron. Which, given the art of the Krozair swordsmiths, was as it should be.

The woman said, "So, Jikai, you prefer your sword to me?"

Prepared to be gracious to a gracious lady, I contented myself with a churlish: "Perhaps."

Well, she was beautiful. There was a kind of mesmeric force attached to her beauty. Everything about her appeared to be perfect, and that, very often—not always—adds up to a lack of perfection in the totality. Her hair was bright gold, long and rippling free over a turquoise dress girdled with gold. Her figure would take the breath away from any man who has not seen my Delia. Beside my Delia, this beautiful shining woman looked artificial. She was overwhelmingly aware of her personal attraction, of the force of her beauty, and the power that beauty conferred.

She smiled alluringly at me. Her teeth were very white—they would have to be, seeing the list of perfections she possessed—and her lips were of that melting red that gets in under a fellow's ribs and twists about like a white-hot knife.

I made her a small bow. I was still wrought up, with the smoking corpses of dismembered men casually tumbled about.

"My lady—"

"You call me majestrix."

"So you're Queen Mab, then?"

She smiled.

"Release my servants. We must leave here at once."

I used more caution in opening the first cage holding a fat fellow with three quivering chins and a pot belly, garbed in black and green and with a great golden chain around his neck. I remembered the pit where we had freed Milsi.

"Open up the rest, dom," I said, and ignored his affronted dignity. The queen merely smiled.

Yet, in that smile, I thought I sensed rather than saw a puzzlement, as though she could not understand my attitude. She couldn't grasp why I hadn't been bowled over by her beauty.

Well, people like her no doubt bathed in blood every day. A few poor fellows butchered meant nothing to her...

As though carrying on that thought, she said, "You fight exceeding well."

"When I have to."

She frowned and the lightning flashed. "Majestrix!"

Her own guards were crowding out now and running to pick up the malkos' fallen weapons. I had no desire to get into another fight. "Majestrix," I said dutifully.

She smiled.

Then I realized what the smile was for—it was certainly attractive, lighting up her face, as they say—it was designed to render me totally her slave, bound to her by adoration of her beauty. I did not laugh. I wasn't that far sunk in boorishness, by Vox!

She said, "Anglar! Move everybody out. We go that way." And she pointed to the black door at the end. So, the black door was the way we all went, fussed over by our fat friend in the black and green, and the chins, and the gold chains, Anglar the majordomo.

The corridors through which we walked were wide and well-lit, only a little dusty, and quite free of traps.

Feeling in no mood for conversation, I replied when spoken to and nothing else. She grew a little restive.

"You ask me nothing of this place. Have you been here long?"

I had to bite my lips to keep from shouting with mirth.

I eyed the guards she employed. They were all hulking great fellows, of a variety of races, and they carried weapons, and although I could probably put up a good show, I had no desire to fight them. So, because of that, I did not reply, as I ached to do, "Do you come here often?"

Mind you, by the disgusting diseased left eyeball of Makki-Grodno, had I done so, things might have turned out a little differently, by Zair!

Probably because of that feeling that I was reacting in a typically boorish way to a woman too conscious of her own powers of beauty and rank, and wishing to make amends, I said, "Majestrix. I am covered in the blood of those poor malkos, and I, perhaps, offend you. I must clean up as soon as possible."

And she said, "Jikai—you are very dear to me as you are. Do not fret."

Unable to make anything of this, or unwilling, I managed to mumble something and we walked on. In the next chamber we found a series of magnificently spread tables laid ready for us. And, in a small room in the corner, a bath.

I washed myself clean. I gave no thought to the oddness of finding a bath, where before we had traveled in our own muck, sweat and others' blood...

She had prepared a chair next to hers, on her left hand, a chair smothered in chavonth pelts and ling furs, a chair almost like a throne. It was not, I saw as I sat down, quite so bountifully supplied with the symbols of rank as the chair in which she sat. The food smelled wonderful, looked marvelous and tasted delicious. It was, without question, superior to any food I'd come across before in the Coup Blag.

She spoke with her mouth full of basted chicken leg.

"You called those diabolical warrior malkos 'poor malkos' after they tried to slay you. They are very fierce. Do you feel guilt over their deaths?"

"Yes."

"But why?" She sipped wine, a red superior vintage, and swallowed. "They are fit for carrion."

"They are guards, paid to do a job."

"And are you paid to do a job?"

"I have been, in my time."

She leaned back against the pelts, and poked into her mouth with a bejeweled little finger. She spat a scrap of meat. Then she remembered.

She sat up.

"And you call me majestrix! Do not forget."

I said, "I will not forget, majestrix, if you do not."

For an instant I thought I'd gone too far. Then she smiled. That smile was a marvel, truly!

"I forgive you. I have never met a man like you before."

By Krun! If platitudes had been invented on Kregen, which they were not, she would have been first in the line.

It occurred to me that she would be pleased if I told her I'd never met a woman like her before. As this was almost true, I compounded the lie and told her. Her smile dazzled.

"Yes. I know. I am something special..."

"Oh, yes," I said, taking up a deep rosé with just a hint of purple around the edges of the goblet. "Very special. Something quite else again."

And, as I thus foolishly ate and drank and tried to think of what to do next, I gave no heed to what was actually taking place around me. All I could see was a queen, and with her her retainers and guards, supping well. We had a walk to go before we escaped. But we would escape, I was certain. As I say, I overlooked the most elementary of questions. I offer in my exculpation only that the horror of this place must have worked on me, that I was worried over the fate of Seg and Milsi and the others, that I was tired—well, no, being tired is a sin, and I have no truck with it.

She said, "I had a map, a certain route through the Coup Blag. But it was lost."

Still no alarum bells tingled in my stupid old vosk skull of a head. This Queen Mab quite clearly knew what she was about, was used to wielding power, and I felt a dim stirring of surprise that so powerful a party as hers had been taken up. At least, our group were still free... At least, at the least—I hoped and prayed they were.

"I think," she said. "I think I shall enjoy walking with you." Very gallantly, waving the goblet aloft, I said, "And I with you, majestrix."

So, off we set again. There was a marked absence of traps in the corridors and rooms. I mentioned this. Two rooms later three of the guards were squashed against the roof as a stone block in the floor reared up on springs. Queen Mab just looked, tut-tutted, and we walked past on the other side.

She talked in a fine free way, animated, a flush across her cheeks. She displayed a queenly indifference to the horrors in this place. As we walked and talked, and what I said remains mostly a mystery to me—mainly a pack of lies about the romance and thrill of being a wandering adventurer and paktun—she would say, "Just so," and, "I see," and look suitably wise, bending her head graciously.

The slave girls in their silks and bangles looked bedraggled, and dragged their feet. Noticing this, I remarked that we were all tired, and that I hadn't slept in a long time. At once she lifted her hands in the air, looking toward her servants. Then she half-turned, halting, to look at me. At the time we were passing through a dim chamber suffused with a wan greenish light, and stuffed with piled coffins, from which stray wisps of cloth and desiccated limbs protruded.

"Tired? Oh, of course they are." She lowered her hands to her sides in a helpless gesture. "The poor things."

"We'll all march the better for a rest, majestrix."

"Most certainly. But let us find a more pleasing chamber than this."

The corridor, only a little dusty, turned and we walked up an incline. The next room, which was duly prodded by guards in what I could only take as a perfunctory manner, yielded nothing save a giant stone statue of some multi-limbed beast, standing on one leg at the center and trying to reach, with his tentacular trunk, a bunch of hanging fruit. The thing was grotesque. We hurried past.

The next room opened out into a blaze of light from crystal chandeliers.

I looked up, gaping. I expected the things to break free and fall on our heads, trying to slash us to ribbons.

A gigantic bed, big enough for a regiment, occupied the center of the room, masked by hanging damasks. Sweet scents cloyed on the air. Tables were laid with fruits and evening meal delicacies, and wine stood in amphorae.

The queen clapped her hands.

"Rest, everyone. Take your ease."

Everyone immediately flopped down on the cushions and rugs strewn about the floor. I looked about.

"Guards?" I said. "Majestrix."

"Guards? Oh, of course. Anglar—set guards."

He bowed deeply, his black and green robes flapping. He flourished his ivory wand at a hulking great Chulik, whose tusks were set with diamonds. The Chulik looked savage.

"Nath the Kaktu! Set guards as commanded. Bratch!"

Nath the Kaktu bratched, bellowing fiercely at his men. They went off and lolled at the entrances to the chamber. I decided that I'd sleep lightly and keep my fist wrapped around my sword hilt.

Now some of the three or four-armed folk of Kregen, and some with tail hands, who look like apims as far as faces are concerned, have been known when down on their luck to dress as apims, with their extra arms hidden. They may then wander through bazaars and markets, looking all innocence, and use their extra hidden hands to seize food and goods from the stalls and secret them inside their capacious clothes. One has to watch for rogues like this everywhere.

So—one of the guards, who looked like an apim with bad teeth and a ferocious haircut, standing guard by a door opposite the head of the bed, twitched his tunic around under his armor. I glanced across, caught by the movement, and Queen Mab called to me, lazily, a husky note in her voice.

Immediately, I walked toward the enormous bed, not wishing to give gratuitous offense, and the guard was forgotten for the moment.

A young fellow was in the act of walking away from the bed curtains, which were half-drawn. His skin was a clear smooth bronze; he had a pretty face, with crinkly hair and a rosebud mouth, and he looked sulky. His sulkiness turned to a look of hot resentment as he passed me. I ignored him.

A group of the slave girls gathered at the foot of the bed and began playing musical instruments and singing. The slaves carried enough boxes and bales to explain the instruments as well as the sumptuous clothes the queen wore. You may judge of my condition, a condition obscured from me at the time, when I say that I found the music enjoyable.

Now Delia can play the harp like an angel. Often of an evening in Esser Rarioch we would have musical sessions, and Jilian Sweet-Tooth would play her flute. Jilian is an accomplished flautist, and Delia's friends would gather and play and sing and we'd have a wonderful time. It was refined, of course, and very far from my evenings singing with the swods in taverns; but it was not ludicrous. Aimee could play a Kregen instrument not unlike a zither and the harmonies the ladies produced would have charmed birds out of trees. If I have not mentioned Aimee before it is only that she has not figured in my more hectic adventures up until a little later on.

So, now, I sat on the edge of the bed and listened to the music and enjoyed it, even though they performed that miserable song out of Hamal, "Black is the River and Black Was Her Hair." This is so painful as to be farcical.

The extent of that bed was truly amazing. The coverlet shone silkily, the pillows resembled the thighs of romance, the hanging tapestries and damasks glowed with amorous scenes. I watched as the music finished and the queen ordered her people to leave. Leaving that bed was like departing from a room of itself. The last hanging dropped into place and we were alone in the subdued glow of the lamps.

Well, she looked magnificent, like a wild beast of the jungle about to leap on her prey. She wore her golden hair loose, waving down in deep folds about her naked shoulders. The robe clung narrowly to her waist, slit from throat to ankle, and the golden lace blazed against her pale skin. Her mouth formed a luscious circle as she pouted at me. She stretched out a naked arm.

"Jikai—I am waiting."

Well, now...

Judge of my condition when I found myself advancing upon her across the wide expanse of the bed. Oh, yes! I, Dray Prescot, savage wild leem of a fellow, moving in on this delectable woman who lay back, pillowed in her golden hair, as the robe parted. It was all beyond belief.

The thought of Delia sprang into my mind, and the queen said, "You have loved before, Jikai, I can tell. But they were nothings. Mere trifles. I own that I am surprised—"

I swallowed. Her perfume dizzied me. She was really beautiful, now, I could see that, beautiful and desirable.

The way her skin flushed delicately with rose, the way her body curved, the way her mouth pouted, red and shining with passion...

"Surprised?" I managed to stammer out. "I am surprised—"

"You should not be. I am irresistible! My surprise is for myself, that I have formed so violent an attachment for you."

A roaring thundered in my head. There was only the body of the queen in the whole wide world of Kregen before my eyes. I inched closer, and now I was crawling over that silky coverlet. She lifted her naked arms, white and pink against the blaze of her hair.

"Irresistible! No man can resist me, not even you, Dray Prescot!"

"Majestrix," I mumbled.

"I am tormented with longing for you," she went on, her face flushing now, her body rising as I neared her. "I am prepared to—no matter—you are the luckiest man alive..."

She was very sure of herself. Well, she had every right to be. She *was* delectable. And she was arrogant with her power, conscious of her sway. Women have this power, it is undeniable. They use it; that, too, cannot be gainsaid. No doubt they boast of their conquests, woman to woman, in their private moments. I cannot stand a man who talks about women, and I usually withdraw when men start their boring conquest stories. As for women who boast to men...

The image of Delia rose before me, scalding.

I stopped moving forward.

She saw. Her face lengthened, her eyes brightened in the lamplight, her gaze fastening on me like the teeth of a shark, a remora, leaching away.

Two things happened, one a memory, the other a movement. I truly believe and would stake my immortal ib on it—I saw through her and jerked back before those two events occurred.

One—the memory—was what she had called me, without a Llahal or the pappattu between us.

The other—the movement—an insolent brown and red scorpion waddled out from under the pillows and stood, balanced, waving his stinger at the lush and naked body of the queen.

Saved by the bell?

No!

Saved because I understood all too tardily just what went forward here. And, then, many men would not call it being saved; they'd call me all kinds of benighted idiot. But I knew—and could guess—and in that moment the full horror hit me.

She saw the scorpion.

She screamed.

That scorpion was real to her, if not to me, real and not a part of the mumbo-jumbo.

She was off the bed and scrabbling for the curtains and they parted as Anglar thrust in, and, with him, the bulky form of the Chulik, Nath the Kaktu. Anglar swept a massive green and black cloak about the woman, massive in that it concealed her body and hooded up over her head and turned her into another being. The golden hair fell away, ripped free. Dark hair, dark and shining, swooping down to a peak over her forehead lay revealed. Her face blanched with vicious temper.

She stood and a trembling finger pointed at me.

"I shall not slay you, Dray Prescot. You resist me now. But you will submit—you *shall* submit! If it takes all your life, you shall submit!"

I said, "I do not know who you are. You are not Queen Mab. But I do not know you."

"You will, Dray Prescot, you will!"

I took a breath. The spell was broken. I said, "You seem to call me by a name you know. How is that?"

"Fool!"

"Well," I said, equably, "that is true, and I do not deny it. You say you have formed an attachment for me. That is your misfortune, woman, for you should know better—"

"Beware—"

"Oh, I'll beware all right. You are not Pancresta, that is sure. But you know of Spikatur Hunting Sword?"

Anglar laughed. Even the Chulik, polishing up his tusk, grimaced—and Chuliks and a sense of humor are light-years apart.

"I know of the creeping worms! Spikatur! We took them over, and made them do our will—*our* will! And you, you ruined it all, you and your wizards! I know! Why I do not condemn you to a life of torment I cannot say—" She put a hand to her forehead, a white naked arm snaking from the black and green robe. She looked suddenly bewildered.

I looked for my ally, the scorpion, but he had vanished.

The curtains of the bed parted as Anglar and Nath the Kaktu assisted this woman to step away from the bed and out to her chair. This throne-like chair was pushed into a cleared space. I crawled off the end of the bed and thought to take up the Krozair longsword from where I'd shed it as I'd gone slinking forward under the spell of this woman. For, spell it truly was.

And then! By Zair, I tell you, my heart turned over and all the blood rushed to my head and I was almost sick, sick as any poor beaten cur dog...

A tinkling tintinnabulation of golden bells...

The woman closed her eyes, sitting erect in the throne-like chair. Her eyelids were covered in gold leaf, and not unusually in the way of that kind of cosmetic fad, the leaf split along the lines of creases. In that moment all the beauty of her face dissipated, so that the pallor of her skin and the golden eyelids resembled a corpse face, painted for the last death journey to the Ice Floes of Sicce.

The multitude of tiny bells tinkled and tingled, and I felt the blood rush from my heart.

Stiffly, I turned about. A procession entered the crystal chandelier-lit chamber. A familiar, a horribly familiar, a blasphemous procession...

"You fool," whispered the woman, naked in her green and black robe. "What you have thrown away..."

Instead of sixteen Womoxes, bulking in their black tabards girt with green lizard skin, horns all gilded, there were but twelve. They bore a palanquin smothered in decoration and with its golden cloth of gold and embroidered curtains half-drawn. Against the red-gold sliding gleam of silks within a small shape showed, in shadow. The massed golden bells, tiny, spine-chilling, tinkled into the enveloping silence.

There were Katakis in the procession, savage, evil, predatory men, slave-masters with their low-drawn brows and snaggly teeth. Their whiptails curled boldly above their black-haired heads, and each tail was strapped with bladed steel. There were Chail Sheom, beautiful half-naked girls, chained and decorated, painted, whimpering. There were all manner of strange and obscene creatures, fashioned from nightmare, not of the Kregen I knew. There were, in this procession, things I had not seen before, and there were things missing.

The voice I had heard in that room of the blue doors, that had, all but one, turned red, whispered now.

"Mother," said that fragile voice. "Why do you tarry? What ails you?"

The woman opened her eyes. They were now of a deep pellucid green. I looked from her to the procession, and the palanquin, and tried to discern the creature within.

I remembered the warning, burned into the portal of the Coup Blag. But he was dead! He had been blown away in the Quern of Gramarye. He had to be—he was dead, dead, dead!

"You—" I choked out. "You are dead!"

"Silence, Dray Prescot." The woman spoke on a hiss, my name long-drawn with evil, and yet, and yet—she looked at me with those green depthless eyes, and I shuddered.

"Mother—we have won—why do you wait?"

So, then, I saw it, or thought I did, and trembled anew for the fresh evil loosed upon the glorious and forbidding world of Kregen.

Again I tried to peer past the cloth of gold curtains into the interior of the palanquin. Man or woman, boy or girl? How tell, in that eerie whispering voice?

Then, among the retinue of people following the palanquin I saw Pancresta, walking not proudly, but in a resigned, shoulder-drooping way. And I saw that we had been deceived. Spikatur Hunting Sword, we had been told, had been taken over by some new leader, some person with fresh ideas for evil and murder. And I thought I knew who that person, that devil, was; and yet I knew I did not know.

For Phu-si-Yantong was dead.

He was not in that palanquin, so like the one I had seen him ride in before. He was a mighty Wizard of Loh; I did not think he could come back from the grave.

The woman must have read a deal of the appalled thoughts on my face. Truth to tell, by Zair, I am not sure what I thought, what I imagined, in that moment of horror.

"Yes, Dray Prescot. Yes. You are trapped. My child rides in the palanquin that was my own and only wizard's. You and your vile sorcerous friends slew my wizard. I tried to aid him and could not. You have much to answer for, and yet, and yet..."

"Mother!" The weird whispering voice, so like its father's voice, sharpened. Still I could not tell if the creature borne within the palanquin was wizard or witch. "Mother! The time is now. We have played the game well, and we have joyed in it. But, mother—*now*!"

Yes, they'd played their games with me. The woman had given me no Llahal when we met, and not inquired my name, had not, in her impersonation of the queen that I had fostered, inquired for news of the king. She had known. She had known all there was to know about this place from the beginning, for she and her wizard, Phu-si-Yantong, had constructed it themselves.

No wonder the power of this place was wielded with such consummate ease!

I had to hold onto the fact that I was not dealing with Yantong. The child in the palanquin was aping her—or his—father. The woman was speaking again.

"My name, Dray Prescot, is Csitra. Mark it well. I owed you a score such as any woman would hunger to avenge. Yet I would have spared you, as you know. I would have raised you up, against the wishes of my child, the child of Phu-si-Yantong. Know, now, that I, Csitra, am a Witch of Loh, and you are doomed!"

Twenty

A Voice Speaks

I found a voice. If it was my voice, or another's, if it spoke from the grave, or from my love for Delia, if it was fostered by some lingering aftereffect of the counter-spells worked on me by my comrade Wizards of Loh, I did not know. If it came from the Star Lords I did not know. That, even then, seemed to me so unlikely as to be a foolish wisp of a whim.

That voice issuing from my throat spoke up bravely.

"Now wait a minute!" said the voice. "Now, just hold on—hold on a moment! You say you would have spared me, would have raised me up—and this after what you say was done to your wizard. Well, and what have I—here and now—said or done that offends you? Tell me, Csitra the Witch, tell me—if you can!"

"What—" She put a hand, again, to her head.

The long golden hair she had worn as part of her disguise, when I had forced on her, by my assumption, the identity of Queen Mab, lay abandoned. Her own shining black hair, peaked over her forehead, sweeping tightly past her ears, suited her better. Her beauty remained; but now in a strange and, indeed, frightening way, the artificiality had vanished. She was herself, Csitra, and the depth of terror was—she looked and was the better favored for that.

"What do you mean?"

"Mother! Waste no more time. The tormentors await and I must slake my just vengeance first!"

Her head rolled from side to side. Her voice faltered. "Phunik! Wait, wait—there is more here—"

"The man is mortal, he is Dray Prescot, and he is doomed! *Queyd-arn-tung!*"

That means no more need be said, but more did need to be said, and said damned quick.

I found that voice speaking again. "Since when does a mother, even a witch, sit still under insults from her own child? I have not insulted you. I treated you with courtesy—"

"You slew my wizard!"

"That," said the voice, "was before I met you."

"Do you know, Dray Prescot, what you are saying?"

A shrewd question. I did not. But I was in no condition to argue. I went on with that voice issuing from my mouth: "I have known very few Witches of Loh. I detest braggarts, pushy people, the vainglorious of the world. Perhaps had I known you were a Witch of Loh, and not a mere queen, I would have understood. Do you, Csitra the Witch, understand that?"

I, myself, was under no delusions. I was fighting for my life. Instead of cold steel, I used a voice and a tongue that welled up from some unsuspected source of deceit deep within me. And, anyway, of what use a warrior's sword against a witch's spell?

"*Mother!*"

Her green gaze left me and centered on the palanquin.

"Wait, my uhu, wait."

So, now, I understood what the creature in the palanquin was. Uhu—a hermaphrodite, half man, half woman, a person cursed or blessed with androgynous characteristics that could make its, hers or his life a heaven or a hell—uhu.

"Why, mother, why?"

"Because I say so!"

And the green eyes blazed with an awful occult power.

Asinine, my remark—rather, the remark of the voice issuing from my mouth. "Young, the uhu?"

"Yes, Dray Prescot. Young and unformed, a coy among wizardly witches. But able to destroy you—if I please."

"But why—*now*—should that please you? You see I do not prevaricate. I am what I am, what the gods fashioned me. I mistook you. That was a mistake, but an understandable one. What is past is past. Even a witch cannot alter that."

"You think so?"

I refused to rise to that bait.

I felt the cold in me. I was shivering. If talk could keep me alive, I'd talk the four hind legs off a vove.

She looked at me as though I were a frog's leg, to be dissected. "How can I trust you?"

I breathed a shaky breath. Those words told me I had won a small space, a tiny moment of time in which to operate.

The uhu from the palanquin spat out vicious, tumbling words, adding up to a demand that I be handed over—instantly.

"Phunik," said Csitra the Witch. "A flyer remains unsaddled." Which is to say that there is unfinished business. "Leave me. Go and play with your creatures. I will call when I have decided—"

"Mother!"

"Go, my uhu, go."

She turned her shoulder to the palanquin and the retinue of grotesque and ghastly retainers mingled with the chained slave girls and the warrior guards.

The moment hung charged with tensions that I, a mere mortal man, would never comprehend. It seemed to me the crystal chandeliers twined together and rushed upon me. The sweetly scented air cloyed and tried to suffocate me. The very floor rolled like a leaky seventy-four after four years' blockade off Brest. I saw the people staring at the palanquin, at the witch, and at me. I thought I would fall from the clamor in my head.

After three or four centuries of black emptiness, the tiny golden bells began to tinkle, and the procession turned around, and the Womoxes lifted the palanquin. Sheened in red-gold, glittering, and yet black with an indrawn power, the palanquin bearing the uhu, Phunik, the child of

Phu-si-Yantong and the Witch of Loh, Csitra, moved away out of my sight. I saw it go. I did not believe it had gone, not really; but the witch and I were left alone with her own people.

"Now, Dray Prescot, I think you must prove to me in deeds what you say in words."

Overcoming the first spell of allurement she had placed on me had been accomplished only through my Delia, and the scorpion, and my own wits. Could I hope to defeat a second and far stronger spell?

The chamber with its dangling chandeliers spun about me. I felt the nausea rising. I fell down. I, Dray Prescot, Lord of Strombor and Krozair of Zy, fell down in a faint. Well, to be honest, I performed the fainting act well; but that act needed little assistance, by Krun! Like any poor unfortunate girl cramped into too-tight clothes and paying the penalty for fashion, I fainted away.

As I toppled to the ground, I remember thinking that the girls who fainted to order were rather cleverer than stupid...

Cold logic—now—makes me sweat in retrospect. She could so easily have thrown a spell of true cognizance upon me and so suspected that I but shammed. Her slaves lifted me up and bore me off, and she cooed and aahed over me, with my poor lamb this and my poor dove that as to make the nausea rise almost uncontrollably in my guts. But I held fast, and was carted off.

In my struggle against Phu-si-Yantong I had always imagined and hoped that there was in the wizard a streak of goodness. I had found it difficult to believe that any man, Wizard of Loh or not, could be entirely evil. So, now, I fancied that in this witch-woman, Csitra, some tenderness for others than herself or the objects of her desire must exist.

I profoundly hoped so.

All the same, until I had been revived I was of no use to her. She called for someone named Pamantisho the Beauty, and heard an answering shout of joy and the quick patter of feet. That would be the pretty boy who had passed me with so sullen an expression. Csitra the Witch would be occupied for a bur or two, then...

No doubt the length of time I had to plan and execute my escape depended on pretty boy Pamantisho's staying power.

Having had no orders either to bind me or knock me about a bit, the guards just dumped my lax body onto a pile of cushions in a corner. They talked among themselves, and I gathered they were not happy here, and those few from Loh wanted to get back there very quickly. They said they were going for some booze—their words were highly colorful—and then they might hunt up some fun elsewhere. Guards in a witch's retinue ought to be superfluous. What their fun would be I did not care to guess.

I cracked an eyelid open.

It goes without saying that when a warrior falls down in a faint he will grip tenaciously onto what he is holding. The guards had passed a few uncomplimentary remarks about the longsword; but it was still there, and someone had tucked it down into the scabbard. I did not think this merited any comment on the quality of guards Csitra employed; they did their job and no doubt were paid, and they had seen the witch's powers, and the way she and I had, at the end, got on.

Now I was about to test the witch's powers again...

The guards began some of the usual warrior nonsense down at the wine tables, and others shouted at them to shut up, Shastum! and then someone shied an empty goblet at a chandelier.

This appeared a typical scene. For me, it represented just about the only chance I'd get.

So, now, I had to stand up, get out of here—and run.

By Krun!

I wanted to lie there. Just to lie there and rest. My body felt as though a sixteen-ton weight had rolled back and forth along the length of my spine. My eyes were red raw. My mouth was like—well like some disgusting part of some disgusting creature's anatomy. I just wanted to lie there and go to sleep.

Metaphorically, the snowflakes whirled about me and the deep snow formed my couch and pillow, and I could close my eyes and drift off, peacefully and gently and wonderfully.

No. Not good enough, not for a craggy old Krozair of Zy who had comrades to think of, and a world to save, and Delia at the end... My joints sounded like frozen twigs going bang bang bang under the iron hooves of horses. I stood up. I nearly fell down. And then, somehow, I was in at the back of a hanging arras, and breathing dust and cobwebs, and feeling my way along the rough stone wall.

By this time there was just me, a scarlet breechclout and a Krozair longsword. All the rest of my gaudy trappings had vanished.

With a scarlet breechclout and a Krozair brand a fellow is as well dressed and equipped as he needs to be, save at the poles, on that marvelous and terrifying world of Kregen.

Along corridors and passageways, avoiding traps, stumbling across rooms where specters gibbered, climbing stairs where the decomposing corpses of unfortunates told of sprung traps, hauling myself along by willpower, I dragged a painful way. Do not ask me if I would have escaped. I try not to boast, for, as I had told Csitra, I do detest the braggarts and pushy people of two worlds. Perhaps I would have been caught and moldered away in a fiendish trap, or been melted down in an acid bath, or been chewed up in the fangs of a monstrous beast from nightmare.

But, somehow or other, there is in my thick old vosk-skull of a head the fixed idea that I would have escaped.

I think that being a Krozair of Zy played a major part in that thinking. Poor old Phu-si-Yantong—he'd come unstuck before against a Krozair Brother. It was quite clear that no Brother of any Order of Krozairs had been through this maze before.

But the people of Spikatur Hunting Sword had.

Down low on the corner of a doorway the sign, cut into the stone, showed the heart pierced by a line. That line not only showed direction, it was the sword, the sword piercing the heart that was the sign of Spikatur Hunting Sword.

Staggering, making a sketchy attempt to prod the floor with my own sword, and glaring up with bloodshot eyes at the roof and around the walls, I tottered on. I followed the sign, the sign of Spikatur, and I followed it back the way we had come.

How long would it be before the uhu, Phunik, tired of playing with his creatures? How long before Csitra wearied of her amorous sport? Then they could go into lupu and descry objects at a distance. They could use the signomants they must have located in the corridors and tunnels. Then they would see me. Their vengeance would be swift.

Stumbling, I staggered on through rooms I recognized.

The carved doorway through which we had entered could not now be far off.

With great caution I entered a circular chamber. There were twelve doors, paneled and colored. Halfway around the chamber lay the mummified corpses of two werstings and two strigicaws with slit throats. Opposite them, near a splay of bones and skulls, the body of a Chulik sat propped against the wall. Of the hellhounds and the Pachak there was no sign.

I breathed with an open mouth, panting, my eyes wild, my hair falling over my forehead, gulping for breath. The Krozair longsword in my fist trembled.

The streaming mingled lights of Zim and Genodras, the Twin Suns of Scorpio, never reached down into this subterranean gloom. The crystal shed its radiance upon the scene. Under the Suns the Wizards of Kregen flourish, and are of many kinds. Some pretend to powers they yearn for and may never attain. Others make little show and can blast you where you stand. Some are not yet in possession of the secrets of thaumaturgical art they will later acquire. I had known Wizards of Loh who had been successfully kept prisoner by barbarians, by maniacal lords, probably because those Wizards of Loh did not number among their arcane arts those of blasting and destruction. Some, whom I had rescued, had later learned the awful secrets.

Most Wizards of Loh could go into lupu and see at a distance. I sweated and gazed about, seeking the doorway through which our party had first entered here. The feeling of unseen eyes watching me oppressed me with a palpable weight.

We had uncovered the mystery of Spikatur. Originally formed to combat the crazed schemes of Hamal in the person of poor old mad Empress Thyllis, Spikatur would have ceased to exist once Hamal had been defeated and was now being reconstructed. The conspiracy had been taken over and given a new and darker impetus. Once powerful forces containing our own wizards came to the Coup Blag, this place would no longer support those who directed Spikatur Hunting Sword. By Sasco, no!

In those whirling moments of darkness as I stumbled across the chamber, heading for a way out and into the light of day, I felt the absolute conviction that Seg Segutorio would win through. He would not lose his life down here. He would succeed. Good old Seg!

I could see the door I wanted. The sword piercing the heart wavered as my gaze faltered. Everything was going up and down. I staggered on.

The door opened.

Things rushed through, a crazed cloud of kaotim, Undead, decomposed corpses shedding their grave wrappings, skeletons clicking and clanking, beasts and half-beasts, risen from the tomb to sink their spectral fangs into me.

Shuddering, I threw the longsword up before my face.

If this was to be the last fight, it would be a fight, by Zair...

Without waiting for the revolting mass of Undead to reach me, I let rip a long ululating scream and raced forward, sword flaming, ripped into them in a wild surge of fury and despair.

Yet, despair? That charge was wild and ferocious, an onslaught of murderous precision. The Krozair brand sliced and hacked, bits and pieces of corpse flew, bones sundered and crunched to powder. The things whirled about me. Yet, fiendish though it was in sheer blattering headlong fury, my charge was aimed. Hacking a way through, I did not stop. I cut and slashed and went on, unstoppable, heading for the door I needed.

There was no slaughter here, for these foul creatures were already dead. In that breakneck onset I merely sent them back to where they had shambled from. Strange, too, to witness the superb Krozair longsword slicing and cutting and bursting gross bodies asunder and remaining steel-bright and unsullied. Yellow bones cracked and flew into spouting chips. Sere skulls gaped emptily at me, and cracked open as one cracks an egg open with a spoon, and nothingness gusted out...

Only a few long paces separated me from the door. With a howl of such savage ferocity as would wake the dead, if they were not already awakened, I burst through the last of the kaotim. A single smashing backhanded blow and I was through the door.

To slam it shut was the work of an instant and then I hared on tottering legs along the corridor. I could recall the layout—I could dodge the traps—I could take the correct twists and turns, and fight my way through the miasmic spirit-sucking atmosphere of this place. I could!

Mind you, memory ducks and dimples hereabouts. I recall some of the passageways and I think—I am almost certain—there appeared a pair of Kataki twins who were left in four or five pieces. But that could have been a dream. I thundered on.

I came to the foot of an enormous spiral staircase. I gulped air, tasting the flat stale dustiness of it where there was no real dust upon the floor, and started up.

What I expected, I do not know. Surely, by this time, Csitra or her uhu, Phunik, must have disengaged themselves and be watching me? Perhaps they continued to play their wicked games. They had turned Spikatur Hunting Sword to their own ends, and been discovered. Their pleasures were of the dark and ghastly kinds. They but toyed with me, I thought, and then came out to the top of the stairs and so hurried through the corridors. No, they could not be free yet, could not be spying on me, I thought, and tried the passageways and so came to the last chamber. Here we had all entered in, apprehensively, boldly, fearfully, but we had all gone in. And the Pachaks had entered cheerfully, lusting after plunder. I was glad they were still with Seg. More than ever I was confident he would get out safe, alive and well.

The radiance of jade and ruby, streaming in through the archway!

Ah! The supreme blessedness of the Suns of Scorpio, shining refulgently, beckoning me on!

Outside lay the jungle. That was a mere nothing to a man in my mood, a man who had dared the dangers of the Coup Blag and beaten them. I'd swing through the forest to freedom.

I would have, too... I am confident of it...

Mouth open, hair flying, limbs aching, eyes glaring, I stumbled on toward that beckoning radiance.

The brilliance of Zim and Genodras thickened and tinged with blue.

The blueness grew about me, dazzling me and a chill touched my skin. I gaped upward. Hovering, bloating, enormous, the outline of a Scorpion, radiantly blue, leered down upon me.

"No!" was all I could gasp before I was sucked up and whirled away through unguessable dimensions.

I opened my eyes.

I was sitting in a chair, and the chair, hissing, rushed along a lighted corridor. But I knew I was in no corridor of the Coup Blag.

I unfurled my tongue and wet my lips and managed to husk out: "Star Lords!"

The chair rushed around a corner and into a wide room. It hissed. It swiveled. It deposited me before a blank wall, and stopped, and I remained, sitting. It is most unlikely, whatever the necessity, that I could have stood up.

A voice: "Dray Prescot."

"I know that," I said. And, then, I thought to say: "The Shanks. They have reached Paz?"

"Not yet. There is time. There are things you must witness."

"Aye," I said. "There are things I *have* witnessed!"

"If you are to serve both your will and ours, if you are to save Paz, watch and listen."

I opened my mouth, but the effort was too great, and I closed it again, clamping my black-fanged winespout shut, and I watched as light bloomed on the wall before me.

By Beng Dikkane, the patron saint of all the ale-drinkers of Paz! I could do with a wet right now!

The glow grew like an unfolding flower. The light showed me a picture within the flower shape, a picture of color and movement and sound, and thought. I stared and listened, enthralled.

"You see what may happen, Dray Prescot."

Seg! Seg Segutorio, and with him Milsi, and Kalu and his Pachaks, and Fregeff! And complaining old Exandu, helped along by Shanli, with Hop the Intemperate to look out for them. They moved along a stone corridor, and the radiance of the suns lay before them.

"Thank Opaz!" I said.

"Remember, what you see is only what may happen."

"It will... It will!"

And then the weirdness of hearing the inner thoughts of the people in the picture overcame me. Seg was tortured by guilt—guilt over abandoning me—and yet in his thoughts the strong belief shone through that he knew of me, as I knew of him, that we would both soldier through.

And Milsi's thoughts overcame me also, and I hungered for Seg to know the truth.

And the others... I shut my mind to their thoughts. This was eavesdropping! This was contemptuous invasion of privacy! This was, this was—

"It is necessary, Dray Prescot, onker of onkers, that you *know*."

"Know what?"

"Know what it is needful for you to know. No more."

"I needn't really have asked, need I?"

And then all the foolishness was swept away.

The picture changed.

The voice said, "This has happened, this is smoke blown with the wind."

I saw a small and secret chamber banked with flowers. I could smell the scents, heady, intoxicating. A woman sat at a low table, gracious in the way she bent to untie the last thong on her calf-high boots. She was garbed in hunting leathers of russet, and propped against the table stood a rapier and scabbarded to the other end of the belt and lying on the table, lay the matching main gauche. A shimmer moved all across the picture and now the woman, still with her back to me, was dressed all in sheerest white. Her shining brown hair fell softly in gentle waves, her form dizzied me. She lifted her arms to unfasten the white gown, and I realized that time must have passed since the moment, a mere heartbeat or two ago, that I had first seen her. A night had passed in that short interval.

She turned to face me.

Yes—yes!

I had known, known from the first moment I had seen her. And now my Delia smiled, that smile that can twist me up and wring me out and deposit me like a limp dishrag at her feet—when she chooses. She smiled in welcome.

"You know I must leave you now? I wish it were otherwise, but—"

She spoke to another person in that secret flower-bowered room. The shadow moved across the table as the other person approached.

A fierce voice said, "I know you must leave, and I hate it!"

"I have to, so no more need be said. And I am late already."

A man moved into the picture, his back to me, and all I could see was a hulking great fellow, naked to the waist, with the muscles like boa constrictors, and a stupid yellow breech-clout. I stared. I tasted ashes.

Delia said, "You will not fret when I am gone—no, no—of course you will. Well, now you know what it is like."

And the man's obnoxious bellow said: "I know! But, before you change into your hunting russets, and your black boots, and do on your rapier and dagger, I think—my heart, I really do think there is time."

And Delia of the Blue Mountains, Delia of Delphond, laughed, delightfully mocking at the great hulking brute of a beast. She rose, glorious as a woman who knows she is a woman, and knows a woman's power and does not abuse that privilege. Splendid she was, so splendid as to catch the breath in the throat. Nothing else in two worlds mattered to me save Delia, and this ugly brute took her up in his arms as a leem might seize on its prey, and held her close; and I saw the way he held her, the gentleness and the tenderness so extraordinarily at odds with his appearance.

And so this—this person—swung Delia about and I saw his face.

And it was me.

So I remembered, this scene I was watching, recalled it with a pang as just one of the many many times Delia had gone off about her secret affairs for the Sisters of the Rose.

I collapsed back into the hissing chair of the Star Lords, and I shuddered. For I could sense the flowing thoughts as Delia mourned for the parting, mourned as I mourned, and we poor wights caught up in the toils of duty that sundered our paths. Pitiful, yes, of course; but there was more to this life of ours than that, a great deal more...

"Watch, Dray Prescot," said the voice. "Watch and listen."

"Spikatur—"

"You have smoked out their lair. You know how they will be dealt with, how they must be dealt with. These pictures before you now, they are your new reality."

Wrought up as I was, bloody, tattered, exhausted, I could not leave alone the horrors through which I had been.

"And that uhu brat of Yantong's?"

"Shastum! That is to be. Watch and listen and learn!"

So I watched.

I watched as Delia, the Empress of Vallia, put on her russet hunting leathers, and pulled up her tall black boots. I saw the professional way she strapped her weapons about her: rapier and main gauche scabbarded at her sides, the Lohvian longbow built for her by Seg over one shoulder, the quiver of arrows, fletched with the superb crimson feathers of the zim-korf of Valka, angled cunningly to hand, the long narrow Valkan dagger down one boot. She disdained the cape the pictured representation of myself offered her, throwing her head back so that the lights caught and gleamed in those outrageous chestnut highlights in her hair, reckless, glowing, filled with life.

Had she been with Seg and me as we tramped through the Snarly Hills she would have been more dangerous than either of us, than both of us put together, I did not doubt, by Zair!

Sitting sunken in a daze of longing wonder, exhausted, I watched the pictures, fired with passion, shaking with fear, exhilarated beyond reason, as the moments passed.

I, Dray Prescot, watched and suffered and triumphed with my Delia, my Delia of the Blue Mountains, my Delia of Delphond.

The fate of our Vallia was being decided as I watched and hearkened, and through the terrors that near drove me insane with fear for Delia I saw how she marched so blithely along and I thought I understood a little more of what the Star Lords wished me to know.

What the Everoinye did was done with knowledge and forethought, and what few mistakes they might make had no effect whatsoever on their plans.

A table hissed up from somewhere and brought refreshments. I sat, sunken, gripped by terror for Delia, watching. At last, the picture died. I had touched nothing of the food and drink on the table.

When the enormous blue Scorpion of the Star Lords came for me I cared nothing for Spikatur Hunting Sword, nothing for the Shanks. One thought, and one thought only, possessed me.

I stretched out my arms and soared into the blue infinity.

"Lallia the Slave Girl"

This is a story told on the world of Kregen, which orbits the twin suns of Antares, four hundred light years from Earth in the constellation of Scorpio. This is a story sung and mimed in all the great halls of the cities of Loh and Turismond and Havilfar of Vallia and Pandahem and sung and danced around the campfires of the hosts in Segesthes but it is not told or sung in any smallest part of the continent of Gah.

It tells of Lallia, a chained slavegirl, one of the beauteous chail sheom. Most gorgeous of all the women in the city was Lallia, golden-haired and emerald-eyed, of a form to dizzy the senses and of a sweetness of touch that would not bruise a flower. Every night her master would chain her to the iron slave bar at the foot of his couch with iron chains. He would smile on her with a smile of very cruel fondness before he reposed himself to sleep among the silks and furs, and she stretched upon the marble floor at the foot of the couch.

Not by a full arm's length could Lallia reach her sleeping master. Night by night she worked beneath the couch, with a broken shard of pottery, a lacquered hair pin, a discarded comb.

Lallia laughed in her captivity and lifted her sweet rose-red lips to her master, and in her heart she stored her purpose and in her mind she planned her course.

Night by night she worked until at last from beneath the hidden inner rail of the couch she stripped free a long and sharp splinter. Like the tongue of a risslaca, that splinter, like the horn of the mythical brumby in length a full two arm's width stretched wide, at one end as thick as Lallia's calf, at the other jagged and sharp and cruel.

Night by night with the deadly splinter in her hand she waited for her master to turn on his couch, sleeping so indolently with his purple mouth open, his veined purple cheeks puffing, waited for him to twist and turn until he was within reach and she knew she would make no mistake.

For three waxings and wanings of Kregen's largest moon, which in Gah is not called the Maiden with the Many Smiles, Lallia waited patiently on the cold marble.

For one hundred and sixty two days rising and setting of the twin suns, the crimson and the emerald, which in Gah are not called Zim and Genodras or even Far and Havil, Lallia waited.

Her master would boast of how much his chained slave girl, his chail sheom Lallia, loved him and of how she liked to feel the touch of the slave chains upon her rose-pink skin. Like his fellows he believed that her nightly sojourn naked upon the marble floor of his bedchamber made her love him more.

On the one hundred and sixty second night after she had torn the splinter free, Lallia saw her master's bedclothes slide back from his turning body. He had suffered an ague during the day and was restless. He lay exposed. More, he twisted sluggishly down the bed. She could see the thick white skin over his heart moving with a slow and heavy pulsation. Carefully she selected the space between two certain ribs. She pointed her wooden splinter between the two ribs at the dull white skin where it sagged and puffed, and she kneeled up tall, for she could not stand in the chains shackled to the iron slave bar, and she thrust with all her strength.

Who can say what emotions coursed through her breast as she struck? Who can say what primitive beast-senses were aroused and slaked in that delicate girl-body? She struck in silence and the wooden splinter penetrated the thick white skin and pierced through and embedded itself in the beating heart.

Only then her breath broke through her clamped lips in a long and shuddering revulsion. For a moment, after her master's huge gasp and lapsing gurgle, Lallia remained taut, high-strung, trembling. Then, with all her strength once more, she dragged free the splinter. Thick blood gushed in a stream onto the bedclothes and the couch and the ornate rugs of Walfarg weave upon the floor.

Carefully, Lallia drew off a sheet from the bed, carefully she wiped the gory splinter, and the sheet's whiteness turned a lurid crimson. Carefully she made sure that not a single spot of blood had splashed her naked body. Who can say what feelings of triumph filled her breast as she wadded the sheet and hurled it towards the window? Blood speckled a trail between couch and window. The stained sheet lay crumpled beneath the curtains. Perhaps Lallia smiled as she bent to replace the murderous splinter in its secret cavity beneath the couch. And then—and then her face lost all its smiles, her eyes glared, her breath came quick, her breast rose and fell in spasmodic horror.

For from the end of the splinter its tip, a full three inches long, was broken off, was gone, was nowhere to be seen—instantly her eyes turned back to the sheet and she saw with deadly anguish what she had done. In that sheet, proof positive and damning evidence, neatly wrapped and waiting to be found, lay the broken splinter tip.

She dragged at the chains and shackles, she tugged at the slave bar; but she could not break free. No slender slave girl could break the chains that bound her to the foot of her master's couch.

All that night as the seven moons of Kregen passed overhead against the constellations, and the samphron oil lamps burned low, Lallia lay huddled in her chains and her nakedness at the foot of the couch, shackled to the slave bar, helpless, waiting for the morning and the discovery and the wrenching away of the splinter from its cavity and the matching of the blood-soaked tip. The heady scent of moon blooms dizzied her. Then would follow the instant call for the torturers, and then if she still lived, the executioner.

Who can say what agonies passed through her mind all that long night?

With the first light of the green sun falling through the window past the thick drapes and painting an evil patina upon that blood-bedappled sheet, Lallia roused herself. Her fate lay blood-soaked and wrapped in a gory shroud. She prepared to play her part to the end, as she had planned, even this late. She set up a wailing and a screaming.

The retainers and household servants and slaves rushed in and fell to shrieking and moaning at sight of their master lying dead in a rimed crust of his own blood.

The trail of blood stains was found. The window was tightly shut—an assassin! A master stikitche, it must be, who had entered here, for the closed window proved that no ordinary criminal could have done the deed. The sheet was snatched up.

The smell of blood overpowered Lallia. She could not close her eyes and look away. The steward lifted the stained bundle, calling that the assassin had wiped his blade before he left, as a master stikitche would do, another proof, if any was needed. The steward took the upper edge of the sheet, where the golden threads and the scarlet and blue embroidery shone with a more sinister luster. He lifted it high.

Lallia's heart must have beaten faster. How she must have dug her teeth into her lip, her breath coming fierce and short. Now they would find the wooden splinter tip and guess, at once, what she had accomplished. The steward lifted the sheet high, and shook it out, and—lo!—it was empty.

Lallia was sold to a more kindly master, who by his lights pampered and petted her, allowing her to wear robes during the night and who did not always chain her to the slave bar at the foot of his bed. And when he did so he used silver chains. Her beauty and allure were so great that any man would dare much for her sake. As for her old master, he who had perished because he believed a folk myth, after a magnificent funeral and much officious weeping, he was buried in the family's ornate tomb, laid to rest with three inches of wood buried in his heart.

I have also heard a further ending to this story. In some places of Kregen it is often the custom among the high born, who are superstitious in these matters, to be embalmed after death, in the fashion of the Ancient Egyptians. As you will understand, the allure of Lallia was so great any man would risk much to gain her. It was the embalmer of her late master who bought Lallia the Slave Girl.

DELIA OF VALLIA

Delia of Vallia

Delia of Vallia, the story of a lady of quickness and passion, of cool irony and high resolve, is complete in itself and separate from the saga of Dray Prescot.

The Star Lords who brought Dray Prescot to Kregen appear to be changing in their attitude to him, even though he is a mere mortal man. They have favored him with an insight into their plans for that marvelous and mysterious world four hundred light years from Earth, where men and women of many different and exotic races mingle and strive to work out their own destinies under the red and green fires of Antares.

The destiny of the island Empire of Vallia at the moment is one of faction and disarray. Mercilessly savaged by outside foes, both physical and sorcerous, and rent by internal rivalries, the country is slowly gathering itself again after the Times of Troubles. But some unscrupulous people feel that now is the moment to strike and that one more push will bring them to the summit of their ambitions.

Against this background of color and action, intrigue and sorcery, the Star Lords have afforded Dray Prescot the privilege of vicariously sharing in the headlong adventures of Delia—Delia of Delphond, Delia of the Blue Mountains. As the narrative unfolds we know Prescot suffers. The cassettes on which the tale is told are often fuzzy and faint. But love and devotion for Delia, and pride in her courage and resourcefulness and her joyful onslaught against every challenge, stand forth clear and unashamedly. We, too, are privileged to share the story on these cassettes and go alongside Delia of Vallia as she hazards the perils of Kregen under the streaming mingled lights of the Suns of Scorpio.

Alan Burt Akers

One

From the Ochre Limits

The woman prostrate on the desert sand moved with the lax tremble of imminent death under the vulture's outspread wings. The bird inclined his stiff black wings, circling in the air, and regarded the woman with unhurried patience, awaiting the moment of her death.

She rolled sluggishly onto her side and Rippasch the vulture curved above her, his twin shadows flickering across the sand. The woman opened her eyes.

The bird lifted and the polished beak, sharp and hooked, caught the radiance of the suns and glittered. The woman's eyes half-closed. Watchfully, Rippasch dropped lower. Now she lay still, sprawled and supine, a last quiver of her limbs signal enough.

The ochre sand stretched to the horizon unbroken except for the line of footprints, faltering as they neared the point where the woman had fallen. The twin suns burned high, red and green, drenching the barren land with heat. The bird flicked his wings and curved in to land on outthrust claws. He cocked his head to one side.

The woman's arms lay loosely, her left hand across her breasts where torn russet leather revealed tanned skin, her right open at the side of her thigh. That open right hand rested limply on the hilt of a heavy sailor knife. A roll of sand partially covered the broad blade where she had fallen.

No breeze blew to muffle the scratching sound of the vulture's claws as he strutted toward the woman. His beak pointed. Her eyes remained half open.

Cracks disfigured the softness of her lips and dust stained her face into the semblance of an idol's death mask. Her breast moved in shallow rhythm, slowing, dying, stilling to quietness. Rippasch fluffed his neck feathers and strutted forward.

The woman remained motionless.

Reassured, Rippasch fluttered out his wings and hopped onto her body. His claws dug into the tanned skin; they did not break through into the flesh or draw blood.

For two heartbeats the vulture poised on the woman's breast, a black wedge against the sunslight. For two heartbeats only—then his sharp beak darted forward for the feast.

The woman's left hand struck straight up.

Her fingers closed around the thin and naked neck. Any squawking shriek of fear or astonishment Rippasch might have uttered was mercilessly choked off.

The woman's right hand closed. The knife glittered once as it swept in a flat lethal slash.

The vulture's head flew off.

Instantly, the decapitated body was turned, was twisted upside down. The spurting flood of blood cascaded out in a jutting stream. That warm wet blood splashed over the woman's face, coursed into her mouth. Greedily, she lapped the blood, swallowing, feeling the moisture wet against her parched skin—wet wet!

She drank greedily, thirstily, gulping the red blood like a savage beast crouched over its prey.

At that moment the woman was a savage beast, ferocious and cunning, skilled in the arts of survival, and she devoured the goodness of the kill her prowess had brought her.

Presently she licked the sailor knife clean. Moisture was so precious not a drop must be wasted. She replaced the knife in its rawhide sheath at her right side, below the main gauche that snugged sweetly against her hip. The matching rapier—plain of hilt and guard, slender and yet not too slender, not a fancy weapon—remained in the scabbard swung on plain steel lockets from her left side. Her waist was narrow and the lesten-hide belt with its silver buckle, dulled from much use, was hauled up to the penultimate slot.

Standing up, she picked the sucked-dry carcass from the sand and shook it. Her hunger was not so great, yet, that she needed to fall upon the raw flesh. But she would, if she had to.

In her present situation she was sorry that she could not husband some of the blood. But that would be the first to go. Moisture was all important. And, again, from her experience she felt regret that the vulture had not chosen to attack her corpse toward evening. She might begin to sweat again, now, and that was sheer waste.

She looked about the hostile horizon.

Her airboat had decided to crash here in the Ochre Limits after a short, sharp and nasty onslaught from beastly flutsmen, murderous slavers who thought they had sighted an easy prey. She had shot three of them with her longbow and skewered a fourth. Poor Pansi had died with a javelin through her throat and big, bluff, laughing Nath the Jokester had died with a barbed spear through his guts. Clearly, the flutsmen wished to take her alive.

After she'd taken the left eye out of the fifth—Nath had dispatched two—the remnants flew off. She'd sent a last shaft after them and taken little comfort and only minimal satisfaction from the shriek of pain from the rearmost.

So, from a wrecked airboat and two dead friends, she had begun to walk out of the desert.

Had anyone asked her if she was afraid she would have told them in her cutting way not to be such a nurdling great fool, and then ignored the question and got on with the job of survival.

If you kept on stirring blood in a bowl you could stop it from congealing; but she had no bowl and the effort would probably have taken more energy than she would lose by drinking all the blood at once and accepting the consequent loss later. She walked carefully, not hurrying, minimizing her movements, wasting nothing of her strength. Normally she walked with a grace that turned heads, not in a voluptuous hip-swinging fashion, but as though she trod moonbeams. Now she went along as though walking a tightrope across the sand.

Since the reiving flutsmen had downed her flier and slain her friends, she had maintained her direction. She knew where she was and within a few miles of just how far she had to walk to reach the river. Otherwise she would have been forced to hide up in the daytime. She cocked a brown eye up. Up there, circling high, a black dot regarded her.

She considered this new Rippasch.

No. Not yet. She still had strength and the blood had revived her. Time yet to cover more distance, get off the sand and onto the gritty dust and rocks, before she need fall down and so take off the head of that insolent creature up there.

Mind you, she said to herself, in the way her husband talked, mind you, the vulture was only being himself and acting out his nature. Rippasch was hungry and thirsty, too. And, he did help to clean up the desert...

The Ochre Limits, uncomfortably thrust between the provinces of Falinur to the north and Vindelka to the south, existed mainly because the soil ran poor and sour. True desert they could hardly be called, although they would kill you from heat and thirst as finally as any of the great deserts of Kregen. The woman walked carefully as the gritty dust beneath her sandals more and more supplanted the shifting sands. She peered under her hand, looking ahead to the horizon.

She was too determined to acknowledge even to herself how much she longed for the first sight of the trees, glimmering in ghost veils through the heat whorls, to herald the river. Firmly though she might push down her feelings, they surfaced, from time to time. Then she had to fix her gaze on the shimmering horizon, and hold herself just so, and put one foot in front of the other, and march, march on.

Boulders showed here and there as she went along, and a few lizards skittered. The water table began to give sustenance to incredibly hardy growths, dusty ochre and umber like the Ochre Limits themselves. This gave her fresh heart. Those plants grew roots long enough to reach down to a Herrelldrin Hell; she'd exhaust herself trying to dig down for water. Best to keep on walking, one foot in front of the other, over and over again.

That Opaz-forsaken river had to be getting near by now, surely?

A bush of a size to reach to her knees went past as she walked on, and then another on the other side. Soon the ground, hard and dusty, could no longer be called barren. It was still useless for agriculture, fit for the wild creatures of the world. Folk said that only madmen or leem-hunters—and they were by nature mad, too—ever tried to live in the Ochre Limits. Her tanned fingers reached for the hilt of the rapier. Leems were nasty, ill-tempered, eight-legged beasts of ravening destruction and huge appetite. A rapier would be of scant use against a leem...

Scurryings among the bushes caused her to keep her head turning, her eyes alert. And the twin suns sinking down the sky ahead began to dazzle, casting long double shadows from bush and rock. Her mouth was afire. The blood had made her more thirsty than ever. The pebble she picked up to roll around inside the cavern of fire that was her mouth alleviated the problem a little; a little, not much.

Small animals ran away from her now. Tiny, furry little beasts, tiny scaled beasts, tiny naked-skinned beasts, they all ran. On them the larger predators preyed, and on them the bigger, and, finally, the leem preyed on all. One of these fine days, no doubt, there would be a leem hunt on a grand scale. But other things came before that. She found herself wishing that the grand leem hunt had taken place in the past.

Reality supervened. This wild, hostile badlands could not support life enough to maintain many leems. They would be solitary, each with her or his own area, mingling only during the mating season. She was, in all sober truth, unlikely to run across a leem. Should she do so, she'd do more than many and many a leem-hunter did in a season.

The thought occurred to her that she could be walking into a vast loop of the river. If she turned to left or right, to north or south, she might meet the river in an amazingly short time. Resolutely, she thrust the thought from her. She marched on, due west.

This river, the River of Shining Spears, ran from the Blue Mountains south-southeastward into the Great River, called Mother of Waters, She of the Fecundity. It marked off the southwestern edge of the Ochre Limits. The idea of water, sparkling, splashing, *wet*, tortured her.

The Great River ran on southward in generous loopings, through the capital city, Vondium, and so on into the sea. The river, the canals, the sea—all were wet.

This wonderful island empire of Vallia had seen perilous and terrible times recently. Enemies, overseas and within the island, had sought to topple the country and seize the reins of power. Well, many of those enemies had been dealt with, and those remaining would be dealt with in due time. She could not concern herself with problems of others at this time; survival meant keeping a tenacious hold on the reality about her, the drifting dust, the sloughs of sand, the scattered bushes from which might spring deadly peril.

Seasons ago the idea that reiving flutsmen could wing freely in the skies of Vallia would have been ridiculous. The emperor maintained order in his domains. But since the Time of Troubles and the revolutions and insurrections and invasions, times had changed. The old emperor was dead and the new struggled to hold together the tattered remnants of the people loyal to Vallia, sought to bring back the old days of peace. Much of his time, perforce, was spent overseas hurling back the challenge of enemies, carrying fire and destruction into their homelands, instead of the fair island of Vallia. The emperor of Vallia, who was also King of Djanduin and Strom of Valka and lord of many broad lands, carried within himself a dream of unity. Many people followed him with fanatical loyalty, and many more opposed him for their own advantage.

The woman continued to walk on across the badlands with a determination that would not surprise those who knew her.

Her legs must have dropped off a long time ago, she felt. Weird ideas kept whirling in her head. Leems and water and flutsmen and the state of the country, all muddled up with annoyance that the trip to Delka Ob, capital of the province of Vindelka, had been interrupted. She admitted to herself that she was tired, deathly tired; but, also, she would not admit that fact. As her husband said, tiredness is a sin, particularly for people with work to do.

The first tree sprang at her, quite unexpectedly.

It appeared to be a tall, leering presence, black against the suns' glow. The sky sheeted in jade and crimson, in ochre and gold, in delicate tendrils of mauve. So there were clouds left in the world, after all...

She moved aside to let the tree pass.

The next clump had to be rounded more cautiously. The fantastic notion was lodged in her head, along with the bells and the clamor and the hollow silence: the trees were sentient and walking and out to clasp her in their barky embrace.

She tried to stop, to take a breath, to force herself back to sanity.

Her legs refused to stop walking.

She went on, walking with her purposeful gait, walking on, unstoppable.

As she marched on with all the clamor bellowing away in her head and the muffled silences bellowing the edges of that uproar, she began to wonder if she had made a disastrous mistake. She knew where her airboat had been attacked, where her friends had died, the point from which she had begun her march. Perhaps she should have remained with the airboat until night, and then started. But she had had all day... Perhaps that was the trouble. She fought the devils of self-doubt, and mistrust of her own judgments. She knew she was not unique in this. He who did not doubt, she who did not mistrust, must be lost.

But she had been so sure, so confident!

The distance to the river, the speed at which she walked, her own strength and determination... The equation was not going to balance. Soon she would lie down. Then she would be finished.

If only those devils of flutsmen arrogant astride their saddle birds had not smashed the water jars! If only her flier had not been attacked at all... If only...

She marched on, and now her head was high, her shoulders back, chest out, and she strode on, not as though drunken but as though forcing her way forward against a whirlwind that sought to hurl her back.

She was used to marching. She'd marched through the Hostile Territories. She'd marched with armies with banners. But now the pain in her feet and ankles had ceased. She could not feel anything in her legs at all, so that *proved* they'd fallen off long ago.

The long shadows dropped down.

She had completely miscalculated. The whole thing was a miserable fiasco—a fatal fiasco.

A sound obtruded.

A tinkling, running, *splashing* sound...

She couldn't run.

And in those last few moments as she forced herself on toward the river she knew she had not miscalculated, and, too, she knew she was not marching on, striding out, rather she was staggering, toppling, near falling, desperately trying to reach the water before she collapsed.

Blindly in the last of the light she marched straight off the edge of the bluff and plummeted headlong into the river.

She hit with a divine splash and wetness surrounded her in bliss.

Then it became imperative to reach the little shelving beach under the bluff at once.

Jaws and claws lived in the river.

A few powerful over-arm strokes took her to the bank. She pulled herself out and lay on the mud, dripping, her wetness a cloak of benediction. The fourth Moon of Kregen, She of the Veils, rose to cast down her fuzzy pink and golden light. The woman lay on the bank, in the mud, her brown hair spread and shining and the glory of her body abandoned to wetness. Magnificent, she looked, lying there, rounded and lissom, abandoned, sprawled, her tanned skin glowing through the rents in her leather russets.

Something hard squelched in the mud at her side.

A voice said: "By Vox! I'll fight any man who says I'm not first!"

Her eyes snapped open. She took a breath.

"Well," said another voice, thin and nasal. "She's not dead then, Hirvin."

"Out of the Ochre Limits," said another.

No one offered to fight Hirvin.

The woman turned and half sat up, leaning back on out-thrust arms. The clustered men, six of them, caught their breaths. They sat their mounts at the top of the bank. Moonshine glittered on their metal. Shadows ran and concealed their faces beneath the helmet brims.

She had been concerned lest she encounter a wild and savage leem; what she had encountered was far more dangerous.

Their lances spiked up from stirrup boots, the pennons indistinct and unrecognizable in the hazy half-light. They bestrode totrixes, and the ungainly six-legged riding animals stood docilely enough, proof of harsh discipline in their management.

Hirvin cocked a leg over his saddle and dismounted.

Automatically, he took a hitch to his belt.

"Fetch her up here," he said, and the order was obeyed with betraying alacrity.

Three of the others dismounted and slid down the bank. They seized the woman, who did not resist. They brought her up to the top of the bank. The light of She of the Veils shone down. By that haloing golden light the hard hawklike faces came clearer, harsh with incessant patrols of the badlands, harsh with imposed discipline, harsh with unrealized ambitions and denied wish-fulfillments.

"A Beauty," said Hirvin, and he sucked in a breath. His face congested. An old scar shone lividly against the browned skin. He put a hand to the cheap and ornate clasp of the first of the belts girding him.

The woman put out her tongue and—as though exploring forgotten territory—licked her lips.

She swallowed and shook her head. She opened her mouth and a strangled cry changed to a wheeze. Then she could speak.

She said: "Llahal. You should know that—"

Hirvin bellowed laugher. He threw the first belt down and the axe it carried clashed against the hard packed earth of the higher bank. He roared.

"Polite, this one! Trained, I don't doubt! By Vox—Llahal to you, shishi, and play your part well, and—"

"I am not—"

"That's of no consequence." His voice sharpened. "Hold her!"

156

She moved her arms, in a particular way, and the two fellows grasping her were grasping thin air.

The rapier cleared scabbard sweetly. The main gauche slapped up, crosswise, in her left hand.

"You would do well to go your ways. You are swods, soldiers to be ordered. You are not brigands, murderers—"

"We are swods and we've had no fun for days on end—"

Hirvin saw something, something in the way the woman held the rapier and left-hand dagger, that made him rip his own sword free. It was a clanxer, a straight cut and thruster. He rushed, with a yell, aiming to smash past with superior weight and strength and knock the woman down with the flat.

He struck. The woman was not there.

But her rapier passed through his upper right arm.

"Do not make me kill you," she said.

"Howling Hakkachak the Hungry!" he screeched. His left hand clamped around his arm, pressing, and still a dark blot of blood stained out over his fingers. "Get behind her, you fools! Grab her! By Vox, I won't be denied my pleasure from this beauty—"

The first fellow to grab her, the one with the broken nose and the silly sly grin, fell back, staring stupidly at the dark wet line across his forearm. That was blood. He looked up, starting to yell, and Hirvin roared again.

"You miserable stupid onkers! Get around her! Trip her up! By Vox, do I have to do everything myself!"

The other two men climbed down from their totrixes hurriedly. They fanned out in the moonlight, circling the woman. She turned at once and ran toward the bank, ready to dive in and chance the jaws and claws of the river.

She was amazed at her own weakness. A hand clamped on her arm, and a fist grabbed her brown hair. Her head was cruelly jerked back. A foot struck and knocked her legs from under her. She was aware of realizing that she did have her legs, and that was interesting, as she fell. They dragged her up to Hirvin.

A knobby fist hauled on her hair, forcing her to lift her face. She stared up at the man who looked down on her, gloating. He gloated as much from pride that he had won, as for any anticipation of what he intended. The scar moved as he spoke.

"You stuck your sword into my arm. Two can play that game."

The others—dutifully—laughed at the sally.

"Lial, do you go up to the hut and get things ready. Hot water and bandages."

The fellow with the freckles and snub nose ran off at once. The woman was dragged up by her hair. They held her, hard and harsh, and they took the rapier, main gauche and sailor knife away.

"A pretty thing like you oughtn't to play with men's weapons." Then Hirvin roared out again, his good humor restored, the sting from the rapier thrust ebbing. His men guffawed, genuinely, and they dragged the woman with them along the bank.

Their guard hut abruptly showed a light through the window as Lial struck flint and steel and caught the tump ready for the lamp. That was a cheap mineral oil lamp, and would no doubt stink all night. The place contained bunks for ten men, an audo, with a curtained alcove for the leader. The light showed his rank markings. Hirvin ranked as a ley-Deldar. The woman was pushed down on a bunk and the men stood back, staring at her.

She sat up. Sly looks passed from swod to swod. Young Nal swallowed, visibly trembling.

She said: "You are—"

"Say nothing, shishi." Hirvin held out his arm without looking as Lial bustled up with a cloth to wipe away the blood. "As soon as this little pink is bandaged, then you and I will try a fall or two, and not with Beng Drudoj, either."

Chuckles sounded in the little hut. The mud brick walls were hung with cheap and garish cloths such as could be bought for a silver sinver in any bazaar. A cooking stove built into the wall stank of grease. The bunks draped grayish bedclothes, heaped like stranded and decaying fish. The lamp, inevitably, smoked.

An arms rack, built of mud brick with some wood, held spears, stuxes, axes and short swords. The men, watching the woman, began to take off their weaponry. Outside sounded the clatter of hooves as the totrixes found their own way into their stalls.

"Watch her!" snarled Hirvin, then winced as Lial slapped a steaming cloth onto his wound. "Careful, oaf!"

The water stood ready on the stove, and it was clear the men were willing, very willing, to forgo their evening meal until afterward. Patrolling the river and the edge of the Ochre Limits was a miserable existence.

When Lial finished bandaging Hirvin's arm, the Deldar took a breath, sniffed, drew in his stomach and flexed his arm experimentally. He looked at the woman.

"Will you scratch? If you do you will have to be tied down."

"I will do more than scratch—"

Hirvin shouted.

"Get the clothes off her! Tie her down! By Vox! No little shishi balks me—"

She kicked the first one so that he turned green and rolled about the floor. The second only just missed having an eye removed. The third got a grip on her hair and then keened in agony as two fingers struck up his nostrils. The other two fell on her, bearing her down by weight, and Hirvin simply leaped on top of the lot.

The door of the hut opened and the growing night breeze blew dust across the floor. Hirvin, sliding forward and hitting his wounded arm a crack on the edge of the bunk, yelled.

"Shut the door, Tandu, for the sake of Beng Dikkane! And keep that brat of yours outside if you don't want him to see man's work."

He reared up and swung about as his comrades grasped the woman, holding her. Now she struggled unavailingly, lissom, supple, her brown hair aswirl.

The four-armed man in the doorway said, curtly: "Stay outside, Dalki. See to the totrixes."

Hirvin's momentary distraction as his wounded arm cracked against the bunk edge, and from shouting at the four-armed Djang, gave the woman a tiny moment in which to act. The two men holding her felt her movements and could not hold her. One wrung his hands as the wrists poured molten streams of pain up his arms, the other reeled back with blood spurting from his nose. The woman leaped up onto the bunk, panting, brown hair wild, and from the last of her assailants she snatched the fighting man's dagger. Heavy, unadorned, designed to be a gut-spiller, the dagger menaced the men in the hut.

She looked a magnificent savage beast of the jungle, broken free of her chains, uncaged, no longer shackled for the delight of the passing trade.

The Djang, Tandu, used his upper left hand to sweep the dust-covered cloak up over his shoulder, out of the way. His height overtopped all. His broad, ferocious, open Dwadjang features congested with blood. He stepped forward and knocked over a three-legged stool. He did not notice. He stared at the woman, poised on the bunk. She did not brandish the dagger; she held it as a person holds a weapon they know well how to use.

Some of the swods were over the first shock of their injuries at the hands of the woman. They gathered themselves together, and stood up and wiped the blood away. They looked at their leader, at ley-Deldar Hirvin, and murderous intent disfigured their faces. They were mercenaries, hired for a mind-dulling task; they would not be balked of their prey.

"She's only a woman!" yelled Hirvin. "She will not stop us with a dagger. Get behind her, throw a blanket over her, bear her down!"

Young Nal, trembling, scampered around the end of the bunk and Lial and Long Naghan snatched up a blanket. Tandu, the Djang, stared at the woman.

His hand, his upper right, whipped out one of his swords. His lower left drew a long dagger. He advanced, he did not shut the door as he had been ordered, and his boots scratched on the blown dust. His hip collided with the edge of the nearest bunk and dislodged a marching pack there, which fell and emptied its contents onto the dusty floor. He did not notice.

He stared. His face, congested, broad, a furious ferocious frightening Djang countenance, empurpled.

He shouted. He roared in such a voice as would bring the very stars out of the sky.

"Do not touch her!" His lower right hand caught in Vogon the Amsant's hair, and jerked the bulky mercenary back. He thrust himself on, sword lifted, dagger snouting. He was visibly shaking with passion.

"What nonsense is this?" screeched Hirvin.

Tandu the Djang drew himself up. His sword swept in the ritual salute to the woman and then flickered out, a bar of lethal steel, to menace Hirvin.

"You fool! This lady is my queen! The Queen of Djanduin!" The Djang sword darted for Hirvin's throat. "This is the Stromni of Valka! The Empress of Vallia! Delia of Delphond, Delia of the Blue Mountains!"

Two

The Djang Tandu and His Son Dalki Stand Watch

Deldar Hirvin staggered back, away from that reaching Djang sword. His eyes opened wide. His mouth thinned into a bitter line. He spat his words when he found his voice.

"The empress? What is that to us, now? If it is true, Tandu—"

The Djang swirled his sword to encompass the others. Young Nal, behind the bunk, froze, ashen.

"True? Aye, you nidges, it is true!"

"Then," said Hirvin, spittle slobbering, "then we are all dead men. What I say is so!" He twisted away from the point of the sword, gestured to his men. "It matters nothing to us, empress or queen. If she lives—we die!"

"Down on your knees!" thundered Tandu. "Down on your faces in the full incline!"

He knocked the bowl of water over from the table, and sent the table flying after it. He bloated with the enormity of his own rage, his harness straining under the immense swelling of his ribcage. He looked—he was!—frighteningly formidable.

"Thank you, Tandu," said Delia. She spoke levelly. She was in control of her breathing now, and fighting off the dreadful tiredness. She smiled.

At that smile Tandu almost exploded.

"Do we kill her first," said Sly Oswalk, "or after?"

Tandu roared his contempt.

"First, nidges, you will have to slay me!"

"That, Tandu the Onker, we will accomplish," said Hirvin, and leaped.

Delia threw the dagger.

Heavy, simple, cruel, it passed clean through Hirvin's neck.

His eyes crossed as he vainly attempted to focus on the steel transfixing his throat.

"Hai!" bellowed Tandu, and then, remembering: "Dalki!"

Swords snapped up, and before Hirvin, tottering, fell under their feet, the men were at handstrokes.

It was a poor contest; when Dalki, a younger edition of Tandu, burst in raging, it was no contest at all.

Sly Oswalk, alone, managed to slip through the open doorway and escape into the night.

Tandu and Dalki were all for following and cutting him down without mercy.

"Majestrix! He deserves to suffer in the deepest of Herrelldrin Hells, to wander screaming among the Ice Floes of Sicce forever!"

"Aye," said Delia. "Probably. But he snatched a bow before he left. I value you, Tandu, and your son Dalki, too much—"

Tandu, stumbling over a corpse, had the sense to make no otiose reply.

Delia sat herself down on the edge of a bunk. She put a hand to her hair, smoothing the wildness back. In that brown hair, caught and embellished by the lamplight, outrageous chestnut and auburn tints glowed. Tandu, breathing hard, beamed down on his queen.

"I remember you, Tandu. Yes, I assuredly do. It is Tandu Khynlin Jondermair, is it not?"

"Yes, majestrix, may Djan Kadjiryon have you in his keeping."

"And you married one of our girls in Valka, I recall, when you came from Djanduin to train our young men to fly flutduins? Yes—Valli, I remember, beautiful Valli of the violet eyes. And Dalki is your son."

Tandu breathed so that his bronze-studded harness creaked. "Valli died, majestrix. Slain by those Djan-forsaken cramphs of aragorn. When we fought in Valka."

"I am sorry, Tandu. We have been through terrible times together."

"That is true. But there is my son, Dalki—"

As Dalki, shorter, and by a fraction less formidable than his father, bobbed his head in awed respect for this famous and indomitable woman— the Empress of Vallia! The Stromni of Valka!—it was clearly apparent that he had heard of Delia of Vallia, heard of her and shared his father's fanatical loyalty. Yet Dalki drew his harness over but two arms; he was not a true Dwadjang with four powerful fighting men's arms. He was a miscegenation; yet clear-eyed, strong-faced, proud and upright, a true son to his Djang father and Valkan mother.

"Can we stay here tonight, Tandu? I am tired."

Instantly, Dalki was at the bunks, picking up blankets, bashing straw-filled mattresses, hauling all the pillows about to find the finest.

"You are hungry, majestrix, thirsty?"

"I could drink the whole of the Sunset Sea, were it sweet water."

"A meal! Dalki, a meal for the queen!"

The mercenary frontier riders provided poor food; but the Djang and his half-Djang half-apim son rustled up the best. They brewed strong Kregan tea and heaped a pottery dish with the golden yellow paline berries. Delia sipped the tea and chewed a paline as the meal was prepared. She leaned back against heaped pillows, and looked with her brown eyes level and curiously unimpassioned upon the scene. She had come through a bad ordeal. She had done so before. No doubt, in Opaz's good time, she would do so again.

The corpses were thrown outside to be cleared away in the morning. Tandu and his son would not sleep all this night. Not, by Zodjuin of the Silver Stux, when their queen slept and they stood guard.

Simple though the ingredients might be, the meal Dalki cooked up smelled delicious. It tasted very fine, also; although Delia would probably have chewed on passe biltong and sour water with her hunger. She did not consider it strange that the Djangs had not asked her why she was here, marching out of the Ochre Limits, instead of living in her great palaces—any of them—surrounded by luxury. They knew she was a woman well-used to the hard trails of life.

That lack of curiosity on their part did not make her quench her own curiosity about them. When she had finished the meal, which she had insisted they share, she said: "Tell me, Tandu. You came to Valka to train young men to fly flutduins. You were an ord-Deldar, I believe. At any rate, you would soon have passed out of the Deldar grade to become a Hikdar commanding your own pastang. Why is it that you are here, riding guard on the Ochre Limits, chasing bandits for the Kov of Vindelka?"

Tandu let his gaze linger briefly on his son. His broad, high-colored face suddenly took on lines Delia had not noticed before. Tandu looked, for an instant, sad.

Then he said: "Because I married my Valli."

Delia felt the shock.

"In Valka? Where I am Stromni and my husband is strom? In our Valka?"

"Aye, majestrix. In the Time of Troubles, when you were away fighting our enemies. A few people only, but enough."

"My husband and I much mislike folk who do not look on all Creation as one. Djang, apim, we are all Opaz's creatures, all men and women under the hand of Djan."

Softly, Dalki said: "You suffered under many enemies then, majestrix."

His strong face, so like his father's and yet inlaid and softened by his apim ancestry, betrayed the awe and elation he felt at actually speaking to the Queen of Djanduin and the Empress of Vallia. Delia smiled.

"You were not born, then, Dalki, I know. But, you are right and have learned the lessons of history correctly. But, in one thing, there is more to learn. I have many enemies still."

"May Djondalar of the Twisted Staff strike them all low!"

"A happening devoutly to be wished," agreed the queen. She did not so much yawn as indicate that she would have yawned if she allowed yawning to figure as a part of what she tolerated in life. Instantly, the two Djangs—for Dalki thought and talked more like a Djang than a Valkan—fluffed about preparing the best bunk and smoothing the pillows and spreading extra blankets. Then, tactfully, they withdrew so the empress might complete her toilet in privacy.

Delia put her head on the pillow and went at once to sleep, confident in her Djangs and their strong right arms, all three of them. As ever, her last thought was for her husband who was—well, who the hell ever knew where he got to?

He was probably out somewhere outlandish bashing hostiles over the head with his great Krozair longsword and, as ever, thinking always of her.

What a pair they were! And then she was asleep.

Outside the guard hut the Kregen night breathed easy in the glitter of stars and the golden and roseate light of She of the Veils, soon joined by Kregan's first moon, the Maiden with the Many Smiles. The Djangs prowled watchfully. Any beast or human of evil intent would find short shrift at their hands.

Shortly after the hour of dim, which is the opposite to the hour of mid on Kregan, Delia awoke. She stretched and knew instantly where she was. She sat up. She stretched. Then she stood up and girt on her rapier, which Dalki had carefully cleaned, and went outside the hut.

Instantly, like a black shadow, Tandu stood at her side.

"Majestrix?"

"I'll stand a few burs' watch, Tandu."*

"But, majestrix—"

"Dalki needs his rest."

Tandu mulled this over. He had heard the stories concerning Delia of Vallia, so many of them true, so many far-fetched as to be fantasies; but, this!

"My queen, to stand a watch like a common swod—"

"Swods are not common, Tandu. And I have stood sentry go before."

Tandu, for one, well believed that.

---

* bur. The Kregan hour, approximately 40 terrestrial minutes.

163

"As my queen commands."

Dalki wanted to be mutinous until his father told him the queen commanded. Then he went into the hut and threw himself onto a bunk, and went to sleep dreaming of Delia of Delphond.

The high star glitter picked out the familiar constellations of Kregen. Delia sighed. Her husband had told her of other constellations and stars that he saw from his own funny little world with only a single yellow sun and a single silver moon and only apims, as he and she were, and not a diff in sight. Odd! Perhaps, one day, if the Star Lords ordained, she might herself go to that funny little world he named as The Earth. Odd.

They stood watch, queen and swod, scanning the riverbank and the trees and aware of the changing patterns in the rustle of leaves in the breeze, the smell of river and mud, the tiny scuttlings of creatures of the night. And to Tandu Khynlin Jondermair came the absolute conviction that to stand a guard duty with his Queen Delia was to confide half the safety of their mutual watch into hands as strong and capable as the toughest Djang in all Djanguraj, in all of Djanduin. He breathed easy, did Tandu the Djang.

Presently, in a soft whisper that reached only the Djang's ears, Delia spoke.

"And you never returned to our Djanduin, Tandu?"

"No, majestrix. I thought—I did not think my son Dalki would be... be well received there, either."

"Mayhap you were wrong in that."

"I do not know."

"I trust you were. One day, Tandu, we will put it to the test." She did not look at Tandu as she spoke; rather she kept a lookout along the river and the trees, watching for others like Hirvin or Sly Oswalk, who had escaped, to come seeking their fortune with the queen in the guard hut. "And so now you serve Vomanus, the Kov of Vindelka."

"Aye, majestrix. I had a letter from Panshi, the strom's chamberlain in Esser Rarioch. Kov Vomanus received me kindly. But that was just of him, and as he was—"

"As he was?"

"Times have changed in Vindelka, majestrix, as they have elsewhere in Vallia."

"Before those damned flutsmen brought down my flier and killed Pansi and Nath the Jokester, I was on my way to Delka Ob. I chose to fly over the Ochre Limits, for that was the shortest route. I am sorry, now, that I so chose. But I must get to Delka Ob. Vomanus is to be wed, and I must be there for the ceremony."

She did not add that when Vomanus, her half-brother, had been wed the first time she had not only not been invited, she had known nothing of it until later. Of that union had been born Valona, who was not Valona the Claw. Vomanus's wife, Saenci of the Locks, had died. Delia had felt grief at that, even though Saenci had not been of the Sisters of the Rose. Her daughter, Valona, was of the SoR. Now Vomanus was to be wed again, to a woman unknown to Delia. Natural curiosity as much as family pride impelled her to attend this wedding and, in a pathetic time-binding way, perhaps, make amends to Saenci of the Locks.

"I must get to Delka Ob, and quickly."

"We hear little out here, majestrix. We performed the ritual mourning for the kovneva. We do not know that the kov is to be married again."

"Well, he is. So, good Tandu, first thing in the morning I set off for the capital."

He turned, slowly, to regard her.

"Yes, Tandu. You and Dalki shall go with me."

He said, simply: "You do me honor, majestrix. But—what of our guard duty?"

"At your back is the River of Shining Spears, and across that the zorca grasslands of the Blue Mountains. At your front the Ochre Limits. If bandits appear, they will do little before the men we shall send arrive."

"Quidang, majestrix!"*

Not for a four-armed Dwadjang the puzzlements of command or the complexities of operations. Give a Djang his weapons, point him in the right direction, and very little if anything in the whole world of Kregen would stop him and his fellows from trampling on. But present him with a conundrum, a difficult problem in logistics or operations, strategy, and he was lost. Then he would turn to the two-armed Obdjangs with their gerbil-like faces to make the decisions and to take the command. Obdjang and Dwadjang, they lived together in fraternal friendship in Djanduin.

A long screeching cry cut through the night.

Delia cocked her head.

"A wherezik has found its prey," quoth Tandu. "Poor victim, swimming in the river at this time of night."

"No doubt," said Delia briskly, "the victim's belly was stuffed with its own victims."

"Aye. Aye, majestrix. That is the way of the world."

"Has there been any report of leems lately?"

"Not one."

"I am relieved to hear it. On the morrow we take all the totrixes and march downriver for Mellinsmot. There we should be able to find a flier, or zorcas if they have no airboats."

"Whatever the folk of Mellinsmot may have, they will gladly yield it for their empress."

---

* Quidang!—Kregish for "Very good!" "Aye aye, sir!" "Your wish is my command and will be obeyed instantly."

"That, I hope."

"Oh," said Tandu, easily, "they will." In the star-shot darkness the lights of the moons shadowed on his hand, instinctively reaching for a sword hilt, without thought. Delia half-smiled and half-sighed.

"The Hikdar will be surprised," said Tandu, out of nowhere.

"The Hikdar?"

"Aye. He brings a patrol along the bank, on a regular schedule. Just to see we are not all dead or run off."

"Oh!"

"Hikdar Leomer ti Vindheim will expect to see Deldar Hirvin and us— and he'll find another audo of guards." Tandu made a small breathy sound on the night air that was as near a laugh as a sentry would permit himself. It was clear that to the Djang this was a great jest. Delia felt pleasure in Tandu's enjoyment of the situation. This was a simple enough example of one of the reasons she loved her Djangs so.

They lived in Djanduin, a sizable country in the southwest of the vast continent of Havilfar, down south of the equator. Up here in the north, the large island of Vallia with the clusters of smaller islands around the shores, had seen the coming of many Djangs since the Strom of Valka became King of Djanduin. This free movement and mingling of peoples was a dream near to the heart of the Emperor of Vallia, for he foresaw the time when all of this grouping of continents and islands, known as Paz, must fight for life against enemies from overseas, the detested, despised and dreaded Shanks. So if anyone thought to question why one man should at once be strom, kov, hyrkov, king and emperor, the answer did not lie in the reply that the man was a remarkable person. He was, of course, and Delia had married him; but deeper than that, more touching the core of the future on Kregen, lay this determination to resist enemies and create a whole, free, full life for all.

A dream. Of course, a dream. But without a dream you are without everything.

The night passed. Delia said: "Before we ride for Mellinsmot there is a task I must perform. We will take all the totrixes and all the water we can carry."

A fighting man grasped the meaning without fail. A warrior maiden, a Jikai Vuvushi, probably understood even more rapidly.

Tandu cocked an eye aloft as they finished up the first breakfast of the day.

"Yes, Tandu. I know. Rippasch will be there before us. But—I must."

So, with all the saddle animals loaded with skins bulging with water, they set off into the badlands, out across the Ochre Limits.

Three

A Burial Is Completed

Delia and Tandu stood, heads bowed, looking down at the wreckage of the airboat and the strewn bones. Dalki stood in a respectful way; but his eyes did not stare downward. His right hand rested comfortably on his belt beside the feathered shafts in their plain quiver, and his left hand, held down, grasped a bow. He looked up.

Presently, her private commendation to Opaz for the ibs of her friends completed, Delia said: "It is sad. But we will give them a proper burial. They will surely reach the sunny uplands beyond the Ice Floes of Sicce."

"Without doubt," said Tandu.

Scraping a grave was simple enough. It would blow streaming sand, later on, no doubt, and the graves might be stripped for the bones to lie bare and bleached under the radiance of the suns; later on, the sand would blow back.

Tandu moved with caution inside the wreckage of the flier. He only knocked a few broken things over. He came out with Delia's box which he and Dalki strapped onto a totrix. That contained, besides a fine dress and other feminine essentials, wedding gifts. An earnest only. She had determined to let Vomanus see she was not pleased with him. Later on the full and lavish caravan stuffed with wedding gifts would be sent to Delka Ob. Later on.

She felt relief she had managed to persuade herself to return. Her friends had to be buried, and their ibs commended to Opaz, although such a commendation had no need of bones, corpses or graves. She controlled her shudder. She detested illness, sickness, the stink of the sick room, the fatuous smiles of people watching friends die. When her father had been ill—poisoned by secret enemies—she had managed to hold on long enough to attend to him. But if there was a flaw in Delia of Delphond, a failing, it was this, that she had to force herself into the tasks expected of people in dealing with sickness.

She had not in her life escaped those tasks.

She had been born a princess, married a prince, who had made her a queen and an empress. But she had been slave. She had emptied the golden chamberpots of those who enslaved her, and had, on and off, chopped them up into diced meat for it.

The simple ceremony over, her belongings piled on the back of a totrix, a last look at the smashed airboat, and she nodded to Tandu and they set off.

Away over the scorching wastes of the Ochre Limits lay the Dragon's Bones, a vast collection of monsters' bones of many descriptions. The place was a giant cemetery for giants. There a notable fight had taken place, where her husband—before they were married—had saved the life of her father the emperor. She thought of those long ago days as the totrixes waddled along with their six-legged gait, and she sighed. Life had been—simpler—then.

And, for all that, it had been complicated, too, Opaz knew! Just that the size of the problems these days was so much greater. Now they had half a world to ponder over.

She itched. She was used to discomfort as well as comfort; but the wash she'd managed in the river to rid herself of the mud had not been sufficient. Now dust caked over all. She longed for a wallow and a brush and a soak and a swim in the Baths of the Nine. Mellinsmot would boast such an establishment, no doubt a provincially grand place, full of gilded stout statues and flower garlands. But it would boast, also, piping hot water and steam rooms and freezing pools and an exercise salle. Yes, she closed her eyes and fought the itches, refusing to scratch, yes, she much longed for a session in the Baths of the Nine.

When the line of little dots appeared in their rear, high in the sky and winging strongly on, Delia frowned.

Tandu said, "Damned Djan-forsaken flutsmen."

The skein bore on, and Delia counted six of them.

If the flutsmen wished to attack there would be no escaping them. The Ochre Limits extended in barrenness all around. If they attacked, if they did not attack, all were as one to Tandu and Dalki.

Dalia said, and the note of crossness in her voice was not unremarked: "Why in the name of Vox do we allow these thieving murdering flutsmen so free a rein? Does not the Kov of Vindelka sweep his province clean?"

Hesitantly, Tandu said: "I know nothing of these high matters, majestrix."

"But you can see the flutsmen up there?"

"Yes, majestrix. They have grown worse just lately—"

"I thought we'd cleansed the land of them, and the aragorn and the mercenaries. I thought all our enemies were being driven back into the north. I don't know what Vomanus is playing at."

Tandu and Dalki might not worry, one way or the other, over six flutsmen—for themselves. But Tandu caught his son's eye, and for a moment they reined in to ride knee to knee as Delia trotted on ahead.

"The empress does not care for flutsmen, father."

"So I gather. I do not care, either. But we have the empress with us—so—"

"So we protect her. I know that."

"Shoot as many of the devils as you can before we come to handstrokes. After that—it is the empress, alone, who matters."

Riding up ahead, Delia wondered if the two Djangs were laying bets in the way her husband and Seg Segutorio had the habit of doing. Thoughtfully, she drew out her longbow. This was a Lohvian longbow built by Seg, who was, in his friends' opinion, the finest bowman not only in all Loh but in all Kregen. She had thought she was a good shot having been trained up by the Sisters of the Rose, until Seg had given her of his learning and experience and expertise. Seg had trained her to shoot, as he had trained her children. She had no doubt she could feather two of the flutsmen up there before they landed; but the flutsmen would shoot back.

They'd use crossbows.

Delia half-turned.

"Crossbows," she said. She spoke in that cross way, reflecting her worries, and then instantly hoped the Djangs would not think she was cross with them. Some empresses of Kregen, in this situation, would blame their retainers for any misfortune.

"We will shoot them, majestrix, before they land."

"Before they shoot us!"

"Aye, majestrix. As you say, before they shoot us."

The thought of cruel iron bolts punching into the bodies of the Djangs upset Delia. It was bad enough to think of quarrels smashing into the totrixes. In all the marvelous diversity of life on Kregen, Delia joyed in the warmth and variety and very profuseness of life, each one precious. Except, perhaps, for inimical forms who wanted only to rip her up and eat her. Then, of course, she had to harden her heart and see they did no such thing.

Now, and with a heavy heart, she gave her orders.

"Dismount. Make the totrixes lie down. I do not like this; but it is a thing known and done."

The Djangs knew, had done it, and instantly understood.

Even then, it was nip and tuck.

The flutsmen swept on, the wings of their fluttrells beating with a pulsing rhythm that drove them through the air and sent them diving down at the little party on the sand. The totrixes didn't mind in the least that they should stop trotting along, and were no doubt highly pleased that they were actually being allowed to lie down. But, being six-legged saddle animals of contrary natures, they wanted to lie down where they wished, and not where their masters intemperately pushed and pulled them.

"Giddown!" rumbled Dalki, hauling a totrix around so that his head jutted over the rump of the one ahead.

"Stay there!" roared Tandu, as his totrix started to lumber up and move to a different place where, it was altogether probable, the sand was much softer and more comfortable.

Delia laughed.

"We must make a comical spectacle!"

"Aye, majestrix. And here come the flutsmen."

Three bows lifted and three arrowheads snouted up.

The Djangs did not have the Lohvian longbow; but their Djang bows were superb in their own fashion. Shooting at a flatter trajectory their shafts could carry almost as far as those from a longbow, and at shorter ranges they were deadly.

Delia shot in her longbow first.

The leading flutsman, his feather-streaming hair blowing wildly behind him in the wind of his passage, his accoutrements glittering, his tall aerial spear slanted up and aft, screeched. The rose-fletched shaft pierced him through his face. Delia did not stop to congratulate herself on a fortunate shot, for she had aimed at his body, but whipped out the second arrow.

Tandu loosed and then Dalki.

Neither Djang missed.

Five in ten, six in twelve, were gone.

Four crossbow bolts thudded viciously into the sand and two of the totrixes. One animal was killed instantly; the other, screaming, reared to his feet and tried to bolt, and fell over tangled legs all fouled up in his reins. Delia shut her ears to the sounds.

If these reivers of the sky were the same as those who had slain Pansi and Nath the Jokester, then her heart would harden even more. Either way, she shared most of the philosophy which attempted to stop people from killing her.

Her second shot was flailed away by a stupidly flapping wing. Tandu scored no better and Dalki's arrow skewered into the feathered underside of a fluttrell. The bird toppled forward. His rider went feet-first over the bird's awkward head vane, hit the sand, and was up, raging.

He was the first to land and whip out his sword, abandoning crossbow and bird, and come racing across the sand toward the three in the meager cover of the saddle animals.

Delia put a shaft clear through his bronze-studded leathers. He stopped running forward, yelling like a demon, waving his sword. He stopped. He stood up, the arrow through him. Then he fell down.

The remaining two flutsmen leaped from their birds in gouts of ochre sand. Their faces, hard, grimed, contorted with fury, bore a vague resemblance to human faces. Delia with those faces before her eyes was in no further doubt or wonder that these two had not flown off when their comrades had died. These flutsmen were driven to kill, they had been using kaff, and they were drugged past all reason. They spat foam and screeched, and rushed.

Delia's hand lifted to her right shoulder. Her hand, unblemished by a single ring, snapped forward.

The terchick crossed the lessening distance to the first charging man in a blurred streak of steel. The little throwing knife, sharply-pointed, cunningly balanced, left Delia's hand and sped through empty air and pierced through the right eye of the flutsman. The steel skewered on into his brain. He gyrated for a few foolish moments before he fell down.

The last one barely hesitated—if he hesitated at all—before Tandu's swords went through him and chopped him, both together.

Dalki said, "You always were greedy, Father. I was about to loose—I could have shot you."

Tandu roared, and wiped one of his swords in the sand. "My hide would have turned your shot, Dalki!"

"Well, Father, and mayhap. Next time, allow me to get a look in."

Delia refused to feel faint. After all, what were six dead men more or less in this world of suffering? She was well aware that flutsmen had kissed their families good-bye long before they took up the aerial reiving trade, and the only folk to mourn them would be the members of their own marauding band.

Still, once upon a time, under a certain moon, each one of them had had a mother...

For the sake of Pansi and Nath the Jokester, Delia felt no incongruity in wishing that those mothers had never conceived, or had miscarried, or had drowned their babes in infancy...

And, even that was no good. Had it not been these flutsmen, then it would have been others... You couldn't solve all your problems by killing. That had been tried. It worked for a time; but in the long run you simply finished up with nobody.

"Majestrix?"

She had not spoken; bluff old Tandu was wily enough to know when to jolly even an empress along.

Dalki said: "If ever it was needed to be proved, which it never was and never will be, by Djan, then the queen is a true queen of the Djangs!"

On that, Delia felt it time to gather up the totrixes, make a check, and mount up. Tandu, having come from Djanduin to teach Valkans to fly flutduins had never been a true mercenary, had never become a paktun. Similarly, Dalki was no paktun. They started to mount up.

Understanding this, Delia sighed and then laughed.

"Make a check first. See what these flutsmen have on them that is interesting to us. And, if they have gold, it is ours. Is not this so?"

"Yes, majestrix—"

"Tandu! Now hearken. You and Dalki may call me 'my lady' as well as this tiresome majestrix. You know that."

"Quidang, my lady!"

With that settled, the corpses rifled—they turned up nothing of interest and six leather bags totaling a hundred and twenty-one gold pieces, two hundred and thirty-five silver pieces and not a copper ob among them—the two Djangs and their queen set the totrixes in motion. They walked the animals, husbanding them, and so took their way out of the Ochre Limits.

As they rode Delia pondered. Portents in what had happened alarmed her. Affairs, in her half-brother's kovnate province of Vindelka, were quite clearly not running smoothly.

Flutsmen? Paid guards who attacked unfortunate women?

One would think this was some wild and barbaric land instead of civilized Vallia!

Of course, much of Vallia's civilization had been stripped away during the Time of Troubles, and even now the country was not fully restored. But in Vindelka? She grew a trifle warm at the thought of some of the words she would use when she met Vomanus.

When they reached the river she was again forcefully reminded that this latter-day Empire of Vallia was not the same as the Vallia into which she had been born. She could not plunge in and go for a good long cleansing swim. Jaws and claws... When she was a young girl the rivers had been made safe. Well, as in the case of the prowling leems and other savage animals, one day the rivers and the land would be made safe again.

Reaching a pleasant glade above the riverbank, they camped and cooked a meal. The men brought up as much water as they could in every container that could be pressed into service, and the queen gave herself a thoroughly good wash. Trusting in the glowing radiance of Zim and Genodras, the twin suns, she washed her hair. Some of the scents and unguents that poor Pansi would have used had been smashed in the crash of the airboat; enough remained for her to perfume her hair—subtly—and to make herself feel a little more like Delia. Despite all the titles she had had hung about her, she tended to think of herself just as Delia. Some of her titles she loved; others she was ambivalent about, and a few—a very few—she could not summon up enthusiasm for. She was too sensitive of what they meant actively to despise any one of the collection.

Tandu was fussing.

Delia eyed him.

He started to bang the fire out. "If we leave now, my lady, we will reach Mellinsmot before nightfall."

"Excellent! Then we leave now."

As the twin suns slid down the sky, and the western horizon smoked into jade and ruby flames, it was pleasant to jog along the riverbank, in the sweetness of the late afternoon and early evening, and see ahead the lights of the town waiting to welcome them.

Jogging along, Delia thought of her husband. There was no particular reason not to think of him, and the time of day made no difference, for she thought of him at any time, as, he had told her, he thought of her. Each had to go one way, for a space, until all the dangers were past. Then they would be together and not let anyone or anything part them again, ever...

Riding jolting along on a saddle animal all day, biting on sand and dust, fighting off murderous flutsmen, trying to keep clean and get enough to eat, all this took a toll, drained a girl, set a dull fatigue into her bones so that the prospect of bath and bed pleased her far more than they would ordinarily. Just to wash herself clean, eat a gargantuan supper, and then stretch out and go to sleep!

Marvelous!

Of course, one vital ingredient would be missing tonight; but then he was so often away she had fashioned a life for herself that, half of a full life though it might be, had, perforce, to suffice. He felt exactly the same way.

In the last of the light as the totrixes quickened their six feet, some of the pleasure of the evening waned.

They reached an avenue of tended trees; considerable cultivation had been passed in the gloaming and now they approached the northwest gate of Mellinsmot. The gates stood half-closed and a handful of travelers scurried through, dimly seen figures, to hasten away into the gathering darkness. The people were leaving Mellinsmot and heading along the beaten path by the river.

Tandu offered no comment.

Delia swiveled in the saddle. "Odd," she said. "Folk usually enter a town at night, not leave it."

"Going back to their holdings, my lady," ventured Dalki.

"Probably."

The brick archway echoed their totrix's hooves, and the guard detail would be springing out to challenge them—

There were no guards on the gate of Mellinsmot.

"Odder and odder," said Delia.

Tandu loosened one of his swords, and brought his bow forward, holding it half-drawn, arrow nocked in the practiced archer's grip. Delia brought her own bow up. Dalki, at her back, followed the example of his father and the queen.

Echoes rustled from the brick walls. The streaming radiance of the suns was almost gone. Shadows, plum-colored, bruised with darkness, fell about them.

"The Feathered Risslaca is a comfortable inn, my lady, so I have been told." Tandu did not turn to face Delia as he spoke. Beyond the next edge of twin shadows might lie danger. Tandu kept his gaze darting about, taking in everything, watching for the first suspicious movement. By now they all knew something was wrong in the town of Mellinsmot.

"Or," went on Tandu, "perhaps my lady would sooner go straight to Strom Dogan's villa, here?"

When the strom, who held this town and surrounding lands, his stromnate, at the hands of Kov Vomanus of Vindelka, understood that he was to host the empress, lavish hospitality would be immediately forthcoming. Delia, looking about at the deserted streets, the boarded-up windows, wondered.

A dog slunk away into the enveloping shadows. His tail dangled between his legs. Dalki rode with his head screwed back, alertly scanning every window, every shadowed doorway.

"D'you smell it?" demanded Delia.

"Aye, my lady." Tandu's broad face lifted. "By Djan! Like intestines left out in the suns."

Delia made a face.

"Apt, if unpleasant, Tandu."

The way lay ahead through a crossing, where the houses stood back. One side of the road lay swathed in blackness; the other was mildewed with a ghostly glow of fading red and green. A door opened and a lozenge of yellow light burst across the beaten way. A voice screamed.

A figure fell out of the door, was hurled out, for the violence of its movement sent up a swirl of dust in the half-light. The figure tottered forward, twirled about with flailing arms and as the door slammed shut fell to lie sprawled in the dust.

Delia nudged her totrix forward.

"Caution, my lady!"

Tandu was there, before her, dismounting to bend over the dark sprawled figure. He twitched away a corner of the raggedy blanket that concealed the figure's face.

He jumped back. He jumped back a clear three feet, and stood, frozen.

Delia looked down.

The face had been that of a young girl. No doubt it had been comely, with smiling eyes and smooth cheeks. Now that face was smothered in suppurating sores. The stink broke up as fresh sores burst, to run in greenish pus.

"The Affliction of the Sores of Combabbry!"

Dalki said, his voice high, "Do not touch her, my lady!"

"No." Delia's voice shook despite all she could do to hold herself steady. "This explains all. Mellinsmot is a town of contagion and death!"

Four

Affliction

Serried in rows beneath the gilded ceiling of Strom Dogan's Great Hall the suppurating sufferers lay festering in their sores. Twin white half-moons shone beside Delia's mouth; to disappear instantly as she smiled at the person for whom she ministered. Pus, vomit, blood, excrement, filth and muck—all were as one to Delia. She bathed foreheads in the approved stiffly starched yellow romantic way; she scraped the muck off the floor and scrubbed the strom's boards clean.

He, Strom Dogan nal Mellin, having cowered away in his topmost tower with his family, too frightened to risk contamination even in the short distance out of the town, had been hauled out of it by the empress.

The hauling had been done by Tandu.

"You will give orders to your people, and you will help, Dogan." Delia had spoken in such a way that Dogan's chattering teeth had almost splintered in his frenzy.

Then: "Tandu—you have my permission to pull the strom out by his ears." "Quidang, my lady!"

So—Strom Dogan and his people had, unwillingly and fearfully, been pressed to assist the empress. The Empress of Vallia ordered, organized, controlled. She also wiped up filth and scrubbed floors.

Sickness—the very idea of sickness nauseated her.

When, as a young girl, she had been thrown by a zorca, her immediate reactions had been of fury at herself for so lamentable a display. The second thought had been one of surprise that her zorca, so brave and patient, a marvelous saddle animal, should have thrown her at all. But it was accidental.

Only then—as the third reaction—had she discovered the injury to her leg. She had been made a cripple. She dragged one leg after her like a stamped-on crab.

Getting over that, as her only way of phrasing it to herself, had involved a secret visit to the Swinging City of Aphrasöe arranged by her father the emperor, and then a surreptitious dip in the Sacred Pool of Baptism of the River Zelph arranged by the wild and savage clansman who was to become her husband. So she knew about these things.

The stink in the strom's Great Hall was prodigious.

Sweet Ibroi was burned by the bushel. Water was continually sluiced down over the floor, to be swept away in foaming sheets of brown and yellow and green. Sometimes the water swept away red—when someone's sores burst past all enduring. All the anti-pollutants available were used.

How the contagion spread even the needlemen could not swear to. Better not to touch a sufferer. Better not to breathe too close to the air he or she had breathed. But, after that, what gods or demons hurled the sickness from one poor wight to the next?

Pungent ibroi, a capital disinfectant much used to wash down slaves' quarters when Vallia dealt in slaves, before the present emperor outlawed slavery, was consumed in vast quantities. At least, along with its sweet-smelling fellow it freshened the atmosphere.

Strom Dogan, a bag of lard in Delia's private opinion, quivered and shook. His wife, the Stromni, was made of sterner stuff. Her fears were for her family. These, Delia excused from caring for the sick on the understanding they would roll bandages. The town was dying. Someone had to care for the sick.

If that person happened to be the empress—well, and wasn't that one reason she was empress at all?

"But, majestrix—your poor hands!"

"Do not worry about my hands, Stromni. They are used to hard work."

Stromni Elspa shook her head and her soft brown Vallian hair slipped a little from the retaining pins. She could not understand the majesty and might of an empress in these conditions. By Opaz! If she, Stromni Elspa nal Mellin, was empress, she'd get the servants to handle the mess and take herself off into the country very smartly. If her husband had a little more moral fiber, they could have galloped through the infected streets and been clear away by now. They would not have been caught by this domineering woman and forced to act like common servants. The only reason Stromni Elspa tolerated the disgrace lay in the half-comforting thought that she must be storing up favors for herself with the empress.

Cartloads of little blue flowers were brought in. They trundled in through the open gates. The flowers had been culled from where they grew in weed-like profusion among the cultivations. Dalki rode out with the carts and rode back with them. No one ran away.

There were two sorts of little blue flowers. One sort possessed a tiny silver heart on each petal. These were vilmy flowers. The others were fallimy flowers.

From the vilmy flowers was made up a paste that soothed the sores and eased the pains of the sufferers.

From the fallimy flowers was made up a paste used in the normal way to scour cisterns. Now it scoured and cleansed everything that came into contact with the sickness.

Delia did not personally inspect every flower petal to make sure. If some soothing ointment paste went onto the floor, not too much harm would be done. If scouring paste was rubbed into a sore—no, that would not do. Delia gave strict—very strict—orders about that.

Stromni Elspa looked puzzled.

"But, majestrix! I mean—whoever heard of anyone putting fallimy paste on their body? It would—it would—"

"It would scour their chest most thoroughly."

"Majestrix?"

"You'd be surprised. And I laughed."

At Elspa's bewildered expression Delia bustled into caring for the next row of patients. If the sores could be kept clean, if the patient could be kept cool, there was a chance of recovery. Much of the sherbet drink, parclear, was consumed. Three days of terrible suffering, with suppurating sores breaking out all over the body, and three days of fighting to contain them and keep the patient cool, and then, if the gods smiled, the worst was over, the crisis past.

And, anyway, Delia couldn't explain about the little silver heart on the little blue flower petals. Poor Thelda! She always meant well...

To think about the past was as fruitless now as to think about the future. All she could do was work and work and go on working. She took this dreadful attack of pestilence in the town as a personal affront. Detesting every moment of it, fighting nausea, biting down on vomit, she forced herself to care for the sick.

Tandu made her rest. He did this with such auspicious tact and understanding for a Dwadjang as melted Delia's heart. It was clear, if she did not let herself rest and sink her abused body down into sleep, then Tandu would feel personally responsible for the consequences. Knowing her Djangs, she was aware that it was not beyond the bounds of probability that, in order to save his Queen of Djanduin, he would personally slay every last sufferer. Then, the queen could rest.

For some folk, and for Djangs, that was a normal way of thought.

The dead were burned.

Covered of faces, with gloved hands, the people dragged out the corpses and piled them up. The smell was not really tolerable; but with Delia, Empress of Vallia, standing so tall and firm, grasping a ghastly limb to help haul, gently pushing a twisted body up onto the pyre, no one could hang back. The strom and Stromni, gagging, took their part. The bodies flopped, some already swollen, some with tongues jutting, some just indescribable lumps of offal.

The flames licked all clean.

The bodies melted and ran, sloughing away. Hair frizzled. The corpses crisped.

When the last were burned, there were more. In the town of Mellinsmot the doctors had been the first to die. Only one needleman remained, and he looked shriveled at the enormity of the catastrophe. As one batch of dead was burned, so another was dragged out. The process deadened the mind and calloused the spirit.

But the avenging spirits of whatever gods or demons had sent this torment upon the people would not be appeased. Townsfolk huddled in the churches and the temple, and there the Affliction of the Sores of Combabbry sought them out, and consumed them.

The needleman shook his head helplessly. His face looked like a chunk of indigestible meat after a dog had chewed and rejected it. His eyes lurked in shadowed pits beneath his eyebrows.

"We can do nothing, majestrix, nothing."

"You can, Agron the Needle! You can alleviate their pain."

Agron's leather wallet shook as he reached in to fetch out fresh acupuncture needles. In the cunning Kregen way he could insert a needle and twirl it and banish pain. He could not halt the onset or the course of the disease.

One of the churches, the structure of crumbly brick dedicated to Flamdelka the Gatherer, commandeered as an emergency hospital, was crammed with sufferers. Flamdelka the Gatherer was one of the older spirits of this part of Vallia, only half-believed in by most folk, still worshipped by many whose business took them across the Ochre Limits.

Dalki walked his totrix up slowly and dismounted. He, like everyone else, looked exhausted.

"My lady. My father bids me to remind you that you promised to rest now—"

"Yes, Dalki. Later." Delia pointed up. "Look, Dalki. A warvol flying over, looking for food."

The black wings spiraled over the church of Flamdelka. Dead bodies were being carried out and placed in carts. The smell did not offend the warvol. He was a kind of vulture, not nicknamed Rippasch, and he was hungry.

"Very good, my lady," said Dalki, and lifted his bow.

Agron the Needle nodded. He did not know how the disease was communicated. But if the warvol fed on a dead person and flew away—who knew where he might go and who knew where he might carry the disease? If he did at all.

Dalki loosed. The shaft pierced the shining black feathers. Without a cry, the warvol pitched onto the roof of Mother Hansi's Banje Store, and fell plump into the street. The corpse would be thrown onto the pyres along with the other corpses.

If she was honest with herself, Delia felt she ought to admit that some venom for Rippasch impelled her in that deed. The warvol, like Rippasch, cleaned up dead bodies, prevented the kind of disease under which they now suffered. But, in stripping an already diseased corpse, the bird might spread the contagion. Of course, it could be spread on the air, by the skin, through tears... No one knew.

She was persuaded to rest only by the consideration that if she collapsed then she would only be hindering the efforts of the others. Out of pride could come blind selfishness.

"My lady?"

"Yes, Dalki. I will rest."

Walking slowly back along Fruiterer's Street and so across the dusty square of Palm Kyro, she could feel the way her legs ached. Her back ached, too; but in a different way. Dalki, tight-lipped that the queen had chosen to walk back to the strom's grand villa instead of riding, walked a few paces in rear, leading his animal. His father had no need of dinning into his ears every few hours the sobering thought of how lucky they both were in being able to attend on the queen. As a Djang and a Vallian, Dalki needed his queen and his empress, and he was perfectly well aware of his good fortune.

There were no airboats in Mellinsmot. Most of those in private hands had been used by their owners to fly away to safety. There were very few of those. The strom's two fliers, of which he had been inordinately proud, had been commandeered by the soldiers and the mercenaries had robbed him, taken off in his airboats, and not even wished him a remberee. The black fliers used by a local Company of Friends to ship in ice had likewise all been seized. Delia was informed that in four days' time a flier might be expected bringing ice. In that time those sufferers whose temperatures rose too high would die.

Stromni Elspa wanted to fuss. Delia was brisk with the woman; not unkind. At last she could stretch out in the bed in the room they had placed at her disposal. Either Tandu or Dalki, or both, would remain just outside the door and not even an earthquake would shift them.

She thought of the poor people of Mellinsmot, of Opaz, of her friends, of her children and of her husband. Then she went to sleep. She awoke early, washed and dressed, ate a huge breakfast, and stuck straight into tending for the sick, of caring and cleaning, of soothing and swabbing. The routine established itself. Until fresh cases ceased, the routine would continue.

As for herself, she had no fears. She was concerned for her two Djangs, and kept them away from any too close contacts with diseased victims. If the damage was not already done, they might escape. Not everyone caught the Affliction of the Sores of Combabbry. The stench hung over the town. She had bathed in the Sacred Pool in far Aphrasöe. That had conferred upon her a miraculous ability to recover rapidly from wounds and to resist infections. No, she had no fears for herself, and in this knew she cheated. Naturally, this made her take on greater burdens, exposing herself recklessly. In turn, this distressed her friends. It was all a mix and extraordinarily difficult to find the correct path of conduct.

On the day when the airboat bringing the ice arrived only ten people were so close to dying that the ice would make no difference. The three days of sores and the three days of temperature rise followed by a decline to death had already spelled destruction for too many souls. Now, the ice would make all the difference.

Even then, Tandu and Dalki with a couple of the strom's retainers only just managed to hold onto the airboat and persuade the crew to land. The smell warned them. Dalki, in particular, was most fierce.

He waved his sword under the nose of the skipper of the airboat.

"Put this voller back down, dom! Or you'll grin from a mouth under your chin!"

"It is death—" The skipper, a fat and jowly man, quivered and sweated.

"For you—yes! Down!"

The voller landed and at once the ice was unloaded.

Delia said to Tandu: "Your son cuts a fine figure, Tandu. When all this is settled, what will you two do?"

"Why, my lady, go back to guard duty, I suppose."

"We shall see. The emperor has need of good friends. I think a place will be found for you—if you so choose."

"I would choose so, my lady."

"Good. And Dalki shall be a Deldar at once."

Tandu beamed. The ice smoked as it was hurried away covered in sacking. "That pleases me, my lady. I give you thanks—"

"Of course, one cannot really have a son outranking his father. It is known. But, in this, I think you will have to be a Hikdar. I can see no other course."

"My lady!"

Delia turned away abruptly. Often and often she had discussed this thorny problem with her husband. How easy to dish out ranks and titles! How much pleasure it gave to reward good friends! And how selfish it was, giving of honor and seeing how easy it was, and taking the pleasure. Tandu was pleased and Dalki would be pleased and she was pleased so where was the error? Yet she worried over this as she knew her husband worried, also.

With the coming of the ice a crisis point was passed. From that moment no more people who could be saved died. And, significantly, there were no more outbreaks. Those men and women who had remained to fight the disease and care for the sick ceased to be stricken in their turn.

That evening by the light of a samphron oil lamp, Delia composed the necessary letter.

It was brief, said all that was appropriate, expressed regrets that she had unavoidably missed the wedding of her half-brother Vomanus. Early next morning she sent off the ice flier with the letter, charged strictly to fly at once to Delka Ob and seek audience of the kov. Her seal, stamped across the ribbons fastening the letter, would be proof enough of the importance of the errand of uncouth icemen.

She could not leave yet. There were still sufferers to be tended. Two days later a voller flew in. A girl dressed in leathers stepped down, the rapier swinging at her side, her face bright and eager, her color up, her head high.

"Majestrix!" she said, advancing with her lithe step. Then, in a softer tone, she said, "May Dee-Sheon have you in her keeping."

"Yzobel!" said Delia.

"This is a dreadful place. You are safe?"

"Perfectly. And happy to see you."

Yzobel wore white leathers. Her body complemented the beauty of her face. Yet her rapier and main gauche that hung from silver lockets were practical, hard weapons. This was a girl who could turn her hand to fighting as well as nursing. In that, she mirrored others like her.

Walking with Yzobel into the shade and already looking forward to a glass of parclear, a plate of miscils and palines, and a good chat, Delia was not surprised that Yzobel had arrived. Once the ice-flier had reached Delka Ob, the disappearance of the empress would be explained. One of the sisters, at least, would be immediately sent.

"I came on ahead," said Yzobel. "The others will be here very soon. They were gathering medicaments. But I have a message, majestrix."

"Oh?"

"The mistress wishes to see you. You are summoned to Lancival. We should leave at once."

"Of course," said Delia, Empress of Vallia, Sister of the Rose. "I am ready. Let us go now."

Five

Lancival

"Returning to Lancival is like feeling your mother's arms enfolding you." So had said a long-dead sister, and despite the sentimentality of that, Delia admitted its truth. Other sisters had said similar sentiments. Delia likened the feeling of going back to Lancival to resting her head on her mother's breast. This Delia regarded as sickly sentimentality—and, also, admitted of its truth. Her own mother had died when she was young, a tragedy she believed she had surmounted.

Lancival. Lancival of the red roofs and the ivy-clad walls. Lancival of the calmness and the peace, the singing and the quietness and the harsh banging of steel on steel and the panting exertions of girls in combat. Lancival of the Disciplines known only to women. Lancival of the Whip. Lancival of the Claw.

Not because she was the Empress of Vallia, but because she was an initiate of the SoR of a certain exaltedness, Delia possessed her own room in one of the collegiate buildings. A mere cubbyhole, it contained a narrow bed, a set of bookshelves, a dressing table with brushes and combs of plain wood and bristle unadorned and decorated with not a single stroke from a paintbrush, a single design from a chisel. A wardrobe held various robes required by the Order, a selection of undergarments of the most Spartan kind, sandals and fighting boots, a cloak and an enveloping black leather hat with a black band. The sheets were plain yellow, the pillowslip plain yellow, the towels draped over the washbasin plain yellow. The mirror set above the dressing table was not quite large enough to reflect all of her face at the same time. She was adept at tilting her proud and imperious head about, like a gawky girl, to see what was necessary to see.

This room was one of a double row along a third-story corridor, each cubbyhole like its neighbor as a pea in a pod. This particular room had once been occupied by a sister of the SoR, now long dead, renowned in the sorority's annals as Velda the Tempestuous.

The stories clustered about Velda emphasized the usual normality of her character, even her sweetness of personality. The stories told those who listened that when Velda met injustice she could not control her temper. Her temper was fierce, vicious, intemperate. A mistress of the Claw and Whip, no accurate tally had been kept of the unseemly wights she had dispatched to the Ice Floes of Sicce, she clawed and slashed them all indifferently if they offended her keen sense of justice.

This room was, therefore, always known as Velda's Room.

Just why the mistress had seen fit to assign Velda's Room to Delia of Delphond puzzled Delia. Now, she no longer concerned herself over that order of puzzlement. The room represented a haven at certain times, a sense of penitence, a place where she might strip away everything that was not Delia.

She was always glad and relieved to sink down on the narrow bed in her room at Lancival, and always ready and relieved to close the door upon that room and leave to go about her business in the wider world.

High on one wall hung a portrait of Velda the Tempestuous. It showed her in the full regalia of white leathers, long-legged, scowling of face, the Whip coiled along her arm, the Claw extended menacingly. Her rapier and left-hand dagger snugged about a narrow waist. Her hips flared in her arrogant, menacing pose. Her long white leather boots were mud-splashed. This small touch had always to Delia brought the image of Velda alive, as though the sister could not be dead but ready to answer the summons to prayer, to be met in the refectory, to be engaged in discussion at any of the formal functions of the SoR.

The Sisters of the Rose were mindful of tradition, and looked to the future, and kept themselves secret in the world in which they labored.

Beside the head of the bed stood a heavy wooden chest on legs which, in that austere room, were incongruously carved into the likenesses of rose trellises. The doors in the front of the chest were locked. The top supported a few essential items of toiletries.

Now Delia took off her raggedy russets and threw them into the wicker basket by the door. Novices would collect the laundry by rota, and wash and repair her clothes. Once, she had labored on those duties here.

She went to the end picture of the row that hung beneath the portrait of Velda. Before she opened the picture on its hinge away from the wall, she stood, brooding on the line of portraits. Each was mounted in a narrow plain frame of varnished wood. There were fifteen. As always, she gazed at the face tenth along. That frame, like the first six, was surmounted by a small nosegay, a posy, of roses carved and painted. The face looked back with its brown Vallian eyes, gentle, sweet, stunningly beautiful. Delia sighed.

Life was brutal.

You tried. You attempted to make what you could of this puzzle Opaz had given you. Yes, her grandparents, represented in the first four portraits, were dead, and it was seemly that after full lives of better than two hundred years, they should be gathered into the Benediction of Opaz the Everlasting. And her father and mother; death had claimed them. As for the seventh portrait—a little frown dented Delia's forehead. She'd left him after the Battle of the Incendiary Vosks in Hamal, unwillingly, but committed. No doubt he was off swinging his damned great Krozair longsword and adventuring in places she would rather not hear about until afterward.

As for her son Drak, in the next picture, he was being groomed to become the Emperor of Vallia and take over from his father. When he did so, Delia fully intended to speak rather intemperately to the mistress, and demand that she be allowed to join her husband in whatever nefarious goings on he was up to. They owed her that much, the SoR, surely?

She held the first picture open, still pondering.

The picture after Drak's showed Lela who was known as Jaezila. Soon there would have to be a further portrait placed below that, a picture of Prince Tyfar of Hamal. And the quicker those two decided to marry the better and so put every one of their friends out of their tantalizing frustrations at the idiocy of two young lovers.

And so to the tenth portrait.

Below it, almost a part of it, had been fixed a much smaller portrait, practically a miniature. This showed a man with black curly hair bunched on his head, with a hawklike face, bold and arrogant, with two blue bolts for eyes. His chin was like the ram of a swifter. Delia had never met this man, this Gafard, Rog of Guamelga, the King's Striker, Prince of the Central Sea, the Reducer of Zair, Sea-Zhantil, Ghittawrer of Genod. He had married her daughter Velia and their daughter's portrait was affixed as the last in the row. This showed a babyish face, and Delia resigned herself to having a fresh portrait commissioned, for little Didi was growing up.

The small posy of red roses was echoed by a single rose fixed above the portrait of Gafard, the King's Striker, Sea-Zhantil.

Delia swung the door that was the first picture back and forth. Still looking at the face of Velia, she reached into the space beyond the picture and took out a bronze key. The handle was cast into the form of a stemmed rose.

Next to Velia her twin brother's face stared in powerful authority from the painted panel. This was Zeg, who had been called Seg in honor of Seg Segutorio. Now Zeg was King of Zandikar, and the face of his wife, Queen Miam, smiled from her own portrait. One day she and Zeg would have to visit Vallia, or Delia and her husband would have to make the long journey to the inner sea of Kregen, the Eye of the World.

As for the next portrait—and here Delia sighed in a way far removed from her patient long-suffering anguish over Velia—this was her daughter Dayra, ferocious, mischievous, led into evil ways. This was Dayra, known as Ros the Claw. She it was, surmised Delia, who was the cause of this summons to Lancival.

Dayra's twin, Jaidur, known as Vax Neemusbane, looked out from the next picture, and with him his wife, Lildra. They were now King and Queen of Hyrklana. Jaidur had served the SoR very well on secret errands, many of them not even known to his mother. Now he was settling down nicely with Lildra in the island kingdom of Hyrklana. A touch of real responsibility had worked wonders for his wildness, a wild streak he shared with his twin sister and which she showed no signs of outgrowing.

The penultimate portrait, of Velia, a daughter born later, loved and named for the older Velia, again would soon require replacement, for Velia was growing up. Delia hoped the mistress would allow a visit with Velia here in Lancival, for Velia was being educated and trained by the SoR. It might not be possible. Discipline sometimes imposed a harshness well-nigh insupportable to a mother.

She held the bronze rose-key in her hand.

She knew—she had been told—that her dip in the Sacred Pool of Baptism in far Aphrasöe had conferred upon her a thousand years of life. She did not age. She had seen to it that her children and her friends and loved ones had also bathed. Like her husband, she had for the moment pushed aside the unanswerable questions this longevity aroused. If the time ever came for drastic measures, she, at least, would be ready.

Crossing to the chest with the rose-arbor legs, she opened the front doors.

She took out a silver-mounted balass wood box, the wood hard and black and shining. She opened the box. From it she took a thick, black, snakelike whip. This she put on the bed, quickly.

From its velvet bed she lifted her Claw.

Shining, razor-sharp steel, clawed with talons, the thing fitted up her left arm with steel splines. She turned it over. It shone with oil. With it she had been trained to rip a person's face off.

She put it back, quickly, replaced the whip, shut the lid, and pushed the box back into the chest.

Despite what the mistress might say, Delia did not intend—just yet and so soon—to wear the Claw and carry the Whip.

"Not," she said, half to herself, "not yet, by Vox!"

She shook her brown hair free about her naked shoulders. Then she picked up two fluffy yellow towels and walked along the corridor to the bathrooms. She left the door of Velda's Room open.

Steam engulfed her in the suite of bathrooms. Naked women walked about, took the steam, talked, swam in the pool. Delia was quick. At this time she wished merely to wash off everything she could of her stay in Mellinsmot.

She was not sure; but it seemed more than likely that Tandu had also written a note, sent by the icemen. He had expressed no surprise at her sudden determination on departure.

"Yes, my lady. We can do all that is necessary here until the sisters arrive."

"May Djan go with you, my lady," Dalki had said, looking up as the flier lifted.

They had called the remberees, cheerfully. Yes, Delia reflected, toweling herself briskly and bringing up the circulation, yes, it was almost certain. Her two Djangs must have said that the empress needed to be hoicked out of the plague spot at once. This was the only way she could be commanded to leave Mellinsmot.

But, all the same, she still would bet that Dayra was the cause...

Many of the women splashing about and gossiping and taking the steam were known to her. Many more were not. You could not expect to know every single girl personally who went through Lancival. And, of course, a goodly number of highly respected sisters of the SoR never went through Lancival at all.

She exchanged a few words with women if they talked first, giving not the Lahal form of greeting of the outside world, but the SheonFaril—the Sheonli in its usual abbreviated form. Two women near her under the hot air funnels which teased the hair into a glowing sweetness were wrapped up in each other's news.

"Taken her off, my dear, without consent."

"Did you have to castrate him?"

"No. I'd have liked to, but it was thought not necessary. The poor girl— well, she was only a Sister of Samphron, but they're not too bad."

"And her parents?"

"Everyone suffers after the Time of Troubles, although the new emperor has worked wonders. Oh, yes, they were only too happy to make a gift to the SoR. I think the mistress has dedicated that sum to some new curtains for the refectory."

"We need some of the targets to be restuffed. The girls seem to knock them to pieces wonderfully quickly these days."

"I know! It is these new bows. They are so much more powerful and accurate than our old ones."

Delia smiled and let the warm air flow over her head, turning her shoulders to feel the grateful heat spreading down. Soon she was dry and her hair, carefully prepared by one of the superior novices, gleamed with its auburn tints through the Vallian brown. Naturally, she wore no jewels.

Walking back to Velda's Room she saw Yzobel waiting inside. Yzobel wore a rose-colored gown with a silver belt and dagger. She looked splendid.

"The mistress is waiting?"

"Yes, Delia. She says that she thinks you have had enough time to cleanse a regiment of Jikai Vuvushis."

"If ever you become the mistress, Yzobel—and you might, you might—I trust you will be as intolerant. It tones up the muscles."

Yzobel laughed.

Delia put on her underthings which were not of sensil, not even of silk, but of a plain smooth cotton. They happened to be scarlet. Had she been intending to wear her pale lemon-colored dress—in the color called laypom of which she was fond—she would have worn appropriately colored undergarments. As it was, when she put on the rose-colored gown, fastening it with bone buttons, what she was wearing underneath would remain a mystery.

Her sandals were flat of sole and heel, fastened by a mere three latchings of simple leather. Her belt, like Yzobel's, was fashioned from silver links. Her dagger was the long thin dagger of Vallia. She took no other weapons of steel.

From a drawer in the chest she took out her two brooches.

One was the regular circlet of roses of the SoR.

The other was small and neat, a jeweled representation of a hubless nine-spoked wheel. Delia owned more than one of these brooches. She pinned it to the rose dress firmly.

She saw Yzobel's little frown, a dint of her lip as her teeth caught.

"I know, Yzobel. But the mistress cannot deny my womanhood."

"She would be the last to do that!"

Delia nodded her head, agreeing. "Do you really need new curtains in the refectory? I heard Keshni and Lovosa talking."

"So you heard of Lovosa's latest? She was most wroth they did not let her unman him. He deserved it."

"Probably. I was not there."

Again Yzobel's lip dented under her teeth. "Yes, and we do need new curtains. A thousand orphans were discovered wandering in the Lower Mai Hills—"

"Wandering?"

"Yes. They fondly imagined they were a war-band ready to fight the invaders. Some of them were barely seven years old."

"So they proved expensive."

"That is one reason we are here. As for the curtains, we do need them. I, for one, do not care if the old ones fall to pieces."

"Nor I."

Going along the corridors and down the stairs, Delia was well aware that by saying that was one reason they were here, Yzobel did not mean that Delia had been summoned here by the mistress to contribute gold. Yzobel meant that succoring orphans was one part of the reason for the existence of the SoR.

One part, an old and original, of a surety, but in these days a part that had to share resources.

She was the empress. Well, for what that was worth when set beside the work these women did to the glory of Opaz and Vallia, she had already dedicated that part of her life. The mistress would be the first to explain that a sorority that did not exert every sinew to gather in revenue from everyone, high and low, rich and poor alike, would wither. The Empress of Vallia, in great fashion, could bestow a chest of gold. Had done so. But if every sister did not make her contribution, then the feeling of responsibility died. Unpalatable facts to some, these were, and Delia knew that. As for her own financial affairs, she had never considered herself to be a rich woman. Training with the SoR had engendered in her an understanding of the satisfactions of simplicity. That was just as well, considering the troubled times through which the country had gone and was still, by Vox, going through right now. Every copper ob they could scrape up had to go to the Treasury to pay for the upkeep of the country, pay the army, buy saddle animals, both of the ground and the air, pay for education, pay for a thousand clamorous demands of empire.

She put a hand to the plain white leather pouch on the silver belt. Among the items there—a comb, a kerchief, a few pins, odds and ends—could be found not a single bottle of scent.

Scent cost money. Perfume cost more. The SoR relied on gifts together with some income from their holdings in Companies of Friends to keep them going. The lands around Lancival within its mellow valley supported them in the way of most of the food they required. They did not squander their money on resources.

All the same, perfume was a vital part of a woman's style; the SoR were not foolish enough to prohibit its use.

Natilma na Stafoing passed Delia in the shining hall leading to the lavender court. Natilma smiled. A remarkable woman, robust and yet elegant, with long hair done into coils, she wore hunting leathers and there was blood on her gloves.

"Sheonli, Delia! How nice!"

Delia smiled and spoke for a few moments. Natilma was one of the more senior sisters, and was well spoken of in the line of accession to the mistress. As they talked with the radiance of Zim and Genodras, all a lake of rubies and emeralds, flooding about them, Yzobel fidgeted. Natilma observed, and smiled again, and went on talking.

Lansi ti High Ochrun came by, and stopped to talk. She, too, with her copper hair and heavy mouth, was high in the councils of the SoR, another prospective mistress.

Yzobel shuffled her sandaled feet.

Taking pity, Delia laughed, and said: "I must really go. The mistress is waiting."

So, lightly, Delia walked out into the lavender courtyard into the radiance of the suns.

"If I were mistress," said Yzobel ominously, "I wonder what I would do about those two."

"Well, you are too young. And when you reach your hundred, they will probably not be here."

Then Delia checked herself. It was extraordinarily difficult to reconcile herself to this unexpected longevity. She was not at all sure that she wanted it. When Yzobel reached her hundred she would enter the ranks of those sisters who might look, one day, to become mistress. She would look very little different from the way she looked now. Only by the tiniest marks could one Kregan judge the age of another.

And Delia would look the young girl she truly was until she was a thousand. Was that nice? Well, time would tell.

At least four of the women who happened to be passing and stopped for a moment to chat as Delia made her way to the mistress's tower did not, she judged, happen to be passing by chance.

Yzobel clicked her dagger.

"Brazen," she said, and her nostrils pinched in.

Yzobel could get away with outrageous behavior, and Delia knew it. In the normal way of the Discipline, no sister could speak thus of another without reprimand. But, there was something planned in the way the ranking sisters just happened to be walking meekly along as Delia went toward the mistress.

Nothing overt was said. Just making their marks, as it were. Delia fancied there would be more making of marks yet, before they ranked their Deldars and got down to the politics of the affair.

The mistress of the Sisters of the Rose could have her apartments in no other tower than the Tower of the Rose.

Thither Delia went.

The grey stone walls, ivy clad, appeared to her to shed a cooling benediction from the heat of the suns. The archway closed above her head. The rugs upon the floor were not all of Walfarg weave; there were many lesser carpets to cushion the feet. Up the blackwood stairs, a single sharp ring upon the bell, and the door opening and old Rosala smiling and beaming and stepping back to usher in the sister come to see the mistress.

"You are well, Rosala?"

"A touch of gyp in my left elbow, my dear. But I'm as chirpy as a cricket and shall be two hundred and ten next birthday."

They went along the carpeted corridor whose walls were adorned with the trophies of various past deeds. The mistress's room at the end looked just the same to Delia. Then she frowned. In one corner a curtain was half-drawn across a bed. It was a proper bed, as anyone could see with half an eye, not a day-lounger.

That bed was a new touch, an addition to the usual.

That did not, of course, mean it was abnormal.

Most of the drapes were of that pale sheer rose color that verged on the opalescence of a Zimful sky at evening, when Genodras had sunk below the horizon. When Zim sank first in the long cycles of alternations, then the evening sky held overtones of quite different natures. Against the walls and drapes the furniture stood as ever, the familiar pieces, polished, cared for, each one in its place and each one fulfilling its own duty. The desk, of balass wood, still angled across the curve of the southwestern tower window.

The mistress did not rise to greet Sister Delia.

She used one pale hand to gesture to the seat set four square before the desk. Delia sat.

Winsome to suggest this brought back vivid memories of herself as a young girl. Trite to suggest that, and trite to ignore the feeling.

The scent of flowers banked in their troughs along the wall brought back the memories! The flick-flick plant on a windowsill, set there to catch flies, would as ever have to be hand fed. A new tang hung in the air. Delia, gently, tested its meaning. Medicaments. Well, then, and perhaps now she understood a little more of the chance meetings and the markings of marks that were no chance.

"Faril Sheon, Delia," said the mistress in all formality. Her voice breathed more memories; but the tone was weaker, the full bell-note fallen away. Delia sat straight, heels together, hands in her lap, head up. She looked at the mistress.

Here in the heart of the heart of the Sisters of the Rose there was no need for the small secret sign.

"SheonFaril, mistress," said Delia.

"I am more than glad to see you. You have worried me."

The mistress had once been able to lift a full-bodied man above her head and throw him up a flight of stairs. Now she could do that, perhaps, to a fair-sized dog. Her face, unlined, bore only the marks of wisdom and experience and pain engraved upon it in the planes and the shadows. Her eyes were as bright and brown as cobnuts as ever they had been.

Like Delia, she wore the rose-colored gown. Her belt from which swung the long Vallian dagger was of plain rope, untwisted, raw. Her hair, brown as a thrush's wing, held her face in a composition at once peaceful, dominating, gentle and harsh, all in that puzzle of vaol-paol that is a woman's face. In that eternal vaol-paol, the Great Circle of Universal Existence, was to be found more than mere philosophy.

"I grieve to have caused you concern." Delia's gaze lingered on the half-curtained bed in its alcove corner. "I apologize for my daughter Dayra. I assume that is why I am here."

At the mistress's expression, Delia added, annoyed at the tinge of alarm in her voice: "It is not little Velia?"

"No. Velia is a rose beyond price. Nor—this time—is it your Princess Dayra, who calls herself Ros the Claw."

Delia felt the breath in her. If this was bad news, she must find the strength to bear it. She said nothing. She waited as the Disciplines taught.

"You have seen my bed. I use it, in here, rather than waste my meager strength retiring to my chamber in the evening and dragging myself here in the morning."

"Mistress—"

"Wait, my daughter, wait. Once I was as you now are. But that was long ago. It is time I sought peace with Opaz. Time I handed over to stronger—"

"Mistress!"

"Do not grieve, Delia, who was Delia Valhan, and is now Delia Prescot, Empress of Vallia."

"You know that means—"

"It means a very great deal. But I am going, no one and nothing can halt me, and you, Delia, are my chosen successor. You are to be the mistress of the Sisters of the Rose."

Six

"Take this gift away from me."

"No."

"You have been selected by me, Delia, to be the mistress. Your election will follow."

"No." There was no hesitation, no doubt, in her. This was not for her. "No, mistress. I am aware of what this means. You know I am aware. But I cannot."

The mistress placed a plain square of yellow linen to her mouth. Her coughs were tiny scrabblings, as of nestlings.

"How can you refuse?"

"I do not know how. I know only that I must."

One narrow hand, doubled over, ridged and veined blue, crept onto the desk top. That hand trembled.

"Delia—"

"I cannot—I feel pain, and shame, and dishonor—all foolish feelings, I know. But take this gift away from me."

The mistress said: "Once I had a husband. He was all the world to me. But he died. Once I had children. One is still alive—somewhere. All you will need of husband and children you will find here, in Lancival."

"That I can believe, yet cannot—"

"Once I was called Elomi the Shining. I was born in Valka. Did you know that?"

"I knew."

"Valka is so beautiful it can break the heart. Yet Lancival is—"

"I cannot be the mistress, mistress. Do not ask it of me."

"And if I—?"

"You would not command. It is not in—"

"But if I did?"

"You will not."

The mistress sat back in the wide-armed overstuffed chair. She appeared to shrink. "No," she said in that forlorn whisper. "No. I would not."

For a moment, silence enfolded the two. The mistress looked across at a side table where stood a crystal parclear set, the glasses sparkling. Instantly, Delia rose, crossed to the table and poured a glass of parclear, the sherbet drink fizzing in crystal abandon. The mistress sipped, and then drank. Her neck looked fragile as she swallowed.

Delia made no move to pour parclear for herself until the mistress nodded.

A moment later, the fizz stinging her mouth, Delia was ready to battle on against an unwanted fate.

Like any general swinging his troops across a battlefield to search out a fresh opening for an advance, the mistress took up a fresh subject.

"Your husband is well?"

"When I last saw him. We had just won a great battle—"

"A disgusting business of Incendiary Vosks. We heard. The SoR must do all we can against these Shanks that raid us and seek to enslave us."

"That is one of the great aims in our lives that prevents me from accepting."

"Are there not secret societies of men? They may not lay claim to our prestige. But they exist."

"That is true. My husband has never belonged to any of them in Vallia—"

"I hear differently, Delia!"

Delia smiled. This tack would not take the mistress far along the road to converting her.

"You mean the Kroveres of Iztar? Men said, when the KRVI was formed, that my husband was too proud to join one of their already existing secret orders, but must create his own. That, I need hardly say, was not true."

"No. I imagine not. And Zena Iztar would not be fooled by mere men."

"Assuredly not!"

"I have grave news concerning new Orders. There is a new Order that troubles me."

"I would have thought we women had enough already."

"In view of the new one, I agree. In some of the continents of Kregen women are not regarded in the same way they are regarded here in Vallia. In some places women have to find themselves, understand their rightful place, think of themselves as people, grow in understanding. In some places they are not treated as equals."

"Yes."

"You chose to take your husband's name when you married. You need not have done."

"I wished it. My husband is as much a Valhan as am I."

"That is true. In some places women have only a given name until they marry. They are locked into a way of thinking about themselves that—in our eyes—demeans them, and yet which they, themselves, fail to grasp. When women in those places revolt, the consequences can be ugly. Of course, in the end, it will come all right. But the learning process is painful."

Delia knew the mistress was saying this as a part of her tactical advance. She listened dutifully.

"They overreact, hate everything that is male, and carry on in ways that, while ugly, are perfectly understandable. That is the nature of revolution."

Delia found herself saying, "We have had experiences of revolutions."

"Two, at least, involved women. There was Queen Fahia of Hyrklana. And the Empress Thyllis of Hamal. The SoR played some part there."

"I know and joy in it."

"I wish first to speak to you of your friend, Jilian Sweet-Tooth."

Delia waited.

"She is a sister. She is a consummate artist with the Whip and the Claw. She is a good friend to you and your husband and those of your children she has met. Yet she sorely worries me."

"Tell me, mistress."

"I will! Do not deceive yourself on that! This new order of which I spoke. Jilian is being drawn to it. Most of the sisters composing this Order come from the SoR. There are a few from the Sisters of Samphron, the Sisters of the Sword, one or two others. Even the Little Sisters of Opaz have been sucked in. This could prove a most grave crisis."

"If they adhere to our principles—"

"That is a matter of conjecture. They are taking a new and hard line. They call themselves the Sisters of the Whip. They place the symbol of the Whip above all others."

Thinking of that thick black lash of vileness safely locked in its box, Delia felt the ominous forebodings.

"You know, mistress, I prefer the rapier and main gauche, the bow, the terchick—and this new sword my husband and his armorers have developed, the drexer."

"Yet your friend Jilian is very apt with the Whip."

"Very—apt."

"We shall not cease from teaching the disciplines of the Claw and the Whip here, at Lancival. But the Sisters of the Whip..." The mistress stopped speaking and put her narrow doubled-up hand to her side. Her face remained unmoved. Delia stood up at once. She could see the mistress was in great pain. Without hesitating, Delia crossed to the desk and rang the silver bell.

Rosala hurried in, cackling and clucking.

Delia called as she might call an order to her soldiers in a bloody affray.

"Yzobel!"

When Yzobel ran in, between them they carried the mistress to the bed and made her comfortable.

"Send for all the needlewomen!"

"Yes, majestrix."

From her tone of voice, Delia might have expected the swod's cracked-out answer of: "Quidang!"

After that it was a matter of arranging affairs, of seeing to protocol, of making sure the mistress was given every attention and left in peace.

She would recover, for her time was not yet. Delia did not believe this was a cunning scheme to attract sympathy and sway her to the mistress's wishes. These women were above petty schemes of that contemptible nature.

Mind you, some of the schemes of the ladies who wished to become mistress would frizzle the hair. Delia firmly intended to have her say in all that. But that time, also, was not yet. There was so much to do in Vallia and in all of Paz that at times she felt as though she was shut up in a box of feathers.

She felt an extra pang of disappointment that she could not see Velia. That sprite was out with her classmates on what was euphemistically called An Educational and Recreational Trip for Young Ladies. The description might fit a startling variety of activities. Velia might be picking wild flowers to press in her album, joying in the wonders of nature; she might be stalking another party of girls and both parties deadly determined to spot and attack the other first; she might be working in some tavern all heightened color and watching hawklike for the people she had been sent to spy on; she might just be indulging in simple swordmastering, perhaps snapping her Whip at stuffed targets, or slashing with the practice claw at opponents armed with a variety of weapons. Delia had given strict instructions that young Velia should be taught the bow to the highest standards attainable at Lancival. After that, Uncle Seg would put on the final polish that would turn an excellent archer into a superb archer. You could not start too young learning the bow.

Sosie ti Drakanium, who was a captain of messengers, stopped Delia on the long marble sweep of staircase leading up to the Reading Rooms of the Laypom Hall. Sosie, a bright and lively girl with cropped brown hair and those deep brown Vallian eyes, hailed from Delphond.

"Majestrix. Is the mistress—?"

"She is overworked, Sosie, and needs rest. That is all."

"Thanks be to Dee Sheon! I am bid to ask you to see the Lady Almoner as soon as possible. She did not know of this dreadful news, of course, but—"

"She will certainly have more important things to do now than worry over me, I know." Delia let a small smile curve her lips, a small smile only and enough to respect the proprieties.

"As the Lady Almoner, Wilma Llandrin will be particularly busy trying to fill the shoes of the mistress until she is well again."

Sosie's bright face remained serious.

"Or until we must choose a new mistress."

"Oh, I wouldn't worry over that for a long time yet."

"But I do worry. So do others. There are some sisters who are undoubtedly most worthy and yet I would not wish to see them as the mistress. But, there is one sister I, and many others, would so wish."

Delia simply rode this as though flying a saddlebird high above the clouds.

"I am sure every sister has her own particular favorite as candidate, Sosie. You are young yet—of the junior chapel, I know—so at least you do not have the alarming thought that someone might wish to elect you!"

Sosie looked away.

"Quite, majestrix," she said. And said no more.

To rescue Sosie, Delia smiled again and said: "I will go straightaway to see Wilma. You are on your way to your Jikvar class?"

"Yes. I have to work at it. The rapier is more my weapon."

"And mine." They reached the corridor where the tall windows patterned sparkles across the carpets and marble. At the far end triple bronze-bound doors gave access to the working apartments of the sorority—working only in the sense that their work was generally regarded as work, as distinct from things like gardening and sewing and cooking and nursing which were not-work work. The distinctions were kept up, although at times they appeared nonsensical hangovers from another age.

Sosie wore black leathers instead of her usual tan tunic and she pushed the balass box straight under her arm before bidding Delia remberee in the SoR fashion of remberee, and swinging off with her long stride after the au revoir. Delia looked after her and shook her head. Sosie had an hour or two of strenuous exercise before her. The rules of the sisterhood demanded exact obedience to a rhythm of work, play, instruction and sleep. Periods of service in the outside world came as a culmination of and an enhancement of the training. Many people could not distinguish between the Discipline of such an order and ordinary discipline. That was their misfortune; sometimes it led to petty little squabbles and misunderstandings from women outside the sorority. Despite the claims made, and the undoubted truth of many of them, it was also manifest that all women were not considered equal with men—very far from it in some places and in the eyes of some men.

As a jikmer, a captain of messengers, Sosie had particular functions to perform. Yzobel, also, was a jikmer. Delia was aware that many men believed the women had set up a rank structure of delmer and hikmer and jikmer and chukmer aping the grades within male armed forces. That this was not so did not fail to amuse her.

Yzobel favored white leathers. This was her privilege. Trouble with white leather was that in moments of activity, stretching to days of action on end, it tended to become grubby. Only the very best quality leather and finish could be employed to resist dirtying; all the same, it looked splendid, no doubt of that.

The interview with the Lady Almoner was short. Wilma Llandrin did, indeed, have much to occupy her. Sisters did not go around calling each other sister this and sister that all the time. Delia expected to be called Delia; if girls chose to address her as majestrix, that, again, was their privilege.

"Delia! This is dreadful—before I can get away to see the mistress there are a thousand and one things I must do. Yet—"

Wilma, who called herself simply Llandrin, dropping all her worldly ranks and titles within Lancival, was a small, plump, meticulous woman. She could not be called fussy. Her hair was not pure Vallian brown but contained admixtures of a darker hue. Her face, which in the normal way was a model of understanding and rectitude and calculation, now revealed the turmoil occasioned by the collapse of the mistress.

"If there is anything I can do—?"

"Oh, everything here is under control. But thank you. I wanted to give you more information on what we know of the Sisters of the Whip and of Jilian Sweet-Tooth. But that must wait a moment."

"Of course."

Here in the wide office, with many girls at their desks organizing every detail, Delia was well aware of the arcane expertise employed. Wilma could do sums in her head that lesser mortals could never do, not with all the fingers and toes Opaz gave them, not with a regiment of girls and each one with an abacus. The sisters said that Wilma could look at a set of accounts, scanning each page as fast as her fingers could turn the leaves, and tell you at the end about every misplaced copper ob. That was a gift perplexing in its subtlety and, at least in many girls' eyes, of downright torment.

For Wilma Llandrin herself, the reverse was true.

Looking at this wonderful woman before her, remembering her as little Delia Valhan, she was amazed at what the passage of time could accomplish, although this was a mere part of what the mysticism of the rose taught. Much speculation had followed Delia's accident that left her a cripple, and more when she had returned, strong and fully fit and even more beautiful than before. No—looking at the woman before her, Wilma Llandrin gave thanks to Opaz that she, Wilma, had not been called to become Empress of Vallia.

Details of protocol were easily settled, as the two sisters talked for a moment only. Then Wilma, looking down at a ledger before her, said: "Of course, Delia, the mistress is actively seeking a successor. I must tell you I do not seek that honor."

"Honor? Yes, it is an honor. But, also, it is—"

"Yes!" Wilma picked up a pen. "It can create and it can destroy. We all know that. The choice must fall upon a sister who is not only worthy, but one who can bear the burdens."

Delia started to say something that might open Wilma's confidence to her; then she changed her mind, and said: "I have so much to do, as you can imagine, and much as I love Lancival, I do not wish to remain here longer than I must."

"I am sorry to hear that."

"No more than I am to say it."

There, said Delia to herself, perhaps that will clear the air a trifle.

The pen twirled. Wilma Llandrin was not the Lady Almoner for nothing. She looked up. "You have heard about the new curtains for the refectory?"

"Yes."

"I am not going to ask you for a contribution to pay for them—or the thousand orphans."

Delia held her smile in check, inwardly bubbling with joy at dear Wilma's machinations. This method of exerting power, traditionally belonging to women down through the ages of a male-dominated world, need not be thrown away in a more modern age of equality. Some women conditioned by events and not by reason, saw only cheapness in trying to hang onto women's role as the swayers of men's actions through hidden and persuasive means. Any weapons were good weapons if they fitted the hand. Delia detested the idea of men and women having to deal in terms of weapons to oppose each other. But until all was in all, as the saying went, needs must.

Men and women were just different. That was all. It was nonsensical to claim they were the same. Provided each received fair dues from the other, and, in more enlightened areas, each received as much help and sustenance one to the other, one from the other, then Opaz would shine upon them. Men and women could get on if each had a fair crack of the whip. That reminded Delia.

"I have to attend Aimee's grakvar class in a quarter of a glass." She glanced at the clepsydra; the water was rose-colored. "I then have a jikvar class and then a hikvar—and after that I think I shall expire in the steam of the Baths of the Nine. Unless—?"

"No, no, Delia. You must conform to the rhythm. I shall call a conclave this evening."

"Very well." As Delia turned to go, she looked back. "And, Wilma, don't you overdo it. Lancival cannot spare you. You may not believe it, we all do."

Wilma Llandrin smiled and then took up the first of the incessant stream of requests for orders and instructions. Being the Lady Almoner, she had the last word. She caught Delia just as the empress's fingers trailed from the door handle.

"Oh, Delia. I am not going to ask you for a contribution for the refectory curtains. We are opening a self-denying week for that. Nor for the orphans—that has been covered. I am going to ask you for a contribution for the repairs to the hospital of the Meek Sisters of Mercy. It has been in ruins since its destruction during the Time of Troubles."

"And they cannot finance it themselves?"

"Quite out of the question. The MSM are not a wealthy Order, and we have helped them in the past. They are worthy women."

"Very well. I will see to it, sell some jewelry, something like that. At the moment I do not have any saddle animals to spare. They are still dreadfully short."

"All these wars! I know."

"When my husband returns from these wars I will have him dip into his pocket. There are other projects in mind."

"He is successful, thanks be to Opaz. Surely, Delia, he will return with caravans of loot from our defeated enemies?"

Delia, one hand on the door, shook her head. Her face remained perfectly grave.

"No, Wilma. The emperor is not in the habit of plundering cruelly. And our late enemies in Hyrklana and Hamal are now our allies. As for the Shanks—"

Wilma's face reflected her stated distaste for them...

"As for the Shanks, they stink of fish and have little of value that we prize. They may have, in the future."

Proving she was the Lady Almoner, Wilma said with a sniff, "Even if gold stinks of fish, it is still gold."

Seven

Unwelcome News of Jilian Sweet-Tooth

Being conscious of her own faults, Delia often became extraordinarily tired of trying to correct them all the time. She'd remained sweet and reasonable in dealing with her two Djangs, Tandu and Dalki, when all around she was almost overwhelmed by sickness and filth. Now, in the muted light of the arms salle where as a small girl she'd often thought this was how the world must be below the sea, she went through the regulation exercises with her Whip.

She slashed and bashed and knocked the stuffing out of the dummies. She did not sweat. Some of the girls at practice regarded her askance, and this, too, annoyed her.

She was the empress, true. That had no bearing on the way she ought to be treated here. Here in Lancival they were all sisters.

A robust girl straining her leathers like any heavy male Deldar, flicked her whip, took out a patch of canvas on a dummy's head representing an eye, and then looked over a shoulder at Delia. Delia was about to flick at her own dummy.

"You wanted to ask me something?" Delia let her whip trail across the polished wooden floor.

The girl—Delia didn't know her—flushed up in a bright wash of blood.

"No—no, majestrix—"

"And you may call me Delia like any sister."

"Ah, yes—ah, Delia—"

"Now get on with your practice."

The girl did as she was bid. She did not cry, for that was a practice frowned on except in the most special of circumstances. But her next three blows completely missed the target.

Delia felt mean—and she also felt liberated.

By Vox! She was no angel, no spirit of perfection. Do 'em good to get the rough edge of her tongue now and again.

Anyway, her bad temper was not just because she had to slash her whip about, and then slash her claw about; she was far more worried than she liked over Jilian. Whatever was to be said about that young lady, or what had not been said so far, seemed calculated to distress her friend Delia.

Since the evening she had arrived, there had been all a hustle and a bustle, what with the mistress collapsing and the consequent preoccupation with the consequences. Now, when Delia had finished up with the Whip, the Claw, and passed a pleasant period throwing other girls about the mat, really tying each other up in knots, she could go along to the pro-marshal.

Thalmi Crockhaden, the pro-marshal, stood up as Delia entered the small study room. Thalmi's hair, which remained a bright yellow despite all, marked her out as being different from the usual run of Vallians. She was of Vallia, of course; but somewhere back along the line an ancestor had strayed, given the mores in use at the time. She was not overlarge, not over-pronounced, not over anything. It was not just because of her position within the SoR that she reminded Delia of Naghan Vanki the emperor's chief spymaster. To most of the junior sisters, Thalmi spent her time arranging the most awkward timetables for training sessions. And, even then, they'd say, her assistants did all the work.

Precisely. Thalmi spent her time organizing the ramifications of the spy net operating from Lancival and elsewhere.

"You are well, Delia?"

"More or less. And you?"

"Too busy, as usual. The mistress—pray Opaz she quickly recovers—has told you, I'm sure, why you're here. It's this friend of yours, Jilian Sweet-Tooth—a remarkable product of the SoR and now about to desert us."

There seemed to be no accusations in Thalmi's straight stare, as she felt for the armrest of her chair and sat, nodding for Delia to sit. But Delia decided to get the undercurrents out of the way first.

"Before we talk of Jilian—have you any news of Dayra?"

"None. The princess has not been brought to my attention of late. Not since she and her friends looted an abandoned temple—to a monastic local godling, to be sure."

"She has been swayed by bad companions. We know that. But I take the full blame—"

"Oh, no, Delia! Oh, no. I know better than that. Your rascal of a husband who calls himself the emperor—he is far more to blame."

"I choose not to believe that."

"Believe what you like, sister. You will not alter the truth—or, at least—" And Thalmi smiled widely, delighted at her own idiotic words. She and Delia knew that the truth was what was believed, and what was believed could be manipulated. "At least, you believe in error."

"And yet," said Delia, putting a barb of her own, "Dayra was educated and trained by the SoR."

"Yes. If she becomes embroiled with these fatuous Sisters of the Whip, we must expect even greater disasters."

"You'd better tell me about Jilian."

"She has sworn to have the manhood of that rast, Kov Colun Mogper. She will not talk of the indignities she suffered. I gather from my reports that the Sisters of the Whip can promise more than we can in the way of vengeance upon men."

"Vengeance upon men—all men?"

"Aye."

"Well, some of them deserve that, a lot of them. But all? This does not sound like Jilian to me."

"Nor me. But I am assured that she has gone sour."

That rebellious yellow hair of Thalmi's, which she was at pains to cover with a brown wig from time to time, could not spoil the effect she had of being insignificant. Her tongue might destroy the effect. Delia sat up.

"You sound bitter, Thalmi."

"I've every right to be. As Dee Sheon is my witness! When these Sisters of the Whip poach from other Orders, I feel sorrow; but it is no concern to me. When they take our girls it is my concern. And I'll tell you why they want them—it is because of the Claw. Only we can manipulate the Claw."

"Sometimes I wonder if that is so marvelous a gift—"

"Delia!"

"Clawing a man's eyes out tends to become fun to some girls—"

"Never fun. But a redressing of the balance of nature—yes." Thalmi sat back and waited a moment before saying, "Don't worry too much about Dayra. I do not feel the apprehension for her, despite all, that I do in others. She has not gone sour in quite the same way."

"All the same," said Delia, shaking her head and feeling stubborn. "I find this very hard to believe of Jilian."

"I must confess disappointment. I was hoping you had news of her. Something timely to give me a lever to win her back. There is still a chance. But every day that chance grows more slim."

Leaning forward and helping herself to a yellow paline from the wooden dish gave Delia time to gather thought and strength. She looked up, the paline poised—she was not in the habit of popping a paline here in Lancival. "You say the Whip women need our expertise with the Claw. That I can understand. But by their title—?"

"Yes. They worship the Whip. To extremes."

"One then has to feel sorry for them."

"Oh, aye!"

The pro-marshal spent a few moments expressing her feelings on the subject. Presently, Delia said, "This means you do not know where Jilian is, either? Or where the Sisters of the Whip may be found in conclave?"

"We run across their handiwork from time to time. No, I don't know where Jilian is." Thalmi sounded personally offended, and Delia saw the spymistress *was* personally offended. She had a right to be, in nature. "We managed to trace a chapter in Vondium. But one would expect some to be found in the capital. Others exist in your own Blue Mountains—"

"It grieves me to say that does not surprise me. The Blue Mountain Girls always have been an independent crowd."

"And in various other provinces—Vomansoir, Falinur, Quken, Vindelka, Ogier—"

"Clearly, then, a locus of infection exists and is spreading." All the provinces mentioned occupied a compact area in the center of Vallia. "What other objects, do you know, are the aims apart from humiliating and killing men?"

"That, my dear Delia, is what I would dearly love to know."

The webwork of intelligence thrown over the country by the SoR was not infallible. And, in any case, the sisters were far more concerned about their rigorous pursuits of excellence in service to the generality of people to take kindly to rooting out a rival Order. Looking after a thousand orphans, rebuilding hospitals, tracking and dealing with men who thought they could kidnap girls—these were everyday pursuits, sadly enough, after the Times of Troubles.

The pro-marshal pushed the dish of palines close toward Delia. "There is one other thing that, perhaps, might give us more concern than all the rest." At Delia's delicately raised eyebrow, she went on: "Sorcery. We believe witches and wizards play a prominent part with the Sisters of the Whip."

Slowly, Delia spoke some of her mind.

"I believe I can grasp some of Jilian's thinking in this. The SoR offered me the chance of taking Witch's Vows, and as you know I declined. I am not sorry for that. We are not an Order biased heavily toward sorcery—"

"We can produce competent thaumaturgists when there is the need, Delia."

"Oh, yes, we can, of course. It could be that Jilian believes she will receive more help from the Whip Women."

"If that is all it is..."

Delia took another paline, looked at the clepsydra, and said, "But it is not, you think? Well, we will see. Now it is time for us to eat and then I must attend the Fifth Sheon Service of Praise."

"I attended the Third. Very well, Delia. I will see you at Songs later."

When she'd left the pro-marshal's study, Delia realized this unwelcome news about Jilian had made her bad-tempered again. Despite her dislike of the Claw—although dislike was too strong a word: distaste, perhaps?—she was minded to fill in a private study period with a good rousing slashing session with her Claw. But she did not. Instead she read of the heroic deeds of Benga Kathyn of Tezpor, which had happened so long ago they were probably mythical.[*] After the Service of Praise and the study session, Delia was relaxed enough to attend Songs and join in with a will. This was one of the magics of Lancival, this capacity to soothe and calm the most unbridled passions.

And, while that was undoubtedly true, and sweet to the mind and spirit, the truth also remained that she could not spend very much longer here. No message had been received from her half-brother Vomanus yet. This was not surprising, in view of the circuitous route communications would have to take to reach Lancival. No man in all Vallia, in all Kregen—as far as the sisters were aware—knew of the location of Lancival. It was under their noses, of course; but that made the secret that much sweeter.

She determined to remain halfway cross with Vomanus.

Quite apart from her position as empress—a position which always

---

* Benga: saint.

amazed her—which in the most general and particular terms gave her some privileges in the knowledge of just who people intended to marry, Vomanus was, after all, her brother! He'd gone off and married before, and young Valona was the result of that. Valona had gone through Lancival like a divine wind. Well, who was this new lady her brother was marrying? Had married now, by Vox.

Many seasons ago, Delia could recall with the utmost clarity using all her influence—which even then was considerable as the Princess Majestrix of Vallia—to send out expeditions to search for the wild barbarian clansman who was to become her husband. It had fallen to the lot of Tharu of Vindelka and Vomanus to find the man so eagerly sought. Tharu had been slain in that service. Vomanus, in his open, reckless, careless way, had later on passed some casual remark about it being better had he, instead of Tharu, who had willed him his kovnate province, been the one to die. His wild and reckless ways distressed Delia. She saw Vomanus as a man as well as a half-brother. Some other, deeper, hurtful, more prodigious reason impelled Vomanus in his wild ways. He had gone through a string of women, friends, acquaintances, always laughing, always reckless, never caring—he seldom bothered to clean his weapons properly after a fracas and one day his sword would snap in the midst of combat because it had rusted away undetected. Delia suffered for Vomanus because he suffered and she could not understand why.

She could not allow herself to believe the obvious answer—for in that she would sense in herself a rebellion against the mercy of the Invisible Twins made manifest in Opaz.

Her thoughts jibed with the words of the hymn that moment being caroled out to the raftered ceiling of the Lesser Hall. "In the Light of Opaz we see our beacon guide through the darkness of the world." Trite words, perhaps, but words always fervently sung and believed. Delia could not quite imagine breaking away from these beliefs, except and only in circumstances arising from her marriage.

In the course of the evening as the songs and hymns were sung, she contrived a few quiet words with people she wished to gauge. Sounding out their minds, as her old tutor, Rose Mandeling, would have said. She said with a trifle impatience to Thalmi Crockhaden, the pro-marshal, "And that is all you can tell me of this Nyleen Gillois?"

The pro-marshal did not tear that yellow hair; she looked as though she might have, had she been other than she was.

"By the Rod of Halron and the Mount of Mampe!" She took a breath. "I had a first-class agent at Delka-Ob. She provided timely, informative, detailed reports. Nothing from her until this morning—and—"

Delia turned her shoulder on the ranks of singing girls in the Lesser Hall and leaned one elbow on the balass-wood bar. Novices in pretty dresses decently covered by striped rose and yellow aprons served soft drinks like sazz and parclear, and also a wide selection of vintages. The bar area lay recessed from the main hall. The singing served as a pleasant background. Delia saw how upset the pro-marshal was, and half-guessed the cause.

Thalmi nodded savagely. "A single last message, no doubt as a gesture of defiance, perhaps, I hope, as a sign of some remnants of conscience."

"She has joined the Sisters of the Whip?"

"Aye! May Dee Sheon make her run forever!"

"So we know the name of the lady that Vomanus of Vindelka has wed. Nyleen Gillois na Sagaie. Sagaie is in Evir, I think?"

"Yes, right up in the far north, over the mountains, a land of furry savages. They no longer bend the knee to the emperor; they've got themselves a king up there, now, after the Time of the Troubles."

"It will probably be necessary to bring them back into the fold of Vallia, one day. There are other more pressing concerns at the moment." Delia stopped herself. She did not wish to discuss strategy of empire here. She wanted to concentrate if she could on Vomanus, on Jilian, on Dayra. Velia might, with any luck, return from her trip for ladies before her mother left. If not, Delia would not wait...

"Judging by the 'na' in her name, she must be of importance."

Cattily, Delia said, "And Sagaie could be a one-shanty village."

The pro-marshal showed her teeth.

Yzobel could offer no further information. She knew only what she had been told, and had been sent to Delka-Ob to carry a message to Delia, who had been expected to be there for the wedding. As for Thalmi's spy—or, rather, ex-spy, in Delka-Ob, Yzobel knew nothing. Not only did she not know her name, she did not know of her existence.

The capital of the province of Vindelka, Delka-Ob, contained a strong group of the Sisters of the Rose. The pro-marshal was clearly worried about future defections.

"The illness of the mistress could not have come at a worse time."

Familiar words—every time was the worst time in Delia's experience—but they remained uncomfortably true in this situation. Knowledge that the mistress was stricken, rumors of strife over the election—yes, these ugly events could easily sway women who had personal grievances. And who, in this sinful world, did not have those?

"The mistress," said Delia, and she tried to speak with purposeful positiveness, struggling against the dreadful uncertainty, "she is going to be perfectly well again—"

"Of course. But for how long? I do not usually speak frankly, my dear. But I really do think that you—"

"Thalmi, as you bear me some affection—"

"Delia! Really!"

The singing reached those marvelous high notes in the Canticles of the Rose City, and for a space there was nothing any mortal with a melodious spirit could do but sink back into an inner reality and listen. Soaring and lofting, sung with all the purity of girls' voices unbridled by limping fashion, the song told of great days and great deeds. Also, it spoke to those who would hear of famous men and noble women, and, equally, of famous women and noble men. Thalmi sipped her wine and waited until the long cadences sank and died. Silence hung drab and yet pulsing with inner echoes under the rafters of the Lesser Hall.

"The Canticles of the Rose City," said the pro-marshal. "Of course, they mean something extra special to you, Delia."

"And to us all, surely? They speak of the rose, do they not?"

As though instructing a raw novice, the pro-marshal said, "The Canticles of the Rose City are a myth-cycle at least three thousand years old. They concern, chiefly, the doings of a half-legendary, half-historical man-god." She spoke, Delia saw, with meaning. "That person's name was Drak. A name, I believe, not unfamiliar to you—"

"There is no need for this, Thalmi. I know what you imply. My family. Yes, well... My son Drak will be the emperor. That is arranged. And then, my dear, I shall be free to follow my own inclinations. I welcome the day."

"If I did not know you better, I would call this ingratitude and you an ingrate."

"If I am, then I am."

"Who else do you see—do you *feel*—to be right?"

"That is not for me to say."

"Everyone else will have their say—and you will, too."

"Probably." And Delia laughed.

"But, sister, you are in error." Thalmi waggled her forefinger—the forefinger of her right hand. The left hand clutched a goblet brimming with a first quality Gremivoh. "Just because you shuffle off the position of empress—no doubt your son Drak will marry Queen Lush in due time—"

"I think not." Delia spoke sharply, very stiff.

"No? Well, no matter. The point is, whether you are empress or not has no bearing on your duty with the SoR. And, you know that well!"

"That is what I have believed for a long time. Part of me still believes. But I have changed. When I was a girl the idea of being the empress escaped me, for everyone talked of the emperor my father, and of the emperor my grandfather. My mother—we used to call her Lela, out of love—was never, in my eyes at least, an empress. And I truly do not think she ever thought of herself as one. She married my father out of mutual love and was content to be with him. He did not really recover from her death."

Delia would not go on to say that she had felt the joy so strange to herself that her father had, at the last, found a new affection from Queen

Lushfymi of Lome. It was because of Queen Lush's genuine love for the emperor that Delia did not think the ambitious queen could truly love Drak. Anyway, it was planned for Drak to marry Silda, Seg's daughter. That would take careful thought and preparation, by Vox!

Again, she did not care to mention that Vomanus, her half-brother, had been born of her mother's first marriage. There were too many worries and too many tangles. If it boiled down to being mistress of the SoR and nothing else, then she would accept nomination leading to almost certain election. Otherwise, she wanted only to be with her husband, and let the SoR manage without her for a little time.

She rubbed her right hand along her left arm, up from the wrist to the elbow, and back, in a smoothing and soothing rhythm of which she was barely conscious. Thalmi noticed, and smiled again, her teeth white.

"You do not practice enough."

"I suppose you will cite that as another dereliction of my duty!"

"I could." Thalmi sipped her wine and—lo!—the glass was empty. She reached out her hand for another goblet. "It is all one. You keep your Claw here. Have you no others at home?"

With a bitterness that shocked herself, Delia burst out: "Home? What I kept of my own possessions at my home—at my home!—is lost, gone, destroyed. I start again, and a revolution or a war or damned reiving fluts-men fly in and burn and steal! I had a Claw in its balass box in the palace at Vondium. Where it is now Opaz alone knows."

"Drink some wine." The pro-marshal proffered a glass.

"Very well." Delia understood she had overreacted. But every time she thought of the way the homes over which she had slaved had been despoiled it made her blood rise up and demand a safety valve, as the headwaters of a dammed lake used the safety-valve overspill. "At least, my home in Djanguraj is still unspoiled."

"And Strombor—"

"I have some ling furs there, soft and long and silky white, that are tatty now and need attention. I would not like to see those white ling furs stolen."

"Possessions are chained weights about our characters."

"You quote and it is true. But sometimes I know I have changed from the girl who accepted everything the SoR taught."

"I believe it, to my sorrow."

"If you remain true to me, I shall remain true to you."

"Never think otherwise."

Delia sipped her wine. "Then take from me the gift you and others are so eager to press upon me." She lifted her left hand, still tingling from that reflexive massage, and waved. "And here comes Wilma so I suppose she will call the Conclave now."

With the inevitability of their natures there ensued a certain amount of jockeying for positions as the women entered the Conclave Chamber, a certain amount of giggling and stern rejoinders, of quick whispers, and of meaningful glances. The majority maintained a dignified mien. They had work to do and they meant to do it and have done with it.

Thinking back uneasily to those last few exchanges with the pro-marshal at the bar, Delia wished, now, that she had not made so obvious a point about the "remaining true" business. If you had to keep on proclaiming undying friendship then one might suspect that the friendship was in need of continual sustenance. She had made many friends in the outside world and her husband's blade comrades were her blade comrades. Every now and again some little vow, some small indication of the depths of feelings that existed between them might be in order.

Taking her seat in the comfortable but plainly furnished chamber, Delia rubbed her wrist and waggled the fingers up and down. No doubt about it. She was out of practice. The knack of using the Claw was taught at Lancival at an early age and the skill multiplied over the years of continual practice. This applied to most other weapons, of course—most, not all.

Some twenty women gathered in the Conclave Chamber. Those who had made their marks with Delia on her arrival, the various officers of the Order, and short-sighted Nandi ti Rondasmot who wrote down an account of what was said, they sat to their task each in her own individual fashion. Most took the duty seriously; some were conscious of their superiority; some wanted to have the thing over and done with and others wished to go on talking all night.

Rosala, with two novices there to help her unobtrusively, gave her report on the mistress. No change.

"Thank you, Rosala. We are all grateful for your devoted care of the mistress. Now you may leave."

"Thank you, my lady."

"And," added the Lady Almoner, "make sure you get a good night's rest, Rosala!"

A number of items on the agenda demanded attention. Of all the women there, Delia fancied that she alone experienced this unwelcome sense of distancing. Of course, what they did here and what was decided was of vital importance. The Sisters of the Rose wielded power. But, all the same, Delia was overwhelmingly conscious of her responsibilities in the outer world.

Natilma na Stafoing in her robust way was saying: "And so we must deal with these Sisters of the Whip. Deal with them harshly as they deserve."

Lansi ti High Ochrun pushed her copper hair back from her forehead. Softly, she said, "We refer to these Whip women freely and openly, here in Conclave and in Lancival. Might not it be wiser to treat them in the same way we treat that *other* Order, whose name we do not use openly?"

Everyone knew which Order Lansi referred to.

A number of sororities possessed names beginning with S: Samphron, the Sword, Silence, Sensibility, so that their abbreviations took notice of this fact. The Order to which Lansi referred considered themselves a cut above the rest. The old antagonism remained, ridiculous though it was, like two bitches fighting over the same bone in a dusty village street. The rivalries between male Orders were, often, of the same intensity.

This rival sorority had chosen to saddle itself with the title of The Grand Ladies Order of Gratitude. Out of disrespect and mirth, the SoR sometimes called this *other* Order the Grand Ladies. They were, of course, well aware that the GLOG meant that the Order, not the Ladies, were Grand. The GLOG habitually wore green leathers, were stronger in the north of the country—although that in normal times had no significance—and had done good work for the poor and sick, and had fought against the invaders of Vallia. They maintained what was probably a stronger force of Battle Maidens, Jikai Vuvushis, than the Sisters of the Rose. They did not use the Claw but were cunning with the Whip.

Delia's eyes closed. She opened them with a jolt of surprise. The women talked on around her. More than one sister had suggested that they referred to the GLOG euphemistically as the *other* Order because they were frightened of them and their influence. If you don't say his name the bogey can't get you.

In her clear voice, she said: "Let us treat the Sisters of the Whip as just another Order. Are they then so fearsome?"

As she listened to the various answers, reasoned, hot-tempered, cautious, her eyelids dropped down.

As a small girl learning about the Grand Ladies, she had said, "Who are they grateful to?" and had been surprised at the ladylike bellows of laughter from her tutors at the sally.

Rose Mandeling had said, beaming, "Oh, they are grateful to Opaz, of course. But it is truer to say they are grateful *for* all their worldly possessions and positions."

Delia managed to open her eyes. The chamber swam in a blue haze. She was tired—and as a hairy graint of a clansman was in the habit of saying: "Tiredness is a sin."

Well, she was sinning like mad right now, and unable to do a single thing about it.

Some items of the agenda were dealt with. Delia sat, exhausted, eyes closed most of the time, joining in when she could. Nothing was decided about the Sisters of the Whip, about the mistress, even about the new curtains for the refectory.

When, at last, the Lady Almoner brought the meeting to a close, everyone felt restless with dissatisfaction. They recognized that, just at the moment, there was precious little they could decide. Some of the women had used great skill in steering any discussion away from consideration of just who was to be considered for nomination to the position of mistress.

That suited Delia.

She smiled and said the remberees, and trailed off to Velda's Room. A thorough wash, an attention to the necessities of the toilet, an abstention from any further food or drink, and a swift and thrashing kind of onslaught on her hair, and she could fall into the narrow bed, think of all those she could not sleep without thinking of, and then drop down into nothingness.

Eight

Delia Rides the Gale

In the small cabin situated in the stern of the airboat Delia pulled down the top of her russet tunic over her breast. She tucked her chin in and squinted down. She had always had nice skin, smooth and unblemished, and now this—this monstrosity—squatted nastily on her chest like a furry grub. The patch was as big as her thumb. When she looked more closely she could see tiny yellow pimples peppering the angry red of the rash.

She did not much care for rashes and she disliked pimples.

The beastly spot did not hurt. It did not even sting. She could feel nothing even when, distastefully, she prodded it with a finger.

The hateful thing just erupted on her skin, growing larger, sitting there like an obscene grub above her breast.

The flap of the door covering quivered, and a beringed hand showed, about to pull the curtain aside.

A voice bellowed: "Majestrix! I would crave a word with your puissance, your humble servant craves entrance."

Delia made a face.

She slapped the tunic up and latched it and said in a small yet firm voice: "Come in, Lathdo."

The man who entered—he was apim with brown hair—bulked in the tiny cabin with its bench seat and folding table. He wore armor. He carried swords. He bore the insignia of a Jiktar. He half-crouched under the cover and was clearly ill at ease.

"Yes?"

"A storm, majestrix. Since we quitted Delphond the weather has been kind. But Jordio swears he can smell the Riders of Notor Zan about to enfold us."

"We must descend, then, Lathdo. Is Mimi there?"

"Your orders are to be obeyed without thought, majestrix." He half turned his head, the tendons straining in his neck above the gilt rim of the corselet, and bellowed: "Mimi! *Bratch!*"

Delia did not jump. She'd called in to Vondium to see if any letters were waiting for her, and had read all the mail and no letter from him at all, and taken the opportunity to re-equip with a fresh set of clothing and necessaries. No letter from Vomanus probably meant he was as cross with her as she was with him. Most of the urgency to reach Delka-Ob had now passed, of course, since the marriage had already taken place.

She would have to go to see her half-brother and congratulate him and wish Nyleen well. She just hoped she would find her brother's new wife amenable and nice, so she would not have to lie through smiling teeth.

Drak was still prancing around in the southwest of Vallia; the country was still untidy in the view of a girl who had been brought up with the empire as a unit, the factions still plotted and the damned revolutionaries and secessionists still badgered away. The army was very thin in Vondium, what with the strong forces sent into Hamal, others into the north of the country and still others with Drak. The Lord Farris had insisted in his patient way that she must take a bodyguard and added: "Your news of flutsmen so active in Vindelka is worrying, majestrix."

"I suppose you are right. Both Yzobel and Sosie must be about their business." She could not tell a man that they were off about business of the SoR; but that was patently clear. Farris, a loyal friend for as long as she could remember, was the Crebent Justicar for the emperor, and ran things when Drak was away.

"Jiktar Lathdo the Eager has recently been promoted. He is zealous, and a good fighter. He will—"

"Yes, yes, dear Farris. You are right. Mind you send word to me the instant you hear from the emperor."

"Have I ever failed you in that?"

"I am sorry. No, never. Just that..."

"And it was remiss of me to mention it." Farris was of the quality of men of whom an emperor could never have enough. His loyalty to Delia personally was beyond question. The only serious trouble with the Lord Farris was that he was approaching old age.

So she'd taken one of Farris's small but encouragingly growing force of airboats and started off. She'd gone by a swing back through Delphond to make sure a little matter at Drakanium was in order, and then set course for Vindelka. With Jiktar Lathdo the Eager, the pilot, Jordio the Hawk, and Mimi the Smile, she'd taken off with the dismal hope that she would get through this quickly and fly back to Vondium to some good—some marvelous—news.

When Mimi put her ringletted head into the tiny cabin Delia was in two minds whether or not to consult her about the rash on her chest. Probably it would go away soon. She would rub some ointment on tonight. That should do it.

Mimi looked upset.

"Very well, Mimi, my dear, I shall speak to the Jiktar."

"It is so—so—degrading!"

"I agree."

The word *bratch*, which meant jump to it, although in no way as vicious as the infamous *grak*, addressed to slaves to make them hop about their work or be slashed by whips, was often heard in the ranks of the swods as the soldiers drilled. It was not, at least in Delia's hearing, addressed to her people. Mimi, young, still under training, had been overjoyed to be plucked out of her humdrum routine in the palace in Vondium to be chosen as personal handmaid to the empress. It was a tremendous boost to her ego, a real start on her career, and, more than all that, of supreme bliss to be able to be with the Empress Delia of Vallia. Mimi believed this without coaching.

"But," said Mimi, with a little return to the smile that gave her her cognomen, "I do not want to make trouble."

"I shall, if that big froth-blower Lathdo does not learn to speak to you properly."

"Thank you—"

"He is new to his position, you see. He has just been promoted ob-Jiktar from zan-Hikdar, and he is—well, he is Eager..."

"Oh, yes, majestrix. Very Eager."

Delia wished that her two Djangs, Tandu and Dalki, had been in Vondium. She would have welcomed their support and protection. But they had both been sent up to Vindelka with a letter from the Lord Farris, in explanation and also instruction. The Djangs would find a snug berth in Vomanus's bodyguard rather than riding patrol along the Ochre Limits.

The flier shook as wind gusts rattled past.

Mimi looked uncertain.

"This Jordio the Hawk is a good pilot, Mimi."

"Oh, yes, of course, majestrix."

"You are not afraid of fliers?"

"Oh, no, majestrix."

Delia did not smile. "You have heard the old tales of how the airboats we bought from Hamal were always breaking down. Of course you have. But now we are friends with Hamal, we can buy proper vollers, and from Hyrklana, too."

"My mother told me." Mimi moved to the topmost chest stacked along the side of the cabin and picked up a hairbrush. Delia saw that the girl wanted something to do. "Also, my mother would be amazed that the empress does not travel with a great retinue—"

"When it is necessary, I do. We shall not be away long."

Delia submitted her hair to the brush. Mimi had a nice stroke, but Delia missed the delicate touch of Rosala or Floria. But Floria—who was just as brilliant and beautiful as Rosala—was off being married, at last, and Rosala had gone, too. Since Delia's adventures in Hamal had taken her away from her handmaidens, she had not worried overmuch. And, now, poor Pansi was dead, along with Nath the Jokester, and she was going to have to train up this Mimi.

As she lay back, letting the brush stroke through her hair, she reflected that Mimi was one of the girls greatly affected by the recent Time of Troubles. The bad days had muddled up girls' education in far worse ways than boys, for a lad need only shoulder a spear and march off with the army to make a name and fortune for himself, if he did not get himself killed. For girls it was different, unless they were Jikai Vuvushis. Mimi came from the province of Forli and had not been educated by any of the sororities, at least, not to Delia's knowledge. Her mother, a shrewd woman with ambition, had applied for a place for her daughter Mimi. She had backed her application with a letter from the Kov of Forli, Lykon Crimahan. He had once been at loggerheads with the emperor, and had proved himself if not a good friend at least a man prepared to set to and work for the new emperor and let bygones be bygones. That had tilted the scales in Mimi's favor.

A slender, meek girl, Mimi's choice of career had been wisely chosen by her mother. At Mimi's age, Delia had been stomping around in black leathers slashing with her Claw and foining with rapier and main gauche. That would not have been practicable for Mimi. She was set on a career, now, and ought to be successful. In pursuance of that, Delia decided, she'd probably let the Little Sisters of Opaz have Mimi for a spell, sharpen her up, teach her the tricks of the trade. All that would help Mimi's prospects. So many girls applied and so few could be taken, Delia felt the burden upon herself. This, as with so many other aspects, was one of the abiding oppressions of being empress.

Delia was a very proud woman; but she was not so foolishly proud as to believe that being handmaiden to an empress was the summit and achievement of a girl's life.

But, by Krun, it was a damned good start.

The flier lurched again and then started a gentle descent. A consummate flier herself, Delia recognized the masterful handling. Jordio must be trying to avoid the worst of the blow by diving and attempting to find a layer of calmer air.

The brush snagged in her hair.

Delia winced.

Mimi gasped.

The brush began to stroke again, tentatively. Delia said nothing. She did not pride herself on her tolerance for not biting the girl's head off. She was sorrowfully aware that by saying nothing, she punished the poor girl far more than a swift epithet and insult ever could do.

The flier swung bodily sideways, was caught and held, and swept back onto course.

Delia said: "That is enough, Mimi. Perhaps you would like to see about that hole in the hem of the turquoise gown? You discovered the hole, which was clever. And, be careful not to stick the needle in your finger. Jordio has his hands full."

"Yes, majestrix."

As she ducked out onto the deck, Delia reflected that it was as well that not yet, not quite yet, the gentle intimacy of handmaid and empress had been established between them. Mimi would learn the empress's funny ways in time.

The wind blew her thoughts away.

Jordio, a wild shape in a flapping cloak, stood at the control levers like some phantom operator of a ghostly sky-mill. Lathdo clung to the rail at his side. Both men peered ahead, into the wildness. The sky pelted down at them, lowering, dark, massy with wind and clamor.

Delia hauled herself along the rail until she stood with the men. They were startled to see her, as though an apparition from a Herrelldrin Hell had jumped up to drag them away.

"Majestrix!" The rest was lost in the howl of the wind. Something to do with not being on deck and being in the cabin.

She said nothing. She held on. Her lips opened and the wind rushed past. This was glorious!

The flier leaped up and down like a crazed sliptinger, that beautiful salmon of Western Vallia, and Jordio met each leap and lunge and held her. Delia looked ahead and down. Were those lights below?

She banged Lathdo on a bulky armored shoulder and pointed.

He nodded.

Jordio inched his controls carefully, and the flier, responding, lunged down and kept at the angle, sweeping in through the gusts. The lights grew firmer. Wind struck into her face as a force, tearing, liberating. But however much she might exult in fronting the elements, those same elemental forces could take the flier and twist her end over end and shred her and cast her down as a mass of tumbled wreckage onto the ground below.

Her hair blew back in a whiplash of abandon. Poor Mimi! The lights brightened. A village, perhaps a small town, huddled against the fury of the storm. The place was somewhere in Vindelka, on the way to the provincial capital.

"... get ... down!" bellowed Lathdo. He looked furious in that dark light, his jaw muscles bulging. If aught happened to the empress!

Delia could guess his thoughts. She could feel a small sorrow for him; after all, he was new to the job and the big blow-hard was eager to do what he imagined to be the right things around an empress. He, like Mimi, could be trained.

Nothing of any of the seven Moons of Kregen could be glimpsed in that wracked sky. The darkness lashed with the wind, and the wind scourged with the darkness. No one saw it.

One moment Jordio was bringing the flier down in a steep descent, angling her to catch the wind, and the next they'd slammed slap bang into the roof of a building.

The flier simply broke up.

Upside down, whirled on the breath of the wind, Delia caught a fantastic glimpse of Mimi flying out of the aft cabin like a kite.

Something hard struck Delia across the back. It was probably the edge of the guttering. Bits and pieces of destroyed airboat whirled about her. She saw nothing in the clamping dark of either Lathdo or Jordio. She fell off the edge of the roof, her back aching like the devil, her eyes filled with tears of pain, of fury and frustration, and her mouth wide open and yelling blue bloody murder.

She hit the dung heap.

Well, Seg and her husband knew about those kinds of adventure. She sat up, spitting straw, and glared about with such a look of savage hatred as would have fried a leem.

She could barely smell the stink, for the wind lashed it away. Her hair blew all over her face when she turned to look downwind. All she could see was the whole world leaping up and down. Then she realized this uncanny movement was merely a tree, blowing bent, and straightening, and so bowing once again to the power of the storm.

She stood up and went a dozen staggering steps to leeward. She bumped into a wall, grazed her fingers, and held on. She dragged in a few gulps of breath. That she kept on her feet meant that her legs weren't broken. That she gripped to the wall meant her arms weren't broken. That she remained upright meant her back wasn't broken—although it damned-well felt like it. And because her head did not roll off and get blown away by the wind, her neck wasn't broken.

She gulped more air, shook her face free of hair, and crabbed along the wall. Her groping fingers felt the door long before she saw it. It fitted snugly into the jamb.

The exhilaration she'd felt at the touch of the wind faded. She felt exhausted.

She was feeling far more tired lately than she should. When the rain began she knew she'd have to cave in, or, being a Sister of the Rose, think about giving in and then go marching on, stupid though the marching might be.

But the tiredness dragged at her. This was frightening, the way she could feel the fatigue deep within her bones. This was something new to her, and nauseating, unnerving.

Holding onto the edge of the jamb and getting her breath, resisting the tug of the wind, she recalled herself after she had fallen from the zorca and become a cripple. Yes, there had been something of that feeling then. Certainly, she'd never felt like this when she'd been carrying any of her children.

She put her teeth together, bit down, hunched up her shoulders, and swinging her leg vigorously, delivered a thumping great kick at the door.

She had to kick three times before she roused any answer.

The door cracked the space of a narrow nose and one eye. She put her mouth to the slot of light and bellowed.

"Let me in!"

Another thumping great thwack with her toes reinforced the demand. She was prepared to lay about her with her tongue, get 'em jumping, have a fire and a hot toddy, a meal, find a decent bed, and—first and most important—stir 'em all up into going out and scouring everywhere to find Mimi and Lathdo and Jordio.

The door slapped open. She tumbled in. An oniony sack clapped over her head. Whoever they were in here, one of them hit her over the head. The smell of onions faded with everything else, faded and went away, went with the wind.

Nine

A Walk in the Radiance of the Suns

She supposed, with deep rancor and considerable soul-searching, that this was what happened to girls who grew to think themselves too important. They had given her a tunic, and a breechclout. Both were of grey.

Slave grey.

Well, she'd been slave before. She had helped to outlaw slavery in Vallia. But, here she was, trudging along with a forlorn group of other slaves, all following a coach down a long and dusty road, going from where to where she had not the slightest idea.

After the onion sack, she'd been kicked awake to find herself stark naked chained in a bed. And that damned spot on her chest had changed into a swelling. The swelling was ugly in her eyes, a bulging lump. A cautious swivel of her eyes revealed other lumps. When she could touch her face she felt more.

So these people, whoever they were, had led her out to the waiting coffle of slaves, and taken their chains off and affixed the slavers' chains. She trudged along with the others, and no one wanted to talk to her.

She was merchandise.

The day sparkled about her. The streaming mingled radiance of Zim and Genodras, the twin Suns of Kregen, touched everything with fire. She half-shut her eyes. The road was ochreish, dusty and dry. Her feet, naked, did not pain her, for empress or no empress, she was hardened to going barefoot. Perhaps, toward the end of the day if the march was long, her feet would pain; but, then, she was in all truth a little out of practice for this particular brand of adventure.

Her latest escapades had been more in the nature of riding a superb saddle animal at the head of armies.

The road, like most roads of Vallia, was atrocious. Relying mainly for transport on her magnificent system of canals, Vallia neglected roadworks. This specimen stretched out between fields of Strafin and Chawinseed, all glowing purple and orange above the green in the rays of the suns. If these slavers put her to work in the fields, she'd make a break and run for it.

The guards who marched beside the small column, only occasionally flicking their whips, were not apims. They were diffs, Fristles whose cat faces bristled with whiskers, and whose fur showed the patternings of various races. They did not look so much bored with their job as indifferent to what they were doing. They continually scanned the sky.

If they expected a patrol of Vallian aerial cavalry to sweep down and rescue the slaves, they would, in Delia's opinion, be expecting nothing. She trudged on. The coach up ahead swayed and jolted along. Over the heads of the intervening slaves Delia made out the ornate gildings on the coach, the real glass in the rear window, the rail at top retaining a piled mass of boxes and trunks. To trudge along as a slave at the back end of a handsome coach? There was an incongruity here.

The other people taken up into slavery smelled less than sweet. The dust stung her nostrils. The suns blazed down, pouring a conciliatory warmth upon the world for the violence of the storm. The coffle passed through a village which she did not recognize. Every door was bolted, every window shuttered; nothing moved save the gilded coach and the slavers and their merchandise.

The woman who slouched along beside Delia twisted a narrow neck to peer with filmed eyes upon the scene. Her hair straggled, dust smothered, unkempt. It was, surmised Delia with distaste, just like her own.

"All run off. Bad cess to 'em, says I. More of us there are, the lighter the work."

"Where are we going?" Delia responded with a quick eagerness to the advance. But the woman relapsed into the indifferent silence chaining them all.

They trailed on, a hopeless, miserable crew, bound for the horrors of the unknown.

Delia eyed the nearest Fristle guard who marched along with wilting whiskers, his cat face sullen, the dust staining the brass-studded leather jerkin. He carried an axe at his belt, and a spear sloped over his shoulder. Every now and again he tilted his head up, so that the leather flaps of his cap dangled free, scanning the sky.

Suppose she were such a guard, herding slaves along? And one of the slaves in her grey slave tunic and breechclout accosted her, saying something like: "I am the Empress of Vallia. Release me at once, or your head is forfeit"?

What would she think; what do?

A swift thwack with the spear, an insult? Perhaps a taste of the sharp end to keep the cramphs in order? Certainly, it would be a surprising guard who would immediately leap into a torrent of majestrixes and unshackle the chains and bow and scrape.

There was no hope there.

Not yet. When she reached their destination, and managed to gain converse with someone in authority, then would be the time. The person riding so grandly in the gold coach, Delia surmised with a chill, might believe, and, believing, dispatch her out of hand.

The aragorn and the slavemasters chased out of Vallia bore a sullen resentment against the emperor and empress for depriving them of a livelihood. Not all people welcomed the manumission imposed from above.

Only a short time after leaving the village the slaves began to falter. Soon some dropped to the ground, unable to continue. Chains clanked and dragged in the dust.

Delia was pulled down by the woman at her side.

Instinctively, she tried to help the woman up, a hand under her armpit. The woman's head lolled. Other people began to drop. The guards used their whips, and shrieks lifted, cutting in the bright air. But the coffle stopped.

A totrix came lolloping back from up front. It bore a rider in silvered armor who flourished a whip and swore most vilely. She slashed at the slaves and the guards indiscriminately, shouting at them to go on.

"Grak!" she shrieked. "Grak, you useless bunch of tapos. Grak, or you'll all have your throats cut!"

A second totrix appeared from the front of the column.

Dully, Delia wondered how many more cavalry trotted so grandly as advance guard.

The second rider reined in beside the first.

"Easy, Chica. It is clear they must have water—as I said in the village."

"Since when does anyone listen to you, Nath the Muncible? They must be whipped into marching."

"They will be whipped to death. Then who will pay you?"

"Ah—your piddling ways sicken me."

Despite this altercation, the coach up ahead rumbled to a halt and presently a few tame slaves brought pannikins of water. Delia drank. She was not at all surprised that she drank as the other slaves drank, huge greedy gulps, grasping and jostling. After a bur or so the whips snapped and the coffle slowly resumed the march.

Slavery had been outlawed in Vallia and the slavers and aragorn banished, if they failed to take up an honest living. So this nightmare could not be happening—should not be happening. But it was.

She was far stronger than most of the people in the slave coffle. She could march. She had to retain her sense of identity, bide her time. There was great danger for the empress in this situation, paradoxically, far more danger than for a citizen. Her death would be well rewarded in the circles of her enemies. By keeping on, attracting no special attention to herself, keeping herself to herself, she could survive until she met someone to whom she could talk. If the gods favored her, it would be someone she knew, someone who was a friend.

She was far more frightened of the horrible swellings disfiguring her body. Her thoughts had to be kept under control. She made her legs go up and down and carry her on as she had in the Ochre Limits. But, truly, this trudging along, even loaded with chains, was nowhere as bad as that experience. These lumps and bumps, these rashes speckled with yellow pimples that grew into obscene blemishes upon her body, growing into smooth hard lumps... No. If she thought that, then she would have infected all of Lancival, those in Vondium and Drakanium...

No. No, that could not be the cause of the swellings.

And, if she thought rationally about this march, it was far far worse than struggling across the Ochre Limits. Then she had been a free woman, able to make her own decisions and affect, in however small a way, her own destiny. Now she was slave.

Did she have the Affliction of the Sores of Combabbry?

This pimple-speckled rash, those smooth swellings, were unlike the suppurating sores of the disease. But she had bathed in the Sacred Pool in far Aphrasöe. That would make a difference. Must make a difference to the course of the disease, surely? Perhaps she was a walking bed of infestation.

When she had spoken to the woman who dragged along at her side, her own words had sounded odd. A lump swelled beside her mouth, distorting the shape, slurring her speech. Another lump had joined those on her breast, and her face matched the general lumpiness. She must look a sight!

One leg—the left—was fully half again the size of her right leg. How odd it looked, to see one fat and one thin leg, striding forward under her!

She was growing light-headed.

Careful, girl! she said to herself, and bit down, and closed her eyes against the glare of dust, and marched on.

The course of the Affliction of the Sores of Combabbry was known. She would never have allowed herself to be taken to Lancival without complete conviction that she was free of the disease. A period of quarantine would have been necessary, and because she had not taken the disease and it was being checked in Mellinsmot, she had, along with the doctor, taken it that she was free. *Was* she free?

Just because these horrible lumps were different from the sores might not mean the disease too was different. If this woman at her side caught the infection—she would erupt in suppurating sores because she had not bathed in the Sacred Pool. All the mixed emotions experienced by Delia at thought of that magical baptism tormented her anew.

The trudging progress of the coffle degenerated to a shuffle. They made little better than two or two and a half miles an hour. When the suns at last slid down to the western horizon and the air cooled and the coach halted and tents were erected, they'd covered perhaps twenty miles or so. The slaves fell down in their tracks at the side of the road, and slept.

Those who remained awake kicked the others awake when a thin gruel, hard bread and pannikins of water came around. Then they all slept. Delia was not molested, although a few of the younger girls were removed from their chains and then, later, returned. A man slave, husky and with a mop of dark hair, was taken and likewise returned, much later than the others. He staggered in, groaning, was chained up and fell full length into an exhausted sleep.

The next day they made another twenty-five miles or so, and picked up half a dozen new slaves from pinched-face people at a crossroads inn. Gold changed hands. The newcomers were shackled up and the dreary procession resumed.

On this day the watching of the sky, although it persisted, was far more perfunctory. From this Delia deduced the coffle must be nearing its destination.

She still could not recognize where she was. She was in Vindelka—the kovnate province of her half-brother, for Val's sake!—but that was the extent of her knowledge. When you flew so fleetly high above the ground, details below blurred. An hour or two in the air could cover all and more, far far more, than a girl could walk on her feet in a day...

The cultivated fields were left behind. The coffle entered woods which thickened and deepened, cutting off the light. The track wound unevenly over bumpy ground. At the thought of bumps Delia touched herself, and winced. She was more lumpy than the ground upon which she walked.

If these damned slavers erupted all over with putrescent sores and boils, she did not think she would grieve overmuch ... If her three companions who had crashed with her in the airboat were infected, she would not only grieve, she would have to face her own guilt.

Common sense told her that she could not be held to blame. Medical opinion held that she could not have contracted the disease. But medical opinion was unaware of the existence of that Pool in the River Zelph of far Aphrasöe. Common sense might tell her all it liked; she was Delia and she was weighed down by self-recriminations far outside common sense.

Although she had been unable to see everyone in the coffle, she was confident that Mimi, Lathdo and Jordio were not there. The two men with her in the forward part of the voller must have gone slap bang over the other side of the house. As for Mimi—she had sailed off like a kite in the cabin. Where she was now, Opaz alone knew, and Delia consigned the little handmaid's fate to that manifestation of the Invisible Twins in trust and hope.

Then she fell over a snaggly root and pitched full length.

The woman chained with her fell on top of her. Metal clanked. Guards appeared with whips, ferocious. Delia managed to wriggle around and drag the chains up so that the links took most of the blows. But some struck through, and stung, stung like liquid fire.

The thought burst into her head...

If I had my Whip now...!

The guards sorted things out with blows and lashes and the coffle moved on. Delia felt a rising terror at her own fatigue. She was just so damned tired! She stumbled along in her chains as the shouts of "Grak! Grak!" beat about them. The woman she had dragged down said nothing. She walked as though encased in ice. Blood glimmered through a rent in her grey tunic.

Delia's legs began to turn to jelly, the fat left one and the thin right one. They were still attached to her body and they continued to go up and down and forward and back; but she was sure they were jelly. She couldn't feel anything of them, and nothing from her feet. The world around her grew dark.

Just keep on marching. That was all she had to do. Keep on going forward, head up, chin in, chest out, striding on and on, and not shuffling along with her head hanging and her back bent and pains running all over her except below her thighs.

The shadows of the trees mingled with the shadows in her eyes. Nothing underfoot except clouds. The chains would soon wear away the skin. She had nice skin. Before the blotches and the lumps appeared. She couldn't see much.

The earth under her rustled with leaves. She could not remember falling down again. She was not being whipped, so she could not have fallen down. A bowl was thrust into her hands. They were resting for the night!

She drank off the gruel wolfishly and wiped her finger around the bowl, and licked it. Almost, she had been likening herself to Pakkad, who in Kregish mythology stood for the downtrodden, the pariah and outcast. If she could sleep through this night, she would gather strength for the morrow.

And on the morrow anything might happen.

Ten

Alyss Carries Water

Carrying water remained one of the chief occupations of slaves.

With the yoke cutting into her shoulders carrying two tubs of water, Delia walked into the stone-flagged kitchens. Greasy Nardo the Water Master shrieked at her.

"Grak, you useless lump!"

Some of the water spilled, and Nardo shouted again.

Delia took no notice. Since the end of that frightful march in the slave coffle and her selection to become a water-carrier, she had spent a sennight here and already had worked out a scheme of escape. She continued to feel fatigued. The tiredness dragged at her. Her strength was barely enough for carrying the water. And her lumps and blotches turned her reflection in the water into that of a hideous nightmare.

From all this she took hope.

No one with whom she had come into contact had contracted the Affliction of the Sores of Combabbry.

Hurrying to the trough and pouring water in, with great care so as not to spill a drop, swinging the yoke first left and tipping and then right, she emptied the tubs and started back for the kitchen door. Nardo watched her with his greasy face glistening and his switch flickering.

Outside the kitchens the wooden stockade enclosed a yard and stabling and the well, with the tops of trees showing over the palisade. Sentries prowled there. Where she was she had, of course, no idea. None of the slaves knew that.

Silly Nath at the well had already cranked up a bucket and he stood, lanky and lopsided, ready to fill the tubs.

"Smells like roast ordel today," he said, spittle glistening on his narrow chin. He was cross-eyed. He wore a grey slave breechclout. The water shone silver from bucket to tub. Silly Nath did not spill much.

"Not for us," said Delia.

A totrix in the stables shook himself and stamped.

Four slaves staggered past under bundles of kindling, and more followed, dragging a lurching cart piled with logs.

"Can't you steal a little for me, Alyss?"

Delia sighed. "I'll try, Nath."

The tubs were filled. She settled the yoke so that it rested on the least sore parts of her shoulders, and started back for the kitchens.

Looking down at herself she thought—she hoped—that her left leg was not quite as fat as it had been. Was it? The skin glistened where it stretched taut. Thin white lines showed cutting in under her kneecap. Perhaps the lumps were going down at last?

Fat left leg or no fat left leg, she could ride a totrix. She marked the beast, stamping and snuffling in his stall, pampered and fed. There were six altogether, and she hungered for this particular one. When she was astride his back she'd be out through the gate, clear away if it was open, bashing it open if it was closed. After that—well, as she carried the water she descended into scarlet images of what would happen to this place when she returned leading one or two of her regiments.

No. No, that wouldn't do at all. That was quite silly.

Oh, no. She'd come back here leading one or two armies.

There would be very little left of this place by the time she and her people were finished with it.

On this mental fare she subsisted as the days passed. No one offered to molest her. The slaves slept higgledy-piggledy in dormitories above the kitchens. Facilities were primitive. From the yard looking back over the kitchen and superimposed dormitory a view could be obtained of a stone tower crowned by battlements and with a flagstaff. The pole raked up, bare.

A hint of more battlemented walls and towers beyond the first indicated that this place—wherever it was—had considerable defensive strength. Even the richest people looked twice before deciding to build castles in stone. They cost fabulous sums. This place probably consisted of a stone tower or two, and the rest of the fortifications would be of timber. Probably.

On the day that Nan the Bosom announced she was pregnant and the inevitable arguments started about who was the father, Delia really did think her left leg was just about its right size again. Nan the Bosom, outraged that the contraceptives she had paid for in kind had failed her, flailed about with her largest ladle. She was Soup Mistress, and her largest ladle was large. It cracked alongside three or four flea-bitten heads, and thwacked half a dozen grimy shins—and Nan had hardly begun.

"Not me, Nan!" and: "Musta been Nardo!"

And so on.

Delia waited outside until the water in her tubs stilled to mirrors. She had no wish to become involved. The tub-mirror showed her face as a nightmare to her, still, but not so much a nightmare as before. The lumps *were* going down. Her hair! To laugh in these circumstances could only indicate despair. It was just as well that she could view herself with some dispassionate analysis. Yes, she always tried to keep herself neat and tidy, that was true. But she did not think she was a vain woman. Just as well. The sight glaring back at her from the water mirror would have driven a vain woman past the verge.

With a savage thrust of her shoulders, she shattered the image in the water.

Putting the yoke back on, she went into the kitchens. The uproar continued. Nan, it was clear, didn't care who the father was. She just wanted to hit everybody with her ladle.

When Delia turned back from the well, Silly Nath said: "Smells like ponsho today, Alyss. Will you steal me a bit?"

"I'll try."

She turned away toward the kitchens in the never-ending drudgery. A flag flew at the flagstaff.

Instantly she stopped.

The flag flapped, infuriatingly twirling itself from side to side and pointing away from her. She could make out only the colors, not the devices. The colors were white and ochre.

Well, and what else had she expected? White and ochre were the colors of Vindelka. And that was where she was.

She remained utterly convinced that the devices on the flag were not those of her half-brother Vomanus. He would never run a degenerate hell-hole like this. A touch around her waist, a fingering pressure, brought her back with a thump from the considerations of an empress to those of a slave.

"Give us a cuddle, Alyss—"

"What, with me, Nath?"

She was so startled that was all she could think of.

"I like you. You're nice."

"But—" She moved away. Silly Nath would not leave the well and the crank handle. He'd been flogged silly for doing that—twice. "Look at me!"

Silly Nath twisted his head on one side in his ecstasy of cleverness. "They call me Silly Nath. But I've seen you, Alyss. You're different. You're lovely."

"I'm all lumpy."

"Yes. You gimme a cuddle tonight."

Because slaves lived in squalor perhaps anything only slightly less hideous than the ugliness around would appear lovely to them. Delia was aware of the incongruity of responding to an amorous advance by denigrating her appearance. That verged on the coy. Here she was, dressed in slave grey, carrying two damn great tubs of water, her hair a mess, her lumps making her grotesque, arguing with a simpleton about cuddling. It was enough to make a girl say a rude word.

And then, amazingly, vouchsafed from Dee Sheon herself, wonderfully, she realized what that last limping thought meant. She was coming back to life. Not because poor Silly Nath felt her attractive and wanted a cuddle, but because she could see the funny side of the situation.

"Nan the Bosom is pregnant, Nath."

"'Twaren't me."

"Now's your chance. I can't cuddle you, Nath." Then the limping humor changed, and the words whiplashed. "Stay away from me, Nath. For your own good."

All the same, on the morrow the kitchen slaves kept asking Silly Nath where he got his black eye from. He didn't say.

He looked more miserable than sullen when he filled the tubs. Delia had no need to harden her heart. Some things were done in her world and some things were not done. The question of soft or hard hearts did not enter the equation.

And the flag still flew.

When she reached the kitchen door a voice she did not know was saying: "...no concern. We expect some more in a few days. Until then you'll have to manage as best you can."

Greasy Nardo the Water Master wiped his forehead. He looked at once angry and chastened. The man speaking to him wore slave grey, but his tunic bore a white and ochre patch, and his switch was larger and thicker than Nardo's. His face resembled that of a half-starved water rat, with pimples.

"Is this the woman?"

"Yes, Master Uldo. This is the woman."

So, said Delia to herself, so this is the First Water Master, Uldo. He was doing a thorough job of frightening Nardo.

Uldo switched his stick at Delia.

"Alyss. Come with me." As Delia instantly obeyed, the feel of the switch on her arm, he shouted: "Onker! Do not bring the water tubs." Delia, acting as a slave would act, instantly put the tubs down and cowered away.

Surprisingly, Uldo said, "There are men in the treadmill to bring the water up. You will carry it from there."

She nodded. She did not say anything. She knew how to act like slave. She wondered if she might let this Uldo live a little longer than the others when the time came...

The First Water Master strutted along importantly, slashing about with his switch, and Delia trailed along after. They went through the yard, where she gave her usual quick scrutiny of the totrix stables, and so through the open barred door beyond. Sentries looked down, mercenaries by their appearance, as the two walked into the shadows and began to climb wooden stairs into the interior of the building.

They went by flang-infested stairways and dusty corridors until they reached a panel, jutting from the wall. These back stairs and runnels were to be found in most of the palaces and castles of Kregen. Uldo pushed the door open and they went through.

The room was low-ceilinged and the walls were stone-faced. Very little could be seen, for the room was filled with steam. The sounds of rushing water mingled with the hoarse thump of a bellows. A blurred halo of reddish-yellow light and a wash of heat told of a furnace being stoked to greater output. A faint cloying taint of heavy scents hung on the steam-laden air.

Uldo pointed with his switch.

"When you are told, Alyss, you will take the hot water into the bathroom. You will make sure it is very hot."

"Yes, master."

Then, again surprisingly, Uldo said, "Ninki fell and scalded herself. You will do her work until she is well."

"Yes, master."

"And there is time for you to comb your hair. Velia!"

At this Delia started, and turned pale.

A gross form waddled on stumpy legs from the steam.

The woman was vast. Her arms were dripping wet. She wore only a grey slave breechclout. She would have made a middling-sized vosk look small. She ran with moisture. She shook. But her face with its multiple chins and piglike nose and small bright eyes smiled.

"Come on, dearie. I'll make you look presentable."

Uldo brushed moisture from his eyebrows. His expression remained that of a worried man run off his legs.

"We're short-handed, Velia, and Ninki scalds herself. I wonder if she did it on purpose. Remember, Velia, you'll have to see to it. You're responsible."

"Oh, that's all right. My lady knows me." Velia's enormous body quivered with amusement. "She trusts me."

"More than me—"

"That's because I'm a woman."

"So," said Uldo, turning to leave the steam room, "I see."

When he had gone, Velia drew Delia off to the side where curtains concealed an alcove where the steam coiled less thickly. A few shelves with unguents and scents, a truckle-bed, a chest, toilet articles, indicated the place where the Steam Mistress spent her entire life. Scraps of food drying on a plate would have fed a couple of the slaves down below. Delia repressed the growl from her stomach.

"Now, let's have a look at you, dearie."

The Steam Mistress produced a cheap but ornate comb and started to tear away at Delia's scalp. Any protest would have been futile. Delia, perforce, allowed her hair to be dragged into some semblance of order. With that out of the way—"A start only, dearie, a start only, for it's in a terrible mess!"—she was washed thoroughly. There was, in any event, a copious supply of hot water. The grey slave tunic and breechclout could only be brushed and the worst of the spots either got off or rubbed over with a grey chalk. The chalk slicked in the heated atmosphere. Delia touched her face.

She had been speaking normally. The lump at the side of her mouth had disappeared. She looked down. Her legs looked the same size—almost. She fancied the left was still a teeny weeny fraction fatter than the right. The lumps noticeable on her two days ago were now quite gone. She felt and looked all over. She could find not a single blotch.

"All right dearie, all right. You're fine. There'll be plenty of that, later on, I don't doubt."

Delia chose not to inquire what the Steam Mistress meant.

She could still feel the shock that had flashed through her when Uldo had called out the Steam Mistress's name.

Suppose her little Velia should be slave here!

"Now, Alyss. You must be quick. My lady will have her bath hot. You must run. And don't spill a drop."

"Yes, Velia, no, Velia."

"H'm," said Velia the Steam Mistress, "you'll do."

After that they waited. The water boiled in the pans. Velia gave a series of thunderous strokes upon the bellows and the furnace roared and the steam spouted. Everything was drenched in moisture. Delia adjusted the yoke, a smaller and more refined version than the one used in the kitchens. She balanced the copper pans. If they splashed and the water hit her, she'd be scalded red. They waited until the very last moment, until a bell jangled, before the boiling water fumed into the copper pans. Then Delia ran.

The bathroom next door was hot. It smelled of exotic perfumes from the far corners of Kregen. Ceramic pots of Pandahem ware bulged with flowers. Drapes hung artistically.

The bath itself lay sunk into the marble flooring. Velia had given Delia a pair of wooden-soled slippers, for the floor heated by ducts was far too hot even for a slave to walk upon barefoot. A woman wearing a long white gown and carrying a silver rod beckoned imperiously. Delia poured the water into the bath and then raced off for more.

By the time she had completed four trips she was beginning to glow a trifle.

The water in the copper pans now bubbled all the way to the bath.

"Hurry, you ninny!" commanded the woman with the silver rod. She looked harassed. She darted to a curtained doorway and peered out, the door just cracked ajar. She turned back.

"One more, and hurry, girl!"

Delia flew.

When she returned, the water bubbling and steaming, the woman looked surprised. "Very well. One more. *Grak!*"

Delia grakked.

She was just pouring the last of the water into the bath when the flunkey woman opened the door, bowing, and a woman walked in who, immediately, took Delia's attention. She stood back, holding her copper pans still, partially concealed by the fronds of a fern, and watched. As usual with many great ones of the world, they took no notice of a slave, the grey slave clothing blending with the background.

This woman walked with studied poise. She was attended by a handmaid clad in pearls and little else, a fashion Delia considered either offensive and decadent or just plain tasteless. Some people liked the fashion, though.

Clad in a draped white gown, the woman reminded Delia of a lazy cat, curled before the fire. The latent sensuality concealed by satisfaction in her face was perfectly complemented by the perfection of her form as she threw off the gown. Her hair was not chalk-white, not silver, but of that platinum luster that so often occurred in Vallian women. The blondeness sheened platinum in the overheated atmosphere.

Her face was not remarkable for beauty, and perhaps its own icy perfection marred any warmth that lack of external beauty might have lent it. She was, judged by almost any standards, a remarkable woman.

Poised, posed, she stood on the lip of the bath. She extended one foot, the toenails painted and polished a deep purple. Her foot arched. Clearly, this moment of the bath was for her a moment of sensual pleasure.

In the next instant, she would have plunged her foot into the water.

Quite without thought, perfectly instinctively, Delia darted forward.

"Careful, my lady! The water is boiling hot—you will scald yourself!"

The woman hesitated, and in the same moment, tottered. She began to overbalance. If she went full length into that water she'd be parboiled. Delia ran. She got an arm around the woman's waist, locked into the swell of the hips, and pulled back.

In an undignified tumble of naked arms and legs, the pair sprawled on the matting surrounding the bath.

The flunkey woman shrieked.

She rushed forward and yanked Delia up. She thwacked out with her silver rod, striking Delia about the shoulders.

"Imbecile! Onker! Look what you have done!" The silver rod slashed. "Now you will be flogged jikaider until you are shredded to death!"

Eleven

Nyleen Gillois

The silver rod struck again.

Tangled up with a naked woman as she was, Delia had to make up her mind.

Her instinct was simply to get up and take the silver rod away and give the flunkey woman a taste or two. That was also the act of a slave who wished to commit suicide. The flunkey woman, dragging at her to pull her off, hit again.

With a twisting heave as though struggling to get free, Delia half-hunched around and so took the silver rod into her left hand. Naked flesh, pink and glowing, bulged up before her eyes. Concealing her movements, she gave the rod a hefty pull and then instantly rolled the other way. She started to yell, adding to the shrieks from the other two.

"Your pardon, my lady! I was trying to help!"

That vicious pull on the rod yanked the flunkey woman forward, caught unexpectedly and off balance. She staggered. In the next instant she would go head first into the bath.

Delia considered enough was enough.

She got her body in the way, rear-ended the woman off, and then bent to the other who screamed in her nakedness upon the matting. Delia hauled her up.

"There, there, my lady. It's all right. You are unhurt, praise be!"

She did not care to give the praise to any particular deity or spirit until she knew a little more of this platinum-haired woman's predilection in religious matters.

"You touched me, slave!"

"Yes, my lady. You would have been boiled—"

"Silence!" screamed flunkey-woman.

"Oh, do hold still. Ilka, do!"

"Yes, my lady."

"Now you, slave. What is your name?"

"Alyss, my lady."

"Alyss. I see. And you saved me from the boiling water?"

"I could do nothing else, my lady."

Let her chew on that one. Delia had the idea that too great a pressure on a sense of gratitude would be wasted on this woman.

"Let me look at you—" The great lady stood up, gave herself a genteel shake and, oblivious of her nudity, sized up the slave before her.

At that moment the opposite doors burst open and three hulking great warriors burst in, swords drawn, shields up, glaring and spitting, ready for blood. They skidded to a halt on the marble, and then began to hop up and down.

"My lady!" the Hikdar shouted.

"I'm perfectly all right, thank you, Nadia. You'd better leave. Otherwise you'll burn your feet off clear up to the ankles."

"Yes, my lady!" And: "Quidang!" The three Jikai Vuvushis bashed their swords against their shields, turned smartly, and trotted off. Smartly.

As though the antics of her guards cleared the atmosphere, the great lady unbent graciously. A dent at each corner of her mouth might have been mistaken for amusement. Delia stood, unmoving, silent, waiting for events. Great ladies were unpredictable—by Krun! who better than her to know that?—and it might be very necessary in the next moment or two to be cunning, groveling, tearful or grateful.

The woman flunkey, this Ilka, came forward with the white robe, which she wrapped about her mistress. All the time the pearl-clad handmaid had remained in a stasis of terror, her hands clasped together on her breast.

The great lady settled the robe about her shoulders. She drew her head up so that the platinum hair sheened.

"I have taken a liking to you, Alyss. I think it will be amusing for you to serve me. If you continue to do as well, you will do well." And she laughed, delighted at her own quip.

"Yes, my lady."

"Do you think the water of the correct temperature now?"

Delia did not hesitate. If this was how the fish felt when the hook whipped out of his mouth, she did not know. But it was a chance, and she grabbed it.

Going to the edge of the bath, she knelt down and tested the water with a tentative finger. It stung only a little.

"It stings only a little, my lady."

"Then I will chew a palmful of palines. Sissy!"

The pearly maiden jumped and blushed and ran to fetch the yellow berries so that her mistress might savor their flavor while she waited for her bath to cool.

Ilka, the flunkey woman, glowered at Delia.

When the water reached the right temperature, and Delia reported the fact, the great lady once more removed her gown and stepped forward. She dipped that purple-painted toenailed toe into the water, and smiled, and sank down into the depths. The water sluiced away from under her. Perfumes were poured in, and soft scents filled the room. The place stank rather too high for Delia's tastes, but she had been told by other ladies that her tastes were far too refined in some directions, and far too coarse in others.

Gently laving the water about her breast, the great lady looked up.

"Ilka. See to it that Alyss is taken away and bathed, cleaned up, her hair combed, given decent clothes. I think Sissy cannot teach her very much, but let her try. Then bring her to me."

"Yes, my lady."

This was done.

As they went through the performance in an adjoining and less splendid bath chamber, Delia said: "Who is the lady, mistress?"

Ilka, superintending the operations upon her new charge, sniffed.

"Why, you fambly. She is Nyleen Gillois na Sagaie, who is now Kovneva of Vindelka."

In an even voice, Delia said: "She is newly married to the kov, is she not?"

"Oh, him," said Ilka, and slapped her silver rod at the slave braiding up Delia's hair.

"Is he here?"

"No. And speak properly, girl!"

"Yes, mistress."

Presently, when they were clothing her in silver tissue and dangling strings of pearls about her in strategic positions, she said: "Mistress. Is there something I might eat?"

"Eat? You cannot be hungry?"

"I am hungry, mistress."

Ilka sniffed, as though the clepsydra had sprung a leak. "Oh, very well. You, slave, fetch food. And Grak!"

The slave girl prodded by the silver rod ran off, to return shortly with a copper bowl of bread and bird's wings, roasted in brown gravy and smothered in Tarnton dressing. Delia made herself eat it all, although she was not overfond of Tarnton dressing with its rich mixture of fruits and honeys.

She liked fruit and she liked honey; but she liked them as they came and not adulterated by would-be culinary artists.

As she ate she reflected that it was sheer bad luck that her half-brother was absent. Any appeal to this Nyleen would, in her judgment, prove fatal.

Quite clearly, Nyleen ran this household of slavery and Vomanus could know nothing of it all. He couldn't, surely? No—Delia would not believe that of Vomanus, despite all his feckless ways.

She consoled herself with the hope that this removal to a higher sphere within the castle would afford her better opportunities for escape.

In the old evil days when slavery was the norm in Vallia, if slaves ran off they were usually recaptured very quickly, simply because they had nowhere to hide. Once Delia ran off she'd have a very different future. Oh, yes, very different, by Vox! As she rearranged the strings of pearls and pulled the silver tissue straight she dwelled for a time on what might happen here when, say, Nath Karidge, the commander of her personal bodyguard, turned up with his cavalry...

"Grak, girl!" Ilka, frowning, harassed, shooed the slaves away. These slaves appeared to be a poor lot, pinched and hollow-eyed, and reserved for the most menial work. That they were employed this close to the great lady reinforced the impression of emergency everywhere apparent. At the same time Delia winced within herself at her own categorization of these poor creatures, and then she chastised herself again for that demeaning thought. People were people in the light of Opaz.

The emergency, to put it in overstatement, was easily understood. This Nyleen was from Evir, and that northernmost province of the empire had broken away, revolted, got itself a king and carried on the practice of slavery. Nyleen expected to be served by slaves. Just how Vomanus had happened on her was beyond Delia's grasp at the moment. But he had and he had married her. So here she was, kovneva of the kovnate, and damned-well determined to go on being a slavemistress. The countryside was being raided for human merchandise. Until the stock of slaves could be built up, they'd be short.

Delia fumed, hurrying along with Ilka through corridors showing every sign of new and uncompleted furnishings. This place had probably been just three or four stone towers joined by short curtain walls, an ancient sax, a frontier fort. Now they'd built new timber halls and walls and kitchens and were furnishing the whole up like a palace. Well, Delia felt even more convinced as they hurried through the antechamber that Vomanus could know nothing of all this.

Two bulky female slaves wearing just grey breechclouts and carrying a sofa with gilded legs and upholstery of a bright green and yellow shrank aside to let Ilka pass. The flunkey woman—she was called with respect Silver Rod—pushed past without noticing. Delia followed.

Through the antechamber, the great lady's retiring room beyond was not quite what Delia had expected.

Yes, there were quantities of furniture in dubious taste, and feathers and fans and drapes, and side tables bearing wine and munchables. The carpets floated one ankle deep. The air stank of perfume. All this was tiresomely normal for women suddenly catapulted into affluence. But, also, there were more tasteful refinements. Three or four good pictures adorned the walls. The mirror was a marvel, tall and cunningly swiveled. In an alcove stood a harp. The instrument had not been tampered with in the sense that many women ordered grotesque carved representations of gods and goddesses to be applied all over the frame. This specimen stood upright and was there to do what it had been built to do.

Delia recognized the handiwork, of course. This one had been built by Master Nalgre the Strings, for there was no mistaking his supreme craftsmanship. He was dead now for over three hundred seasons. If she cared to look down low at the side of the soundboard she would find a name scratched into the varnished wood. Her mother had been cross. Harps, young Delia, she had said, are for playing on and not for writing your name on, as though you can claim the instrument as yours. And, in her strict old-fashioned and loving way, her mother had sent the harp to Vomanus and brought in a new one. Well, that was all a long time ago.

"Stop gawping, girl! Arrange your clothes. And recline on the lowest step of the divan!"

Stopping gawping was not too difficult, for the harp brought back a gush of memories. And reclining on the lowest carpeted step of the divan was easy. The divan itself, smothered in silks and furs, waited under its freight of feathered fans. But arranging her clothes—well, now, how did you arrange a scrap of silver tissue and a few strings of beads?

She finally decided to get a string each side and the rest down the middle when Nyleen walked in. She came with her retinue. This was small. Sissy hovered, still unsure of herself. A big strapping wench waved a feathered fan, for the overheated atmosphere needed to be siphoned off and fresh air imported to make any real difference. Nadia, the guard Hikdar, led her pair of fighting women. They wore silvered breastplates, deeply curved. Delia had always thought girls comical when they adopted brass breastplates, but these girls in their breastplates, corselets, breast and backs, looked likely in a fight.

"Parclear, Alyss!"

In a weird reprise of her actions with the mistress, Delia rose and poured and fetched the sparkling drink. Nyleen slouched in her divan and the others took up their ritual positions. A large dark girl wearing the black and white skin of a wersting led a couple of werstings in on leashes. These black and white striped hunting dogs had been thoroughly tamed. They hunched together for comfort, and rolled their eyes. No doubt their fangs had been blunted.

Wondering what was to happen next, Delia resumed her reclining position on the lowest step. She had seen queens and empresses in their thrones, with slaves and chail sheom, chained slave handmaids, and savage beasts chained, with handlers to control them, and enormous slaves waving faerling fans. This Nyleen aped her betters and aimed high. It was, Delia decided, comical and also farcical. Also, it was dangerous.

A bell rang. A woman wearing a deep green gown and girded by a belt from which hung many keys, entered and began a long conversation with Nyleen. The kovneva listened, pettishly, every now and then sipping her parclear or taking a biscuit crumb from Sissy and throwing it to the werstings. Delia lay and schemed plans of escape.

Then she discovered what her main duties for the kovneva were to be.

She was not at all surprised.

After all, hadn't she been along this road before?

Fat Queen Fahia of Hyrklana had used golden bowls. As for that poor unfortunate wretch, rumor had it she'd been chewed up by her own vicious black neemus. In any event, as Delia's son Jaidur was now King of Hyrklana, with Lildra as queen, Fahia would never again be queen and snap her fingers for her golden pot.

Nyleen, Kovneva of Vindelka, favored silver pots with a furry rim. Much, my dear, more comfortable.

At least she retired behind a screen to wash. Delia did all that was necessary. In truth, compared with the muck and mess she'd scrubbed up in Mellinsmot, this was a mere tiresome chore. Throwing the soiled linen into the basket and washing her hands before fetching fresh, she debated if she should break this Nyleen's neck now. No. Perhaps it would be better to unriddle the puzzle first. Nyleen, aloof, her platinum hair in the almost capable hands of Sissy, returned more than once. Delia soldiered on, nursed on, sistered on.

There were no men in close attendance on Nyleen.

She managed to snatch a bite to eat now and again, for any idea of the Kregan's regular six or eight meals a day was quite out of the question. Only when Nyleen slept was Delia free to sleep. Common sense made her decide not to escape that night. Sleep was the first priority. After all, she wouldn't run far when she could barely drag herself to her new cot and fall, flat out.

The next few days witnessed a gradual improvement in her bodily strength. Soon, she bubbled with confidence, soon she'd be back to her full natural vigor.

Kovneva Nyleen's routine varied but little. When she went out riding she left her handmaids in the fortress and rode with Nadia and an escort. No banquets were held. Dancing was arranged for the next evening. On the appointed hour people began to appear in the wide hall which, now cleared of its benches, normally served as the refectory. Not a single man was present.

Being cut off from news of the outside world always gave Delia a claustrophobic feeling. What was going on, right now, in Vondium, in Valkanium, in Delphond? Had there been any news of her husband? Were her children still well?

Had the Shanks attacked again from around the curve of the world? There were a million and one items the answers to which she desperately required. Yet during this time she remained calm. She planned her escape. She stole food and clothes and found a loose flagstone and scooped a hole and hid her loot there. She was ready on the night of the dance.

The slaves with whom she had worked in the kitchens could only stare enviously. Only Silly Nath yelled out, some nonsense about cuddling that night. Nan the Bosom thwacked him over the head with her second largest ladle.

These slaves had been trundled in to stoke up the fires and provide hot food from a railed area at one side. They kept looking at the piles of food and racked amphorae, and licking their lips. Depending on what manner of slavemistress Nyleen was, they might this evening get a wet or get a thrashing.

Nan the Bosom started a racket among the slaves, fiercely accusing some scoundrel of stealing her best onion-slicing knife. "How can I make soup if I can't slice onions, and how can I slice onions if I don't have my best onion slicer?"

The knife—it had a black handle and was thin and exceedingly sharp—was not found. Naturally. By that time it lay snugged under a flagstone.

If any wight was foolish enough to try to stop Delia, then she or he or it would serve in lieu of an onion.

Nyleen showed no great discrimination among her women as to rank. All those who were free danced. The slaves slaved. Forming an opinion about the inclinations of Nyleen, Delia grasped at another thread. Nyleen detested men, clearly, and surrounded herself with women. That was her privilege up to a point. But Silly Nath was here, and other male slaves. They were not seen as men. They were seen as slaves.

The orchestra proved abominable.

Five women scraped and blew and banged away, and Sissy jangled on the great harp made by Nalgre the Strings over three hundred seasons ago. The superb instrument had been carted down to the converted refectory. Delia chose not to listen to the so-called music. But it served to provide a background and a tempo for the various dances. The lines formed and broke apart and reformed, hands joined and parted. Couples gyrated in the waltz brought to Kregen by the emperor. Eyes sparkled and teeth glistened and the glowing aromas rose.

They were circling in the dance called the Broken Vaol Paol when Delia slipped away unnoticed. In this dance the circle is broken at a certain point and a general excuse me follows as partners change in order to reform the Vaol Paol, the great circle of life of the philosophers. Delia hurried away.

Down through ways she now knew well she pattered on bare feet. Her flagstone would yield a pair of stout sandals one of the Jikai Vuvushis had spent one hell of a time yelling over and searching for. Torches cast their streaming orange hair in the night breeze. Stars prickled above. In the yard the well looked lonely without Silly Nath as its constant companion.

The kitchens still operated, pre-preparing the food for its final cooking aloft in the refectory. Delia avoided the light, skulked over to her flagstone. She put on the drab brown clothes, girded up the belt, fingered Nan the Bosom's black-handled onion knife. She put on the sandals and made for the totrix stalls.

The far doors opened on the yard and many torchlights glittered through, blowing in the breeze. The sounds of zorca hooves, the noise of totrixes and the groaning protestations of wheels reached her. A procession entered the yard. She shrank back into the shadows, cursing this inopportune interruption. Now she would have to wait until these idiots had taken themselves off.

The ornate coach which had led her coffle of slaves ground to a halt a scant dozen paces from her. Totrix riders reined in and zorcamen jangled to a halt. Lances slanted, their pennons whipping. The sound of armed men and women surrounded her. She lay as quiet as a woflo from a chavnik.

"They have begun the dance already, blast your eyes, Nath! We are late!"

The coachman turned his head. "Yes, master."

"You will be given ten strokes, Nath. Ten."

"Yes, master."

The coach disgorged a man wrapped in a cloak, a helmet upon his head, an air of force and bluster about him. He stamped booted feet. A totrix rider dismounted, flung the reins to a waiting Jikai Vuvushi, and approached this blustery blowhard of a man.

"Chica! Go and tell my sister I am here. Bid her send her tame slaves to attend me before I dance!"

"At once, jen," said that same Chica who had been so severe to the slaves in Delia's coffle on the way here. She strode off, long-legged, virile and potent, a fighting maid from sole to crown. A nasty customer, that one, judged Delia.

Looking from the shadows, listening, cursing these fools for interfering with her meticulously planned escape, Delia waited as the man Nath the Muncible approached this stamping blowhard who was Kovneva Nyleen's brother. A right pair, then. She eyed the zorcas. One of those, now, under her, and they'd never catch her... Few animals on Kregen were as fleet as a zorca over ground.

"Your orders, jen?" Nath the Muncible spoke in his even voice.

"See to the men. Keep them well away. You know how my sister detests all men."

"Aye, jen. All save you, thanks be."

"She cannot do without me." The words came out big and puffed. Delia felt it time to begin to creep away in the shadows and see about a zorca. The big man went on talking, spitting his words out with venom. "She married that fool Vomanus and so we are one step nearer the throne. The moment the empress arrives and can be killed the quicker we can take the second step."

Twelve

Just Delia, Playing the Harp

The empress stopped moving.

Breathing evenly, alert, motionless, still as a reptile waiting to strike, the empress crouched in the shadows and the words she had just heard reverberated in her brain.

"The moment the empress arrives and can be killed..."

Escape this night, then, was out of the question.

Delia fancied she wanted to know a little more of the plot to kill her. If she ran off now...? Well, she could always return with the armies, as she had planned. That way something might be decided. But she was Delia. She was Delia of Delphond, Delia of the Blue Mountains. She was Delia of Valka, and Empress of Vallia, and also queen and princess of this and that, and kovneva and Stromni of other fair places on Kregen. She was honest enough to admit to herself that, while all these fancy titles might mean more to her than perhaps they ought, they weighed evenly in the scales beside her sisterhood in the Order of the Rose.

She could remember her father the emperor continually complaining because his advisers and pallans and counselors would protect him and not allow him to go running headlong off into danger. She had had a fair share of danger. But she was Delia. Of course, she was well aware that she had been influenced by her husband. He, the great hairy clansman, had been powerfully influenced by her, to their mutual joy, and he was adjusting nicely to being emperor. In this situation neither of them would be likely to run off.

The blood in their veins might boil hotly at injustice and they would do what they could to set things right. But they were no plaster saints. If they scented adventure, they were after it like a leem after a ponsho.

So, now, Delia waited quietly in the shadows, her decision taken and her mind firmly made up.

She'd dance attendance on this woman and her brother, these two Gillois, and not only would she find out what they were up to—the pair of scoundrels!—she'd see to it that their precious schemes came to nothing. And if the pair of them ended up dead, that would be their misfortune.

Nath the Muncible moved quickly to the steps of the coach. Watching, Delia saw how he moved in a fussy and yet hesitant way. He assisted a cloaked figure to alight. Delia watched avidly. Another member of the cutthroat gang, clearly, come to join in the plot. Well, he'd lose his head as easily as the others.

The face in the hood of the cloak lay in shadow. Torchlights struck twin gleams from the person's eyes. The Lord Gillois na Sagaie stamped and turned, his sword swinging.

"Everything will be prepared for you, Sana, immediately."

The woman in the cloak acknowledged the information. The hood twisted around. For a moment, a matter of a half dozen heartbeats, she looked directly at the spot where Delia hunkered down in the darkness. Delia held her breath. The world fined down to that hooded face and those twin gleams of light from hidden eyes.

The hood turned away.

"Very well, Cranchar. I am in need of a bath and clean clothes. I do not think I shall attend your sister's dance. Convey my regrets."

"Yes, Sana, of course."

Movement followed as the Sana was escorted away by two serving girls from the coach and by Nath the Muncible. If the Sana was a wise woman or a witch, Delia could not tell, the ancient title of sana being used indiscriminatingly for any woman whose powers were beyond those of normal folk.

Time to be moving.

Nyleen would be calling for Sissy and Alyss to go off and assist the new arrivals. Delia moved like a hunting cat of the jungle, smooth and feral, soundless in the shadows.

The flagstone made a faint chiming gong note as the last corner dropped. Motionless, clad once more in her silver tissue and beads, she glared around. A hard shadow moved against a distant torchlight.

"Who's there?"

Armor clanked. A broad form blotted out the light.

"A Chail Sheom? What are you—?"

Delia leaped.

She was not fussy. She was quick and professional.

The guard's armor and helmet and sword and shield did not save him. He had marched in with his lord, and now he lay on the ground with a broken neck for all the good his zeal in guarding had done him. Delia flexed the muscles in her arms and shoulders. The fellow had needed a shave. She ran fleetly away, skillfully taking the shortest and darkest route, fled up the backstairs.

She made it back to the refectory with a second to spare.

"Sissy! Alyss! There you are, you ungrateful girl. Attend the lord my brother. Mind you are punctilious."

"Yes, mistress."

"Well, then—grak!"

They grakked.

Luckily for Lord Cranchar Gillois na Sagaie, he wanted nothing more from the girls than attention to his well-being. Hot water, towels, wine— these they provided. Anything further would have distressed Delia, for she wanted to find out about the plot against her before she slew him.

She had to allow Sissy to deal with the mysterious cloaked figure addressed as a sana, and when the two girls could talk afterward, she asked the obvious question.

"Oh," said Sissy, tossing her head, for all her uncertainty determined not to allow this new girl Alyss to oust her from her position as the number one handmaid, "Oh, she's a witch. No doubt about it."

"Ugly?"

"She had nice hair."

"Beautiful?"

"Her body was too thin."

Delia did not really care what the witch looked like; what counted was her power.

This gave credence to what she had heard at Lancival about sorcery being employed by the Sisters of the Whip, for Delia believed she had stumbled on a hotbed of that order here.

"She complained there was only one handmaid to wait on her. She was horrible." Truth to tell, Sissy did look upset. "You were lucky with the Lord Cranchar. Now he is here we shall see a few things!"

When they returned to the refectory the dance was the Pandamon Jut Gallop, a dance brought over from the island of Pandahem. Delia did not dance. She wondered just what those few things might be that Lord Cranchar would show them in a household of women. The music grated on her, despite her shutting her ears. Presently she stood up and went across to Sissy. Nyleen was prancing with her brother.

"Sissy. Don't you want to dance? I'll play the harp."

"You can?"

"A little."

"If you make a mess of it, my lady will have us—"

"Don't worry. Look, here is a chord—" Delia swept her hand over the strings, and then pressing the round of her palm against two strings finished up with that thrilling vibrato with all its mysterious over and undertones that only a harp can fetch forth from the soul of music.

"We-ell," said Sissy. "All right."

So Delia played the harp.

The Strom of Valka had once told her in genuine and abashed amazement that he'd no idea at all that she could play the harp. Well, by Vox, and hadn't she sweated blood for season after season learning the mystery? She played divinely.

Presently the other musicians stopped scraping and blowing and banging.

Presently the dancers stopped dancing and crowded around.

Delia played on. Her repertoire was vast, culled from many races and cultures of Kregen, and she played now with a release of her feelings, letting herself, for the moment, forget her problems in the spiritual uplift and the earthy chuckle of the music. She forgot she was slave, she forgot she was empress; she was just Delia, playing the harp.

When she finished and the strings thrummed into an echoing silence, she sat back, at once filled and exhausted.

No one said anything until the Lord Cranchar, slapping his thigh, exclaimed: "Sister! You have a slave there worth a sack of gold!"

"Yes," said Nyleen comfortably approving of this new source of wealth dropped upon her. "When I decide to sell her."

In his decorated evening robes, flushed from the dance, high of color, Cranchar might consider that he looked splendid in the eyes of many a woman. The women here, except one or two including his sister, kept away from him. He always had ample body space. They did not look squarely upon him, and if by chance their glances happened to meet his, they would look away with a furtive sliding motion to which he could only respond with a bear-like roll of his shoulders.

In looks he superficially resembled his twin; but his hair was of the darker Vallian brown, and his face, far from being of an icy complexion was fiery, choleric, and with the veins sprouting blue. He stamped his feet a lot. Delia rose from the harp and, demurely, made her way to where she had been bidden to sit in attendance upon the kovneva.

From then on Delia was commanded to play the harp as a regular part of her duties. She still had to run with the fur-rimmed silver bowl and the towels. But more and more as the days passed, the harp-playing overtook all her other work.

Fresh batches of slaves arrived, and a certain amount of readjustment took place in slaving duties. The fortress was being turned into a luxurious palace, and remaining a fortress despite all. She was unmolested, and as she played she listened to the conversations between brother and sister, between the kovneva and her cronies—and she learned no more of the plot against the empress.

The witch, who was called Fiacola the Gaze, remained closeted in the chambers reserved for her use. She was regularly attended by Sissy and some of the newer slave girls whom Sissy attempted to train. Delia was content to remain with Nyleen, play the harp, and listen. But, she promised herself, she would not wait forever. If nothing more transpired of this famous plot, she'd escape and bring the army down on this decadent place. If they were all swept away down to the Ice Floes of Sicce, there'd be no more plot. Yes, by Dee Sheon!

Thirteen

Nyleen Enjoys Herself

When Delia was thrashed she told herself that she had had enough and that as soon as her back stopped hurting she would escape.

The afternoon before had not appeared any different from any afternoon. The twin suns shone. Food was eaten and wine drunk. The harp was played. Toward evening the woman in the green gown, girded with keys, Paline Pontora, the chatelaine, told her mistress that a batch of male slaves had been brought in. Nyleen nodded. Her teeth caught up her lower lip. A slumberous look about her eyes and a marked flush of her cheeks denoted a greater significance to this information than was at once apparent.

This time the refectory was cleared of tables and benches, not for dancing but for games of a more sinister nature. The Lord Cranchar did not attend. He bore the cognomen of Cranchu, and this, alone, was enough to mark him as a man of savage temperament and cruel ways. Yet he did not attend.

The bewildered men slaves, stark naked, were herded in by Jikai Vuvushis, armed and armored. Spear points prodded narrow buttocks, whips licked expertly around shanks and backs and ears. The men yelled in pain and shuffled on in their chains. They were an unremarkable collection of men, some tall, some short, some fat, some thin. They stood in a bemused huddle as first two and then another two of their number were selected. The ladies sprawled in fascinated attention on divans and chairs about the cleared central space. Guards stood at alert, waiting for any rebellion. No doubt some of them relished the chance to lick a whip around a fellow's bottom. The sports were varied and ingenious.

All of them meant pain, humiliation and indignity for the men, and death at the end. That death was not quick in coming. The screams bouncing from the ceiling of the refectory would have chilled a listener's heart. The men were not gagged. That, it transpired, would have blunted the women's pleasure.

Delia watched not so much in horror and pity, as in a dull and futile rage.

Whatever of inhumanity woman could show to man was performed there, in iron and lash and blood, in sporting events that led through agony to fresh agony, until death could be the only winning post.

The races of the iron spikes, the hurdles of the sawed blades, the fights between men who believed that the winner might be allowed to live— only to discover their mistake when they screeched their triumph—the whiplash contests between girls who prided themselves on the skill and cunning of their whip arms—all these passed in a miasma of distant horror to Delia. She had to believe what she was witnessing. After all, many a girl had said in a passion that this was what she'd like to do to a man, to any man, to all men. It was understandable.

Nyleen craned forward on her chair, anxious to catch the moment when a man with a shock of fiery hair decided he had had enough and would beg for his death.

She snapped her fingers at Delia.

Dutifully, Delia brought forward the silver bowl.

She did not care to look at suffering and death. Also, she did not much care to watch Nyleen. The kovneva moved. Just how it happened, Delia was not sure. Nyleen was sure.

"You stupid bitch! I'm wet! Look—" Nyleen lifted herself. She shouted: "Ilka! Drag her off. Stripe her! Thrash her!"

"Yes, mistress. How many?"

"How many? There cannot be too many..."

Ilka lifted her silver rod. "The harp, my lady?"

"Oh, yes, of course. Sissy, bring a fresh towel. Give the bitch twenty, then. Mind they are good and strong—no, wait. In the morning. Yes. I will watch myself in the morning."

So, in the morning, they stretched Delia's naked body out and chained her down and so thrashed her with a thin and whippy rod. A Jikai Vuvushi hit her. Ilka counted on her slate. And the Kovneva Nyleen watched.

Because she was acting the part of a slave, Delia shouted.

Truth to tell, she was not sure that she possessed the fortitude and willpower not to scream her head off.

She felt terrible. She did not faint, but the world went away from her for some time. The fire traced scorching fingers down her back. Liquid agony poured into her. Each narrow stripe shocked through her, as though some devouring monster closed his fangs on her head and chewed her right down to the soles of her feet and then back again—each time.

They let her rest all that afternoon. In the evening she was expected to play the harp.

The harp badly needed tuning, which was a difficult task. She did not consider herself to be particularly adept at tuning, although, of course, this she could do. Nyleen came in and watched her for a space, and then said: "And are you sorry, slave?"

Delia was sorry, all right. But not for what Nyleen imagined caused her that sorrow.

"Yes, mistress."

"You will not be so clumsy in future."

"No, mistress."

The girl wearing the black and white skins hauled on her couple of werstings, and the hunting dogs snuffled and followed obediently after the kovneva. There were other hounds in the other ward, opposite the yard holding the kitchens, but just how many couples Nyleen owned Delia had no way of knowing.

The kovneva walked toward Delia. Her icy face showed no emotions of compassion as she said: "They have treated your back?"

"Yes, mistress."

"That is good. You are valuable."

Nyleen put her hand on Delia's shoulder where the pearl beads clustered. She ran her hand down, over Delia's bare and scorching back. Delia gasped. The kovneva turned her hand, moved it down around the ribs and onto Delia's stomach. She rubbed, reflectively.

"When your back is mended I will have other tasks for you. More enjoyable tasks. If you have learned your lesson."

"Yes, my lady."

Nyleen fondled for a moment more and then walked off trailed by her retinue. Seething with emotions that in this situation were ludicrous, Delia returned to the harp. Sissy had said Nyleen was gentle. Given the opportune moment, Delia did not believe that the empress would be gentle.

To make an effective escape she would have to have a riding animal. Those werstings, tame and blunt-fanged though those she had seen might be, could still run down a poor half-naked girl escaping through the forest. Run her down and hold her for the hunters to ride up with their whips and chains and nets.

She could barely manage the harp. She had no great hopes of riding an animal until her back mended.

Because she had dipped in the Sacred Pool of Baptism her back would mend far faster than these slave-handlers could expect. There was need, therefore, to pretend she was worse than she truly was. Well, by Vox, that was not so difficult!

As though her punishment was the signal for jealousy to break out,

Delia found that many hitherto smiling faces were now frowning. Fault was found with her. During this period as her back mended she hoped that she sustained her spirits not by mere thoughts of revenge. She was acutely aware that she could so easily succumb to this nightmare. She could go under without a trace. But she hoped she managed to last out on a little better spiritual fare than mere revenge.

The practical teachings of the SoR as well as their mysticism helped. Perhaps she was most fiercely sustained by her loving thoughts of those dear to her. The idea that she would never see them again tortured her far worse than the scouring pain of her back.

The kovneva's personal needlewoman, a pinched-faced soul who was seldom seen, had been refused permission to practice her arts and insert acupuncture needles to ease the pain.

"Through pain shall the shishi learn to cleanse herself," pronounced the kovneva.

As a principle of life, that was pretty shoddy, considered Delia. That it sometimes occurred made no difference. Pain could so often turn a person inside out and drive them savagely against any form of kindness or human warmth, embitter them, make of them soulless devils.

She took not a grain of comfort from the fact that she had brought this on herself. If she had escaped when she had the chance, she'd have been clear away, this place would be a smoking ruin, and her back wouldn't hurt. So much for going out and seeking adventure!

And then, being Delia, she knew damn well that she couldn't have done any differently. As for doing it all again if the chance should come—well, that she would have to take under advisement, with counsel for the defense her sense of the rightness of the universe, and counsel for the prosecution these damned pains scorching down her back.

Already, therefore, she was feeling better.

Her husband often said that Kregans had a funny old sense a humor. People said that the emperor seldom smiled or laughed, yet with her in the good times he was always laughing and joking. When the bad times came and he put on that expression people called his devil face, her heart ached for him. He had been forced to do many things he abhorred, as had she. Such was the price of being fetched to be emperor and empress. She was coldly aware that without him her career as empress, had she succeeded her father, would have been much harder, more bitter and infinitely unhappier.

She knew also, without pride but with much thanksgiving, that without her he would have been morose, even more savage, intemperate and utterly lonely.

The evening passed. Delia played the harp and was aware that she did not play particularly well. Nyleen remained unrelenting.

"Play, slave!" she commanded. "Do not stop until I give you leave."

A few of her cronies gathered in her retiring room, hard, ambitious, cold women. Most of them came from Evir. They followed Nyleen Gillois in the hope that her schemes would bring rank and riches. "When the empress is dead...!" were words heard more than once. Delia did not catch just what the plans were after that occurrence.

She marked these women, their faces and characters, their names. She had once had a very good friend who came from Evir, and she had been totally unlike this bunch. Thelda, who had married Seg Segutorio, had been pushy and over enthusiastic, yes, always attempting to do the right thing and more often than not ending up in total confusion. But Thelda had been good-hearted, and she'd considered herself Delia's best friend, as she never tired of telling everyone, including Delia. Well, she was believed dead, now, and the last Delia had heard about Seg was that he was just about over his grief for his wife. Now he was making attempts to build a new life—going off adventuring with the emperor, for a start.

One of these sycophants, a woman hard and grainy, with a face like the blunt end of a tent peg, said: "It is a pity, Nyleen, that the fool girl died. She, at least, knew what the empress looked like."

"Do you criticize me, Ethanee?"

"No, kovneva! Of course not."

Nyleen picked a paline from the silver dish. Sissy was most attentive. "That is well. The girl died before I could make proper inquiries. I think the pity is that none of our girls went through Lancival at the time the empress was there, when she was princess majestrix. We must recruit more."

"Assuredly, kovneva."

Nyleen sucked another paline, and her face resembled the outer crags of ice that wall off the Ice Floes of Sicce.

Favoring the scorch that was her back and playing minor melodies, Delia listened. She kept her attention on two items, and two items only. One—playing the harp. Two—listening to what these people said. She would not allow her thoughts to dwell on what had happened to a Sister of the Rose who was questioned about the empress. Not yet.

"There is no more news?"

"Only that the emperor is still absent from Vondium, the Lord Farris rules as Crebent Justicar, and Drak the Prince Majister prances around in the west country fighting the rebels. The army is split between Hamal and the frontiers in Vallia. If only that bitch of an empress would come!"

"And there is no news of her since she left Mellinsmot?"

"None." Nyleen threw a paline at Sissy. She did not laugh, as Sissy, attempting to catch it in her mouth—to pop a paline—missed and the yellow berry hit a wersting, who snarled and gaped blunted fangs. "None at all. I think she went to see her SoR friends. There are rumors that their misbegotten mistress is ill. I hope she is. But—where is the empress now?"

"Lancival?"

"I expect news from there shortly."

At these words Delia hit a false note. The string twanged angrily until she stopped it. She went on playing without looking up. This one false note, apparently, was allowed to pass as a result of her beating.

If these Whip Women suborned a sister who knew Delia and she turned up here, the minions of Hodan Set would be let loose in the cant saying. Both fur and feathers would fly, not to mention silver tissue and pearl beads.

The likenesses stamped on coins, no matter how beautiful the original engraving, would never betray her. Her portraits hung mostly in the homes of friends. During the great festivals of the calendar season she would be seen by thousands of cheering people; but to them she would appear as a distant golden figure, haloed in light. The clusters of nearer nobles and guards would know her face. If she met one of them, they would treat her as the empress. It had been her misfortune to be taken up by a pack of rascally slavemongers who actively plotted against her.

Nyleen was never left alone with Delia.

Always the folk of her retinue accompanied her. Nadia and her guards; the wersting handler, a creature of northern Evir called Rinka the Stripe; Ilka the Silver Rod; Paline Pontora the chatelaine; various slaves to run and fetch and wave fans. Her cronies came and went. Her brother made punctilious appearances. If Delia could get Nyleen alone...

Yes, that was one way she'd extract the information she required. She'd ask outright, fair and square. And Nyleen would answer. Yes, Delia considered, equably, Nyleen would answer.

Her back mended. She gathered other scraps of information. More people were in the plot than she'd at first suspected. The witch stayed close. And then Nyleen announced she was leaving for a visit, she did not say where, and she would be taking her retinue, including Sissy, but excluding Alyss. Recognizing that if she had not completely failed there was no more she could do, Delia made up her mind to escape this very night.

Fourteen

Cranchar the Cranchu Carouses

When she was in a hurry Delia used needle and thread in a fine free way. Her stitches were uneven, rambling, usually overlarge, generous in the amount of material she expected them to deal with. When she had the time—which was pretty damn-well never, by Vox!—she could make herself be a fine seamstress. Then her stitches were marvels of neatness and exactitude, cunning in their beauty.

Now, with the silver tissue on her knees, her head on one side, and her face puckered up into a scowl, she made herself put in neat, precise stitching. An open window in the small room she and Sissy shared let a gentle zephyr play on her half-naked body. Sissy was washing her hair in the corner, making a tremendous fuss with spilled water and splashed suds, chattering all the time.

"You should not, then, have let her tear the tissue," said Delia, and bit a thread, her teeth even and white and sharp enough to bite clean through Nyleen Gillois's jugular.

"How could I stop her—ow!" and Sissy groped in agony for the towel. "My eye!"

Rising and laying the stitching aside, Delia passed across the yellow towel. Sissy came from Evir, from a family who owned land in a small way. She was wrapped up in the fortunes of Nyleen, but she was a scatterbrain, really, and hardly responsible.

"I am sorry you are not to come with us. The kovneva likes your playing. But we could not take the harp with us, and you are in disgrace, anyway."

"You sound pleased."

Sissy stopped toweling herself and one bright eye peered out. "Oh, no, Alyss! I did not mean that!"

"I believe you."

Oddly enough, Delia did. Sissy was too open to nourish jealousy. She was far removed from the hard brittle women who clustered about Nyleen Gillois.

Now, toweling herself vigorously, she spoke in what Delia could only believe was an unthinking way.

"Still. I did laugh when you wet the kovneva."

Threading a fresh needle, Delia felt it politic not to reply. Almost immediately Sissy stopped toweling herself. With her hair standing in spikes she stared sickly at Delia. The handmaid's face shook, her mouth trembled. "Oh," she said and the saying was a gasp, "I did not mean that!"

Delia replied equably. "No one heard you."

"You did!"

"But I am your friend—am I not?"

Sissy nodded with great eagerness.

"Oh, yes!"

"So that's all right, then." The needle was sharp and Delia was careful. The silver tissue was drawing together nicely, but it was fastidious work, demanding great attention. Why these great folk liked to clothe their slave girls in this diaphanous stuff, drape them in exotic costumes, almost escaped Delia. She could see why, of course; but the act reflected scant credit on any warmth of humanity. At least, and for this she was devoutly thankful, Nyleen did not chain them up. They were not true Chail Sheom, chained obedient slaves for erotic pastimes. The chaining of women was just one of the reasons for the reactions of women like Nyleen and her cronies.

"You won't tell?"

"No. I thought you liked the kovneva."

"I do! But—she frightens me. I wish..."

"Yes?"

"I wish I was strong, like a Jikai Vuvushi, and could use a sword! Then..."

"Yes?"

"Nothing. The lady Nyleen is gracious and a true jena, a true lady. I joy to serve her."

"Yes," said Delia, and dragged a stitch through the silver tissue, and so spoke her mind on that, whereat Sissy gasped.

"Alyss!"

Then Ilka stormed in, brandishing her silver rod and uttering threats, so Delia had to cobble the last few stitches together. Sissy brushed out her hair at lightning speed, took the silver tissue and popped it about her shoulders and ran out. Slaves would take down her small traveling bag. Ilka looked at Delia, and switched her rod, and smiled—a smile of no friendship—and went off. Delia threw the sewing things back into their basket, closed the lid, then sat back. A puff of disgust parted her lips.

Tonight, as ever was, by the gracious Dee Sheon!

As for the name Alyss. She had used the name before in some of her nefarious schemes for the SoR. Her husband had chanced upon it, and had laughed immoderately. When Delia asked him what caused this merriment, he replied that, yes, by Zair, Alyss did live in Wonderland.

So she was left behind as Nyleen Gillois na Sagaie, Kovneva of Vindelka, rode out with her entourage.

The kovneva's brother, the Lord Cranchar Gillois, known as the Cranchu, remained in the castle. Almost at once a change came over the place. Instead of the light sound of women's voices, the heavier beat of men's voices echoed along the passages and halls. Serving wenches stayed close to their slave mistresses, and a wary look entered all their eyes.

Chica the battle maiden brought in a new bunch of slaves, garnered from some hell hole. The men were sent about learning what the whip could do to their backs. The women and girls were reserved for a different fate. As Delia discovered, what Cranchar and his henchmen planned would not happen if the kovneva remained in the castle.

Within a slave structure differences of status must exist. Delia, because she had been born into a slave-owning society, understood the hierarchy. She had renounced and denounced slavery. But she knew that these women dragged into the castle stood on the lowest rung. Slaves like Sissy were very near the top, and she would not have been slave at all if her parents had not run into debt and sold her. Better for Sissy had they found her a decent husband; but then, some folk could not trust gold at second hand.

Four hulking great fellows blundered into the kovneva's retiring room and took the harp down to the refectory. Delia waited for the summons. She donned a clean yellow breech-clout and a tunic, old but serviceable, of a dull brown color she'd found wrapped around a silver bowl in a wooden chest. Her biological rhythms seldom gave her trouble—sometimes there was a little discomfort but almost never any pain, she was far too active a girl. She did not think that would make much difference to the slave girls below. There was much to ponder and think on as, summoned by a girl with a black eye and half her grey tunic torn off, she went down to the refectory.

The stink of spilled wine and sweat and cheap perfume stung her nostrils as she entered. Many torches blazed from sconces along the walls. The tables had been pushed to either side to form a cleared area in the center, and along the walls sat Cranchar's retainers, supping and drinking and shouting and banging their goblets on the tables, roaring.

Four girls stood at the center wearing layers of variously colored veils, and shivering. So it was to be the Dance of the Nine Veils. Each girl, of course, would be wearing only eight.

Nath the Muncible looked up from where he sat at Cranchar's right hand. His face flushed. "Here she is!"

Cranchar did not turn around.

"Play, girl... You know the tune."

Without a word, Delia went to the harp, sat down, tilted it into her knees, rested her hands on the strings.

Well, now...

The refectory had at a stroke been turned into a male province of hell. Half-naked wenches ran with brimming pitchers. The heat poured from the fires in the alcove where Nan the Bosom laid about her with her ladle. The food heaped high on silver platters. Many amphorae had been overturned in some tussle, and their contents ran and spilled between the cracks of the floor. No one took any notice. The stink of wine and greasy food, the yells and bangings on the table, the fights that broke out here and there and which ended in a thwack and a curse, all this pandemonium formed the background to the playing of Delia of Delphond.

She touched the strings, and brought forth that mysterious, heart-searching note from the soul of the harp.

Everyone turned toward her.

Cranchar wiped his lips and bellowed.

"Dance!"

The girls had probably been picked up from some low tavern, even a dopa den. They knew the dance, and performed it with a trembling languor that changed with the tempo into a most vigorous demonstration. Their limbs flashed. They smiled. They twirled their arms, pirouetting, posturing, and the veils flew off and floated free. When it was finished and the men set up a crowing racket of approval, the girls ran out, more drink was poured and drunk, and the next item began. This consisted of girls contorting themselves in weird and wonderful ways. Again, observing not so much with distaste as a deliberate blanking of her feelings—for now—Delia saw that these girls were professionals. They'd quite clearly been trained from very early ages to contort and twist themselves so. They were clever and agile, no doubt of that.

There was a difference in the performances of the contortionists and the dancers that did not escape Delia.

The men applauded wildly, shouting and drinking and roaring, enjoying themselves. They could not see anything odd in a girl shedding veils in a dance for their delight. The more beautiful she was, the more artful in her dance, the more they appreciated her. They did not see that to a woman who danced in this way an act of indignity was being forced on her. There were pros and cons, of course. But Delia was well aware that the Kovneva Nyleen would see in this spectacle only a familiar story of men persecuting women. She would fill her mind with thoughts of revenge, and fail to look deeper at the fundamental relationships between men and women.

The revenge taken by Nyleen here in this very room was her way of striking back. That it would solve nothing did not matter. There were ways to redress the balance; Nyleen's way was not one to be recommended. Delia sat back from the harp as the contortionists finished, wondering if her grandiose thoughts were all to be proved wrong when the next item wheeled in.

Chica must have stumbled on a traveling fair, a troupe of perambulating actors, for now a play was presented. That it was bawdy in the extreme and thus caused enormous merriment probably accounted for the gang of ruffians watching. They were scarcely followers of the playwrights acknowledged as masters and mistresses of the boards. It was all pretty crude stuff, with a deal of bladders and feathers, false noses and tails—the impersonation of a Kataki was particularly splendidly done—and a deal of falling about and head thwacking.

Delia glanced across to the alcove where the kitchen staff gawped away, fascinated. Nan the Bosom, no doubt, was busy picking up techniques of head thwacking.

During the short interludes between acts and scenes, Delia was called on to provide incidental music, which she did. While the players postured through their buffoonery, she studied this Chica and this Nath the Muncible. She very soon came to the conclusion that what Sissy had said was right. They did not get on. Chica, so Sissy had said, awed, would slit a man's throat as soon as kiss him.

"And has Nath kissed you, Sissy?"

Whereupon Sissy had giggled in her own not-silly way, and left Delia with the assumption that Nath the Muncible and Sissy were farther along the road of romance than anyone suspected.

The atmosphere thickened. Smoke from the fires began to twine tendrils into the refectory, and a subsequent tremendous racket sorted out the damned stupid incompetent whip-fodder slaves to attend to their fires. Some of the men enjoyed that. They flexed their arms afterward. The fires were attended to; but Lart the Boil had a broken arm and Nath the Turnips had not one but two black eyes, and others of the slaves nursed their bruises.

Catching Nath the Muncible's eye as he looked at her, Delia half-smiled, and made an unmistakable gesture that she wished to leave. Nath bent to the lord. Cranchar Gillois did not turn around. Nath straightened up and shook his head.

Delia would stay and play until she was given leave to go. That was the word of the lord.

In the nature of the fight that broke out at the far end, no one knew exactly what the cause was and cared less. Two men leaped into the center, swords whickering as the players might have said, and started to knock seven kinds of brick dust out of each other. Their comrades applauded and bellowed, and bet on one or t'other. When the first lay senseless upon the floor and the second staggered with a broken left arm, the bout was considered ended.

More wine flowed, the slave wenches were chased, more wine flowed, and still no one had struck up a song. And more wine flowed. Half a dozen more fights erupted, more wine flowed—and still no singing.

"Shishivakka!" someone yelled and fell over backwards off his stool. His wine pot fell on his head.

Most of the cutthroat crew in Cranchar's band were apims, but there were a few diffs, a Khibil, a Rapa, and a Fristle whose catlike face blazed up as he yelled, "Fifivakka!"

Nath the Muncible spoke again to Cranchar. In the Muncible's posture was eloquence and urgency. Cranchar hoisted his goblet—of gold and encrusted with jewels, a pretty piece of ostentatious bad taste—and laughed and shook his head.

"Let them race," he shouted. "And a bag of gold on it!"

"Hai!" the men roared. "Hai for Lord Cranchar!"

"Clear that harp out of the way," directed Nath.

Despite his romance with Sissy, the Muncible was, Delia had little need to remind herself, a traitorous slave-mongering acolyte of Cranchar Gillois. She could expect no favors from him.

The Vuvushi Race, where girls ran and used sharpened steel to hinder their opponents, was one thing. Down at the end of the hall girls were herded in for quite another.

Slaves lifted the harp. For the first time Delia became aware of the stain in the wooden floor as a rug was skidded away. She knew how that stain had come there.

The man who had been impaled, early on in Nyleen's own games, to have bets wagered on just what he would do, the quantity and caliber of his screams, the amount of blood, and of course how long he would last before he died, had died in the end and the floor under him had been stained. Slaves had scrubbed; the stain remained. Delia moved away.

The harp was set up again to one side, nearer to Cranchar. Delia walked slowly across, carrying her stool. She did not hurl the stool at Cranchar the Cranchu. She did not wish to throw her life away uselessly.

He wore a rapier and main gauche, the Jiktar and the Hikdar. They were overly ornate. Now he took the left-hand dagger out and rapped it on the table before him.

He obtained a degree of quiet.

"Strip them. You start *there* and you finish *here*!" and he flung the dagger into the floor before the table, where it stuck and quivered. "That is your winning post."

Rapacious fingers ripped the tattered clothes from six girls, who tried to cover themselves in the uproar. The men were all jovial now, more laughter and jokes flying. If they gave a thought to what the girls were feeling the Ice Floes of Sicce might go up in steam.

Disputes arose among the men over who would be the first six. A tall fellow staggered out, ripping off his own clothes, shrieking he would ride, damn you all, and fell flat on his face, out to the world, drunkenly snorting. He was kicked aside and the six men who elbowed their way to their mounts prepared. The race was simple. The girls would gallop, run, crawl on hands and knees to the winning post, and the men would sit astride their backs and whip them on.

That was the race known as the Shishivakka.

A bag of gold pieces jingled for the winner.

Cranchar need turn his head the merest fraction to see Delia. That florid face, brilliant and flushed, swung toward her. The mouth, crimson and full, parted.

"Play for the race, girl."

"No," said Delia.

Fifteen

Shishivakka

In the general uproar, Cranchar barely heard her. He most certainly did not believe what she had said could be what it sounded like.

"We'll have 'The Agate-Winged Jutmen'—that's a good rousing tune. Play, girl."

"No," said Delia.

He heard her.

He still could not believe what his ears told him this slave girl said.

"Play!"

"No."

The noise at the far end of the refectory bounced off the ceiling. The caterwauling mingled with the jingle of bottles, the crash of overturned benches as men crowded to get a better view. Cranchar put a hand to his ear, and sticking a finger in rubbed vigorously. He shook his head.

"You say you will not play for the race, slave?"

The blood rushed and collided in that already fully blown face. He gave her no chance to reply, spilling out words in a froth of passion.

"You refuse to obey? You are slave and you will obey!" At Delia's small shake of the head he roared on: "Then you will be flogged jikaider until your back is a pudding! Hai! Chica!"

But Chica was no longer in the refectory. At the first shouts of shishi-vakka she had gone.

A bright thrumming thrilled through Delia's head. She felt like one of the strings of her harp just touched by a cunning finger, vibrating and resonating through her out to the whole world. She deplored, at the same time laughed at, the pretensions of women like Nyleen Gillois; but she felt as a woman that she could not bring herself to play for this race. That unpleasantness would ensue was without doubt. She acted as a slave; this showed her that, despite all, she did not possess a slave mentality.

Cranchar the Cranchu bellowed his outrage. He surged to his feet, roaring. His men stopped their own roaring to stare stupidly at him.

"The slave harpist refuses to play!" The words rattled around. The men stared. And, suddenly, Delia saw this as a direct confrontation with the will of the master. The lord had ordered; a slave had disobeyed. In so petty a matter, surely, the men would say, the lord will brook no opposition.

"The whips!" screeched Cranchar.

Nath the Muncible stood up. He spoke swiftly into his master's ear. Cranchar gestured irritably, as though brushing away a pestiferous fly; but then he listened.

With graphic gestures, Nath indicated Delia's back, the harp, and then—so Delia guessed—mentioned the amount of gold the slave was worth to the kovneva. "If," no doubt Nath was saying, "if you have her whipped, how will you explain this to your sister the kovneva?"

"Very well!" Abruptly, Cranchar erupted into jovial good humor. He laughed widely, swinging his arms. "Very well! The slave will not play for the race. That is of small consequence. She shall race herself!"

Before his men had time to digest any suggestion that their lord had climbed down before the fear of his sister, Cranchar was roaring again.

"Fetch her down!"

"Make room!" shouted the Muncible. He was leaping for Delia before anyone else moved. His face blazed with anger and passion. He looked a remarkably ugly customer. He took Delia by the upper arm. He bent close.

"Listen, my girl!" He looked ferocious; he spoke softly. "You're in for a thrashing if you make another mistake. I cannot save you. You are alone. Do as you are bid and no worse will befall you."

Quietly, Delia said: "I will race; I will not play. And I do not stand in debt to you."

"Women!" said Nath the Muncible, and dragged her off.

He treated her gently. They reached the waiting group of female steeds and male riders and the old brown tunic vanished in a twinkling, torn off by greedy hands. When calloused fingers reached for the yellow breech-clout, Nath struck them away. He bellowed a raucous comment on the beauty of this steed. Then he roared: "I'll do the honors. We don't want to damage the merchandise."

The yellow breechclout whisked away. Delia stood forth.

A broad hand thrust against the small of her back. She was aware of the room and the ranked tables and the inflamed faces of the men, of brandished wine goblets and heat and uproar. Then the hand knocked her over and she was on all fours on the floor.

Nath appeared in front as she twisted her head up to see. He held a rapier aloft. This would be the signal.

A hard yet soft bulk squashed down on Delia. She let out an involuntary gasp. Whoever was straddling her was broad and heavy and hot. Hands grasped her hair. A thick and hairy leg stuck forward past her left ear, and its fellow jutted forward past her right ear. She almost squashed flat into the floor. But that she would not allow.

She bunched her muscles and fought back against the weight.

The bedlam in the room continued unabated. The heat puffed into her face. The man sitting on her back felt as though he weighed as much as the Heart Heights of Valka, mountain upon mountain. She drew two ragged gasps, and Nath slashed the rapier down.

Instantly a thin, hot, scorching pain laced across her buttocks.

The bastard up there had a switch and was whipping her on.

She started to crawl forward. The floor razored off a layer of skin at every movement, or so it seemed. She felt as though she was pressed down as flat as a sheet of paper. She struggled on, her mind a blank, hearing a shrill continuous uproar, seeing only the floor ahead and the next painful place on which to put down her hands and her knees.

Seven naked girls ridden by seven men, they scrabbled their way along.

Her knees were pits of fire.

Through the blankness of her mind the idea that this just would not do rose up in letters of flame. She stood up.

The man on her back yelped and wrapped his legs around her body. He held on, one hand in her hair, the other over her shoulder. If he'd fallen off that would have been his hard luck. Delia stood up, swaying, feeling the weight. She bowed a little forward, got her breath, and then started to run.

The run was more in the nature of a stagger, a lurching struggle from side to side, one foot after the other. She knew how to put one foot in front of the other when every instinct screamed at her to lie down, roll over and die. She kept on.

The noise grew prodigious in the refectory.

The man on her back shifted his grips, deliberately, dragging on her. So that confirmed his chances.

She stumbled on.

No other girl and rider preceded her. As for winning this disgusting race, that was nothing. She just wanted to get to the winning post and free herself of this incubus.

What she looked like she had no idea. She was aware of the table at the far end, slowly, as she neared it. Cranchar was roaring with the rest, waving a wine goblet, inflamed.

She began to think she could never complete the course. Her body felt as though it were being crushed down into the floor with each step she took. The man on her back held her in such a way that it was difficult to breathe. If he pulled her hair out by the roots she would not be surprised. On and on she struggled, and her doubts grew. She could never make it to the far end! Never! But she would. Pride—damned stupid pride. What had pride ever done for her? Now—all it did was make her struggle on with this man on her back instead of falling face down, to be kicked and whipped on like anyone else.

Something like ten strides remaining. Strides! Ha! More like ten feebly tottering steps. Lurching, rolling like a dismasted vessel in a gale, she staggered on.

Eight steps, seven and six. A splinter in the floor jagged her heel wickedly, and she barely noticed.

Five and four.

Now Cranchar, drinking his wine at a gulp, tossed the goblet over his shoulder and reached for a fresh. Three steps, two...

The left hand dagger stuck up from the floor.

That was the winning post.

One last step...

Beneath her feet the floor seemed to her to be swooping up and sinking down, nauseatingly. The man on her back clawed at her, yelling in her ear, thrashing her with the stick. She ignored him. The whole world fined down to two objects, circled in roseate fire, limned, coruscating, beckoning.

One—Cranchar Gillois the Cranchu.

Two—the left-hand dagger.

The first waved his new goblet so that the wine flew like golden rain, his face a scarlet bloom, his mouth open and bellowing. Sweat clustered on his face.

The second jutted up from the floor, its point stuck, its hilt ornately chased, and its blade a silver length of death.

The limpet on her back with his legs wrapped about her had to be dealt with. The matter scarcely warranted comment. She had not dislodged him before, and she knew why. Now she gave a rolling twist to her shoulders, smoothly shining, and shed him as she might shed a sack of laundry. He went over, spilling untidily onto his back. She gave him not a glance. The throw was merely a throw taught any girl who went through Lancival.

She lunged for the left-hand dagger.

Astonishment gripped her.

She was slow. Agonizingly slow.

A fierce and condemnatory anger suffused her at her own lethargy. Her muscles shrieked protest. Her body felt as though she were forcing it through molten metal.

Her right hand scrabbled for the dagger.

The main gauche would not fit comfortably, the quillons and the pierced and scrolled shield baffling her desperate attempts to take up the dagger as a fighter would. She had to turn her hand over and take up the blade with her thumb to the pommel and her little finger to the blade. Upside down for a rapier and dagger fighter...

Cranchar gaped for only an instant. Then he was leaping backwards, dropping the wine goblet, groping for his rapier.

Delia leaped for him. The main gauche glittered as she struck.

A long thin rapier blade slashed in from the side. That licking splinter of steel struck the dagger down. Delia lurched on and the dagger struck ferociously into the wood of the tabletop.

Cranchar shrieked insanely.

"Spit her, Nath, you fool!"

Nath the Muncible held his rapier down over Delia's outstretched arm. She panted, heaving with the effort of drawing air into her lungs. Her legs and arms trembled. Her hair swung forward over her face, half-obscuring the fury and desire to kill blazing there.

"Lord! Your sister—"

"Then if you will not, I will!"

Cranchar's rapier was in his fist. It snouted up.

Delia drew in a painful lungful of air, twisted herself around. Nath's rapier withdrew. For a horrid instant, as she lay sideways against the table, panting and naked, she thought he would thrust her through.

The next instant, as Cranchar drove forward savagely, she slipped away, fell along the floor, and the dagger remained fast wedged in the table. Cranchar's rapier hissed past her head.

As she rolled over she saw a pair of thick and hairy legs above her. A bloated belly jutted above. A red face lowered toward her.

"Stay there, slave!"

The man who had ridden her in the race shouted. He shouted hard and high.

"The gold! Lord! I won—the gold you promised!"

Cranchar looked bewildered. His rapier flicked back, ready for another thrust when he could see his target. The slave girl had vanished beyond the table. Now he shook his head.

"The gold? Magero? What gold?"

A bedlam of shouts broke out at this from the men.

Magero hollered louder than all the rest, bloated, red-faced, triumphant, and not to be cheated of the gold he had fairly won.

"The bag of gold for the winner. Lord! I claim my right!"

If she'd had the dagger now she'd have stuck it straight up and Magero would have been less of a man than he was.

But he had told her to stay there, to lie still. Now he was yelling angrily that, by Vox! he'd won the gold promised. He reached for the bag upon the table, near where the dagger jutted.

"My gold!"

Something soft crashed into Delia and she sprawled half-under the table. A naked girl with limbs flailing fell with her and the man riding the girl's back toppled over them. The rest of the field followed. Most of the girls dragged forward in complete exhaustion. Blood stained the floor in their tracks. One girl, with blonde hair and a heavy body, screamed and screamed as the man riding her whipped her on.

Magero was yelling for his gold. Cranchar was shrieking for the slave wench to be dragged up for him to spit. The girls were crying and sobbing, two or three simply flopping over and sprawling still, and their riders were fiercely arguing that Magero's mount had cheated. Nath the Muncible appeared.

The whole scene sickened Delia. She felt nauseated.

"You said you do not owe me anything, Alyss. This may be so. I do not stand to suffer for you." The Muncible's face was pale, his nostrils pinched. He reached for her and took her shoulder in a firm grip. "Up! And speak small before the lord."

She was standing, swaying with Nath's hand on her shoulder. She realized she would probably fall if he had not supported her. That made her think. She had thought very little since she'd first said "No!" to Cranchar the Cranchu.

"The girl won fair and square," said Nath. "Magero has won the gold, lord. Your sister the kovneva—"

The rapier in Cranchar's fist glittered in the torchlights. He moved uncertainly, scowling.

"I know, Muncible—and you run in peril—"

Nath let go of Delia's shoulder.

Instantly, she fell down.

Truth to tell, that collapse was not entirely fake. She felt as though she could not have stood up a moment more. She fell and sprawled on the floor, covering herself, and so lay motionless.

Let the bastards sort this one out!

A considerable commotion persisted, with catcalls and yells boiling up as men argued intemperately among themselves. Delia lay still. Some said she had won fairly, others that she had cheated by standing up.

The man who had come in second struck his girl.

"You stupid shif! Why did not you run?"

The girl held her knees and crooned in pain.

"I could not, master—"

"My gold!" Magero would not be put off.

"Cheat!" shrieked the man he had beaten.

"Say that again—"

"Cheat!"

Magero roared into action. He and the man who had come in second, Naghondo the Squint, tore into each other.

In a wild and unscientific flurry of heavy-handed blows they started to bash each other about the head. Magero landed a pile-driver and Naghondo staggered back, only to yell and spit out a tooth and come windmilling in again. They wrapped their arms about each other, massive hairy bodies fast locked, and fell down, struggling and writhing and trying to throttle each other. Delia lay still.

Nath hoisted her up.

Over the din he shouted: "The slave has fainted. You!" to a scared slave girl, whose pitcher of wine slopped in her terror. "And you!" to another, who dropped her platter of palines. "Take this stupid slave girl to her quarters! *Grak!*"

Helped by Nath, the two girls somehow heaved Delia up and started to carry her off. The fight between Magero and Naghondo rip-roared on. Men ran out from the tables to form a ring and cheer. The girls, trailing blood from their knees, staggered away. The bag of gold lay on the table by Cranchar, the left-hand dagger sticking up at the side. Cranchar stared hotly at Nath and the two slave girls, at Delia's form as she was carted off, a limp and lovely burden.

"I haven't forgotten!" he said. He slapped the rapier down. "She will recover from her faint. Then we will see."

Nath, bent over, hurried on. The two slave girls, whimpering, grasped various portions of Delia's anatomy and helped.

Swinging back to the fight, Cranchar, his blood up, bellowed his bull roar over the noise. He was caught up at once in the new combat.

"Fight for your gold, Magero! If you win, you win the gold. If you lose, then your mount cheated!" He looked enormous, bloated, scarlet-faced, once more in command. "Let the gods decide!"

Sixteen

Magero's Gold Piece for his Little Paline

Most of the next day Cranchar spent with his women closeted in the chambers of the tower reserved for his use. His men rampaged within this tower, and the noise broke over the walls and roofs of the fortress like surf driven before a gale. Slaves cleared up the refectory and put the place to rights before the kovneva returned.

Of the other three towers built of stone, one contained Nyleen's quarters and the small rooms of her handmaids and slaves. The next contained her fighting women bodyguards. The last tower's contents were unknown to Delia.

She felt humiliated, dirtied, her pride grossly affronted.

She tried to tell herself these were irrational reactions. They left her alone that next day to recover. This was, she surmised vaguely, because Cranchar was either roistering on or sleeping it off, and there was no one left prepared to take action. As for her own feelings, these were murky and passionate.

Some of the girls, apart from the pain in their knees, had accepted the Shishivakka race as a mere part of entertainment, what men expected, and therefore tolerated because there was nothing else they could do. Certainly, and to Delia incongruously, Magero sent up to her by a little slave girl a single gold piece.

"Magero the Obstreperous bids me give you this, Alyss," said this girl, wiping her nose. She was scrawny, unkempt and as appealing as a cold haddock. The gold piece shone on her dirty palm.

"Put it on the table, Limi," said Delia. "And go."

"Do you not send thanks?"

"Get out!"

The door cracked shut. Poor Limi... And, this gold piece in thanks from Magero meant he had won the fight with Naghondo the Squint. He was big enough, the hairy monster.

So then, of course, to add to her woes she had to feel guilty about shouting at poor Limi, who was just a skinny little slave girl. As soon as she was up and about she'd make it up to her; probably an extra helping of whatever was the tastiest dish of the day would soothe Limi's hurt feelings. Delia was only too well aware that slaves had feelings.

Jumbled up with her own feelings about the race were the problems surrounding this Nath the Muncible. Certainly, when she brought her armies down on this place, this sink of iniquity, why should he not die along with the rest?

He had gone out of his way to afford her what protection he could. He had run perilously close to disaster. If this puffed-up bladder, this Cranchar, had been half the lord he fancied himself, then Nath would be walking around headless. Had Cranchar been of that breed of lord of Kregen who did not lightly tolerate interference with their desires, Nath would be done for.

Only the thought of Nyleen, the kovneva, kept her brother in check. Nath had played on that. Delia found, and with alarmed surprise, that she was actively looking forward to the return to Nyleen.

Almost unimaginable!

During the late afternoon she found strength enough to rise. She bathed and washed her hair and brushed it out. The thought of that flagstone with its loot hidden beneath tempted her. Well, and why not? Surely there would be fresh unpleasantness when Nyleen got back. Cranchar would fabricate some story to have the impertinent slave girl up to her neck in trouble. Gold was gold, and pride was pride. The two Gillois hungered for the one and allowed the other, perhaps, to overpower their actions. Once Nyleen was persuaded, Cranchar would have a free hand. Delia did not relish that prospect. Tonight, then, and may the luck of Eos-Bakchi the Five-handed be with her!

She prepared herself, physically and mentally, for the tasks ahead. Stealing a kerchief of food was not over difficult, the most dangerous part being to dodge the swipes of Nan the Bosom's third largest ladle.

Silly Nath was all agog about the race; but Delia shooed him away—very gently—and skulked back to the room she shared with Sissy. The odd thing was, without the girl there the room appeared bare and lonely. She locked the door with Sissy's bed jammed against it, put a pot to hand in case anyone tried to break in, and then composed herself on her own ramshackle bed.

Obnoxious.

Yes, that was the word she would use about this place. The slaves were cowed in their fashion, and full of energy when a master or mistress appeared. They carried on their own way of life, as it were below stairs, and contained their own febrile strengths. But this place was obnoxious. She did not know its name, although she'd heard Nyleen and her cronies speak of Veliganda as though they might be referring to this fortress. Anyway, whatever its damned name, it was obnoxious.

She lay on the bed, then she got up and prowled about the room. She picked up the earthenware pot, and hefted it, and swung it through the air a few times.

Here she was, cowering in her room until dark, frightened of every footstep in the corridor outside, wondering if some drunken lout would break in. It just wasn't fair. Girls could learn tricks, stratagems, cunning twists and grips to deal with men, but a man's brute strength remained a man's brute strength. By Vox! If any drunken bastard broke in here he'd have a smashed head and caved in ribs and go reeling out clutching himself and with a face as green as Green Genodras!

It was all very well taking a lofty world view when you sat on your throne in your palace wearing a crown and with regiments and fleets and aerial forces at your beck and call. But when you sat in a little room with only an earthenware pot to defend yourself with—world views reduced in importance and took a back seat.

Cunning, intelligence, skill and courage. They were just about the only weapons she had. She might have taken a pride in her use of the old standby of women through the ages down in the refectory. Women who were blinded by anger, like Nyleen, would condemn and have only contempt for that particular stratagem. But the faint had been splendid. She'd fainted clean away, swooning beautifully, and that had got her out of it.

Footsteps passed in the corridor, and she tensed up, and then only half-relaxed as the heavy tread passed on.

If she could have taken on in a fight all Cranchar's men, and bested them, she would have. But that behavior did not belong in the logical world, that was of the stuff of the shadow plays and mimes hawked along the souks of the great cities of Kregen. Actors might fight whole armies and win, tiny girls might put to rout regiments; she was a mortal girl.

The slot of light falling from the window in mingled streaming jade and ruby slanted further along the floor, began to creep up the wall. The Suns of Kregen were declining. When the shadows fell, she would move. And woe betide anyone who got in her way!

With these brave thoughts to make an attempt to sustain her, she waited.

Once, and once only, she allowed herself to think of her husband. If he was beside her now, had he been there, last night, in the refectory—well, and perhaps the shadow plays would have been proven true.

Even though he had changed greatly, she knew with utter conviction that before anyone bestrode her in the Shishivakka race, her husband would be dead. And, equally, the refectory would have been awash in the blood of Cranchar's men. As for the Cranchu himself, a Krozair longsword would make his head leap from his shoulders... Idle dreams, girl! she told herself. It's all up to you, and you alone...

The gold coin sent up to her by Magero lay on the table. It gleamed erratically as the slanting light of the suns glanced across the surface. It showed a worn portrait of Delia's grandfather on the obverse, and a trophy of arms on the reverse with the exhortation to Support Vallia.

She did not touch the coin. The exhortation to support Vallia reminded her that these people here causing all this woe were Vallians. She had demonstrated her reactions to Magero the Obnoxious and his gift by shouting at a poor little slave girl. Limi had jumped with fright. That reaction, it seemed to her, was perfectly natural. But, wait a moment... Magero had bothered. He had shouted at Cranchar. There seemed the distinct possibility that he held some petty rank, that he was not as cowed as the other henchmen. This gave her to ponder.

When he'd changed his grip on her, she had promised to chop him. But he might merely have been making sure of his hold, not wishing to fall off. That reading of what had happened was admissible, grotesque though it might seem. The way nature had constructed men and women with only two arms meant that certain holds could not but fail to fall in certain places, willy-nilly.

She glared at the kerchief of food. That would be required after the escape. But she was hungry. Slaves were entitled to eat, for they had to maintain their strength in order to serve their masters and mistresses.

Going down the backstairs to the kitchens this time called forth a greater degree of resolution. She felt as a small animal must feel, penned at the end of its burrow, knowing the savage predators approached nearer and nearer with every passing heartbeat.

A new chief cook was on duty. The old one, Naghan the Meats, had been ill and unable to work, and Nan the Bosom had stepped in. Now she showed her feelings about being relegated back to her soups by thwacking about with her various-sized ladles, each increase in size a measure of her mounting displeasure. The new man, a slave with uppity airs, was Ornol the Rasher, for his specialty was vosk rashers served in a hundred and one different ways. He looked at Delia as she came in, and Silly Nath darted across with an urgent query about the well.

"You should be out there, Silly Nath, not lollygagging about here!"

"Yes, master. But the handle is split..."

Ornol the Rasher threw his hands up in despair. He looked porcine, flabby, with a sheen to his skin. His grey slave tunic bore a yellow and ochre favor. "All right. I will look."

Nan the Bosom, when they had gone, said: "He'll never last." Delia ducked the swing of the third largest ladle.

She found a hunk of bread and a bowl of soup, and Nan looked the other way. As any slave would say, a slave has to eat.

Had she cared to consider the matter, it was a measure of her own personality that these kitchen slaves had not turned hostile and jealous when she'd been promoted out of the kitchens, rising in the slave hierarchy, to be harpist.

The soup was good, a thick ordel, and she wiped the bowl with the crust of bread and wolfed the lot down. She decided not to return to her room but to wait out the last of the Suns here and then steal out into the yard.

Then she made a mistake.

Thinking to take herself out of harm's way, she went off to one of the small storerooms. This one held flour sacks. She spread a few empty sacks and lay down, continuing to build her strength for the night's operations. There Magero found her.

He was not drunk. He had been drinking, and he carried a flagon of good red, and he was flushed and jovial and sweaty, but he was not drunk. He smiled. His teeth were gapped. He wore a lounging robe of a lurid pink and blue, and he carried a basket of food of better fare than slaves were provided. Quiveringly alert, Delia was aware of his bulk, and of his belt of plain leather—with cheap bronze fittings—and of the rapier and main gauche. The belt also swung lockets for a clanxer, the straight cut and thrust common sword of Vallia.

He called her his Little Paline. This was a compliment.

"You ran well, girl. I won the gold. That buffoon Cranchar could not deny me, not after I knocked Naghondo's squint straight for him. Ha!"

She said nothing. She drew herself into herself, warily.

"I like you, my Little Paline. For a slave you are beyond beauty—I have never seen anyone to match you." He put the red wine down and spilled some food in placing the basket. "I feel we are soul mates. We have much in common. We serve a master who does not appreciate us."

Delia wet her lips. "The kovneva—"

"She will whistle, and Cranchar will come groveling like a beaten cur. I have seen it." He smiled gappily. "But I have not come here to talk about onkers like that. You had the gold piece? Or did that slave shif steal it away?"

"No, no," said Delia. She did not want to bring more trouble on Limi's head. "I had the gold piece."

"You see! You see how generous I am. And I can be much more generous. Much more, if you are nice to me."

Delia decided on a course of action that would have aroused contempt in women like Nyleen Gillois.

"You are so big and strong, and you fight well. Yet you speak ill of the lord. Perhaps it is not safe to know you."

"Safe? Of course it's not safe! Cranchar fears me, for I can see through him. Come here, girl, and take off your tunic."

"Should I not dance for you, first?"

"You have no veils, and I am sharp set."

He reached for her, and she slithered away on her bottom. Standing up, and making herself smile, she undulated around him, keeping out of the reach of his hairy arms. This was ludicrous; she had to have him dead to rights before she hit him, he was such a great lummox.

"You entrance me enough! You need not dance for me!"

"Oh, Magero, you great zhantil of a man! Do I not dance well?"

She was gyrating and swaying, and weaving her arms about and smiling, her head on one side. Magero gaped. Sweat stood on his brow.

"By vox! You overpower me, my Little Paline!"

She reached up to the latch on her tunic, and undid it, and flapped the grey cloth down and then up. The tunic was one of Sissy's, and was a tight-ish fit. She danced lightly around, avoiding him, and he lumbered after her, sweating with passion. Now if she'd chosen the firewood shed, there'd be a handy length of lumber to hit him over the head with...

"Come here, sweet! I am ready for you!"

Despite the desperate appearance of this situation, Delia felt close to hilarious laughter. It was comic, this tantalizing of this great man mountain. She'd have to take him with bare hands, get him in a grip, and hope to finish him quickly. But he was so big, and—unfairly, unfairly!—so mannish brutish strong.

Her plan was this—she undulated around flapping the grey cloth down and up tantalizingly so that his eyes boggled out on stalks—she'd come in close, let him slobber all over her, and she'd have the rapier and main gauche out quicker than he could think. Then the weapon used would be up to her...

She circled to face the door and advanced. He broke into a great slobbering smile and opened his arms wide to enfold her. She moved in quickly, and felt his paunch slog into her stomach with a grunt. Her hands dropped to the hilts of the weapons. He was kissing her neck—and over his shoulder she saw the door open and Naghondo the Squint appear. The man's face bore an expression of vicious hatred. He lifted the bludgeon and brought it down with savage and unerring accuracy on Magero's head.

Magero dropped soundlessly, sliding away from her.

Naghondo leaped in.

"That'll teach the bastard! And I'll carry on where he left off! C'mere, girl! You're mine now!"

Seventeen

A Zorca for Two

To speak thus to Delia when she was unarmed was one thing. Even had she been wielding her earthenware pot, perhaps. But to speak thus to Delia with a rapier and left hand dagger in her fists was to commit a grievous error.

The point on which she chose to check this Naghondo and show him his error amused her. It created a pleasant frisson.

"You claimed I cheated in the Shishivakka race, you great blowhard oaf! Draw your rapier and we'll see if I cheated."

"Do what?" He looked completely flabbergasted. The billy lowered. He looked stupidly at the rapier and dagger whose points hovered before him. Then he let rip a great bellow.

The roar was compounded of amusement, not even of contempt.

"C'mere, girl! I'll show you what fun is!"

Had she been of the truly murderous kind she sometimes thought she was, Naghondo would have been dead by now. When she thrust, he had time to skip back to the doorway. He looked puzzled. Then his face cleared. "You wish me to show you? Right!"

He whipped out rapier and main gauche and bore in.

"I'll show you a few things, my girl, and then I'll show you a few more. Hai!"

She realized he intended not to spit her but to hit her with the flat, punish her for her effrontery. That was his misfortune. She did not stop to curse herself for not having the courage to stick him through on the instant. She set herself, met his first attack with ease, set up her own attack, and missed the final thrust as he stumbled away and only took a sliver from his ribs.

"You bitch!"

Now he came in with more deadly intent.

Circling him, feeling the strength of his wrists, the speed of his reflexes, sounding him out, she was aware of faces looking in at the door. Well, this was a free show. Come one, come all. She'd have to remember to put out a hat or a bowl to collect the copper obs after the show.

Then she banished thought and allowed the transparency of the sworder to enter her soul.

Naghondo was a fair hand with the rapier, but he was not in her class, nowhere near. She circled his bald attacks, checked his twinned onslaughts, the left-hand dagger held and deflected out of the true line. She stuck him through the arm and he yelped. Then she stuck him through the other arm, and he yelped again. He staggered over Magero's prostrate mountain of a body and twisted and fell. She stepped in, smoothly, rapier ready to dart down and finish him.

Hands grabbed her shoulders and waist. She was dragged back. A rapier pointed at her midriff, and Chica said: "Enough, girl. You think you are a sworder—well, desist, or you will meet someone who knows the Jiktar and the Hikdar."

"Treat her gently," said Kovneva Nyleen, over Chica's shoulder. "She is worth gold. Bring her to me when I summon. The rest of you carrion crows—back to work! *Grak!*"

The rush and scurry to obey cleared the area outside the door of the flour storage. Nadia with her bodyguard crowded up, carrying their weapons. Nadia's full-fleshed face looked savage.

"Let me at her! I'll show her what rapier work is!"

"Yes, yes, Nadia, you are very good," said Nyleen. "But the girl is deranged. She is a harpist. Not a Jikai Vuvushi."

"All the same, my lady," said Chica, taking the rapier and dagger from Delia. "She seems to know one end of a sword from the other."

Nyleen looked scornful. "Naghondo cannot make a fist of rapierwork. He should stay with his clanxer. That is more his mark. And I shall want to see my brother over this."

"Quidang!"

Nadia looked disappointed she was not to have a bout, and Chica led Delia off. Nyleen did not even bother to speak to her slave harpist.

As for that same slave harpist, she was so savagely condemning herself as would have made all the saints in The Golden Grottoed Halls blush. *Why* had she been so stupid? *Why* hadn't she just got on with escaping? *Why* hadn't she killed these men instead of trying to be so clever? The excuse that Nyleen had returned and so scotched any escape plans was merely an excuse. Damn the woman! *Why* had she skulked in the flour storage? It was all so—so *infuriating!*

Also, it was deadly...

Nyleen was saying in her hectoring voice: "What's that there, Magero? Give him a kick and rouse him. Is he dead? That would not worry me. He is getting too big for his boots. My brother will have to watch him..."

The sound as of some leviathan of the deep breaking the surface and uttering a distress signal would be Magero the Obstreperous regaining consciousness.

Naghondo the Squint, carried off, complained loudly and bitterly that the fool girl had only stuck him because he'd fallen over that oaf Magero. Since when did a slave shishi know anything about swording?

The reason for the puzzlement and clash of sympathies in these women was perfectly plain. They were women. A man, a common brutish man, had attempted another woman, who had defended herself—and with naked steel. But the woman was a slave, a nothing, one of the grey ones. Where should sympathy lie?

The last Delia heard before she was assisted up the stairs was a fruity bellow from Magero, frothing.

"The girl was my steed, Naghondo the Squint! Not yours! And she has a fire you don't understand." The spluttering voice pounded out words that must have caused Magero's aching head to throb even worse. "If you touch her I'll have your tripes!"

Stupid to warm to man-mountain Magero the Obstreperous... Still, the idea of having Naghondo's tripes spilled out wasn't altogether a bad idea, at that...

When they'd dumped her back in her room, Nadia looked back, scowling, and said, "One of my girls will stand outside your door until my lady sends for you. Keep you out of mischief. Mind you behave yourself, slave."

She stretched out on the bed, feeling her bruises, and contemplated with thoughts that were exceedingly hot the fiasco of the evening. What a leem's nest she'd made of it all!

Not being in the habit of feeling sorry for herself, she didn't lament over that end of the mess. And to start longing for what might have been was worse. She'd just have to start over.

But it was cruel, damned cruel, by the disgusting diseased left eyeball of Makki-Grodno!

So that little memory of him made her feel even more determined and, truth to tell, even a little better.

Then Sissy waltzed in, prattling on, all agog, and with a few words upended all Delia's plans. Delia experienced a piercing shock. She trembled and went pale. Sissy, chattering on, did not notice.

"Yes, Alyss, I know you have had an exciting time. But my lady is fond of you, as she is of me, of course. And dear Nath will do all he can." Sissy's rounded shoulders drew back as she thought of Nath the Muncible. Then: "And with the poor kov so near to death in the Lud Tower, who knows what is to become of us?"

"Kov?" Delia's words croaked.

Sissy, busily unpacking, rattled on. "Poor Kov Vomanus. He is like to die, and the needlewoman can do nothing. It is very sad."

Delia stood up. She swallowed down and some of the bile went away. Vomanus was a reckless scamp; but he *was* her half-brother.

"In the Lud Tower?"

"So dear Nath said. Alyss! You cannot go out. There is a Jikai Vuvushi, and she was very strict with me when I came in. Alyss!"

Delia opened the door.

The Battle Maiden was hefty, big-breasted, thick of thigh, with a high color. Delia put an arm around her neck, above the gilt-rimmed corselet, and twisted. She did not kill the girl. She dragged the unconscious body into the room and, unheeding Sissy's squeals of terror, stripped the armor. She put it on. It fitted here and there, for, and she would not say it herself, there were few, very few, women in all of Kregen with so perfect a figure as Delia of Delphond. She strapped on the weaponry.

Sissy, hand to mouth, face green as Genodras, watched. The girl's eyes rounded into enormous terror.

Delia tied up the Battle Maiden herself.

"Now, Sissy, you know nothing of all this. You will not tell anyone, not Nath, not anyone. If you do, I shall come back and cut off your head."

Sissy started to cry.

Delia resisted the impulse to put her arm around the girl's shoulder and chide her for a silly goose. She looked very fierce, said, "Remember, Sissy, your head!" and marched out.

The helmet was of that curved pattern that both allowed freedom of movement of the neck and shielded the cheeks. Delia's face was, therefore, partly shadowed. She tilted the helmet forward. She marched with a swing, just like any of your battle-hardened Jikai Vuvushis. She stared with utter contempt and loathing upon Limi who was creeping along carrying a linen-covered bowl. Limi shrank away. Delia strode on.

Sissy ran out after her, distraught, and then raced off in the other direction. If the girl had any sense she'd have stuffed the Battle Maiden under the bed first. And, if Sissy babbled out her news—why, then, that would mean that Delia would have to start fighting in real earnest. Somehow her blood was up. Somehow she was invigorated. And, she told herself sternly, that could not be just because she was concerned about someone other than herself, could it? That was to admit to a silly kind of perverse self-love.

Making her way to the Lud Tower at this time of evening when some of the torches were lit and others were not was not overly difficult. No wonder she'd not discovered what existed inside the fourth tower. The ward rang hollow under her Battle Maiden's sandals with the iron studs. Her equipment clanked. That wouldn't do for any regiment Delia commanded. A guard stood at the lower doorway. The torch was lit and helped by contributing its quota of shadows to conceal her face.

"What do you want, dom?" inquired the guard in an unfriendly voice.

"Why, dom—nothing that concerns you—" The blow was swift, unexpected, and hard. The girl collapsed. Delia dragged her into the shadows inside the doorway and then started up the stairs. The place stank of damp and dust and disuse. Nyleen hadn't as yet gotten around to redecorating in here, then.

The kovneva was very sure of the kov. There remained only two more guards and a couple of werstings on the second landing.

The guards, being human, could be knocked out without trouble. The werstings presented a more formidable obstacle...

The black and white striped hunting dogs snarled at her, exposing yellow fangs. Their tongues lolled. They were chained through slots in the wall so that she could not pass without putting herself within their range. Their fangs had not been blunted. She took out the Jikai Vuvushi's terchick, hefted the little throwing knife, hurled. Even as the first wersting yowled at the steel sliver in his neck, trying to bite and scrape it off, so the long slender steel of the rapier slid into his mate. Feeling disgusted, Delia stepped back.

With the blood-stained brand in her fist she ascended the last flight of stairs and pushed open the door at the top.

In the dimness she could see little apart from a vague rectangle of radiance from a door in the room's far wall. Something moved, and a trembling voice said: "Majestrix!"

"Quiet," said Delia.

A chain clanked. The voice said: "I would give you the full incline, majestrix, but these cramphs have chained me up."

He spoke in a low voice, heeding her injunction to be quiet. Evidently, he knew her. She said: "Kov Vomanus?"

"In the inner room, majestrix. I fear he is near death."

She went in, kicked over a stool, peered about. Her eyes could make out objects better now. The man was, indeed, chained. His straw pallet was filthy. A few scraps of bread in a wooden platter looked stale. His hair stood up in spikes.

The far door beckoned her. But she paused to say: "You are?"

"Larghos Ventil, majestrix. I serve the kov—"

"Yes. I will see what I can do for you."

She went through into the far room. She put a hand to her nose instantly, gagging.

The light from the arrow-slit fell across the haggard face. Vomanus did, dreadfully, look close to death. She held herself within herself. Sickness... Suffering... Disease! How she loathed all this ghastly business!

"Delia?" The fluttery voice barely stirred the stifling air. "Delia?"

"Yes, Vom. It's me. I'm taking you out of all this."

"Yes, but—Nyleen—?"

"Do not fret."

Vomanus looked as though he might be in the process of being starved to death. That would be like the dark revengeful soul of Nyleen. He tried to rise, and she shushed him, and turned back to the outer room.

"Larghos—the keys?"

"The guard, majestrix—with the werstings."

"Yes. And do not call me majestrix, as you love your life. If you must, call me Sishu."

"Yes, my lady, yes, Sishu."

She went out and down the stairs, the rapier held just so and ready to rip into the throat of anyone attacking her up the stone stairs. The guards still slumbered. The werstings looked pathetic, slumped in their own blood. She tapped the two guards again, just to make sure, wondering when the guard Deldar would come by to change the sentries, snatched the keys off the uglier girl's keyring and darted back up.

She had been gone a bare score of heartbeats, but already Vomanus was querulously demanding where Delia was.

"Hush, Vom. I'm here." She threw the keys at Larghos Ventil and went through to bend over her half-brother.

"Nyleen," he said. "She tricked me. I thought she was—"

"Yes. Where are your clothes?" Then, berating herself, she looked. The clothes, splendid wedding gowns, lay bundled in a chest. She dragged them out and then Larghos was with her and they began to dress Vomanus. He was wasted to skin and bone.

"Nyleen is a wicked woman," he babbled. "She is mad, quite makib. She plans to be empress of Vallia."

"Yes, yes, Vomanus, my dear. Put your arm through here. Larghos! Do up those laces! Hurry!"

"Yes, Sishu."

"She plans to kill you, Delia. Kill you!"

"I know."

"She sent the wedding invitations, all smiling, and she waited to kill you and you didn't come. I was glad."

"How did she manage to bring you to this?"

He shivered.

"Fiacola the Gaze... Sorcery!" He glared up, and reached out a withered arm to grasp at her dangling pteruges. "Witchery!"

"If you don't let go I can't dress—there, that's better. Larghos, a blanket! And how was she to be empress?"

"Why, she plans to marry the emperor. Then, she will kill him, too. She and her brother—"

"Kill the emperor!"

And then Delia saw the comic side of that. "*Marry* the emperor!"

"When you are dead."

"Well," said Delia, Empress of Vallia, lifting the shriveled form of her half-brother off the bed. "Well, we will see about that!"

"Oh, she will marry him. Her witch is strong. I—I—"

"Yes. Now keep quiet. If there is any fighting to do I shall have to drop you."

"Sishu? Should not I carry the kov?"

She laughed. A small gurgle in the dimness. "So that I can do the fighting myself? Unimpeded? Why, Larghos Ventil, I was hoping you would help with the fighting."

"Yes, majes—yes, Sishu."

Down the stairs they went. "Give those two another tap, Larghos. Do not kill them."

He picked up the girls' abandoned weaponry, and tapped them, and then crept on. The guard at the bottom still slumbered, for Delia had dealt with her more severely, but Larghos tapped her, just to make sure. A big fuzzy pink moon floated above, the Maiden with the Many Smiles, and this did not please Delia. The overpowering scent of moon blooms reached her, strong on the night air. Sounds of the usual fortress business floated up; there were no shouts of alarm.

She started off for the tricky business of penetrating back to the yard and Larghos said: "The stables are this way."

She stopped. Of course there would be other stables. She said nothing, but followed Larghos as he led off in the opposite direction, skirting the tower, heading for the far corner where the stone walls ended jaggedly and the new wooden ramparts joined. In the angle stood a small door. At the side leaned sheds. A zorca stamped his hooves and blew.

There was one zorca.

Delia let fall an unladylike remark.

A girl slave passed carrying a bucket. The moon shone. The moon blooms drowned the night in perfume. And there was one zorca.

The girl slave vanished around the corner. Delia lifted Vomanus into the zorca's saddle which Larghos, with practiced skill, had already cinched up. The saddle animal was a splendid example, belonging to the guard on perimeter patrol, and, like all zorcas, was so close-coupled as to make riding two up difficult. With a little give and take and a squash it could be done. She had felt the strength flowing in her arms and back and thighs when she'd lifted her half-brother. He would have to go, of course. But she could scarcely ride off and leave Larghos Ventil. She could do so, of course, and he would understand and accept the proprieties of her decision. For she was the empress. And that was the kind of thing empresses did.

Delia was not and never could be your ordinary mundane kind of empress. If she wanted to do something and it didn't hurt anybody else, she'd damn well do it. If it didn't discommode them too much, she'd do it... But in this...?

Torchlights blazed up from the darkness. Through the gateway separating this ward from the next, lurid light flickered. Orange highlights bounced on the stonework of the tower. Shouts raised, heavy angry bellowings. The heavy beat of war-sandals cracked out, iron studs ringing against flagstones.

"Up with you, Larghos. Hold the kov firmly."

"But, majestrix! Sishu!"

"Up, man! Hurry."

"But I cannot leave the empress—"

"Do as you are commanded. Escape and fetch help. Now, Larghos, when I open the gate, ride as though your hide depended on it. For by Vox, believe me, it does!"

"Quidang!"

The wooden gate opened easily enough and the faint squeal vanished in the increasing uproar beyond the other gate. Larghos bent his head, Delia gave the zorca the subtlest of taps, and the superb animal, responding, leaped through. Delia swung the wood closed. No time to lean against it for a gulp of air and a moment's respite. Truth to tell, she doubted if she could have brought Vomanus safely through to the other stables in his condition. Larghos would care for Vomanus, stop him from falling off, and, the sooner the better, return with help.

By that time Delia planned to be long gone. Her confidence nerved her; she trusted in herself for a very long way, but what others might never see or suspect in her she was very well aware of herself. Her confidence and self-assurance were frighteningly thin. Her nerves had been scraped raw. By Krun!—all she had to do now was get across to the stables and select a mount and ride off. That was all.

She suspected she had just about enough courage left for that.

Through the open gateway ruddy light flared, like the single enormous eye of some diabolical pagan idol drowned in the jungles of Chem. Two guards catapulted through, to land with twin crashes on the flags. Furious bellowings reached her. The coruscating lights of the torches reflected in whirling radiance from the weathered stones of the tower. Iron studs gonged against the flagstones, and guards appeared. The two who had been thrown through staggered up. The group hesitated, and then with naked steel turned.

Clutching her bloody rapier, Delia peered about into the shadows, desperately seeking a place to hide.

Eighteen

The Artistry of a Sword Mistress

Hunkering in the shadows next to a shed that contained something unmentionable—something best left undisturbed judging by the smell—Delia glared out into the ward. Torchlights cast ominous flashes and gleams of fire. Silhouetted and animate, the guards gathered themselves. Evidently a new coffle of slaves had just come in and someone retained spirit enough to resist. More than one slave was being loaded with extra chains and bashed over the head in the next ward. Delia had to cross that space and then get past the kitchens to the stables. Setting themselves, the slave handlers rushed back through the archway and the noise increased.

Delia glared. She glared in a veritable passion of frustration and sheer bad temper.

By Vox! By Krun! By Dee Sheon! By all the gods and goddesses and spirits of Kregen! Just when she'd got Vomanus away and at last—at long damned last—things were going reasonably well and she could envisage herself astride a zorca and speeding away, this maniacal crew of idiots had to come shouting and scattering torchlight and whipping on packs of yowling werstings.

As a man she knew might have said, it was enough to make her throw her hat on the ground and jump on it, by Zair!

The rumpus and the lights drew back from the archway. She waited, seething, feeling her temper boiling up and scalding away her doubts and uncertainties.

She could remember her mother in her strict yet loving way saying: "Now, Dilly, you will say you are sorry to Opaz every time you lose your temper, and no sweets for a week."

This pack of rasts here in Veliganda led by Nyleen and Cranchar were like to have her off sweets for the rest of her life.

Her mother used to call her Dilly. That was a long time ago. At least

Vomanus had called her Delia, even if, so distressed she had been, she'd called him Vom. They were the affectionate names of their youth.

If her mother had married her father first, instead of Vomanus's father, then young Vom would have grown up to be emperor. That would have saved a very very great deal of grief for her and for the hairy clansman she had wed.

The snarling racket of leashed werstings made her react. By Krun! She felt invigorated, the action driving the blood through her. She felt capable of anything. At first, she had guessed the alarm to be raised because a sentry on the battlements had spotted Vomanus and Larghos riding off astride their zorca. Then she had fancied it must be because missing sentries had been found. But the torchlight, spilling in through the gateway and bouncing in lurid reflections from the stone of the tower, remained stationary. It did not advance menacingly. And the snarling growls of the werstings spat no nearer.

She took a breath, and spat. That shed reeked. Standing up, she hitched up the weapons belt. Gripping the rapier, she advanced out from the shadows.

The surge of confidence brought her to the gate. The flagstones glistened with the running fire of torchlight, orange and golden in the night. The diffuse pink lighting from the Maiden with the Many Smiles washed away, haltingly, before the harsh glow of the torches.

One of the male Fristle guards hovered by the stone arch. He was ill-at-ease. Like most Fristles who are not armed and armored by their masters, he wore a leather jack, brass-studded. The racial weapon of the Fristle, a curved scimitar, kept slipping up and down in its scabbard as the catman pulled and pushed. He looked ready to run, given half the chance.

Silently, Delia approached.

The uproar beyond the gateway markedly reduced. One or two words spurted up. They might have been key words, they might mean nothing. "Decadent... Take them away... screws... error... ways..."

Delia marched on. She angled her head so the torches threw deep shadows across her face. The rapier, unwiped, went back into the scabbard. She made herself take the long and exaggerated steps some Jikai Vuvushis affected. Her accoutrements jangled.

The Fristle jumped.

"Out of the way, man!" snarled Delia, and strutted on.

The pecking order of this fortress was made transparently plain, as Nyleen made it plain dealing with her brother, when the Fristle said nothing but shuffled away. He waited until the Battle Maiden had stalked past, and then he resumed his place. He, it was clear, would prefer to be very far away.

Apart from the noise going on around the group of people who were moving—spasmodically—away beyond the wall, another and altogether different species of noise emanated from the kitchens. This noise seemed to be, first: Nan the Bosom thwacking, second: Ornol the Rashers screaming ineffectually for obedience, and, third: Silly Nath bellowing that someone had stolen the bucket from the well.

The stables were so filled that some totrixes and freymuls were tethered outside. The animals did not care for the noise, and blew and stamped. Delia had her heart set on a zorca, for obvious reasons, although if she had to steal a freymul, the so-called Poor Man's Zorca, she would do so. Saddle animals were scarce since the Time of Troubles. The general busy scene around her afforded some protection. The mob of people kicking up the most noise vanished into the fortress. The kitchen hullabaloo sounded louder. Then Silly Nath ran out, all awkwardly scrambling, and Nan the Bosom chasing him, with her largest ladle going like a slave-powered trip-hammer used to break stones.

"Give me back my bucket, Nath!"

"Shan't! Need it for the well!"

"I'll stuff you down your well, head first!"

With a smart side-step, Delia darted out of the torchlights. She moved fast around the edge of the yard in the shadows.

In the stables she drew in a breath redolent of straw and droppings, pungent with liniments and sweat. She put her hand on a zorca, gentling him. His single spiral horn jutted up to a fine length, well-proportioned. Not all first-class zorcas possessed large horns; some zorca-copers claimed it as an infallible sign of breeding. She put her hands on the animal, not bothering to saddle him, and a thin and scorching fire slashed around her legs.

She fell down, and was dragged to the door.

Struggling over, she tried to rise, and another whip joined the first about her, and tripped her. She lay there on her back, glaring up helplessly at Chica, who stared down in mocking triumph. Chica's atra swung on its golden chain from her neck, and the little good luck charm glittered in distant torchlight. The amulet was of a particular kind, the golden ornament a miniature of a man in agony being transfixed most unpleasantly by a stake. Chica smiled.

"Alyss. So this is where you are! We did wonder."

She snapped her orders and the two whips withdrew. Jikai Vuvushis seized Delia, stripped away her weaponry, dragged her up with her arms twisted behind her back.

"The kovneva sent for you, Alyss, and you were not there. Only poor Thafti with a bruised neck, all tied up. Why did you do that?"

Delia just stood there and said nothing.

"You were going to escape! Of course. That's it. Poor girl. You were going to run away from the kovneva. How ungrateful." The mockery was crude, heavy, and cut with the effect of a blunt wooden lath upon steel.

The grips the two Battle Maidens fastened on her were efficient; she could have broken them with a trick taught by the SoR. Then she could have started to run off into the darkness. Waiting at the side stood three Jikai Vuvushis. Each one held a bow. The bows were of the compound reflex type, short and sharply curved. Three arrows were nocked, three strings were partly drawn. Three steps, three arrows, no more Alyss the slave girl.

Chica flicked her whip. The black length of the lash, shining, thick at the butt and tapering to a thin and evil slenderness, writhed up. The tip struck Delia upon the thigh.

The Battle Maiden's pteruges absorbed most of the sting; the shock remained.

"Bring her along. The kovneva is indulging us in a small entertainment tonight. This will add to her pleasure."

Coiling her whip up along her arm, Chica swung about, a tall, agile and commanding figure.

Forced along by the guards, Delia considered this Chica. She was called Chica the Fangs. Her legs were long and sturdy, and she walked with a step lithe and free, almost bouncing. She favored dark clothes, with the silvered corselet shining bravely, and she looked very much like a desert reptile, quick and sudden and deadly.

With sword points at her back, Delia was woman-handled into the refectory. The tables were pushed away to the sides. Stakes were set up. The saw-edged barriers were in place. Nyleen was preparing another entertainment for her cronies.

Swathed in a profusion of gems and feathers, her silver hair glimmering in a net of emeralds, Nyleen sat in the high-backed chair where her brother Cranchar had sat for his entertainment. Her pallid face twisted with grotesque pleasure when Delia was brought in. Nadia, full-fleshed, lumpy with passion, half-drew her rapier.

"Ah, my dear," said Nyleen. "So they have found you. I do not think you will play the harp for me this evening."

Delia made no reply.

"No. No, I thought not. But we will find other amusements. Do not fret over that."

Nadia pushed forward. She looked ugly. "This shif thinks she can handle a rapier, my lady. Let me teach her—"

"Tsleetha-tsleethi," said Nyleen. "Softly, softly. Let us first enjoy a small spectacle."

That small spectacle disgusted Delia. She closed her eyes. Presently the screams of the men faded, and their tortured bodies were dragged away.

"Ah!" said Nyleen, and she helped herself, daintily, to a handful of palines. "That has quite refreshed me. But then, of course, it is no more than men deserve."

The keys jangling from her chatelaine, Paline Pontora walked swiftly in. Her green gown rustled. She bent and spoke urgently in Nyleen's ear. The kovneva sat up straighter in her chair. She looked murderous.

"So the kov my stupid husband has run off! Well, the worse for him. He will soon be brought back and punished."

She bent her gaze on Delia, who stood to one side of the table. "And you, Alyss the Harp. Did you know of this? Why else would you wear the armor of a Jikai Vuvushi?"

Delia just didn't bother to answer the unpleasant woman.

"You—!" shrieked Nyleen.

Nadia drew her rapier. "Let me teach her, my lady!"

Nyleen slumped back. Her eyelids half closed, and she smiled. Her teeth closed over her lower lip. Then, slowly, she opened her mouth and half-turned to her Battle Maiden Hikdar. This Nadia quivered. She served in the office of cadade, captain of the bodyguard, and she was raging.

"Yes, Nadia, my fighting leem. Let us see what she can do."

"Rather, my lady," said Chica, and she spoke with some regret. "What Nadia can do. I would welcome a chance to claw her."

"That chance will never come, Chica the Fangs!" Nadia drew her left-hand dagger. "I will cut her up artistically..."

They removed the armor Delia had donned. They thrust a rapier and main gauche into her hands. Wearing only a slave-grey breechclout, she was thrown into the center between the tables.

The feel of the hilts in her hands did, with the natural magic of any mistress of the sword, feel good. If she was to die, why, then, she would do so and seek to find the sunny uplands beyond the Ice Floes of Sicce. But, before that, this rapier and this dagger would no longer glitter pure silver.

She turned, almost casually, with a lazy movement, and lifted the weapons.

"I am ready," she said in her small voice. "Bring on your vermin, Nyleen the Vile."

A gasp ran around the watching women. For an instant Delia thought she had overstepped the mark, had overdone it. But Nyleen laughed her pearly laugh and waved her hand. This spectacle, it was clear, would excite her, would be wonderfully enjoyable!

Nadia did not waste time. She leaped forward with a parade, her steel flashing. She was determined to show to all that she was the greatest swordswoman there, and to cut up this stupid and impertinent slave girl with great artistry. She would make the silly shif suffer. She was supremely confident.

Whoever had trained Nadia had been efficient and thorough. Of necessity, for her to have risen through the ranks of the Jikai Vuvushis to become a Hikdar meant she knew her business. To be chosen to be the cadade of a kovneva's bodyguard meant she also understood the management of women—and men, too. She fought with great competence and skill. But, very soon, Delia felt her out. She was wooden. She did not possess that spark, that indefinable transparency of the great sworder. Soon, dreadfully soon to the bewildered Nadia, her attacks failed, her cunning feints vanished, and blood stained along her arm, her thigh, over the rim of her corselet.

The sighing sound of the watching women susurrated, and faded. Entranced, unbelieving, they watched.

Delia was not cruel. Once she had the measure of Nadia she did not cut her up out of spite. And, too, she found that she had no interest in merely killing the overblown woman.

There was little need to exert herself unduly. The steel scraped and slithered, chiming with the unholy carillons of combat. Blood flowed. Nadia's blood flowed...

Presently, with a sweet little passage she remembered with some fondness, she stuck Nadia through the thigh, and, withdrawing, instantly stuck her through the other. The armored pteruges could not deflect thrusts of that degree of skill.

Bleeding, in pain, unbelieving, Nadia sank down to the floor. Her weapons slipped from her hands. Delia put the point of the rapier at her throat.

"Yes, Nyleen?" she said, still in her small voice. "And?"

Silence for a moment, for two moments, and then amid a babble of expostulations, Chica leaped forward.

"Let me!" screeched Chica. She snapped her whip.

The lash snaked toward Delia. With a single contemptuous flick of her dagger, Delia checked the strike, lopped the tip off the whip. The women gasped.

Nyleen called above the hubbub. Everyone stopped to listen to the kovneva.

"Vile men have their Jikordur and their hyr Jikordur, in which the ritual of personal combat is sanctified. Well, and are we any the less? What is there a man may do that we cannot?"

The howls broke out then, women screaming for blood.

Delia stood, the rapier and dagger held ready, watching.

The kovneva motioned to two Battle Maidens, who stepped forward and leveled their bows at Delia's breast. In this the kovneva showed her cruel streak. She joyed in her power, and what she could command. "Chica, you have been challenged, I think."

"Aye, my lady! Let it be done!"

Nineteen

The Whip and the Claw

Nyleen Gillois na Sagaie, Kovneva of Vindelka, torture mistress of untold numbers of men, would-be murderer of her husband, would-be wife and murderer of the emperor, had studied long and assiduously in the histories of Loh. With her lip caught up between her teeth, as a young girl in cold Evir, she had read of that mysterious continent of Loh and of the Queens of Pain.

To be a Queen of Pain of Loh!

She had never considered herself to be a cruel woman. She was merely the instrument chosen to redress the imbalance between the sexes. The witch Fiacola the Gaze had perhaps contributed more to her success than Nyleen cared to admit. But, in this coming confrontation, she saw more than mere revenge.

The satisfaction on her icy features reflected her inner joy that she had the power thus to test Chica the Fangs. Nyleen was always conscious of the necessity to preserve and display her power. This slave girl had skill with the rapier. Well, then, let Chica the Fangs discipline her, cut her, and let Nyleen take the frisson from Chica's lash, from her Claw, and the risk the Fangs ran!

Nadia the cadade was carried out, groaning, wondering what cyclone had hit her. Delia was stripped of weapons. She regarded Chica the Fangs warily. She could feel a pulse in her temple. She well understood what was in store. Her chin lifted.

"Very well, then, Chica the Fangs. You stand challenged."

"Give her a whip, and fetch my own old Fang. And bring the balass boxes." She turned, a hard, bright, agile woman, to face Delia. She sneered. "You challenge me, you fool! It is not only whips."

So, Delia knew.

Well, perhaps if she'd practiced more she wouldn't have this fluttery feeling in her chest.

They brought her a whip, a long snaky length of vileness. They gave Chica her favorite whip, old Fang, and she flicked it out. It was long and hard and supple, and it could strike in the pain ways and in the death ways. And Chica was its mistress.

The balass boxes were brought. Bronze bound, triply-locked, they were placed on the table before Nyleen. At once, Chica threw back the lid of one and took out her Claw. She held the thing aloft, a marvel of cunning linkages and bright steel and lacings and razor-sharp talons.

It glittered, held aloft in the torchlights. "Hai!" she cried, exulting. "Now you face death!"

From the second box Delia took out the Claw. It was a good, serviceable model, and when she tested it with a tentative thumb, reasonably sharp. There was no doubt that, if she had to use a Claw, she would prefer to partner it with a rapier. But a Whip would serve. Would have to serve, seeing that was the forte of this Chica. She held the Claw for a moment, and Chica laughed contemptuously.

"Help her strap it on. I will give her every chance. But it is clear she has no idea of a Jikvar, no idea at all."

Leading her cronies, Nyleen gloated. The Claw was strapped on Delia's left arm and hand. She flexed her muscles, rotating her arm, pulling back and jerking forward. The Claw fitted her surprisingly well. She looked at Chica the Fangs. That need not be her real name. She had gone through Lancival. Once, she had been a Sister of the Rose. That was the sadness in this, for Delia; that and the thought that sorcery had been used to debase this girl and deflect her from her vows.

Nyleen leaned forward. She was breathing more rapidly.

"Alyss. You do understand? You are to die. The manner of your death will be more unpleasant if you do not stand up to it. We here are all Sisters of the Whip. We know. The Claw has its uses, as you will discover." At this the women laughed, sensing the mood of their mistress. Nyleen went on: "But it is the Whip that must be used to chastise all men, everyone who stands against us. Why you set free the kov my husband, if you did, is of small consequence. What matters is your death here. Try to use the Claw. Use the Whip. Die like a woman!"

Then she sat back and with her cronies settled down to enjoy the spectacle of a half-naked girl being cut to pieces by an expert.

And, of course, Chica the Fangs was an expert.

In the desperateness of this situation, Delia had time to reflect on the comicality of her instinctive reaction. To herself, fervently, she said: "When I get out of this I promise Dee Sheon most devoutly to practice more regularly!"

Then Chica's Whip flicked and the fight was on.

As any bully-fighter might do, Chica sought at first to torment Delia. The Whip snapped and hissed. Twice she struck Delia in the pain ways, and Delia gasped with the shock. Once, in Lancival, seasons ago, she had heard a girl describe Delia as the Flower of the Sisters of the Rose. And, like any silly empty-headed girl, she had hugged the description to herself, mightily proud. Later she had seen the folly of that, and had been displeased. Now, had her sisters been able to see her, they would have seen the Flower with petals drastically wilting.

When Chica's whip flicked like a surging ripple of black destruction in the next passage, she got the Claw in the way, twisted, and yanked. But Chica was not to be caught like that. She disengaged and struck back, and Delia only just had time to skip sideways.

"The shishi learns!" crowed Chica. "This is becoming more enjoyable!"

Delia circled. The Whips abruptly leaped, and struck, and twined, and parted. Both girls leaped back.

The thing to do, Delia reasoned as she circled warily, was to get rid of the Whips. They fouled the issue. If these women followed the strict procedures, if the Whips were wrenched away and discarded, rapiers would be thrown into the ring. Chica would be as good as, if not better than, Nadia. That was probably the cause of the cadade's open desire to excel with the rapier and dagger. Probably.

On the next sudden onslaught, Delia swirled away from the tip, snapped her own Whip and slogged the lash into Chica's side. It was not as clean a blow as she had hoped for; it slapped against the corselet and made Chica jump.

"You bitch!"

Delia said nothing but reeled the Whip in, coiling, ready for the next attack.

When Chica, incensed, struck again, Delia jumped forward. She let the thicker section of her antagonist's Whip coil about her body. Its major force spent, it merely stung. She cracked her own lash up, high, sliced it down in a rippling line of destruction. The tip blazed across Chica's face.

The girl screamed and spun away. Her own Whip began to uncoil from Delia's body. She clamped it with her left hand, dragged it savagely back. She rippled her own Whip, and struck again. Again Chica screamed.

That damned helmet! It blocked the major force. But those two blows had opened up two vivid weals across the girl's face. Chica's lash snagged in Delia's left-hand Claw. She dragged again and the razor-sharp steel sliced through the Whip. A length as long as a girl's leg fell away.

Instantly, Delia leaped. She slashed with fury with her Claw. The blow hissed past Chica who stumbled back, shaken, off-balance. She staggered. And then she had recovered and come screaming back, her Claw gouging for Delia's naked side.

With a routine block and twist, Delia checked the onslaught and instinctively slashed back. The return missed only just, only just—and both girls stood back, panting.

"What, Chica?" called Nyleen. "Do you toy with her still?"

Chica bit down on her lip. She looked frighteningly savage.

"She will rue these blows, my lady!"

"Then, Chica, my dear, pray let us see. We are waiting."

The next passage was not quite the same as that preceding. The Whips became entangled. Chica, relying so much on her lash, took a moment too long to attempt to untangle the lines, and Delia stepped in. The Claw razored down.

Only a woman in the Jikvar of Chica's skill could have twisted herself away from a stroke of that expertise.

The Fangs slid the blow. Just. One steel talon ripped across the shoulder, slashing through the metal-studded leather of the latchings. Around the watching women ran the gasp of excitement—of pleasure. Who among them was dismayed that Chica was meeting her match?

A man had once said to Delia that the sight of women fighting did not so much disgust or offend him as sadden him. To which she had replied, tartly, that if a woman has to do a certain thing in life, then a woman will do it.

Delia did not proceed to demolish Chica. For one thing, the Fangs was too good for the slightest chance to be taken. But Delia did, having seen that first latching go, cunningly contrive to slash the other shoulder. At that, the return blow whispered past her face and only a last minute wrench away and recovered lunge saved her from losing half her features.

The Fangs took three steps back. The black length of the Whip rippled to stillness along the floor. Her silvered corselet sagged away, held by the waist belt and rib-straps.

"Very well," said Delia, flicking her Whip and making Chica jump. "I will give you a few moments to make yourself comfortable."

Sucking in the sight, Nyleen felt her insides deliquesce. This was better sport than she had ever imagined!

Furious, still not accepting that she had met a superior in the Jikvar and the Grakvar, Chica ripped away her breastplate. She wore under the padding a thin supple-leather vest. She was not a big-built girl, being of the wiry and agile variety. But she was a woman. For that, alone, Delia was cautious...

Waiting quietly for Chica to get set, Delia reflected that just about the only truly authenticated example of a man using a Claw came from the Life of Velda the Tempestuous, whose old room Delia now lodged in at Lancival. The man—apparently his name had been Nath or Naghan the Flute—had hungered after an initiate of the SoR. He had broken into one of the provincial colleges to an assignment with her. Everything had gone wrong, and in the ensuing fracas he had slain a sister. He had snatched up and donned a Claw. Then he ran into Velda.

If Delia did to Chica what Velda the Tempestuous had done to this Naghan or Nath the Flute, they'd have to carry the Fangs out in baskets. Or, rather, to make less mess, in buckets.

Chica slished her Claw through the air. She snapped her Whip.

"I am ready, dom."

Delia, using the Disciplines to relax herself in this pause in the fight, deliberately slowing down some rhythms so that others might be speeded up, smiled.

"You call me dom, Chica the Fangs. Strange address, surely, from a Jikai Vuvushi to a mere slave girl?"

The Fangs rippled her Whip. "Yes, you are a slave girl now. But you have, I think, been through Lancival."

"As have you."

"I am done with them! They betrayed me. Now, I am a Sister of the Whip!"

"That is your misfortune."

Nyleen shrilled from her chair: "What are you two standing lollygagging about for! Get on with it! Chica—cut her up. Bratch!"

Delia made a small elegant gesture with the Claw. "That, Chica the Lost, is your mistress."

"She is what she is. Like me, she hates men. So—"

"So you hate everyone? Indeed, you are Lost."

"Fight, you bitch, and have done!"

In the moment before the Whips rose and leaped Delia said: "I think, my girl, it is you who are done."

"*Bratch!*" The shriek from Nyleen made her cronies start.

Chica the Fangs put out everything of which she was capable. Perhaps, Delia had just time to consider before surrendering herself to the demands of the Whip and the Claw, just perhaps Chica had grown soft in whipping poor defenseless slaves instead of facing opposition.

Leaping streaks of darkness, the hiss and crack of cunningly applied lashes, the quick intake of breath, the sliding scrape of feet upon the floor... The glitter of the Claws blinded. The Whips coiled and struck, withdrew, rippled, slashed again...

Chica put the lopped tip into Delia's ribs, and she gasped with the dizzying pain. On the next passage she sliced the supple-leather vest from Chica, spilling it away in two clean halves. Without waiting, she roared in, the whip slicing and the Claw slashing. Chica just saved herself. And, in stumbling away and avoiding that savage attack, she entangled her lash with Delia's. The two Whips writhed together.

Both girls reacted instinctively. Both hauled back with all their strength. Chica was brought staggeringly forward, off balance, gasping, as Delia reeled her in. At the last moment the Fangs released her grip on her Whip and flopped away.

Delia threw the entangled mass onto the floor.

She stared at Nyleen.

"Well, Nyleen?"

Nyleen chewed her lip.

Now it should be rapiers...

Chica screamed at the kovneva.

"Kovneva! My lady! *Daggers!*"

Nyleen nodded. She felt sweet and moist and satisfaction coursed through her. She would like Sissy to be here to minister to her. But the fool girl was missing... She'd be in for a flogging, of course. But, now, Nyleen gloated and would not miss a single moment of this fascinating passage at arms.

Two Jikai Vuvushis threw two daggers into the center.

They stuck, quiveringly, light splintering from hilt and blade.

Chica leaped, ripped the nearest dagger free, brandished it. "Now, sister, you will understand!"

Delia took the other dagger. It was a Vallian dagger. It was long and slender and sharp. Its quillons were marvels of curious ornamentation. It was not, most certainly was not, a left-hand dagger. The major problem with Vallian daggers was to find steel of the quality required. So long, so thin the blade, inferior metal would snap. These looked to be weapons of quality. Delia felt the hilt in her hand, and she held the dagger in her own way.

Delia was accounted a mistress of the bow, having been taught by Seg Segutorio. She was a mistress of the rapier, having learned much from her husband. She was a mistress of the churgur's art, the use of the battle sword and shield, having been taught by Balass the Hawk. She was a mistress of the Whip and the Claw, having been through Lancival. But of the Vallian dagger—ah! Of that superbly cunning instrument of death there was no one in the whole wide world of Kregen, it was said, who could teach Delia a single tiny thing.

The Fangs used her own Claw to rip away the two parts of her supple-leather vest. She ripped them and tossed them down. She fronted Delia.

Catlike, she half-crouched, and began to circle. Delia circled with her. Like two primordial felines out of the mists of time, the women circled each other, seeking an opening, panting only lightly, their legs long and supple moving them with infinite grace.

Now there would be no long-range work. Now they would meet, body to body, arms and legs thrusting, seeking to rip and claw. Their skin glowed in the torchlights, sleek and rounded, the hollowed shadows tinged in violet and carmine. Chica tossed her head back, and weaved left and surged right, and Delia let her go past and used her Claw to rip a bloody chunk out of that glowing skin.

Chica screamed.

She threw herself at Delia, dagger and Claw lifted.

With expertise that spurted from her inmost depths, Delia feinted, blocked, caught the Claw and let her dagger slide on. The stroke was cunning, perfectly delivered, superb. It would penetrate between Chica's ribs, slice on unerringly, burst into her heart.

Infallibly...

Why? Why did Delia turn the dagger slightly, turn the direction of the thrust? Why did she let the blade score along Chica's ribs instead of rupturing her heart? Why?

Again, Chica screamed, and fell back, and Delia was on her like a leem.

The Claw flamed before Chica's eyes. The talons, each razor-sharp, each capable of dragging flesh from bone, of gouging out an eye, hovered over the Fangs' face.

Among the watchful women were many who understood the techniques of fighting. They might not practice; they could judge. They saw. They saw the diversion of the blade. Now they saw Chica's horrible disfigurement, her death in agony.

Chica glared up, froth on her lips, her eyes wide and yet blank, drugged with the awful knowledge of impending destruction.

"A fight, dom," she said. "A fight."

"And you have lost, Chica the Lost, as I said. I will not kill you. I have other plans for you."

With that, Delia turned the Claw and used a blunt and heavy edge and knocked Chica the Fangs backwards. The girl sprawled limply across the floor. The Claw flopped with a clank of steel. And the dagger flew from her hand, skidded across the floor to smash into the kovneva's feet.

Standing up, Delia let Claw and dagger dangle. She stared at Nyleen, and her face expressed contempt. Splendid, she looked, Delia, Empress of Vallia who was just Delia. Only a light sweat glinted on her body. She breathed deeply. Superb, superb, and consummately deadly...

Nyleen was staring past her, at the door, and the kovneva's eyes opened wide. An expression of great joy filled her icy face. She smiled. Then she giggled, as at a supreme joke.

"Slave! You fight well. You have skill. Chica was good, in my service, very good with Whip and Claw. But now, I think, now you will face a greater! Now you will be tested to the utmost!"

Delia did not turn. Hell and damnation! She'd fought and fought well and won. If they shafted her, well, she'd try to deflect the arrows in the way her husband had shown her. But that was difficult, by Vox! When the door bashed open and this newcomer entered, she had felt the flicker of a hope she had resolutely refused to acknowledge. An obvious hope, a pent-up desire that would burst out like flame. He had done it before. She'd been naked, chained up, staked out as a sacrifice, menaced by steel and talons and fangs. And he'd come storming in like the maniac he was, and rescued her.

But not this time.

She'd won, and she could feel the tiredness creeping up on her, a fatigue she pushed aside and ignored which yet insisted on trembling her legs and jerking her muscles. And now the bastards were bringing on another champion.

From what Nyleen said, from the expression on her face and the satisfied oohs and aahs from her cronies, this newcomer was going to be very good indeed.

If she was better than Chica—and she would be, she would be!—she'd be the very devil to handle.

Oh—why hadn't she practiced more!

"Drag Chica away!" commanded Nyleen. "Give the slave her Whip. Now we shall see some *real* Whip and Claw."

She called along the length of the refectory, a glowing, commanding woman, joying in her power and enjoying her own joy. "Come in, my dear. Lahal and Lahal. You are more than welcome. Now you can show us how it should be done. As you can see, the onker Chica could not manage it."

From the swiveling movement of the watching women's heads, Delia realized they were watching the newcomer walking from the door toward her unturning back. She did not hear her. That, alone, boded ill. If only she'd put in more practice sessions... Chica had not been easy. And the dismal truth of the coming encounter was made crystal clear as Nyleen crowed her own pleasurable anticipations.

"Here is a slave shishi for you to—well, my dear, I hardly dare call it fight—for you to cut up. Step forth, my dear. For you are supreme, far far better than Chica with Whip and Claw."

"Cut her! Cut her!" screamed the waiting women.

When a Claw struck and cut it could rip your face off...

Delia turned around.

She saw the woman walking down between the tables. She saw. The newcomer, this redoubtable champion, lifted her head and spoke.

"You wish me to fight this silly little slave girl and cut her up for you?" said Jilian Sweet-Tooth.

Twenty

All for Vallia...?

Jilian swirled off her enveloping black riding cloak. Dust stained the hem. She wore black fighting leathers, trim, taut, still shining although scuffed. At her waist the belted rapier and dagger swung to hand. Terchicks snugged across her shoulders. Her Whip coiled up her right arm. Somewhere in her baggage would be her bronze-bound balass box. She did not look at Delia.

"I do not think, kovneva, I shall fight this girl."

"Not fight her, my dear? Oh, of course. You are tired from your journey. I see! Well, this shif must be tired, too, since she has defeated Nadia Woodraven who used to be my cadade, and Chica Trevalmin ti Alvondsmot, whom we used to call the Fangs."

Jilian let her dark intense gaze pass broodingly across Delia. She drew off her left-hand glove, supple and black. She did not remove the right, for the Whip coiled its sinuous lashes about the leather gauntlet.

"If Nadia and Chica are both defeated, have you not found yourself a Jikvushi who would serve you and fight for you—if you treated her well?"

Giving the kovneva no time to reply, Jilian gestured with her right hand. "Slave—bring me wine, a light yellow, for my mouth is as parched as the Ochre Limits."

The slave girl thus addressed scuttled to obey. Delia stood motionless. Jilian looked almost just the same. Her pale face bore its normal look of brooding intensity, her dark hair cut low over her broad white forehead setting an added luster in her dark eyes. Her whole face looked almost the same; pleasing, broad and well-proportioned and with a warm and mobile mouth. But there hung about Jilian Sweet-Tooth an air of dejection, of more than usual brooding hurt. She took the wine and quaffed it and threw the goblet at the slave girl as Nyleen arched her back, like a cat, her face rigid in its icy smile.

"You have been unsuccessful, Jilian?"

"Yes and no. I have almost certain news of the rast. Almost certain. But I must follow up even this slender lead. I came to advise you that I leave for Pandahem tomorrow."

"Do not forget to bring back his head—or some other part of Kov Colun's anatomy—for our inspection and delectation as you tell your story."

"If there is anything of him left."

"Ah! And, now, Jilian, mayhap you will cut this slave shishi up for our inspection and delectation—*here and now?*"

Still Delia stood motionless. Truth to tell, in all their practice bouts together, she and Jilian had never settled the issue—who was the better. It had not mattered. They had joined in combat, joying in the tussle, in the skill and expertise. In the nature of practice bouts they had used rebated weapons and heavily padded Claws. Whips, one against another in practice, were uncommonly difficult to manage. Delia just did not know who would win, if she and Jilian fought in the Jikvar and the Grakvar with razor-edged Claws and Whips that could flay.

Again, truth to tell, she was aware of the odd trifling deficiency in Jilian's technique. She had told her friend. And Jilian had told her, in her turn, of Delia's mistakes. Perhaps, if it came to a fight to the death, just perhaps, Delia felt she might win. But that victory would leave her a ruin. Then she thrust those thoughts aside. So Jilian had renounced the Sisters of the Rose and had joined the Sisters of the Whip. Very well. That did not mean she had renounced her friendship. Being Jilian, she would do what she wanted to do, and Delia found herself confident that Jilian would unravel a way to settle this without fighting.

She hoped so, she devoutly hoped so...

Moving with her lithe easy swing, Jilian crossed the open space and hitched herself up onto the edge of a table. Her body sat erect, and one long leg swung backward and forward, backward and forward. If anyone here could think it of anyone else, then that swinging leg in the tall black boot was a most insolent gesture, most insolent indeed.

Jilian took up a goblet of wine. She said: "Let me compose myself, kov-neva. As I said, I have ridden hard and long."

She drank the wine down. Then, with her bare left hand, she wiped across her mouth. Deliberately, she said: "By Mother Zinzu the Blessed! I needed that!"

Delia showed no startlement. She just hadn't given a thought to the idea that Jilian would tell the kovneva and her cronies who this slave girl was. Delia showed no startlement; but she was profoundly moved. Jilian, a member now of the Sisters of the Whip, could so easily have told, so eas-ily done what would amount to a betrayal of her friend. But, by saying what she had after she drank, Jilian was reassuring Delia. Jilian had never, to Delia's knowledge, visited the inner sea of Turismond, the Eye of the World. But she had heard the emperor, many times, say those words when he was dry and downed a draught.

"By Mother Zinzu the Blessed, I needed that!"

Yes, those words had been used many times, and Jilian was reaching out to Delia. Now, she went on in a conversational tone: "People call me Sweet-Tooth. Many people—and, I think, all men—believe that because I was born in a Banje shop and like sweet things, I was given that name. That the Tooth does not refer to any tooth I have in my head is so; men do not know."

Nyleen's frustration grew visibly upon her. Now she took what Jilian said in an entirely different context from that intended. Jilian was speak-ing to Delia, reassuring her that her secret was safe; Nyleen imagined she was making excuses for not fighting this slave girl.

"Do you tell me, Jilian, that because she is a girl you will not fight her?"

"Give me the moment I ask, kovneva. Then, as surely as a leem takes a ponsho, you will see..." She pointed negligently at the length of whip sliced from Chica's favorite Fang. "Chica relied too much on her Whip. You did

287

well, kovneva, when you brought her away from the Sisters of the Rose, for she spied for them in Delka Ob. Now, they know nothing of our plans."

The horror hit Delia then.

Could Jilian be a party to the plot to kill the emperor?

That did not seem credible to the empress.

The emperor had rescued Jilian and brought her out of humiliating bondage to a position of respect. Jilian was a loved and valued member of the household, who had raised her own regiment of Jikai Vuvushis to fight for Vallia. At first she had known the emperor only as Jak the Drang, a now famous cognomen. Delia understood well enough the ties Jilian might form.

Between the emperor and the empress existed ties that had not been broken by the sundering of four hundred light-years, by the interference of superhuman beings, immortals, godlike beings of supernal power. Those bonds had not been broken by the petty slanders of evil tongues. Other attachments, for these two, were matters of supreme indifference. Yes, considered Delia, poor Jilian might well have formed a romantic attachment in her mind. Perhaps that had gone sour.

Perhaps she *was* in the plot to kill the emperor.

If so, then she was going about it in a remarkably peculiar way...

Also, this explained what had happened to the spy sent by Thalmi Crockhaden, pro-marshal and spy mistress of the SoR. A girl of Chica's caliber would be needed for that work. Yet she had turned sour, gone rotten, been suborned, turned herself over to the Sisters of the Whip.

The cause of that rapid overturning of the beliefs of a lifetime and the embracing of inferior beliefs, now entered the refectory.

The witch, Fiacola the Gaze, walked in on the arm of the flunkey woman, Ilka the Silver Rod. Following, spitting and snarling, prowled two couples of werstings straining the leashes held by Rinka the Stripe. The intrusion of the witch brought everything else to a halt.

Even so, in the respectful hush, Nyleen called crossly to Ilka: "Where is that tiresome girl Sissy? I shall surely stripe her when she comes crawling and sobbing to me."

Ilka made a small gesture with her free hand. "I have not seen her, my lady."

Fiacola the Gaze kept her face hidden by the deep folds of a dark blue hood. She moved heavily to a chair quickly vacated at the side of Nyleen's chair. She sat, and Ilka fussily arranged her robes. The hood was not thrown back.

Only those two eyes caught the torchlights and gleamed a deep crimson in the shadows of the hood.

Not for nothing was the sorceress Fiacola called The Gaze...

Standing quite still, Delia took note of what went forward. She was able to feel amusement that amid this respectful hush, Nyleen still could react in her cross way, and Jilian could still swing that long booted leg back and forth in her insolent fashion.

When Fiacola spoke her voice surprised Delia. That voice sounded deep and clear, like a note from a woodwind, like a sonorous chime.

"Does Jilian Sweet-Tooth forget what she now is?"

Jilian's booted foot stopped swinging.

"She says she is tired, Sana—"

"I am aware, kovneva, of what goes forward here."

Delia clamped her mind shut. Witches did have powers; of course, this Fiacola could merely have been listening at the door. But, all the same, it was a mightily powerful performance.

The witch's hood turned and inclined and Delia was aware of that sliding crimson gleam upon her. In the silence the hoarse breathing of many of the women sounded like the scraping of sword upon shield, the grating of a badly balanced spinning wheel. Even the werstings slobbered into silence.

The witch spoke again. "You promised me a diversion tonight, Nyleen. I do not object to seeing women cutting up other women if they deserve it. But that does not compare."

"You are right, Fiacola," responded Nyleen instantly. She lifted her right hand and gestured. She made of the gesture an imperial demand. "Begin!"

"Leave the slave girl to me." The ominous ring in the words was not lost on Delia.

The two Jikai Vuvushis with half-bent bows shepherded her away to stand near the side table. Jilian sat on the edge of her table across the central space. And, into the space from the flung open doors, on the kovneva's command, advanced a familiar, a sorry, a horrible procession.

The women who used their whips upon the naked bodies of the men were careful. All the shuffling men wore chains loading them down. There were various sizes and weights of chain in common usage among slave-masters. Sometimes they would refer to a slave as a one-chain man, or a three-chain man. This gave an indication not only of his troublesomeness but also of his strength and the care they took over restraining him until he was brought to heel and trained into the ways of slavery.

Most of the men wore one set of chains.

One man wore two. One man was a three-chain man. One was a four-chain slave. And one was loaded down with no less than six sets of chains. He could walk upright, which he did, defiant, arrogant, his four arms cruelly chained up his back.

"Oh!" said Delia to herself. "My poor Djangs!"

The two-chain man was Jordio the Hawk. The three-chain man was Lathdo the Eager. The four-chain man was Dalki, and the six-chain man was Tandu, his father.

So Jordio and Lathdo had fallen safely from the storm-wrecked airboat and had been taken up, at last, and so, eventually, brought here to be tortured to death. And her two ferocious Djangs? Surely, she reasoned, surely they must have ridden up to take service with the kov, bearing the letter from the Lord Farris, and had been sent on, and so been entrapped. They would not have been taken easily...

Dragging their chains, herded in a mass of suffering, the four men did not see their empress and queen beside the table at the far end. They saw the prepared stakes, the saw-edged barriers, the instruments, and they understood what was to be their fate.

Now the excitement rippled around the watching women. Everyone brightened up. Nyleen and her cronies prepared themselves for a pleasant divertissement. Only the witch kept her gaze bent on first Delia and then Jilian. She looked from one to the other, and back, like a reptile measuring its prey.

The occult powers of sorcerers and sorceresses could be very real, or could be shams to rook the gullible. Delia believed this Fiacola must be mistress of some of the arts, for to suborn away a Sister of the Rose from her vows must take thaumaturgy of a high order. Perhaps Delia could not answer for the integrity of every Sister...

But—Jilian! No, that was certain sure. Witchery had ensorcelled Jilian, quite apart from glib promises of help in tracking down Kov Colun Mogper of Mursham to his just desserts. If Delia could not believe in and trust Jilian, then her whole concept of integrity was proved valueless and ridiculous.

The first men were prepared for blood, agony and death. Delia put one hand on the edge of the table. Sticky wine fouled her fingers, but she did not grimace with distaste. Spilled wine, sticky and unpleasant though it be, was as nothing beside the spilling of blood now being enacted out there on the floor. The Claw still strapped up on her arm fit her hand like a glove. The dagger, blood-befouled like the Claw, hung limply in her fist. The two Battle Maidens kept on taking their surveillance away, kept on darting looks at what was going on out there among the shrieks and the vomit and the blood. But they did not relax their vigilance. One movement, and one or other of the Battle Maidens would shaft her...

Aware of the grisly scrutiny of the witch, Delia deliberately kept her own gaze averted. She did not look at the suffering human beings out there; she looked at her Djangs, and at Lathdo and Jordio. They stood sullenly, chafing their chains, so overloaded they could barely move. Their clothes were in a mess, ripped and stained, and their faces were bruised and bloodied. But they did not look cowed. In this, at least, they were prepared to face a ghastly end with fortitude.

She noticed an odd circumstance about Dalki. He was the four-chain man. But, somehow, he seemed only to have three chains lapping his body.

As she watched a loop of chain tumbled free of his tunic. Weirdly, like the trunk of a mammoth beast withdrawing, it slithered up and vanished from view. Delia blinked. Dalki seemed to be in movement although he remained still. Most odd. Another chain dropped, and was checked, and so drawn back. She felt the pulse in her throat. In some unaccountable way, Dalki was freeing himself of his chains. He must have been working on them from the moment they were first loaded upon him, and, no doubt now, he was cursing away that it had taken so long, and that he was in sight of freedom when he was also in sight of death.

A victim shrieked and died. He was glad to die, and the women were sorry that entertainment was over. But they looked eagerly for the next. Nyleen stood up. She walked with her smooth gait out onto the floor to inspect personally the gruesome wreckage. Other women crowded up. The guards moved forward.

Nyleen liked, now and then, to take a hand herself. She could flick and slash her Whip, and although she would have been cut to shreds in short order by any mistress in the Grakvar, she still liked to posture.

"Chain some to the posts," she commanded. "We will have a competition."

"Oh, yes, kovneva," chorused her cronies. And, still, Delia found it hard to hate the silly woman. Her craving for power and glory, her mimicry of the ways of the Queens of Pain of Loh, as Delia shrewdly surmised, her genuine belief that she had a mission to chastise all men, all these things added up to a woman bereft of essentials and adrift on tides of unchecked emotion. That was unfortunate, reprehensible, and in its effects evil; but Nyleen, Delia guessed, was also the victim of sorcery.

"Chain up some fine specimens, strong ones." Nyleen pointed. "Those! They are sullen enough, by the Breath of Evirani! We will make them wish they had not been born men."

Lathdo, Jordio, Dalki and Tandu were chained up. In an odd way, Dalki managed to conceal his handiwork and was chained up with the others. Delia marveled. Three other hard and hairy men were chained up alongside to the stakes. Nyleen preened herself and took the whip a girl slave ran out and proffered.

The first blow missed. No one laughed. Jilian's booted foot quivered; but it did not swing. The second blow chunked into one of the hairy men, and he yelled. The third blow almost took Nyleen's eye out. She glared around pettishly. She threw the Whip down and drew a long Vallian dagger.

"I have a keener way with men, my dears!"

"Yes, kovneva!"

She advanced with the dagger held aloft.

"Wait!" The deep bell-like voice of Fiacola the Gaze caught everyone. Nyleen stopped and looked around. The dagger slowly descended.

"Yes, Sana?"

"The Jikai Vuvushi, Jilian, will now fight the slave girl."

"But, Fiacola—"

"Fight! *Now!*"

Jilian put her feet on the floor and stood up slowly.

She turned to face the witch. On Jilian's pallid face that brooding look compressed into a deep and intense absorption.

"And Sana, if I do not choose to fight?"

The witch cackled. The mellow voice broke into a harsh cackling croak, as of great enjoyment.

"I did not think you would. Would you fight some other girl? Say, that Jikai Vuvushi there?"

Delia felt her heart contract.

"Oh, Jilian!" she said to herself. "Careful!"

But Jilian tossed that dark hair back. "If I was commanded," she said, carelessly.

The Witch nodded within her hood, and the sliding crimson gleam came and went. "Take the dagger from that slave girl. Take the Claw away from her. Why, Kovneva Nyleen, do you think Jilian Sweet-Tooth will not fight this one particular little slave shishi?"

Nyleen looked bewildered. "Why, she says she is tired. But she will fight. We will see to that."

The hood swept back. Fiacola's face was revealed. Delia saw the smooth round plump features, like those of a young girl who in all innocence and purity follows the sacred procession, clad all in a long white gown, trembling with the spiritual fires of devotion. A clawed hand lifted, and a black fingernail pointed.

That hooked talon pointed directly at Delia.

"Jilian would fight another, if you commanded, Nyleen. But you will not make her fight this one! I know! I have the power. I have the Gaze!" Her voice rose, booming around the refectory, echoing, demanding. "For that silly slave girl is Delia, Empress of Vallia!"

Into the stunned silence Delia's scornful laugh rang like a sword striking stone. "The witch is deranged. I am just a poor girl caught up into slavery—"

"It is useless, Delia of Delphond! You are the Empress of Vallia."

A massive bull bellow smashed above the sudden chatter. Over the exclamations of wonder and surprise, and then of understanding and satisfaction, that gargantuan roar broke like a hurricane.

"My queen!"

Tandu turned into a writhing onslaught of flesh and bone and sinew, striving against the chains.

The witch laughed. "This woman is, also, as you will doubtless know, the Queen of Djanduin."

Her pure childlike face turned toward Jilian. Brightly she looked upon the Sweet-Tooth.

"Jilian. You are a Sister of the Whip. I have said the kovneva will not make you fight your friend, the empress. But, for me you will fight her. For me you will cut her and cut her again, and slay her into little pieces. For me, for Fiacola the Gaze, for I have the power over you, Jilian Sweet-Tooth."

Watching her friend, Delia felt the agony for her, the sorrow. Jilian trembled. She swayed. Her pallor now turned her face more icy than Nyleen's. Sweat dropped.

"You have the power, Fiacola. And I believed you."

"Continue to do so. What is there that can stand against what I may make you do? Fight the empress, Jilian! Fight and cut and kill!"

As though a mere inconsequential irritation in the clash of wills, Nyleen chattered out quickly: "If this is true! It must be true! Then we have won! But, Jilian—fight her as Fiacola commands. But I do suggest you do not kill her. Let us chain her up and let her die—differently—yes?"

"Chain her up?" said Jilian. She swayed. "Fight Delia to the death and then not kill but turn her over to you for..."

"Only if Fiacola approves, of course."

Watching her friend, Delia said nothing.

Jilian's bare left hand brushed the dark hair back from her forehead where it immediately fell back into that curved line above her eyebrows. "Lace up her Claw," she said to the Battle Maiden plucking at the lacings. "Fetch my balass box."

Delia sucked a breath.

The box was rushed in and placed upon the table, and all the time Tandu struggled and writhed and roared. No one paid him any attention. Jilian unlocked the box and threw the lid back. She withdrew her Claw. That glittering fang of death was a supreme example of the Jikvar armorer's art. She glanced across at Nyleen.

"You would do what you say, kovneva?"

"Of course. What else? Now, Jilian, my dear, do as Fiacola commands and let us get on with this evening. It is going to be absolutely splendid now. Now that the empress will be dead we can all go forward with much greater heart. It is so exciting."

The Sweet-Tooth moved as a bamboo and paper puppet moves behind the screen in a shadow play. Always a girl of a brooding and intense nature, she now seemed to draw in upon herself. She spoke in a slurred way. "You command me, Fiacola the Gaze?"

"I command, Jilian, and I have the power over you."

The Claw turned in Jilian's right hand, turned and lifted and positioned ready to be fitted snugly up over her left hand and arm. Each steel segment, cunningly curved, articulated, oiled, catching sparkles of fire from the torchlights, would be honed to razor sharpness. Once that hand of death fastened on Delia's face...

Delia said: "Fiacola claims she has the power, Jilian. And you have been led into a belief she speaks the truth."

Fiacola's head swiveled from her rapt attention upon Jilian to stare in a liquid crimson gleaming upon Delia.

"Silence! Shastum!"

"Fiacola the Gaze," said Delia, and she felt a stroking pressure upon her, like spider silk drawing and tightening. She lifted her head. "You claim to be a witch. But there are powers of which you know nothing." The contempt in Delia's voice flayed as the lash flays in a flogging jikaider. "You do not feel. There are powers beyond your puny comprehension."

"I command this girl, and she will surely cut you and slay you into little pieces—"

"You, Fiacola the Malignant, command nothing. You may deceive this pitiful creature Nyleen and her abhorrent cronies. I do not think you can command against those powers of which you know nothing."

The childish features contorted. "I am Fiacola the Gaze! I have powers! Jilian—cut her, kill her, slay her into little pieces! I command you!"

The crimson gleam remained fast set upon Delia. She faced that Gaze, unflinching. She could feel the spider strands drawing upon her mind, and she resisted. There was no other chance of life beyond this...

"Jilian," said Delia, and her voice rang and soared. "Jilian!"

Instantly, Tandu's roarings subsided. The witch, her gaze fixed on Delia, flinched. The Sweet-Tooth moved her head in a peculiar sideways motion.

"There is no hope for you, Delia of Delphond, Empress of Vallia." The witch chattered and her childish features twisted in concentration. The spider strands tightened.

Jilian said: "You command me to destroy my friend, witch. Your power is great. But Delia and I have a power, too. It is a power you fear and abhor because you cannot feel it."

And Jilian Sweet-Tooth reached her left hand up to her neck and drew one of the three terchicks that snugged in their sheaths over her shoulder, and threw. The throwing knife glinted just once as it streaked. The point penetrated Fiacola's right eye, and the blade went in up to the hilt.

Had the witch turned into a puff of blue smoke, Delia, for one, would not have been surprised.

The spider strands slithered unpleasantly, like cobwebs brushed aside in the dark, and vanished.

Nyleen shrieked, purple-faced. Her shock at the revelation that Alyss the slave who played the harp so divinely was the empress had been followed by joy that the woman was under her hand at last. And now—now the witch was dead. All her icy pallor fled. Engorged, she screamed orders. In a trice Delia and Jilian were overborne and chained. Nyleen cast a single glance at the crumpled body in its hooded gown. Fiacola the Gaze was dead. There were other witches. The scheme must go on. She must have the empress killed—kill her herself!—and then marry the emperor and destroy him. Then she, Nyleen, would be Empress of Vallia. The scheme *would* work...

The dagger held aloft, she advanced upon Delia.

Tandu roared at her. His magnificent Djang head lifted and he told her something that brought the breath short between her teeth.

"Your tongue will be cut out, rast, I promise you!"

Dalki shouted across, adding to what his father had said, amplifying, going into graphic details. His description of Nyleen drove the color from her face. Her body shook in its panoply of gems and gold and silks. She looked like an Ice Queen of Myth, a Queen of Pain of Loh. The dagger trembled violently.

Delia heard Jilian say: "Once we get out of these chains we will make a bonny fight of it. Delia—I knew nothing—"

"Yes, Jilian. I know."

"How can you know? How can you trust me—?"

"I thought I knew my Jilian Sweet-Tooth. And I was right. I did. Fiacola the Gaze did not, for all her sorcery."

"... pasty-faced, impotent, sag-chested, knock-kneed, moustached, bladder of a woman," quoth Dalki, merrily, going on into further disparaging descriptions of Nyleen.

She rushed at him, foaming, the dagger lifted. She struck wildly at his head. He moved his head sideways and the dagger gouged into the wood of the stake and stuck, lodged fast.

Nyleen pushed in against the chained man whose two arms were viciously chained around the back of the stake and whose legs were chained all the way from thigh to foot. She reached up past his head for the dagger. The next time she would not miss.

She reached up, her body straining in the silks and tissues, looped with gems. She remained there. She lifted a little onto her toes. Dalki's arms, chained around the back of the stake, quivered with some intense exertion. Nyleen did not reach farther for the dagger, did not move, just stood there on tiptoe, pressed against Dalki.

Delia saw the Djang's face. He was not a real Djang, for he had but the two normal arms; but he thought and acted like a Djang. That face was compressed with effort, the eyeballs starting, the veins throbbing in the forehead, the mouth clamped and white with strain. Sweat rolled down Dalki's Djang face.

And the kovneva remained on tiptoe, pressed against him.

The women began to fidget, to call out. Ilka left the body of the witch and walked down the line of tables. The werstings snuffled and yowled. Jikai Vuvushis began to chatter among themselves. Some looked around in a bewildered way, as though wondering where they were.

And, still, Nyleen, Kovneva of Vindelka, remained unmoving on tiptoe, straining against Dalki.

Delia saw an odd movement at the kovneva's neck.

Something lifted there, like a collar, lifted and withdrew.

Nyleen fell.

She collapsed and sprawled to the floor.

Ilka reached her, bent, looked, turned and screamed: "*The kovneva is dead!*"

Jilian said, "And about time too. I am ready to throw off my chains, Delia."

"And I."

Delia, about to discard the chains that the inattentive guards had allowed to loosen, steadied herself. Just before she broke loose she looked not at Nyleen, dead upon the floor; but at Dalki. She saw.

His father was a Djang, no matter that his mother had been apim. Dwadjangs have four arms. Dalki, too, had four arms. But the second pair of arms were truncated, tiny, as long only as half a forearm each. But the hands were broad and powerful. Those hands withdrew into the rents in his tunic. They might have looked pathetic, muscular hands that could only just touch each other across his chest. They might have done. But those hands had taken Nyleen's throat between them and choked her out of this world.

Dalki had worked on his chains with those hidden hands, and now he stepped free and raced for his father as Delia and Jilian cast down their chains and raged out. Jilian's Claw went on in a twinkling. Her rapier licked out. Delia found the first rapier to hand, for the guard would no longer require the blade, and the two girls ranged shoulder to shoulder.

Not a single woman in the refectory would care to challenge one of them. Now there were two...

"This will be a bonny fight," said Jilian. "If we are lucky it might be dubbed a Jikai."

"It is nice," said Delia in her decisive way, "to have friends."

There was little need to spell out to Jilian what Nyleen had intended. She made no further attempt to explain away her conduct. There was no explanation this side of the black arts.

Delia said, "Now the witch and Nyleen are gone, I think these poor fools will come to their senses. I hope so. I would like to avoid more fighting."

"So would I," said Jilian, making her Claw catch the lights of the torches and splinter back silver stars from each razored talon. "So I dearly would. But someone has warned that cramph Cranchar. Here he comes."

The doors burst open, and Cranchar and his henchmen rushed in, brandishing weapons, roaring for the devils who had slain Fiacola the Gaze.

Over the uproar, Delia called: "Cranchar! See to your sister."

He saw the limp gaudy form, cradled in Ilka's arms. His face bludgeoned. He stood stock still. He put the gauntleted hand gripping his sword to his forehead. In a low mad voice, he said: "Then are you all dead. Dead!"

"No!" shouted Nath the Muncible, striding forward with Sissy defiant and yet palpitating at his side. "There has been death enough to warm the Ice Floes of Sicce with spilled blood."

Tandu ripped the last of the chains free as Dalki helped him. Tandu stared up, engorged.

"My queen! Is this the chief rast?" Without waiting for an answer he leaped for Cranchar.

Cranchar was a dead man then. But Tandu caught his foot in a loop of chain and tumbled head over heels, all four arms going like a windmill, rolled into the tables and brought two or three down with pots of wine cascading onto his head. He roared.

Nath the Muncible was pushed out of the way as Cranchar hared for the door. He screamed at his men. They stood undecided, or followed him, or started to attack. Those that chose the latter course no longer figured in the annals of Kregen. Jordio the Hawk and Lathdo the Eager, freed, snatched up weapons.

Delia called above the hubbub, commandingly, as befitted an empress.

"I desire no further bloodshed. But I think Cranchar the Cranchu should not be allowed to escape. He did plan to kill the emperor, and that cannot be allowed to pass."

Men—and Jikai Vuvushis—ran out after the Cranchu.

He was a poor figure, Delia considered, broken now that his sister was dead. But anyone at all who attempted ill against the emperor her husband must know he ran in peril of his life. Some of the Jikai Vuvushis came forward, and some made the greetings of the SoR, and some of other Orders, and they bent the knee to Delia, Empress of Vallia.

She had to put up with this. For one thing, it meant the girls were getting back to sanity and order could be restored. For another, it was a visible proof that the thralldom imposed by the witch was passing. Some of Nyleen's cronies might not be happy, might plot revenge; they would have to be handled with tact and firmness.

Nath the Muncible walked forward. He held Sissy around the waist.

"Majestrix," he said. "I crave your forgiveness—"

Sissy goggled up. "Alyss! Are you really the empress?"

"Hush, dear heart," said Nath, discomposed. Jilian laughed and Tandu and Dalki bristled up. Lathdo the Eager bustled forward, ready to perform his duties.

Delia quashed it all.

"Yes, Sissy, dear, I am the empress. And if you and Nath are as happy as the emperor and me—" Then she stopped. That was a poor promise for a couple. Of course, these two would not face the near-inconceivable horrors faced by the emperor and empress. "You must be happy, Sissy. Nath, I believe I do understand your problems. You have done ill, but that, too, will wash away with time. Just take care of Sissy."

"Quidang, majestrix!"

Then they came back with the report that Cranchar the Cranchu had jumped off the topmost turret of the tower rather than be brought back to the empress to face his just punishment.

Delia sighed.

"He wasn't much of a man."

In the refectory as elsewhere in the fortress the rapidity with which order was restored was a result not so much of the fact that Delia was an empress as from the force of her personality, the way she instantly decided and commanded, the air of complete confidence she radiated. No one could suspect her own inner doubts. The Sisters of the Rose gathered, still dazed, yet forming a formidable force to support not only their empress but the Flower of the SoR.

A quivering lump of male humanity hovered around at the back of Nath and Sissy. Stertorous breathing and the creak of harness—and a man mountain of flesh, sweating, shaking, totally shattered, protruded into view, and dodged back, and so shambled forward again. Delia did not laugh. What happened here could be taken as the signpost for future actions, and people who did not know the ways of her husband and herself might easily react with the cynicism born of harsh life under authority.

"Nath! Tell Magero to step forward."

Magero the Obstreperous shambled up and fell down plump on his nose in the full incline. His rear end pointed skyward. His nose rubbed in the spilled detritus upon the floor.

In the normal way, Delia much misliked this groveling. Now she pursed up her lips and let Magero grovel. She was in half a mind to leap on his back and give his rump a few cuts with the rapier, just to remind him.

Presently she said, "Jilian. Will you please lend me a golden talen. I promise to return it as soon as possible."

Without question Jilian withdrew a gold coin from her belt purse and handed it across. Her white face brooded on the scene, interested and yet sadly detached. Delia caught her breath. This scene was over. Now Jilian hungered to find Kov Colun...

"Magero. Stand up!"

"Majestrix!" he blurted, and fumbled and stumbled, and stood up, and so could say nothing.

"Here is your gold coin." She flipped it to him. "I shall do nothing. For in you I sense a poor strayed ponsho, who does not think but acts. This is your misfortune. I shall not kill you. But I think—remembering what you have done—it better for your health if you go far away. Probably out of Vallia. Go overseas and become a mercenary, and you may turn into a fine paktun, even a hyr-paktun. Perhaps, in a number of seasons, you might return to Vallia."

"Quidang, majestrix!" and: "Thank you, majestrix!" and a slobbering gulp of air. Magero the Obstreperous might, Delia considered, make some attempt to think—next time.

As for Naghondo the Squint, he lay in the side doorway with a hole in his head. Delia refused to say the obvious—that made two—and turned back to what needed to be done.

The plot against Vallia had been broken.

Vomanus would recover and resume his lordship of the province. There were friends to be rewarded. There was a lot to be done. Jilian... Ah, well... The Sweet-Tooth would go her own way, by Vox, and all Delia could do was commend her friend to the good graces of the Invisible Twins made manifest in Opaz.

Jilian heard the whole plot, and made a grimace. She had been not only a tool of sorcery; but an unwitting accessory to crimes she could not commit. That, of course, had been the undoing of the witch.

"So Nyleen had it all planned out. With an ordinary empress and emperor it would have worked, I think." Jilian slowly unstrapped her Claw to lay it aside in the balass box. "You have won for Vallia, Delia."

For Vallia? Delia smiled. For Vallia also, of course...

She watched where the remains of Nyleen were being carried out. "Think of the emperor. What he would have endured." She spoke very firmly, most decisively. "Oh, no. I couldn't possibly have let that dreadful woman marry my Dray."

FIRES OF SCORPIO

Fires of Scorpio

Fires of Scorpio chronicles the headlong adventures of Dray Prescot on the marvelous and mystical, beautiful and terrible world of Kregen, under the twin star Antares, four hundred light-years from Earth.

Dray Prescot's own words convey most strongly the sense of a powerful and dominating personality. He claims he is a "plain sailorman" and, certainly, he received his early education in the horrendous conditions of Nelson's Navy, but his character is complex.

He is described as a man above middle height, with brown hair and level brown eyes, brooding and dominating, with enormously broad shoulders and powerful physique. There is about him an abrasive honesty and an indomitable courage. He moves like a savage hunting cat, quiet and deadly, sudden.

The bright lands of Paz are threatened by the Shanks, reivers from over the curve of the world; yet most of the peoples of Paz continue on in their own feckless ways. As an adventurer who, among a list of titles, has collected the job of Emperor of Vallia, Prescot knows that he faces a dark future. At the moment he is on the island of Pandahem after a brush with adherents of Spikatur Hunting Sword and their witch leader in the many recesses of a mountain, about to go hurtling into a fresh series of adventures.

Facing a dark future? Yes... But we know from what he says that for Dray Prescot no future can ever be totally dark, that he will never give up hope, while life holds Delia, Delia of Delphond, Delia of the Blue Mountains, and he may clasp her in his arms under the mingled streaming lights of the Suns of Scorpio.

Alan Burt Akers

One

Seg learns what frightened me

Stumbling around at night in a jungle alive with ravenous monsters is not a pastime to be heartily recommended. Particularly when that jungle sprawls hungrily on the horrific if beautiful world of Kregen four hundred light-years from Earth.

The fetid stench of the place choked from rotting vegetation, putrid stink-flowers, decomposing—things—of indeterminate character. The darkness pressed down as black as the armpit of a demon from hell. All I wore was a scarlet breechclout and all I carried was a longsword. Those two items have seen me through many fraught adventures in the past. There is no doubt whatsoever in my mind they will see me through many more in the future.

Each step was a probing forward venture. Dagger-sharp spines, a mass of corruption, a razor-edged leaf or a killer vine all could lie waiting for the next unwary step.

An incautious movement might precipitate me into a spiny-ribcrusher, and the spines would close with a meaty chunk and the juices would melt me down to a puddle.

Ahead in the pervasive darkness a faint line of pinkish radiance fuzzed into view and a coughing roar growled menacingly at my back.

Instantly, I was down on one knee, crouched, glaring back. To anything following me I would be silhouetted against that faint wash of moonlight. The sword snouted.

Breathing lightly, unmoving, poised, I waited.

Waiting, patience, silence, these spell survival in the jungle.

The coughing grunt smashed out again to be followed by a piercing scream and a thrashing crunching pandemonium of noise among the trees. Whoever or whatever had hunted, stalked, leaped and fastened fangs on his victim had seized a tougher prey than he had envisaged. Bad cess to the both of you, I said to myself, and cautiously rose and shuffled along to the slot of light.

Keeping bent over to make myself as small as possible against the radiance, I moved on and I did not press too close to any vegetation.

A tentacular looping horror, a spiny vine insensate with blind hunger, slashed. There was just time to see the whiplash against the rosy moonlight. The longsword switched up.

The killer vine coiled and thrashed and half of it swished back among the trees and the other half wriggled underfoot like an overturned can of worms. I stepped over and went on.

Shadows moved across that slot of fuzzy pink and golden moonlight. I stopped stock still.

Without a sound, without a movement, I peered from the blackness of the jungle out into the moonlight of the tangled clearing.

A face showed clear in the radiance. Sharp, in focus, the face turned directly toward where I stood.

The skull-face, covered by a tightly stretched pebbly skin of gray and green granulated texture, was blunt of jaw with the roots of the teeth exposed, the nostrils sunken slits, and the eyes, overhung by bony projections, of a smoky sullen crimson. The radiance of the moon fell full on that face, illuminating the rotting teeth, the decomposed nose, the crimson demon's eyes. Out of nightmare, that face, out of the deepest levels of subconscious horror...

I stepped out into the clearing.

"Hai!" I said. "Now I am mighty pleased to see you!"

The rotting teeth parted in a gasp. A sword flashed.

Then: "Lahal. I thought you were dead."

"And I, you."

"You are alone?"

"Yes. I was told a falling block of stone parted you from the main company. Your people are nearby, Skort?"

Skort nodded that ghastly head which was merely the normal head and face of a Clawsang, one of the many magnificent races of Kregen who are not made in the image of *Homo sapiens*.

"Yes. I think we are thoroughly lost. It seems to me that block walled us off from the rest of you and when we followed obvious tunnels in the mountain we came out into the jungle through a cave exit. We are lucky to be alive."

His people clustered a little way off and they had a shielded fire flickering. The smell of roasting meat made my mouth water. Skort saw the way I licked my lips.

"Come and sit down. It is little use trying to move off until dawn. Eat and drink."

"Thank you."

They had cleared an area of unpleasant jungle inhabitants of the smaller and creepier kinds, and I sat down on a tuft of dry ground. They made me welcome, and soon I was chewing on a bone. It was pointless to inquire what the meat might be. Some of Skort's men were patiently cleaning their swords and spears. They were a hardened lot, tough and experienced, and by reason of their graveyard faces inured to the askance look, the repressed shudder. I asked Skort what he intended to do now.

He paused for a moment, and the moonlight caught in those crimson eyes. "First, tell me what befell you in that place of horrors."

"The party adventured farther after gold and treasure. Some were killed. There is a Witch of Loh in there." I stopped. Skort flinched back when I mentioned a Witch of Loh. That is a very proper reaction to any reference to those powerful wizards and witches. Mind you, they are not your Satany black-magic kind of witch, who is not really a witch at all. A witch is merely the recipient of the old religion, attempting to carry on in face of the newer religions, abhorring the blasphemies of those who take her name in vain. Skort motioned for me to go on, and I pushed the finer nuances of nomenclature away for the moment.

Here we were, trembling in a clearing in a horrendous jungle outside a cave-riddled mountain in which lurked untold treasures and untold horrors. Any normal man would be forgiven for wishing to be gone from this accursed spot as fast as possible.

I said, "I have to go back in there to find out what happened to my friends."

In the short time I had known him, during this expedition, Skort had said little. He appeared anxious to talk now. His crimson eyes widened.

"I, too, must return. But—not for friends."

Waiting, not wishing to probe, knowing if he wanted to tell me he would, I gnawed on my bone. The Star Lords who had brought me to this wonderful world of Kregen to help in rearranging the planet's destiny had lifted me out of the caverns and tunnels to show me a vision of Delia. She had gone through experiences that had made me shout and bellow like a callow child, made me tremble and shudder. All I wanted to do now was leave this accursed spot and return to Vallia where I would find my Delia, as she would find me. But, first—and I knew Delia would approve—I had to make sure Seg was alive and well. Seg Segutorio was a blade comrade. He and I—well, we'd been through the fire together, as the saying has it.

Skort addressed himself to some of his people, and they stopped making too much noise.

"You do not ask me why I wish to return."

"You have your reasons. I have told you mine."

His skull face turned fully toward me. He said, "Did you find the queen?"

"No. We found a cell block and a lady, the Lady Milsi—"

He nodded, quickly. "She is handmaid to the queen."

Slowly, I said, "She is well but saddened. There was another woman in an adjoining cell who was dead. The Lady Milsi was sorely disturbed."

Skort put a hand to his head.

"That then, is the end of my duty. I serve Queen Mab. She and the Lady Milsi were seldom parted. I sorrow for a great one of the world."

He was moved, that was clear. Also, this did serve to explain why he had joined the expedition to venture into the area where first the king and then the queen had disappeared.

I spoke a few words of condolence, and then said: "This means you will not be going back with me?"

"I think not."

Before I could make a fool of myself, or a faux pas, or say something else stupid—for Skort's decision was so eminently sensible it warranted no comment—a shrill shocked scream ripped across the clearing. In a boil of shrieking confusion men spilled away from the fire.

A thing reared above them, swarming from the jungle in tendrilled bunches of horror, smashing down on waddling clawed feet, sweeping with those tentacled clumps. A man was seized up and stuffed whole into the maw slung low and rimmed in writhing feelers which swayed all together and so closed on him.

A smell as though a compost heap had been opened up prematurely belched from the monster. It reeked. And it scooped up men and stuffed them into its insides.

Skort ripped out his sword. He flung himself forward. He had a rapport with his people, and would account for every one. I did not fling myself headlong after Skort.

Instead among the bedlam of yells and shrieks and the confusing criss-crossing of shadows as men ran and fell and the monster-thing swept its tendrilled bunches of horror upon them, I dived forward. I kept low. I skirted the damn thing with its gray rotten hide and its hairs and its swing-ing tentacles. My target was the fire. That had been abandoned at once as the thing burst in from the jungle.

A whiplash flicked at me and I went head over heels along the ground. My ear went into a plate of cold porridge and I skidded. That—proba-bly—saved me. The tentacle that slashed down to seize me completely misjudged my distance as I went sliding along on my ear. I hit the ground, let out a great "Ooof!" and then was up. The longsword flamed into my fist and a single slice cut the tentacle into a little wriggler upon the ground.

But there were far too many tentacles for one sword to amputate in time. The fire! The longsword snicked back into the scabbard, blood and ichor or not, and I seized up a flaming branch and flung it full at the ghastly monster-thing. Another followed, arching in a wheel of flame, spitting fire. I tried for the thing's eyes; but they were well-protected under hanging mats of coarse hair. Tentacles flicked my way; I burned the first one off.

After that, Skort's men saw what was needed, and we simply threw firebrands at the monster-thing until we drove it off. Either that, or we'd have burned it up. It was, said a man who knew about these things, an oiklt, and not a very big one at that. It made a strange mewling cry at the end, drawing off. It had lost tendrils, and much hair had been burned off, and it was discomfited. But the oiklt had eaten four of Skort's men, and this was cause for lamentation.

Despite that, we had seen the thing off relatively easily, and—truth to tell—I had experienced no feelings of imminent doom when we fought. Perhaps that was merely the after effect of our experiences within the mountain.

Carefulness for other peoples' feelings, as well as sheer common sense, made me draw away from the Clawsangs as they set about their tasks. They would observe all the necessary rituals for their lost people. This was all a part of life on Kregen, as of any world where men and women of sensitivity are to be found. Their religious observances, although obscure to me and entailing a quantity of wailing and of plastering mud upon themselves and of doing nasty things with twig-made quirts, still conveyed their own deep appreciation of the sanctity of human life and of their grief that life had been wantonly spilled.

I kept an old sailorman's eye open in case the monster's mate happened by, or the first oiklt decided to come back and risk a burning for some more dinner.

The night passed thus, and presently Skort came across and said that having remembranced the dead, he would post guards and I could therefore go to sleep—if I wished.

Odd, the way a boon is presented. Of course I was deathly weary. Of course I wished to sleep. But if I did so I might never wake up. If I did not, I would insult Skort. All a pretty little entanglement of motive and feeling, race and race.

Eventually I thanked Skort and sat myself down and closed my eyes and Skort put a hand neatly on my shoulder and I woke up and it was full daylight. I had slept.

In the mingled streaming radiance of the Suns of Scorpio slanting into the clearing and lighting up the world for us, the dark events of the night passed away as though mere dreamstuff. I stretched and sniffed and Skort made that hideous grimace, all rotting teeth and glaring eyes, that is a Clawsang smile.

"Yes, you smell correctly. Breakfast."

As we ate, I sensed some reservation on Skort's part. He clearly wished to say something, and nerved himself to utter the words, and then withdrew and said some inconsequential observation of our present situation.

So, guessing what he wished to say, I said: "I wish my duty was concluded, as is yours."

The green-slime around the exposed roots of the rotting teeth glimmered. Skort nodded. He was well-pleased.

"Yes. I must return to report the queen dead. It is a sad duty."

I swallowed the last of the food and took a last mouthful of tea. I stood up. All I owned was—one, a scarlet breechclout, and, two, a Krozair longsword.

Skort stood up. His people looked on. They were travel-stained with ripped and torn clothing; but at least they had escaped from the mountain intact. What my friends would be like—well, that I had to find out.

"Remberee," said Skort.

"Remberee," I said, and struck off along the trail leading from the clearing toward the mountain.

The face of the mountain, caught at this early morning sun angle, bewildered by its vastness and variety of carvings. Vines looped and trailed across the rock; but the very profuseness of decoration could not be concealed. The lake opened out to my left with the usual activity on the brown sandspit. One proceeds with caution under these circumstances. I did not leave the concealment of the trees at once, and with daylight and the twin suns I could see the damned vines that sought to loop my neck and throttle me. I could see the nasties and the creepy crawlies, and that, by Vox! is a great help.

My skills as a hunter and stalker are not inconsiderable. Well, to stay alive on Kregen in some of the more robust spots such skills are de rigueur. But I have known men and women who can move through any terrain like ghosts, unheard, unseen, unsuspected until they strike. I do not profess skills of that high order; but, crouched unmoving in the cover of leaves that did not seek to choke or chew me, I was at a considerable advantage. So in the long level streaks of suns light as Zim and Genodras, the great red and the smaller green suns of Kregen, rose over the treetops, I blinked my eyes with shock.

A figure appeared soundlessly beside the track. It was concealed from all observation except from where I crouched, I judged, and that due to a casual alleyway between the leaves. I most certainly had not arranged that slot of vision. The figure did not move, made no sound, and had made no sound in reaching its present vantage point.

Often my comrades joyed in stalking one another, seeking to leap out with a joyous shout of surprise. Seg Segutorio was our master and our mentor. Inch and Turko and Balass—Balass the Hawk!—and Korero were very good indeed, and Oby had learned much. When we could we played pranks, one on the other, and led a riotous life. But that very life had sent us off about business in the world, and our days of laughter in mutual comradeship were circumscribed by duties reserved to nobles and lords of the land.

So now I watched that alert figure beside the trail. The man carried a bow. The bow was a Lohvian longbow. It was held in a certain way. I own it, although the superhuman Star Lords had shown me a picture of Seg and the others escaping safely from that deadly maze within the mountain, I had barely dared to believe. Now I believed.

I pursed up my lips and fashioned a bird call. That bird would never be found in this jungle, here on the island of Pandahem, maybe; the call fluted across the space and the man beside the trail did not move, made no sign—but the return call whistled out, true and golden on the morning air.

Presently, after a long space of waiting, unmoving, silent, watchful, we judged that no one spied on us. We met in the shadows of an aromatic bush whose small blue and white flowers brought back the memories.

"What in a Herrelldrin Hell happened to you?"

"And you! I found a tunnel which led to the jungle—"

"As did we," said Seg. He stared at me accusingly. "You were going back in there—"

"It seems to me you were in front of me going back—"

"Well, my old dom, I thought you were still in there somewhere."

Seg's dark hair brustled up, it seemed aggressively, and his fey blue eyes looked wild. Tough, competent, kind-hearted, the best archer in all Kregen, as I devoutly believe, Seg Segutorio was not about to become maudlin over me. Rather, he'd take a deuced mocking line, and cut me down to size in no time.

"So you were going back into that ghastly place to look for me." I shook my head. "We're all maniacs, Seg, all of us, and I verily believe you are the biggest maniac of all."

"Well, Dray—it seemed like a good idea at—"

"Aye," I said, dryly. "I don't doubt it."

"The others are waiting farther along. I simply said I'd scout a little—"

"The Lady Milsi?"

"Fine. Still very quiet, of course, over the death of the queen. I think you saw how—"

"Yes." I knew that Seg and the Lady Milsi had, as they say on Kregen, been shafted by the same lightning bolt. I told him what Skort the Clawsang had told me. Seg looked thoughtful.

"There is a power vacuum now, in this kingdom."

"Well, Seg, I've told you. If you wish to become Emperor of Pandahem—now's your chance."

"Cretin!"

"Yes. I agree."

"Which hole did you discover? I saw only the one, and we came through that one. You could not have done."

I looked at Seg. We were blade comrades. Why should I not confide in him? I said: "There are things that I wish to tell you, Seg, and that you will not believe at first. When you get home to Vallia, ask Delia. She will confirm what I have to say."

At once he was almost serious, and made only a few mocking remarks about the chuckle-heads. I told him that I was never born on Kregen, that I came from a planet called Earth and, moreover, a world that possessed only one little yellow sun and only one silver moon and only apims, *Homo sapiens*, without any of the splendid array of diffs that make of Kregen so wondrous a world.

He shut his eyes and leaned back when I finished speaking.

"I believe you, my old dom. You've always been more than a trifle apt to go flying mysteriously off somewhere. Next time you disappear, I refuse to worry my head about you. If you prefer one little yellow sun and one silver moon—"

"No!"

"—and only looking at people with faces like our own, then the best of Eos-Bakchi to you!"

"The Star Lords constrain me, that is all."

"That is all!"

"No, Seg." I made up my mind. As so often happens when confidences begin, others spurt out like a flood. "When I was up in Falinur of which at the time you were lord—"

"Yes, I was the Kov of Falinur. I am glad I gave it up and let Turko take it on."

"When you returned to us from your adventures, I met a man called Lol Polisto."

"Oh, old Lol," said Seg. "I knew him—only a little. Something to do with wanting to be a farmer and having nothing to do with politics or fighting. I marked him as a good likely man."

I looked straight at Seg.

"He is now married to Thelda. They have a fine child. His Thelda is—"

Seg stared back. His expression stopped me.

Then he said, "You are hard on a man, Dray. When I had that great wound in my back, then, was it?"

"Aye."

"Funny thing. I sensed there was more to your concern for my back than I could fathom—"

"Look, Seg. If you'd gone rushing off up there—you'd have killed yourself—"

"I wonder now—and this shocks me—I wonder if I would have gone rushing off. I thought Thelda must be dead. She was cut off in Evir; I had searched for her there." He stopped speaking, and shook his head. Then, quickly, like a reptile striking: "She was happy with Lol Polisto?"

"Very. She thought you dead. She would never have married Lol if her first husband was alive. You know that."

"I loved Thelda, in a funny way. Then she was dead. And I stopped loving a corpse, a ghost, and merely cherished a memory. Now there is the Lady Milsi. And, as you know, she is the first..."

"I know." Then, to soften the stupid arrogance of presuming to know all of Seg's life, I added: "That you have told me of or that I have seen." And then, in case Seg began to feel something of what I'd expected him to feel in this, and therefore to give him a chance to slang me, I said: "Anyway, a lot of folk predicted that you and Jilian would—"

"Jilian? Jilian Sweet-Tooth?"

"That's right."

"She's a bonny lass, what with her Whip and her Claw. But—not for me." We sat more comfortably now under the leaves and we watched the trail both ways as we talked, and no one beyond three or four paces would have heard our voices. "And, I tell you, my old dom, I knocked out a fellow's teeth who linked your name with that of Jilian's—"

"One expects that kind of foul-minded slander from the meaner sorts of intellect. You've probably heard many filthy rumors of Delia—"

"So far," said my blade comrade Seg Segutorio in a flat and neutral voice. "So far I have only had to kill four people who mentioned Delia in that connection."

I was surprised. I stared at Seg.

"Killed four!"

"They were well rid of."

Massive emotional overtones are not for Seg and me. But I knew. I swallowed. Good old Seg!

But, all the same, four deaths for mere words...!

If that is Kregen, as it is, it is, then, perhaps...?

"If it was my wound," said Seg, in a ruminative way. "But, why didn't you tell me?"

"I guessed you'd say that."

"Well, why?" He wanted to know why I had not told him that his wife Thelda was not dead but was married to another man and, apart from her mourning for Seg, was very happy with her new child. "Why?"

"I could say I don't know why. That was true, once, after your wound had healed. But I'll tell you the truth."

"Yes?"

"I was frightened—"

"Frightened? You, Dray Prescot, *frightened*!"

"Too right, my old dom, too bloody right. I was frightened. Scared right through to the soles of my feet."

He shook his head in amazement, a small gesture that would not be observed should hostile eyes be watching.

Now Seg is a man of parts. No one with normal human emotions is going to remain unaffected under the impact of news such as had just hit Seg. He had suffered a shock. He had loved Thelda, and she had, he thought, died, and he had gotten over that, and now had found the Lady Milsi. Life was going to be exceedingly unpleasant for Seg in the next week or so, or for however long it took him to adjust. That his marriage to Thelda was now over admitted of no question. That Thelda was happy with Lol Polisto was important. That Seg might find happiness with Milsi was also important.

I knew Seg would also consider as vitally important the happiness of the Lady Milsi. She, he would say, must not suffer on account of Seg's past thrusting itself awkwardly into the present.

Eventually he heaved up a sigh and said, "When I tell the Lady Milsi, I believe she will understand. I've already spoken to her of Thelda, and she has told me that her husband is dead. Opaz rest his ib."

The mention of Opaz made him go on: "And this story of yours of a world with only one sun and one moon—that is blasphemy in the eyes of the religious. What of Opaz? What of the Invisible Twins made manifest in Opaz, in the glorious light of Zim and Genodras?" He squinted up. The red sun and the green sun shone refulgently, and the streaming opaz radiance poured down splendidly.

I said, "Gods are not suns."

"Agreed. But, all the same—"

"All the same, we'll have to get back to the main party before they start after us and raise devils better left sleeping."

Quickly, slurring details, I told him of the black sorcery within the mountain. "So we'd best be off. Nothing remains to detain us here."

"And when you vanish in a puff of smoke, you'll be gallivanting about somewhere else on Kregen?"

"Or Earth."

"Aye."

A lightness of spirits affected me now that I had told Seg. Two items of news had been dovetailed into a seeming one; and that economy pleased me in its use of emotional resources to the best advantage. Seg had killed to protect the honor of Delia, had filled a fellow's mouth with blood and broken teeth in defense of mine. Deplore the violence though I might, in hard times on a hard world, honor—that tawdry bauble—sometimes has to be upheld to the utmost.

I'd do the same for Seg. That went without saying.

We went along the backtrail like a couple of savage hunting beasts—no. No, as I have said before, we were not *like* a pair of savage hunting beasts. We were.

Yet the chill conviction remained that against the dark sorcery within the tunnels of that gargoyle of a mountain, all our warrior skills would not prevail. We'd escaped, and had achieved a kind of victory. Now we had to make good our escape.

Seg's reference to my disappearance in a puff of smoke was uncomfortably close to the truth. When the Star Lords sent their gigantic blue Scorpion to fetch me away from wherever I happened to be and plonked me down somewhere else it must in all seeming appear to any onlookers that I did vanish in a puff of blue smoke.

The problems we faced immediately were simple. We had to get out of this pestiferous jungle and back to civilization. Seg had to see the Lady Milsi safely home. I wanted to return to Vallia and Delia. The Star Lords had shown me that she was safe and handling her problems—handling them! She'd smashed the opposition that had enslaved her, and had taken command with all the imperial majesty and grace that makes her the supreme Empress of Vallia.

So that although Delia was safe and well, I hankered to get back to my island empire of Vallia and try to unify the place and make the place a real empire again, as it had been in the old days before the Times of Troubles.

"One sun, one moon," Seg said to himself, half disgustedly, half with the pleased confrontation with a new idea that sounded impossible.

"And no diffs."

"I can't see how a world can have only apims like us. It is against nature."

"Yet the apims of Earth might call the diffs of Kregen menagerie men—"

"Bone-skulled idiots! Ask your pal Unmok the Nets about that. He's in the beast-catching business."

"Probably," I said, cautiously. Unmok the Nets would for a surety be on a dozen different schemes at once, if I knew him. A small animal broke cover ahead of us, and darted away to vanish into the greenery to our right. A thin screen shielded the lake here, the carved wall of the mountain lay to our rear, and ahead stretched the way we must go to win free.

"You are a kov without a province to govern," I said. "There are provinces in Vallia. Will you take the Lady Milsi there—if she wishes to go?"

"If she wishes it—yes. I regard Vallia as my home."

"As do I..."

"But I shall have to fight for my province."

"Would you wish it another way?"

He heaved up another sigh and slapped his bow up and drew the arrow already nocked, and let fly. The rumbling bulk of the dinosaur that broke the screen of bushes and started for us took the shaft clear through one yellow eye.

Before the enraged beast's bellow crashed out again a second shaft followed the first. Seg loosed a third time. Blinded, stuck through the pulsing skin of his throat, staggered, the dinosaur—all scales and fangs and claws—screeched and turned tail and blundered back into the bushes. A tremendous sloshing splash sounded. After that a succession of sucking noises, and splashes, and a screech or two, indicated where the denizens of the lake were feasting.

"Quick," I said.

"No. The first shaft hit before I loosed the second."

"True. Slow, then."

"No. The third was in the air before the second struck."

"True." I cocked my head judiciously. "There was no wager on it, though. Had there been—"

"One, two, three," said Seg.

And I laughed.

More than one person had judged this little foible of ours—of gambling on the outcome of shots in battle—as degrading, decadent, altogether horrible. In truth, it was some of those things. But, also, it served a deeper and more fundamental purpose in the horror of battle. My daughter, Princess Majestrix of Vallia, the Princess Lela whom we called Jaezila out of love, had instantly perceived the inner truths we men so clumsily sought to express by this betting on shots.

We had gone adventuring across the face of Kregen, Jaezila and I. Now, as Seg and I walked along the path leading to the camp where the rest of the party waited for us, I reflected that I was like to do much more of this adventuring than of ruling as an emperor. And, I would have it this way. My son Drak, the Prince Majister, would run the Empire of Vallia, and run it well. We had superb advisers, men and women we could trust.

Echoing my thoughts, Seg said: "So we'll be off adventuring again, then?"

"We will, Seg, if the Star Lords do not demand some fresh service from me. There is no way, as yet, that I can stand against them, for they are superhuman. But I am working on some few ways of attempting to resist them. One day, I hope, I shall be able to take charge of my own destiny."

The smell of woodsmoke reached us. In daylight, away from the jungle, the air was freer, we could talk, and not feel the pressures of instant destruction all about us.

Seg laughed. "It seems to me you've run your destiny pretty much as you willed it. By the Veiled Froyvil, my old dom! Look what you've accomplished!"

"Titles, ranks, some property here and there. They mean little, all save one. I count as far more important the family and our blade comrades."

Pursuing his thoughts, Seg said: "And you've no idea where you will be sent by the Everoinye?" He used the word Everoinye, Kregish equivalent to the Star Lords.

"None whatsoever. If I disappear, do not think harshly of me. Just remember I do all in my power to rejoin my family and friends."

"There is a great deal still to be done in Vallia—"

"Yes. But the Star Lords pursue their interests over all of Paz, over all of this side of the world. To them, Vallia is no more important than this island of Pandahem, of the continent of Havilfar, or any of the others."

"They must be a right weird lot. And you've never seen them?"

"Not one. They are superhuman. But not, I judge, immortal."

"I wish," said Seg, "I wish they'd take me along with you—"

"So do I!"

"A scorpion, did you say?" Seg pointed. "Look!"

He strutted out from a rock beside the path, reddish brown, glitteringly black, his stinger held arrogantly aloft, waving from side to side—waving at me.

I felt the familiar constriction in my throat.

The scorpion of the Star Lords—would he herald the Scorpion, the phantom blue Scorpion so huge he encompassed the world?

He did.

Blueness caught me up in a chill embrace. Unseen winds howled. I was falling. End over end, stark naked, winded, I was seized up by the Everoinye, tossed end over end and dumped down blinded and gasping upon some other part of Kregen to sort out a problem for the inscrutable purposes of the Star Lords.

If... if they had not contemptuously tossed me back through four hundred light-years of space to the planet of my birth.

Two

Of the donning of a Silver Mask

The sea bellowed and roared less than a hundred paces off across a sandy beach, spuming in white foam fountains against jagged rocks that stuck out into the surf like the teeth of a Clawsang. Inland the jungle began where the beach ended, its greenery lush and profuse and deadly. Was I, then, still on the island of Pandahem?

The Star Lords make no great fuss over the people they select to do their dirty work for them. As usual, I was stark naked. The scarlet breechclout and the Krozair longsword were gone. No doubt Seg was even now stooping to pick them up, bewildered by my disappearance. Well, now he knew who had taken me up and why I was gone...

Farther along the beach a headland walled off what lay beyond and the jungle dripped over the beach. In the shadows lay an upturned ship.

She was an argenter, a broad comfortable trading vessel, and clearly she had been there some time. Her upper works were vanished away—I did not think they extended down into the sand—and her keel was well-covered with green growing things. A group of people clad in brown robes hurried toward the ship and vanished into the dark opening cut into her side.

Feeling exposed, I ran swiftly up the beach into the treeline. The vegetation here based on sand was sparse; I wondered which would win this eternal natural battle, the sand or the jungle.

A pathway opened out onto the beach a few paces along and a further group of people walked out from the trees into the radiance of the suns shine. They talked together quite naturally, their voices a mere rumble, so that I judged they had no fear either of hostile denizens of the jungle or of enemies lying in wait for them.

Now, being dumped down naked and unarmed to sort out a problem for the Star Lords has been my lot for a long time. I was not prepared to take it for granted. An order of precedence had to be established. First—just what was it that the Everoinye required of me this time? Second—I had to find a weapon. Oh, I am privy to the Disciplines and can throw people about in unarmed combat; but on Kregen a man without a weapon in his fist remains at a disadvantage. Only last would I worry about clothes.

Edging closer to the trail, I stopped as three people walked along, deep in conversation. Their words came muffled. But, clearly, striking out as a risslaca's tongue licks out, the words hit me.

"My Flem! It is not to be borne!"

And the quick answer uttered in temper: "You are right, By Glem! We will tell Pudor and have done."

"I am with you, in the name of the Silver Wonder!" said the third.

I felt sick.

Now I knew what I was up against. These people were worshippers of Lem the Silver Leem, an evil cult—evil as judged by ordinary people with ordinary morals and outlooks on human life—a cult dedicated to the overthrow of every other religion and the enslavement of all those who did not bow down to Lem the Silver Leem.

The three men wore brown robes, decked with silver.

They carried weapons.

In that upturned ship they had set up their secret temple. Their confidence was plain. No one was likely to interfere with them here. And, also, if they were acting as they always acted during their religious observances, they'd have a baby in there, a child, and they'd slit its throat and disembowel it and offer up its heart to the blasphemous silver image of the leem.

The task of stopping them from indulging in their other obscene practices and their orgies could wait. Right here and now I had to get that child away to safety. If this was not the task the Star Lords had set to my hands, then it was the task I set myself.

And, as usual, this would be a task of the most difficult and dangerous nature.

Once I had rescued the child and restored it to its mother—it, of course, because the baby could be male or female and of any race of diffs or apims—then I could set my face to the north and start off for home.

The three men stepped out onto the sand and began slurping their way toward the ship temple.

Belted to their waists they carried swords. A glance showed me these weapons were the Pandahem pallixter, a straight cut and thrust weapon very much like the familiar Havilfarese thraxter. More often than not these swords were called thraxters. It seemed to me that I would need a sword in the immediate future.

The chance of cutting these three down had gone. They were in sight of anyone watching from the ship. I turned quietly back to the jungle. Some more of these perverted worshippers of a vile creed would be along soon.

The next two worshippers came in sight along the trail not long after, and of the two one was a woman. Well, as women claim equality in most things and more than equality in the rest, that made no difference.

The man went to sleep most peaceably, and the woman followed him before she had time to cry out. I dragged them off the trail into the bush. They would slumber for some time but I judged it best to tie them up. The brown robes ripped easily enough—I used those from the woman—and I gagged them for good measure. Pulling on the robes and adjusting the fastenings and the silver tassels, I quelled a feeling of distaste. From a leather pouch I drew out the man's silver mask. This was a quality item, stamped and fashioned into the likeness of a leem's snarling face and covering forehead, eyes, nose and cheeks and sweeping down to cover the jaw bones. It was held by leather straps. I put it on. I fancy my eyes glared as madly from the eye slots as those of any leem.

The suns shine lay warm and mingled in radiance across the sands, mocking what went forward in that upturned ship. There would be guards, heavy men, sweaty in leather harness, and well-armed. They would have to be dealt with.

The woman carried a canvas bag of provisions—white bread, cold meats, cheeses, fruits, and the man a straw-wrapped flagon of a middling Stuvan. Their purses yielded golden deldys and silver dhems, and a mixture of other coins, so what with the Pandahem pallixters, I judged I must still be on the island of Pandahem.

From the position of the suns I was on the south coast of the island, and the jungle at my back confirmed that. Where I'd left Seg at that

Opaz-forsaken mountain was in the southeast corner of the island, so I was farther along to the west. So, very well. After this little lot I'd simply walk along toward the east. If I could find a riding animal, even better. I would not, I fancied, find an airboat very easily. They were still rare in Pandahem.

Sounds reached along from the trail. More worshippers were hurrying to their blasphemous rituals. I heard a heavy voice saying: "And after we've conulted him, we'll sew him in a sack and dump him in the sea."

"Agreed!" cried a second voice.

If they were talking about this fellow called Pudor the first group had been contuming, he was in for a bad time. Conulting someone is to deliver him a tremendous buffet about the heart, either physically or psychically. It is not a pleasant experience.

Conulting, though, was just the kind of experience that would suit these worshippers of Lem the Silver Leem.

Letting this next batch go past and keeping well down, I waited until they were well out across the sands. With a most careful check of the back-trail, I rose to my feet, stepped out onto the sand and started off for the upturned ship.

She had once been a fine craft, broad and bluff-bowed and high-pooped, able to breast the waves and send the white spume scudding. Now she was just an upturned keel. It seemed to me there was another sacrilege going forward here, that a once-fine ship should have sunk into so low and degrading a function.

The followers of Lem have themselves branded upon a sensitive portion of their anatomies. Down south in the city of Ruathytu, capital of the Empire of Hamal, I'd once been dragged out of a nasty situation by Nath Tolfeyr. At that time he was still a figure of mystery to me. He'd hauled me into a secret temple of Lem, and there I'd perforce gone through the disgusting rites to make me an initiate. The brand I'd suffered had long since worn away, owing to my immersion in the Sacred Pool of Baptism in the River Zelph. That was in far Aphrasöe, the Swinging City of the Savanti. If anyone asked to see my brand—and I much doubted anyone would—then the action would begin that much sooner.

The thought occurred to me, as it had done off and on, that perhaps Nath Tolfeyr was a Kregoinye like me, a person doomed to serve the purposes of the Star Lords. I did not think so. But he could be...

Anyway, all that mattered at the moment was that I was in possession of the ritual information that would allow me to pass muster as a follower of the Silver Wonder. The priests and the acolytes, the initiates and the hierophants, all had their grades and ranks. They had their secret signs and secret formulae. My knowledge was of a temple in Ruathytu down by the aqueduct by the Jikhorkdun of the Thoth. Well, what I knew would have to serve.

The silver mask proclaimed me as a Hyr-Jik, a fairly middling rank in the cult. I'd have to browbeat those below, cringe to those above, and stick anyone who argued.

The ship neared. A little breeze got up and blew grains of sand in silken patterns before me. The twin suns would soon be gone, down past the western horizon. Already the sea sheeted with crimson and jade. I fancied there came a touch of coolness upon the air. I breathed in deeply.

Once in a temple of Lem the Silver Leem a fellow would breathe the stink of incense and the raw choke of spilled blood. Thinking back to that unpleasant interlude with Nath Tolfeyr in the temple of Lem, I realized that in all probability the reason the Star Lords had chosen me to handle this situation was precisely because I'd gone through that initiation. The Star Lords, although they had done me a deal of harm in the past, had done so through sheer indifference. They were not actively malignant. They were not chuckleheads, either. They knew a good sound tool or weapon to be used in the heat of combat when they saw one. And, by Zair! they'd used me!

A movement beside the opening cut in the hull of the ship took my attention. Two guards in their harness of brown and silver stood there, spears slanted, on guard.

They passed me through without comment and I brushed aside hanging curtains of brown with silver tassels and so entered the antechamber. Racks and hooks were here provided for the impedimenta not required within. I stacked the canvas bag and the flagon. I drew the robe about me, and, a hand on the hilt of the sword, marched on.

The place was just the same as the temple in Ruathytu, and vastly different.

Constrained by the shape of the upturned ship, the temple had been cunningly laid out. The arching ribs of the vessel lent the space the appearance of a fane. Brown and silver hangings covered the old wooden hull. Torches flared from tall silver stands, four and five torches arranged around each stand in brilliant clumps. The incense was being burned in strength. I kept my mouth shut and tried not to breathe too deeply.

The people stood about in casual attitudes, talking quietly. Every now and then a star glitter would strike from the corner of a silver leem mask. The air of ease here struck me painfully. These debased characters waited for their diabolical rites to begin, and as they waited they chatted together, of this and that, and took a delight in the expectation of coming pleasures.

To one side of the altar stood the tall iron cage. It was not empty.

The sacrifice was a girl child, not above three or four years old. She wore a white dress, short to her knees, and flowers in her hair, which was left free and shining softly brown in the lights from the cressets at each side. That light shone on the black basalt slab.

I looked away. High over the altar reared the shape of the leem—silver, glittering, rampant, ferocious. The image, I judged, was formed of beaten silver over a wooden core. The sculpture was not of the first quality; but it captured the sheer ferocious impact of a leem. Leems have wedge-shaped heads equipped with fangs that can strike through solid oak. They have eight legs and two hearts and they are feral beasts who kill and joy in the killing.

A normal weasel-shaped leem is of the size of a full-grown large leopard; this image was over one and a half times life size. The torchlights glittered from its ruby eyes. I looked away.

The sacrifice was not crying. She was eating sweets of some kind, trifles of sugar and honey and candy in brilliant sticky whorls children love to buy from the local banje shop. Sticky goo ran down her chin.

I tapped the heel and then the toe of the sandal I wore, a simple enough artifact suitable for hot climates. The fellow, now tied up in the bushes, from whom I'd taken the sandals favored solid leather soles, with rope thongs. The sole made a sharp tap through the sand strewing the floor.

These people had used the deck of the ship, then, as their floor, interesting.

Priests with golden decorations superimposed upon the colors of Lem moved about, preparing the knives and flails. The congregation talked in hushed tones, at ease, the incense stank and the torches and cressets burned brightly. I kept the hood of the brown robe half across the silver mask.

A vivid, a scarlet, lightning bolt of memory hit me. I could see just such a scene as this, out in the open air with the priest about to plunge his knife into the body of the sacrifice. And then a flier swooping in with me whirling a Krozair longsword and Barty Vessler leaping out and severing the child's bonds. An elegant, refined, very proper young man, Barty Vessler, the Strom of Calimbrev, a man with high ideals of honor and duty. A fine young man now dead, struck down by the cowardly blow of a kleesh whose come-uppance had been too long delayed. Vengeance is for fools. But some redress for Barty's death was long overdue.

Moving slowly, head half-bent, I approached the iron cage. Chains lapped the stone slab. The light threw contorted shadows from the bars across the girl child within the cage. The sweet stickiness ran down from her mouth and shone.

She had to be freed. Also, to perform this duty properly, another act must be done. I eyed the priests.

One of them, bulky in his robes, wore more gold than anyone else. He would be what they called the Hyr-Prince Majister, or some such nonsensical title. I marked him. Keys swung at his waist, and he wore a sword.

An under priest approached.

"Not too close," he warned.

"I would have words with the Hyr-Prince Majister—"

"Who?"

"I said—" Then I stopped. I saw that I had blundered. That was not the title of the chief miscreant.

A cresset flared in its bronze cage hard by my left shoulder. Another stood a few paces to the right. Between them stood the cage. The basalt slab under the idol stood to the side of the cage, at the center of attention by the altar. I moved forward, striking like a leem.

I kicked the priest twixt wind and water. The left hand cresset went over backwards from a single sweep of my arm. Without pausing I slashed across to the right-hand cresset and knocked that flying. Live coals hissed out to scatter across the floor. The stink of smoke thickened.

I took the chief priest's neck in my left hand and I stuck a finger in his eye.

"Open the cage, rast! Move quickly and quietly, or you are dead."

He could not gobble his fright because his air was choked off in my fist. He scrabbled at the keys. He was useless. I dumped him down, raked off the bunch of keys and selected the largest. It did not fit the lock.

Now shocked shouts burst up in the confines of the ship's hull. People were running and screaming. I intended them no good. I did not look back. I sniffed. The smell of burning grew. There would just be time...

Three keys later the lock snicked open.

The girl child looked up, past me, staring in wonder past my shoulder. Brown drapes burned fiercely. The fire spread. If the floor was well alight by now, fine. The ship was old, her timbers tinder-dry. She should burn well. That would be a more fitting end for a proud ship than this blasphemy.

I scooped the girl up. She started to cry.

Flames broke up in my face as I swung back from the cage. The uproar was now prodigious. So far no guards had burst through the smoke to find out what was going on.

And, still, I had not drawn a sword...

"It is all right," I said to the girl. "I am taking you home."

She just cried.

Cradling her in the crook of my left arm I took hold of the chief priest by the ear and dragged him along.

I spoke to the girl again.

"What is your name?"

She did not answer; just cried. Perhaps she had been chosen with smiles and garlands of flowers and had been happy to be given sweets and taken off. Perhaps. That could be attended to. I gave the priest a kick up the rump as he wriggled and dragged him along past the wafts of black smoke.

Ahead hung a blue and brown curtain, in checks. The way lay forward. Through that curtain extended the bow section of the old ship. My plan—such as it was—was to make my way forward and escape through the hawsehole. I had not failed to note that the hawsehole still existed, just a few feet above the level of the beach.

Once, years and years ago upon this planet Earth, I had clawed my way through the hawsehole to stand, brave in gold lace, upon the quarter-deck, an officer in Nelson's navy. That effort had been immense. It differed merely in kind from the effort needed now to escape from this stinking den of iniquity.

Two guards blundered up through a narrow corridor lit only by a torch in a becket. They looked wild. Their leather brass-studded armor was spattered with grease.

It was necessary to let go of the chief priest to deal with the two guards, that and shield the child. The guards went over, yeowling, and I trod on them as I dived after the chief priest. He tried to duck and scuttle away, screaming.

"C'mere, you rast!"

The collar of his robe felt hot and greasy. I hauled him back. He squirmed like a trodden-on lizard, and howled, and held one hand to his injured eye. His noise did not muffle the ululations and hullabaloo going on beyond the blue and brown checked curtain. The two guards rolled away as I kicked them out of the path and went on, head down shielding the child, dragging the chief priest.

At the end of the corridor an open door against the roof reminded me the ship was upside down. A narrow slot had been sawed in the bulkhead to allow passage. I stepped through and dragged the priest after. The space out there, dark and suddenly chill, stank of old rast's nests. I forged ahead.

From some way to my rear a sudden burst of shouting indicated the congregation had recovered from their surprise.

Just how long it would take for the ship to catch well and truly afire, or for the Leem lovers to quench the flames, I had no way of telling. Certainly, the flat tang of smoke persisted, slick on the tongue among the stink of rasts.

Knowing your way around a ship comes naturally to anyone who has served some long time at sea; even upside down as the old vessel was, the ways remained familiar. Up ahead, in the sweep of the bows, lay the hawsehole I sought.

Through the darkness ahead a light glimmered. The light was sickly, sallow; but it shone as a welcome.

I hurried on.

Hurrying was a mistake and there was no welcome awaiting me when I debouched into the forward hold and saw what lay in wait for me.

The stench of leem filled the air.

The chief priest was shrieking in soul-destroying fear. I took a pace forward—and stopped.

There were two leems.

They snarled. In that sickly light their jaws opened widely, and the blackness of their gums showed their yellow fangs in glistening horror. They hissed and leaped.

Three

Of two leems and one torch

The girl child cried and dribbled. The priest shrieked and writhed. The stench of the leems belched foully in that confined space.

The leems leaped. In that instant I dropped the priest and switched the girl around behind me. I drew the thraxter. The sword cleared scabbard— and the leems hauled up in midair, choked on broad silver chains and collars about their necks.

They crashed to the floor and were up in an instant, howling, spitting, all a bristle of fang and claw.

I glared at them. Foul beasts! They'd come sniffing around the chunkrah herds to cut out a straying animal and chew her up for their dinner. The priest tried to run.

I twisted the sword about and let him see the point and he cowered back, shaking.

"They are death—death, you fool!"

"Aye! Your death for certain."

He slobbered.

The leems were chained one each side. The sweep of their claws at the ends of the chains practically met along the center-line. There was no way past them while they slashed at anything that approached them there, and while there was probably a wheel and ratchet mechanism for drawing the chains back taut, there was certainly no time now to find it and put it into operation.

There was no way back through the fires and the enraged worshippers, and there seemed no way ahead.

The chief priest fell to his knees, wailing. I lifted the child higher on my arm. The leems snarled and slavered, the foam frothing upon them. Their hides hung loose and matted, slimed in filth. The sickly light fluttered as the fires at our backs sucked air past and made the shrunken torch-light waver and fleer.

With the child to protect, the sword would not serve here. The blade snicked back into the scabbard. The torch was a greasy, poor affair, not one of the great torches of Kregen. But it would do its duty. It must.

The leems leaped against their chains, snarling, and fell back. I pushed the child more securely—yet again!—into the crook of my arm. I kicked the priest. And I thrust the torch ahead. The flame sizzled hair. The nearest leem yowled, desperate to get at me and tear out my throat and sink his fangs into me.

"Back, you misbegotten creature!" I yelled, incensed.

The torch thrust again, burning him about the muzzle. He shrank back. My own back was to his mate; now, with a single step forward, I dare not step back.

Shaking his head from side to side to avoid the flame, the leem tried to burst past that fiery barrier and get at me. The torch thrust and withdrew, flicking him with fire. His frenzy mounted, as did my own fury, so that we were just two enraged beasts, fronting each other.

Each step must be judged and taken carefully. The floor, which was in reality the underside of the old ship's deck, was rotten in places, treacherous with splinters. And there was the priest to kick ahead, like a cringing, mewling football. The leems' chains rattled. Their roars shook the timbers of the ship. The girl child continued to cry, turning her flushed and tear-streaked face into my shoulder against the brown robe. I held her gently—gently and yet with a grip of iron. After all this, I would not lose her.

A dozen paces, and the torch a mere sickly waft of flickering flame and greasy smoke, and we were through.

I hurled the torch at the leem, who yowled and cringed away and the brand struck the far bulkhead and scattered in a pyre of dying sparks.

Ahead shone a small ragged opening of light.

The danger of the leems passed, the priest appeared to regain some of his senses. He stood up when I kicked him and hauled him by the scruff of the neck.

"You are a dead man, unbeliever, defiler—"

"Shut that claptrap! And keep moving."

The roaring at our backs increased as we pressed on for those last few steps. The waft of smoke drew ahead gossamer-like, and the priest choked on a lungful, so that I laughed at his discomfiture. We must have presented a strange spectacle, half-demented with fear, stinking with leem-stench, half-burned, rushing through the decaying hulk of an upturned ship.

Up to this time the priest appeared to have forgotten he wore a sword belted to his waist. Or, if he had not forgotten, he had made no attempt to draw the weapon.

As I pushed up toward the jagged opening where the rim had long since fallen away and the planks had begun their last rotting decay into powder, the priest bethought himself of his sword. No doubt, at the same time, he bethought himself of his own congregation, that he was the chief priest, and of his own proper manhood.

For whatever reason it may have been, he chose that moment, as I bent to peer out of the opening, to draw and essay the task of chopping off my head.

The thraxter whispered its tiny chuckle of metal against metal as it hissed from the scabbard.

The priest was no fighting man. I simply moved—sideways and down and around, the child shielded away—moved so that the priest's blow, delivered with a panting, ferocious, desperate force, struck the timbers. The sword hit and stuck and he could not pull it free. He struggled with the thing, tugging on the hilt, and then he cast a look at me, such a look as would freeze the marrow in his own bones.

I said: "Tell me, why should I not slay you now?"

He blinked and swallowed, still tugging at the sword stuck fast in the timber. "You brought me here from the temple for some other reason than to kill me."

"So I did," I said, as though suddenly remembering. "So I did. Now get through the hole—*Bratch!*"

He jumped at that savage word of command, and hitched his robes up and swung a leg over the rotted opening. I gave him a push and he let out a yell and toppled away out of sight.

The last of the sun's radiance fell past the hole, deeply emerald and darkest ruby, twinned sky colors eternally orbiting each other, in love and in hate. Well, this night I'd have to skip and jump before I was free of the brown and silvers. I took a quick look back, past the waft of smoke and the leem's area. Their racket kept up. It would take time for the Leem Lovers to draw back the chains. Time to be moving before they rushed out onto the beach to cut us off.

A glint halfway up the bulkhead took my eye as I put my foot on the splintered coaming of the hole. I stopped and looked. The last of the suns, breaking for a moment free of cloudbanks low on the horizon and flooding the world with a rusty patina, pierced through the opening. The light fell on the three steel tines of a trident, still embedded in the wood.

The leems were screaming and snarling, which indicated they were being drawn back on their chains; the chief priest was probably running like a drunk over the sands to escape by now; the child was crying harder and was soaking wet; the debased followers of an evil cult were after my blood and no doubt some of them were already out on the beach... I stepped away from the hole, crossed to the bulkhead and reaching up wrenched out that narrow three-tined trident.

Then, and only then, I made for the hole and leaped through.

As I had expected, the chief priest was running for it. He was a dark flapping shape against the sunset glow. My foot kicked something hard in the sands. It was the silver mask discarded by the priest. I picked it up, musing. Shouts lifted past the entranceway to the hull. Time to go. The chief priest had escaped. That was his good fortune. I'd not risk the child's life chasing him—let alone my own.

We set off together, the girl child and I, up the beach toward the trees.

I carried the trident in my right hand, hefting it from time to time. Around the haft, just below the three long narrow and cruel tines, a ribbon of brown had been tied, a silken ribbon of brown with silver fringes.

Once we'd reached the shelter of the trees one problem would have been put behind us, and another and more colorful would face us. I'd not pitch our luck too high, and so did not venture too far into the trees. The jungle remained sparse at the sand's edge. There would be no point in going back to find the man and woman I'd left tied up. For one thing, their comrades, backtracking my movements, would have discovered them by now; and, two, they would have no idea, I judged, from which village the girl sacrifice came.

She sniffled and snuffled. I was loathe to keep her quiet with a hand over her mouth; but after I'd cleaned her up and she'd found a piece of sticky sweet goo in a pocket, she quietened. Cleaning her up did not present a difficult task, not in a forest where there were a myriad different leaves. As they say, in a forest of Kregen you can find a leaf to suit every purpose. They are not far wrong.

The suns at last sank and the sky changed from a sea of rust to an ocean of darkness shot with the stars of Kregen. Soon Kregen's first moon, the Maiden with the Many Smiles, would rise and then her fuzzy pink light would provide illumination enough.

When the second and third moons, the Twins, rose, the light would sparkle most pleasantly—if you were going for a stroll in some pleasure-section of a city, say. If you were trying to escape from enemies, you might not relish such prodigious quantities of light during the night time.

Making the most of the small time of darkness before the Maiden with the Many Smiles rose, I hurried along the beach, skirting the trees. The coolness had not come with the going of the suns; the air sweltered.

Now that the priest had escaped me—and I clutched the trident in my fist—I decided to head eastward. If the girl came from a village to the west, then I'd be unlucky. Wherever she came from, someone would know apart from the priest. Taking him along had been showing off to the gallery, really. And, in the end, he'd given me the slip.

The sand shushed under my feet, and the girl on my arm, lulled by the motion, at last fell asleep. Her tiredness overcame the excitements and fears. And I still did not know her name.

The old ship burned splendidly.

Little though there might be of a Viking funeral in those flames, the thought occurred. Orange light stained the sky. The stars glittered and dimmed—for a space. Dry, that old argenter, dry and tinder for consumption. She burned away and fell into ashes, and so the darkness took her.

I hurried on with my burden into the shadows.

Pausing every now and then to take a careful look around and particularly backwards, and seeing nothing of pursuit, we made good our escape—for I tended to regard the girl-child sacrifice as one of the party. Adventure has that effect. I did the looking around and she slept; but it was we who made our escape.

The beginning of this day had seen me encompassed by jungle, and the end saw me striding along the edge of a jungly forest, skirting the greenery, trudging along in the sand. By the light of the Maiden with the Many Smiles and later of the Twins, I kept going. Tiredness did not touch me. I'd be tired later on. Now I had to find the nearest village or town and see about the sleeping charge the Star Lords had placed into my care.

An eventful day had passed. Perhaps the excitements had come along in fine style, maybe they clustered thickly around each passing hour, but I didn't regard this as an unusual day for Kregen. Well, not too unusual... The truly unusual day on Kregen, that world of beauty and terror, is when nothing happens.

Four

Ashti of the Jungle

The folk who lived in their scattered villages along the brown rivers running through the jungle might not have advanced so far along the so-called road of civilization as many another peoples of Kregen; but they only tried to kill me once and then, when I'd explained, became very friendly.

Three villages along we ran into someone who knew my charge. The leaf-roofed, rush-walled houses were round like beehives in this village. The ground was packed hard by equally hard naked feet; to turn into a quagmire when the rains fell. The headman did not wear a bone through his nose; had he done so it would have suited his regal magnificence well.

A woman wearing a remarkable sarong-like garment of gemmed greeny-blue silk told us the child was probably from the next village. She seemed to recognize something about the cut of the child's jib that must be peculiar to one village out of them all. As for the remarkable garment, artificial though the gems might be and the silk not a true silk, nonetheless, it looked out of place.

I thanked them, and went on. News of my coming preceded me by this time, and, no doubt, a warning that I meant no one any harm. If they wanted to kill me and do a proper job, that would have been very easy. A few arrows, a few darts, a sudden shower of spears from the undergrowth—they could have done for me. But, with the child on my arm, clearly seeking her mother and bearing no one ill will, no one challenged me after that first time.

The girl's mother was not at all pleased to see me.

Her face expressed the utmost consternation. We spoke in the universal Kregish tongue which had been arbitrarily imposed on all of Paz, and she just did not want to know, about the girl, about me, about how I had found the child—whose name, now revealed, was Ashti.

I did not smile at the remembrance of another Ashti I'd known—known only as an enemy—now dead and buried and tried to be forgot. This Ashti yelled and reached for her mother, with her hands nice and clean and her dress white and clean and a shining clean face. The mother backed away as though skeletal plague hands reached for her.

"Ashti is your child," I said. We stood outside her hut with the blue shadows about our feet, the mingled rays of the twin suns falling across the earth of the compound where chickens, dogs, naked children, pigs, led a communal and interesting life of their own.

"No more. Take her away. Take her back."

This woman, whose name was Fischili, wore a remarkable garment, sarong-like, of orangey-green silk, and the gems, artificial though they undoubtedly were, gleamed and glistened splendidly.

So I thought—cautiously—I could see some of the answers.

"Woman! Fischili! Will you take your child Ashti back into your home?"

"Man! No!"

A fellow put his head out of the hut door, pushing aside the reed curtain. He did not wear a bone through his nose either, but he did sport a pair of wondrous gold earrings; maybe not gold, maybe brass, and maybe they'd turn green in his ears before long; but they, like the woman's dress, looked spontaneously splendid.

"Go away, man," he said. "You interrupt my sleep."

"You heard I was coming. Did not the drums tell you?"

"We did not know you brought back the dead to us."

"Ashti is not dead."

He jumped out and stood next to the woman. He shook a spear in my face. He was wrought up and excited. His skin of that superlative golden-red copper color glowed with sweat. I held Ashti and saw that her skin was much paler than her parents' but that, I did not doubt, would glow with that coppery-red tint as she grew older.

"Dead!" he shouted, waving his spear.

"Go away!" shrieked Fischili.

Now when I'd taken the spear away from Fischili's man and thrown it into the earth of the compound, and started to shout, a most wicked and selfish thought occurred to me.

If I did not persuade these two to take their child back, and why they refused was obvious, I'd stand precious little chance of persuading anyone else. The damned Leem Lovers had gone sniffing around and had bought the child. Bought a living human being with tawdry dresses and brass earrings. Well, slavery was a fact of life on parts of Kregen, and we'd do for it one day and banish slavery. But this was different. If the law did not proscribe this act, an act common enough on Earth, then I had no rights at all. The parents had sold the child; ergo, the child was dead.

And the selfish thought was this: What was I to do with a little girl child if I went hopping and skipping under the Moons of Kregen swinging a damned great longsword?

What, indeed...?

Common sense told me that I could easily knock sense into Fischili's man, if not into Fischili herself, and make them take Ashti back. Oh, yes, that would be easy.

But what would Ashti's life be like after that?

Far better for me to find her a good home where she was wanted.

And, of course, I realized where—if the Everoinye left me alone—I could find such a home. I hoped.

So, instead of doing anything else, I said: "I will go now."

I turned and walked off. Then, pausing and turning back and shouting so that not only Fischili and her man heard me, I yelled: "I shall care for Ashti. If you try to follow me I shall probably kill you."

Ashti had stopped crying some time back in our short journey. She did not cry when we left her mother and her—probable—father. I believe little affection had ever existed there. Ashti had been pleased to be back where she recognized faces and places; from now on I would have to see that the faces and places she saw were all friendly.

Continuing eastward seemed the best bet at the moment, for the jungle folk mentioned a town as being situated on the estuary of a river in that direction. I did not think it would be any town I knew—Mahendrasmot was well over to the west—but I stood a chance of picking up passage in a ship.

No one appeared to want to change the life-style of these folk who lived in the jungle. They were not primitives. Their style was simple, with quantities of home-made products and a living based on minimal cultivation and maximum hunting and gathering. Mahendrasmot was a steel town, as its name implies, and there was no lack of metal implements among these folk of the jungle, which suggested that iron and steel manufacture might also figure in the town I approached.

I should perhaps mention that very early on in this jaunt I'd ripped up the brown robes to make a breechclout for myself and a sacklike holdall to carry the two silver masks. With a sword at my waist, Ashti on my left arm and the trident in my right fist, I looked an odd character, I judge, from the expressions on the faces of those people I spoke to.

There had been some serious trouble with Ashti when I'd wanted to take her dress off to wash it. It was pretty sticky and grubby by that time. She wore nothing else. So, very firmly, and chattering away all the time to her, I got the dress off. We happened to be beside a stream at the time, which seemed the logical place to be if you wanted to wash a dress, and I washed dress and child at the same time. This was just before we reached her own village and was in honor of meeting her parents. Ha!

Anyway, by the time we reached the town of Hukalad we'd reached an agreement. Ashti could talk well enough; but it was going to take a little time to loosen her tongue into full confidence. I recognized that. Also, at this time I was not an altogether wonderful forager in a jungle. If you don't know what to look for you can starve in a jungle. If you do know, and find the things you seek, you can live like a lord—at least, like a lord of the jungle.

I must confess that by the time we approached the outskirts of Hukalad I was mightily looking forward to unending cups of superb Kregan tea, real steaks, real vegetables, palines and, quite probably, quite probably, a glass or two of wine...

The money I had without any compunction removed from the Leem Lovers, would keep us well enough until we could find a ship. Sailing would be far the quickest way of reaching Vallia—the only way—in the absence of airboats, or saddle-flyers.

Ashti said, "I'm thirsty."

"We'll soon find some parclear—"

"Want sazz. An' I'm hungry, too."

"So am I, isn't that funny," I said, and smartened up my pace. She wasn't above giving me a kick or two to keep me going. Parclear is a refreshing sherbet drink, and sazz is the same with the addition of fruit juices that make it colored. Either one serves its purpose.

We attracted only perfunctory interest. Most of the buildings were of wood, the road was unmetalled and would be a quagmire in the rains, and there were no proper walls as such around the town, merely a stockade. This was of a good size, and sturdily built; but I had seen what sea rovers could do against wooden stockades.

The biggest buildings looked to be temples and palaces—overgrown villas with three stories, really—and inns and taverns. I chose a modest-looking place that stood on the corner of an open space, and, going in, concluded for a meal for two, lots of sazz, lots of tea, some wine, and a room for the night. Gold changed hands.

Always there is the problem with gold in a strange town.

That night I wedged the door shut, stuffed pillows in the bed, made Ashti sleep on blankets by me—and that was a luxury compared to the jungle—and so sat half-awake all night. The precautions were unnecessary; I felt tired, but I'd recoup the lost sleep somehow.

"Ship out, dom?" The landlord, bleary-eyed and with a runny nose, sniffed. "No ships looked in here since the bar silted up."

I used some bad language.

"They've took all the trade, them down the coast," went on the landlord. "Hukalad is finished. I'm selling up myself, soon, and moving to Tuscursmot."

My ears went up like those of a leem scenting ponsho.

"Tuscursmot!" I said. "Is the town far off?"

"You'd do better to ride, rather than walk. I can sell you a fine freymul—or a hersany—I have a splendid pair of hirvels—"

"Stay, stay, landlord! No doubt you could lay your hands on a zorca if—"

He shook his head.

"Gold dust."

"Well, my feet have carried me this far, they will carry me the rest of the way."

As the rascal hadn't told me how far it was, and as Tuscursmot must be in a position to benefit from the unfortunate happening to Hukalad's sandbar, I judged the next town to be not very far off at all. I'd buy myself a saddle animal for a half a day's ride, if I listened to this sales talk.

In the end I found that Tuscursmot stood on the eastward arm of the river on whose western stood Hukalad. So, after an enormous breakfast of vosk rashers and loloo's eggs, quantities of tea, heaps of palines, bread done in the shan'feran fashion, with red honey, we set off. We walked, and in the early suns shine, tripping along, Ashti walked for a time, too. She danced on ahead, a sprite in a little white dress, and we talked and laughed as we made our way to Tuscursmot.

Five

Ashti plays in The Swod's Revenge

Tuscursmot turned out to be a charming town, strung out along the banks of the River Curstouran, as the waters were called here, and extending for some distance north and south. The houses were not all wood, many were of mudbrick and stucco-finished, with tiled roofs. As of nature, they were bowered in greenery; but there was a considerable agriculture around the town, and it was clear that these cultivations were prodigious in production and also, I judged, needed constant damned weeding.

The white houses thickened toward the town center into a regular crisscross of streets and avenues. Temples rose. There were hotels, with signs proclaiming the joys to be found within. Palaces dedicated to the Baths of the Nine indicated that Tuscursmot well understood the refinements of culture. The theatres might tell a different story, true...

All in all, Tuscursmot was of that species of town that is your comfortable, county, provincial, market, well-off town, and highly satisfied with itself. Somnolent, perhaps, sleepy, filled with scandals of the frilly petticoat and the embezzling kind.

All, that is, except for the stout brick walls encircling the central portions of the town, the watchtowers manned by bright-helmeted men bearing spears, and the way no houses or vegetation were permitted within a bowshot of the walls. Mind you—the bowshot was a short bowshot; the impression was gained that as bows improved the folk of Tuscursmot had not bothered to keep their killing zone in step with changing technology.

So, an interesting town. Industry was decently concealed away in a curve of the river out of sight of the town. No doubt there were shanty towns down there. If this was true of Earth, it was no less true of Kregen.

As far as I knew, the name of the street I wanted had been Lower Squish Street. This ran from the cleared space fronting the South Gate down alongside the river bank and so trailed away at last when no more houses were built beside the track. Bushes—even trees—loaded with squishes grew everywhere, and I thought of Inch, and sighed, and went along to a neat little tavern halfway along Lower Squish Street, under the trees.

Carts pulled by krahniks passed, loaded with produce. The air smelled sweet with that particular aroma that is of Pandahem South—much invigorated here, I might add, by the scents of squishes. This close to the equator they'd get ripe harvests on a regular basis. A gang of Rapas wearing striped aprons busily unloaded a cart of its barrels. Grapes could be produced readily enough, but ale—that might present a problem. The Kregans have ways of producing wine and ales in the most unlikely circumstances—which is a thirst-quenching miracle.

"Hai, doms," I said pleasantly. "Warm work."

The beaked faces turned to me, the feathers bristled, and then the biggest Rapa—the one with the yellow feathers beside his beak—contorted his face into the grimace that passes for a smile among Rapas.

"Aye, dom, warm work. You'll be quenching your thirst inside." He nodded toward the tavern into which he and his mates were unloading the barrels. The sign said, beside the swinging flagon, The Swod's Revenge.

I smiled. I liked that name.

"Aye. If the ale is good."

Ashti decided it was time she took a hand in all this chatter that wasted time. After all, she had walked quite a long way before I'd picked her up.

She jumped down and started for the tavern steps, her white dress like a flitting moth in the suns light. The Rapas smiled. Truly, Tuscursmot was a friendly place.

"Come on, Jak!" she admonished me over a shoulder. "I'm thirsty."

"You're never anything else."

The tavern, low-ceiled, seemed to me of that order of establishment that would boast a cheery mine host, a good wine list, an ample cellar, good honest plain fare that melted in the mouth, and, if you stayed, beds that enveloped you in soft slumber. Well, I was half right.

The landlord greeted me in a friendly fashion. He was a Khibil, and his fox-like face with the arrogant moustaches and that air of supercilious superiority that most Khibils have did not, in this context, set my teeth on edge.

All the same, in the tap room I recognized as being either a copy of or an attempt at a tap room of Hamal, I wouldn't come to the point at once.

He put the jar of ale on the counter. There were two Ochs giggling in a corner, a couple of Fristles playing dice by the window, and three apims at the other end of the bar. I sipped.

"By Beng Dikkane, I needed that," I said.

Ashti piped up.

"Sazz! Sazz! Sazz!"

The foxy landlord poured and placed the glass on the counter. I gave it to Ashti, who drank it off like a trooper. I wondered if I was getting her into bad habits. Well, she was nearly four years old. Kids are tough at that age, far tougher than I was likely to be.

The silver winked as it lay on the counter.

The two Ochs stopped giggling and, hand in hand, went out. The landlord picked up the silver dhem and bit it. Well, that was fair comment on the wicked ways of the world.

The two Fristles stopped playing dice, and went out.

The three apims pushed away from the bar. They looked nothing special, although two wore their hair colored and tortured into the fashionable towser cut—I say fashionable... that towser-cut had been fashionable in Ruathytu, capital of Hamal, some seasons ago. No doubt the style had just reached this outpost. The three of them wore tunics and trousers cut short and ragged to the knee, mostly of greens and browns. They carried knives and cudgels. Their faces—well, now, as I glanced at their faces I realized that not all the people of Tuscursmot were friendly to the wandering stranger in their midst.

The trouble was, I had Ashti to look after. And she'd as lief walk down and start to talk to these three bully boys.

So, I tried to handle the affair as though it wasn't happening. All these snaggly-toothed, leering-mouth three had done was stand up away from the bar. And the diffs, the Ochs and the Fristles had left. I put my back to them, with my ears flapping, I dare say, to listen for them, and looked hard at the landlord. He was a Khibil.

"Landlord," I said.

"I am called Palando the Berry."

"Palando the Berry. Can you direct me to the house of Scauro Pompino ti Tuscursmot? You know, Pompino the Iarvin."

The Khibil landlord said straight into my face: "Duck!"

He had no need to warn me. The sound of the footfalls on the floor, the way in which tunics rustled when arms are lifted, the sound of a wheeze on an indrawn breath, all these betraying things told me what the three tearaways were trying to do.

I not only ducked, I went sideways, turned around and looked at the situation.

The cudgel smashed onto the counter, the fellow with the towser cut in green and yellow quite unable to halt his blow. I kicked him twixt wind and water and before he fell down screeching I hit the other one with the orange and vermilion towser cut in the ear. That happened to be nearest. The third fellow swung his cudgel and I swayed away and knocked him down inside his blow. The three of them lay on the floor like three little fishes, stranded, gasping and wheezing. It was all not very clever, a trifle messy—the last one sprayed blood from his nose everywhere—and of no real credit to anyone. I should have spoken up first.

With that feeling strong on me, I said: "I crave your pardon, Palando the Berry. There is blood on your floor."

"Rogoglopher!" the landlord bellowed at the top of his voice. Moments later the chief Rapa looked in.

"Yes, master?"

"Heave these outside, Rogoglopher. They met more than they bargained for this time."

"My pleasure," said the Rapa, and bellowed for his mates to give him a hand. I sensed undercurrents of local conflicts and politics here. Maybe these were just locals, terrorizing their local tavern. Maybe they were more. I did not care; it was of no concern of mine.

"Pompino?" I said.

"Aye. You know him?"

"Yes." My voice sharpened. "Ashti. Stop playing with that blood. You'll get it all over your dress. And it's hard work to get blood out."

The landlord leaned forward and looked over the counter.

"Rogoglopher!" he bellowed.

The Rapa came back from dumping senseless bodies.

"Yes, master?"

"Get that floor scrubbed out."

"Yes, master."

The Khibil landlord brushed his whiskers. "I keep a clean house here, in the Swod's Revenge."

"Aye, Palando the Berry. Pompino—"

"Oh, aye, Pompino. He is away at the moment."

I compressed my lips.

"Just tell me where away lies his house. That is all I ask."

"It's no good going there. There are only his wife and twins—"

"Two sets of twins, I believe."

"That is right. I see you do know him, then."

"Look, Palando. If you are trying to protect Pompino—forget it. He is a friend. If you were to turn me away he would be most wroth, believe me."

Palando nodded. "I remember the way you put those three Durkin brothers out. Nasty customers. Oh, I believe you. But he is away—"

"Just tell me where his house is."

"But he is not there."

I looked at the counter. I looked at the low ceiling. I studied the rows of flagons and bottles and glasses. I saw the amphorae in their tripods in the area beyond the bar. Many were stacked against the wall all leaning like the drunks they might make. I looked back at the counter, where Palando the Berry swiped with a cloth.

I said, "I may have to start at the beginning and go to every house in Lower Squish Street. I should find the right house then. But it would be easier—do you not think, landlord, it would be easier?—if you told me which house."

"Would you care for a refill? Your glass is—"

I did not grasp the landlord. I did not touch him. Nor, for that matter, did I blow up. I said, "Ashti—leave that Rapa's bucket alone—"

Too late.

The Rapa, swabbing at the floor with his mop, let out a yell. The bucket spilled. Bloody water swilled across the clean floor. Ashti laughed delightedly.

I took a breath.

"Palando the Berry. Tell me. Where does Pompino live? I ask for the last time."

He said: "I will tell you before that little she-pinki destroys my tavern and my relationship with my servants."

Ashti laughed as a Rapa coming in the door slipped on the blood and skidded into a table and so brought that down on his head. Truth to tell, Ashti hadn't done anything yet. I would promise Palando Ashti's full resources of mischief if he didn't cooperate.

But, in the end, he said: "The fourth house along. You can't miss it, it has a red door."

"Oh? Why red?"

"I thought you said you knew Pompino?"

"Maybe his fondness for red is something new."

Ashti was red now, the hem of her dress, where she was banging the bloody froth. I bent down and hoicked up the squealing, kicking, struggling handful—the reason I hadn't pulled her out of it before. There would be a stern contest of wills in the immediate future between clean dresses and having further mucky fun.

"Well, he did have that front door repainted when he came back from one of his excursions, recently, I'll say that. It always used to be a decent blue."

Having at least wormed out the secrets of Pompino's whereabouts from his fellow Khibil, and having sorted out all I could in the way of Ashti's dress, and not being in the frame of mind to hang about in the Swod's Revenge any longer, I hoicked up the struggling handful and said the remberees and started off along Lower Squish Street.

Eventually I had to let her run ahead. And then I noticed that although she wanted to get down and run, freely, off, she didn't go over far. She ran and played within easy distance. She, as it were, kept her radius of action located on where I happened to be. I own I felt highly perked up at that, and, also, dismayed.

The fourth house along stood within what was obviously a pleasant evening stroll down to the Swod's Revenge. Pompino was not one to miss a trick like that. The house looked charming, white-walled, freshly painted, with two stories and with highly polished windows. The roofs were blue slate. That was probably imported, for Tuscursmot had a busy trade, and was a clear indication of conspicuous wealth. If the jungle folk could use honest leaves for roofs what was the need to import slate? Well, there are ways among men and women not explicable by logic.

The area before the house was set out as a gravel garden. The gimmick—no, that is the wrong word—the art in a gravel garden is not to let anything grow. It is all stone and gravel and chipped flints, split rocks to yield a fascinating spectrum of colors. The suns bring out the shine and the glitter of mica and the fleck of semi-precious stone. Cunning sculptors earn vast sums designing gravel gardens, and contractors earn vast sums laying them out. When it comes to the slave who goes around uprooting the weeds, vast sums are conspicuous by their absence.

So Pompino did all right for himself. By the word "ti" in his name, meaning "of" he was a man of importance.

I walked up the gravel path through the gravel garden, and an enormous one-eyed, one-tusked Chulik stood up from the porch and glowered one-eyed at me.

He was taller than me, yellow-skinned, his pigtail hanging down his back dyed blue. He had only one tusk thrusting up from the left corner of his mouth. I judged he'd taken a back-handed slash in some old fight. There was a scar above the gap in his jawline. His piglike eye regarded me solemnly. The missing eye was decently covered by a blue patch on a string around his ear. He wore a leather kax and pteruges, and looked uncomfortable in the warlike costume.

"Llahal, dom!" I called, getting in with the friendly greeting early. "I am a friend to Pompino the Iarvin."

He said: "Go away, master. You can do no good here."

I felt the astonishment. The Chulik spoke as though I had come forewarned of some disaster. All I wanted to do was pass the time of day with my fellow kregoinye, Pompino, chew the fat about old times in Jikaida City, and then take off. I also, I must admit, hoped I'd get him to help in the way of transport. So I said: "I just want to have a word with him. We have not seen each other for some time."

"Best leave now, master."

He carried a short spear and that was all in the way of weapons. Now I knew he'd be expert in the use of the spear, for Chuliks on their islands are trained up from birth to become mercenaries and to handle any kind of weapon. They usually adopt the weaponry of their employers. But this little spear which looked as though it would snap the moment the Chulik put his strength behind it?

Despite all the comicality of getting through locals and their clannish close-mouthed remoteness, I suddenly began to fancy there might be something amiss, after all.

"Are you servant to Pompino, Chulik?"

"You had best leave, master. Go—now!"

He was speaking in a hoarse penetrating voice, as though desperate not to be heard. And, he did not sound like your true overpowering Chulik would sound like, telling a mere apim to do something. He sounded like a slave. I judged that if Pompino was as important a man as, suddenly, I conceived him to be, he would have Chulik servants, and, also, that very much could be amiss with him and his family.

Thinking that perhaps my kregoinye comrade Pompino was in serious trouble, and prepared to go barging forward to sort it out, I became aware of an absence.

I looked about, sharply.

"Ashti! Ashti!"

But the girl was nowhere to be seen.

Six

Puzzles for the Brown and Silvers

No sign of Ashti in the gravel garden... The left side of the path was walled off by a profusion of flowering shrubs twice man-height... To the right the path led around the side of the house. That way, then...

The Chulik regarded me somberly. I started off, going along the path right-handed.

"Hold!" he called in a stronger voice. I looked back. He hefted the little spear as though about to cast.

"For a little girl, dom?" I said. "You would not try to stop me, surely?"

His one good eye rolled in its socket, making a hideous grimace. He rolled that eye toward the solid door. In the door and at about eye-level for a well-built man the slot of darkness suddenly winked silver. I paused.

The Chulik, in his small un-Chulik-like voice, said:" Aye!" Then: "You are a friend to Pantor Pompino?"

"Yes."

I have said many times that Chuliks are ferocious fighting men, and their women as well. I have also said that they know little of humanity. Well, I'd met a Chulik in a wrestling booth on the south coast of Panda-hem, in Mahendrasmot, who approached a good long way to humanity. And his tusks had been barbarously sawn off. Maybe this Chulik also had glimmerings of humanity?

I said: "Your name, dom?"

"Men call me Chenunga the Ob-eyed—"

"Well, Chenunga the Ob-eyed, I must find the little girl. If you wish to try to stop me you must make up your mind to it." I waited, glaring at him. I would not wait long.

He must have seen that in me. The spear lowered.

"I will cast." His voice barely reached me. "You must run fast..."

Without another word, without a signal of movement, I took to my heels and belted around the corner of the house. I did look back as I passed the corner of the stuccoed brickwork. The little spear flew past. I smiled. So something was amiss...

At the side of the house a small arbor of climbing flowers, hung and limp in the heat, cast a welcome blue shade. A small green door showed, half-open. If Ashti had ventured in there I could well be at a serious disadvantage. If I knew the little minx, and I was coming to know her ways better each day, she was after sazz and biscuits, palines, anything sweet and sticky. I ignored the little green door and went on looking for an alternative way in.

A trap door in the gravel was flung back on its supports and two amphorae lay there, propped against a wooden tripod. Wine stained across the gravel from a third amphora smashed and leaking. I realized that if Ashti had seen that she, with her nose newly accustomed to the scents of a taproom, might well decide that down there lay the drink she loved. Sherbet drinks, sticky sweets, they would lure her on. She might be a child of the jungle, and trained already to take care of herself there, as a modern day child of Earth is trained to take care crossing the busy road and dodging traffic, but she would be lured on.

The head of a ladder thrust through the trap. I looked down, quickly, scanning what lay below and immediately withdrawing. Barrels, boxes, amphorae lay neatly stacked against the wall I could see. Also, there was an open door...

With a single bound I went up in the air, caught the ladder, slid down it as a sailor slides down a companionway. I was running the instant my feet hit the stones. The shadows engulfed me. I crouched beside the open door, unmoving, scarcely breathing, and I cocked an eye aloft to see if the Chulik had retrieved his spear and followed me. The trap gaped bright and empty against the sky.

The only other person in the cellar was a dead woman who lay against the far wall, half in shadows. She wore a decent blue dress and her face upturned in a hideous grimace. She was a Fristle, and her cat-face looked ghastly. Both her hands were clasped about the broken haft of a spear deeply embedded in her chest.

I looked away, through the open doorway. The corridor was just a corridor, with doors to either side and a staircase at the end. These were the cellars to Pompino's house. Up aloft, then, I judged the mischief—and, also, Ashti.

I unslung the narrow trident from my back and held it over my right shoulder, tines forward, my fist gripping comfortably at the point of balance, ready to thrust or throw. If I had to switch grips into a two-handed hold for some foining, that could be done in an instant.

Padding silently along, wary of each door, I reached the staircase and looked up.

The door at the top, over a small landing, did not look particularly inviting. Down in the cellar the coolness struck in gratefully, and the shadows up there concealed enough to make me wonder if the door was locked or not. Up I went, rapidly, silently, wondering if I was making a fool of myself. But one does not ordinarily find dead Fristle women in cellars unless there is something seriously amiss...

I kicked the door open and leaped through the opening, ducking away and to the side and colliding with a fellow about to open the door. He looked more surprised than I was. He carried a big sword—I say big, the thing was like a falchion, curved and single-edged, and he instantly slashed at my head.

The trident caught the sword. I twisted. If I made a mistake I could only take comfort in the thought that he might mistake me for one of the desperadoes causing the mischief. I put my left fist into his mouth and nose and knocked him over. He was an apim and went flying back.

Farther along the passage, which was paneled in light woods and with rush matting upon the wooden floor, two men appeared from the corner. They were armed and armored. They carried tridents not unlike the one I wielded. They wore brown tunics trimmed in silver.

They rushed on and then halted, staring in perplexity at my trident. The brown breechclout might not show much silver; enough did show to slow them down.

Now, therefore, I was certain.

"Hai!" shouted the first fellow. He wore a large black beard, and I say wore for it looked false to me. "Hai! In the name of Lem the Silver—"

He did not finish, for my trident took him in the throat. He pitched back, spraying blood. His companion shrieked and rushed, slaying-fury in his eyes. My sword snicked out, I slipped his first thrust and then the thraxter slid between his ribs. He sank down, gasping.

The stink of spilled blood gusted up.

I do not slay wantonly. The man at my back, his face a bloody mask, tried to stab me. I slashed back, and he fell.

The noise must have attracted attention by now.

Nothing else for it... A straight bash on, sword whirring, a hefty charge into whatever lay around that far corner...

What lay around that corner and through the doorway was a tableau. There were four of them, an apim, a Brokelsh, a Rapa and another fellow whose race I did not then know. They brandished weapons and wore leather jerkins studded in brass. Their faces were mean. The Rapa's feathers bristled around his beak. The thick body hair of the Brokelsh gave him that particular spiky bristly Brokelsh look.

The apim said: "Stand still!"

I stood still.

In a chair sat a Khibil woman of exceptional grace. She was quite clearly in a long-gone state of fright. But she held her head erect, her foxy features composed, and her hands were folded in her lap. There was a bruise beside her cheek, near her mouth, and her white dress was torn from one shoulder. She looked at me without expression.

I saw her—and then I saw past her and past the legs of the four hulking ruffians. Another white dress showed there, and two twinkling feet, and Ashti ran out, through their legs, yelling.

"Jak! Jak!"

I said, "You are the lady Scaura Pompina?"

She nodded. I do not think she could find the spit to moisten her mouth to speak.

The big apim with the whiskers and the scar down his left cheek snarled at me again as I went to move forward.

"Stay there, unless you want to see this woman dead."

"I do not know who you are," I said, and I kept my voice down, kept it even, kept it un-Dray Prescot-like. "I have no quarrel with you." This was not true. "Just let the lady go and walk away, and we may consider this thing finished."

They laughed. Well, they would, of course.

The Rapa reached out and caught Ashti by the dress and reeled her in as a fisherman reels in a catch. He held her most familiarly, and she writhed and kicked and yelled.

I held very still.

Ashti had come to mean a great deal to me in our stroll along the shore of Pandahem in the past days.

There had been a man at the front door with a crossbow bolt aimed at the Chulik. That seemed clear. The Chulik must be servant to Pompino. He had tried to warn me off, knowing that his mistress might be murdered at any moment if he did anything foolish.

I said, "The children? The two sets of twins?"

The bearded apim guffawed.

"Tied up in bed. Now, dom, before we kill you, tell us where this rast Pompino is."

I nodded at them. "You carry tridents and wear the brown and silver." I put a snap into my voice. "By the Silver Wonder! Are you then all fools?"

They gaped, not grasping what was going on. If I leaped now—but Ashti squirmed and kicked and yelled, and the Rapa clouted her on the bottom. At this she let out an almighty yell and almost struggled free.

He took a fresh grip on her, and turned her so that her head lay inside the crook of his arm.

"What do you know of—?" said the apim.

"Lem must be witless to employ loons like you," I said, and the snap in my voice lashed at them. "If you have harmed the children or the lady—or if you harm that child—you are all dead men."

The Brokelsh looked past me. I did not turn. I'd left three dead men there, and heard no one else.

"Where are Halki, and Nath?" he said.

Things were just beginning to get out of hand. If I did not leap soon I would be too late. Yet a single slash and Pompino's lady would be dead, and Ashti too. I looked at these four, and I held the thraxter at what must appear a negligent angle. I said, "Which question do you wish me to answer first?"

This puzzled them. While it was clear they were not over-bright, they were deadly dangerous. I moved forward a few paces, and I managed to summon a grimace that might pass for a smile. "Pompino, or Halki and Nath?"

The apim said, suddenly, high, screeching: "He is not one of us! Slay him!"

So they tried.

There were four of them. An apim, a Brokelsh, a Rapa, and the other fellow.

The big apim, all whiskers and scar, remained with the lady Scaura Pompina. The Rapa held Ashti. That left the Brokelsh and the other fellow to shriek and leap at me.

If I give the impression these lay brothers of Lem the Silver Leem were not over-bright, I do them no injustice.

Hard, they were, brutal and rapacious. Serving their masters who were the initiates of the cult of the Silver Leem, they aspired to no more than to bash a few skulls, skewer through between a few ribs, take a few purses of gold, get drunk a few times. They bristled and snarled and hurled themselves at me.

Just the two of them—the Brokelsh and the other fellow.

Descriptions of fights are not boring if you consider the circumstances. In this case, if I dealt with these two in too rapid and summary a fashion, the big apim might just slit the lady Scaura's throat before joining the fight. And the Rapa would have no compunction over Ashti, none whatsoever...

The whole affair had to be balanced on a pivot of exceeding smallness.

So, of course, being more than a trifle warm, I hit the other fellow on the nose. I hit him hard. His nose opened up like one of those gorgeous scarlet and orange and blue flowers of Balintol. He tried to blubber through his mouth, which was of a large, squarish, full character, highly purple in color—even before I hit him. His eyes were most prominent and affixed somewhat high on his face, so that his cranium partook of a very shallow dish. I left that alone. I didn't want to risk my knuckles on bone of that evident sharpness. The frills stuck up around the top of his head like the defenses of a dinosaur, or the frilled fins of a fish. As he carried on blubbering, I ducked away from the Brokelsh's blow.

The thraxter in my right hand clicked across. I had, of course, struck the other fellow with a left. The Brokelsh looked for me where he expected to see me, and I wasn't there. Well, of course I wasn't. Who wanted to hang about when swords whickered—as they say—for your guts? I gave the surprised Brokelsh a cheerful kick up his bristly Brokelsh rear and launched myself for the apim and the Rapa.

Seven

The four terminations of the Lady Scaura Pompina

From somewhere the sweet smell of squishes wafted into the room. The taste twined in the warm air. For a single and scarlet moment, I recalled Mefto the Kazzur, who had featured in my life at the same time as Pompino. Mefto the Kazzur, who had bested me in sword fighting.

The headlong leap left me no time to brood on past misfortunes and mishaps. The apim's hairy face screwed up. He dragged back on the lady Scaura Pompina's head and his blade glittered.

The Rapa bristled. Ashti squirmed. I caught a glimpse of her face, golden, shining, furious, and then it seemed her face disappeared behind two rows of teeth. She opened her mouth and bit. The Rapa screamed.

"Good for you, Ashti," I said and went full tilt into the apim.

My sword flicked away his blade. The hilt lifted and descended and thunked, and the man toppled and sprawled, his eyes crossed, his mouth glugging open.

Without pausing to see if the lady fell off her chair or not I whirled. Ashti was doing all right; but the feathered Rapa with his vulturine beakhead would soon master her. So I tapped him on the back of the head and snatched Ashti from him as he pitched onto his beak.

"Jak!" she said, chattering. "He hit me!"

'And you bit him."

"Serve him good—nasty man."

The Brokelsh, all hair and uncouth roaring noises, recovered from the kick up the backside, charged at me. He was brave if not over-bright. When he, too, lay slumbering with his three comrades, I took stock of the situation.

There was the fellow with the crossbow at the front door who, it seemed to me, must come running in to investigate the cause of the uproar. Cautiously, I poked my head around the other door and looked along the corridor. The light glimmered from side windows, fell across the floor and across the humped shape beneath the far door. That had to be the front door. The shape did not move—but the door jerked against it, opened and pushed, and then closed, only to open and push against the shape once more.

Very carefully—just in case there were more of these bandits—I walked along the corridor. The shape on the floor was the dead body of a Stroxal, with a spear through his face. I recognized the spear. I pulled the body away and called out.

"Hai! Chulik! You got him. It is all safe now."

You will observe I called Chenunga the Ob-eyed merely Chulik, and not by his name. Even then, after so many seasons on Kregen, I remained still bristly around Chuliks. As for Katakis, with the exception of Rukker— and he was a marginal case—I'd so far never met a halfway-decent Kataki. Which was a tragedy, for all of Kregen. And Chuliks—the door opened and he came in, looking suspiciously around. He saw the body and he saw me.

"Yes," I said. "The others are unconscious."

"The mistress—?"

"She is safe."

"The children?"

"Bound in their beds, so I am told. I have not seen them."

"I will attend them at once."

All the deference dropped away as he asked his questions. Something of the old coldly ferocious Chulik manner broke through, an echo of the time before he lost his eye and his tusk.

The quick light patter of feet along the corridor brought the Chulik around. His hand reached for the spear.

"All right, Ashti," I said. "The Chulik is on our side. Don't bite him."

She turned her head. She looked sorry not to get the opportunity to fasten her teeth into the Chulik.

"They will wake up in there—" she said.

"Then we must tie them up."

Chenunga the Ob-eyed went off to find the two sets of twins and Ashti and I went back into the room where we'd had the fight. We stopped on the threshold. The stink of spilled blood gusted up, raw and vile.

Ashti looked quite calmly on the scene.

The lady Scaura Pompina was just about to rise from her knees. The front of her dress was a mere red shining mass. There had been four of them, an apim, a Brokelsh, a Rapa and the other fellow.

Scaura Pompina had slit all four throats.

Ashti wandered across and picked up a discarded trident. She started to poke at the Rapa's dead body.

"All right, Ashti. He's on his way to the Ice Floes of Sicce now. He can't feel you sticking him."

"But I can feel me sticking him."

Against logic of that kind it is difficult to argue.

The woman laughed suddenly, throwing her head back, letting her hair swirl, laughing.

"The child is right! Look at the four bullies now! Dead! May Horato the Potent thus destroy all scum like that!"

"What were they after, my lady?"

"After?" She drew herself together and took a look at me as though seeing me for the first time.

I had to be patient. Faint sounds of yells drifted in, so that meant the Chulik was releasing the twins.

"They were after Pompino," I said. "I came here to see him, also. But what could they want with him?"

"Lem," she said. By the way she spoke I saw she was not an adherent. "The Silver Obscenity."

The ways of the folk along the southern shore of Pandahem varied enormously. The jungle people lived quite unaffectedly cheek by jowl with constant danger and death, the jungle their home also their mausoleum. Death was merely another stage to them. Ashti, already, held a contempt for other death that just might, I considered, just might extend to her own.

The people who lived in the towns and cities had, it seemed, settled there. They were not indigenous. The jungle folk tolerated them up to a point. A clash of cultures had not happened, which was not to say that, this being Kregen, it would not do so.

So I could harbor a vile suspicion of my comrade Pompino. Maybe he had become an adherent of Lem the Silver Leem?

It was possible. He was a kregoinye, like me, a man picked out by the Star Lords to go about the world for them and pick their hot chestnuts out of the fire. Unlike me, he believed the Everoinye to be some kind of god, and he was bursting with pride that he had been chosen. All Khibils share that feeling of conscious superiority, of course. But for Pompino, pride upheld a shrewd understanding of his own worth. He might have been dazzled by promises. Maybe the adherents of Lem had caught Pompino at a bad time. If he did not get away about business for the Star Lords from time to time he brooded and fretted. He had told me this himself. If he felt slighted, and the Leem Lovers happened by... Oh, yes, it was eminently possible.

Then the two sets of twins burst in, all a-yelling and a-screaming. They threw themselves on their mother. If they noticed the blood and the dead bodies, they were not as important as making sure their mother was unharmed.

I grabbed Ashti and went off, out of the room.

There remained a considerable quantity of clearing up to be done, and I had no desire to become involved in that. Ashti kicked—once—and then said: "I'm thirsty."

"Good," I said. "We will find some sazz for you."

Chenunga the Chulik came out and started up the corridor. He was going to retrieve the little spear and begin the disposal of the dead. He saw Ashti and me.

"Master?"

"We're off to Swod's Revenge for a wet."

"But—the lady Pompina will require you to dine here."

"Undoubtedly. But I dislike the smell of blood with meals."

His Chulik face grew more yellow. "Everything will be cleaned."

"Then we will return later. Tell me, Chulik, where is your master?"

He spoke up openly.

"From time to time he is called away on business. He is on a trip now. I do not know when he will be back."

"And why did these Leem Loving scum wish to see him?"

"I know that—"

"Then, Chenunga the Ob-eyed, tell me."

His pigtail wiggled as he spoke. His one piglike eye regarded me with what appeared to be a baleful stare.

"They wished the master to join them. He refused. On the last occasion he slew three of them. This was their way of revenging themselves at the same time as they forced their wishes on him."

"It seems to me they do not know Pompino very well."

"No, master."

"Well, you did your duty as you saw it. And you caught that Stroxal in the end, thank Pandrite. So we will be off. Remberee."

We went out, and I was conscious of the construction that could be put upon my actions by those with limited vision. And to say I wanted Ashti out of that house of death, while true, was also laughable as a reason. A jungle child, she'd seen far worse already in her four years.

At the well in a secondary yard, walled in at the rear, we washed off. Ashti's white dress was, once again, in need of laundering. Also a large rip was spreading along the hem. And, it seemed to me, the cloth was decidedly thin under the arms. Ashti, of course, being perfectly used to running about without the encumbrance of clothes, was resolutely determined not to be parted from her white dress.

Eventually, looking as spruce as we could, we set off along Lower Squish Street for the Swod's Revenge.

The thraxter, cleaned up, snugged in the scabbard. And I'd taken a couple of tridents. If they represented ill luck or a talisman of good fortune, I did not know. But they would act as a catalyst, that seemed certain sure...

The dusty road had no appreciable affect on Ashti's bare feet. And I'd been going barefoot when I was her age—aye, and much later, when I was a powder monkey in Nelson's fleet and, later still, in my adventures on Kregen. The vegetation bordering the road gleamed a brilliant dark green. Each leaf appeared freshly polished. Humming from the greenery and the quick flitting darting of insects told of the myriad life forms all fighting and struggling for existence. How life mocks us all! We fight and struggle and think ourselves grand and proud and mighty because we achieve a few shining goals, and, in the scheme of things, each one of us is just the same as any one of those gauzy-winged shining insects, flitting among the leaves.

And so, with these maudlin—if arguably true and demonstrably banal—thoughts echoing in my old vosk-skull of a head, I trudged on along the dusty road and a high and a fierce voice roared: "Duck!"

So, grabbing Ashti, I dropped and rolled full length. Ashti let out a startled yell.

The flung billy hissed through the air where my head had been a heartbeat ago.

She was quick on the uptake.

"Durkin!"

"Aye." One of the Durkin brothers—the one without the towser cut—dodged back into the leaves.

"Who shouted?" demanded Ashti. She wriggled around and half-sat up. "Hai!" she called. "Durkin cramph!"

"Ashti!"

The fierce, dominating voice that had told me to duck, roared again: "Still in trouble, then, Jak! I don't know how you've survived without me to look after you."

So I stood up. Ashti clung to my fingers. A man flew up out of the bushes and landed on his head. He landed, to be accurate, on his towser cut. His brother followed. Then a Khibil broke through the screen of leaves dragging the man who had flung the billy at me. He was being drawn along by an ear. He was not very happy about the situation. The Khibil landed a soggy kick and the third Durkin brother reeled away.

"Clear off!" ordered the Khibil, not even bothering to gesture. "Schtump! Before I lose my temper."

The three tearaways picked themselves up, groaning, and slouched off along the road. It had not, all things considered, been their day.

"I don't know," said Pompino. He looked full at me.

I looked back. It had been some time.

He was grandly—no, no, sumptuously dressed. He wore silken robes of a brilliant blue, emerald sharp, sapphire soft. A quantity of gold chains hung about him and bullion and lace decorated the cunning curves and folds of the garment. He carried a thraxter and a dagger in jeweled scabbards. His hat was a broad floppy feather-fluttering creation. He looked, in short, splendid.

I said, "You look splendid, Pompino. Been to a fancy dress party?"

"And you, apim, look as though you've just been in a fight and not come off well."

Very calmly, and quickly, I said, "Ashti. Do not bite the Khibil—no! Do not kick him, either. He is a friend and he just saved our heads from being knocked off."

Ashti swung back. Pompino looked at her. He smiled.

"Ashti, is it? I shall like you, Ashti. You are smart and quick."

Ashti just glowered at Pompino. She said, hard and determined and with a mind made up: "I'm thirsty. Sazz."

Pompino's ferocious whiskers bristled up. His foxy face with that supercilious curl to his mouth and the damyoutohell eyes regarded me with lofty scorn.

"You keep a lady waiting for a drink, Jak? What has become of your manners?" Then, very gallant, very polished, he bent down and crooked his arm. "My lady Ashti. Pray, allow me to escort you to the Swod's Revenge, where my good friend Palando the Berry will provide sazz in abundance."

She gave a swift, liquid, upward glance at me. I nodded. Then, and only then, she took Pompino's arm. They set off for the tavern.

Time enough when Pompino was settled with a drink under his belt to tell him of the attack on his family. They were safe now, there was nothing Pompino could do. Ergo, let us get comfortable in our relationship again before we opened up new problems.

Palando the Berry looked at us, swiped his cloth at the counter, and said: "So you found them, then, Pompino."

"Aye, Palando. The child fooled me."

We sat in a corner and it being almost time, wine was brought. Ashti looked at the flagon, and I said: "Stick to sazz or parclear for as long as you can, my girl. They bear less hard on the stomach and the purse."

"My girl?" said Pompino.

So I sketched in how I'd run across Ashti. Then I said: "We parted on a scheme to steal a voller. I know you took her. I also can guess you waited for me. But, I was otherwise engaged."

"We waited for you, Jak. Then the Kildoi, Drogo, became impatient. It was not wise to argue with him."

"No. I can see that. Anyway, no harm was done." I told him what had happened and how I'd indulged in Death Jikaida, and then I said: "And you've been working for the Star Lords again?"

"Of course. It is all that keeps me sane. My wife—well, enough of that. And I've been importuned by these confounded idiots of Lem recently."

I told him what had chanced at his house.

He did not jump and go rushing up there. He held his glass steady. He said: "And the children are safe?"

"Yes."

"And the lady Pompina?"

"Your wife is safe." I put a fist to my chin, and then said, "There were four of them, as I have told you, an apim, a Brokelsh, a Rapa and the other fellow. The lady Pompina slit all their throats."

"Well, Jak, what else did you expect?"

I drew a breath. "What else, indeed?" Still talking, finishing the wine, we brought ourselves up to date. Then Pompino rose. "Well, I shall have to go home some time. You will be dining with us, of course. Chenunga will have the place cleaned up by now if I know him. Come on, Jak. Let's go and eat and talk. Maybe, if we are lucky, the Star Lords will send us out on an adventure for them."

Eight

Pompino and I plan a Jikai

In some societies on Kregen, custom demands that a host and hostess sit at either end of a long table with their guests between them. Other cultures ordain that a host and hostess sit side by side with their guests around them. Others place the host and hostess each within a circle of guests in semi-obliviousness one circle of the other. Where there are more than one host and one hostess—as in the quadrim people of Loghrangipar—more variations ensue.

In Tuscursmot, wherever originally the people had traveled from to settle here, they held dinner parties with style. And you have to remember that on Kregen, besides the differences of location and culture, you have also the differences of racial stock in a form far more violently different from anything here on Earth.

The Khibils of the inner sea, the Eye of the World, accustomed to the ways of the folk there, might have been surprised at the social mores of the Khibils of South Pandahem. The Khibils of other parts of Paz would have their own customs. The variety remains enormous.

The three of us—the Lady Pompina, Pompino, and me—sat each at a small separate table facing three long mirrors. We sat side by side, and could see one another in the mirrors. Ashti had been sent to a comfortable bed along with the two sets of twins, who were growing apace.

This custom does have advantages; it is also diabolically inconvenient. But Pompina insisted on high culture. Everything had to be done perfectly and by the strictest code of etiquette. Pompino looked fed up.

The greeting between the two Khibils had been casual to the point of exiguity.

Satisfied that his wife was safe, and his pairs of twins still whole, Pompino seemed—to me at least—to lapse into a private world of his own. He acted the host as the strict etiquette demanded by Pompina dictated. Beyond that he spoke only when spoken to, and shortly. He drank sparingly. So that wasn't the problem. The servants served a fine meal. That one of the cooks had been killed, that the place had been reeking with blood, that the mistress had nearly been murdered, could not be allowed to interfere with the proper entertainment of an honored guest.

That I was an honored guest followed in the nature of the events. Being a crusty old shellback, I could handle that kind of attention, and keep a hand over my goblet when the flagons came around.

Pompina did not so much become drunk—and I would be the last to blame her had she done so—as merry. To use a technical word known to the sorority, she became sloshed. She uttered fervent thanks to a variety of gods and spirits, and Beng Dikkane, the patron saint of all the ale drinkers of Paz, got in there along with Pandrite and Opaz and Shenorveul the Sceptered Scourge.

Pompino caught my eye in the mirror opposite.

He made a face.

"My wife is happy, Jak. I must—"

"Don't, Pompino."

"Yes. You are probably right. I think the Star Lords picked me for my last mission because of my familiarity with this little problem in life's rich armpit."

"Oh?"

"Later."

I nodded, and allowed a charming Fristle fifi—all the servants, after the death of the woman in the cellars, had been locked in the woodshed in the yard—to fill my goblet.

The wine was not Jholaix, from the northeast corner of Pandahem. It was a clear golden Markan and highly prized.

"Captain Logan brought it in from his last cruise," Pompino told me. He twirled his goblet, looking at the clear golden liquid. "A successful captain, Logan. He commands *Tuscur Castle*."

My ears pricked up. If Pompino knew someone connected with shipping I'd put in for a passage out. That would be far faster than riding or walking around the coast. Already I envisaged myself back with Seg and my comrades.

"You did not seem particularly surprised to see me, Pompino."

"Palando the Berry told me a hulking great brute of an apim, with a little golden child, sought me. I'd an idea, from his description, that hairy apim brute must be you."

"I have a confession—"

"Yes. You did not just happen to be here and thought to look up a fellow kregoinye."

"The Everoinye sent me on a mission along the coast." I outlined what I'd been up to, from a more professional angle this time and in more detail. Pompina hiccoughed and her head touched her breast. She started erect, and then stood up. We mere men rose also.

"I shall now retire, Pompino. Good night, Jak. I am in your debt. Please partake of my hospitality for as long as you wish."

"You are very kind, my lady. I do crave a boon—"

"Ask."

"Ashti. You have heard how she came into my care. I do not relish taking her with me into danger—"

"Of course. She has a home here for as long as the gods allow. I like her." Pompina chuckled and tears squeezed from her beautiful foxy eyes. "I loved the way she bit that stinking Rapa."

"Again, my thanks."

When she had gone, Pompino walked across to a lounging chair and flung himself down. He did not spill a drop. "Very grand, the lady wife. She lives partly in a world of her own, a world of fantasy. I have done well, as you can see. But Pompina affects the ways of the nobles. She feels she should be a vadni, at least. And I am a mere horter..."

He used the word for gentleman—equating with the Vallian koter—used mainly in Havilfar which was used also in many other places. A horter was a cut above your ruffianly riffraff. Yet Pompino had that word "ti" in his name, and therefore was of importance.

I turned the subject back to shipping.

"Tell me, Pompino. What chance is there for me to ship out? I have to get—"

"You've only just arrived!"

"Aye. But I have unfinished business—"

"Everyone who is not yet dead has unfinished business."

"That is true, by Zair."

"Must you go so soon? I want to tell you what the Everoinye had entrusted to me. Because of that I've been pestered by these vile Leem Lovers."

"Oh?"

He nodded and quaffed his wine. His whiskers were marvels of grace and proportion, ferocious when he brushed them back.

"Aye! I was sent up north to smoke out a temple of Lem, and although I had the place gutted, I was not satisfied with my work or that I had finalized my commission."

Thorough, Pompino, when he got his teeth into a problem. Unlike me, he was devoted to the Star Lords. Although, to be fair, I'd come to a much better understanding of those remote and superhuman beings in these latter days.

He went on: "They passed information down through their network to the south here. I'd masqueraded as an adept of Lem, having gained some insight to their foul rites, and the local temple insisted I join."

"They didn't know you'd worked against them, up north?"

"Of course not! But, with this last ugly attack it seems they may have discovered that."

"So the unpleasantness is likely to recur?"

He did not look pleased, sitting erect holding his goblet, his foxy face compressed and fierce.

"Maybe we will have to discover what they know." I ruminated. "If we follow up the local temple, and—"

"It will be razed to the ground tomorrow. I have passed the information to the town governor. We are an independent town, and soon we will be a city and will cease to be Tuscursmot, and become—I think—Tuscursden. But even so, some of the rasts may escape."

"Would it be possible for us to attend the razing?"

"Yes, it would. It would also be not a politic act. The main source of infection stems from the north."

"Where you were?"

"Aye. In Tomboram."

To say that I was shafted by a bolt of illumination might be extravagant. I did not gasp. But I know my craggy old face drew down into that frightening beakhead some folk describe as the devil's frown.

Pompino said: "What—?"

I said: "In Tomboram, a kingdom up there in North Pandahem. To the west lies Menaham, whose people are called the Bloody Menahem by their foes. Aye! And your wife—and you said the Everoinye selected you because you were married to her and understood her ways—you went to the Kovnate of Bormark. The kov is, I guess, Pando. And his mother, Tilda the Beautiful, Tilda of the Many Veils! That is it, is it not? Tilda is much like your wife—"

He gaped at me.

He licked his foxy lips.

"How—?"

"There is no magic in this, Pompino. I knew Pando when he was an imp of mischief, seasons and seasons ago. And his mother—" I paused. I would not stand condemned in my own eyes over Tilda the Beautiful. If she had begun to drink because I treated her correctly and as a great lady, had helped her to gain the kovnate for her son Pando, and had then left—I would not feel guilt. All my affection, love and life are dedicated to Delia.

"Pando, Kov of Bormark," said Pompino. He drank hugely. "Well, he may have been an imp of mischief when you knew him. I tell you, my friend, he is a right tearaway now."

The last time I had to my knowledge seen Pando and Tilda was right after the Battle of Tomor Peak. After the Battle of Jholaix, where Hamal had, for a time, been sent reeling back, I had not stopped to see Pando and Tilda but had flown directly back for Vallia and Valka.

Any king or emperor must keep a finger on the pulse of his world. I had kept abreast of much of the news out of Pandahem. I knew that King Nemo of Tomboram had reinstated Pando as the Kov of Bormark. Nemo was now dead and a relation, a dark and narrow-minded man from the distaff side of the family, now reigned. This King Nemo the Second had confirmed Pando in his estates.

I kept my voice even.

"How fares it with them, Pompino?"

He drank and refilled his glass.

"Bormark is not a happy kovnate, Jak. It is sour. I think—and, mark me, I have no proof—that the cult of Lem the Silver Leem has taken the heart out of the province."

"And this temple you burned? It did not—?"

"No. That will not settle it. There is more to be done, in Bormark, before the place smells clean again."

Slowly, I said, "I count Pando and Tilda as friends, Pompino. Even though I have not seen them for many seasons."

I did not add, as I might once have done, that when those two in their rags and misery had been dragged up before me, all clean and sweet in fresh clothes, and they had not recognized me after the battle, I had felt hurt. I had kept a straight face. But they had not recognized me as Dray Prescot, their old helpmeet. If that did cut me, I had passed it off, had taken the blame and the guilt to myself.

In all these years there had not been time to go to Bormark. All that could be done by the agents I had sent, I had thought done. But Tilda

She just did not see why she had to stay here, even though the Pompino pairs of twins looked likely, and would prove a source of sazz and sweets and practical jokes. She insisted on coming with me. I had to say no. And there was a funny old lump somewhere in my throat as I tried to explain. But explanations were impossible. In the end, stony faced, I had to shout the remberees and walk off, and leave Ashti struggling in the gentle grip of Pompina and the twins.

"And make sure you mind her carefully until we are gone. She will escape and try to follow else."

"*Jak!*"

She was crying and struggling, a wild, biting, scratching jungle girl. I walked off. I felt terrible.

But a little four-year-old girl had no place in a world filled with the deadly glitter of naked steel.

Although... Mind you... If Ashti got those teeth of hers fastened in your leg you'd not go skipping about so easily, no, by Vox!

The difference in the Pompino of his home and the Pompino of the outside world was remarkable. He came alive among his ships, their people, the impedimenta, the bills of lading, the tarry rope, the barrels and amphorae—in short Scauro Pompino ti Tuscursmot, known as Pompino the Iarvin, turned out to be a consummate shipping magnate. Well, if not with five ships in quite the magnate league, at least a man of substance.

I took a great interest in the technical side of the business, having been away from the sea for some time. I was always amused by a culture which produced barrels and amphorae, one from the north, the other from the south, in the northern half of the world, reversed in the southern, and took that fact for granted. The ships themselves, too, in their ranked mast-raking mass alongside the wharves filled me with a delighted sense of well-being. We went aboard *Tuscurs Maiden*—Captain Linson, master—and were made welcome.

"We shall be sailing in Captain Linson's vessel, Jak. So get settled in."

Linson, master of *Tuscurs Maiden*, did not appear to be of the usual run of sturdy old sea dogs. He was an apim, which was not at all unusual for shipmasters, and looked to be in the prime of life, clean-shaven, sharp-eyed, hook-nosed, very erect and correct. But, all the same, there was about him an air of devilment I found intriguing—and bracing.

As we stood on the quarterdeck with a tiny breeze fanning our cheeks, watching the busy bustle of provisioning ship, a black smudge rose into the bright midday air. The source of the fire was an old ship, an argenter whose days were long past for sailing the high seas. She lay in an abandoned area an ulm off, and she burned, black and stinking to the sky.

Linson looked disturbed, as any man looks disturbed at a burning ship.

"Do not distress yourself, Captain," said Pompino.

So I knew that was the temple of Lem the Silver Leem going up in flames. No wonder the wind brought down a sharp unpleasant smell.

Walking across to the rail with Pompino, I said: "I hope they take them all. I do not like leaving before we know there will be no more attacks."

"Should one or two wretches escape, I do not think they will harm my family, or Ashti. I've arranged for a more strict watch. By Horato the Potent! I've paid good gold to buy guard paktuns. Can a man do more?"

I was not going to be drawn into that discussion.

"All the same," said Captain Linson, joining us and tucking his telescope under his arm. "Fire is a mortal fearful thing in a ship, by Heisha of the Fiery Flukes!"

"You are right, Captain," I said pleasantly. And then, copper-bottoming the bet, added: "You run a fine ship."

Despite that air of sharpness about him, he looked pleased. His sharp eyes sharpened and this time with pleasure.

"Thank you, horter. You are kind." And then, like a rapier going in: "You perhaps have some knowledge of ship craft?"

I liked it.

"Some, Captain."

"I am glad to hear it."

No flies on this one, by Krun!

Pompino and I had adventured across the land dry enough to make men kill for water. He wouldn't know how much knowledge of ship craft I possessed. I caught a sly pleased smile on his face. The crafty old devil was lapping this up, thoroughly enjoying it. I made up my mind that, if a chance of showing how clever I was at sea occurred, I would resolutely refuse it. I'd show 'em what a landlubber I was, and joy in fooling them.

A Relt stylor came aboard and Pompino was closeted with him, going over the accounts. Linson went off ashore. I was left at a loose end. We were due to depart with the evening tide, for you do not just step into a ship and close the door and whip up the horses. You have to wait for nature's pleasure in matters of the tides and weather and the state of the wind. We had no oars, being an argenter. So I explored the ship.

Like all argenters she was broad and round and high and comfortable. Her sail area, as usual, was just sufficient to send her along at a stately pace without any danger of capsizing or of proceeding at a dangerous heeling rate. The gimcrack work and gilding were not ostentatious. Her lines were full and she was capacious. I found only a couple of places where the carpenter must be called to cut out rotten wood and replace it with new. Her rigging, not taut, was in good condition. She carried her artillery well-positioned and the varters snouted their menace out from her fore and stern castles. These ballistae could shoot either darts or stones. Her armory was tightly locked up and a Chulik mercenary stood there, armed with a boarding pike and a sword, and after a few words I found I had no burning desire to inspect Pompino's ship's resources in the way of weapons.

"If we are attacked by renders, no doubt you'll see inside," said the Chulik. He wore leather and blue and green feathers, and an iron cap, and he let the boarding pike hover around my midriff.

"No doubt," I said, and took myself off.

Up on deck gulls flew across, shrieking either cheerfully or menacingly depending on the mood of their auditors. They were headed for the fish quays farther along the shoreline. Tuscursmot lazed under the heat of the twin suns. My feet had no difficulty in leading me to the staterooms aft, where I found Pompino just finishing his business with the stylor. The Relt was packing up his satchel of papers and files, his feathers much ink-stained. Pompino sounded brisk.

"You will take a glass before you go, Rasnoli. Ah, Jak! You have come just in time. All arrangements have been made." He went on to say that *Tuscurs Maiden* was now cleared for a voyage to the north, some trifles of cargo for the south having been cleared from the ship. She had just taken on a parcel of local produce. We were all set to go with the tide.

"Just in time for what?"

"Why—I do not believe in paying mercenaries to lollygag about. You shall sit with me when we hire on our paktuns for the voyage. They are waiting on the quay."

This seemed an interesting prospect, for being an old fighting man myself, I take a delight in observing fellow mercenaries. On Kregen, that trade is not held in the low esteem it holds on Earth. For some mercenaries, perhaps, it should be. Masichieri, who are little better than bandits, are bad news anywhere.

But your correct and upright paktun is—or should be—a man or woman of honor. Once they hire out, they take their pay and keep and fight to the death. In theory.

I said, "Are there any Pachaks?"

He screwed up his face. "Four only, I'm afraid."

"H'm. How many do you take on?"

"I would like two dozen." In the Kregish he said jikshiv, which is one way of saying twenty-four.

"So you have to find twenty more?"

"Aye. And not a Khibil among them."

So, up on deck we went and sat on the folding chairs on the quarterdeck, in the shadow of the sterncastle, and watched as the mercenaries trooped up the gangplank.

"That Chulik of yours guarding the armory," I said. "He looks likely."

"Nath Kemchug. He costs a lot; but he earns his hire."

The first two mercenaries up the gangplank and onto the quarterdeck were twins. They wore leather, iron caps, were barefoot, and their hair was cropped short. They were varterists.

One said, "I am Wilma the Shot and this is my sister Alwim the Eye. We know our business, and—"

"Yes," said Pompino. "I have heard of you. You are welcome and will be paid the top rate. Next."

The four Pachaks were in no hurry to come aboard. They guessed we would hire them, for when a Pachak gives his nikobi he will fight for his employer until death or a formal renunciation releases him from his vows. The next fellow was a Rapa, big, beaked, feathered, clad in mail, carrying three swords and a dunnage bag over his shoulder. Also, he carried a shield, an oval thing of wicker, bronze rimmed.

"Rondas the Bold," he said. Indeed, the feathers around his beak and eyes were red. Sometimes it is difficult to judge if a Rapa's feathers are his own or decorations. "Churgur." This meant he was a sword and shield man.

"You have served in ships before?"

"No. But I can learn."

Gently, Pompino said: "I am more in need of archers."

"I can shoot—"

"You do not carry a bow."

"That is true. Try me."

Pompino leaned a little toward me and spoke softly.

"I like his style, the blowhard. Your thought?"

"If you can get him cheap, hire him. I judge he can fight. Although he may wish to remove that mail and don leather."

Now that the enormous conflict between the Empire of Hamal and what seemed to be the rest of Paz was over, there were many unemployed fighting men. They sought employment where they could. To be tazll, unemployed, was unpleasant.

Eventually we hired on twenty-five paktuns. In fact, only five were real paktuns, that is, mercenaries elected by their peers to wear the silver mortilhead, the pakmort, at their throat. This marked them as renowned fighters. We did not sign on a single hyrpaktun, who could wear the golden pakzhan at throat or on shoulder knot. But, as I have said, in these latter days almost any mercenary, if he—or she—was not an obvious youngster, a coy, tended to be called a paktun.

Of the twenty-five, fifteen were apim and ten were diffs.

Smells of cooking made all our mouths water, and everybody went off to their various quarters to eat. The aft staterooms were partitioned off so that, as Pompino said, we could indulge in privacy when we wished. My cabin was small, clean, smelling of sweet ibroi, and would serve admirably. I own I craved for the evening to arrive and the tide, and then we would be off. A tug, a low many-oared vessel, came to haul us out past the boom. I remarked on this extravagance.

"Yes," said Pompino. "It is a waste of gold pieces when you have stout arms and backs in your crew. But it keeps the harbor master happy—he is a distant cousin of my wife's—and the crew feel I intend to look after them."

With the feel of the ship under me, the sky darkening above and scintillating with the myriad stars of Kregen, I felt a tremendous liberating gust of spiritual well-being. We were off. Off to start the Jikai against the Leem Lovers.

There were many other undertakings I might be about in Kregen right now; but this was a task set to my hands. Apart from Delia and my family and friends, it seemed to me I did not do wrong in thus setting my face toward this adventure.

Ten

Decision at the Mermaid's Ankle

No compunction troubled me in allowing Pompino the Iarvin to outfit me in style. We were kregoinye. When it came to push of pike we shared our possessions, and made the best of it. At the moment, Pompino held the money and goods; ergo, he outfitted me.

I wore a decent blue tunic, and grey trousers cut to the knee. I went barefoot. I had a red scarf tied around my head. I swung a thraxter from a broad leather belt. If we got into a fight I would have the choice of Pompino's armory to arm and armor myself.

The days passed sailing along the coast. We sighted a few other vessels, and all was well.

Tuscurs Maiden rolled along, breasting the swell with a deal of white smother from her forefoot. The breezes blew and the weather remained fine. To keep from idleness was not difficult.

Pompino himself supervised the handling of the mercenaries, the marine component of the ship's complement.

Captain Linson, the master, kept his seamen well in order. They were a bright bunch, and the sails went out and came in in a handy fashion.

The Ship-Hikdar, the first officer, knew his duties and played a mean game of Jikaida. He did not drink. He had a tongue that could cut, in a figurative sense, as well as the Whip of any Sister of the Rose. The Ship-Deldar, the Bosun, an enormous man with an enormous red beard and enormous belly, rejoiced under the name of Chandarlie the Gut. The Ship-Hikdar, Naghan Pelamoin, ran a taut ship, and the Ship-Deldar used his rattan rarely. *Tuscurs Maiden* was, I judged, as happy a ship as one might expect to find, given the misery of much sailing ship life.

More rather than less of the coastlines of Kregen are festooned with myriads of islands. Here lurked danger. We sailed well out into the offing, and Captain Linson knew these waters. We were stopped by a swordship off the town of Hanmensmot where we were due to offload some cargo. Everyone crowded to the bulwarks to stare across the water as the swordship closed.

Pompino chased his Relt stylor to have the papers and passes ready for inspection. The swordship, long and low in the water, hauled her oars into a smothering wash of foam and lost way. A boat lowered and started across for us.

Studying the swordship, I became aware of Pompino at my side. He nodded across the suns-glinting water.

"A prickly lot, the citizens of Hanmensmot. But I suppose they have every right to be. Pirates are active."

"They cannot imagine we are renders in *Tuscurs Maiden*!"

"Perhaps they can. Towns have been sacked by renders pretending to be honest seafaring merchants."

The boat bobbed closer. She flew a huge blue and green flag in some exotic design. The swordship was smothered in flags. Her oars rested, quiescent. Her thole pins were arranged in groups of three, very close together. There were nineteen banks, giving the ship a total of a hundred fourteen oars. She was, thus, propelled on the old system of alla sensile. Sometimes it is rendered as zenzile.

Pompino sniffed. "Not like my swordships. I admit that *Whitefang* is old; but she rows on the modern system."

By this I knew his swordship *Whitefang* employed the style known as al scaloccio, that is, more than one man to an oar. Less than three men on an oar is a system not as efficient as three oars each with one man; four or five or more men to an oar yields much greater rewards in propulsive effort. I use Terrestrial terminology here, not Kregish, for the sake of simplicity.

I said: "If we are to sail up to the Koroles, and those islands, I understand, are infested by pirates, we might do well to have *Whitefang* with us."

"Do you think me a ninny? My other four argenters sail in company with fleets of my associates. *Whitefang* must serve her duty with them as guardship." By his way of talking I knew he held back a secret. Guessing that was easy enough.

"So your other—and your wonderful new modern slap-up-to-date swordship—waits for us farther on?"

He growled. "Of course, fambly."

We discharged our cargo and took on water and so weighed and set off eastwards once more.

Where there are islands and where the governments are weak or divided, then pirates tend to flourish. At the next port along, Febranden, a large and sprawling city up a sizable river, we joined a convoy bound for the east. We all felt easier in our minds as we set off, one among a press of sail. Counting ships, I made the convoy to be twenty-three argenters, ten of the small coasting type vessels, a few oddments of ships—boats, really—tagging along for protection and no less than ten swordships and risslacters spreading out around us. This was impressive.

Also, it was alarming.

"If they provide this many warships, Jak, it must mean they anticipate trouble."

"Aye. You had no news in the marketplace?"

"Only the normal scares, price fluctuations, scandals. Maybe this is standard practice for a passage through the Koroles."

I lifted one eyebrow.

"Well!" he flared out. "As I am kept so busy for the Everoinye I do not often have the opportunity of sailing in my own ships. Much as I would like to."

We consulted Captain Linson.

He was affable in his piercing way, aware of his responsibilities and position. "I have known a convoy of this size to warrant five swordships, or eight or so risslacters. But not, I must admit, six swordships and four risslacters."

"Your conclusion, Captain?"

"We are headed for trouble."

"Nothing more specific?"

The air of devilment Linson carried, with his hooked nose and clean-shaven darkness, sparkled strongly now.

"Yes. I picked up a scrap of gossip in the masters' saloon ashore. They were talking of a render called Quendur the Ripper. The topic was one not popular. But his is active at this time. They said he had put together a squadron of pirate vessels. This is the answer to honest sailormen."

Pompino looked across the gunwale. Across two argenters, bluffly bursting the sea asunder as they wallowed on, the sleek shape of a swordship showed, almost lost under the sea as she cut her way through. His arrogant Khibil head lifted.

"Over there is my new *Blackfang*. Let this Quendur the Ripper taste her steel!"

"A fine craft," agreed Linson. "And captain Murkizon is a fine skipper. As for his crew—"

Pompino rounded on the master.

"Well?"

Linson spread his hands in a tiny gesture.

"They are not what I would like to see. I would not tolerate them in *Tuscurs Maiden*."

Pompino bristled up his whiskers. His foxy face looked fierce, and then shrewd, and then alarmed.

"D'you know how much I paid for that ship? And what I gave Captain Murkizon to sign on a top-class crew?" Pompino breathed heavily. "By Horato the Potent! If he has played me false—"

"No, no, horter!" Linson, in his turn, looked alarmed at the damage his words had wrought. "Captain Murkizon is a fine officer. Just that he did not have the best opportunities for picking up a good crew, and the ship is not yet run in. Give him time, and plenty of rope's end, and he'll have them all shipshape and Vallian fashion."

This expression was not new to me—it was much of a muchness with "all shipshape and Bristol fashion"—but it did indicate what the sailors of Kregen's outer oceans thought of the splendid galleons of Vallia.

"I hope so, by the Merciful Pandrite, I hope so."

I walked away across the quarterdeck to take a better look at *Blackfang*. As the days progressed in convoy I was able to size her up, her and her sisters in the escort. She was indeed a superior swordship. Her hull was painted an entire jet black. Her flags were the blue and yellow of Pompino's sailing house. She pulled twenty-nine oars a side, and Pompino told me that six men hauled on each loom. More could be assigned in moments of emergency to haul on ropes fastened to the looms. Her upper deck bristled with artillery—varters and catapults. Her end castles were not overlarge, and her beakhead lifted long and slender. Her ram cut the water ferociously, and Kregan sailors have the knack of using both ram and beak. Perhaps, although superior, she was not the absolute best of her kind, but she was a fine well-found vessel and one I'd joy in the command.

Very soon now we would call in at Mattamlad, a town situated at the mouth of the River of Bloody Jaws.

Over that river, going northwards, Seg and I had flown in pursuit of a voller carrying adherents of Spikatur Hunting Sword. We had not heard the last of that little lot yet, I felt sure. It seemed to me that after I had been snatched away from Seg on that jungle path by the lake and the great carven rock face, he and the party would backtrack. Eventually, they'd arrive here, at the mouth of the river. The Kazzchun River was a place where one did not go swimming. Everyone was extraordinarily careful getting into or out of boats. We went ashore as soon as we arrived, and I made inquiries.

No. No, horter. Our apologies. We have not had a party—or a man—as you describe through here. I started at the customs office and went to the local government bureau for foreigners and then from various taverns to various inns along the waterfront. No one had heard of Seg or the party.

So, I was in a quandary.

If I just went charging up the river and hoped to run across them I could easily miss them. Then we would just go on and draw farther apart. If I stayed here I'd miss the adventure with Pompino. If I went with my kregoinye comrade I might be leaving Seg in the lurch. So—a conundrum.

A fellow with one ear and a hang dog expression followed me out of the Mermaid's Ankle, accosting me with a leer and a sniff. I looked at him stony-faced. Oh—and the tavern's name merely gave expression to that warped Kregan sense of humor. The story was simple; the mermaid was no mermaid but a shishi dressed up in a skin of scales, which had rotted through and exposed one shapely foot. Where the ankle and its gold bangle came in follows on—but I will not repeat that.

"Your pardon, horter. If you want to go upriver I'm your man."

He wore skins, his hair was a stringy mess, and he carried a long knife—in his belt.

"I am not sure," I said.

"I have a canoe and ten willing paddlers. I whip them only to keep them happy. You will not regret hiring me, horter. By the Bloody Jaws of the Brown River Herself!"

The offer was tempting. A few gold pieces—croxes they were called hereabouts—would hire him. If he tried treachery his knife would avail him nothing. And I did want to know what had happened to Seg...

And then common sense prevailed. "Sink me!" I burst out. "Seg can take care of himself!"

"Do what, horter?"

"Nothing. Here." I handed over a single gold piece. "Thank you for your concern. Have a wet on me."

I walked off, feeling that I had behaved like a fool. Seg was probably the toughest orneriest critter in this part of South Pandahem. He'd shaft anyone who tried to harm him or the lady Milsi.

Going back to the ship I met a fellow who looked to be wider than he was tall, an optical illusion enhanced by the vast leather carapace he wore. His face appeared to have been cut ruggedly from the side of a barn. Brick red, bewhiskered, sharply blue of eye, that face bore the marks of a man accustomed to throwing his weight about.

"Hai!" he called, rolling up to me. "Horter Jak! We've been looking everywhere for you. I've looked in all the sleaziest stews this side of Hamal!"

I stopped. "Llahal, Captain. You are?"

"Why, Lahal, Horter Jak! I'm Cap'n Murkizon of *Blackfang*. Who else, by the Black Moustache of the Divine Lady of Belschutz!"

"I do not have the honor of the lady's acquaintance, Captain. But thank you for looking for me. I am on my way back to the ship."

"Aye! To that Cap'n Linson's sea-scow!"

Any ideas I might have entertained of going aboard *Blackfang* were quashed by Pompino. As I went up onto the quarterdeck, observing the fantamyrrh as I did so, Pompino hurried forward.

"Jak! We were all worried. Thank you, Captain Murkizon. I shall want to see you later. Now, Jak, listen—"

"It might be amusing if I shipped in *Blackfang*—"

He looked stricken. He drew me aside. "What, Jak, have you lost your senses? I lead our partnership. Do you think I intend to endure the miseries of a swordship when I can sail in comfort in this splendid argenter? And we must stick together. You know that."

In the end I acquiesced. Thereby hang the threads of our fates.

The smell of mud permeated this place. Mattamlad slumbered under the suns. The heat rotted everything. Sweat was copiously shed. The quicker we were away the better. At last, joined by seven ships from the port, we weighed and let loose our sails and picked up a breeze and so set forth to confront the pirates in their lair.

Eleven

Cap'n Murkizon mentions his Divine Lady of Belschutz

"What do you make of her, Captain?"

Captain Linson did not for the moment reply to Pompino's question. He balanced easily, staring at the speck infuriatingly rising and falling on the horizon. The fleet sailed around us, and every glass would be trained on that distant dot of mystery. Linson lowered his telescope.

"Impossible to say. But a single ship would not sail these waters voluntarily if she was crewed by honest men."

"Ah!" said Pompino, and brushed up his whiskers.

I looked around at the fleet. The crowding ships presented a marvelous spectacle, a sea filled with sails. Around our flanks patrolled the swordships and risslacters, long and low and lean, their oars driving them half the time through the water, it seemed, the other half over it. Their rams snouted hungrily. The commodore in charge of the convoy was reputed to know these waters thoroughly, and had given guarantees to the owners that he would get their ships through. Certainly, we had sighted nothing suspicious, and had penetrated a goodly distance into the Koroles, maintaining a course through deep water and avoiding too close proximity to any island.

All the same, that vessel hovering on the horizon was clearly a spy, sent out to keep observation on our progress. The charts we had of the area were sketchy, and Linson explained this in the old and timelessly frustrating way.

"The local people feel their waters should be charted by them. It is difficult to come by reliable charts of these waters."

So now we would have to wait to be attacked. Sooner or later, and no matter how well the commodore guided us, we would have to pass near to one or other of the islands. When we did, then we could be pounced upon and devoured piecemeal.

We now sailed the Sea of Chem, although strictly speaking we had left that sea to enter what Vallians called the Southern Ocean. To me, a fellow accustomed to dealings with the southern continent of Havilfar, the idea of the Southern Ocean being north of Havilfar remained as a reminder of the strong parochial natures even of great peoples of Kregen. The people hereabouts, including the commodore, called the stretch of waters the Pandakor Sea. It would make no difference what the name of the water happened to be if it closed over our sinking hulls.

Pompino in his affronted way, said: "Why doesn't the commodore despatch a swordship to sink or drive off this pestiferous fellow?"

I left it to Captain Linson to explain something of the arcana of the sea to Pompino who was, to be sure, a landlubber who happened to own a fleet of ships.

"She hovers away there upwind of us, Horter Pompino. She has the weather gage. She can control how far down to us she runs before beating away. And a swordship would never catch her—"

"Why not? A swordship has oars, does she not?"

"Against the wind, the oarsmen would be destroyed in the amount of time required to pull that distance. And when the swordship reached that spot, the shadower would be long gone."

"It is not," Pompino delivered himself of the opinion with considerable force, "like riding a zorca."

Low down and to the northeast appeared a wide dark smear across the horizon.

Pompino borrowed Linson's glass and studied that dark streak. He braced his shoulders back.

"If we are to sail this close to an island, we must prepare."

Forgetting all about my cunning scheme to pretend ignorance of nautical ways, I was jolted into saying: "That's no island, Pompino. That's foul weather."

Captain Linson pivoted to regard me. His sharp face with that damned great hooked nose tautened. "Without a glass, horter Jak? You are so confident?"

So, of course, I had to say, "Well, out in the desert that's what bad weather looks like sometimes."

The lame explanation passed, and I contumed myself for so petty a deception. Truth to tell, despite the companionship and keeping myself busy, I fretted. The Leem Lovers waited, and I wanted to get about this private venture for the Star Lords.

The gods and spirits of the oceans evidently decided to balk me a little further. The gale was due. Judging by the extent of that ominous bar of blackness across the horizon, she was going to be a big blow.

Swordships are cranky and wet and uncomfortable craft. Something like a galleass of Earth, a swordship pulls her oars as her main propulsive element; but she has masts and canvas and can sail reasonably handily. Not so a risslacter. A risslacter is closer to the galley of Earth, even lower, even leaner—and far wetter and more uncomfortable. They'd have to run for shelter if the blow steepled the waves to overtop their freeboard. That would not take much of a wind.

Linson shared that view.

"The commodore is signaling." Bunting broke across the flagship's rigging; this brought back the memories. Perhaps I was taking this whole naval excursion too matter-of-factly. I had simply drunk in the naval atmosphere, feeling back at home, and had taken for granted the romantic and dangerous elements inseparable from sea voyages on Kregen.

The signals brought a change of course. I judged the commodore had no thought of avoiding the storm; he must be heading to gain the lee of an island. I scanned the horizon to larboard. No sign of land broke that shining surface. And the blackness of the gale reached higher and higher into the glowing sky.

Presently the outriders of the storm arrived. The sea got up. The sky darkened. *Tuscurs Maiden* began to respond to the sea and her motion increased. The warships pulled ahead, angling their yards, trying to make a run for it. We watched them go, and lumbered along after.

Thunder and lightning pelted down. The sky grew black. The sea writhed, and still no rain came sizzling down. Safety lines were rigged. The hatches were inspected. The canvas was reefed until we ran under a storm jib and a scrap aft. I would have preferred to have taken the canvas off the yards altogether; but Linson was the master.

Pompino went below. The Relt stylor, Rasnoli, who to his surprise had been included in our expedition, took a bucket below. He, too, did not look too happy about the feathers. Poor Pompino.

The gale, when at last it struck full force, was not as bad as I had expected. We managed to creep into the lee of an island and so rode out the worst. The darkness persisted. We heard a tremendous crash and the following yells and shrieks, and guessed two ships had collided. Linson looked calm and confident; but he strode his quarterdeck at a more rapid pace, trying to be everywhere at once.

The gale lasted the rest of the day and most of the night. Linson handled his ship well. We kept up against the sea, only running away at the moment when to do anything else would have seen us dismasted and swamped. Toward morning the motion of the sea appreciably abated. A few stars pricked out above. We had lost no one overboard. The mercenaries were packed away below and no doubt were as green faced as poor Pompino.

As the dawn broke luridly across the horizon and the sea, churned into long deep green rollers, bore on away ahead of us, *Tuscurs Maiden* began to resume her status as a sea-conquering vessel and not a mere half-drowned scrap of driftwood.

A man climbed up onto the deck and, crossing to the side, looked over. He was apim, a paktun—he wore the silver mortilhead—and an archer. He wore a green tunic and gray trousers, and he looked useful. He saw me watching him.

"Good morning, horter."

"Morning, Larghos." His name was Larghos the Hatch, not a talkative man, and hired at the top going rate for a mercenary bowman who was not a Bowman of Loh.

He pointed over the side. "I think he is done for."

I joined him and looked where his finger pointed.

A man floated in the water. He clung to a splintered spar, and the sea spumed over him as though he were a submerged rock.

"I do not think so. If he has been afloat all night—"

"Then," quoth Larghos the Flatch, stripping off his tunic, "he may be saved." With that, he jumped over the side.

The lookout was already yelling. Everything must be done nip and tuck, or we would lose Larghos. I could not fault his conduct; but Linson would probably rave.

The air struck sweet and crisp after the gale. The Suns of Scorpio rose in their blaze of splendor. The sea opened out—empty of ships. We sailed alone upon that hostile sea in the dawning light.

Linson and Naghan Pelamoin, his Ship-Hikdar, proved themselves fine seamen as they took way off the ship and rounded her to in the swell. A rope's end was chucked down and Larghos the Flatch was hauled inboard. With him was pulled up a cursing, sodden, raving barrel of a man who shed water all over the deck and glared balefully about.

"Welcome aboard, Captain," said Linson. He spoke with great urbanity, but the transparency of his enjoyment was lost on no one.

The fellow sputtered, spraying water. His hair hung plastered to his scalp. He looked obsessed with fury. Brick-red his face, ferocious his whiskers, brilliantly blue his eyes. He stamped and water squelched.

"Aye, Cap'n Linson! You may laugh, by the Cross Eyes of the Divine Lady of Belschutz!"

Pompino, looking gaunt, hurried on deck. He stared, appalled.

"Captain Murkizon! *Blackfang!* Where is my beautiful *Blackfang*?"

"Do not upset yourself, Horter Pompino! *Blackfang* still sails, Pandrite rot 'em! Sailed off and left me when the damned sea washed me overboard. I'll have 'em all, I'll trice 'em all up and strip their skins off jikaider—so help me!"

"Fell overboard, did you, Captain?" said Linson. He radiated enjoyment.

"Not *fell* overboard, you—you—" Murkizon dragged in a great breath of air and swung his arms. "*Washed* overboard!"

I said casually, "Better get below, Captain, and dry off. Although you may have trouble finding dry clothes to fit you."

He swung to regard me, must have recognized me, must have practically decided what to reply, when the masthead lookout sang out, high and clear.

"Swordship! Swordship!"

"Thank Pandrite," said Pompino, rushing to the rail. "It must be my lovely *Blackfang*."

We all stared, but of course we would not see the swordship for a space yet. The suns shone, Linson set the hands to their duty with a few dryly cutting words, and Murkizon took himself off to the galley to dry out. I perked up. Life was undoubtedly going to be more entertaining from now on.

I was right in that. But the entertainment was far different from what I was expecting.

The lookout called down information on the estimated course and speed of the swordship. He could not distinguish her colors at the distance, even with a balanced telescope, and her build meant she was low in the water and much like any other swordship—not all. I fancied that if some men I had known in my career were in command of *Tuscurs Maiden* they'd be up the ratlines like monkeys to take a damned good look at the fellow for themselves. Old Abe would, for a certainty.

The breeze veered and backed uncertainly. Towards the hour of mid it settled down to a stiff westerly breeze. I sniffed the air. This amount of wind would be just about the maximum a swordship would tolerate. Here an interesting feature of the ships of Earth and of Kregen came into play, for ships and their rigging are designed in different ways on different coasts where the prevailing winds dictate what is the best sail plan. The argenters of North Pandahem usually carried a crossjack on their mizzen mast. Whilst the lateen was not unknown on Kregen, down south, instead of a pure lateen they used a kind of standing lug on the mizzen. The effect was to enable the argenter to sail a little more stiffly and keep her head more up into the wind. We were thus able to steer a good northerly course, resuming our onward progress.

The lookout bellowed down that the swordship had disappeared. Pompino looked worried.

"If my beautiful *Blackfang* is sunk..."

"That could have been a rascally render," I said. "If so, let us hope he is sunk."

Presently the lookout, a new man relieving the old, shouted down that smoke wafted over the horizon.

"There," said Captain Linson. "She was a Pandrite-forsaken render and she is burning one of our convoy."

Truth to tell, these distant events did seem to bear out that theory.

Captain Murkizon came on deck wearing a long roll of blue cloth swathed about him. His hair bristled everywhere. He rolled as though he was a part of the ship.

He and Larghos the Hatch put their heads together and spent some time talking. Although I saw no gold change hands, I felt sure a man of Murkizon's stamp would for the sake of his own honor richly reward the man who had jumped into the sea to save him. This seemed fitting.

A vague shape on the larboard horizon that vanished astern was probably the island under whose lee we had sheltered during the earlier part of the storm before we had at last been blown downwind. We sailed on, a fine bluff argenter, smashing into the sea, leaving a broad creamy wake aft.

Pompino was so far recovered as to sit down to a light meal toward the latter end of the afternoon. He made a number of uncomplimentary observations upon the habits of waves and storms, and mentioned that his insides must have been reamed out cleaner than a milk churn before milking time. We were all, in our various ways, kind to him. I managed to refrain from mentioning fatty vosk rashers; but with Pompino to goad into a frenzy the temptation was sore.

Captain Murkizon reassured him, insisting that *Blackfang* still floated and was a perfect sailing and fighting instrument when he'd last seen her— in everything except her captain.

Linson put a hand to his face.

"It is a pity, Captain, that you did not have the time to knock your crew into shape." He kept his hand half-concealing his smile, very sharp. "I'll allow that if it had been me I'd have been tempted—with a crew like that— to have *jumped* overboard."

"Why, you—!" began Murkizon in a strangled scream.

A sailor burst unceremoniously into the cabin.

"Swordship!" he shouted. He looked wild, clinging to the door. "Swordship! She broke through a squall—she's right on top of us!"

In a yelling rout we broke for the deck. Sure enough, a squall feathered darkly away across the sea. Ahead, all her oars rising and falling like the wings of a bird of prey, the narrow shape of a swordship hurtled down on us.

"Beat to quarters!"

The scurry and rush, the slap of bare feet across planking, the clang and scrape of metal on metal as the varters were prepared, the insane racket of the alarm drum, all these things blended into a pandemonium that ceased as the Ship Deldar, Chandarlie the Gut, blew a long trill on his pipe. The ship stilled.

"Cleared for action, Captain!"

"Very good, Hikdar," said Linson to Naghan Pelamoin.

The hush laced with the slap of the sea, the creak of rigging and groan of timbers, impressed us all. One had to admit that Linson ran a taut ship.

"Who is she?" demanded Pompino. He was clearly agitated. "She is not *Blackfang*?"

Linson handed across his telescope.

"See for yourself, horter."

Pompino studied the racing shape ahead.

"All I can see is a black wedge and oars like wings."

"Aye. And her flags?"

I caught Pelamoin's eye. "Your telescope, Hikdar, if I may?"

He handed the brass bound leather wrapped tube across without comment. I put it to my eye and studied the onrushing vessel. Well, yes, she was a swordship, and Pompino's description was apt. The shape of her, wedgelike, low, with those banks of oars glistening and rising and falling, beating her on. The smother of white around her ram passed swiftly away aft. Her flags? Blue and green, with gold devices, stiff in the wind, difficult to make out.

"You know her, Captain?"

"She is not one of our escort, horter."

"I see."

Bearing to quarters was not a precautionary measure, then. I handed the telescope back.

"I'll just fetch a few weapons from the armory, Pompino. Maybe we can fletch a few before they board."

At this he changed completely. From a landlubber who had recently bought a fleet of ships—with the gold given him by the Star Lords, of course—and in constant anxiety for the well-being of his beautiful vessels, he became my companion of old, a rough tough fighting man contemptuous of opposition, ready to fight with the best. Out of his element he had been becoming almost querulous. Now there was the prospect of a few handstrokes in the offing, he reverted to his usual arrogant happy Khibil self. He brushed his whiskers up fiercely.

"Aye Jak! We'll show the cramphs!" We fetched weapons. We prepared. With the men at their stations and the girls at their varters, the complement of *Tuscurs Maiden* waited for the coming attack.

Twelve

Concerning the Swordship Redfang

The Suns of Scorpio hung low above the horizon streaming their mingled opaz radiance across the sea in paths of viridian and vermilion. A scattering of sea birds screamed and swung away. The dark blot of an island showed stark against the sky as the squall whisked past. The swordship had shot from the island's shelter. The squall had concealed her. Now she bore down upon us with her cruel bronze ram slicing through the sea as it would slice through our timbers.

Although clearly Captain Linson was a consummate seaman, the task of handling *Tuscurs Maiden* in battle against a swordship was of the order of scaling a mountain peak with your hands tied behind your back and wearing skis.

His sharpness was never in more evidence.

His orders rapped out. The hands rushed to obey. The yards braced around, the argenter's head fell off, and with the wind up her tail *Tuscurs Maiden* took off directly eastwards. The evolution was conducted smartly. With a vessel of even moderate speed, speed equal to that of the swordship chasing us, or the speed of a Vallian galleon, he would have outrun our pursuer. But the vessel was an argenter, slow and lubberly.

The swordship balked in her first initial rush to ram, swung about to follow, sheeted in spray, like a crocodile smashing through the water.

Pelamoin said: "Nogoya. She's a damned swordship out of Nogoya."

Pompino shook his sword at the pursuing vessel.

"That Pandrite-forsaken island is too big for its boots. They think they own the seas."

"At least, they control the seas here, and we have strayed into their area. They will not seek to destroy us, Horter Pompino, but to board and enslave us. They use slaves."

"Then my hand is turned against them," I said.

Captain Murkizon swaggered forrard from the after castle. He carried three swords in various hangings from his belt, and he swung a vicious looking double-headed axe.

"The best way to deal with these rasts is to hit 'em before they know! Hit 'em, knock 'em down, and jump on 'em!"

This seemed an eminently sensible idea. As to its practicability, that would have to be proved.

On a dead run to leeward the swordship hoisted a scrap of sail on her foremast. She leaped after us. I walked aft, up through the sterncastle, and peered out alongside a varter which snouted from its port.

Wilma the Shot said: "I'll guarantee to land a rock right on the head of that fellow up front."

A light laugh from the gloom of the aftercastle drew my attention to Wilma's sister. Alwim the Eye patted her varter. A heavy and exceedingly ugly-looking dart lay in the trough. The dart was of iron, and multi-barbed.

"And I'll shove this right down the gullet of that archer next to your fellow, sister."

From the armory I'd taken one of Pompino's bows. It was compound, reflex, a sound weapon if without the range of a Lohvian longbow. For the kind of work we envisaged, this boy would suit perfectly.

"And what do you ladies leave me?"

"Why—that rast at their bow varter."

"I see him." He wore a leather jerkin whose brass studs winked brightly in the dying light. As I watched he bent to the weapon. "He is about to loose."

"More fool him," said Wilma.

The rock struck somewhere below. The water muffled its force. The brass-studded figure bent frantically to his windlass. In only a moment more, as the ships neared, the range would be admirable. Had Seg been here, with his bow, he'd have shafted the whole forecastle party, the whole lot of the prijikers who clustered ready to leap onto our deck.

Pompino joined me with Murkizon. We watched as the swordship swept in on our tail.

"He'll have a job trying to ram and board from there," said Murkizon, "may the Crooked Left Arm of the Divine Lady of Belschutz smite him."

Chandarlie the Gut appeared, squinting over the stern.

"The cap'n says for me to shout when that damned swordship is about to ram."

"Aye," said Murkizon. "Then he'll swing his stern. He'll make the cramph miss, if he's lucky and fast enough."

Pompino looked at me and I said: "Don't pin your hopes on it. Swordships have a habit of sticking their teeth in."

"I do not relish being made slave."

"Who does?"

Men clustered above us on the open top of the stern castle. Their feet drummed on the planking. Wilma bent to her varter. The arms were drawn fully back, the string taught, the rock positioned. Her sister called across. "My dart first, I think, sister."

"Aye, sister."

The dart flew.

The archer took the dart in his midriff, and the fellow abaft of him took the dart, also, as well as the third in that group. Alwim the Eye let out a delighted crow and bent to the windlass. The Rapa, Rondas the Bold, bulky in his mail, bent to help her. I felt surprise, and then pleasure.

The other varter clanged. The rock squashed down on the head of the fellow Wilma had pointed out. She, too, let out a pleased cry. I lifted the bow. Before I loosed, an arrow streaked across the narrowing gap and pierced through the varterist who had been my target. Someone on the top of our sterncastle, with the advantage of height, had loosed first.

That, then, was where I should have been—as an archer. As a swordsman I would be better where I was.

My own shaft took the varterist's mate.

Then a shower of arrows whistled toward us, and some stuck in the wood and a few shrieked through the stern ports. No one was hit. I nocked another shaft and loosed. The varters clanged again. The ram of the swordship foamed on, drawing closer and closer. The shadows angled more levelly across the deck from the stern ports, and soon the swordship would be a mere lump of darkness against the suns set.

"We're lit up like puppets on a stage," grumbled Pompino.

A huge midriff bumped me and Chandarlie craned to get a better look. He was wheezing like a runner dragging his feet out of mud at every stride. His eyes screwed up as he measured distances. If our vessel could be swung at precisely the right moment we stood a good chance of letting the swordship overrun us and of smashing up his oars. Chandarlie poised, watchful as a hawk above a sparrow.

If the maneuver was not carried out correctly, by employing the headsails rather than the rudder, the argenter would simply present her quarter and beam to be rammed. Maybe, I was thinking, just maybe it might be better not to try to be clever and swing at all—just let the fellow's rostrum go into our stern and hope it would be forced down below us. He could be swamped, then...

"Now!" bellowed Chandarlie.

In the midst of drawing and loosing, of picking likely targets and moving with the swing of the vessel, the first sideways swing went unnoticed. Then the ram of the swordship veered away, the foam of water spouted up. A rock hit the wood near us and splinters flew. A shriek from aloft and a heavy thump on the planking told of one poor devil who'd been shafted on our sterncastle.

Had Linson's topmen been quick enough—had he backed his main topsail and maincourse, and thus, in taking way off us suddenly, allowed the swordship to swoop past and smash up his oars—had this happened we might have gotten away with it. But the helmsman, no doubt hoping to hasten the swing of the vessel, put just too much rudder into the evolution. It happened very rapidly. One moment we were sensing the swing, watching the bow of the swordship and the cluster of prijikers there, the next the whole ship shook with the crunch of the ram hitting us.

If the swordship skipper observed our movements and compensated by turning into us must remain conjectural. I grabbed for support, regained my feet, and saw the whole howling mob of warriors come swarming inboard.

"Hit 'em!" Murkizon foamed and roared into action.

There was a dead feel to *Tuscurs Maiden*. We met and fronted that first savage attack. Swords blurred down. It was hard brutal work in the confines of the after castle. We had a great advantage in that the attackers must force their way through the ports. We cut them down as they strove to gain entrance. In a sudden and deathly affray we stopped them and flung the remnants back. Murkizon peered out, ignoring a few shafts that winged toward us.

"By the Tangled Lice-Ridden Hair of the Divine Lady of Belschutz," he raved. "I'll settle your hash for you, you—!"

With that he leaped bodily onto the small forecastle of the swordship. Pompino, shoving forward and whirling his bloody sword, leaped after. The Rapa pressed up. There was little I could do but follow. We had smashed their first attack, now we could carry the fight to them. We stood a good chance of smashing them utterly.

So, over the stern I went and down onto the swordship's forecastle. The jump was steep. I landed agilely enough, but a rolling lurch of the ship toppled me forward. Pompino's sword flashed above my head. I rolled, hacked the legs from under a fellow with a pike, dove headlong at three men clustered together and wielding axes. Three blows, mingled with two feints and a duck, disposed of them. I looked about, the sword dripping.

Wilma and Alwim extended their swords, and both were as bloodied as mine. Three of our Pachaks, their tail-hands gripping gory daggers, finished off the last of the swordship's forecastle party.

Naghan Pelamoin raged up, shouting.

"*Tuscurs Maiden!* Look!"

There was a moment, before the next assault, to look back. The argenter, under full sail, was drawing off. The swordship's oars ceased to beat. In the heat of the combat, the skipper and the oarmaster had ordered the men to stop pulling. They would be near exhaustion after the pursuit, and no doubt it was felt that the swordship had rammed and the prey was theirs.

Well, in that they miscalculated. The turn had done enough for the ram to strike obliquely. *Tuscurs Maiden* was not decisively rammed. The bronze rostrum had not smashed through her timbers. Now she sailed on—and we were left stranded in the swordship.

The imminent approach of suns set struck me forcibly. With the argenter sailing so grandly off, we'd be more than likely to lose her during the night. So there was nothing else left for it.

"Forward!" I yelled, like any storyteller's tin pot hero. "Hit them! We must take the ship!" With that, and a rousing yell of: "*Hai! Jikai!*" I bounded down onto the catwalk.

Soldiers clustered by the foremast, and someone shot an arrow. I flicked it away and went bullheaded on. There was an awareness of bodies at my back, pressing on swiftly after me. We hit the group at the foot of the foremast and swept them away and roared on aft. Up on the stumpy stern-castle the wink of steel glowed crimson and jade in the dying light.

"Jikai! Jikai!"

We smashed up the ladders, they were hardly companion-ways, and roared in a shouting, struggling melee across the scrap of deck. The men at the whipstaff went down like sickled wheat. A confused impression of uplifted arms, of striking steel, of men shrieking and blood spouting, and we staggered back to our senses. We looked about. A man ran away from us, ran forward along the gangway, screaming. He threw himself off the beakhead over which we had entered his ship. He was the last.

Pompino said: "Well, and what now?"

Darkness fell about us.

Murkizon boomed: "We showed 'em, the cramphs!"

"Aye, Captain," said Pelamoin. "But, as Horter Pompino says, what now?"

"Why, we take possession of the ship and rejoin that imbecile Linson. When I see him I'll—I'll—"

"Yes, Captain," observed Pompino, gently. I saw that my comrade was fully himself, ready to put the boot in or ready to soothe, as the mood took him. I did not doubt that I would have to listen to an account of his exploits in thus taking a swordship—and from an argenter. Indeed, this would mightily enhance his own prowess in his eyes. Veritably, so!

The oarsmen were slave.

Chained to their benches, eight to an oar, they sat slumped in the apathy of exhaustion. It took some time for them to understand that we would not enslave them in our turn.

Lanterns were lit. Some of the people who had leaped into the ship with us went off to see about food. Wine was discovered and brought on deck. Chandarlie the Gut went off to inspect for himself the forepart of the vessel. She might not have rammed in the sense of a real ram; but she could have sustained damage there. He came back to reassure us. All was well...

Pompino said, "Then this is a new addition to my fleet. Very well. You, Captain Murkizon, will take command. Naghan Pelamoin, you will be Ship Hikdar. Chandarlie, if you can get your gut about the narrowness of the vessel, will be Ship Deldar."

We all laughed. It was the aftermath of battle, and men and women do strange things at those times.

The two varterist sisters took up goblets of wine and went off to inspect the ballistae upon the forecastle. We had lost one of the Pachaks, and only the three remained. Larghos the Flatch had a scratch down one cheek. A Brokelsh was stuck through the guts and would die by morning. We made him comfortable. Then we totted up accounts.

There were twenty-one of us, twenty-one fighting men and women. Well, that was ample to run the swordship if we were cautious. I do not think anyone of us had much idea of being cautious. Incessantly the paktuns and the seamen went over the details of the fight. By Vox! They seemed to remember far more of it than I did, or cared to do...

We were in the process of unshackling the oarsmen, slaves no longer, when Rondas the Bold came on deck prodding with one of his swords. So the fellow who had run the length of the gangway and flung himself overboard had not been the last, then...

"Found him cowering and mewling in a little cubbyhole," announced Rondas. He poked. "I thought I'd get some shut-eye and this confounded miserable specimen woke me up."

Someone yelled, high and delighted. "Chuck him overboard!"

"Hold on," I said.

Now I was well aware that my position was an ambiguous one. I had no obvious function aboard. I was the friend of the owner; that gave me no right to question the captain or his officers.

"Why should we not chuck the scum over the side?" demanded Murkizon. He looked ready to bristle up.

"He can give us information. And," I said, nodding to the rowing benches where the poor naked shock-headed mass of humanity was groaning and coming back to life. "It might be amusing to let him pull an oar for a time."

"Aye!" roared our fellows.

"Well—"

"Ask him," said Pompino, and that settled that.

The fellow turned out to be the purser, the officer Kregans call the palinter, and his stomach, while no rival to the splendor of Chandarlie's, bespoke a man who lived well. He was in a dreadful state. He looked as though his world had crashed in ruins about his head. Well, in a very real sense, it had. He told us that this swordship was out of the island kingdom of Nogoya, which we knew, that her name was *Flame of Nogoya*, which made us laugh and jeer, uncaring. We inspected the name, and found it to be painted over an area of woodwork planed clean, so this ship had been taken from somewhere and renamed by the Nogoyans. The palinter, this miserable Nog the Rations, also said that we would all be taken and hanged by the heels by his king, for his king was puissant upon the oceans and demanded tribute from all who sailed his waters.

"I see he keeps slaves," I said conversationally.

"That is all they are good for, to pull an oar."

"Are they criminals, prisoners, of your country?"

"No. They have been taken at sea for not paying the just dues demanded by the king, and—"

"And that is what would have happened to us peaceful seamen if your Pandrite-forsaken captain had taken our ship!" bellowed Murkizon. "All the honest sailorfolk know of your rotten island kingdom!"

"The pirates—"

"You're no better than pirates, yourself. At least they pull their own oars."

So, after this Nog the Rations had told us things needful for us to know, he was taken down to the rowing benches and shackled up. I abhor slavery. But I viewed this in the light of sentence passed by a court of justice. At least the fellow had his life, such as it was. He'd be set free at the end of this adventure, if he still lived.

Murkizon and Pelamoin, with the ready paunch of Chandarlie, sorted out the oarsmen. When it was put to them, they saw the justice and wisdom of continuing. After all, if we were to succeed in our mission, we needed strong backs and arms to haul the oars. They were no longer slaves. They were free men and women with us, consigned to fetching up safely at a port and there resuming a life of liberty. They cheered.

We collected up the whips and threw them overboard.

More cheers greeted this. And then a hairy wretch with many scars across his naked shoulders shouted out fiercely, "And where is the whip to lash on Nog the Rations?"

"Leave him to me," said Chandarlie the Gut.

Pompino announced, with a flourish of his whiskers, that for good and sufficient reasons—and obvious ones, to boot—he intended to name this ship *Redfang*. The name pleased us.

Thirteen

The Star Lords call for action

Redfang sailed north. We were now entering waters where in the old days sailors from Pandahem kept a ceaseless lookout for the swift raiding galleons of Vallia.

During the Time of Troubles in the island empire of Vallia most of her splendid galleon fleet had been dispersed or destroyed. Then we had built up our aerial squadron. Still, galleons were being built once again and much trade was carried on, and every now and again some venturesome Vallian captain would snuff about looking for an enemy to board and plunder.

If my dreams of uniting all the lands of Paz became the reality it could be and, by Zair, ought to be in any decently run world, fellow seamen from Pandahem and Vallia, instead of fighting, would join in opposing the fish-headed Shanks who raided us all. Vallia had concluded treaties of friendship with a number of countries after the defeat and expulsion of the Hamalian forces; diplomacy must continue to bring forward fresh treaties. And making treaties is an activity to drive a fellow to exhaustion. Down in Ruathytu we'd had some...

"Sail ho!"

The yell brought everyone hurrying up, in the usual way, when only the lookout perched in the cross-trees could see that distant speck of the horizon rim. This time, I did go up and have a look myself, carrying one of the telescopes we'd found in the swordship's miniature charthouse.

Once the far-off sail had been centered in the glass, a single look told me she was no galleon out of a Vallian port.

"What d'you make of her?" bellowed up Murkizon.

The lookout screeched down what information we had, that the vessel was on a reciprocal course and appeared to be of sufficient size to warrant a goodly crew of renders changing course to intercept and cut her off and cut her up and devour all her goodness. I stared at the lookout, not so much shocked as in surprise.

He saw me looking at him after his outburst.

He wore nondescript clothes, a blue shirt and a breech clout, was bare of feet and with a green scarf knotted around his head. His face, of the narrow kind, held a taut constipated look, as though he seethed impotently within.

"You've been a render, then, dom," I said.

"Aye. This swordship—with a fine gang of cutthroats. We could make a fat living for ourselves here."

"Well, Asnar the Grolt, you would have to speak to Horter Pompino on that score—aye, and your comrades."

Watching the distant speck of sail, we continued this odd conversation. "As to the owner," said Asnar the Grolt, "we signed on to serve, and that is why we sail north now. But—"

"There are more important things to do in life besides piratically storming peaceful ships."

"You, then, have never roved the seas in search of plunder."

I did not disabuse him. I'd been a render in my time fighting with that remarkable lady pirate, Viridia the Render. She operated among the Hoboling Islands, off the northwest of Pandahem. As always, as always, I wondered what had happened to her and her cutthroat crews.

The sail vanished over the horizon rim, but I did not descend to the deck. The motion of the vessel, the light, the glorious tangy Kregan air, all combined to detain me. I thought of Viridia the Render, and naturally this led me on to think of many of those other folk I had met during my life on Kregen.

During that life on Kregen, I have met very many people of all kinds. Some of them simply wandered across my path, busy about their own purposes and impinging only to the extent that their actions, thoughts and emotions affected mine. Then they drifted away. This fact of life is generally learned by children when they first lose a bosom friend whom they met yesterday or the day before. Nursery and Primary Schools, First Grades, are filled with these tragedies. People just encounter, communicate, part, like vollers passing on a night of Notor Zan, ships passing in the night. Sometimes we spend a fraught period in the company of fresh acquaintances, and then call the remberees and go our separate ways.

Some folk, particularly on this Earth, still have not caught up with this simple fact of life. They complain when what one might call minor characters appear and disappear. One can only suppose that these critical complaints are voiced by people who are in constant communication with every single person they have ever met in their whole lives.

Bringing me back to the cross-trees of Pompino's *Redfang*, Asnar the Grolt observed: "The breeze is turning fluky."

"Aye. We're in for a spell of calm—"

"I think so, too. At least we have oars."

"And that is interesting in view of your comments about renders—"

He laughed, narrow-faced, dark, mocking himself as much as the concept of piratical brotherhood. "You mean we all take our turn at the looms?"

"Precisely."

He lifted his telescope and trained it forrard.

"What do you make of that?"

I looked. A dark wedge of smoke lifted above the horizon rim.

"A ship burns."

I swept the circle of the horizon. The line lay bare of all save that ugly blot of smoke.

Something was happening and we could not see, could not know what that might be. We could only guess. This situation where one saw little clues, caught faint whiffs of reality, this was the very stuff of life to an old ship captain, a tactician and strategist in naval matters. Piracy? Or something more sinister? Even as that thought occurred to me I heard the raucous squawking from over my head.

The old feeling of resentment hit me, to be immediately brushed aside. I knew that Asnar the Grolt could not hear that mocking croak. He could not see the glorious scarlet and golden bird that planed on stiff wings down out of the suns glare, circling around my head. I looked up. I shook my fist. Asnar sat, rigid, unmoving, a lump carved from stone.

Circling in the air the giant raptor from the Star Lords regarded me from bright black eyes. This was the Gdoinye, messenger and spy for the Everoinye.

"Well, you bird of ill omen," I roared up, "and now what do you want?"

"You act as though you carry the approval of the Star Lords, Dray Prescot. You and the kregoinye, Pompino."

"We act because we wish to act, bird!"

The screech mocked. "Onker! There are more than one brand of Leem Lovers—as you know—"

"I know!"

"The Everoinye do not wish you to fail in this."

Staring up at the gorgeously glinting bird, a blaze of gold and scarlet, I wondered who was the onker, the idiot, in this situation. There was no sign of the white dove from the Savanti to keep an eye on me. I bellowed.

"By Makki Grodno's disgusting diseased liver and lights! D'you think Pompino or I wish to fail? Onker!"

"Make sure you do not."

With a final insulting screech the bird winged up, turning, shimmering in light, vanishing.

Asnar said: "There is a sail," and then he roared down to the ship: "Deck below! Ship ahoy!"

No time had elapsed in the real world since the bird appeared up to the point he vanished. Now life jumped into motion again. Above the horizon rim showed the speck of a sail, glinting in the suns light. I steadied the telescope. I looked.

So...

So I understood what the Gdoinye had been saying, and why he had visited me at that particular moment. Leem Lovers, he had said, there are more than the one kind... Oh, yes.

I recognized the shape of the sail approaching us.

Tall, narrow, more planing with the wind than catching it as an ordinary sail does, that tall shaft of canvas on a polacre mast indicated clearly—and terribly—just what that ship was.

Asnar the Grolt bellowed down, "Can't make her out yet."

Without wasting any more words, I shinnied down the backstay and jumped onto the deck. I went across to Pompino and Murkizon. They saw my face, and a muscle twitched beside Pompino's eye. Murkizon almost— not quite—took a step back.

"What, Jak? What is it?"

I didn't shilly-shally.

"Shanks."

The word whistled around the ship like wildfire.

Shanks!

Fish-heads; rapacious, murderous, merciless sea rovers from over the curve of the world. They were called, among many insulting names, Leem Lovers. They were not of Paz. They were diffs, alien, enemy, who would slay us and glee in the slaying.

"We cannot fight them," said Captain Murkizon.

The silence that ensued, punctured by the slosh of the sea and the dying sough of the breeze, the slap and bang of loose tackle, reminded us all of the importance of this moment. No one was going to suggest that Captain Murkizon was frightened of the Shanks. We were all aware of the ferociously formidable reputation of the Fish-heads. It took twice the normal amount of killing to slay one of them.

Pompino cocked an eye at me. Quietly, I said to him, "You saw the Gdoinye?"

"Aye. We have been summoned."

"Yes."

"Well," demanded Murkizon. His face resembled a sunset of the great red sun Zim. He burned. "What do you say?"

Naghan Pelamoin and Chandarlie the Gut looked at the captain, and away, and then at Pompino. Pompino did not hesitate.

"We may not wish to fight the Fish-heads. It is true they raid our coasts and slay us and burn and kill. It would be feeble of us not to try to stop them."

"Have you fought the Shanks before?" demanded Murkizon.

The Rapa, Rondas the Bold, shouldered forward.

"I have. They may be killed like any other man."

The two girl varterists said, more or less together, "We have shot them before."

Murkizon shook his head. "You said, Rondas, that you had not shipped as a marine mercenary before. So you fought the Shanks ashore. I tell you, they are a very different proposition afloat and in their damned magical ships."

"Their ships are not magical," I said, very sharply. "They are well found, with good lines and a remarkable sail plan. But they are only ships. They may be rammed and sunk."

"Have you tried?" boomed Murkizon. "I have. They sail fleeter than the wind itself."

"Well," declared Pompino, brushing up his whiskers. "You may not wish to fight them as I said. But they are sailing down upon us with the breeze. Look!" He pointed. Sure enough, the Shank was foaming along, the bone between her teeth spouting only a little, her tall narrow sails all slanted so that the breeze sucked her along. "She seems to fight *us!*"

"And she'll be upon us very soon," said Pelamoin.

The hesitation in Murkizon was undermining the resolution of the crew. They respected the barrel-like captain as a fighting man who knew his business. If he hesitated, the dangers must be immense.

The moment hung with dire consequences. These men had to face the hard facts of life, and that life spent on the marvelous and terrible world of Kregen. The Shank bore on, creaming down on us, and apparently bringing the wind with her. Her superstructure was of the square, boxlike construction favored by the Fish-heads; her underwater lines would be sweet and clean and of a very high order of marine expertise.

"They will be on us!" I bellowed. "Beat to quarters! Captain Murkizon, I respect your decision. You may go below and keep out of it if you—"

He didn't let me finish. I thought he would explode.

"Go below!" he fairly foamed. "Not hit 'em and knock 'em down and jump on 'em! I shall remember that! I only said we should not fight them if we did not have to!"

"Well spoken," said the Rapa. "By Rhapaporgolam the Reiver of Souls! Now I shall find out how different fighting them on water is!"

"Aye!" raved on Murkizon, incensed. "And by the Nauseating Nostril of the Divine Lady of Belschutz! My axe will drink their green slimy blood before they send me down to the Ice Floes of Sicce!"

At the moment I felt any mention of Makki Grodno would be superfluous. But I stored away Murkizon's colorful remarks about his Divine Lady of Belschutz.

"Then let each of us offer up a prayer to the gods," said Pompino. "Pandrite and Opaz shine on us this day."

"Aye!" And then they started to yell: "Jikai! Jikai!"

So, that settled it. We were in for a fight, whether we wanted it or not.

The Shank drew on apace. Now we could see the dots of scaled helmets, glimpse the wink of steel. They had various kinds of artillery. Our varters were prepared, the windlasses cranked, the strings drawn back, rocks and darts positioned in the troughs. I saw to the bow I'd borrowed from Pompino, and made sure the quiver of arrows was full.

The breeze fanned our cheeks. That breeze fluttered, died, blew strongly again, vacillated, shifted around the compass—died, and did not blow again.

The Shank sailed on and then, gently, her sails not quivering as ordinary canvas would, she slowed. Presently, we were two ships, idle upon a painted ocean.

Pompino glowed.

"Now we have the cramphs!"

At once Murkizon's attitude changed. He glared.

"Aye," he said. "Aye, Horter Pompino. We have oars. But, look, the damned Shanks are putting out sweeps."

Sure enough, five long sweeps a side slid out from the Shank Vessel, struck the water, began to pull in a long slow rhythm. Gradually, she began to move through the water toward us. Her progress was painfully slow. She would take some time to reach us at that speed.

"Any man with sense would pull away from her," said Murkizon. He cocked an eye at me.

The Rapa, Rondas the Bold, and the Chulik, Nath Kemchug, stood talking one to the other. Not races of diffs who ordinarily got on, Chuliks and Rapas. But it was clear they both shared the same opinion here. The archer, Larghos the Flatch, joined them. The girls remained at their varter positions on the foredeck. Chandarlie the Gut prowled the ship. I spoke to Pompino.

"We will have to talk to the oarsmen, Pompino."

"We will. I'll tell 'em. That will be the end of that."

He went below the gratings. *Redfang* pulled a mere twenty-two oars a side; but eight men pulled and pushed on each. We could turn up a fair rate of knots. The drummer we had appointed, a seaman with a shock of black hair and a face with a nose knocked out of shape, went below. Nath the Slide would keep the time going, hammering out the rhythm.

Murkizon was drawn into the conversation on deck. He waved his arms about. His face shone. Then he stamped his foot, hard, and bellowed so that all could hear.

"That is the best plan! I agree! But if you are all killed do not come whining to me that it is cold on the Ice Floes of Sicce!"

Intrigued by this talk of a plan, I felt inclined to add fuel to this flame of enthusiasm. I shouted, in a high mocking voice.

"Ice Floes of Sicce! And the Shanks? Why all of the demons and devils there wouldn't have the Fish-heads—not if you paid them!"

That raised the kind of groaning laugh it deserved, and Pompino reappeared on deck. "Plan?" he called. "I heard. What plan?"

They left Murkizon to spell it out.

"The Shanks make slow progress. With all our oars pulled by willing hands we can run rings around 'em. We use our superior speed and turning circle under oars, dart in, ram 'em on the broadside and pull clear. Pull clear quick, mind! Instanter! So they don't get the chance to board. Then—" and here he spoke with evident relish. "Then we stand off and watch 'em sink."

"Aye!" went up the full-throated roar.

Against that vociferous approval, I had to be the idiot to say, "And what about the treasure they carry?"

That was shouted down in a tumult of yells. The gist was that the only treasure aboard was likely to be stinking fish.

There was no arguing with them now, and with Pompino agreeing to the plan, that motion carried the day.

The oarsmen who so recently had been slave agreed that for this business they'd pull their hearts out. They could make the ship move! They'd show what they could do as free men hauling at the hated oars...

A terrible anger at those who had oppressed them became evident in this, as though the ex-slaves were happy to strike out at this new foe in lieu of the old. They were perfectly confident that they could carry out their part of the plan. On the instant of ramming they would be ready. Those who had been pulling would push, those who had been pushing would pull. They'd backwater with such skill and precision we'd be out of the hole our ram had made, the proembolion would help us to back free, and we'd be away and laughing before the first Shank recovered from his fright. So help 'em all the gods and goddesses of the Sea!

Our motive power thus secure, we set about preparing ourselves for the coming ordeal. For ordeal was what it would be. People stood to their posts. The varters were manned. The prijikers stood tensed, ready to repel any attempt at boarding that might, despite the plan, eventuate. The drummer gave his preliminary warning rat-tat.

Pompino called.

"Redfangs! Are we ready?"

"Aye! Ready!"

"Then—Hai, Jikai!"

The drum roll smashed out, every oar rose as one, struck in a welter of suds.

Like a stone flung from a catapult, *Redfang* shot across the sea, leaping for the sinister shape of our foe.

Fourteen

We drop in on the Shanks

Smashed into a million splinters of light, the sea sprayed away from the thrusting ram of the swordship. The vessel heaved herself through the sea at every stabbing thrust of her oars. Straight as an arrow she hurled herself for the flank of the Leem Lover's craft.

Somebody on the forecastle began to sing those outrageous verses from the more boisterous sections of the song "The Worm-eaten Swordship *Gull-i-mo.*"

Others took up the refrain, beginning low-voiced, building as *Redfang* surged onward into a full-throated chorus. A chanted paean of defiance, flung before us at the Shank, rolled across the sea.

The breeze remained dead. The sweeps across that narrowing gap of water churned with a motion betraying the frantic efforts of the oarsmen to propel their craft out of the killing crunch of our ram. Spray flew back like fabled diamonds flung across sable velvet. We stood braced against the speed and we roared our defiance in a rollicking barroom song, chanting out the defects and the mishaps of that nauseous swordship *Gull-i-mo.*

The flags fluttered. Roughly fashioned from scraps of colored cloth we'd found aboard, they flaunted Pompino's blue and yellow. The air tasted like wine. Everything swam into a focus brilliant and brittle. Every sound spurted with meaningful force. Onward we plunged.

The Shank was turning.

Murkizon shouted his helm orders. The men on the whipstaff braced themselves, and the head of *Redfang* swung with a barely perceptible motion to line with deadly accuracy on the enemy beam. Now we could see the heads of men over the bulwarks. We could see the suns glint from scales. In only short moments the arrows would rise, the varters loose.

The two varterist sisters, Wilma the Shot and Alwim the Eye, bent to their ballistae, taking a cool sight, lining up. When the moment was right—and not before—they would loose. Larghos the Hatch lifted his bow, not yet fully drawn, waiting his moment. I followed his action, taking as my mark the head of a man near the afterdeck who looked as though he might be the helmsman.

Many heads crowded above the enemy bulwarks. Spears showed, a few. Mostly they used long narrow tridents. I knew about those tridents.

Pompino scrambled up to join us on the forecastle. He looked inflated, wrought up, brilliant of face.

"By Horato the Potent! We're going to catch them slap bang in the middle."

"Amidships," said Asnar the Grolt, hefting his boarding pike. He wore three thraxters in his belt, and three daggers.

Naghan Pelamoin, ready to return to his post as the Ship-Hikdar, spoke sharply.

"Remember, we do not board! We ram, backwater, and leave the cramphs to sink."

"Aye!"

Asnar the Grolt shook his pike again; he made no comment further.

Rondas the Bold and Nath Kemchug stood together, not speaking but clearly standing shoulder to shoulder. From this sign I took heart. When Rapa and Chulik stood side by side against a common foe, then perhaps all of Paz would come together in common union far quicker than I had judged. The breeze of our passage blew in our faces. The suns shot shards of fire across the sea. And the side of the Shank drew nearer across the water.

A rock rose from the Shank. Turning over and over in the air it arched up to splash into the sea twenty paces short. A howl of derision sparked from our prijikers.

The two girls remained calmly at their varters.

Another missile flew to drop short.

Again that derisive yell broke from our ranks.

If one of those rocks hit our group, there would be yells aplenty.

Wilma said, "I will take the forrard varter, sister."

"Aye, sister," said Alwim. "And I the aft."

A couple of spare men apiece had been detailed to wind the windlasses for the girls. Wilma and Alwim were by way of being Varter Chujiks, a corrupt term and a slang way of saying they were gun captains in Earthly parlance. By this time I had formed a high opinion of their accuracy and expertise. If they could knock out the enemy artillery we stood a much better chance of carrying out the plan.

The next rock sloshed down just overside to larboard. The spray went whipping aft.

We roared on, with the ship leaping under the thrust of the oars. The Shank's waist ahead of us swarmed with men. Her sweeps lashed the water, clumsily trying to turn her. For a single instant only a flashing remembrance of the time we went roaring down to attack a Shank leaped into my mind. Then we had smashed into the Shank and after a tremendous fight had bested him. But then we had been fighting with hardened Vallian seamen from a Vallian galleon, and we had a strong contingent of Chulik marines. Now we had a swordship and a handful of fighting men.

No, this time was going to be far different, if they got aboard us, from the time of Captain Lars and his splendid galleon *Ovvend Barynth*.

The two girls let fly their varters and the rocks crunched in. Then the arrows began to crisscross. We shot all the way in. And we were shot at all the way in.

Unlike the shanks in the ship *Maskinonge* we'd fought in the old *Ovvend Barynth*, these Fish-heads had two arms. We could see them busily drawing and shooting their reflex bows. Our archery replied. Arrows fleeted in. They were yelling over there as the ships closed. Rather, the noise was that thin devilish screeching any man, hearing, must shudder at. My shaft glanced off something in the way, and missed my aim. Philosophically, I drew and loosed again. One cannot always hit one's target with the first shaft. Not like Seg.

Asnar the Grolt said: "Uhoongg!" or something that sounded like that. I gave him a quick glance. A long barbed arrow pierced his face, tearing away his cheek and exposing his teeth and eyeball. Blood ran. He did not speak again; but fell down onto the deck. In those closing moments as we bore in to ram, all a fighting man could do was commend poor Asnar the Grolt to his particular gods, and turn more sternly to face the enemy.

A rock appeared to me to be aimed straight at me.

It lolloped on like a friendly puppy about to lick your outstretched hand, only this puppy would rip off that hand and pulp the body attached to it.

The rock skimmed over our heads. In the din I did not hear it crash. The screams ripped out as though tearing men's lungs with them. The stink of fish grew as we closed with the Shanks, that odious fishy stink that makes any man of Paz wrinkle his nose in disgust.

From our perch in the forecastle we could look down on the waist of the Shank. That space was crowded with men, with beast-men, man-beasts, halflings, all with scales and stinking fish heads and squabby fish tails. There was no drawing away as we foamed in to ram. Pompino saw that.

"Remember!" he yelled, hoarsely, making himself heard in the uproar. "Keep them off. We do not board."

"Aye, horter," said Rondas the Bold in his vulture's voice. As a paktun his humor tended to the macabre kind. "We might not want to board; they will."

"Then," said the Chulik, Nath Kemchug, "we stop them." Their sense of humor is atrophied, Chuliks; but they have voracious appetites for a fight. "By Likshu the Treacherous! I will take a double handful of them with me if I go down to the Ice Floes this day."

"We just need to keep them from getting aboard in the few moments between ramming and drawing off!" shouted Pompino.

My Khibil comrade had not, I judged, seen a very great deal of sea-borne action. If those devils of Shanks got their hooks into us, we'd have the self-same devil's job to break free.

An arrow sprouted suddenly from Wilma's arm. She gave a scream of shocked surprise; then tried to carry on. She bent to her trigger as her crew finished winding. Pompino saw.

"Wilma! Go off the castle—"

"If someone will snap the arrow it can be drawn—"

"Go down, Wilma. D'you want to look like a pincushion?"

A rock hissed past so close it stirred our hair.

And, all the time these incidents had been occurring, little splinters of hardness in a sea of noise and stink and movement, we had been forging on and on toward the Shank.

"Prepare to Ram!" screeched Chandarlie the Gut. His voice bashed back to Murkizon. The drum beat increased, a frantic blam-blam that got into the blood and vibrated the nerves.

Redfang fairly leaped the last few paces into the flank of her quarry.

Those last few moments before we hit passed as though I observed them in a dream, and all the fighting that followed, slow, hazy, almost perversely unreal, while the real events took place swiftly and in stunning flashes of rapid action. This strange dilation of time meant only that one lived through the horror for longer than it really lasted.

We hit.

The ram struck shrewdly along the Shank's underbelly and so nicely timed were Murkizon and Chandarlie's commands, that the oars flurried into powerful backwatering on the same instant.

Everything lurched forward. People clung onto whatever happened to be close. The jolt of impact juddered through *Redfang*. Some careless idiots lost their grips and sprawled headlong. Ropes strained and some parted. The ship jolted as though she'd run head on into a brick wall.

The Shank rolled. Now we should slide off neatly and our proemblion prevent the ram from entering too far into the side of the rammed vessel. Our oars, smashing the sea into foam, would haul us off.

Grapnels soared up against the sky.

Hard three-hooked iron shapes, they swung up and over and slogged down to bury their barbed fangs into *Redfang*. We had been hooked.

"Backwater!" Chandarlie yelled and heaved his gut around. "Their lines won't hold!"

The drum rolled and rattled.

The oars dug deeply, all in perfect rhythm, all pulled through the sea together. The sea roiled away, churned into suds, and *Redfang* did not move.

"The ropes hold us," said Pompino.

A boarding axe was grasped in my fist. Do not ask me how it got there, and my thraxter stuffed away in the scabbard and the bow discarded. The axe was there. I leaped from the forecastle down onto the beak. Grapnels stood there, their arms stuck, their shanks up and taut with the strain of the ropes. Like any sensible sailor who wishes to grapple a ship, the Shanks had used chains for a goodly length before bending on their ropes. I'd have to crawl right forward to get past the iron chains and slash the ropes. There was not a chance in hell of prying the grapnels loose under the strain on them, and the axe wouldn't look at the chains. An arrow stood up by my head, going thwunk into the wood. Damned arrows! They would have to be ignored. I went on crawling forward.

"Cover him!" Pompino must have shouted that before he jumped down after me. I guessed it would be him.

The first grapnel rope parted—and believe me I hit the thing only a hand's-breadth up from the link to the iron chain!

The second went and an arrow struck the blade of the axe as I withdrew. The haft vibrated like a harpstring. I held on to it and struck at the next. By this time I was beginning to become a trifle warm.

The height of *Redfang* over the Shank waist meant they had to shoot upward from there. The archers in the ungainly square end castles were shooting down on me. This was not, I may say, a particularly comfortable position. I hit the next grapnel rope and she parted, and that cleared all along the beak. At the time I was doing that, others of *Redfang's* company were busily parting grapnels nearer to them.

And, just as I was about to congratulate myself on a job well done and to feel satisfaction that we'd denied the Shanks the chance of boarding us easily, I looked down over the enemy's waist.

As I looked down on that crowding mass of scaled helmets and scaled men, a rock swathed through them. It chopped down five of them and mangled them in spraying green ichor. At least one of the girls was still in action, and archers as well, as the shafts spat in. Down there on that alien deck they were screeching their chants, waving their tridents, desperately trying to stop us from pulling back.

"Ishtish! Ishtish!" they screeched, in their own tongue, fishy and hissing and nasty as it was.

Then, as I looked down on that scaly mass a Fish-head somersaulted away from a door that evidently closed off a companionway leading below. He sprawled on the deck. In the doorway stood a man—an apim. Naked, hairy, he glared madly upon the scene on deck, and then looked up. He stared directly at me.

"Help!" he yelled over all the din, a ferocious bellow. "Help!"

The Fish-heads heard him. Tridents menaced him and the other apims and diffs of familiar features of Paz who came trooping up from below. It took little deductive skill to deduce these men were slaves, maintained to pull the oars in the fluky winds off the coast. No doubt when the Shanks were finished here they'd hurl the apims and diffs of Paz overboard.

Chandarlie the Gut bellowed at my back.

"That's Quendur the Ripper! And I'll wager that's his foul pirate crew with him!"

"Leave 'em!" someone else shrilled. "Pull back!"

"For the sake of Opaz!" screamed Quendur the Ripper.

"Let the renders go hang!"

An arrow scorched past my ear.

Pompino spat his words out in the uproar. "What now, Jak?"

"Why, Pompino, we cannot leave a fellow human to these fishy horrors, can we?"

"Back!" Chandarlie was yelling, and I could imagine him waving his arms, his stomach aheave-ho.

"They are pirates, and would have done us no good had they taken us."

"Aye, you are right. But, by the Black Chunkrah, I would deny the worst fellow you could imagine to these Shanks."

With that I threw the axe at a tall Fish-head who looked important and knocked his head all sideways, and snatched out my thraxter, and leaped down onto the deck.

Pompino's despairing yell bounced after me: "Jak—you get onker!"

And then he was jumping with me and, as we had been before, we were in action shoulder to shoulder.

All a mad bedlam, a welter, a chaos, a leaping and skipping and slashing... We battled the Shanks on their own deck. Tridents against swords, the Fish-heads tried to bring us down. The rescued renders were not wholly helpless, for they had snatched up weapons in their escape. They began to bash their way from the companionway door toward us.

A little fellow with a droopy moustache and spaniel eyes screeched and flopped forward with a trident lodged in his back. He'd go no more a-roving across the wine-dark sea...

Our Rapa and Chulik comrades joined us, and we battled on. For a space it was touch and go; but the very audaciousness of the hairy filth, as the Shanks called us, leaping down into the attack confused them in their own onslaught. We had, as it were, thrown a spanner into the works, and now we had to extricate said spanners without loss. We could see no crossbows among the Shanks, and so they had none to span, but they'd know what a spanner was in this context—a fellow of Paz to be slain.

Fish-heads hissed and gibbered away around us, scales glistened. They wore ornamental branches of coral of various colors in their helmets. They carried spears and swords as well as tridents. They used heavily-curved bows. And they knew how to fight. By Krun, they knew how to fight.

We lost more men from the render crew before they could be hoisted up at our backs. The muscled body of the pirate chief, Quendur the Ripper, covered with the weals of the lash, pressed past. His face was a single black blot of anger. He held a trident and he stabbed and thrust and slashed with it as though a demon jerked his muscles.

"Fish-heads," he kept on saying, over and over. "Fish-heads. Fish-heads."

Saliva spittled his lips. He looked mad enough to be loaded with chains against himself.

"Get aboard, dom," I called across. "Sharpish."

He kept on alongside us, slashing his trident about, and croaking out: "Fish-heads. Fish-heads."

I put some snap into my voice. My words were interrupted twice by the need to knock a Shank over in the interim.

"Quendur! Get aboard the swordship! *Bratch!*"

He glared sideways at me. A trident hissed past and I grabbed it out of thin air, reversed it, hurled it back.

"You—!" he croaked.

"Get aboard." I did not repeat that harsh word of command, bratch, for he had the message. He turned and leaped for *Redfang*. I didn't know him. Maybe he knew me, or thought he did... Unlikely...

"Get going Rondas!" I bellowed it out. "Up with you, Nath Kemchug."

They were both still alive, which was miracle enough, although both wounded. Pompino was still untouched. We fought for long enough to get the mercenaries away and then it was the old duel between my fellow kregoinye and myself. I was not prepared to make an issue of it. To do so would get us both killed.

"Are you going, Pompino, you stiff-necked Khibil?"

"I am in command here, Jak, you pompous apim. Get aboard and leave the man's work to me."

"Fambly," I said, and leaped for *Redfang*. Before I hit the beak I was yelling for archers. Larghos the Flatch and his comrades laid down a carpet for Pompino, and I contributed as soon as I laid my hands on a bow, and the two girl varterists shooting superbly, swathed away the raging Shanks. Wilma's wound was barely bound, and leaked red blood. But the mercenaries of Kregen are not quite like your mercenaries of Earth. The outmoded concepts of honor and pride and service rendered for payment given are not outmoded on Kregen. Perhaps the nearest to that you'd get on Kregen would be the masichieri; bandits who call themselves paktuns, to their shame.

Pompino was hauled inboard. He was laughing. Well, let us not go too closely into the question of why he laughed.

And, on that instant, *Redfang* began to withdraw from the wound she had inflicted in the side of her foe. The Shank began to heel. As we drew off, she slowly turned over and sank.

Fifteen

Of a galleon, a rapier and honor

In an outward wash of foam-tinged green bubbles the Shank vanished.

Subsequently we carried out those necessary rites and services for our dead, consigning each to his or her own god or pantheon and releasing their bodies over the side.

Wilma recovered of her wound; many of our wounded did not. Captain Murkizon remained a most subdued man. Everyone felt sympathy for him. He had been right—of course he had been right!—yet such is the contrary nature of humankind that right though he was we felt that deep undercurrent that in this case being right was not the right course. Do not ask any explanation. I deplore racial hatred, as you know. I deplore slavery. In the dealings of the folk of Paz with the raiding sea rovers from over the curve of the world, Fish-heads called by many unpleasant names, rights and wrongs and instinctive feelings jumbled and became confused.

We put into the free port city of Matta, where they charged us exorbitant docking fees, the mercenary slit-eyed devils, and saw to our needs. The released oar slaves naturally wished to return home. We were sailing north. Those sailors contracted to Pompino would continue, and the mercenaries indicated they would remain hired to him. We could hire oarsmen, and they were not cheap, we could buy oarslaves, or we could see about a different vessel. The knot was cut by the timely arrival of what was left of our convoy. They straggled in over the space of three or four days, those that had survived, and among them to Pompino's gratitude, sailed *Tuscurs Maiden* and *Blackfang*.

He went up to the most imposing temple to Horato the Potent and registered his thanks. The priests reciprocated.

This free port city of Matta maintained a sizable fleet of swordships, and they swept their part of the seas clean of pirates. After the Koroles the seas were not so infested by renders; but wherever there are coasts and islands, no less than extensive trade routes, there will, it seems, be pirates.

"So, friend Jak. What next?"

"You ask me?"

"Aye. I saw the Gdoinye, as did you. But I am puzzled." Pompino's haughty Khibil face expressed concern, and by the way he brushed up his whiskers I knew he was troubled. "We are adventuring as it were on our own account. You and I, together, are setting about work for the Everoinye. Yet we must pay our own way, make our own passage, suffer all these delays. I ask you, Jak, is that right?"

"You should know that nothing is right, when you want it to be. Life is not fair."

"Oh, I know that, fambly!"

"It would probably be best to sail in *Tuscurs Maiden*."

"You think so? I confess, I am beginning to wonder if I was altogether wise to invest in a fleet of ships. They are a great worry to a man."

"Oh, aye, assuredly."

"But we saw the Gdoinye. He has a sister, the Gdoinya, who is, as I and Neil Tonge can testify, as great an onker. That must mean the Everoinye wish us to continue."

"Yes."

"I just wish—" And here Pompino sounded positively petulant. "I just wish they'd set us down where we are to set about our work for them!"

I almost laughed, for Pompino's expression and attitude were downright comical. But this was serious business. And that, as any sane man knows, is comical in this insane world, anyway.

"As they have not, we must make our own way. And, Pompino, my friend, think of the things we have done, to fight our way through the pirates of the Koroles, to have taken a swordship—to have saved our lives."

He sniffed. "You think these things constitute a Jikai?"

"Oh, no. Nothing as grand as that."

"To tell you the truth, Jak, I am not sorry to get out of a swordship. The noise of the oarslaves distresses me, the way they all rise up and then hurl themselves backwards, the clashing of their chains, their grunts of effort. I did not think it would be like that."

"You do not mention that sometimes they stink—"

"Not in my ships! I pay good gold for sweet ibroi—"

"You may disinfect their smell. You cannot disinfect the blot that slavery imposes on civilization by its very existence."

He stared at me, taken aback at my tone.

Then: "I share much of your philosophy, Jak—by the Pink Cheeks of Dandy Pullhard, I must do for we both serve the Everoinye!"

"Aye."

His words reminded me of the reaction of John Evelyn when in 1644 he went aboard a galley out of Marseilles. He was "amazed" at the "discomfort" of the galley slaves. He mentioned their rising and falling as one, the noise of the chains, the splashing crash of the "beaten waters" and how the slaves were "ruled and chastised without the least humanity." Yet, he said, for all this they were "Cherefull, and full of vile knavery."

The vile knavery my comrades and I had been up to, when we'd been galley slaves, had been, besides conjuring a better share of food and water and ponsho fleeces, dreaming up ways of escape.

With an intake of breath and a gusty sigh, Pompino said, "Very well.

We sail in *Tuscurs Maiden*. And I think Captain Murkizon will return in *Blackfang*. As for *Redfang*—"

"You could do worse than give her command to Naghan Pelamoin."

"My thought, exactly. Captain Linson has trained up a new Ship Hikdar to replace Pelamoin. But Chandarlie the Gut will sail with us."

We walked down through narrow streets to the jetties where Pompino's little squadron was moored. The air struck fresh and sweet, the suns shone. Now this free city of Matta was interesting to us—well, almost every city, not all, is interesting—by reason of one singular fact. The latest fashion craze here was for men to wear tightly restricting corsets. They were made from various bright materials, boned and laced, and worn over a tunic. The men strutted about with wasp waists. The women strode about uncorseted and free, swinging, lithe and limber. As I say, fashion is a tyranny best steered clear of.

A breeze curled in off the sea. We rounded the last warehouse corner and Pompino stopped. He shaded his eyes.

"Now *that*," he said, "is a *ship*. If I could buy the likes of her for my fleet, I would be a happier man."

I turned the corner. A Vallian galleon sailed into the port. Her flags flew bravely, the old Vallian flag, and the new, the new Union, with the yellow cross and saltire on the red ground.

"Yes," was all I could say. I felt myself responding to that ship from my adopted homeland. She sailed superbly, her canvas trim and taut, a curl of spume under her forefoot. We watched as she took in her canvas and noted the smartness of her evolutions. Later on I managed to make an excuse and left Pompino to see about stores while I had myself rowed out to the galleon. Her name was *Schydan Imperial*, out of Vond. I knew her master, Nath Periklain, and my first words hushed the welcome on his lips.

"Jak, majister?"

"Aye, Cap'n Nath. Jak. Now let us go below and you must tell me all the news of Vallia."

This he did when we were ensconced in his stateroom, with wine and palines upon the shining table. The array of stern windows let in the light. Everything was as smart and spick and span as was to be expected in a galleon of Vallia. These beautiful ships were being built again, and were now venturing on trading missions to places—such as here in Pandahem—where seasons ago they would have been regarded as enemies.

The news Nath Periklain conveyed reassured me. Vallia might still not yet encompass all her lost domains, but what we had prospered. Our enemies were contained. Time alone would see the whole of Vallia once more united. He had nothing to tell me of the Empress of Vallia, and while I grieved over this blankness in my life, I felt strengthened. If mischance occurred and there was ill news of Delia, I would hear. Also, and this I did not forget, the Wizards of Loh who were our comrades would apprise me should events take place that would necessitate my immediate return. I could breathe easier. By Zair! I'd not spend another moment adventuring out in these foreign lands if Delia or my own country needed me. And there is no pretension, no pride, in this, merely a sober matter-of-fact statement.

I took the opportunity of writing letters, many of them, for Nath Periklain to deliver when he returned to Vond.

"An argenter?" he said at one point. "But, majister—I mean, Jak—my ship is at your disposal."

"Thank you, Cap'n Nath. But you have your duty and your living. I have my own duties to perform." I sipped the wine, a splendid Gremivoh. "Our foes thrive in north Pandahem."

"May Opaz in his glory strengthen your arm, maj—Jak—as you strike them down!"

"I do have a request—"

"Name it!"

I did not smile; but these crusty old seadogs dearly love to display their adaptability, and their capacity to produce miracles. "All I would ask is a length of scarlet cloth."

He called in his steward and in no time a length of high-quality scarlet cloth was produced. I nodded, pleased.

"My thanks, Cap'n Nath."

"And is that all?" He nodded to my waist where the thraxter hung. "A rapier and main gauche?"

"We-ell..." I was tempted.

They were brought in by the steward, a matching pair in a balass box. They were fine work, balanced, sprung, elegantly finished. My resistance crumbled.

"A gift, majister, a token of esteem."

To refuse would have insulted him. So with a single guilty twinge, I strapped them on. They felt good.

"More wine?"

So we talked and drank companionably and the suns descended across the land and the lamps were lit. Presently I rose.

"It is time for me to go, Cap'n Nath. I give you my thanks for your hospitality and your gifts. I shall not forget."

"And you are for Tomboram? Bormark? I have been there but once. The folk do not much care for Vallians."

"Unfortunately, that is so. But do you not think that after we helped eject the Hamalese they will look more kindly upon us?"

"By Vox! They should!"

"Well, that I shall soon find out. Rembaree, Cap'n Nath."

"Remberee, majist—Jak!"

He'd told me a little of his history, for he was known as a captain among the Captains of Vallia. His eldest son, having gone for a mercenary, had been lost to all knowledge until the Times of Troubles. Then he'd returned to take up sword in defense of his own country. He was now, this strapping son of his, said Nath Periklain, a shiv-Hikdar in the 2EYJ—the Second Regiment of the Emperor's Yellow Jackets.

"A rapscallion bunch," I said. "And with the ESW the best fighting fellows an emperor could have around him."

Examination of the rapier revealed the neatly incised mark of the Brudstern, that magical flower shape, on the forte close to the guard. Magical or not, many a fighting man of Kregen will not handle a weapon that does not bear some such mark to draw mysterious forces into the blade.

"By the Blade of Kurin!" exclaimed Pompino when he saw the matched set of the rapier and left-hand dagger, the Jiktar and the Hikdar. "A fine weapon, indeed, and the dagger also."

We had talked of the fashion—new to these parts—of rapier fighting, and Pompino was aware that up north the fashion had been well-established over the seasons. "All the same, I doubt these rapiers in the midst of a battle."

"Sometimes," I said. "It depends on the battle and what your opponents are using and doing. A rapier can be extremely useful. But, of course," I added with some judiciousness, "it is always a sound principle to carry a second battle sword."

"Oh, aye."

My suggestion that I'd picked up the matched set from a sailor down on the docks who had no real idea of the true worth passed muster. Pompino merely indicated that, if it pleased me, he would like to foin a little and see how this rapier went compared to others.

We only got into two fights during that short stay in Matta, and they were scrapes, hardly worth the mentioning save for the fact that in the second Pompino used the rapier and main gauche. Afterwards, as we strolled along in the moons light with the scent of Moon Blooms in our nostrils, he confided: "A handy weapon, if a trifle long. I think I may take it up, for I have seen, and you have told me—"

"Sometimes a rapier is perfect, sometimes it is a fool's weapon. Just be prepared for all eventualities."

"We sail with the tide on the morrow. So?"

"So a further wet would seem to be in order."

"By the pot belly of Beng Dikkane, you speak sooth."

We found a tavern smothered in Moon Blooms, the sign cracked but still with enough paint to tell us this was The Spotted Llancrimoil. In we went. The ale was good and the wine a trifle better, all imported and not cheap.

We sat back and stuck our feet out and surveyed the company. These folk were mainly seamen, a few merchants and the sprinkling of rogues.

Captain Murkizon found us there.

He had been drinking. His red face looked like the monstrous countenance of Zim witnessed through a sandstorm. He blurted out the words he had evidently been storing up in his heart.

"Horters! I am being sent back in *Blackfang* in disgrace! I hew to my own convictions. If events prove me wrong, that does not dishonor me! Horter Pompino! I crave your forbearance."

I remained very quiet, pushed back in my seat against the paneled wall. No one took any notice of us, and a fight was developing further along where a thief had been caught with the coins between his fingers.

Speaking quite mildly for him, Pompino said: "We sail with Captain Linson in *Tuscurs Maiden*, as you know."

"Very well! Let me sail in her. I will serve as Ship Hikdar, Ship Deldar—I will hand and reef and steer!'"

"Captain Linson—"

"Oh, I know!" Murkizon vented his bitterness. "He dislikes me. He considers me a loud-mouthed buffoon. But I know what I know. Let me sail with you, Horter Pompino. You will not regret the decision."

Pompino hesitated and cast a look in my direction. I leaned forward. "It is a matter of honor," I said, and sat back.

"This means, Cap'n Murkizon, that Larghos Standur, who was Ship Hikdar in *Blackfang* and has been acting Captain, must now be confirmed in that rank. You understand that?"

"I understand, Horter Pompino. I agree!"

So the deal was concluded. Murkizon would sail with us. Pompino exhibited his customary Khibil skill and avoided any argy-bargy overposition by taking Murkizon on as supernumerary.

During this whole interview, Captain Murkizon had not once called upon any part of the anatomy of the Divine Lady of Belschutz.

Sixteen

Of the recantation of Quendur the Ripper

One Kregish word for coward is Jikarna. This is a compression of the universal word Jik for martial matters, and arna, which means the absence of. Captain Murkizon by his manner clearly realized and feared that the imputation that he was jikarna would be made against him. I, for one, and Pompino for two, knew he was no coward. He had been right. But he was in that truculent, bellicose mood in which he might do anything foolish and reckless to redeem himself in his own eyes.

"I shall go with you, Horter Pompino, and you may rest assured that—"

"Queyd-arn-tung," said Pompino, and the brick-red-faced barrel of muscle had the sense to know when enough had been said and to shut his black-fanged winespout.

So *Tuscurs Maiden* joined a local convoy and sailed north.

Having formed an opinion of Captain Linson I was not at all surprised that however sharp-tongued he was, however cutting, and however amused at Murkizon's expense, he did not make any capital out of Murkizon's clear inner turmoil. Linson, like us all, respected the red-faced barrel of a swordship captain and understood the reasons for his conduct vis-à-vis the Shanks. He and Larghos the Flatch spent a deal of time in each other's company. The argenter sailed on and with various ports of call astern of us we rounded the northeastern corner of Pandahem. We sailed along the coast of Jholaix.

Ah, Jholaix! No need to elaborate on the thirsty comments made by the hands as we watched the land draw near, and headed the moment we made port for the nearest tavern. Jholaix!

Here it was that we had put a first check to the crazy ambitions of the Empress Thyllis of Hamal. She'd started up her insane schemes again, of course, with the help of the Wizard of Loh Phu-si-Yantong, whom she knew as the Hyr Notor. Well, both of them were dead and gone to the Ice Floes of Sicce. There was the uhu, the hermaphrodite, Phunik, to concern the future. We had not heard the last of her, him or it.

Because even in the lowest taverns of Jholaix the wines were superior—except for the dopa dens, of course—the hands might reel back to the ship yodeling their hearts out yet never have a black-dog the next morning. Hangovers were bad for trade, said the folk of Jholaix.

Due north of where we now sailed lay the island of Valka.

A mere miserable thousand miles or so away—Valka! No, I would not think of my paradise island stromnate, and always I thought of that jewel island, of the high fortress of Esser Rarioch, of the gardens and calmness and the joyousness, the laughter of my friends and family. No. Those days would come again, they must, in the belief of the light of the Invisible Twins made manifest in the glory of Opaz.

"Dreaming, Jak?"

And, sunk in thoughts, at first I did not recognize my chosen name, and so turn to smile at Pompino.

"Dreams? Aye, Pompino."

"Well, you are lucky you have no wife to get away from."

I turned away, sharply, and concealed the expression on my face.

But willy-nilly, the days passed. We passed the border between Jholaix and Tomboram, and the port city and capital of Pomdermam lay ahead. We had been shuffling along in convoy and doing the usual business of tramp ships, picking up cargo here and discharging it there, hiring our carrying capacity and earning a living. For Pompino and me, this chartering was mere cover to our deeper designs.

For Captain Murkizon, this chartering and carrying and chaffering—not to mention chattering—seemed an affront, a mere matter of base business to a swordship captain.

For Captain Linson, master, this was how he made his living, and he was sharp at it. For every copper ob that was recorded in the accounts meticulously kept by the Relt stylor Rasnoli and which would, after necessary deductions, arrive in Pompino's coffers, perhaps as much as a quarter ob reposed with Captain Linson. This was not to do him an injustice. He, like any sensible skipper, looked out for an early retirement.

Expressed in latter-day terms, twenty percent was a fair rake-off.

Pompino was as well aware of this habit as any other shipping owner. He closed that eye. He had to. So we sailed on westwards. The northern coast of Pandahem had been a fairy-tale place to the reivers from Vallia. In the old days the galleons and swordships prowled these coasts, snapping up prizes, and the enmity smoldered between the two islands, to break into flames of violence and hatred when interests clashed.

At the least, the ambitions of Hamal and their frustration had brought a cessation to most of the hostility between Pandahem and Vallia. I say most. Men and women do not change their ways overnight, in normal life, very easily.

Westward lay the country of Menaham, and its people, the Bloody Menahem. They posed problems for the future. They had welcomed the arrival of Hamal, had cooperated, had sought to conquer and enslave their neighbors. Their next-door neighbor to the west, Iyam, had suffered. Beyond them, in the northwest corner of the island, lay Lome. Now there reposed a puzzle for me personally.

Queen Lushfymi of Lome, known as Queen Lush, had sought our aid and protection in Vallia after she had managed to throw off the yoke of Phu-si-Yantong. She was quite clearly determined to marry my son Drak. Delia did not approve. We would like Drak to marry Seg's daughter, Silda. Well, the future held some thorny projections there, assuredly...

At the moment my attention must concentrate on trying to rid Pando's kovnate of Bormark of the vile Leem Lovers of Lem. If the cult was widespread in Pandahem, then that would be a beginning of a clearance. And you may well and easily guess at some of my dark thoughts and apprehensions. Pando, whom I had known as a young imp, might so easily have been swayed, turned, drawn into practices that in other circumstances he would have spurned. If Tilda the Beautiful was drinking as heavily as rumor suggested, Pando would receive no support from his mother.

Captain Linson was anxious to get into Pomdermam, the capital and chief port city of Tomboram. *Tuscurs Maiden* was in need of an overhaul. She had sailed a goodly distance and her bottom, although not as foul as would have been the case on Earth, was still in need of cleaning. Pompino pulled his moustache and frowned at the news.

"Does that mean there will be a delay, Captain?"

"A careen will take time, horter."

"I see."

I wondered if Pompino did see. Shipping magnates tend to move the colored markers on their maps and expect their ships magically to move from spot to spot about the globe. Mere fiddly details like fresh rigging and clean wood and careening to scrub the bottom somehow often fail to become integrated into the calculations.

"We can take passage in a coaster to Bormark," I suggested.

"Four days, perhaps," said Linson. "To take off the worst."

Difficult to judge. That, to me, indicated a reasonably thorough job, given the area of the ship's bottom. I kept my mouth shut.

Most of the pirates we had rescued from the Shanks had disappeared in the port of Matta. But Quendur the Ripper and three of his fellows had elected to join us. Their swordship had been burned. They had nothing else. Captain Linson, in his acid way, had sniffed and acquiesced, and appointed Nath Kemchug among others to keep a damned sharp eye on the renders. During a long life on Kregen a man or woman might do many things between birth and the Ice Floes of Sicce—hoping as ever to advance to the sunny uplands beyond. Quendur had once been an honest sailorman, and he fitted in, having been severely shaken by his experiences with the Shanks.

Now he stepped forward on the deck to speak.

"Four days, horters. It is not long. And a coaster is subject to many perils here."

"You would know, indubitably, by Horato the Potent!"

"Aye, horter."

The odd fact about Quendur, known as the Ripper, was his continuing perplexity in the face of life. One took the impression that life had rushed on him, taken him unawares, driven him into deeds and adventures that were as much a surprise to him as a challenge. He'd explained how he'd become a render, a familiar story of unjust oppression and the lash, of chains and starvation, and of a breaking out and a lusting after revenge.

He conceived he owed Pompino and me, as well as the company, a debt of gratitude. Well, he did, after a fashion. That we had not had him strung up in Matta was no doubt a weakness on our part. But he proved himself a good fellow, once he'd got the dark bitterness out of him. The bloodlust died after his experiences with the Shanks. Only the bloodlust against the Leem Lovers remained.

Salvation does exist.

A great shock, a traumatic experience, the realization that one has thrust one foot over the abyss, this can haul a person up short. It makes them look afresh at the situation, makes them take stock. Salvation? Well, in Quendur the Ripper's case he forswore his old ways, vowed with a sincerity we took as genuine to hew to the ways of honest commerce upon the high seas and among the islands. He was transformed.

The three who elected to stay with him, two men and the woman, Lisa the Empoin, appeared to share his views. Lisa, in particular, clearly relished this fresh chance at life as an honest woman. And, make no mistake about it, they were useful about the ship and excellent seafarers.

Lisa and Quendur made plans to earn enough to buy an old ship and so go into the merchanting trade themselves. I fancied they would receive substantial, if surreptitious, help.

So we drew near the port of Pomdermam. One of the two lighthouses lay in ruins. The pharos had the appearance of having been struck by lightning. This was not the pharos built and operated by the Todalpheme, the wise savants who monitor the weather and the tides; but the one owned by the king. Its ruins depressed me as we glided past.

Was this an omen, a reminder of what had happened in Tomboram, a portent of a future dark and ominous?

Pompino's own view of his achievements here I knew would be harsh to himself, strict in his ruthless disparagement of any performance less than perfect. He had had a temple burned and scattered the worshippers. He'd told me enough for me to grasp at what he had achieved, and, also, at what was left to do. Down in Tuscursmot the adherents of the Silver Leem were in confusion; up here they still needed attention.

How many more were there? How many others of the abominable temples were there scattered about Pandahem, about the other lands of Paz? Now that I believed the Star Lords had turned their faces against the Silver Wonder, it seemed to me I stood a good chance of finding out, a damn good chance, by Krun!

"Brassud, Jak! Brace up! You look as though you've lost a zorca and found a calsany!"

"Finding the calsany," I said in a voice far too heavy, "would be a triumph."

"Oh!" Pompino put his crafty Khibil head on one side, very foxy, very bristly red, very shrewd. Ahead of us the dock area of the port opened out. "Oh? You're a close-mouthed fellow, all right, full of secrets. So you won't tell me—"

"If there was anything substantial to tell, I'd tell."

"Just a feeling, is it? A deliquescence of the bowels?"

"A hollow insides, Pompino, hollow."

"A breath of the Ice Floes has touched you, my friend." Pompino spoke briskly, perking up, his whiskers arrogant. "You need a long draught and a laugh—although a laugh would, I think, crack your face to pieces."

He was right, of course. On Earth we say that someone has walked over our grave; on Kregen they refer to an icy breath from Sicce. I shook my shoulders, saw that we'd take a bur or two to get in, and went below with my kregoinye comrade. We downed a few glasses; but they made no difference. I was awash with reluctance to carry on, to see Pando and Tilda again, to fight the Silver Leem, to carry out the wishes of the Star Lords. I had to do these things. But I felt I would do them unwillingly.

Yet I would like to see Pando and Tilda again and hear their news and find out how they fared. I hungered to see Lem the Silver Leem and his evil cult banished for good. And I was achieving a better understanding of the Everoinye with every meeting. So—why?

Ridiculous to suggest I felt this unease because I was going into the future without a plan and with no idea of what I was up against. By Vox! That is my usual situation!

Yet—yet that is not quite true. I do have plans, quietly tucked up my sleeve. I eyed Pompino.

"If we just burn the first temple we run across—"

"We will burn the first and the last, Jak!"

"Oh, aye. We can do that. By ourselves or with help. But—what then?"

"Why, then we go home."

"Yes, but, if the temple burns, the beliefs will linger on. They'll rebuild—"

He drank and poured fresh and did not answer.

I went on: "We can hardly kill them all."

"This King Nemo the Second. I hear he is a flat slug. If we can sway him, make him see with clear eyes, he will see to all that end of the business for us."

"If."

"Well—" and here Pompino spoke with some brusqueness. "Have you some better scheme?"

"No."

"Drink up! We will find the temple and burn it and then see what the Leem Lovers do."

Privately, I wondered just how far this haughty Khibil comrade of mine would get with fat King Nemo the Second.

Tuscurs Maiden duly picked up her moorings, and discharged her cargo, and then the master and the hands set about the task of cleaning her bottom. A small creek an ulm along the coast provided a nicely sloping beach, and there were careening lines and stakes provided. Pompino did not hire slaves for any of the work, whereat a few dark looks drifted about the ship. I hung about taking a note of what went forward, a professional interest not blunted over the years giving me an insight. Pompino just imagined you simply tilted the boat over and scraped away.

"There is more to it than that."

"Well, I am for the races. Some fool is backing his sleeths against zorcas—"

"Then he'll lose his money."

"Assuredly. Quendur the Ripper is going along, for he has business—I did not ask. So is his woman. They have been given leave. You're coming, of course—"

"Perhaps."

But, in the end, I went along with them to see the races in Pomder-mam's merezo, the race track carved out of the side of a hill. The view was splendid from the terraces. As was duly surmised, the idiot's sleeths lost to the zorcas. Well, I ask you, in this day and age, to find anyone who still thought a sleeth could outrun a zorca!

Then we hied ourselves off to the town to find a wet.

On the shady side of a small tree-bowered square a tavern swung a sign proclaiming it to be The Trident and Crown. An interesting name, although I took scant notice of it at the time. Just as we were about to enter, Pompino's eye was caught by the shop abutting. A smaller sign said that this was the time of opening. Pompino looked and walked across. Above his head on bronze brackets a down-at-heels signboard creaked as though ready to fall apart. The paint flaked everywhere, and the boards warped. Originally the sign had read NALGRE THE EDGE. At some time past, judging by the fractionally brighter paint, the word EDGE had been obliterated and the word POINT substituted.

Rapier and dagger work were well established here in North Pandahem.

"I left here somewhat hurriedly," commented Pompino, pushing open the door. "I've a mind to buy myself a good matching pair, similar to those you swindled that poor sailorman out of."

I hung my head, and we went into the swordsmiths.

When we emerged into the suns light Pompino swung a goodly rapier on his left hip and a matching main gauche on his right. I gave him a wide berth.

"You'll do me an injury with those things," I said. "After you've done one to yourself, of course."

"I've handled these pig-stickers before—"

"Oh, aye."

In the Trident and Crown we found a quiet corner by a window and ordered up ale. This was not particularly fine ale, and Pompino made a face. He leaned back, and then came out with what had been on his mind, among other things. "Anyway, that rascal Quendur, oh, yes, he may have repented of his evil ways. But he spoke up against going on by coaster just so he could see about his business here."

"I don't doubt it. He is a reformed character; but he is still as cunning as a leem." I sipped. "What was the business, do you know?"

"I've no idea." Pompino leaned forward to the window. "But there he goes now, with his woman. He looks hangdog enough. Let's ask him."

Pompino shoved open the window and called. Quendur looked up as though stuck in the rump by Pompino's new rapier. He saw us in the window of the tavern. He smiled, took Lisa's arm, and hurried across. When he sat down at our table with Lisa, he and she both looked bright of face, flushed, and they breathed rapidly.

When the serving girl brought ale, Quendur drank the lot off in one go. He rubbed his right hand reflectively. Lisa smiled.

"Business all settled?"

"Aye, horter Pompino. Settled and settled well."

"That's good, then."

"Aye. And bad for some." And Quendur laughed.

A brightness about him kept breaking through that hangdog look. He bubbled with some inner excitement, as though still high on adrenalin, as though he'd just pulled off a deed to remember. Lisa hung on his arm.

Not too long after that a carrying chair borne by four Brukaj diffs with patient bulldog faces and liveries of blue and white halted outside the Trident and Crown. The curtains were half-drawn. A Rapa stuck his beaked nose toward the tavern door, twirling a thick stick. Two more Rapas, following on, halted. One immediately turned back and ran off. I watched this byplay in the drowsy square with faint interest, trying to summon up some enjoyment from the thin beer and making up my mind to take off and find a better eating establishment.

The lead Rapa turned to the curtained chair and spoke to the occupant. The Brukaj chair-carriers squatted down, resting. The square rested, too, in the declining suns.

Presently a double file of soldiers marched up, wearing the king's livery, as I recalled. They were led by a Hikdar, who strutted on in a way at once important and grotesque. The men halted by the palanquin and the Rapa spoke to the Hikdar.

Just about then, I suppose, the old itch breezed. I should have suspected mischief sooner. But the air here breathed sweetly, conducive to ease. Guards could be lowered, it had appeared. On Kregen—most parts of Kregen—that is a mistake.

I stood up.

"What, Jak—?"

"Quendur—was your business of—?"

Before I finished he leaned past me to look out the window. His face drew down. The woman put a hand on his arm.

"That is the rast!" he said. "I gave him a good hiding and the impudent cramph returns for more! Well, I can accommodate him!" With that, Quendur leaped up and fairly hurled himself through the open doorway. He roared straight at the carrying chair, screeching his fury and hatred...

Seventeen

Cash for Lash?

It was all our own fault. Well, it was really Pompino's fault. That fiery Khibil turned into a real tearaway when he sensed his honor was imputed. But, then, no. No. Really it was my fault. As usual. I ought to have tripped Pompino up as he roared out of the tavern after Quendur while we sized up the situation.

As it was—here we were.

In chains.

No novelty for me, for that intemperate Dray Prescot who ran headlong and foolishly into danger. But for Pompino the harsh iron chains galled with much more than mere physical restraint. His honor was affronted. He felt degraded.

The occupant of the carrying chair, one Pamcur Ovin, a notable merchant and slave dealer, had been the business Quendur had occupied himself with. Pamcur Ovin had received a thorough thrashing. Now he brought up the king's guards, the law and order here, and sought revenge.

When the guards restrained Quendur, we might perhaps have made a case for ourselves and argued it all out. But when they callously beat Lisa and knocked her to the ground, Pompino's hot Khibil blood sent him passionately to her assistance. So I'd been drawn in. And the iron nets and the chains had risen and fallen, and here we were, bound by chains and lying in a stinking dungeon cell awaiting punishment.

Quendur attempted to apologize; but Pompino, his whiskers electric with fury, would have none of that.

"Had I known, Quendur, I'd have been more forceful with them! You are not to blame. When I see this King Nemo I'll let him have a piece of my mind. Aye, by all the devils of Armipand!"

"This Pamcur Ovin is the rast who ruined my family and had me sold into slavery." Quendur's savage face bore the marks of bruises. The single torch outside the cell fluttered dark shadows across his eyes. "But I think the law will not bring you to that, horters."

"They've put me in chains," said Pompino, with a wealth of evil meaning in his words.

"Yes; but that is because you resisted, and you too, Horter Jak. I will be sold again; you may receive only a flogging and a fine—"

"Only!"

"It will be painful."

"Wait until I get my hands on that cramph Ovin!"

"That is what I swore."

I said, "What are our chances of escape?"

His mouth twisted. "Precious few."

"Still, there must be a way."

Lisa, hanging in her chains as we were, said, "I will offer to—"

"No," said Quendur.

Pompino and I, sensibly, said nothing on that score.

Our jailer brought in pannikins of water and rinds of dry bread and moldy cheese. His name was Trai Naghan. The atra swinging on its chain about his neck was large and ornate. This amulet afforded him great comfort. He was in body long and thin and wiry. There was, really, only half a body there, for his left ear, eye and arm were missing, and he limped favoring his left leg. He'd been chewed up by a leem in youth, and had escaped with his life. Trai is one Kregish word for luck, so that he was called Lucky Naghan.

"They're putting up the flogging frames now," he said in a cheerful voice. "They've a left-handed Brokelsh and a right-handed Rapa."

So we were to be flogged jikaider, until the lashes crisscrossed over our backs and diced our flesh to the bone.

"And the woman?" Pompino said.

"Maybe. She kicked the Hikdar of the guard where it did him no good." Trai Naghan spat reflectively. "I wish I'd been there to see that."

We drank the stale water and ate the hard bread and green cheese. It kept us alive. They were in no hurry to deal with us, and we heard from Trai Naghan that they awaited a great lord to oversee the proceedings. This made no sense to us, and so we hung and suffered others' pleasure.

"Of course," he told us in his chirpy cheerful way, "If you cannot pay the fines, they will not flog you so hard."

Quendur emitted a nasty-sounding snort of disgust.

Pompino lifted his head. "Oh. Why?"

"Why, dom, they won't want to damage the merchandise."

That was explanation enough. If we couldn't pay the fines, the authorities would chastise us in some unpleasant but not too-damaging a way—and then they'd sell us as slaves.

We had to pay to be flogged, and to be thankful we could afford that punishment.

A nightmare quality of incongruousness in our situation afflicted me either with a sense that this could not really be happening or that it was a typical Dray Prescot imbroglio. Here we were, storming up to Tomboram to put down the followers of the Silver Wonder, and finding ourselves smartly locked up in chains awaiting chastisement for a stupid brawl. It was enough to make a fellow spit granite chippings.

The torch sputtered and banged and smoked and dimmed. Quendur let out a groaning laugh in his best sound-effects way.

"Even our light is to be taken from us."

Kregans grow up accustomed always to objects having two shadows, the word for shadow is singular but refers to the two—one reddish, the other greenish—cast by the suns. In a surprisingly large number of countries the folk are psychologically disturbed if there is only one light. One torch, one candle, is a catastrophe not to be borne. I have seen a family cut a rushlight in half, shaking, to light both ends and reinstate normalcy in the world of their home. The Great Death and the Great Birth of the Overlords of Magdag, when they cower away in their newly built and dedicated megaliths, is occasioned perhaps as much by the eclipse of the suns' effect in throwing just one shadow, as by their dread belief that the red sun swallows up the green. I'd seen the horrors then, and had escaped, somehow. I recalled that I, Dray Prescot, was a Krozair of Zy. I'd broken free then. Was I any less a man now that I'd done so much on Kregen and gone through so many ordeals, and discovered such happiness with Delia?

Was I less of a man than that foolish, headstrong Dray Prescot who bashed so intemperately against anything and anyone who sought to do him a mischief?

The feeling of self doubt was—at first—heightened by what then passed between Quendur and Lisa. This fear of a single light source and a single shadow, so odd to terrestrials accustomed to having just one little yellow sun in their sky, is not explicable by geography, nation or race. Some people experience the fear; others do not. Those who do make a point of staying safely indoors with two lamps burning when there is only one moon in Kregen's night sky.

Now Quendur said: "Lisa. They must kill me before any harm comes to you."

Even as I wondered if that could be any comfort to Lisa the Empoin, she turned her head to stare at Quendur. His eyes were fast shut.

"Quendur," she said. "We will survive, as we have before and will again. You will see, mishme, I promise you."

When she called her man mishme a host of memories rushed to torture me. It seems to me that in reporting on the languages of Kregen I have leaned heavily toward insult and harsh command, of the harder and uglier aspects of that beautiful tongue. Maybe this is a mere result of many of my experiences there. The languages are filled to overflowing with words of love. Expressions of respect, affection, comradeship, admiration, fill page after page of the dictionaries, the hyr-lifs of the spoken and written word. If I neglect them, often substituting terrestrial terminology, that may perhaps be because tenderness comes to me only from a few, a very few people. Mishme. What does that word mean? My love, my heart, dear one—all these and nothing of sickly sentiment about the meanings, either. Kregans—or most of them—are robust when it comes to talk of love.

So I thought of Delia, and hungered, and felt lost, and so grew a fresh resolve that was almost shattered as Pompino burst out with all his fiery Khibil passion:

"Pay good broad red gold pieces to be flogged! That is a strange custom! Do they think I'll pay to have my back striped?"

"If you do not," said Quendur, still with his eyes closed, "then, Horter Pompino, they will sell you as slave."

"And so they shall!" bellowed my comrade. "I'll be a slave and slit the throats of the guards and disembowel the damned slavemasters and slaveowners, and all that before I escape!" He swung his reddish whiskers at me. "Are you with me, Jak?"

"Oh, aye," I said in a desert-dry voice. "Oh, aye. I've been slave and escaped. But think on this, Pompino the Rash. Here in Tomboram the king will send you to the swordships, if he wills. You have seen the oarslaves—"

Pompino blinked his eyes, twice, very rapidly. Then: "Oarslaves! Oarslaves! If I set my mind to escaping no miserable whip-deldar will stand in my way! I tell you this when by our comradeship there should be no need."

"There is no need. As you very well know. But—"

Quendur interrupted, in a hoarse breathy voice.

"Think on, Horter Pompino! A flogging is one thing, but to serve in the swordships at the looms..."

"Oh," I snapped out, somewhat tartly. "Oh, he'll survive, Quendur, he'll survive."

Pompino bristled up his whiskers and looked murderous.

Lisa spoke in her turn, hushed but tart with it. "As San Blarnoi says: 'Blowing the frothy head off is one thing.'"

Quendur let out his gurgling groaning laugh and Pompino sniffed with audible affront. I did not laugh. By Zair! This was no situation in which to break down. There were things we could do, one of which was to pray, which we did fervently; the other was to work on our chains, which we abandoned very quickly. Apart from that we could only think and talk.

Each country of Kregen has its own peculiar little ways, in large things as in small. Customs strike across geographical boundaries irrespective of creed or race. As in this devilish business of flogging. Ol' Snake appears in many hideous guises. The Cat's claws are variously unsheathed. Over in the Flower Country in Balintol they pronounce ferocious sentences larded with intimidatory inventories of thousands of lashes. The victim is stripped and tied up. The whip-deldars use what they call the lintash or the tashlin depending on who wields the instrument. This lash consists of a bunch of full-petalled flowers of many varieties. When the victim is struck the petals caress his body. Each petal is counted as one stroke. The velvety flowers do not break the skin, do not sting, do no physical harm whatsoever. But the victim is shamed and chagrined, scored by mental blows far more savage than any lacerations of the skin. The Flower Country of Balintol is a peace-loving, gentle land, with its own concepts of integrity.

Here, in North Pandahem, we were to be flogged jikaider, criss-cross like a chequer-board, and we'd be lumps of raw sausage meat at the end.

The lord who was to oversee our flogging turned up and we were dragged out into a courtyard where the stone walls overhung in menace and the suns did not shine. The flogging frames awaited their human freight. There were many guards.

We were tied to the flogging frames, mother naked.

The lord appeared. Well, he was a notor of Tomboram. His black beard was trimmed short, and pebbled sweat drops studded its edges against his skin. He looked just a man, an apim, handsome in a cruel way, sharp of feature, haughty of demeanor, sumptuously clad. Something about him reminded me of Pando, a mature version of the Pando I had last seen as a bedraggled young man dragged from under the feet of calsanys.

This was the way Pando would look in these latter days...

Pinned to the front of the lord's ornate robes a small silver device glinted. I looked closer, squinting. A silver leem, a small imago of a silver leem, and with brown and silver ribbons...

Well, now...

Clearly, he was there in his official capacity as overseer of the king's justice. In this, Tomboram aped the ways of law-ridden Hamal.

The Rapa and the Brokelsh, wearing black breechclouts and stripped to the waist, rippled their lashes. Big, burly men, powerfully muscled, they took up their positions one a side to strike alternately. I looked at the lord, magnificent in his plumage and gold lace, and wearing that silver leem with the brown and silver ribbons. Just an ornament? I did not think so.

I turned my head a little and spoke to him gently, putting meaning into my words.

"By Flem! This is a poor pass. The rast Pamcur Ovin spoke against the Silver Wonder. He was justly chastised, by Glem—"

The great lord allowed a single ripple of surprise to disfigure his face. He did not look at me. He lifted a beringed hand.

"*Shindi!*"" He pointed at the whip-deldars and the guards. "Retire. I will interrogate the prisoners. Move!"

The guards and the two floggers stiffened up. With habitual unthinking obedience to a great lord's commands they obeyed instantly and trotted off. The lord turned a hard eye on me.

He used a formula I had heard in the temple in Ruathytu. I was able to give the correct reply. He said: "You are not of Tomboram?"

"No, notor. From Hyrklana and about the business of the Silver Wonder. I am honored to meet you. Llahal and Llahal, my name is Jak." If lying would prevent my back being bashed into mincemeat I'd lie like a trooper.

"Llahal. I am Murgon Marsilus, Strom of Ribenor, Pallan of Prisons."

"Ah!" I said, with a wise air and foolishly. This did explain a great many items. It did not, for the moment, get us down off the flogging frames.

"In Hyrklana the man I wish to see is called the Hyr Prince Majister—"

"As here."

"Good, notor. Apart from fraternal greetings there is a message I carry—"

"Tell me."

"Well, notor—"

He gestured in an irritated way. "You are in Pandahem. You call me pantor, not notor."

"Yes, pantor. But if you are not the Hyr Prince Majister then you will appreciate my difficulty."

He may have been hard, a trifle vicious in his overweening authority; he was not a fool. He saw the situation.

"Agreed."

I said, "You will see, pantor, that we are in a somewhat unfortunate predicament here through no fault of our own."

He did not turn his head. He simply called out: "Lart!"

A Relt came running in, ink-stained, fluffy of feathers.

"Yes, master."

"The punishment has been carried out. So enter it in the records. Dismiss the guards and the whip-deldars. Bratch!"

The Relt stylor bratched, and this Murgon Marsilus took out his dagger and cut us free. Pompino would have jumped on him there and then. Luckily for Murgon Marsilus, he cut me down first because I was nearest, and so I was able to trip Pompino up and tip him onto his Khibil nose.

"He is wracked by cramp, pantor," I said, swiftly, and took a good grip on Pompino's shoulder and so held him.

"Traitor!" he said with an evil look.

---

* Shindi: wait.

"Keep your black-fanged winespout shut, you fambly! We are in with a racing chance here."

Marsilus cut down Quendur last. Quendur and Lisa were well up with my scheme, empty-headed though it might be. We chafed our wrists and ankles. Lisa made no attempt to cover her nakedness; anyway, it would have been ridiculous after what we had been through. Marsilus marched us off through a tunnel doorway and into a square stone-walled room empty of everything save a table. On the table stood a jug of parclear. We drank—thirstily, damned thirstily, by Krun!

"You will have to pay the fines," said Marsilus.

Pompino started to bristle up again at this; but I managed to stick an elbow into his ribs and he whoofled for a space. I sighed. "My comrade is still feeling the effects, pantor." Holding down Pompino was like trying to stop a starving cat from a bowl of meat and milk.

"If you cannot pay—"

"We can pay, pantor."

"Then that is settled."

I did not think, then, what he was going on to say.

Our clothes were brought in by a small fellow, an apim, with a loose, wet-lipped mouth, whom Strom Murgon treated as a part of the furnishings. He was called Dopitka the Deft. With him came a hulking great Chulik wearing armor and weapons, breathing hard, his trunk a barrel of muscle, his tusks gilded and polished, his pigtail a dangling length of brilliant blue. His name was Chekumte the Fist, and he looked it, too.

"You may strap on your weapons," said Strom Murgon. "These men are to be trusted, seeing they owe their livelihood to me. We shall go up to the temple and I will make the arrangements." He looked around on us, brilliant and commanding. "And walk small. I risk much by my actions here."

"They will not go unrewarded, pantor," I ventured to say. I ventured successfully, for he nodded briskly and marched us out of the door. We entered another courtyard where a closed carriage waited. The driver sat in a blue cloak, hunched, his whip over his shoulder. We entered the carriage and Dopitka the Deft closed the door.

Just as Marsilus sat down opposite me, I glanced out of the window. A man passed across the courtyard, walking fast, short cape billowing. He was dressed grandly, more grandly than Strom Murgon. The strom's face drew down into a black scowl.

"A friend of yours, pantor?" said Pompino, before I could kick him.

Murgon Marsilus, Strom of Ribenor, Pallan of Prisons, did not react as I expected. He continued to stare from the carriage as the man crossing the courtyard swung away and vanished in the arched entranceway.

"Friend? He is my cousin, Pando Marsilus, Kov of Bormark, and I shall surely kill him if he does not kill me first."

Eighteen

"Dray Prescot! Let me go and I will surely kill you!"

Strom Murgon opened the door and jumped out. He bellowed up to the coachman: "Shindi!" and went loping into the entranceway after Pando.

Pompino looked at me. His look would have curdled steel at a hundred paces.

I said, "At least your back is not diced up."

"You degrade my honor, Jak! Why, I would have—"

"Quiet. Coachmen have ears as well as whips."

Quendur leaned forward.

"I did not understand all that went on. But whatever it was, horter, I thank you. I could not bear to see Lisa flogged."

"It's about time you called me Jak, like everyone else. As for what is going on, it is why we came to Tomboram. Now, Quendur, and you, Lisa, will take off as soon as we can get free of this handsome young Strom Murgon."

Pompino scrubbed up his whiskers.

"If that was the Kov of Bormark, he has changed mightily since I last glimpsed him."

"But we cannot leave you now!" protested Lisa.

"Your quarrel with Pamcur Ovin may have smoothed our way, Lisa the Empoin. Now you must not run more needless dangers."

"But—!"

I said: "Quendur, you must take care of your lady. We thank her. But this is our affair."

Quendur sat back. He looked suddenly raffish, like a pirate about to pounce. He looked—cocksure.

"Your affair it is and may be, Jak. But I will take thought about that."

"Mightily changed," said Pompino. "He looked as though his best friend had died and his worst enemy had gained a crown."

My own view from the opposite direction had been of Pando's cape flowing out as he almost ran. Now what had that young imp of deviltry been up to?

We four sitting in the darkened carriage were still recovering from the shock of our recent experience. I took heart from Pompino's clear determination to push that aside and to concentrate on the future. Quendur suggested we do a mischief to the coachman—"Blatter him good and proper"—and take the coach and disappear into the city.

"Pompino and I have business with this Strom Murgon. He will prove of great use to us. We will play him along like a salmon." We four spoke in conspiratorial whispers, there in the half-darkness of the carriage.

Pompino the Iarvin was not a crafty Khibil for nothing. He favored me with a quick bright glance of those shrewd eyes.

"Aye, Jak, we can do that. And then we burn the abominable temple. Then—"

"Then," I interrupted with some warmth. "Then we see what this flat slug of a King Nemo can do. Is that your plan?"

"Aye."

Quendur and Lisa were listening with rapt attention.

"This Strom Murgon must be the son of Murlock Marsilus, brother to Marker Marsilus, who was Pando's father. Murlock usurped the kovnate; but Pando won it back." I did not elaborate on the part played by Inch and myself in that. "I would guess this Murgon hankers to take the kovnate and succeed where his father failed. He is a strom of some potty little stromnate or other, this Ribenor. That will not satisfy him."

They stared at me as I whispered.

"He is a villain, then," said Pompino.

"Probably. Certainly, if he is mixed up with Lem."

No reaction from Quendur or Lisa convinced me that Lem the Silver Leem was able to conceal the activities of his devotees from the ordinary folk. We were privy to the secrets only because we already had information enough to let us pry past that initial veil of secrecy. "If we destroy the temple and scatter the devotees we will materially aid Pando against his cousin."

"He seems," said Pompino, "this Pando, Kov of Bormark, to mean a great deal to you."

How reply? I cursed my loose tongue and then attempted to brazen it out. "A great deal? Only as a tool to crush Lem."

Pompino sniffed. "You said you knew him—"

"When he was small. He would not remember me."

"It's always a chancy business dealing with great lords," said Lisa.

Given the nature of lordship on two worlds, the instability of power, the corroding effect of authority, this often—too often—was Opaz's Literal Truth.

"And I'll tell you what this strom's face reminded me of," said Quendur. "It was just like a sculpture in our temple of the demon face of the Devil of the Ice-Wind who guards the north shore of Gundarlo."

Something in this Strom Murgon's actions made me say: "Oh, come now, Quendur. He is not much like a Kataki, is he?"

"No. But the likeness was there, all the same."

"Each sculptor has his own ideas," said Pompino, impatient at this talk. "Why do we wait? I agree with Quendur. Let us blatter—"

"Here he comes now," said Lisa, quickly. We quietened.

Indeed, if the strom's face did not quite remind me of that of the Devil of the Ice Wind who hoots so mournfully and menacingly along the north shore of Gundarlo, he most certainly did bear a marked resemblance to any one of the host of minor demons whose portraits are so faithfully recorded from the bad dreams of artists all over Kregen. This was a trick of the indentation of his eyebrows over his nose. He breathed heavily.

"May Armipand take him!" he said, more to himself than us but not giving a damn if we heard. "You! Out! The kov wishes to inspect you. Bratch!"

This, I felt, was shouted as a sop to his own esteem. At his shoulder the Chulik, Chekumte the Fist, scowled down, hand on the hilt of one of his swords.

Pompino breathed in my ear. "Let us deal with these now, Jak, and get clear away—"

"Tsleetha-tsleethi," I said. "Softly-softly. We must remember to maintain the aim. We play this fellow and use him to our ends."

Breathing as heavily as Strom Murgon, Pompino stomped out of the carriage. We followed and trooped back into the small bare room. The strom halted his Chulik outside and did not offer to go in with us. We halted in the center of the room. Pando waited for us.

Well, he did look splendid in everything except the cut of his jib. He'd been a young rip, an imp of deviltry, and lovable through all his pranks. Then he'd become a kov and it had gone to his head, and his mother, Tilda of the Many Veils, had begun to drink. And then—well, and then what? He had seen his army defeated in battle, he had crawled back, somehow, into the king's favor. He had held onto his kovnate. There were lines in his face, of course; but no more than any Kregan who can hope for better than two hundred years of life might expect. There was a nervousness about him, a jerky irritability I did not much care for. He kept rubbing the palm of his left hand over the pommel of his sword. The weapon looked to be plain enough, useful, and at odds with the rest of his gaudy get-up.

He stared at us. His brows drew down in a practiced grimace designed to intimidate. He saw me.

His expression did not change. His glance passed over me, over Pompino and Quendur, lingered on Lisa. We four just stood there like balass blocks.

"You have been allowed to go scot free. This has been done without my authority. What is your explanation?"

Pompino opened his foxy mouth and I said: "The Silver Wonder binds us all in comradeship, pantor."

He let a small twisting movement of his lips convey displeasure, hauteur, disgust with us lower orders—anything we wished to deduce. I own it, I began to entertain doubts about that young imp Pando in these latter grown-up days.

"You claim allegiance to Lem the Silver Leem?"

He didn't beat about the bush; bashed it straight out.

I did not answer at once. Caution in using the name of Lem was habitual to all devotees. Caution derived as much from chauvinistic pride as anything else, I judged, motivated the Leem Lovers in this. Pando nodded then, young, handsome, with betraying blueish smudges under his eyes and that continual rotating rubbing motion of his palm on the sword pommel. Before I'd decided to bash on with the story—in for a ponsho in for a vosk—he said: "You forswear allegiance to the Silver Wonder?"

"No, pantor," I said. "Just that some names are not usually spoken before a Llahal, or the pappattu that Furry Silver and Dried-Blood Brown demand. That is all."

His eyes opened wide and he stood up straighter.

"You speak in a way to have your tongue torn out, rast!"

And, still, I couldn't be sure. Would Pando have joined up with Lem? If he had not, we would be lost to claim allegiance. And yet, and yet—Murgon must have told him, and the strom would not have done that if Pando was not a devotee.

"We mean no harm, pantor," said Quendur, speaking up stoutly. Pando ignored him. He eyed me.

"You are the one called Pompino, from Tuscursmot? That is in South Pandahem." He said that in a cuttingly dismissive way, a North Pandaheem barely tolerating a Pandaheem from the South.

"No. I am Jak."

He started, suddenly taking on a strange, wary look. He inclined his head a little, looking at me with those damned eyes of his bringing back the memories.

"You who call yourself Jak. I think I know you. We have met before."

I made no reply.

"Where was it, tiksum! Speak up. You would not have forgotten me, that is sure. I cannot recall everyone I have met in life. And you are one ripe for punishment."

I said: "I've given your backside a thumping before now, Pando, and I should have given you a few more, had your mother Tilda not been so—"

He rushed and tried to hit me.

I held his arm and we stood, glaring into each other's faces. His whole demeanor took on the frightful appearance of a fellow having a fit. He glared. He tried to speak, and swallowed, and his lips writhed. He spat in my face.

"Dray Prescot! You—you—let me go and I will surely kill you!"

"My name is Jak. I told you, Pando. My name is Jak."

"Yes, yes, yes! That I believe!" He called me all manner of vile and odious creatures. "You pretended to be called Dray Prescot, you pretended to be the Lord of Strombor, and I believed you! And then when the real Dray Prescot made himself Emperor of Vallia, mother and I knew he was not you! You—"

"Behave like a man, Pando, like a kov." I hoped these stupid words might make him empty out his hatred, and then we could start over.

"I've met the Emperor of Vallia, when he was the Prince Majister. A cool, polite, stuck-up cramph—"

"Really? What was he like?"

"Nothing like you. Let go my arm and I shall thrash you and kill you—"

"How is your mother, Pando? Tilda the Beautiful?"

"You dare ask! You dare speak her name—"

"I am told she drinks."

He opened his mouth wide and, now, it was perfectly clear he would shout for his guards. I put my hand on his mouth, and pressed, and said: "We must talk over old times, Pando. When you are yourself again. But if your mother drinks then you had better not blame me."

He slobbered against my hand and tried to bite and I twisted him away. I whispered fiercely into his ear, downbent as I held him. "You remember me, Pando. I was your friend and I remain your friend. If you blame me for what has happened in your life you do me an injustice, and one I will not stand for. Inch was right. You needed to be shown more than I was prepared to show you, out of respect for your mother—"

He got a lip around my palm and slurped: "Let me go!"

That was what he meant; it sounded like porridge slopping from the saucepan to the plate.

I let him go and stood back. I said: "Remember. I remain your friend. If you insist on calling me enemy—"

His sword was out of the scabbard. He held it as though he had no idea on Kregen how it got there. He swayed. He sagged back against the bare table.

"We will see. Because once I—I will not have you killed out of hand. You must prove your friendship, for I have never forgotten you."

"That is something, then, you young imp."

His head snapped up. "I am the Kov of Borm—No. No, kings and kovs never meant much to you, did they?"

"No."

This meeting had not gone as any rational man might have expected it to go. The recriminations—yes, they were expected. After all, as far as Pando and Tilda knew, I'd simply walked out on them. They didn't know that treacherous King Nemo had had me drugged and shipped off like a bundle of washing to slave at an oar in a swordship.

And I was pushing away the central and most dire concern—Pando—Pando was an adherent of Lem the Silver Leem.

That did not bear thinking of.

My three companions had remained silent, and if I suggest this was an awed silence, that would not be too far from the truth. Now Pompino drew a breath and said: "We'd better—"

"Silence," said Pando, and ignored my comrade Pompino and addressed himself once more to me.

"What happened to Inch?"

This did not surprise me. When Pando had been nine or ten—a goodly time ago now—he'd met us and we'd helped him and his mother and secured his kovnate of Bormark for him. Then I'd disappeared, and then Inch had disappeared. Inch had been around longer than I had. Pando, a young rip, would not forget these events of an impressionable youth so indelibly imprinted on his memory.

I said: "I have not seen Inch for a long time."

This was true, Zair forgive me. I went on: "Your King Nemo, the old King Nemo we woke up out of bed with a dagger at his throat—you remember?—had me chained and sent to the swordships—"

Pando flinched.

"Aye! And, after me, he had Inch likewise packed off to slave. Inch escaped, praise be to his Ngrangi. D'you think, lad, I'd have so callously abandoned you or your mother?"

"You should have said sooner—"

"Is all well?" Strom Murgon's voice floated in.

Pando's face took on a dark and hateful aspect.

"My cousin takes good care of me." He shouted back: "All is well, Murgon. We shall be out presently." He spoke without a quiver, a strong young man's voice, used to command. Then, to me: "Very good care. There is a matter between us I do not think can end but with steel."

"You will tell me when you want to, Pando. Now, I would like to see Tilda of the Many Veils—"

That down-droop to his face drew lines around his mouth.

"Yes, you are right, Dray—Jak. She does drink."

"And you do not blame me?"

"I did!"

"I thought so. But—"

"If King Nemo were not already dead and wandering the Ice Floes of Sicce, crying despairingly to find the way to the sunny uplands beyond, I think I would have sent him there."

"There is a new King Nemo, now, they tell me."

"A flat slug. He stands with Murgon against me."

"So you're in trouble—as usual."

At this he gave a small, half-smile that changed his face some way toward the impish look I remembered.

"And you! I need not be surprised that you're in trouble, that is endemic with you. I owe you much, and I have never forgotten. But, now is no time—I have to see the king and discharge tiresome business. Murgon will take care of you. I assume you have talked your way out of this predicament."

"A matter of punishment for a justified chastisement, and the Silver Wonder—"

"Ah! I own I am surprised that you..."

For a moment we stood silently, staring one at the other.

Then he said, "We will talk more on this." He raised his voice: "Cousin Murgon!"

The strom slid in through the doorway, his sword half out of its scabbard. The shadow of the Chulik bulked at his shoulder.

"I am satisfied that you have acted correctly. I shall wish to see these people later. See to it."

Murgon's lips twisted above the beard. But he got out a polite reply. Pando swirled up that short cape, slapped his sword down hard, and took himself off. He strode out, to be exact; but that would convey an impression that was absent. Pompino glanced at me. I shook my head. So—out we all went and climbed once more into the waiting carriage.

This meeting with Pando had gone in a strange, almost eerie, way. What would the meeting with Tilda be like?

Nineteen

Tilda

"But I am not ill!"

"Yes, you are."

"No, Horter Jak! I am not ill—"

"Lisa looks all right to me," said Quendur. "She is a remarkable woman—"

"I agree," I said. "I hold Lisa the Empoin in the highest esteem. Yet she is ill—or, she will say she is ill."

"Ah!" said Pompino the Iarvin.

"I'd never seen the sea until they took me away to be slave." Lisa sat next to Quendur, very close, and his arm lay around her shoulders. "Then

Quendur took the ship I was in, and threw overboard the disgusting wretch I was slave to. Quendur saved me—"

"As you have saved me a hundred times!"

These two looked at each other, and Pompino looked at me with an expression that said they'd forgotten anyone else existed. We were waiting in the carriage by a gateway where Strom Murgon had alighted to see about his business. I wanted to get Quendur and Lisa away, for Pompino and I would have to skip and jump before we burned Lem's temple. For Lisa to pretend to illness after the experience she had endured would be perfectly in keeping and understandable. By Krun, yes!

"They swear by the Gross Armipand up in these parts," observed Pompino in a musing way. "This mass of corruption is the very antithesis of Pandrite the All Glorious. Or so I am told. I think, Lisa, you will have to call most groaningly upon the Witch Mipanda, vile wife of the Gross Armipand, when you are ill. And that will be in short order, believe me."

Lisa half-turned from Quendur's clutch. "Yes. I will be ill." She smiled a pale smile. "That will not be difficult."

Pompino brushed up his reddish whiskers and looked pleased with himself. He was not named the Iarvin for nothing. "Then I shall take it upon myself to blatter this strom with some severity. Yes. By Horato the Potent, yes!"

"Ah..." I said. The caution in my tone brought Pompino's head around very smartish.

"What, Jak?"

"The plan is for us to continue on with the strom."

He looked disappointed.

"So it is, so it is. Well, there is always another tide."

"The Tides of Kregen roll forever," quoted Quendur. "And you have to pull into your moorings sharpish to catch the right one."

"And when this one rolls in, it will not extinguish the fire we shall set." Pompino bristled this out, all red and whiskery and his fierceness quite betraying his shrewdness.

I looked out of the carriage window and then, turning back, said: "As San Blarnoi says: 'Every inch a gentleman and every foot a rogue.' That sums up our Strom Murgon."

"Aye!"

"If it was not for Lisa—" began Quendur.

"We know."

"No one knows much of this cult of the Silver Leem. It is spoken of only in whispers, among sure friends. I know nothing of it. But I have been told not to ask questions." Quendur had been a pirate, a ferocious render of the oceans; he looked sweaty and uneasy as he spoke of Lem the Silver Leem, knowing nothing of that debased religion. Humanity fears the unknown and we all know we fear the unknown, and knowing it is unknown and we fear it doesn't help at all.

A noise of footsteps and distant voices and the shake of the carriage as the coachman roused himself took my mind away from the habitual way Quendur and Lisa had avoided any recognition of the name of Lem when we'd used it before. Not allowing unknown and therefore unpleasant facts into your sphere of cognizance is one defense. The door opened and Strom Murgon climbed in. He looked murderous, as one might expect, and the carriage jolted into movement at once. We rolled out and ground across cobbles, lurching to the right as, I guessed, we negotiated the archway.

No one spoke. The sound of half-suppressed breathing filled the coach with the effect of underground bat caves, geysers of fury, exhalations of menace. I found, as is all too often the case, Zair forgive me, that I couldn't take all this overly seriously. The comic aspects came through too strongly. We were all into a desperate adventure; but it was a real laugh, all the way along...

Then, as we rolled through the streets in the darkened carriage, I fell into an introspection about our motives. Pompino just believed in bashing on and burning the temples of Lem. That would show 'em, he'd claim. The Star Lords would be pleased and would reward him. But—but was this going to do any real and lasting good? The temples could burn; the Leem Lovers could build more. If someone hit you over the head and said: "Stop loving him—or her—and love me instead!" would you switch your love? If something in which you believed was destroyed, would you give up—or would you build again, and stronger?

We believed that Lem the Silver Leem was an evil cult. They tortured and killed little children, and this was reprehensible. But in a slave society where a child was mere property, like a chicken, an otherwise normal and decent person would see nothing remiss in these actions. If you could kill and eat a chicken for the gratification of your physical appetite, then to sacrifice a slave for the benefit of your spiritual wellbeing, to give worship to your god, was a perfectly normal act. It could reflect only credit upon yourself, gain you luster, store up treasure in heaven against the day of judgment.

We, Pompino and I, were committed by the Star Lords to oppose Lem the Silver Leem. We would burn the blasphemous temples and scatter the worshippers. But we had to do more than this. We *had* to do more than this. We had to set something better in view; we had to show the adherents of the Silver Wonder that they erred. That was the true task laid on us. That, then, was the battlefield where our future strife would be fought.

Yet, doubts remained. As I'd once been told, oligarchy was giving way to oligopoly. In religion, self-interest in worldly affairs overwhelmed self-interest in spiritual affairs. Once, Phu-si-Yantong had attempted to obtain domination by his evil and pseudo cult, artificially created, of the Black Feathers of the Great Chyyan. That had failed. Always, the question remained: were the followers of Lem slipping into this materialistic method of gaining power and of retaining it?

Then Lisa the Empoin went into her fainting act, and I was once more in action. Well, by Vox, action is a great anodyne to thinking. And, as they say, wicky-werka.

"What is the matter with her?"

"She is overcome, pantor," said Quendur, grabbing at Lisa who flopped all over Murgon. He drew back, sweaty, looking offended even in these circumstances that someone of the lower orders had touched him. Lisa let out a beautiful groan and clutched at Murgon.

"Stop!" he bellowed, and banged a ringed hand against the carriage roof. The carriage lurched and halted. The door opened and the loose-lipped face of Dopitka the Deft appeared.

"Pantor?"

"The woman is ill! Get her out of here—"

Lisa furnished up a superb slurping hiccough, quite clearly the prelude—at least to Murgon—of being violently sick all over him. Quendur was shouting out a string of nonsense, and Pompino joined in and managed to nudge Murgon along into Lisa. She retched. She brought up an enormous throat-clearing belching roar and opened her mouth wide—right over Murgon.

"Out!" he shrieked and pushed her away. Dopitka caught at Lisa's shoulders and she slid sideways. Quendur, still bellowing incoherently, poised and then pushed alongside Lisa. Together they more fell than stepped from the carriage. Shaking with disgust, Strom Murgon took out a yellow silk square and flapped away at forehead and beard.

The door slammed shut.

Just before the wood hit wood and the lock caught, I heard another bang from outside. Murgon flailed away with his silk. Outside a voice—I did not think it was Dopitka's, but it could have been—shouted: "Drive on, coachman!"

The carriage started. Murgon looked up.

I said: "It is all taken care of, pantor. She was clearly unwell." Then, steeling myself, I rattled on: "It is very kind of you, pantor, to take care of us."

"Humph," he said, or something like that, and wiped away sweat. "Dopitka is not such a fool as he looks. He will make sure they are safe."

If that thump I'd heard was what I thought it was, Dopitka would be in no position to take care of anyone—least all of himself—for some time.

It began to rain, the drops spitting against the roof and hissing at the closed windows.

The sound of rain did not muffle the grinding of metal-shod wheels on cobbles. That changed to a softer slurching as we rolled along a rutted way. Presently the rain stopped. Or, as the door opened and torchlight flared, to be more accurate, we had entered into a roofed enclosure. We alighted.

I looked back through the gateway. Stark against the lowering sky rose a pinnacled, turreted fantasia, a castle glimmering in the rain, frowning down. Between the gateway and the entrance to the castle the rain hung a sheeting curtain of glancing silver. The smell of damp ferns floated from the gate and the drops bounced like sprites.

"The king's palace," said Murgon, shaking his shoulders. He still clutched his square of yellow silk, as though to be ready in case Lisa swooped down on him from the rain, mouth open. "The Chun-el-Boram. I must say it makes a splendid sight in the rain." A stroke of lightning stitched blindness across our eyeballs; the thunder rumbled moments later.

Hostlers saw to the horses and the carriage trundled away. Murgon led us to a narrow door in the far wall. What the building in which we were might be I had no idea. There was no sign of Dopitka, or of the Chu-lik; Murgon made no comment. I guessed they were expected to be quick about looking after their lord. I did not think Dopitka would be so quick.

The place appeared to be a deserted palace. The rooms were large and well-proportioned, full of dust and cobwebs, and echoing our footsteps in a chancy fashion.

The Chulik, Chekumte the Fist, marched in after us carrying a torch. The light in its swirling illumination did ghastly things to the shadows to anyone of a nervous disposition.

"Where is Dopitka?"

"I do not know, master. He was not with the coach when I arrived." The Chulik's face and pigtail glittered with raindrops.

"That tiresome woman," said Murgon, and waved us to follow. Pompino glanced at me, and essayed a cheeky smile, and winked, and I kept my battered old beakhead graven as a heathen idol, and we all trailed off along the dusty corridors after Strom Murgon.

We went down stone stairways into the bowels of the earth.

Well, the adherents of Lem the Silver Leem habitually hid their temples. And the bowels, as I may have remarked before, are conspicuously correct for the adherents of Lem. The torch light fleered ahead of us, driving away the shadows, which clustered again at our backs. We shuffled along, heads down; but there was little need. This way had been traversed many times, and I would not have been surprised to learn the dust was carefully scattered by slaves after each secret meeting.

At the closed leaves of the entranceway ahead of us stood a single Chulik. He was armored, clad in brown and silver, and made a most respectful salute when Murgon appeared. The doors opened. Inside lay the temple.

The layout, all flash and glitter and dread horror, was much the same as in previous temples I had seen. Pompino nodded. He knew, too. Murgon led us to a side door, past the iron cage and the altar and the slab. He motioned for us to enter.

"Wait here. I will see the Hyr Prince Majister and tell him you are craving an audience. I do not know how long I shall be. You will find refreshments."

"Thank you, pantor."

Murgon and Chekumte went and we looked at the waiting room. "Refreshments?" said Pompino, perking up.

The viands were typically Kregan, fresh fruit, crusty bread, a selection of cheeses, light wines and parclear, palines. A Sybli woman smiled nervously, wiping her yellow apron, and ready to wait on us; but we sent her away and she was pleased to be let off lightly. We slumped down in chairs and set to.

I picked up a round and juicy onion and bit. Splendid!

Pompino went straight for the important business and poured two goblets of yellow wine—a middling Pantuvan—and we drank companionably. A small wooden door under a groined overhang opened and a cloaked figure stepped into the room.

The two lamps on the table flamed upon the blades of two swords that instantly menaced that unexpected figure.

"Who are you?" demanded Pompino. "What d'ye want here?"

"Put up your swords, gentlemen," said a woman's voice; mellow and yet bloated with a breathiness I thought might have been occasioned by treading down steep and narrow stairs. "I mean you no harm—"

"I crave your pardon, madam," said Pompino, ever the gallant where women except his wife were concerned. "Pray, sit down. A glass of wine?"

"Thank you, horter—parclear, if you please."

This was a pantomime. I just stood there, glowering, as Pompino did his fussy man-looking-after-woman routine. Mind you, he was naturally graceful and good at the task. The dark blue cloak hood concealed the woman's face; but there was a lot, a damned great lot, of cloak swathing her.

She pushed the hood back only as far as it had to go to enable her to drink. The parclear went down in one gulp and she held out the glass again. "Now, horter, if you please. Wine."

When two glasses of that middling Pantuvan followed the parclear, she held out the glass again. Pompino poured.

So I said, "The kov has not yet arrived, kovneva."

The glass in her beringed hand shook, and some slopped.

And, despite all, she drank that third glass of wine before she spoke.

"How do you...? Who are you...?"

The lamp cast me in shadow, and I was grateful for the space it would give me. Pompino smiled. "We are waiting while Strom Murgon—"

"Him!"

She tried to stand up, and her bulk dragged at her, so that Pompino put a hand under her elbow. He grunted as he felt her weight. I felt the weight of the years crushingly upon me.

"I must see the kov!" Her voice indicated no trace of drunkenness. She spoke with that breathlessness habitual to her. I guessed she was never truly drunk: just permanently in a state of lushness.

I said: "How did the kov—how did you—come to believe in Lem the Silver Leem?"

She twisted her head to look at me, and the hood fell away.

I felt the pity and then condemned myself. This was what life did to people. This puffiness under the eyes, this flabbiness of the skin, this coarsening, this trebling of the chins, glistening like vosk-skin, this whole obscene rendering down of a beauty that had once given this woman the sobriquet of The Beautiful.

"We have not exchanged a Llahal—" she said. "What do I know of the Silver Wonder, save what my son has told me?"

"You do not believe?"

"And you will slay me for that, you will kill me for venturing here, where I am forbidden to go?"

Pompino said, "I see!" And, then, with a touch of excitement he could not conceal: "You are safe with us, Kovneva Tilda."

"Tilda of the Many Veils," I said. "Tilda the Beautiful."

Her face, gross and ruined by drink, closed up, glistening, frowning, her befuddlement struggling under a sudden and impossible conjecture. She stared at me, muzzily.

"You...?"

"Oh, yes, Tilda. It's me. I've spoken to Pando... I've told him why I left—fat King Nemo had me sent to the swordships. And you—"

She collapsed into the chair. That gross body shook under the enveloping cloak. She would never dance again to make a man's blood go thump around his body like a cavalry charge.

"You abandoned me—left me—"

"No. I told you—"

"If you loved me you would have come back."

"But I couldn't come back. And, if I could have done, I would not. You know that. I told you." That was brutal and horrible, and the truth.

Her hand reached for the glass again and in a grotesque parody of gallantry Pompino poured wine for her.

I said, "You do not ask me about Inch."

"I did not love Inch."

Seasons ago—seasons and seasons ago—we had met and in all that elapsed time she might have passed but a single hour. Memory rushed back, fresh and scalding. I had expected drama, histrionics, hysteria, not this befuddlement, this puzzled struggle to understand.

"Inch," I said. "He was sold as slave to the swordships also—"

"Poor Inch... Was that his real name?" Her hand held the glass poised at her lips. Wine glistened there. "Would you tell me your name, if I asked? I often wondered. Pando and I, we met Dray Prescot, the Lord of Strombor. It was not a happy time for us. He did look a little like you; but he was a smooth, distant, sanctimonious prince—"

"Sanctimonious?" And I swear my mouth hung open, foolishly.

She went on as though I had not spoken, sunken in a reverie that encompassed too many memories and too many years. But when I said men called me Jak, she heard, and nodded, and then went on as before, in a low breathless voice, to talk of those days we had spent together with Pando and Inch fighting to gain his kovnate. Pompino shifted restlessly.

"The damned temple's here, Jak. There are plenty of materials. I think I'll take a look around."

"...he wants her for himself and Murgon wants her for himself, and Pynsi is in tears." Tilda's voice droned on without taking the slightest notice of Pompino. Now she began to tell me of the problems facing Pando, of his quarrel with Murgon, which, as is the way of two worlds, concerned the love of a young woman. It all seemed a rigmarole at the time, although frighteningly important later on, as you shall hear, and I wanted to get on and help Pompino. But Tilda held me, held me by what she said, her whole defeated attitude, her dejection. She drank. She drank like a fish. But in that desolate face still remained traces of the beauty that had once conquered without artifice, still she was a woman. I would not admit pity into my thoughts of her—for that would demean us both—I did admit a spontaneous feeling of affection.

The Vadvarate of Tenpanam, whose borders marched with those of Pando's Bormark, had recently lost its vad. Now a young and charming girl claimed the vadvarate. The Vadni Dafni Harlstam—vivacious, quick witted and well aware that powerful men would wish to woo her for the sake of her province—appeared to have settled on Strom Murgon as the man for her. Then Pando, seeing great advantage in uniting the houses of Marsilus and Harlstam, had presented himself as a suitor, so that the issue hung in the balance. And the Mytham twins—Pando's friends of long standing and loyal to Bormark—were in despair; Poldo for the Vadni Dafni, and his twin sister Pynsi for that young scamp Pando himself.

As I say, a rigmarole, droned out by Tilda between healthy swallowings of wine—any wine to hand—and yet a net to entrap the wariest of politicos in the passions and greed of ambitious people.

"I thought Pando, after Shamsi died—a tragedy, a tragedy—would settle down again and marry Pynsi. But no. No, he must aggrandize the kovnate and take this Vadni Dafni. I fear that his cousin Murgon will kill him for the sake of it."

I glanced at the door, there was no sound beyond and I fretted to be with Pompino and about our business. But I had to say: "Shamsi?"

"A lovely girl. She made Pando very happy, and the twins are a joy. But she died, she died. I wept for a sennight."

So Pando had made a life for himself, and it had been smashed up and his wife snatched from him. Maybe there lay one answer. My agents had not kept as full an observation as they might have done; and while this was understandable, I promised myself to find out just why that was. Tilda drank more wine.

"Why did Pando join up with the Silver Leem?"

Her glass trembled. "I came here to plead. Even although I know it to be useless. The foul wretches of Lem would have me killed without a care, if they could. Pando joined so that he might better stop his cousin, who is an adherent. I know a little, a little. Pando has plans for Murgon, and Lem offered him a chance to strike without suspicion..."

I felt much better. Pando had become an adherent of the Silver Wonder not out of love for the Silver Leem but with an ulterior motive. He was using the cult for his own ends; he might yet prove an ally.

Then, suddenly, she said, "Do you remember The Red Leem?"

"Aye."

"I danced in the tavern—I could dance, could I not?"

"None better."

"You saved me in The Red Leem, and we came here back home, and then you left me..." Not quite maudlin; not quite, but Tilda of the Many Veils was fast approaching that state. I could not wait any longer. I stood up.

"I do not think it will serve any purpose for you to remain, Tilda. I have to tell you that this evil temple will soon be burned to the ground, and—"

"But the king!" She was shocked into an emotion I could not identify.

"Nemo the flat slug has no part in this—"

"But you are wrong! The king is the Hyr Prince Majister. This temple lies directly beneath his palace!"

As she spoke I sniffed. Smoke wreathed in under the door. Pompino had been busy.

He came bouncing in and slammed the door after him. He rubbed his hands together briskly.

"We have done that," he said. "Or, rather, I have done it, while you've been chatting away here."

"The king is the chief villain," I said. "And his palace is directly above us."

"Capital! He'll be burned out with the rest of the cramphs. The whole place will go up in flames in a moment or two. No one will get through there. We can leave quietly by the way the kovneva came in."

Smoke billowed under the door, thickly and more thickly.

"Then let us be off," I said. "Tilda, my arm."

She appeared dazed. "My chair—"

I guessed that her gross body would be carried about everywhere; her entrance here must have exhausted her strength. Pompino and I would have to carry her. She weighed a ton.

"The things one does," observed Pompino. And, then, he said, "You have—interesting—friends, Jak."

"Aye. And if the stairway is steep—"

He groaned. "Don't say it!"

We reached the small wooden door set in the shadows of the groined overhang. I tried the handle and it opened outward.

In that instant a torch flared in the passageway beyond. Heavy metalled sandals rang against stone. A harsh voice called out.

"Lock them in!"

The door slammed shut. The grating slide of iron bolts rattled against the door. I gave the wood a savage thrust of my shoulder, and it did not budge.

"We're locked in!"

"And the temple at our backs is a sea of flame!"

Twenty

Fire

When Pompino the Iarvin set the temple of an evil cult alight, he set it alight in no uncertain fashion.

Sea of flames or no damned sea of flames, we wouldn't be leaving this place via that route.

Pompino let rip a few fruity curses, and came up and kicked the door nastily. Tilda let out a single small shriek. Then she fainted clean away. She weighed a ton and a half.

We were in a serious predicament. If we were not suffocated to death, we'd be burned to death, and if we somehow managed to bash this door open, there were armed men beyond ready to cut us to death. And yet, despite the gravity of the situation, I continued to find it extraordinarily hard to take this seriously. I kept thinking of what a ludicrous sight we must make. More than one of my comrades would find the sight we presented comical. Mind you, they'd be up there figuring a way out, ready to blatter anyone who wanted to stop us. But, all the same...

Now I have often mentioned that in these enormous castles and palaces of Kregen the walls are riddled with tunnels and secret passageways and entrances. So I suppose some of my feelings of levity arose from this fact; that I was confident we'd find a way out. We began to search.

Tilda had to be arranged as comfortably as her bulk and the chair and table would allow. She flopped over, a billowy blue mass, and I made sure she wouldn't slip off before I joined Pompino. Now we could hear the crackle of the flames. Heat, although not as yet excessive, began to blast at us through the door to the temple. No sound reached us from the small door under the groined overhang.

"If that is the only way out—"

"If it is, Pompino, there is one desperate way of breaking down the door—"

"Burn it down?"

"Aye."

"Do you continue to search. I will prepare."

"If you do halfway as good a job as you did on the temple, we should be all right."

He favored me with a look that said, more or less, "Go on! Blame me!" and bustled off. I went on tapping at the walls with my dagger.

Pompino wasted no time. Labyrinthine though Kregan palaces are, that is no guarantee that *every* room has a secret exit. He collected up combustibles, the stuffing of chairs, a spindly-legged side table. He had to shift Tilda and place her on the floor, a blue mound, and so break up that table and chair. The pile grew around the door. He sprinkled wine, judiciously— some wine burns splendidly, some fizzes and some would put out the Hell Fires of Shurgurfrazz themselves.

My dagger kept on going "thud" instead of "ching."

By the time I had circumnavigated the walls, Pompino was ready. I called across: "Fire her up!"

The door to the temple emitted jets and wisps of smoke from all over its surface. No flame played directly upon it yet; but it would burn and the heat would lick through in tongues of flame. Pompino struck flint and steel and the pile of combustibles roared. He stepped back, looking pleased.

"It's a race, a race between which door goes first."

"Are you quoting odds?"

"Not me." He twirled up his moustaches. "I started both these runners!"

"As we have to wait and see which lot of flames gallops past the winning post, I am thirsty." I licked my lips. "This is, indeed, thirsty work." The heat in the room was now intense. We moved to the center. Pompino brought over a flagon and we drank. I wiped the back of my hand across my mouth in a deliberate and theatrical gesture, for I saw that Tilda's eyes were open and she was regarding me. "By Mother Zinzu the Blessed," I said. "I needed that!"

"Dray!—Jak! What—I am hot—"

"We didn't have the key of the door, Tilda—no need to fret. We'll be out of this soon. Here, have some wine."

That was an invitation she understood very well. The next flagon we happened to snatch up contained a light rose, Morceling, generally regarded as unassuming and satisfying. The wine all went down Tilda's throat, red white or blue, it made no matter. Her face shone with perspiration. That glorious dark hair that in swirling out as she danced so quickened up the pulse, now lay dank and slick against her skull. I thrust sadness for her away. Very few, if any of us, choose our lives. We just have to make the best of what we get shoved onto us, tough though that may be, tough often to the point where it becomes insuperable. I condemn no one for that.

"Hot work," commented Pompino, and he upended a jug of parclear over his head.

"Hold steady," I said, somewhat sharply. "Have we plenty of parclear left?"

"At least four amphorae, over in the corner. Why?"

"I'm hot," Tilda more moaned than said. She lay gasping, her breath a rattle of desperation. Pompino bent at once, wiping liquid around her forehead and cheeks. She shook that gross head pettishly; but Pompino persisted. The heat now roared at us from the door to the temple, pulsing waves of physical oppression. The door the other way flamed up, burning where Pompino had piled his combustibles. I studied the door carefully. We had precious little time left.

We were trapped between furnaces, flames leaping and shooting up, the very air drying and scorching our throats.

"Come on, come on!" I said, my impatience with the laggard flames turning my voice into that old ugly harshness. The orange and crimson filaments curled upwards mockingly, the smoke puffed impudently, the roar crackled out threateningly.

We waited between fires for fire to free us.

"I think..." said Pompino, at last.

We could scarcely breathe. The air scorched. The pain stabbing my lungs was not confined to me; Tilda now lay puddled and glazed, barely able to groan.

"It's got to be now," I husked out.

If we miscalculated, we'd be done for properly.

Pompino hefted one amphora of parclear, I took another of the sherbet drink. With flaps of our clothes over our heads, we approached the door under the groined overhang. In that instant the door at our backs leading to the temple burst into a gouting whirl of flame. It bellowed and shattered. Sparks shot everywhere. Flames licked in as though deliberately seeking us out individually to burn and crisp and devour.

Black smoke choked into the room, writhing like the coiled hair of demons.

"Bring the kovneva!" Pompino rushed on. "I'll open the door."

I did not argue. My amphora went flying through the air alongside Pompino, hit with his. I swung back without looking again and swooped on Tilda. She weighed, by Krun! She weighed!

With her in my arms I ran like a crippled crab for the door. Pompino had simply put his head down and charged. He wrenched the last few bits of smoldering wood aside, the black charred edges glistening. Smoke wisped. The whole room boiled in an inferno of flame and smoke. We smashed through the door, ripping clothes, leaving a great chunk of Tilda's blue cloak, battled on.

The stone corridor beyond led onto a small room in which the smell of raw blood mingled with the stink of the smoke flattening in streamers after us. Here lay the bodies of four Womoxes, clad in blue with the red zhan-til badge of Bormark upon their breasts. They had been slashed to death. Tilda's carrying chair still stood where they had put it down to allow her to make the last effort to totter into the inner room.

We bundled her into the chair. It had four carrying handles, a wooden varnished roof and hanging curtains. This gherimcal with Tilda aboard was regarded as a fit burden for four Womoxes, large, horned, strong people. Men and women who carry gherimcals are often dubbed calsters, and these four calsters had served their last time for their mistress. Now we two, Pompino and I, had to stand in their stead.

"Don't hang about, Jak! The rasts who did this and locked us in might still be about."

I said: "When you fired up the door I imagine they took it that the fire from the temple had reached there. I do not think they expected a fire."

Pompino laughed. He was very pleased with himself.

"We'll make it even more hot for 'em!"

We took the poles and lifted. We carried the chair and Tilda. We went along the stone corridors. We saw no one. And, by Vox, the chair and Tilda weighed two tons.

Pompino led. He called back: "Those poor devils of Womoxes never carried this lot down a spiral staircase."

"Keep your eyes open."

The scorching feel of the fire still lay on me. I felt as though the insides of my lungs had been scraped out. I still kept coughing to get rid of smoke. My eyes stung. But we tramped on, carrying Tilda, and presently Pompino called: "Stairs!"

The flight of stairs was just wide enough. I got the poles up onto my shoulders, and Pompino kept his end low, and up we went. It was like pushing a boulder up The Stratemsk.

By now the chair and Tilda weighed three tons.

At the top we paused for a breather. I looked back, saw nothing but the dim reflection of the fire, and went to stand by Pompino. Ahead of us the corridor extended left and right, a little dusty, high-vaulted, bare. A few torches here and there lightened the gloom. Pompino jerked his head to the left.

"Is that daylight?"

In the distance, faintly, a wash of light lay across the wall. I squinted. My eyes hurt.

"Probably. Possibly. There is nothing the other way."

Without another word we picked up the carrying chair and started.

The light was not daylight.

Along this left-hand corridor the light glimmered against the far wall to starboard. We reached the cross-corridor where the ruddy light reflected from the wall and looked to our left. We saw what we expected to see, what, in a real sense, we had dreaded to see.

Fire.

Against the orange glow which reached as high as we could see under the roof, distant some two hundred paces, the black imp-like silhouettes of people ran with frantic movements. The effect was like peering down into a demon-haunted inferno.

"That," said Pompino with great satisfaction, "is this flat slug Nemo's palace burning."

"Aye."

"I hope he crisps up with it in bed."

"Any king whose basement catches alight is not going to hang about, now is he? He'll be off out of it. Like us."

The corridors below and above ground had brought us to an exit of the dusty old palace not too far from the entrance Strom Murgon had used. A dozen paces along we were able to assure ourselves that the door really was a door out. Pompino put his end of the gherimcal down. Tilda began to slide to the front until I slapped the rear legs down hard.

"What—?"

"Guards. Why, Jak—did you think we'd just stroll out of here carrying the kovneva?"

You had to hand it to my fellow kregoinye, my comrade Pompino the Iarvin. He had a fine cutting way through all his smartness and fierce whiskery attack on life. I did not smile; but I inclined my head in acquiescence.

"The thought had crossed my mind as a pious hope."

Then he struck a serious note through all the nonsense.

"Pious hopes are for the gods. And if all the Gods of Kregen were against you, and the Everoinye for you, you would succeed."

This remark brought up such a storm of doubt and confusion in my stupid old vosk-skull of a head, I just shook that offending object, and blurted out: "Probably. Come on. Let's knock the poor devils over and take to our heels—"

"I like your sentiments. But I do not think I shall run, taking heels or no taking heels, carrying the kovneva."

In that, he was right, by Krun!

We peered cautiously around that corner. The distant fires as the palace burned limned the space between king's castle-palace and this dusty and abandoned palace with radiance. The rain still wanted to fall, and wetted the stones before us; it would be struggling with the fires, quenching some, over others turning to steam. The smells were a wonderful compound of charring, of wetness, of pungencies released by this commingling of fire and water. And the guards out there were keeping back the crowds who ran up, all agog to see the sight of the king's palace burn.

This scene contained the ingredients of a Walpurgis night, people gyrating around a fire, screeching, some attempting to extinguish the flames, others trying to rescue property, others just gawping, and some making surreptitious efforts to impede the fire fighters. We saw a party of guards in the king's livery dragging two poor wretches screaming away, caught red-handed. This explained the guards' activities. King Nemo the Second was not universally loved by his people. But the guards bore down with hard ferociousness on anyone who stepped out of line.

"There is a way," I said. "Tilda's blue cloak is large. Torn down the middle it will cover both you and me. We can carry her out as just a couple of calsters—"

"Right. But you had better tell her and get the cloak."

"Of course."

When we'd entered this dusty little palace Murgon had commented that the sight of the king's palace, dominating across the way, looked splendid in the rain. Now that palace looked infernal in the rain and fires. Nemo, as the Hyr Prince Majister, kept this palace dusty and empty so as to use it as the entrance to the subterranean temple beneath his own palace. That way he kept the secret of the Silver Leem. Also, it afforded others besides ourselves the means of egress.

"Watch it!" called Pompino in a hushed penetrating whisper. I let my hand whip away from the carrying chair curtain and looked back. Dark figures spilled out behind us.

If we would have attracted their attention, if they would have attacked us, I do not know. A creaking sound from the carrying chair heralded Tilda's head as she forced her body up and opened the curtains.

"What is it now, Jak?"

The glowing reflections of the fires played across her face. That hot light pitilessly revealed the grossness and the wrinkles, the ravages of drink.

A bulky figure rushing up bellowed.

"The kovneva! It is the Kovneva Tilda!"

Another voice, sharp, vicious: "Kill her! Kill her and all with her!"

So that settled that...

With a movement not noteworthy for twinkling speed, Pompino drew his rapier. Then he drew the main gauche. He grasped the weapons and fell into a fighting crouch. I sighed. The fellows rushing upon us carried bludgeons, or stout swords, or pallixters, the Pandahem thraxter. Chekumte the Fist, who urged them on, wielded a thraxter. The big Chulik bulked in that erratic firelight and at his side the slimmer lethal shape of Dopitka the Deft hurried on, the long dagger a glimmer of steel in his fist.

I said, "I won't say 'Is that wise?' for that would be to invite ridicule." I had to step with exquisite care here where the fiery honor of a Khibil was concerned. "But I had hoped that, as a fellow kregoinye and my comrade, you would take care of my back. I see that to be no longer so."

"Oh?" He started to bristle up.

I nodded at the rapier and left-hand dagger. "The work will be brutal stuff, Pompino—"

"Aye, Jak. Aye, you are right." He fetched up a sigh. He slammed the rapier and dagger, the Jiktar and the Hikdar, away into their scabbards, and drew his thraxter. "But I had hoped to get in a few shrewd whacks with my new rapier before they ship me off to the Ice Floes of Sicce."

I did not say, although the thought occurred to me, that he might yet do that if his thraxter snapped.

So, in the lurid glow of a king's burning palace, we fought in the rain.

In the first dazzling onslaught, Pompino hit Chekumte such a wallop with his hilt as sent the massive Chulik over sideways, slipping on the wet pavement, to crash smack onto his nose. Dopitka the Deft, oddly enough, was not in the front rank. We foined them off and split a few skulls, and kept them away from the carrying chair. Tilda took one look, withdrew her head, slapped the curtains to, and—I had no doubt whatsoever—fished out her private bottle and lay back to await the outcome of the fight, however it went.

There were a lot of them, more than I'd thought. They kept scurrying up out of the firelit shadows like glinting ants. Pretty soon the regular king's guards would run over to find out the cause of the fracas, and a very few words would bring them in against us. And yet—we couldn't run off. We couldn't carry the chair and fight. To carry Tilda over my shoulder and continue to fight was something that, although I did not want to do, I could do. Trouble was, she could be killed as she acted all inadvertently as a shield.

The incendiary roaring and spittings of the furnace fires spouted to the dark heavens as the rain fell, soaking everyone and doing nothing to quench that enormous conflagration.

I began to think that this was going to be the last fight of all. Regret touched me that I'd not measured my blade again against Mefto the Kazzur. But that was all a foolishness, dreamstuff fit for the nursery. Here and now on wet slick stone, with a bonfire to light us, the fight was to the death.

"There they are!"

The sound of that voice, so hoarse and menacing, did not reassure me one bit. I was kept busy hopping and skipping in dealing with a couple of fellows, one of whom, armed with a sword and a bludgeon, was intent on either spitting or braining me. It was clear he didn't mind which he did, so long as he did one or the other quickly. I dropped his companion, a bristly Brokelsh, and heard that fruity bellow break out again.

"Hit 'em! Knock 'em down! Trample all over 'em!"

Pompino yelped. "Cap'n Murkizon!"

"Aye," I said, avoiding my man's bludgeon, catching him on the chin with the hilt as I straightened my arm to take another man rushing up. He went down yeowling like a degutted cat. "The gallant Cap'n Murkizon—and him—"

"The ship's company! It is glorious, glorious!" sang out Pompino.

And, I suppose, he was right, in a way...

Various delectable portions of the anatomy of the Divine Lady of Belschutz were remarked on with considerable freedom. Quendur the Ripper was there, yelling, driving on to put a hedge of steel between us and Murgon's followers. These shrank back, at first, at sight of these formidable and high-smelling reinforcements. High-smelling... Quendur and Lisa had marked where Strom Murgon had taken us, had stolen zorcas, and brought up the crew of *Tuscurs Maiden*. They hadn't stopped to wash off the muck. Bilge-scrubbing, careening and scraping, lend men and women a certain effluvium. We sniffed. But for all that it was a bonny fight while it lasted.

Rondas the Bold, his Rapa beak savage, his feathers whiffling, launched himself into the fray, screeching. Larghos the Flatch, running fleetly at Captain Murkizon's side, loosed but the once before getting stuck in with cold steel. The two girl varterists, brilliant, effective, raced swiftly on, Wilma the Shot and Alwim the Eye, battling with superb élan. Chandarlie the Gut thrust that pronounced object into a yelling Fristle and knocked the catman head over heels; someone else kicked him and he did not rise again. Pompino's Chulik, Nath Kemchug, in rushing forward trampled all over the fallen form of Chekumte the Fist, and barely noticed. Oh, yes, it was a fine free-wheeling shindig as the men and women of *Tuscurs Maiden* stormed up to help the Owner.

The rain pitter-pattered down in lines of silver and the fires roared and glinted orange-red in the stalking drifts of rain. Steel flickered and clashed and the uproar was prodigious.

"By the profuse moustache of the Divine Lady of Belschutz! Blatter 'em into the mud! Knock their heads together!"

"This," said Pompino, ducking a wild bludgeon swing and clouting the fellow over the head. "This cannot go on much longer. The king's guards—"

"Get four of your stoutest fellows onto Tilda's carrying chair—then we'll make a run for it."

"Aye!" Pompino yelled orders. His people, caught up in the bedlam and rapture of a knock down, drag out fight, were slow to respond. But, eventually, we sorted things out and having disposed of the immediate threat of Murgon's retainers, were able to pick up Tilda in her gherimcal and go bundling off into the rain. We splashed along, and were stopped only once, and that briefly, by a posse of king's men who melted away very rapidly when we leaped on them. No one wanted any more trouble, that was clear.

We halted just before we reached the jetty to look back.

The whole sky blazed and roared with the conflagration. The palace of Chun-el-Boram burned. And, under the palace, the temple of Lem the Silver Leem would now be a charred and blackened shell. Bad cess to it.

"I trust," said Pompino with a devout mien. "I sincerely trust the palace will fall and collapse into the temple."

"Rely on it."

"By Horato the Potent! I do!"

"I just hope Pando's not foolish enough to get himself trapped in the holocaust. You can still feel the heat from here."

"We will have to let him know his mother is safe."

"Yes. We'll have more dealings with that young rip. And, this time, I'll make sure he understands a little more of what being a kov entails. It's not all wine and palines."

"Quite." And here Pompino favored me with a quizzical look I had to ignore.

Chandarlie wanted to know what to do with Tilda's chair. They'd manhandled Tilda herself into the boat in which they'd arrived. Pompino opened his mouth, and I said quickly, "Chandarlie—if you can bring the gherimcal in the boat, do so. Otherwise the lady will require a formidable amount of carrying."

Captain Murkizon, coming up, roared his merriment. "Aye! I swear the lady here and the Divine Lady of Belschutz have a deal in common!"

Give or take a few anatomical vagaries, you couldn't say fairer than that.

Turning around so that his gut projected magnificently, Chandarlie bellowed: "Quidang!" and bustled off to supervise the loading of the carrying chair. Eventually we all clambered into the boat and pushed off. If there was pursuit, we saw no sign of it.

The hands bent to the looms of the oars. Chandarlie took the tiller up in the little kiosk at the extreme stern. Cap'n Murkizon sat in the stern sheets, and Pompino and I sat a little farther forward where we could talk low-voiced.

"We have accomplished much, Jak. The temple in Pomdermam burns. The Everoinye should be pleased."

"On a private excursion, too. But," I said, "but if Pando's kovnate is infected—"

"Oh, it is, rely on that. Bormark festers. It is nowhere finished yet."

"Nowhere near."

"Unless the Everoinye call us to some other task."

"By the Black Chunkrah! They're unpredictable enough to do anything." With the breeze on my face and the scent of the sea about me, and alive with the satisfaction of a task accomplished, I should be feeling if not happy at least some way fulfilled. As Pompino the Iarvin said, the Star Lords ought to be pleased with us. By Zair! That was a new and strange concept to me in these days.

But, pleased or not, the Star Lords would have other tasks for us. That was not a case of probably, but of certainty. If the Star Lords had turned their superhuman faces against Lem the Silver Leem, then we would be used to the full in that campaign. We had, as Pompino said, accomplished much. Much remained to be done, and I hankered after continuing along the lines my fuzzy thoughts had been taking me. Fire cleansed, but there had to be other ways than by fire...

The oars came in and a scrap of sail ran up the mast. The boat swayed rhythmically and we creamed along. Tilda snored. The hands found their own bottles. I would not—not just yet—think of Delia. In the morning I would think what to do next.

There was Seg to be contacted. The future of Ashti of the Jungle had to be settled to her best advantage. There were the problems of Empire to be considered, there was the next meal to dwell on.

I knew with joy that, despite all, there was just one person I would think of all night, sleeping or waking.

Over all, dominating all plans for Lem the Silver Leem, ousting all my commitments to the Star Lords, dissipating the problems of Empire, the single most important fact of my life remained always and forever as a guiding light my devotion to Delia of Delphond, Delia of the Blue Mountains.

About the author

Alan Burt Akers was a pen name of the prolific British author Kenneth Bulmer, who died in December 2005 aged eighty-four.

Bulmer wrote over 160 novels and countless short stories, predominantly science fiction, both under his real name and numerous pseudonyms, including Alan Burt Akers, Frank Brandon, Rupert Clinton, Ernest Corley, Peter Green, Adam Hardy, Philip Kent, Bruno Krauss, Karl Maras, Manning Norvil, Chesman Scot, Nelson Sherwood, Richard Silver, H. Philip Stratford, and Tully Zetford. Kenneth Johns was a collective pseudonym used for a collaboration with author John Newman. Some of Bulmer's works were published along with the works of other authors under "house names" (collective pseudonyms) such as Ken Blake (for a series of tie-ins with the 1970s television programme The Professionals), Arthur Frazier, Neil Langholm, Charles R. Pike, and Andrew Quiller.

Bulmer was also active in science fiction fandom, and in the 1970s he edited nine issues of the New Writings in Science Fiction anthology series in succession to John Carnell, who originated the series.

For more details about the author, see www.mushroom-ebooks.com.

www.ingramcontent.com/pod-product-compliance
Lightning Source LLC
Chambersburg PA
CBHW020535060726
47499CB00017B/130